Popular Anatomy

By the same Author

Taking Cover, 1982
Foreign Affairs, 1985
Bad Trips, ed., 1991
Worst Journeys: The Picador
Book of Travel, ed., 1992

POPULAR ANATOMY

Keath Fraser

The Porcupine's Quill

CANADIAN CATALOGUING IN PUBLICATION DATA

Fraser, Keath
Popular anatomy

ISBN 0-88984-149-7

I. Title.

PS8561.R297P6   1995   C813'.54   C95-931051-7
PR9199.3.F73P6   1995

Published by The Porcupine's Quill, Inc., 68 Main Street, Erin, Ontario
NOB 1TO, with financial assistance from The Canada Council and the
Ontario Arts Council. The support of the Department of Canadian Heritage through the Book and Periodical Industry Development programme
and the Periodical Distribution Assistance Programme
is gratefully acknowledged.

Represented in Canada by the Literary Press Group.
Trade orders are available from General Distribution Services.

Cover concept is based on a detail from an oil painting by Paul Rasporich;
courtesy of the artist and Keath Fraser, photograph, Al Harvey; photograph
of Canada from space, courtesy of Bill Brooks / MASTERFILE.

Readied for the press by John Metcalf.
Copy edited by Doris Cowan.

Second printing, March 1996.

... He chose to include the things
That in each other are included, the whole,
The complicate, the amassing harmony.

– Wallace Stevens

Of all the institutions that have come down to us from the past none is in the present day so disorganized as the family.

– Bertrand Russell

The end of inflation is linked with the breaking of symmetry between the four forces of nature; there is nothing to say, however, that the symmetry will break in the same way in every bubble.

– John Gribbin and Martin Rees

Of the visible and sub-visible world there is no end.

– Ethel Wilson

Let us worship the spine and its tingle.

– Vladimir Nabokov

Contents

Book Three

BONES

Pilgrim-in-Law

Dedicatory Note

Dear Minna,

No murder on page one, I'm saving that for the end. Anyway, you know what happened to Nan so your interest will be otherwise engaged. I know, without a body in question, you might've liked more science fiction in her pages because you want to be a uranographer. Still, your zeal in helping check Nan's facts against the evidence we uncovered (especially about your distant 'punk' uncle) surprised me. You let me into your life again. So this chronicle of hers is for you. A hope chest? Being in marine insurance, with no experience as an editor or archaeologist, I've tried to see how Nan's obsession with the forces that shaped our family helped her remarry them.

Out of her endless reconstructions I selected and reset a small sample of years from around Nan's birth, to mirror our origins and hers: four years in a decade, during which Vancouver approached its first centenary and lost its underpinnings as a European city. I love this city, with passports to our closed boundary now making us forbidden fruit to the rest of the world. – Mun, let's celebrate as we degenerate, I overheard one longshoreman say recently. I will certainly drink to that. I think age, any age, encourages it.

Your loving father,
Pedro Day
December, 2091

Book One

AGAINST NATURE

The Illusionist Father

Chapter 1

Apocalypse Now

WATCHING A SPIDER wait to net a meal will distract hunger for only so many hours a day. Sooner or later a prisoner has to eat, if he can remember how. This one believes he can. Devouring a lunch that has yet to come, unable to wait longer, he opens up and clamps shut. Muscle memory. Strikes gristle with a molar, grinds at it a while, swallows. He recalls a taste; the idea of a taste. Seems to recall he likes most foods except hot dogs. Still? In this place he would eat the wormiest wiener and consider it a delicacy. In this place the wormiest wiener would *be* a delicacy. In here a gourmet can't separate stomach from mind and he wonders if prison isn't the real guts of imagination.

The spider bounces on its trampoline under the small rusting sink. The prisoner, rarely moving off his cot these days except to pace or poo, meditates wildly on the merits of eating a fly.

Pain of hunger. Worse, diarrhea.

He can recite chapter and verse the slow fragmentation of his body since October. He's still hemorraging pounds, forty or more since his incarceration, and is now a Weight Watchers' pinup. A gorgeous clanking bonerack. Fading muscles continue to eat up his body fat, as water runs out his bum.

Thus the end over means rejoices in . . .

His escapes at this hour are necessarily frequent. Every afternoon, craving food, he breaks out of prison to lose himself. *And lives happily ever after.*

Memo: Bring back some Cheezies.

He reexamines his pale skin. Disease erupting on his right hand, a recrudescence of the old eczema on his Downy-allergic balls, is worse than eczema: looks like a fungus of the heart.

Gloves off, Heart. Be brave.

He concludes this disease has gone wild, having crept from between his third and fourth fingers, up over the knuckle of his middle finger, then down into the forefinger's web, having already spread from the far side of his wrist where it appeared and faded during his first week in prison, returning in an archipelago of crimson blotches over the wrist to this point where he's begun to wonder when it might jump across to infect his other hand. It's like watching lava flow. He loathes its style.

He tries keeping his hands to themselves. Pockets them often to check his bony thighs. His body seems little more than a geography lesson for stupid travellers. Of the ones still alive he would now classify himself among the stupidest.

On the days he judges his skin disease to be in remission, drying up into white scales, those days feel no different from days when its lesions rebloom. The disease worries him, which is its purpose, making him secrete enough bad chemicals for the fungus to feed off his skin and flourish. The disease threatens to encircle his wrist like a handcuff, then slide up his thin arm to squeeze out any blood left above the elbow.

Clearly, hell is the body in decay. His body. A scalp raw and shedding; a scalp he suspects of grey hair amid grease, though he has no access to a mirror. He's allowed a comb but no mirror, toothbrush without paste, a bar of soap but no hot water.

Drained by persistent diarrhea.

Has trouble getting up in the mornings, as if he has septic arthritis in every joint.

Puffed and plugged with stress his middle toe resembles a Bradshaw plum from his mother's backyard.

He wriggles all his toes to improve their circulation inside socks stiff with dirt. The dirty feeling can't be escaped, any more than the hungry feeling.

Once a week he and other prisoners are led to a cold shower. Sudsless, he will rub his loose skin all over with soap and never manage to expunge his b.o. (What he'd give for a hot shower at the Racquets Club, even at the cost of a total thrashing from the ladder's rankest seed: now, probably, himself.) His clothes he is supposed to scrub at his cell sink. But the odour can't be removed from these either. Even if he's lucky, and happens to raise a sink of tepid water, he has nowhere airy in the cell to get rid of the dampness in socks and underwear. Wearing them doesn't help at all.

It's no soap opera, he tells the ceiling. Smileless, latherless, he shaves once a week using the same blades packed to last him the three days he'd intended to be here in Costa Rica.

And speaking of water.

His toilet bowl, cracked and seatless, leaks away between his visits to it in the corner. Should he decide to flush and fill it before using, he must calculate on leaving his waste unflushed for at least an hour, while the prison's weak water pressure refills the tank at a trickle to allow another flush. Meanwhile water in the bowl will leak away, leaving his shit high but far from dry. Should he decide to evacuate and *then* flush he still has problems. Either way he counts on stinking up his lair. Often the water is turned off to fix pipes he can hear being tapped far away in the prison's bowels. This tapping never improves the pressure.

Never is his isolation relieved. Migraines persist.

How he has ached with ungovernable longing for Gwyn, especially on her first birthday in October, but also in the six weeks since. What does her hair look like? How astonishing he can't recall her hair, let alone hands and fingers. He touches his beard and despises its wispy slightness. Memo: Under no circumstances, if released, grow a beard or moustache again.

Desperate and alone. That's the thing, besides what is happening to his body to make it itchy and painful: the idea that he has cut himself off from family and friends, some of whom, like Bartlett, he'd let down by failing to carry on with repayments on his mortgage. Worse is the notion he might've contrived to cut himself off from the rest of his life. Washed up and finished at thirty-four, on an endless beach of failure without rescue or any chance of happiness.

An empty bottle without a message.

His stomach eats at itself. His bowels squeeze to evacuate the mere idea of food. He wants to eat, but can't stand the consequences of appetite. His stomach feels like butterflies in heat. Spastic. What's the difference between diarrhea and dysentery. *Is* there a difference?

Here in prison he has taught himself the saving need of illusion. 'The illusion of end over means,' he reminds his collapsed stomach. He believes this is what has saved him so far: imagining himself out of here, as he used to for clients interested in escaping their own city, except instead of going south he imagines returning north. The idea of home nourishes him. This illusion of an agreeable end is what sustains him, locked inside a spidery jail. How could he believe in any other salvation?

Weak, flaked out on his cot. Unable to rise.

He spots the peephole in his door lifting silently. A moist eye watching him for signs of capitulation. The one lid closes the other.

Faint traffic sounds from downtown San José, other side of the river, do feed his sense of an abiding world beyond brutal concrete walls. Traces of diesel fumes from dyspeptic engines sometimes enter his paneless window, prior to regular afternoon rain and a change in the wind's direction. Through the window he will study the morning's blue sky, before rain comes blowing in. Not that it ever drops below 50°F in this valley of volcanic mountains, where the tourist slogan of 'eternal spring' is all he remembers of where he is. He could've drawn on this city for JetSet. A greenhouse without glass. Doubtless full of parrots.

He can't imagine still being here when the wind shifts and the rainy season, mild as it is, vanishes. As November proceeds to its end, the weather improves daily. He refuses to imagine himself still in jail by the new year.

Thus he rearranges Time every day for the comfort of his carcass.

What he finds to keep his spirits afloat, during these depressed and hungry days, is the illusion that an end to mice, damp and malnutrition is going to come within days or at worst weeks ... that he can see it coming in the distance!

He had set his sights successively on the end of his first week here, then second week, his first month ... finding it impossible, after each disappointment, to think he wouldn't be out before the *next* deadline he foresaw. His dwelling on the end of any story (any potboiler will do) is his way of staying sane. *Pushing pushing.*

'I hang on without recourse inside everybody's funny idea of incarcerated hopelessness. A Mexican jail. Except this one's Costa Rican. Please, Your Worship, deny them their extradition and set me free.'

It has got so bad he focuses not on desserts (for those would be begging him to feel hungrier than he could bear, on the meagre rations given him once a day: rice, beans, water) but on coming to conclusions. He lies here on his cot, or paces the four steps from end to end in his cell, concentrating on what the resolution of this whole comedy, twisted into further soapless operas by his brain, has got to be:

Getting the hell out. What a mournful mouthful.

It's as if someone had torn up all the previous chapters from his Life in Travel, starring himself as ... It's as if his days as Arthur Frommer were over and he'd better start finding out where as a traveller he has come.

Where do stories disappear? Where does his?

He tries to read the Spanish first, then a translation on the facing page. *Y la mujer que has visto es la gran ciudad que reina sobre los reyes de la tierra.*

... And the woman which thou sawest is that great city, which reigneth over the kings of the earth.

Along with his ration of toilet paper (pages torn from local newspapers and shoved through his food slot) he reads *Nuevo Testamento: Español e Ingles*, a Gideon New Testament procured for him by the Canadian embassy man. He finds himself drawn to the ends of its chapters and books, for they're his only hope of life outside walls topped with rusty wire and pieces of broken glass. Once a day he's permitted a brief walk in a walled yard.

He closes his Bible. He opens it.

Trying to tell a tale, any tale, the prisoner discovers himself like a travel counsellor making endless plots on the outside world. 'I don't want to lose my voice from disuse, Your Worship. I'm just a shadow of my old self.'

As in his defunct board game he figures the challenge is to bring the itinerant full circle and discover home as a new place.

He concludes you travel to reach a dénouement. He *has* to conclude this. A force outside is telling him the story.

2.

It goes this way:

He keeps believing the Canadian embassy will do something to get him released. At first he thought the attractive young man who came to visit, to see if he was being treated humanely, J.R. Tocher, was joking when he said the Canadian government had to respect a foreign country's judicial system and couldn't interfere, except to assure itself Canadian citizens were not being mistreated. (The implication was the prisoner should respect it too, despite the government's sympathy for his miserable condition.)

'Not being mistreated?' he wondered, in unshaven despair over having to spend *any* time in prison. This had been his third day here, and already he was weak from the diet. 'I'm not a criminal. I shouldn't even *be* in jail.'

Was there anything the embassy could do for him, asked J.R. Tocher, with regard to the money he owed to – ? The suggestion a Guatemalan hotelier could be begged to give up extradition proceedings, if assured of receiving his money in full, pissed the prisoner right off.

'I don't owe him anything!' Plainly inaccurate, for the extradition proceedings were obviously a retaliatory act in response to money withheld in

Canada months ago by the traveller. He'd come down here in good faith, to see if he could work out a compromise. The hotelier couldn't so much as wait for him to fly to Guatemala; had him arrested in another country. 'Did he think I was going to go back on my word? I didn't have to fly down here at my own expense. Or offer to pay him a dime.'

Tocher examined his fingers. 'That's true, but you couldn't have hoped to do any future business in Guatemala.'

'Exactly. So it seemed worth it coming down to negotiate a settlement, with the proviso I be guaranteed an apology and a promise of dropping all legal action in the case. He's the crook, not me. And the Costa Ricans with their stupid extradition treaty are just as criminal. The bureaucracy, John! I only came to Costa Rica because I got a cheap charter.'

At the time he still possessed all the sureness of righteousness and conclusion.

Tocher nodded, diplomatically. The visitors' room was overseen by a couple of Guardia Civil with old carbines. Costa Rica had no army. 'Every country down here has its problems,' suggested Tocher. 'Death squads and dictatorships. Costa Rica has its bureaucracy.'

Once more he advanced the logical case to counter it: money.

But the prisoner wouldn't hear of buying off a deceitful Guatemalan hotelier as the means of gaining his release. He stuck to his principles – sticking even closer when he later heard Herodotus Tours had finally gone the way of all flesh. Insolvent, broke, unable to meet its debts. So why should he bother making any concession now, assuming the bastard persecuting him could even be bought off? The Canadian had no reputation left to save. By holding out in prison he might begin to earn a moral victory back home.

He refused to accept pocket money from Tocher, for decent soap and petty bribes, determined to embarrass his government into pressuring the Costa Rican authorities for his rightful release. It hadn't worked. The embassy continues to hold out little hope that a matter of personal principle with him is going to make any difference to a foreign government. No, this whole upsetting matter, officer Tocher has concluded, will just have to work its bureaucratic way through the local appeal courts, unless the prisoner is willing to ...

The prisoner isn't. He has nothing left to lose including weight. He twists and scratches. His skin drifts in flakes to the mattress. He's turning into his own dustman. Unless Costa Rica decides soon on extraditing him to Guatemala, only his remains will be left to airmail.

Bony prisoners here tell him he's certain to be worse off in Guatemala. Gringos get no special treatment in Guatemala (as if they get it in Costa Rica). There, say these prisoners, he'll probably die.

'No sweat,' he'd told Reesa at Le Soleil Couchant over goose-liver pâté. They were looking down on Aloysius's hunger strike from a window table last September. English Bay was plugged with grain ships, pointing to Asia. Mountains cupped the far sunny shore. The travel consultant was wondering whether or not to fly to Central America, to keep his market lines open. He was confident after San Francisco. 'In the wake of this bad publicity over threatened lawsuits, biscuit, I need to shore up my reputation. Having bought off clients at this end, I *should* be able to dicker a settlement with Five Stars for very little. Scout out Costa Rica while I'm at it.'

It didn't seem to matter he was sinking under debt or that, if he wasn't exactly named on one of Aloysius's signs, as an exporter of sex tours to the Philippines, he might just as well have been.

He ought to have talked more strongly to that young man about spreading innuendo.

A bright, strange kid. And living on the street just like he used to in Bombay, observed Reesa.

Rad.

The prisoner yearns to be back in his mother's well-lit house. If he can survive this closet, he'll deserve a house. Someplace to rebuild his life.

He spends hours every day touring his mother's home. With exhilarating clarity he sees where moulding on the oak staircase needs repair, what leaded pane should be replaced, where the fireplace requires grouting.

Whether any of this wood, glass, or mortar is actually worn out he has no idea. He imagines the fractures. He sees each so vividly in his ravenous condition, trying to keep his mind off food, that he trusts the accuracy of his imagination to feed him vivid details of the general condition called Life.

Is this the monk's dilemma, he wonders. Memory counting but his having no idea if it matters? And so fabricating the world he knows to be out there?

He conjures up the colour of armchairs, the gleam of floors, the play of light through his old bedroom window overlooking the pool. He welcomes the quiet warmth of things, neglected by him in the past but to be cherished in the future.

The moon is the monk's for the asking.

He fabricates that too. He can see all its seas and craters.

Why should he ever travel to the moon again? He has earned his inheritance by coming through this valley of eternal murk. To help with house taxes, he and Reesa could take in a basement boarder: his mother, say.

He could even start up another business, more modest in scope, possibly an antique business to keep ahead of the next scourge of inflation.

Homesick, he shuts his eyes. Clenches buttocks in a spasm.

He imagines Vancouver in November and finds it glorious. Its rain on his wrist, the smell of forsaken trees and humus, the chop of grey sea breaking in the bay. A black-and-yellow tug in the harbour; parking meters in clean streets.

He considers the general condition. He can't actually remember any particular tug, parking meter, wave, wet smell … only the idea of each, in a more vivid way than if he were recollecting real memories. This faking of his own city feels like his imagining all those others …

It stimulates him. Like imagining a meal. The prisoner sniffs out its subtleties, religiously. His memory growing rampant.

And yet he has no recollection this afternoon of when the rain started streaming down outside his cell, cooling the air. Or of what his daughter looks like, why?

At home he's in the newspapers now. Among other things for being a man without experience. 'What a narrow definition of experience,' writes Reesa, consolingly, of Aloysius's charges against him. She regrets to say he's become more notorious by the week, as news of his humiliating fall has leaked out. At the same time people have started feeling compassion for him. Even Aloysius, still in his tent, is now campaigning to have him released!

The Prodigal Son doing his best for the Prodigal Old Man. Cain unmurdering his brother Abel. Jacob restoring his birthright to Esau. Good grief.

He allows his fingers to rub the smooth pages on his chest.

Squeaky wheels pause at one end of the cellblock, a metal lid bangs. He can hear a door open. Then a hawking throat, a grunt.

'Pronto!'

A guard's voice in the passage, uncustomarily harsh.

Luncheon room service has commenced. The bones of murderers up and down his row are roused to expectation from concrete slabs.

He feels his migraine more painfully now. His scaly hand itches terribly, scalp too. Rain blows into his cell with a thunderous clap. The smelly sleeping pad has worn through at his hip.

Scratching he sheds more skin: he can feel himself slowly disappearing. He plucks the Bible off his bony chest to anchor his mind. He would like to know what happens next.

And the city had no need of the sun, neither of the moon, to shine in it: for the glory of God did lighten it, and the Lamb is the light thereof . . .

The wagon's rusty wheels have arrived.

Moist eye at the peephole. Then the unlocking of his door.

Greedily, the prisoner is expected to rise up and claim his daily bread. But his legs won't work. He can't make his legs work.

'Good bloody night,' his father says, a ninety-eight-pound POW in Hong Kong.

This presence of his father reminds him. The Lord's Prayer ends up differently in the Protestant version.

After the daily bread, before the Amen, comes some kind of glory: a reminder of the Kingdom that will deliver us from evil.

This is the problem with rewriting potboilers, he thinks, no end to the hyperbole.

His goes this way.

June, 2091

I open this up to add a few more lines. That fugitive my doctor has come again, sneaking in after hours, warning me in his quiet voice not to forget that Hygeia is a zoo. How can I forget? I listen for the hundredth time to his soothing prescriptions. His dark eyes sparkle. He has mixed blood, like my grandson, except the doctor is not so respectable. I like him. He is a blend of remedies, none of them cures, most of them wild. Like wasting my time. Go ahead, he urges, the body requires it. I try. My grandson, too, scolds if I don't mistreat my time when I still know better. As if I had the spit left to mistreat it. 'You're still sentient. Take

advantage.' I would like to mistreat it. I would like to paint myself red every night.

Another threat this morning from E. Growled between smacking dentures, about kicking my poor bones to sawdust. Can't understand his venom. Too bad he's not sentient, as we could waste ourselves together. He will pause in the corridor to stare in. It isn't just his loss of control. He has an odious manner hard to believe he was ever lacking. Think he'd like to wheel into my room and bite me. Instead he lurks toothless in the corridor. I suspect he wants a dustup for the same reason I want to be wanton. He doesn't like Hygeia's pictureless

walls any more than the other valetudinarians. My doctor claims the only choice we have is to stir up this godforsaken vacuum, or to sit like mutes. Or is this just me putting words in his mouth? Me wanting to fracture the time left me and give it some grain and shape? Would love to be evangelical about something.

Without me in his road E. might have the media here every year on his own birthday. Asking him the questions they ask me. 'What is the secret of your et cetera?' 'My et cetera is an open book, if you must know.' My birthdays just seem to make his redundant. He's ancient, but I'm more ancient. So they celebrate me. It's not fair to him. But then his jealousy isn't fair to me. Perhaps I should declare myself in cloister and sneap him.

Was listening to myself on tape the other day trying to talk. To my uncle, Bartlett. Diplomacy must be something the child has to learn, before forgetting it again in a wheelchair. Sitting alone in here we're encouraged to sip doses of distilled water. Piss and vinegar. I usually wait for tea, planning the sour bits for my diary. Odd how you glance back in a diary to keep up. No longer recognize yourself in the mirror between lines. Something missing. A link between the younger idea of yourself and the present. I don't think E. has any et cetera left. No wonder he's ignored.

Have made a date with Pedro to take me to the beach. I am taking him. He is taking me. We will go together. So much for the cloister. At

my age these expeditions need a logistical engineer and a porter for the baggage. Since my fall I can barely manage one walk a day, and only along the corridor.

Plotting this short trip with Pedro I seem to have luggage that goes back my whole life. He can of course organize it any way he wants. I just think it important he has agreed to come. Sure, he says, he's interested in history. I wonder. I want to say, 'Don't sound so enthusiastic, my dear grandson. If I could, I would certainly go alone, but the trip is for you.' You would think I had asked him to transport me to Mexico. I think he worries about getting sawdust on his hands.

The plaque will be worth our visit. Must have seen it first with F. ninety years ago. Etched in brass, alongside a huge concrete anchor to commemorate the day when Narvaez sailed into the bay. July 5. The same day I want Pedro

to take me down. We might then kill the rest of the afternoon with a couple of hotdogs. I wonder if the plaque has survived delinquency and storms.

Yesterday our first day of summer. Felt a chill. Don't suppose I feel well enough to enjoy a hangover. A ropy good time should be my reward for longevity, I deserve a hangover. By now I deserve to be senile from a steady stream of hangovers. How I detest the glads I get. Pompous glads have replaced night-after roses, just as commemorations have anniversaries.

E. sitting in the corridor again, balefully. I turn my back on a fribble. The view is lovely and blue. I do love my view. When the power is out, as it often is, the corridor is our valley of the shadow. *Arriba* to you sailboats in the bay. Have talked to Pedro and he is definitely coming. Have

mentioned to him E.'s
worsening abuse.
Getting so I can no
longer concentrate on
my therapy.

   But here is the tea
trolley. *Arriba*. Am a
little leery a salute may
provoke E. So instead
will rub and rub my
forehead, the empty
gesture of diplomacy ...

Chapter 2

Making History

WITH BARTLETT AWAY in Bangkok he decides to rid their shared house of his friend's seed-spilling, mice-luring canary in the following manner:

First, consolidate resolve by sleeping on it. Then rise early, jog down to and around Lost Lagoon. Come back, turn up furnace, shower. Breakfast on English Muffin bread. Upstairs again to listen at Aloysius's door. Enter own bedroom to peck the sleeping Reesa. Return downstairs. Remove empty Barker shoebox from hall closet, puncture air holes in lid with roasting fork. Briefcase, overcoat. Hum a few bars from *Pinafore* in hallway to allay any suspicion of aberrant behaviour. Pause, listen. Enter den swiftly and remove sheet covering cage. Grab groggy but disputative bird, stuff into shoebox. Drape cage again, listening. Leave house with box under arm by 6:45 a.m., entering elevator alone 6:58 a.m. and ascend to office. Put box in desk drawer and work till noon.

He would boot up in the interim, feeding his new desktop computer a fresh diskette, the mechanical equivalent of a croissant, and set to work at his keyboard with an overdue column. *The Best of Years, The Worst of Years ... a year in which your intrepid agent got seasick on Lake Superior, travelled for the first time in a Lear jet, and played tennis in Peru at an elevation of 10,000 feet. Here, with my annual selection of the Best and Worst in Travel for the year just past ...* And so on till noon, when his secretaries would disappear to lunch, bearing static electricity from the tower's dry air all the way up their tights. They crackle, leaving.

Then remove shoebox from drawer. Slip under coat and descend to parking lot. Travel up Cambie to Q.E. Park. On Little Mountain zipper Mikos into pocket. Keep protected from frigid air till safely inside conservatory. *Do not squeeze.* Pay girl, one-handed. *Only squeeze if chirps.* Pause. Breathe deeply ... tropical vegetation, earth. Proceed down sloping path, across goldfish bridge, past first parrot perch. Stop, look up. Pretend listening to birdsong in palm branches. Hope Mikos doesn't answer. Check for any pensioners on bus tours in foliage. Ignore cock parrot at second grotto screaming: *'Hello, Ernie! Hello, Ernie!'* Coast clear, unzip, remove fist gently from pocket. Keep canary out of sight, down by scrotum. Look both ways preparing to let fist blossom. Expect older woman to appear out of bougain-villaea. 'Trying to steal a bird!' Her turkey neck waggling. 'No no,' you respond, 'I'm –' Won't listen. 'Let it go!' Poor Mikos. Won't fly away. You try dropping him. You want him to disappear, into hibiscus blossoms, into Paradise…

2.

But he is saved the embarrassment of detection. This morning upon rising, and before he can carry out his plan to 'disappear' this messy pet like some plainclothes screw, in one of these Ford Falcons in Buenos Aires, he hoists the sheet to discover Bartlett's nuisance lying on the floor of its cage. It must've known of the impending earthquake: been taking precautions by avoiding a potentially shaky perch: positioning itself for trouble only it could divine. Ornithological sixth sense won't save it, however. Dwight con-cludes it's doomed. Not even a fresh broccoli flower he carries in from the crisper and stuffs between thin steel bars will tempt it to rise from the shit-bespattered newsprint. Mikos can't be tempted to perch.

Not till his and many other office towers sway for twenty-nine seconds this afternoon, at 12:43 p.m., when the Lower Mainland and most of the Gulf Islands are rocked by a five-point-six, will the canary's sentience become clearer to him. This morning he thinks the deep freeze invading their unin-sulated old house has simply paralysed the troublesome bird. He expects it to be defunct by the time he comes home for dinner. He replaces the sheet and saves himself an extra five minutes over the shoebox with a fork.

He's on a roll. Slide-lecturing at community centres and public libraries, guesting regularly on national radio; a spring of advice, a welcome oasis in a cold January. He cranks out a syndicated travel-advice column for Canadian newspapers (Southam chain), publishes a newsletter eight times a year (*Afar*), and in spare moments throws off personal-experience articles bylined from the country of his choice and sold to slicks like *Holiday Now*.

But his main job is running a business and counselling clients: business types in office towers like this one, plus off-the-sidewalk trade, and subur-banites who have picked up on his reputation for integrity and experience.

BEST HOTEL – *Hotel Bora Bora in French Polynesia. A tough choice among many outstanding hotels visited this year ... Maybe it was the Polynesian air, but sleep at the Bora Bora was even more delectable than its cuisine. Towels to the thickness of two fingers, service as if by telepathy, and the kind of decor not trying to be somewhere else. No need to be! Tasteful by an obvious absence of taste.*

'Mr Irving?' Candice on the intercom. 'Mr and Mrs Conklin have arrived. Shall I send them in?' Should she? He's already cancelled on them once. '... I didn't realize you were talking to Stockholm, Mr Irving. I'll explain the delay.' WORST CITY *(Foreign) – Dacca. This city should qualify for your charity, not your custom. Hijack any airliner to avoid landing.*

His success in promoting Herodotus Tours relies on an impeccable memory rooted in facts, figures and timetables, allowing his imagination to roam the pulsing green lines of diskettes. He counts on his pearly smile and pleasing tongue. On meetings with bank managers and property agents to finance his scheduled expansion into branch offices. On his never forgetting that selling tickets and booking vacations for the Conklin types are his bread and cheese. His more interesting camel caravans proceed from the premise that only modest successes beget exotic ones.

Frankly amazing are the latitude and opportunities his profession tenders. *Dear Mr Irving,* a letter might go, *re* some new market overseas. *Discreet inquiries into the nature of the Filipino hospitality industry have made it possible for us to offer a confidential package tour to Manila, for the discriminating gentleman with off-the-beaten-track tastes in erotic-seeking pleasures, who probably represents a neglected if limited segment of your clientele ...* He usually took these letters home to show Reesa, who wondered if his semi-anonymous correspondents were catering to pedophiles, or to the meat-and-potato junketeers who flew the connecting hetero/homo flights out of Tokyo and Osaka. She told him to file the letters away in his desk in case her station ever decided to do a show on sex tours. 'Thomas Cook updated,' she mused menacingly. *Not* a tour HT could sell and still maintain its successful family custom.

BEST CITY *(Foreign) – Hong Kong. Disregard what you've heard about noise and pollution. This is the premier world city for shopping, sightseeing, dining: a successful marriage of capitalism and Oriental zip. Star Ferry ride a nickel, restaurants superb, architecture out of the twenty-first century. Most spectacular walk in the world? Paved two-mile path encircling Victoria Peak at top of funicular. I never miss it.*

After several years of knocking round after university, viz. fizzled business ventures, Dwight finally found something to believe in just two years ago: parlaying advice. His devout mother now thinks if travel were religion he'd be a crimson-skirted cardinal. *Best Cathedral – Try Seville's. I fell in love. After your more famous Chartres, Winchesters, Colognes, this stone vault dances on uplifting pillars, as unexpectedly as an elephant ...* Travel had come to him in a road-to-Damascus flash on a trolley bus, heading downtown to argue with a loans officer over a cash-strapped salmon farm of his engendering off the Sunshine Coast. 'What am I doing, fish farming?' Scoop-netting dead coho smolt every morning off the surface of his pens and paranoid about wild-salmon disease. He'd been travelling back and forth to Vancouver and hating it. The world of travel somehow blossomed from there.

Now he sows ideas on a fallow screen and harvests fruit of long hours: riskless, compared to threatened salmon. Travel for the well-heeled and the bargain hunter, travel for young professionals and retired janitors. Travel ranging from a ski trip in the Rockies to desert caravans on a shoestring. Beaches, jungle ruins. Book it, hate it, or else never come back. The opium of the eighties in developed countries (the palliative, the status-breeder, Dwight has concluded) is going to be travel. He realizes nothing gives people greater pleasure than returning home a different person, witness to revolution, or beaten up by the sun. Carting home little black cans of unprocessed images or a new hooked rug. And when you return the city is emphatically fresher, you notice it more, notice life more! Travel rearranges your sense of time. 'Make history,' he urges his public. 'Travel.'

BEST CANAL CRUISE – *A week in Norfolk aboard a fifty-foot barge, converted into a floating hotel of princely comfort. Elsa Line recommended. Cheaper with a party of six. Canapés, glorious wines and delicious pub lunches along the way. A skipper who played Elgar for us on the cello.*

Dwight envisions a chain of Herodotus Tours agencies across the city and ultimately the country. Offices linked by computer, fax, and by a sound reputation based on exceptional service. A network stretching coast to coast, Victoria to St. John's; an empire spun from the brain of his new desktop Apple, a tool expected to revolutionize the industry. He taps into it, researching countries and targeting customers, cross-referencing disks for lectures and interviews with clients in need of instant facts – most of which he carries anyway in his head, with the possible exception of an ocean temperature off Tobago in late February during a leap year. Dwight goes light years beyond the call of duty, because it's never a duty and he hears no call.

3.

He scratches his balls and feels paper: in his pocket a last-minute note from Reesa to call Bartlett's office, to ask his best friend's nurse to their party this weekend. Why Lois and not Megan, Bartlett's steady, isn't clear to him.

'Love to,' responds Lois. 'Just had a card from Bangkok this morning. He mentions going on a side trip ...'

'Pattaya.' Dwight booked the package, Bartlett's first time out of North America. Away since Christmas.

'No,' says Lois. 'Says he's cutting that one short.'

'Oh?'

'Maybe Dr Day is homesick.'

'His canary's sick.'

Lois has an incoming call and puts him on hold. He waits. '... What kind of stove have you?'

'Pardon?'

'Gas?'

'Gas?'

'If it's gas,' says Lois, 'that could be why. We had a budgie when I was little who died from gas. From the pilot light. Canaries, I take it, are even more susceptible. Didn't depraved coal miners used to use them?'

'Uh huh.'

'Any UFFI?'

'Pardon? ... No. We don't carry insulation.' Insurance, for that matter. 'Listen, Lois, got a call on the line.'

'Me too ... Heard you on the radio. Ciao!'

He presses on, categorizing his remarkable travels of the year just past (travels he finds necessary to embroider sometimes in order to supplement his recommendations). WORST CARNIVAL – *Rio's Maybe the most famous and liveliest but also the wildest. If crowds aren't your thing, avoid Rio the weekend leading up to Ash Wednesday. A cacophony of aimless celebration, tom-toms, cuicas ... (alternate suggestion: Adelaide's Festival of Arts, in March of even-numbered years. Don't miss the New Gallery of Aboriginal Art. Or the zoo along the River Torrens with its walk-through aviaries).*

He travels in his office at the speed of light. At his fingertips are railway stations and shipping piers, airports and bus stations. He plots vacations for a public growing insatiable for adventures hitherto neglected: scuba diving off remote islands, helicopter skiing out of high icefields, learning a language in your own flat on the Riviera or a Swiss lakefront. He counts on Candice and Lena to cost-out his ideas, to check on how many different prices are possible for the same ticket. He's into tier systems to broaden his appeal and revolutionize his services. Designer travel on all levels, for all pocketbooks, has so far made Dwight Irving look like a genius.

He won't travel into his computer without acknowledging the risk he runs, regardless of his fail-safe method of leaving neither tickets nor shampoo behind, of carrying only replaceable travellers' cheques and a passport of carefully entered visas, entry and exit stamps. This risk is his secret. His Secret as Candice and Lena know it. Damage control, sure, if it comes to damage control, he can handle that with a system asterisked at vulnerable junctions. He can travel backwards and side to side. He can travel long-haul or short-hop. He feels free to fly off on tangents. He has a built-in shit detector (mainly for his own shit, but not exclusively). If a sleazy hotelier, say, is trying to snow him he'll find out about it from the asterisks that flash. Consistency, that virtue of the small, he shepherds with an imagination large enough to encompass the risk of inconsistency, thereby neutralizing the requirement for virtue.

Part of his Secret is fear. Not the usual fear of terrorists lurking at an unsecured airport, who might take over the plane and spoil the rest of his clients' journey (possibly, too, the rest of their lives). No, what he fears is wasting days inside his computer, following leads that junk out because a coup-threatened country suddenly closes its borders to potential travellers, and ruins whatever equation he's trying to work out in a unique three-country package. Or maybe getting bogged down in a godforsaken hotel whose rates suddenly jump during his tour of inspection over long distance telephone, causing him to scrap these digs and start the search all over for accommodation, even for another country.

Herodotus Tours specializes in small, overlooked countries. Out-of-the-way cities he pulls from memory. He'd rather forget the prosaic bookings to Honolulu and London, but these subsidize the creative side of his operation. What excites him most is trying to introduce intuition and reality and then, having got these shacked up together, to sweet-talk those to whom he hopes to sell a little rendezvous he's carefully figured out for them in Dubovka or La Rochelle. *Pushing pushing* ... Every trip is different. And every day he trips though the lines of his screen's emerald light, splintered into industrial code words, flight and train schedules, and of course currencies ... punts, pounds, pesos ... guilders, bolivars, shekels ... lira, yen, escudos ... and many kinds of dollars.

WORST INFLATION – *La Paz. Avoid banks here when changing money, also street vendors. The latter will give you the going blackmarket rate, a necessity if you hope to emerge from Bolivia with at least some money left, though you risk confiscation of all your cash by undercover fuzz for violating currency laws. Best blackmarket bets are hotels, stores, restaurants. I preferred the stores, especially bakeries with backrooms.*

Luckily, the travelling public have short memories. He has found travellers forget disappointing beds, hidden costs, the food and bad water that gave them the Aztec Two-Step. They forget *not* having had the time of their lives. They forget, after arriving with jet lag and not being able to speak the language, how the joys of travel deteriorate into meals and somehow comparing where you are with home. They don't remember anxiety felt over their holidays slipping quickly away into another year of work. *His* ongoing job is to help them forget jejune travel experiences of the past by expanding their future memories. Why shouldn't people come to think of travel as valuable to them as a retirement pension plan? Investment's his working strategy; travel as a portfolio to draw from in old age. He emphasizes experience *for its own sake.* And writes, for example, WORST DELUGE WITHOUT A BROLLY *(Foreign)* ... Even bad experience in retrospect will take on the interest of a compounding bank account. His satisfying discovery has been the travelling public will connive with him in this mismanagement of memory. They keep handing him blank cheques and refuse to worry about debt or disappointment.

4.

In his tower overlooking frozen city, its azure bay and snow-dusted mountains, the illusionist consults his watch and remembers the Conklins. He calls Reesa.

'Late night for you, I gather.'

'Hmmn. Twelvish.'

'Party?'

'Hmmn.'

'No smoke in your hair.'

'None? Someone must've been smoking. I managed to insult the diplo-mat of a small African country. Too bad I was so gentle with him earlier on camera. *Assassin.*'

'What country?'

'... Death's why I'm calling, actually. I just discovered Bartlett's canary dead in its cage.'

Dwight ponders this. 'The freezing house?'

'Probably loneliness ...'

'Maybe we should send Bartlett a telegram expressing our delight. No, I take that back.'

'Unless you throttled the poor thing. Did you?'

'Give me credit for more style.'

'I'm also calling to mention the pizza I'll leave in the oven for you and the still-sleeping Aloysius to warm up.'

'What's he look like, conked out?'

'I don't go into his bedroom, Dwight.'

'Mikos.'

She has to think. 'Sort of limp on the bottom of his cage, in a deep curtsy with his wings tucked. All that's left is stale air.'

'I was going to buy him a new cuttlebone for Christmas.'

'I asked Aloysius, by the way.'

'Is he going to?'

'He'll think about it.'

'Well, the party's this weekend. Is he likely to steal us blind beforehand, or can he read up something by then on mixing drinks?'

'Teenagers need money too, sweetheart. He's older than he looks.'

'I know, but we can't prove it.'

Hanging up he leans back and pops his suspenders like a harness. The Conklins, yes. He understands the anxieties of inexperienced travellers. When he was nineteen he took a charter to London and found travel a dis-appointing hassle, from packing his suitcase and worrying over what clothes to take, to his anxiety at the airport – whether to sit in the window seat offered him or to insist on a rear seat where, if statistically safer in event of a crash, you had to breathe all that cigarette smoke, which in time would kill you anyway. Travel he found very messy. Aching legs, noisy bedrooms, traffic fumes. Nowhere to relax. To his surprise he'd discovered he was always travelling when he was travelling. Nothing kept it at a distance long enough to let him reoil his wheels. The chain on his wallet made him feel like a callow biker. He didn't need a mirror to know his face had disappeared. Just look at the other tourists: They'd all lost touch with their faces too. Travelling had turned the younger him into a vegetable. Peas, especially. Chips and peas. He became a sop, a blotter, a doormat of impressions and down-at-heel observations. He grew fearful and depressed in London. He got his first migraine headache there. He wanted to go home as soon as British Immigration stamped his passport with an entry *clump*, which dished him the pain he endured night and day till coming home.

He has since circumnavigated the world. He's learned the value of everywhere, claims Reesa, and the price of nowhere. Which is why he finds his screen a godsend. The truth is, over the last year, he hasn't visited any of these cities, hotels or countries on his New Year's list. He hasn't visited any of them in any year. Dwight has not, in fact, left Canada since he was nineteen. An impostor's memory he believes is part of a consultant's success. He travels no farther than his morning jogs take him round the lagoon and into the park's forest – past late-night gays loitering like foreign exchange dealers in a country dependent on its black market, in a virtueless world indifferent to their particular country's survival. This he finds intriguing.

He sometimes wonders why he isn't more worried about exposure. But exposing himself to risk just seems to add to his confidence. Those in on his Secret are discreet. His secretaries, for example, live off the avails and do their best not to break up his trains of thought and flights of fancy. They play along to keep the Conklins and others at bay while he's composing his travels. His personal experiences or lack of them are really secondary to the truth of what he has to say about the past.

His discovery that people enjoy their travels far more in retrospect than at the time of travelling was crucial to his understanding of the business. Easier to sell travel to prospective clients if he can get them remembering their journey before they go. The slides he purchases from abroad help. And his anecdotes and verbal pictures over the radio reap dividends for Herodotus Tours. Even his office posters serve to conjure up atmospheres recollected in tranquillity. 'Look at Machu Picchu, Mr Belknap. I want you to sleep on that picture and come see me in the morning ...' The hypnotic suggestion.

The shaping of experience seems to Dwight a frame around the portrait he cheerfully paints with willing clients in mind. A self-portrait or a portrait of *them* amounts to the same thing. If it's you in the picture – on the steps of that cathedral in Cuzco, or buying dyed cloth in this mountain town of San Cristóbal de las Casas – then the stumpy beggar over there doesn't exist and neither do your exhausted pins. Nor thirst and vapid boredom. A good portrait hasn't a whiff of the baffling and contradictory impressions of travel in the flesh. His special task is to get potential clients remembering what they've not yet seen. Tourism since Thomas Cook has survived on the lie of such history.

Pushing pushing ...

Just because he dislikes travelling himself doesn't mean he can't convince clients like the Conklins of the bankableness of experience abroad. The past is an important illusion. 'Remember, make history. Travel.' What matter if he uses his imagination to make *up* the past? No reason not to trust him: He's a qualified member of ACTA, ARTA, CITC and knows his Bible, *Principles and Procedures of Travel Counselling*, inside out ... 'The travel agency is totally a service industry dealing in intangible products. The consumer pays for something which cannot be returned, unlike clothing or an appliance ... Often, he has no more than a glance at a picture of a hotel or a beautiful landscape.' He has never seen why, if travel is so intangible, he needs to bother with the effort of undertaking it himself. The form is clearly in the packaging. Better he stay faithful to the packaging and deliver a product wrapped up to the last detail. People respond to an honest broker and keep coming back, whether or not he plays the market himself.

The Conklins, yes. Dwight finds himself counselling this retired couple who resemble his usual clientele in law and finance only in their conservative taste. 'Listen, folks. You could visit any city you want to – forgive me, but you've earned it. I'm very grateful you came in today to discuss your dream trip ...'

The Conklins study his framed B.Comm. on the wall. They study him. Blue-eyed young bachelor, deserving of his success and growing reputation. He knows the world and where to go in it. Knows how to listen, they sense.

The retired gentleman crosses his legs, still wondering if he and the wife ought to be bothering a consultant of his reputation with their small potatoes. 'We hear you on the radio. We figured right now seemed a good time to call for a consultation, in case we're missing out on something. Maureen here says we might be – not ever having travelled and that.'

'Well, if I may say so, sir, Mrs Conklin was right. People deserve to taste the fruits of their labour. And a foreign country's the place to start, well away from this weird cold snap we're having. Travel's an investment in yourselves. The future isn't going to wait, believe me.'

He gestures at his walls. 'Pick a poster. A thousand words, yes?'

They look. They look at bright posters beckoning them to beaches, cathedrals, pyramids. Maureen has a feeling her new kneetop boots are marking the carpet. She keeps trying to sit sideways.

'Look at Mexico City ... Splendid destination for an exotic holiday. The Reforma? Chapultepec Castle?' Dwight closes his eyes, recalling many happy memories. He sounds just like he does on the radio. 'Museum of Anthropology, and that delicious restaurant underneath it –' He reopens his eyes in alarm. 'My God, I've forgotten its name – but you'll love the Chilean wine. A fine sauvignon blanc of Errazuriz Panquehue. And of course the Zona Rosa and all those boutiques and smart cafés ...? Not *too* smart, mind you. El Refugio, for examp, with its delicious moué dishes?' Frank and Maureen glance at each other.

'Yes, Candy, what is it?'

'Would you like to see the new buttons, Mr Irving? They've just arrived.' The Conklins turn in their chairs. She's holding up blue badges with white slogans:

MAKE HISTORY

TRAVEL

HERODOTUS TOURS

'Like me to pin one to your lapel, Mr Conklin?'

And she does, a pretty young thing in blonde hair and a maroon skirt. The place seems so casual it's surprising they can do the volume of business the rent must require. Dwight watches Frank taking it all in, as the owner (him) rambles on.

'After two or three days in Mexico City, there'd be no reason not to fly to Cozumel for Easter. Would there?'

Maureen looks at Frank. Would there? A large map is unfolded before them on Dwight's desk.

'White beaches and wonderful hotels, under blue skies?'

'Acapulco?' Frank asks.

'Acapulco on the way back, Mr Conklin. Three or four nights in

Acapulco, or else the quieter Puerto Escondido, watching Pacific sunsets – just to compare them with Gulf of Mexican sunsets – no comparison, in my opinion, but I'd be interested to hear what you folks thought.'

Sandy hair and a nice manner, unassuming. Not watching his watch. Watching them. He seems pleased with his company's new buttons, studying Mr Conklin's lapel.

'Or,' he goes on, 'we could put together a package for you that included Lima. Peru? First Peru – then Mexico to relax in on your way home. We could cut out the pyramids and focus on the beach. Or else forget the humidity and visit San Miguel, in the pretty mountains north of Mexico City?'

'My head is a sponge,' says Maureen. 'I love to hear about all this.'

So Dwight tells them a couple of elegant little anecdotes about tourist life in Lima and Machu Picchu. He could probably find them a tour, if they were interested, which also took in some tortoise-watching on the Galapagos Islands for examp. '... Before flying back to Quito, *then* on to Mexico City?' His clients smile, shaking their heads.

'Listen,' he confides, 'We recently booked a client to Bangkok who's never travelled outside North America in his life. Late bloomers take longer to get going, so what?' He flops back in his chair, palms on desk, glancing at his watch. 'I think it's great the way people are getting off on travel these days ... discovering it for themselves.' He sounds genuinely enthusiastic about his profession, which to a couple like the Conklins is a real pleasure in this age of the fast-buck artist.

They gather themselves in from the horizons of his maps, modestly rearranging their hands so as not to tip themselves one way or the other. They tuck his brochures in their pockets. They promise to give his suggestions serious consideration when they get time to mull them all over, check their bank account, maybe consult the kids. 'Actually, we were kind of just thinking about Disneyland or some place nearer home,' admits Frank. 'She's never been to Disneyland.'

'Oh, *Frank*.'

Frank is teasing. He smiles at Maureen.

'Okay,' he says to Dwight. 'We'll take the sunset package, that one you were talking about in Mexico.'

'Oh, Frank!' The pleasure in her voice pleasures Frank. 'See? You got through to my housebound husband, Mr Irving.'

'We do our research very thoroughly, Mrs Conklin, including husbands.'

They laugh.

This is a way nicer view than Frank expected, even from the sixteenth floor. You can see all the freighters at anchor in the bay. The streets look very tidy from up here, clean.

Maureen says, 'Just look at Stanley Park down there.'

Soon Dwight's gently urging them into his secretaries' office, where he instructs the younger Lena to give these people, these first-ever wearers of Herodotus's new badges, the red-carpet treatment. He passes on his general suggestions about Mexico, and leaves it to her to work out details to the Conklins' satisfaction.

'Thanks, folks. She'll treat you right.'

'Thank *you*, Mr Irving,' says Mrs Conklin. He has such a nice smile.

Later, Candice pops in with a handful of the white and blue badges that glitter with the promise of a nifty idea. But she's wondering about their target market. 'Do we really expect people to wear them on their suits, turning themselves into little sandwich boards?'

No surprise to her that Dwight's on top of it. 'A trip, Candy. We're going to offer a trip for lovers somewhere, maybe Las Vegas, if the wearer happens to be the first person our roving scout spots inside city limits on Valentine's Day wearing a Herodotus Tours badge.'

Candice looks a little doubtful. He can see her hazel irises slightly contract. She keeps a tighter rein on expenditures than he does. 'We'd better order some more then,' she says, 'to make it a blitz that'll pay its own way. Publicity-wise.'

He reassures her. 'I didn't say it'd be a free trip. We'll offer a discount.'

5.

It's on his trek to the CBC studios that the earthquake strikes along Georgia. He thinks maybe some heavy truck has tipped over in the street. He's almost relieved to hear what sounds like a sudden windstorm. When he sees the wide street waving up and down like an asphalt ribbon, he does what comes naturally to him: cowers under his briefcase.

The shock lasts half a minute, a minute. The Birks clock on the corner lurches on its pedestal. People don't know what to make of the city's sudden wooziness, a woman in smart clothes clobbered by a mugger. Sidewalks heave at their feet. Shopping bags drop, scarves dangle, overcoats slide down kneecapped bodies. Nothing seems quite as secure to Dwight now as the past. He takes in the present from under his Dial-A-Lock case: traffic lights bouncing on overhead cables: the jammed green signal blinking, blinking: the thick noon traffic coming to a dead halt. Cracks in the street have opened up in several spots, and in one place the pavement has disappeared down a hole large enough to swallow a Sprint or a Falcon.

The stillness following is like one minute of silence for those lost in a recent war. Dwight's never heard such urban silence in his life. Pedestrians are discovering themselves in foolish postures, rigid with expectation, awaiting the resumption of artillery shelling from an advance unit of East Side guerrillas. They resemble dance partners when the music is killed to spotlight the funniest poses. A woman in red flatties has stepped right out of them on the freezing sidewalk. A lawyer type in a camelhair coat is sitting on the curb hunched up in a ball. One guy in a three-piecer has managed to keep hold of his tony fedora, but his pants have fallen down around his ankle hose.

When another minute passes and the earth in faulty health seems unlikely to sneeze again, motorists, half out of their zigzag vehicles, climb entirely out and circle tires, shaking heads, exchanging excited comments with pedestrians and one another. Bus drivers down Granville are resetting trolley poles to overhead wires, surprised to hear the long metal carcasses start humming again, their lights come on. Dwight discovers his briefcase on the pavement. He bends over and rubs his palm tenderly across the heavy bruise.

'Anybody see what happened?' asks a small-voiced woman with a scrambled hairdo. 'Was it a bomb?'

'Earthquake,' growls an elderly man in a yellow ski jacket.

The bright sun seems unreal now, and people begin stepping back into shoes, pulling up pants. Drivers rearrange stripped seatbelts. Everyone resembles lunchtime adulterers, preparing themselves for an imminent return to the real world. To respectability, thinks Dwight. Nobody quite knows whether to stay on for a chat, light up a post-coital weed, or get the hell back to the office pretending nothing juicy has happened. Nobody, except for one man dressed in a stained raincoat and worn-out Hush Puppies.

This crank on the corner, that Dwight usually sees waving his rosary over a framed portrait of Our Crucified Saviour, has recovered rather sooner than most and is now strolling up and down the buckled sidewalk, holding his beads aloft and saying calmly, 'Jerusalem. Did the earth not shake under Jerusalem?' It's unquestionably this patient man's finest hour.

Dwight rebuttons his coat and adjusts his necktie in the frigid air. With everybody now looking at everybody else, half smiling, shaking heads in hopeful relief, they seem to be wondering who to turn to for confirmation of the event. For once Dwight feels spooky *being* the news: being in it, in the picture. It feels so shapeless. The picture needs some frame, a screen.

Just before 1:00 p.m. local time he claps on headphones and prepares to talk travel with Toronto. He's taping for the next morning, since he refuses to get up three hours early to oblige eastern time zones – give up his jog and hustle down here to stir his brain with the decaffeinated silt the CBC calls coffee. He gets away with this West Coast arrogance. Rupert Wajda insists on having him, possibly because Rupert seldom travels outside Canada himself and relishes hearing how far people are willing to go for a few harsh days in a foreign sun. He'd be astonished to discover Dwight doesn't travel either. That everything Dwight's telling him this afternoon is predicated on a lie.

The only thing he doesn't believe is Dwight's mention of the earthquake.

'Oh yeah?' chuckles Rupert. 'That like your daffodils in January?'

'Not this winter, Rupert. Temporary glitch in the weather. We're playing hockey on Lost Lagoon, believe it or not.'

Rupert chuckles. 'Liar!'

'Hey, it's true.'

'Tell me, Dwight, where should I be heading this week? Gimme some bargains.'

So Dwight Irving does his ten minutes' worth of *Where In the World?* for national listeners looking for hot tips in the post-New Year's market. From his briefcase he usually pulls a list of scoops poached from newsletters of travel clubs he belongs to, whose bargains are available to anyone willing to travel either at the last minute, i.e. after midnight, in the middle of a transitional week between one month and the next; or aboard a Siesta Boeing 707 that hasn't been reserviced since before a turbulent charter flight to Wellington carrying the Irish National Rugger Team to a crushing string of losses throughout the Antipodes.

This afternoon, unfortunately, the quake has rearranged or remagnetized the tumblers on Dwight's lock. He can't get into his briefcase. So he's forced back on memory. Listeners enjoy his appearances not so much for his bargains, anyway (who can afford to cut out for San Antonio at the drop of a hat?), but for personal anecdotes he sprinkles liberally through his interviews: fishing in the Florida Keys and losing his spinning reel; birdwatching in the Argentine with a screwball Swede in a polkadot culotte; eating soup in a Belgrade restaurant. The real perk is the publicity he garners for Herodotus Tours. He hopes to become a national operation inside of five years.

Later, driving home from his office, Dwight tunes in to the local phone-in shows recounting everyone's earthquake. 'Where were you when the Big One struck?' What catches his interest is how the animals behaved. A university behavioural scientist reports how his experimental herd of llamas began to alert him to something unexpected as long as three days ago. They were acting antsy, bunched up in one corner of their pen. This empirical evidence of a lurking sixth sense made the scientist deduce something might be cooking. 'But don't animals also act odd when a rainstorm's coming?' the moderator rejoins. True, possibly just a coincidence, admits the scientist, sounding suitably skeptical of correspondence theory; except his own backbone had started acting up that same day and he'd never had backache in his life! Still on animals, a dairy farmer up the valley where the dikes have broken phones in to comment on the unusually distended udders of his cows at dawn today. 'I knew it wasn't natural like. You understand what I'm telling you?'

No one phones in to say boo about canaries.

6.

After their party Dwight and Reesa crawl into bed at 5:00 a.m. They lie side by side too cranked up on booze, coffee, and conversation for sleep. A hundred people. A hundred and fifty people. Aloysius had tended bar. This spike-haired foster charge of theirs, inherited from Dwight's mother, had consented to barkeep for seventy-five dollars if guests would be willing to tell him how to mix their drinks. Aloysius didn't drink himself, a small mercy for which they were pathetically grateful.

'He asked me afterwards if you can patent a drink.'

'What drink?'

'The Earth Rumbler he called it. He started pouring it and it was a big hit. Everybody was still talking about the quake. Rum. Orange juice. Gin.'

'Is that legal?'

'I actually overheard him telling Sheila Derrick he was a refugee from an Asian region of the USSR.'

This information interests the travel consultant. 'Why, I wonder? What could be more exotic than Bombay?'

'Tashkent, apparently.'

In a bizarre way Aloysius is probably Dwight's stepbrother, except for the fact Dwight is acting as his guardian, a stand-in father for his own mother who found a foster son of Aloysius's generation too much to handle. Dwight doesn't know whether to regard him as Jacob, Cain, or a pain in the butt. He worries about this teenager getting out of hand here in the way he had not so long ago at his mother's. Aloysius claimed her place had reminded him of an oasis for caravans without any Arabs. *Arabs?* That was why he left.

'Maybe it was grapefruit juice,' remarks Reesa, reconsidering. '... With the rum and gin.'

They try to drift off but the early morning air is frigid. He turns the lamp back on, hoping to take the frost off the duvet. He wonders why, with the party's hot air having had all night to rise, their bedroom shouldn't be warmer now, even with no insulation in the walls. The hot air seems to have floated on up to the third floor and through the roof: the party's energy now dissipating in the stratosphere. Where was the spinoff bonus for hosts?

'How come the mayor likes to chat you up in corners?' Dwight hadn't known what to make of the mayor's interest in his wife.

'The only place he can breathe. Says he's allergic to smoke.' She sort of snuggles closer. 'How was *your* party?'

He scratches his stubble. 'Did a little business. Talked some shop. Two stars.'

'Three stars being ...?'

He wonders if this is criticism or mild commiseration.

'Three stars being that New Year's bash last week in London. You read this? Empty five-million-dollar mansion near Hampstead Heath, owned by an absent Arab, which a few squatters crash and decide to welcome in the new year. They start log fires in eight fireplaces and phone friends. These friends phone friends, the word spreads. It's like the rich landlord inviting all the dispossessed he can find to come to his banquet, except there's no banquet. There's no landlord.'

'Sounds to me like an urban myth.'

'I saw it in the paper. The firewood runs out, antiques and Oriental carpets start going up. Party spills out of the house into two swimming pools. When the fuzz arrives, long after auld lang syne, most crashers have left. One of the squatters estimates probably two thousand of them were there at midnight. That's the kind of party you give three stars to.'

'Sounds like an old frat bash.'

Dwight yawns and plumps his pillow.

And wonders if their own landlord wouldn't thank them for throwing a party that trashed this place. Save him serving notice. Give him an excuse to pull it down sooner for a condo tower.

As paying squatters he and Reesa are downwardly mobile, the envy of guests who wish they themselves had the guts to swap mortgages for a month-to-month rent in such a wonderful old house. But it's a house in severe decline. The rent is low in exchange for no lease, no security. They share the rent with his best friend, Bartlett Day, a chiropractor. A once elegant place, with oak staircase and wide landings, gingerbread decorations and odd turrets – all decaying from lack of upkeep. They feel cheap sometimes, but why pump money into something doomed? Water in, heat out. They get admired for choosing to pump equity into Herodotus Tours instead.

Reesa says, 'I suppose we're dead in the water when the bulldozer arrives.' She connives at her husband's illusions. She is her husband's illusions.

'Nonsense. We'll move in with my mother.'

'And have our friends end up with the last laugh? I'd hate to lose my independence.' Most of their friends derive from her four years of interviewing the local movers and shakers on *City, City*, an after-supper TV show.

They lie listening to a car warming itself in the street below. The temperature has fallen to two or three hundred below zero. Dwight sees everybody's espadrilles hibernating in closets waiting for the Ice Age to be over. No snow falling: How could it from a starry sky? He thinks if a climatic change is coming it'll only improve business with its penetrating frosts. Reesa reaches over and puts out the light. 'Sweetheart ...?'

'What is it we say?' he asks her. 'We can snow-ski in the morning and water-ski in the afternoon?'

'When?'

'Isn't it one of our civic clichés?'

'Swim, I think.' She removes his hand from under the duvet and begins to push down his cuticles with her thumbnail. 'Ski in the morning, swim in the afternoon.' But the notion of any heavy exercise mystifies Reesa Potts. 'Why?'

'You mean you think we need a new cliché?'

'No, why do you ask?'

'I've been wondering why I always have to be sending travellers in the other direction. Why couldn't Herodotus corner the market on here, too? You know, *import* tours?'

Pushing pushing.

'... Dwight?'

'Hm?'

'I'd like to have a child before death do us part. *N'est-ce pas?*'

Solemnly, he touches her lips. 'We have Aloysius.' They both snort with laughter. He makes a v-sign and draws her eyelids gently down. 'He can't spell. On the other hand he may be a genius who needs our undivided attention. Not to mention a dreamer and a hustler. It makes him quite exotic, I think.'

'My biological clock is running out.'

'You're only thirty-two, biscuit.'

'I feel older.'

'Smart people do. I read that somewhere about you honours lit types. Who's going to take care of a child?'

'My mother. Maybe a nanny? I'm home most days till mid-afternoon. Families are communal affairs.'

'Your mother's a vegetarian. So's your grandmother.'

'I wish you'd concentrate on the question, Dwight ...' The question at hand is her rubbing him (or so he now feels her) between his legs. She asks, 'What are you talking about, sweetheart. Hmm?'

'Your maternal line. Who knows what drinking carrot juice has done to your genetic potential for breast feeding?'

She withdraws her hand, disappointed. Maybe not. Maybe he is just imagining she is disappointed. He lies here limp and unruffled.

He lies here awake in the black dawn. Where it all ends is usually in bed, for tourists and homebodies alike. Warm air blowing into the structure from all along the base of its geodesic dome, where concrete walls rise up to meet a sky of triangular panes. The palm fronds and fig leaves are storm-tossed at the roof's circumference. The foliage strains at the edges for expansion.

Condensation creates a lovely, humid bubble.

He senses this is the ideal way to travel. Why go to the tropics when he can stay home and smell the same vegetation, the same soft air, the same rich earth out of which all kinds of flowers have been force-grown? He listens to the furnace. He can imagine Bartlett's canary's heart beating with the weight of a damp pea.

May, 2086

Stayed up late last night to watch fireworks over the bay. Can still remember the first centenary, when exploding colours hurt my head. Notably the red, or maybe it was the yellow, stars. Mother, I remember, kept me up late with Granny, to watch the Exposition open. We stood on a shore somewhere with Daddy. In the fuss people buzzed, their faces buttered and jammed in the starry light. After so long, queer how you remember. Little airplanes circling in the dark. Yachts in the bay anchored in close. Earlier that night we paid my great-grandmother a visit, a hundred herself that year. All of them had a

little tipple including Old Granny. Something has given me the same head again this morning.

A wet May. Renaldo calls to say he is off to the races this afternoon. At his age he ought to be in a place like Hygeia too. Calls to say do I know the odds on Piffle Diffle. Some name like that. I suppose I could afford to encourage my own son with the mudders. But his grandfather was a gambler and lost everything.

Renewed threats from this man E. He gets warnings, but only stares at the nurse while teeth shift in his noggin like continental plates. It doesn't figure. I think he has gone to seed and blown away in the wind. Why does he hate me?

Should not discount the possibility he is an old enemy I forgot I had. He smells, sitting in his wheelchair, of the Lysol soap they use to sterilize the floor. Throws tantrums like a baby. I hope he's harmless. But he destroyed the tea trolley last week with one swing of his stick. He has degenerated. We all have. I for example have cut my walks from three a day to two.

My doctor slipped in under cover of the fireworks. In and up the elevator to my keep in the sky. He is furtive around Hygeia, avoiding physicians who call him the Quack. They prefer to repress our diseases in sterner ways, lest we be tempted to view them as piddling. And why shouldn't we, with this view of mountains? He wonders if they miss the point sometimes.

His services are not covered by normal benefits so I pay extra. Head Nurse is skeptical, but doesn't think therapy like his can harm me. I am just salt for his eggtimer, she says. Her medical fashion frowns on elixirs. But I doubt his is an elixir. Not an *end*, he insists, but a means. He pesters me nicely to imagine the future. At my age, good night! It is kind of fun. For example, staring out the window and seeing my city. This is his therapy.

He thinks if I will only see things as if I'm looking back on them, then I should experience what is golden about time as I'm living it. *You will enjoy life more.* God, the earnestness. You have to practise on your own, he counsels, till holistic health becomes a habit. Why does every doctor these days think himself a holist?

'Think of the present as an ideal and it makes the future your reality. That way it can never be an end. Future is the house for your imaginary present.' Oh yeah? Prescribe me another. 'This contradicts the common medical creed that the present is something to be cured by thinking younger. No, you'll feel a lot healthier if you just try to remember what you're looking at.'

He encourages me to keep practising. I sometimes think his therapy makes me feel nothing, except old. 'Precisely,' he murmurs. Is this what I need? 'Exactly,' he reassures, 'how else can you expect to know your age?' I don't really want to know my age. But he persists. 'It's healthy to feel old, if you do it right. Feeling old my way is feeling what I call the glow.' He prescribes all this freely.

It isn't, of course. Neither is the odd bottle

of hootch he smuggles in. I sometimes think this is what he means by feeling the glow – but never mind. 'Treat your body as you do this ideal present. Which means wasting it by daydreaming, unplugging your eyes to see better.' He must think I have a lifetime left. 'I like the way you're a spendthrift with that diary. Keep it up.' It is odd how diligence to one mind is masturbation to another.

He wears a crisp white coat and keeps his thick hair tidy with a hint of oil. No accent, yet I hear the faintest of inflections goading me on. I wonder if this is what I hear when my grandson speaks. Ambition? Conceit?

On the rare occasions when his therapy succeeds it produces a wonderful feeling. I have been practising it going on five years now. Don't quite know if it's doing me any good. My carcass sputters on, so maybe it is.

Pedro my grandson thinks it's loony. But what does a ship insurer know? This is the trouble with middle age, skeptical of the new, trying to reconcile itself with the old. Sometimes think I embraced the new too readily! In public life you had to or you sank. A circus. I wonder if, compared to my ancestors, I ever had a private life?

Those exploding stars can't be stuffed back in their cylinders except in my diary. Following this doctor's roguish therapy I suppose it possible to venture all the way back to the fuse and the unstruck match? Can still see stars in the rain this morning. I think what he intends for me, with so much time on my hands, is to mistreat its laws with impunity and imbibe the glow. Pardon me, the Glow.

Arriba! Hangover is not beyond me yet.

Like H it isn't.

This bleak tower could do with a shakedown and E. seems the only person left to wave a stick at it. A plague on both our houses.

Our cureless disease of aging is the natural law. Is there any court that would decide against such a killer?

My father used to ask me, as he raked leaves, where do stories go? I think it comforted him to speculate about his split life. I honestly think I wondered more where stories came from.

I don't understand my own much better than I understand this city. Evergreen Playground, Lotus Land, God's Country ... The future in paradise has always been with us without our ever catching up to it. And now we've started going backwards. Did I ever look past the posters and our bureau of tourism? Often I was too busy. No metropolis likes to

reflect for long on its past. I found Vancouver vital in too simple a way to bother over in public, when any wonder I might have expressed would've been taken as rhetorical naiveté or political archness.

Still, how can so many people live here when so few resources seem to support them? When did services like garbage collection and the sewers coincide to keep us clean? Who poured and dated our sidewalks?

Electricity like blood courses in the civic body. Cut its supply and we are dark indeed. I still marvel at the power lines and water mains, especially with supplies now breaking down.

Our centennial explosions, yes, I remember them too. To think I was in charge for so long and never understood squat.

Chapter 3

The Question of Our Age

ON HIS DAY OFF DWIGHT sleeps in. But by skipping his morning run around the lagoon, he can overcome his Saturday laziness and get to the office within a half hour of his usual 7:00 a.m. *Stay close to your desk and never go to sea and you all may be rulers of the Queen's navy …* The tenor-doing-the-baritone swanks in from the elevator, surprised to find neither Candice nor Lena quick with his own enthusiasm for travel. His secretaries have yet to arrive. It takes him a moment to remember they don't come in on weekends at all.

He now groans in disbelief. Lena has failed to wrap up the Fatima package: twelve airline tickets left to be paid for, hotels in Lisbon and Albufeira to book, and enough restaurant vouchers for two days along the Algarve. He'd promised vouchers with his own designer signature, in this case a side trip to taste the different ways Portuguese cook fish. Fish? To remind his twelve Catholic pilgrims how they used to eat fish every Friday, before Pope Somebody the First changed the rules, and incidentally drove fishmongers to the brink of blasphemy. *Pushing pushing.*

All this itinerizing to finish before he's free to start the work he came in to do. Saturday is supposed to be his day to think himself clear out to the frontiers. He consults his watch. Reesa claims he loves these excuses to feel long-suffering, it eases his conscience about lying in public.

Today he still hopes to work on his board game. He can finally see where it's heading, or where it should be heading if he intends to finish and copyright it before someone else scoops him. JetSet is a travel game for couch potatoes who'll be tempted to buy it as a substitute for the real thing. He knows travel for most people is two, at most four weeks a year. What happens to their wanderlust during the other eleven months? He wants to tap into the market among travellers stuck at home. Dwight wants © Herodotus Tours to encircle them with a total travelling experience. He wants to encompass whole families in the comfort of their own homes. He boots up his Apple, and overhears Candice's sunny voice in the outer office.

'... *Tours is closed today. But if you have any message to leave, any question about your reservations, or a general inquiry about one of our advertised tours, we'll be pleased to get back to you if you leave your name and number at the sound of the beep ... Make history, don't forget, travel Herodotus Tours!* BEEP ... *Dwight, about a new associate of mine.*' Aloysius. What's he doing up this early? '... *This man was hinting at some business in the travel trade, maybe in the next two months. So I am finding out the best prices to fly groups from Delhi. I want to give you first crack. No hurry. Just be thinking.*'

Incredible. Comes up with this whopper to ingratiate himself after stealing Reesa's car and my mailing list. *What* associate? Memo: Press him some more on why he's harassing my clients: Lay down the law.

Not getting tough with Aloysius reminds him of his other recent delinquencies: a newspaper column overdue, guide books on Italy to read before his next radio program, a late issue of *Afar* to get to the printer. Also a briefing paper to his banker. His banker thinks he needs to be more creative in his financing ideas. He requires a position paper to make sure he (Dwight) has his (the banker's) priorities in order, poised as Herodotus Tours is on the threshold of opening up two new branch offices on the strength of present equity. HT's credit line at the bank is running out. He'll need more collateral. Which is why, speaking of creative ideas, he's counting on his frat-reunion this evening to help him reestablish old contacts.

His plan is to market JetSet and expand his empire with the royalties. Dice-rolling players will aspire by the thousands to reach his ideal city, overcoming hardships along the way, double-bookings and missed planes, bureaucratic delays and foul-mouthed terrorists, to find exotic exile at last. He buzzes with possibilities to this end. Successful players will then be free to live as if they *were* travelling, having found the traveller's equivalent of home away from home in a rapturous city. The thing is, the game should go on till all players have a chance to become citizens.

So it needs to be defined, his imaginary city. Sketched, given some past, framed before marketing. It needs to acquire the cachet of a famous city, known and rewarded by the stroke of recognition among tourists who yearn to visit it. You sell from the centre, Dwight's learned. You go from the known to the unknown. This is the nature of travel and why he personally fears it. JetSet is to begin in each player's home town, go on to famous capitals of the world, before veering off on tangents determined by chance, circumstance, and each traveller's talent for surviving disaster. His ideal city has to be at the edge, not only of a sea, but of public imagination. It couldn't be exotic in any other locale. Otherwise, what reward in finally attaining it?

... and curling streets. No numbered avenues, no grid system. Streets with artists' names. A river winds through from hinterland to sea (cf. map). Plane trees along streets, chestnuts, Japanese plum. Palms too. Flame and neem – why not? – full of parrots. Robins. Where south meets north.

He plans to issue replicas of airline tickets and travellers' cheques, hotel keys, train and freighter tickets, maybe menus from restaurants along the way. The idea is to *avoid* getting delayed at the airport or stranded in a bad hotel ... or losing your travellers' cheques or ordering the wrong dish or making dumb decisions. Avoidance is the key. Having to spend time in a foreign hospital, with insufficient medical coverage and a surly staff, *isn't* one of the cards you want to draw.

Dwight is playing an alternate game of avoidance with finance copyrighters, corporate and trademark lawyers, computer programmers and graphic designers: all necessary, he understands, to market a board game. Where's the extra capital going to come from, when he can barely finance expansion of his main operation? He has to wonder why he's *bothering* to expand it (with interior decorators, real estate agents, new office staff) when he senses the wave of the future is in miniaturization.

Five hours later, still annoyed at Lena, he's falling to his underground car through floors that light up like Ping Pong balls in the lottery.

2.

'It clearly isn't a hoax. That's one conclusion I've come to. The evidence, dear, is overwhelming. I could cite you chapter and verse ...' The old St. Veronica try. Marlene Irving, pouring herself more coffee, unwilling to let her younger son go the way of all pagans. This magazine article will save him. They sit at the pine table in her kitchen, overlooking the swimming pool covered in a tarpaulin. Rain is falling against the bare lattices on the patio.

'If you had *me* on your radio show, as a guest, I'd tell everyone to fly to Turin.'

'Would you? I should have you.'

She narrows her eyes at him, preparing to drag on her Matinee. 'I'm not falling out of trees with money, dear. I thought Herodotus Tours was getting along like a house on fire.'

She taps ash into a glass tray enclosed in a car tire, a Goodyear advertising gimmick from the fifties. He's surprised how unworn the tread remains, considering how much wear and tear she's inflicted on her lungs down the years.

'It is.' He helps himself to one of the last pieces of Christmas cake. 'I say it wasn't?'

'Save some for your brother. He's still glued to his new aquarium. I think the angelfish are playing to his spiritual appetites.' She lifts a quizzical eyebrow in Dwight's direction. He catches a whiff of cheap perfume. Her one concession to economy, apart from tacky ashtrays.

'So what's the big deal,' he asks, pretending interest in her article, 'about your latest evidence? You're saying this is unusual?' He points to what looks like an X-ray image. She has already ticked through the article with a red pen, hear-hearing its margins with 'N.B.!'

'*I'm* not saying it, Dwight. These scientists and engineers from Los Alamos are saying it. Top laser and chemistry men, for heaven's sake, who spent a whole week studying it in Turin, with the complete cooperation of Cardinal Ballestrero and the Sisters of Saint Joseph ... or is it the Holy Clares? ... the ones who've looked after this relic, I don't remember, for five hundred years, ever since it came from France, and probably before that Constantinople, in the sixth century.'

'Probably?'

'Okay, Smart Pants ...' she blows smoke his way. 'So far the important discoveries are about the burial garment. The actual cloth. We can all agree on that. Up till now, the link between the Constantinople shroud and this one is just guesswork. But once the carbon dating is done I fear you among many, dear, will be in for a lot of soul-searching.'

Spoken with the satisfaction of a woman who has consumed her data in delicate, nutritious bites. His mother gives her tinted hair a little pat. She usually pats it before slipping into another voice, as a tip-off. In this case it's her nasal Barbara Walters imitation. 'This isn't another quack relic like a piece of the True Cross, or one of its nails ... Do yourself a favour, Dwight, and take this bombshell home to read. The evidence is *all* here.' She touches her neck self-consciously.

Excessive, even obsessive, she knows he thinks he can excuse his own tendencies in the same direction by pointing to her. Both with the gift of the gab. Both willing to go overboard to gaff a fish. But his mother's also a stubborn lady. She appreciates limits, so religion often enters the picture. Not that the picture's perspective is thereby limited. Not at all, she'd argue. You just have to remember to stay inside the frame. Her neck wattle has begun to wag a little.

'That photograph,' she says, gesturing like a well-bred woman, aware of the knockers on her wedding ring, keeping her palm up and diamonds from view. 'Eyelids, moustache, pigtail – what sort of medieval artist could've faked those kinds of details and gotten away with it around today's scientists? Dwight, even the blood from the crown of thorns. Thirty top scientists, dear, volunteering to discredit the shroud, if they could – all cocks of the walk in their fields – and so far turning up nothing, though they've analysed it chemically, electromagnetically, *even* – would you believe? – three-dimensionally, and not one X-ray has shown it to be a flimflam. These are the same sort of tests that proved Piltdown Man was a hoax, Dwight, in a matter of *minutes*. Except that was 1955, and science today has advanced light years since 1955.' She smiles sweetly at her son, confident of her case. 'Wouldn't you say?'

She inhales smoke, and without releasing it swallows more coffee. 'You were a rookie altar boy in 1955. And this shroud is turning men your age back into believers. That's all I have to say.' Smoke surfaces through her nostrils, curling into little tusks.

'So what happened to the threads?'

'Nothing.' More smoke surfaces, diminished in volume he thinks by the voyage. Yet another layer of soot left behind in darkness. His mother expands, still leaking vapours. 'The threads from the shroud they decided to keep in little glass vials in Los Alamos. In a safe there. The scientists are allowed to borrow them to test every which way you can imagine.'

'But not with carbon, you were saying. There's a holdup for some reason on the carbon.'

Marlene Irving sighs. Swallows more coffee, pokes out her cigarette. Opens her red thermos to check on her level of addiction. Nothing left when she tips spout into mug. She is supposed to cut down on the two c's in her life: caffeine and cigarettes. 'Can't,' she'll say. That's her third c, disinheriting the first two, though her doctor's advice remains the same.

'"*Control and containment*",' she mimics, '"*caffeine and cigarettes.*" Makes me feel like a valve-capper at the water board. I'm always running to the w.c.' Her problem in retaining liquids makes her the thirstiest relative he has. He only has two relatives left.

His father would listen to her out of politeness and then disappear into his greenhouse. He didn't interfere with her bringing the boys up Catholic. English Protestant, a specialist in internal medicine, survivor of a Hong Kong prison camp before his sons' births, he died before Dwight turned twelve. After his death, Marlene was always going off and leaving her two sons with their nanny – out to meetings of the Catholic Women's League, Elizabeth Fry Society, Save the Children – as if in atonement for her husband's death.

'For one very interesting reason,' she now answers, about the delay in carbon testing. She replaces the thermos lid. It's clear to him she thinks carbon dating of the shroud will turn stray sheep like him into lambs of God.

'... On the very morning in Rome that these same scientists had come to the Vatican for an audience with the Pope, to present their preliminary findings, to get *his* support for their dating the shroud with carbon-14 ... that was the *same* morning, Dwight, the Holy Father was shot point-blank in the stomach in St. Peter's Square by that Turkish terrorist.'

By her tone she evidently considers these two events more than coincidental. He's inclined to agree, but for other reasons. The gutsy Pope wanted to avoid carbon dating at any cost. 'Hasn't he recovered by now?' He nibbles a stray maraschino cherry with the texture of a washer.

'Well,' says his mother. 'Read the article and you'll see Cardinal Ballestrero himself is willing to give permission for C-14 tests. But the flock, so to speak, is still weak.'

'You mean the Holy Eclairs?'

'Us. The Apostolic See. The flock.'

'Are you unwilling?'

'I would welcome it.' She lights another cigarette with one of her long matches from the Spanish grill at her favourite downtown hotel, where she meets Monsignor Chucklehead from the cathedral for lunch. 'It would be no blow to me if the whole shroud turned out to be a hoax, Dwight. Not that I believe it will, with this evidence ...'

His brother now backs into the kitchen with folded hands. Inside his caged fingers, slapping faintly, is a goldfish. They watch him walk to one of the island sinks, turn, and push up the handle with his elbow like a surgeon preparing for open heart. The running water begins to steam.

'So you can see,' says Marlene. 'The Cardinal isn't so behind the times as some might like to think. He's interested in scientific truth just as much as you are.'

Dwight is watching his brother's fish. 'I guess I just think it's sad the Church has to confide its family skeletons to the kind of guys who make their living in a bomb factory in Los Alamos.'

Why does he feel like a dragon slayer when his mother suddenly exhales smoke? '*Dear*,' she responds. 'I worry you will *always* find something to criticize. If top scientists – who can't help working for their country – *hadn't* been consulted, you'd say the Church –'

'I think I should rescue that goldfish.'

'Never mind, I hid the plugs.'

'Then it'll die for lack of water.'

'He'll return it soon. He's trying to kill some fungus or something. Damon, take your fish back to its proper home. There's a good boy.'

Damon, who forgot to shave today, is communicating with the creature, his lips imitating the soundless gasps of the waterless fish.

'There's a good boy,' says Marlene, pushing herself back from the table and going over to turn off the hot water. She's holding her cigarette above her head so as not to infect the fish. Damon offers his mother a closeup peek. She smiles sweetly, touching his fingers, before directing him toward the door. Damon smiles back at her, paying no attention to Dwight.

'Maybe,' she suggests, 'you can follow Da upstairs and let him show you his aquarium. Owl has the day off.'

Head cocked, his brother peers through fingers, whispering soundlessly to his fish. The fish appears to be running out of gas. Memo: buy Da a ring for his birthday.

They ascend the oak staircase together, Dwight guiding his older brother by the elbow, a bone he's known since boyhood. Da is easy to guide, a domesticated camel, able to go days, months, years without raising his voice. In fact he has never raised his voice. Never spoken. Never cried, cried out, so much as hummed since birth. He seems to have inherited their father's reticence and carried this to the ends of the earth. His left foot drags, his lip sags to one side, and his left arm isn't one hundred percent. Never a consensus about Damon, except maybe that he'd suffered brain damage at birth. Forceps couldn't be blamed, since none had been used. Which had given rise to Dr Irving's stroke theory: a moment of trauma upon Da's entering the world, a hesitant instant of no blood to the brain, followed by a lifetime of silence. Not complete silence. They think they once heard him whimper, at age seven. His so-called whispering is a kind of reverse image of talking. Dwight thinks with the right sort of mirror they could hear Da. Understanding him, fortunately, is easier. His mouth wide open usually means frustration.

'Da, we'd better get your fish back to water.'

His brother's bedroom is full of ancient fan club pictures of Brenda Lee and the Everly Brothers, carefully embalmed in plastic laminations to prevent shrivelling on his walls. The single bed, covered in a pretty quilt with little wool spikes, seems too small for the large room, too short for the taller brother who sleeps in it. His new aquarium is percolating on the window seat.

Damon gobs on his fish, smears the saliva around on its scales with one finger, then lowers it into the tank.

The fish hangs motionless, threatening to turn belly up and float to the surface. Da watches it waver, urging it slightly with his submerged palm. Other fish orbit in steady, sometimes nervous parabolas, paying no attention to the rising chain of bubbles from the ventilation pipe, or to the motionless fish above. An angelfish makes its erect way magnificently across the glass, seeming to vanish for a heartbeat when the wafer-thin body turns end-for-end to begin its return voyage. Da's fish stirs, its gills quiver. The dorsal fin resembles an aerial. Nearly invisible fins flutter like fly wings. The mouth opens, dumbly.

He watches his brother's face break upward in a smile when his pet drops suddenly to a lower depth, rests for a moment popping its gills, before rejoining the slow merry-go-round of tropical colours.

'I'm glad, Da. You wouldn't want to lose a whale like that. This is a great tank. How do you feed them all?'

Outside in the yard, distorted through the tank, he can see their father's greenhouse, mostly empty now of the tropical blossoms Dr Irving used to cultivate inside. He moves nearer the window. A hungry flock of soaked starlings has blanketed a section of lawn and begun pricking it. The fruit trees need pruning again. Sam and Tom, their Japanese gardeners, will soon return for another season. Sam and Tom never forget to leave Da 'his' section of cedar hedge to trim, 'his' flower beds to weed.

Not that Dwight is forgotten: Marlene is fond of telling him someday the house will belong to him. She also likes reminding him what real estate agents say she could get for a Georgian structure of this size in Shaughnessy. Tempting, she admits, given the cost of upkeep, a swimming pool that cracked in the earthquake, a tennis court that needs painting ... Sometimes she can't imagine why she doesn't put it on the market. Then remembers her insulation might be urea formaldehyde foam. She doesn't want to investigate what she might have had blown into her walls several years ago, before all these revelations about living inside a health bomb. It'd mean tearing the walls out to remove it. It'd mean swearing in writing her house is free of the stuff, if she went to sell.

Dwight wouldn't mind her just remortgaging the place and helping him make history with Herodotus Tours. But she has already sold her cottage on Bowen to help him launch his company. Home she intends to keep squarely in the family.

'There's my whangdoodle,' she says, when both sons reappear down-stairs. 'Da's quite taken with your shoes, Dwight.' Yellow bucks to celebrate spring – or at least this break in the cold snap and the return of warm steady rain. 'I don't know why you'd want to wear those in January. I don't know why you'd want to wear them in July.' She thinks them effeminate. 'Look at your hands, Da. You must have been soaking them like a busy bee. They're all pink and wrinkled. Naughty, naughty.'

She thinks Aloysius's running away has had a bad influence on Damon. The two of them had got on famously. Her new foster son gave Damon the sense of having a brother in the house again. She wanted that. 'They even played cricket outside, like you two used to with your father. Croquet. Ever since last spring he's been very naughty and I blame it on Aloysius.'

'Like teasing the fish?'

'He's like a child looking for attention.'

'He is a child.'

'Yes, but he doesn't have to behave like one. He's going on thirty-five.'

Dwight accepts a mug of fresh brewed coffee from the red thermos. He is happy to inform her that she should be glad *not* to have Aloysius anymore. He stole Reesa's car last week.

Why be reluctant to remind his mother of her orphan's delinquency, when it tends to loosen purse strings? She's already paying for the boy's keep, but enough? She knows Dwight and Reesa had no choice but to take him *in* when he ran away, though Aloysius's ingratitude still puzzles her. She feels he and Sylvia the Owl had got on fine. Sylvia *liked* him. The boy wasn't a lost soul by any means. She still tends to think his Catholic education at the orphanage in Bombay will keep him from going bad.

'Even your upbringing, Dwight ... Do you remember when I used to drive you at five-thirty a.m. to serve mass in the convent? That isn't something you ever lose. That's all I have to say.'

'What isn't?'

She strikes a match and reassesses her vow of silence. 'Your sense of punctuality. Responsibility. I'm willing to bet your sense of service to the public descends in a straight line from serving mass at dawn as a small child. That and a good Catholic education, with the Christian brothers.' She lights another cigarette. 'Didn't they instill discipline?'

'Uh huh.'

'Darn tootin.'

Her house had been too big for the likes of just Damon, her and Sylvia. 'We had room for a refugee and I'm glad we took him in. Even if he didn't turn out quite the way we hoped. Damon, don't dawdle at your fruitcake. Eat it properly, and use your napkin.' She uses her own napkin to dab her mouth, checking her cigarette for lipstick. 'I do apologize again, Dwight. Aloysius is my fault. I dreamt up his coming. I never dreamt he wouldn't like it here.'

To Dwight, this seems as good a time as any to reraise the subject of his visit. (If only he still didn't owe her from as far back as college, for paying off his bridge debts. Marlene will say things like, 'I wouldn't want to think you were deliberately forgetting your debts, Dwight.' But he knows he won't be pressed for repayment.)

'Speaking of fruitcake, Mother ...'

She narrows her eyes again and pulls on her cigarette. 'I thought Herodotus was getting on famously,' she says.

'It is. Reesa and I are pouring everything we have into the company. The bank's all set to give us a big mortgage. The thing is we're *still* strapped, if you can believe it, and can't expand quite the way we *need to* ...'

'You travel too much.'

'Pardon?'

'The money you spend gallivanting ...'

'I don't. I'm very frugal.'

'You mean you sleep on park benches?'

'I stay home.'

'You and Damon.'

'I haven't been anywhere since I went to London in 1968. I enjoy staying home.'

'Listen, dear. Don't lie. We both know you're a big hit on radio, in the newspapers. Learn to budget better. Business must be good.'

'Booming. That's how come this is the time to expand and take advantage. We're at a crossroads. If we ever hope to franchise, it's *now*. I'm on a roll.' *Pushing pushing.* 'Besides ...' He grimaces a little and rubs his jaw thoughtfully. 'Well, the truth is we're thinking of having a baby. We're trying ... We probably shouldn't be ...'

The effect is electric. He can see the smoke come right out her ears. Tactfully, she avoids prying. She puts on her disinterested manner, brushing ash from her cashmere sweater, reaching over to remove Damon's plate.

'What sort of expansion,' she asks carefully, 'did you have in mind?'

He pulls out his position paper. He has it in his brain's hip pocket. And fills her in.

He wants to blanket the country with outlets, he explains, once he blankets the city. It's time to capitalize, expand, cash in on his growing reputation. People are travelling like never before. It's a lifestyle change. It's a wild circle of opportunity. Who could miss a target market like travel?

Puffing, Marlene remains noncommittal.

He consults his watch.

Then she confesses his scheme sounds baroque. '... Could be worse, though. Those old European cathedrals deserve a better press. All their soaring columns and airy light and floating vaults. And everything dedicated to one end, Dwight. The redemption of the striving human figure.'

Before he leaves, she makes sure he has the article to read, especially the parts about the shroud corresponding in every detail to the Gospel accounts of scourge marks, nail holes, spear in the side ... the legs *not* broken.

'Believe me, dear. History is going to find these pages more valuable than the Dead Sea Scrolls. That's all I have to say.'

Memo: Ask Lena to find out if *The National Enquirer* has already passed judgment on the Shroud of Turkey.

His mother sees him out the entrance hall, which smells of floor wax and lemon furniture polish. 'You don't mean to say you pretend all that in the paper, dear, on the radio? I don't believe you.'

'Good.'

He circles the driveway, slows at the crescent to wave at a neighbour raking old leaves, but the rubber-booted Mr Luce doesn't know who Dwight Irving is anymore.

No sweat. When the time comes to market his memoirs, *Scenes From a Life in Travel*, all his old neighbours will recognize him as Mr Herodotus, native son who went on to make history.

3.

The consultant pops a breath mint. Since it opened two years ago, the Racquets Club on Altamira has attracted part-time hookers to the bar, along with good-time Charlies with enough in pocket for social memberships on three-month instalments. There are other members of course. The squash ladder posted on the bulletin board lists names and phone numbers of men serious about fitness and competitive with racquets. Dwight's position on the ladder is nineteenth and rising. He started out nowhere, a year and a half ago, seeded forty-fifth. Satisfaction isn't the word to describe his sense of advancement. Pleasure is. Bliss is.

How anybody like Bartlett, heading the other way, can summon the desire to play puzzles him. He supposes losing (like eating) can get to be a habit. Porkers like Bartlett have a problem because they have trouble staying motivated. Have trouble getting games. Dwight has to play with his own housemate or Bartlett wouldn't bother playing at all. What are friends for? And if he can touch Bartlett for a loan, all the better. Luckily, Bartlett's away playing with beach bunnies in Thailand. So Dwight has a chance to move up a rung if he can defeat number fourteen. *Pushing pushing*. It's a gamble. He could lose. Losing could ruin his evening.

He chokes on his candy, entering the locker room.

'Dwight Irving? Ian Beardsley. Seen you around. That your secretary who called?'

Beardsley is standing on the bench. In his jockstrap. Twenty-five, six. Muscled like a volleyball player. A locker-room regular. Probably lives in a one-bedroom east of Altamira, and works on cloned calculator parts from Taiwan in a makeshift warehouse on Clark Drive. Runs a Skoda maybe, or a Tercel with leaky brakes. Dwight encourages him to reveal more.

'I dress up here now,' says Beardsley. And goes on to explain how he picked up a plantar wart last year and doesn't want another of the buggers. He understands they've finally started disinfecting the floor. He'll believe it when he smells it. 'You go to that meeting when the Acer raised the roof about his operating budget? Guy cares more about bar receipts than the locker room. No skin off his feet, he's not a playing member. I had the bugger burned out with an electric needle. That your racquet?'

Dwight has leant his racquet against the bench.

'Needs restringing, by the look of it.'

Every guy with his own psych-out strategy. Dwight's Slazenger is taut and tuned. There's nothing wrong with his racquet. Cuts air like a whip.

'Yeah,' he admits. 'It's a handicap.'

He senses Beardsley giving his yellow street shoes the once-over. His opponent has removed a pair of neatly pressed sweat socks from a British Airways bag, slipping into them like Minnesota Fats putting on gloves. A cheap London charter, four or five years ago, to judge by the bag's fading letters. Dwight plays out of a Cathay Pacific bag, although he has a line on one from Iran Air, now as rare as a trip to Shiraz.

'What court you book, Dwight?'

'Three.'

Bearsdley pauses with his second sock, unbelieving. 'One is the court I play on. I was careful to let your people know that. Most guys I play with remember that. I thought your secretary understood.'

'She's an airhead sometimes.'

'I'm not big on being watched. It's just a personal quirk. The nosey parkers looking down from the bar, you know, courts two through five ... Sound weird?'

'Them looking?'

'Me, twitching.'

Beardsley looks like he wouldn't mind calling off the game. So Dwight is forced into circumspection. (He did think he had a chance against the younger man, watching him play last week. Playing competitors seeded higher means if you lose there's no penalty, but if you win you have a chance of moving up the ladder. To be challenged by a guy lower down the ladder can also be invigorating, since it means he thinks he has something to take from you. Getting the chance to teach poachers a lesson can be gratifying. Beardsley looks like he fancies himself a pedagogue.)

'I suppose you were counting on it,' says Beardsley, reconsidering his distaste for Dwight's court selection. 'You know, playing a higher seed and that? Like that myself.'

Dwight shrugs, putting his yellow shoes back on. 'Let's call it off. I had a late night last night anyway.' (In fact he went to bed early, in anticipation of this afternoon's match.)

Beardsley quickly shoehorns himself into his court shoes. 'Won't disappoint you, Dwight. Let's give court three a whirl.'

When number fourteen steps through the little door and into the box, lofting a delicate serve to Dwight's back corner, right into a hole where the walls meet, where tweezers could not have dug it out, the ball doesn't even bounce.

'Not ready, Dwight?'

'Yeah. I guess. One-love.' Already losing and yet to swing his racquet. Players like Beardsley love to step through the door and not warm up. They think it shakes out jokers farther down the ladder, only in it for the workout. He scoops Beardsley's next serve out of the same miserable corner with a forehand flick of his wrist, lucky to retrieve it at all, and rallies with increasing authority, gaining good position in centre court, before hitting tin with a hard shot just off the centre of his strings.

Down two-love, he drops another two points when Beardsley, loping casually around, unloads successive lobs into alternate corners and Dwight overhandles them. 'Trust me, it's those strings, Dwight.'

But Dwight wins service with a straight backhand return along the wall, leaving his opponent flatfooted. 'Nice shot,' says Beardsley, not breathing at all hard. 'Your serve, zip-four. Mind your foot on the line.'

Dwight eats sensibly. He drinks only white wine. He jogs. He feels he can take Beardsley. He has this irrepressible confidence. The maple floor, gleaming brightly from the overhead lights, gives him the same rush he used to feel stepping on stage at university. The red lines are just part of his blocking.

The men exchange service with no points won. Dwight keeps challenging the more experienced player for position at the top of the T. Position is everything. Control centre court and the angles take care of themselves: It's like moving protractors around a shoebox. Lean and logical, Dwight soon finds himself on the scoreboard sniping at the lead. Not what Beardsley had in mind, not when his opponent runs off seven straight points.

Number fourteen begins to scan the glass window above for eyes peering down at them.

'You not ready?' asks Dwight, after a very pretty serve laid down like a egg in Beardsley's corner.

'Nah ... but I wouldn't have got it anyways.' He stops to retie his laces and pull up his socks. His sharp nose has a drop of sweat belling off the tip. This pause seems to help his concentration, because he wins back service and takes two fast points, snapping wrist shots of great velocity off the side walls, before Dwight, ahead 7-6, has a chance to run out the game after winning an eighth point in a long and sinuous rally, full of dropshots, volleys, and an unexpected stroke off the left wall from well back in court. Bliss.

The ninth and winning point is almost anti-climactic. Dwight floats through the motions, feeling sure he won't lose after such a gutsy performance on his eighth point. Beardsley refuses to hand it to him, however. He loses, but he loses looking back up over his shoulder. 'Somebody's head put me off on your lob ...'

Dwight can't see anyone in the window.

'I think you're right,' he says. 'My racquet needs restringing.' His serve starts the second game.

Ian Beardsley isn't in the mood to lose again, yet miraculously he does. He spends a lot of time glancing over his shoulder, for evidence of Lucifer himself at the window. Dwight keeps getting stronger. He takes two out of two games, drops a close third game (7-9), then wins the fourth (9-2) and with it the match. He's playing beyond himself, so it seems to Beardsley, who comments skeptically on Dwight's ranking.

'Well,' Dwight answers modestly. 'Work like a navvy and all that.'

'Thought you had a late night last night.'

'Maybe the spectators helped me.'

Spectators? Beardsley seems annoyed the window's still so deserted. Not a single pair of eyes spying down on the debris of his athletic performance. He is sitting on the floor, favouring his surgically treated foot. Dwight is up on his toes, practising backhands down the wall. *Pushing pushing.*

'Just don't walk on that dressing room floor in bare feet, Dwight.'

The winner smiles. Not because he doesn't believe Ian Beardsley's sole may be throbbing from wart-removal, but because Candice did mention (now he recalls) his opponent's careful instructions about court one. It was Dwight who told her to book three instead.

4.

He has noticed before that on public occasions men usually agree not to compete, and watch women do it instead. Women and hair of jostling styles and tints. Women and gowns of a hundred colours and cuts. Tonight in an emerald gown the tall dark Reesa Potts is sensational. Even unrecognized as host of *City, City* she'd still stand out a mile. Dwight feels envy more than jealousy.

He, who hasn't seen most of his fraternity brothers in ten years, wishes Bartlett were back from Asia. For moral support among all these vaguely threatening men. He and Bartlett pledged together; got to know each other shining actives' shoes in the frat house. They'd kept one another sane. Bartlett was an animal back then, admired for being a wild man. And funny, a funny guy among a lot of animals. Now all of the animals look as tame as pets. Dwight has a wad of business cards in his pocket, to hand to old friends like Swaboda, Orsetti, Case ... even as they eye his wife.

Registration, nametags, cocktails before dinner, after-dinner speeches. A fund-raiser full of balding frat rats from an earlier generation, slick brothers from among his own contemporaries, and cleancut students from the generation just initiated. The theme seems to be resurgence, comeback, old values. Frats on their way back in the eighties, ready to welcome students who spurned Greek societies in the decade after Dwight and his brothers left college. Just too bad, announces the alum president, they had to sell the old house for lack of interest among students and alums alike. '... But times are changing, thanks to the American agenda. Thanks to Reagan.' The president wraps up by reading a short list of Theta Phi Beta alums with debt-financing ideas for their local chapter. One of these men, depending on a mail-in ballot, is to be their chapter's next saviour.

Afterward, Dwight's crew gathers at the bar. The rock and roll band strikes up, thumpingly, and dancers hit the floor to frug.

'You're telling me Day is a doctor, Dwight? *Day?*'

'We just booked him to a medical conference in Bangkok.'

Few of Dwight's old brothers have brought wives. The dance floor beyond is hopping with earlier and later generations. Only Leo Orsetti is dancing, with Reesa, to an old Kinks' song. *Girl ... I want ... to be with you ... * Niles Orr, grilling Dwight, is wearing a lapel badge and sipping a double Scotch, both compliments of Herodotus Tours.

'I read somewhere Reesa Potts is a Mensa,' says Niles, watching her attentively. He then laughs as though Dwight ought to feel defensive about this. Same old Orr, with the neatly gapped teeth.

'That the high IQ group?' inquires Stan Case.

'One thirty-five minimum to get in,' says Niles. 'Leaves you out, Case.'

'Barely, Orr. I usually test out at One Three O.'

'With a decimal point,' quips Nick Fussell, 'after the three?'

Niles is trying to recall the name of the Theta who once thought of going into geo-physics. '... Our age like. Bright but lazy. I think he ended up in economics. Potvin? Was that his name?'

'Potvin?' asks Tony Swaboda, beer in hand, his nails clipped.

'His name'd ring a bell. Maybe it was Preston. Peculiar guy, dermatological probs. He used to run laps and work out with a black belt at the Y. Real jock. I came across him recently, for the first time in years.'

'Know who you mean,' says Nick. 'Or one like him.' Blond Nick is watching the dancers. They're all watching the dancers.

'Always on the go,' says Niles, 'eye on the future.'

'Poultice. Something Poultice.'

'Turns out he'd become a big wheel in his association,' says Niles. 'Could've been Mensa for all I know. I think he ended up in Comm. Or else Arts. Hardly any arts students I remember ever stuck us. The only one who stuck, I remember, was an animal. Not Day. This animal was civilized, insinuating himself where he wasn't welcome. Asked me out of the blue once if I'd give him a rubdown in the locker room. I think he was trying to nobble me.'

'Carter,' says Stan. 'Was that his name?'

'The animal?'

'I recall an animal,' Swaboda says, 'in his last year. He kicked up and down frat row for years, landed on our doormat one September evening, the first rush of the season. What did he think we were, somebody asked later, a rehab centre? Loudmouth par ex. Guys in the house wanted to ding him. He ended up pledging us.'

Pause. 'Did he like to fish?' wonders Orr.

'Fish?'

'This animal liked to mooch. Ran around in a Chriscraft called *Matthew*. *Matthew!* Invited me aboard once and I fell off his bridge, my tackle snarled. What a boat. Shit, what a splash.'

They all agree, when the band moves into an old Animals' song, it has really sensed the mood of the evening. They grin, remembering. The way you couldn't dance to it, but how it got you up on your pins. They all watch Orsetti and Dwight's wife among the dancers on the floor. Orsetti like Dwight is wearing a tux. A lot of them are wearing tuxes. The rest like Niles seem to Dwight as competitive as the women, in silk suits, safari jackets, blazers with old Theta crests on their pockets. Jewellery and Whistler ski tans. Everybody doing well.

'Some animal, I remember, threw up over my windshield,' says Dwight, polishing off his Scotch.

'Forster,' says Case. Stan still has a way of squaring himself up when he speaks. He rotates at the waist. 'Didn't Forster's date try to wipe off your glass with her scarf? After a party like.'

'Must have been Lenora,' offers Nick.

'I felt sorry for her,' says Dwight.

'Paxton Lenora. He's in oil now, in another country.'

'She ran out of scarf.'

'No wonder, the way Lenora drank. Fuck. What a gin-guzzler.'

'I thought,' says Orr, 'we were talking about Potvin.'

'Jesus, you guys, this fucking song ... remember?' Nick Fussell has started singing along: '... *and it's been the ruin of many a poor girl ... and, God, I know I'm one ...*'

'I often wondered,' says Niles, 'about Potvin, when we were brothers, supposedly hard and fast, thick and heavy, if I wasn't mistaken in despising him. He was thought civilized by brother after brother. He still is, Potvin. If it's the guy I'm thinking of.'

'He was queer,' says Stan.

'Potvin? How do you know?'

'I got it from Carter.'

'*Carter!*'

'He and Poultice were best buds.'

'Well, listen.' Orr grins. 'He never mentioned it to me. If it's the animal I'm thinking of he never mentioned Poultice.'

'You fell off his bridge. He hardly had time.'

They all laugh at Niles.

'No one liked this animal,' he resumes. 'When he fished me out of the salt chuck and gave me the lowdown on his friends, such as they were, up to that point in time, Poultice never came into the picture.'

I'm going back to New Orleans ... to wear a ball and chain ...

'Time,' says Nick Fussell. '... all seems a piece now. Everything in its place? What an illusion.'

'Parties?' asks Niles.

'Sororities,' says Tony. 'You couldn't beat off the toads with a plank.'

'The cream,' says Case, 'of our generation, and which of us didn't know it, even at the pub, down on the floor, out like a light? Who could forget the brother who shared a Greek motto and a secret handshake, intramural competition, the one who helped you up off the floor, because that's where you'd still be, reposing in your own effluence. A bond is what it was. Pulling us together from the day we pledged, Christ, the hazing. Strokes of the paddle, mopping out the john. Hazed, harassed, stolen from. Our dates were stolen, that's what was stolen, at parties. We got the dirty end of the stick and the actives got our women. Then the new pledges and the cycle all over ... sticking together through thick and thin. We do still. By and large.'

They all look at Stan, like he's impersonating Potvin.

'You mean in professional life?' asks Tony Swaboda.

To Dwight Tony looks like the type with weekend custody rights, who might have preferred to take his daughter to McDonald's for dinner, but instead assumed the greater responsibility to this dim re-creation of the past. He's beginning to bald from the back, like a monk.

'We're an active bunch of fornicators and boozers,' intones Orr. 'Lawyers, accountants ... doctors, I hear.' He peers down at his lapel badge. 'And travel agents. Things going good for you, Dwight?'

Unfortunately, Leo Orsetti chooses this moment to return Dwight's wife, before the entrepreneur can cash in on the opportunity to sell himself further.

'Hey, big guy,' says Orsetti, rejoining Reesa's palm to his. 'Between these two,' he tells Niles, 'they cover the media.'

'Paid to travel the globe,' adds Niles. 'Bigshot travel consultant. Used to be an animal, mind you. You used to be an animal, Irving. What happened?'

Dwight digs down into his cummerbund for a business card. He hands it to Niles. 'Come and see us, Orr, while you can still get in the office for a one-on-one.'

'Yeah? Things going good?' Orr sounds disappointed.

'Straight for the top, Niles.' He tips his hand in an upward angle, flexing at the knees. *Pushing pushing.* Such an asshole, Orr. Dwight finishes off his hand gesture by wiping it casually through his sandy hair, and giving Reesa a peck. He bats his blue eyes at her, smiling his pearls, entwining their fingers. 'We're off, guys. Both of us got shows to prepare, no rest for the famous.'

'Hey,' says Stan, 'a wild and crazy guy!'

Niles says, 'Once a gambler, always a gambler!' He laughs, maliciously. 'About time it paid off for him!'

'I'd like to get in on some of your freebies,' Tony Swaboda tells him. '… Junkets.'

'Eat your heart out, Tony. Say goodbye to my bros, biscuit.'

'Ciao. Lovely to meet you all.'

'Remember, gang. Make history, eh? Travel.'

They groan and make biting motions at the badges on their lapels.

'Men,' comments Reesa on the drive home. 'Why don't I need my contact lenses to read them?'

'Leo a good dancer?'

'He thinks so. He asked me to lunch.'

'What's he doing?'

'I take it oil negotiations. Junketing around the Middle East.'

'Yeah? Wonder who does his reservations?'

'Says he does a lot of bike riding. That and skiing.'

'Good legs for the frug,' says Dwight. 'Married?'

She shrugs. 'Asked me if I wanted to go with him to Kuwait.'

He takes his eyes off the road. 'Orsetti asked you to Kuwait? Dancing?'

'It's farther than you ever take me.'

Dwight smiles. 'We used to be quite a gang.' He mentions stunts they'd pull at initiations. He recalls weekend parties, late beer halls, bridge all afternoon.

'The accumulation of debt?' adds Reesa.

She didn't need Niles Orr's nasty dig to remind her of Dwight's card debts to several frat brothers, his IOUs that a couple of them eventually persuaded Marlene Irving to make good on, after approaching her as a kind of guarantor. Marlene found their cheek presumptuous. Twenty-seven thousand four hundred and nineteen dollars and thirty cents: the sum required to redeem him. At the time, clearing out of frat life around the same month Bartlett left for chiropractic college in Toronto, he didn't care if he was redeemed or not. Now he's grateful for his mother's foresight. He felt free tonight to go to the banquet and ingratiate himself among possible investors in Herodotus. He felt he'd shone tonight and finally reclaimed himself.

For a January night the wind is mild. Drying the streets and popping awnings along Altamira. 'Know what Freud said?' asks Reesa, uncrossing her silken legs under her long gown. 'The pleasure of travel comes from escaping your family and especially the father.' She turns to watch him at Haro in the Morse code of their blinking turn signal. 'You're just the opposite of that. I wonder about you sometimes, Dwight. Us. We're playing with fire.'

They can't find a place to park near their house, and walk back a block and a half. Back to Haro, turning for home under the horse chestnuts, bony against the streetlamps. He can smell damp lawns bordering the apartment blocks. A west wind with all kinds of smells.

In the convent's corridors used to linger whiffs of burned toast and scorched milk, from nuns too old to fast for communion. The rest of them would gobble the wafer like a pastry. His mother would drop him off before six a.m. and he'd climb stone steps to ring a bell at the huge oak doors. A dark January morning, just like this one. A nun no taller than a midget, in her black habit and white wimple, admitting him like a waif. He figured they slept in their habits – tent and sleeping bag combined. He'd step into a black cassock, listening to the priest mutter sleepy prayers as he tied on his surplice, poked his head into the alb, gave his stole a smooch and cinched up the cincture. Then the priest would disappear inside a chasuble and reemerge to crown himself with a black biretta.

They notice Aloysius's third-floor light isn't burning, so maybe he's asleep. They wish he were asleep. But they'd be grateful if he were home, even nosing through Reesa's underwear, and not still out with his band impairing the ears of young people.

Dwight stands on the sidewalk, Napoleonishly, staring up. The pleats of his dress shirt remind him of the starched surplice the nuns kept sharply pressed for their star altar boy. Having the twerp Dwight around to answer Father Sniffles in Latin, to pass him the cruets of water and wine, must've lent a ceremonial air to their sanctuary. After mass the sour smell down the long corridor always made him refuse breakfast. That and the dry mouths on sisters taking communion, for which he held the gold plate to catch their crumbs.

The mouldering stairs squeak in their ascent to the wide veranda.

Dogwood branches slap a peeling pillar in the gently scouring wind. A cone of swallow shit is still glued to the porch boards where it fell from a nest last summer. Only their wide oak door, with its brass trim and bevelled windows, embodies the past unsullied. Their house may be cold and uninsulated, he decides, but at least the insulation it lacks isn't imperceptibly rearranging their cells and corpuscles via toxic poison oozing from the walls.

'That's odd,' says Reesa, pushing open the door. 'It was wide open.'

The stone rolled back he thinks. 'Well, no one can say we don't have an open-door policy with respect to His Royal Lowness.'

'At least my car is still here,' Reesa says, glancing out to the curb. 'Isn't it?'

'The question of our age.'

October, 2081

My birthday today. The Big One. Sprinkled on some rosewater. Didn't know how I felt when reporters asked. Not this old, I supposed. Then remembered my new doctor has counselled me not to think like this. So I told them, 'Old. I can't believe how old I feel.' Not what they came to hear. 'This little chat I'm having with you,' I said. 'To tell you the truth, seems like we had it ages ago. Did we?' They seemed worried I was senile. I could see it in their agreeableness. So I reassured them. 'Déjà vu is what this circus feels like, dear. I love your pretty collar. I could look at it all afternoon.'

Was trying out my new therapy before the microphones.

Then I walked into the recreation room quite briskly, sat down, and began to tickle the ivories. What sayings we once had. I suppose this one originated in fact, for on Hygeia's antique piano the keys really are ivory. They do feel like something forbidden. They are, of course, now. Like cigarettes. Tickle was about all my stiff fingers could manage. In tribute to my new doctor I played 'The End' by an antique group called the Doors. Very simple chords – too simple I am afraid to provoke recognition. Then in response to a very nice toast in my honour I gave a little speech. My first in years.

Parroting my new doctor I talked about

perspective. 'Life is a hospital,' I quoted, 'and the sick keep wanting to change beds, as recovery looks more likely over there. Well, why not,' I said. 'Why not bedhop? Why not drink a little? Noodle if I can? Go to forbidden places in my head?' Noticed the reporters draw back a hair at my performance. They liked it.

Everybody said I didn't sound a hundred. But they don't have a lot to compare me with. They must have thought I was either under the influence of sherry, or a dodderer. A dodderer like the man who has started bothering me. I've heard a nurse call him Eric. An orderly told me Eric used to be a developer. He certainly has a foul mouth from being something of the sort.

He started in this week on me, nudging me from behind in his wheelchair, possibly in reprisal for all the attention coming my way. Once he raised his hand as if to strike me. I think he's playing with half a deck and try to avoid him, on my little treks down the corridor in touch with the handrail.

My time doctor, as I call him, introduced himself two days ago, knocking on my door after supper. He was in the dining room earlier, furtively surveying diners as we fell to like lumps, consulting an inventory sheet of patients he'd picked up at the desk. Later he came into my room and shut the door. No one ever shuts my door. So much seems coincidental on my turning a hundred. I was about to ask him to open it when I noticed his sparkling dark eyes. When he spoke, a kind of musical murmur came out. 'May I sit down, Ms Potts?'

He lifted the tails of his white coat. Smiled. I think he thinks he's pretty special.

That's when he launched into his gentle spiel, arguing that the units we've fractured time into – seconds, minutes, hours, days, et cetera – are just the temporal shapes of cells, blood, muscles, bones, et cetera. 'I think what glues us all together is our common place in time. Don't you?' Me? 'Time is the great healer,' he went on, 'as we've always known but seldom hired. It unifies a lot, time, if only we allow ourselves to mistreat it. Our brains,' he suggested, 'yearn to let us see as if from the future.'

'Brains,' I repeated, beaming ignorance in a little ode to joy. 'Hired ...'

Hadn't the foggiest notion what he was advocating. He sounded like a quack with the patter of a confidence man. Interesting, maybe, but I kept watching his eyes. You can always trust the eyes. He spoke in such a confiding voice I could hardly hear him. Had to tap my hearing implants to make sure they weren't snoozing.

I was all ears, of course, when he started in on having the time of my life. Forgot to ask him to reopen my door.

He claims his therapy is descended from the old holistic medicines. 'The difference is, I don't have an answer for everything.' Good for you. 'I think the law that governs us all is the instinct we have to see things in terms of other things.' He now applied this law to the body – my body, I supposed, not without pleasure. 'The body,' he said, 'is where time gets upset. We have the ability to stop time. By mistreating it, by treating it irreverently. By learning to see the present, as if mirrored from the future, we can treat ourselves to health.' He arched his brows naughtily, inviting me to be his patient. 'Would you be interested in mistreating it?'

My body, as I say, was all ears.

'The full bloom of health comes from the glow that practising my therapy gives ...'

Should maybe have mentioned my taste buds to him. I now stack salt on my food, to taste what I eat. You would think I'd once been a heavy tobacco smoker, before that pleasure got so exotic it disappeared entirely from polite society.

Maybe he understood. 'Feel free to chew over my remarks.' Yes, so much seems coincidental on my turning a hundred. He sounded serious. So I chewed over his remarks. He proposed taking me on as his patient, provided I would agree to see him

on the sly and pay cash. I chewed over this proposal too. I chewed over the proposer. He had amused me. On the eve of my birthday last night I gave him my reply.

Easy to scoff now. But I do need a better way of coping, in my second century. This man Eric, for instance, what a bruiser. And all these questions and expectations on my birthday ... Besides, have begun resifting my trunk in the closet. I have family records I imagine go back to the Ark. At this rate I will never get them down.

Am having no trouble feeling old, no. The chore will be in finding what he prescribes for the bloom. 'The glow,' he corrects me. The city has governed my whole life. What glues the city and me together (to use his locution) is our common place in time. I still have time for my city. My family. This afternoon,

did I remember to pay it tribute, in reply to the tribute to me?

Chapter 4

Against Nature

THE NIGHT SKY IS moonless and filthy with stars. It's all her fault. Enchanted by this horrible spring holiday, she finds his migraine absurd. Tonight she's making him walk on the beach, where the surf pounds in on his pain from a thousand, ten thousand miles out in the Pacific. The vastness of this ocean appalls him. The son of inlets, bays and sounds – of an ocean once removed – and of a cool, temperate climate that nurtures salmon, Dwight doesn't find Hawaii, for all its palms and pineapples, Paradise. It belongs to a country where muggers flock to night beaches like sand fleas.

'Nonsense,' she says, astroll in her muumuu, the costume invented by natives before Cook arrived to soften the later pregnancies of tourists such as herself. 'If you call this a journey, sweetheart, I can't imagine what you'd call one of your expeditions to Papua New Guinea. You write them up so well.' Teasing, she has enjoyed watching him collapse, he thinks, but the spectacle has surprised her. How he grew itchy and desperate before their departure. How he developed tics: a man up against his imposture like the kind of man she often interviews: a man on the edge of his seat, guaranteed to keep the audience on the edge of theirs. But her husband is also a man who can't get up and walk off this set in a huff. He's framed by the horizon and an open sky bearing down on his aching head. *His* fear is a living nightmare. She can't help herself, touching the gold hoops in her ears. She finds it absurd.

Dwight doesn't want any more of Hawaii. The naked sun. The exotic birdsong screaming in his ears like a guilty reminder of professional double-dealing. He wants to draw the drapes in their suite and lie down. He remembers the other time he had a migraine: walking in Brompton Road at age nineteen, from the dinosaur skeleton in the foyer of the National History Museum, when he came across the Church of the London Oratory and stepped inside for relief. It had the same effect on him as the conservatory at

Kew Gardens. It made his head worse. This jibed with his experience of God. The lovely Carrara marble of St. Cecilia – *her* head half cut off – nearly finished him. He has too good a memory to forget the pain of travel.

'Maybe a Kona wind is threatening the trades,' she suggests. 'Which way is south?'

But the weather has been perfect. He wonders how his life since they boarded their plane for Honolulu, since they boarded a second plane for Kahalui, can have flown straight into traction. *She* thinks he must be depressed over the failure of his Valentine Day's promotion scheme, over bad publicity *re* one winner's threat of legal action against Herodotus for conducting its button contest 'in bad faith'. But that isn't it. It's having to listen to this ocean slamming in day and night. It's the stars; the sun. It's the thought of morning sickness (his), when he climbs out of bed and peeks through the drapes.

He has done his best to keep the door to their lanai shut and the drapes drawn. The sound of the birds *out*. He sits reading the travel sections of newspapers flown in every day from Los Angeles and New York, trying to keep up with his lightspeed profession. He scribbles notes, while she sits tanning herself somewhere below in a plastic-webbed deck chair on one shore of a vast swimming pool full of coves and grottos. He's appalled by the tales she brings back. The pool has a bar in a cave you have to swim inside to order a drink. It has a Suntan Consultant. It has suspension bridges linking fabricated rock mountains and a spouting volcano. It has waterslides corkscrewing down the counterfeit mountains. And she brings back reports on the populations inhabiting the shores of this blue lagoon. Cigar-puffing, cardiovascular dentists and wives. Hedonistic, exercise-mad legal secretaries. Blond blue-eyed children in pink and yellow jams. His head aches to listen. To him it's all bad news. He even refuses to go out on the lanai and peer down. She shakes her head. His sundarkened, honours-lit wife shakes her head and tells him to get real. He supposes things could be worse. The electricity in this million-dollar-a-night hotel could cut out and leave him without his morning coffee.

'Sweetheart,' she tells him, 'the good Dr Johnson said travelling is great for disciplining the imagination with a nice dose of reality. *You* must think he meant the clap. I'm surprised you don't find all this illusion and fakery very comforting.'

She must be joking. Their huge complex has only confirmed him in his view that real travel is more artificial than anything he could dream up at home. Dinner for examp. How are you expected to eat in a restaurant surrounded by live penguins, listening to a tropical waterfall, as you watch a floating barge in the encircling lake entertain you with a live floorshow of sequined strumpets in G-strings? A fountain goes off, the black swans head for cover. Tonight, he hadn't eaten so much as a breadstick. Some days ago he'd lost his appetite for entrées when they tried the Early Bird at the Maui Marriott and he broke out in spots. He can't wait to get home to his desk.

'I imagine,' says Reesa, walking him like a dog in the sand, his belt loop in one finger, her slingbacks in another. '... I imagine this phobia of yours has something to do with your father, in the Hong Kong prison camp during a vicious occupation.'

'Fuck off, biscuit.'

Three days ago she'd insisted on his trying to overcome his feelings of revulsion toward travel, by driving him to Hana in a rented Datsun Sentra to look at Lindbergh's grave. Half a day just getting to Hana, snaking along a potholed jungle highway, through intermittent squalls and squashed toads, prickling humidity and backsores (his), with unrelenting glimpses of the stark Pacific. He thought it was time to die. The heat in Hana was gagging, ditto the vegetation. His head had begun to crack open like a clam. He demanded painkillers. Whisky. A knife. She pushed him back into the car and drove them another thousand miles down a dirt track looking for Lindbergh's bones, near a slum called Seven Sacred Pools. They never found the flyer's tomb. But they passed two hundred Datsun Sentras coming the other way, just like theirs, covered in red Maui mud. He refused to come out of their suite the next day. That afternoon the beach had a shark alert. He ordered room service and tried to recover his composure with a hamburger. To be on the safe side, Reesa called in the house doctor. When the doctor learned Reesa was pregnant, she ignored Dwight, except to press a cold stethoscope to his heart. His heart refused to tell her anything. The booming was at his temples.

Says Reesa, kicking sand as they stroll: 'You should try Bartlett when we get home.'

'Bartlett's a quack.'

'Exactly. He's used to your kind of pain.'

Tonight she is taking him the roundabout way to a nightclub in the farthest reaches of their hotel, to see Rich Little. She interviewed him once and thinks he, like the beach, might help to distract his headache. Kaanapali beach is floodlit from the electrified trunks of coconut palms, but close to the surf he senses nothing but darkness. Might as well be blindfolded. He can feel the wet sand invading his sandals like mud. He refuses on principle to take off his sandals, as he refuses to let the world in without pretending he has a choice. He hasn't, of course, not out here at the very edge of the known world. Things are bleak. Past bleak. His thoughtful wife is still hoping to coax him into getting up at four a.m. and coming with her in the car to watch the sun rise, from the ten-thousand-foot summit of an extinct volcano. He knows all there is to know about Haleakala, from having urged clients to drive up there in their thousands, and sees no reason to bother going up himself. He can see how she's begun to make a game of cajoling him.

'As beneficiaries of an adroit travel agent, we're *entitled* to two free night-club tickets along with our half-price suite ... I'm waiting for you to break into a raucous G and S ditty.'

She seems determined to play off his vulnerabilities. Last month, was it, threatening not to return to work after the birth, unless he took her away on a holiday sometime before, she felt his business was going well enough to leave it briefly. She needed a break. He, thigh-deep in branch office wallpaper, appointments, deadlines, didn't see how Herodotus's debts could survive her threatened sabbatical come autumn. She was a contributing partner. At Le Soleil Couchant he watched her watching the waiter, who was just then raising the bamboo curtain to a polite gasp from other diners: a red April sun sliding into the sea. Taking in the anchored freighters, the mountains trailing away up the coast, his wife glowed in the tomatoey light. Four months pregnant, cheekbones full ... 'Look,' she commanded him. 'You hardly ever look anymore.' He didn't see he had any choice but to look, when she asked him. Survival dictated the obligations of partnership. He caved in to the vacation.

He now groans. 'I must've been thinking of your mother. My mother. She'd love this place.'

This place, the Hyatt Regency, seems to sum up the history of tourism. It is a stunning monument to tourism. It is a disgusting simulation of Paradise. Not the kind of destination he'd ever consider for his board game. Who'd want to spend the rest of a life here? Only the historian, Herodotus, starved for wonders, could've found a place like this fascinating. The Mecca of luxury, or what passes for luxury, in the west. A marriage of Disneyland and the Uffizi trying to encompass the known world. Consider the discoveries, thinks Dwight: Beyond the swim-in bars and waterslides lie gardens full of statues and temple-sized corridors with Grecian staircases. At rest in these gardens and foyers are priceless eleventh-century Khmer sculptures of armless kings and sinuous dancing girls. As Reesa commented, on the night of their arrival, 'Bartlett would be interested in seeing these. Remember him telling me about smuggled-out sculptures, from his trip to Cambodia?'

The sculptures, the alien stone figures that struck Dwight like Unidentified Standing Objects, hadn't appeared till the hotel's hallways widened, the lighting dimmed, and the ocean breezes were allowed to sweep in through open walls and down marble staircases. He discovered, when he came closer to the niches and pedestals and glass cases, that these objects *were* identified, on stencilled cards. So that along with the Khmer stuff, he and Reesa found nineteenth-century horsemen from Bangkok temples, Chinese cloisonné vases, Japanese dragon pots, a decapitated Burmese Buddha. His headache worsened. 'You can see what they're trying to *tell* us.' He hissed like a tea kettle all set to whistle. He was warning her. *'This Art Has No Price. It Cannot Be Bought. You Are Staying In A Palace, A Temple To Taste. You Are Having An Experience Reserved For Others Of Your Class And Discernment.'*

'You're such a party-pooper, Dwight.'

'No, I can write the travel poster for this dump. It reads very simply: *'Travel No Farther. You've Arrived.'*

He massaged the shards of his dignity. He knew many destinations around the world aspired to Total Experience but few felt so supremely confident in proclaiming Image Realized as this place. He wondered. All the usual clichés of travel, proclaiming their marriages of Old and New, East and West, were here refurbished as the wedding of Pleasure and Profit in a destination devoted to the replacement of Paradise. On the lower level, where they were heading again this evening, he'd discovered a ten-ton bronze Buddha dominating the concourse at the far end, a great graven idol, where nearby doors led into a Nevada-sized showroom for star acts from the other side of the moon. His migraine had reached an intolerable pitch here. He'd immediately required the closed-in space of their room to recapture his leaking sanity.

They stand on the dark beach, looking out to sea. Homesick for closure, he longs for his computer. For open-endedness within boundaries of a recognizable world. His skin has started to itch again, warning him. This warning reads like a poster for his board game, JetSet: *Venture from the Zone of Safety, Into Outer Darkness, Pay the Penalty.* The pair of them are a perfect setup for a mugging, past the rim of the hotel's beachfront lights. He can feel the mugger approaching, a callous assailant, a Miami-type drug addict on the prowl for cash to feed his habit. Isn't this the land of *Hawaii Five-O* and *Magnum P.I.*? He and his pregnant wife have come much too far to avoid the consequences of imminent retribution. Back down the beach their hotel has faded like an ocean liner, heading in the opposite direction. The future is upon them.

'You're all tensed up,' says Reesa, touching his shoulder.

'I'm dying.'

'Agoraphobia, Dwight, isn't something to be ashamed of. If you wanted to pick a fashionable disease, it's a safe one.'

This is a new tack and he wishes he could be grateful for it.

'Sweetheart,' she tells him, 'fear of open spaces is a recognized medical condition. I've interviewed women who haven't been out of their houses in five years. But *with help* they learn to conquer their fear.'

'I prefer rooms to beaches, that's all.'

'That's natural. I mean if you're an agoraphobe.'

'I'm not. You want me to be. I'm not one. At home I run in the park every morning. Sometimes I walk to the office.'

'Well, downtown you're walled in by high buildings. In the park by tall trees.'

'Christ,' he sighs, aching to return to the isolation of suite and moderation. Disease? What *she's* driving at could apply to anyone who spends most of his or her time in an office, a community library, a computer. Her job seems to encourage a lot of shallow research and cheap psychology. The real world is different. Should his own research happen to prove superficial, travelling clients can end up on the street minus a bed because it was already booked – a bed whose possession by somebody else is nine-tenths of the law!

'The trouble with fashion,' he says, 'is the hemline becomes the party line. It makes out everybody is or should be … the same. We aren't. I'm not.'

She laughs, ruefully. 'Hardly.' She's still touching his shoulder, massaging it a little. '… I found some love letters of yours in the suite.'

He groans and rubs his temples. 'In code?'

'Italics. You'd bothered to underscore every line.'

'I must've thought I was being passionate.'

'You're queer, Dwight. When I'm outside every day, splashing around with our unborn child in the waters of the South Seas, lying around the pool in tropical sunlight and enjoying life to my toenails, you're holed up with the drapes shut writing notes to some city –'

'Oh, that ... JetSet.'

'To frisky maidens, with names like Sonya. And spunky young men around a geranium-couched opera house ... What kind of kinky game are you planning to copyright?'

He reminds her gravely of his objective, a city the travel player will never want to leave. 'Ah, yes,' she responds. 'Your unifying scheme for our children's grandchildren. They will live off the copyright till infinity holes out in the great fairway in the sky.'

She turns her head and listens. 'Hear the music, when the breeze changes? Our orchestra on the barge.'

Snatches of brass, strings. Then nothing but phosphorescent surf curling in, thudding, rushing up toward them in creamy bubbles. Dwight attacks his hands, to relieve their spreading itchiness. His antics she finds absurd.

'Did you ever read the French novel *A Rebours*?'

She knows he hasn't, but manages to appear surprised at this small oversight in his bridge-playing, frat-rat education.

She is looking up at the vast sky that's reducing them to bit players in the fairway rough.

'It seems the son of a wealthy family gets sick of the world and shuts himself away in his house. In his neurotic way he's kind of happy, this fellow, surrounded by his furniture and books. He lives his life in reverse so to speak. He sleeps all day and eats breakfast in the evening. He talks to no one, sees no one except his housekeeper, and he does a lot of imaginative kibitzing. One day, reading Dickens, he finds out how badly he needs some new experiences and decides on a trip to London. Sweetheart, for him this seems like a monumental journey, from Paris to London. He buys a Baedeker and starts imagining what London's like. In due course he sets out. Near the Paris station, where he intends to catch his train, it's pelting rain, so he decides to visit a tavern and ends up having a huge English meal of ale, greasy oxtail soup, roast beef, gobs of mashed potatoes. He's surrounded by sombre Englishmen talking about the weather, waiting to go home. At this stage he starts to remember an unhappy trip to Holland he took as a young man, when the country in the flesh came nowhere near the fairyland he'd seen in Dutch paintings at the Louvre. So, when it's time to pay his check, he sits in his chair wondering if he isn't already in London after all, surrounded by English food, English smells, English weather, Englishmen. The more he thinks about it, Dwight, the more he's convinced he ought to miss his train, since he'd be crazy to risk wrecking the wonderful experience of England he's already had by bothering to leave Paris now. That's how come he decides to return home with all his trunks, all his certainties intact, feeling like a man worn out by a long journey.'

Dwight stares at the surf thudding down, the bubbles popping in the black sand. 'I couldn't agree more – about avoiding London.'

'I'm surprised your paths never crossed.'

'You think my pain sounds like his?'

'He did most of his living in his head. That can build up pressure, sweetheart. You need a *valve* to ...'

'I play squash.'

'Yes, but here your head still hurts.'

Dwight groans to let her know how much. 'Wine sluicing 222s wasn't the answer,' he tells her. 'Neither is Rich Little.'

'Look at the stars then,' she suggests. Squeezing his shoulder she strokes his arm with her fingertips. The itchiness has spread up to his elbows.

'Even if you were to include – you know, to add up – ' she tells him calmly, with the serenity of an Easter Island statue, 'all the dots of light, all the dots now flashing on all the screens, all the impulses temporarily stored on all the diskettes – in all the computers in the world, dots flickering on every TV screen turned on right now across the face of North and South America – and if you took each speck of light to equal one star in the heavenly fairway ... then you know what, Dwight? All these trillions of specks of light wouldn't equal, not come close, to the number of stars above us right now, most of which we can't even see. Let's *pretend* we're a pair of those lovers inside your Apple ...'

Her musical voice lulls Dwight into *wanting* to look up, instead of down into the sand grinding in his sandals. Yes, he wants to look up. He doesn't want to catch out of the corner of his eye some black hole gliding soundlessly their way over the beach at extraordinary speed. It must be a black hole, since the whirling arms surrounding it have the density of stone, one landing on his own ear at the very second another, as he'll hear later, is moving through Reesa's shoulder, separating it from her bag.

Afterward – in the middle of police questions, lost travellers' cheques, lost credit cards, and a lacerated neck where her gold chain was torn off, split lobes where her earrings were torn out – the redeeming thing about getting mugged, to Dwight's mind, is that Reesa has developed a headache too. The hotel doctor, annoyed with him for parading his wife on the beach at night, dabs anaesthetic at Reesa's ears, and hands her Librium tablets. The foetus has thankfully survived. A bit like that skeleton of a hanging whale in Whalers Village: skull, vertebrae, ribcage suspended and preserved in the amniotic air, elegy to a distasteful industry. Who does it belong to, he wonders, the maker or the owner?

What interests Reesa is the way her husband's headache has entirely disappeared with the severe blow he took on the head. He himself assumes the pain disappeared in his instantaneous anticipation of going home. He's relieved to hear her agree to forget about driving them up the volcano tomorrow morning, and to return home a day sooner than planned. He now believes all the bad surprises are behind him.

There is, however, one ... And this will only confirm Dwight in his knowledge that travel is a crock you want to avoid *from beginning to end.* When they arrive home they'll discover Aloysius, their foster son, Dwight's stepbrother, their ward, has thrown a surprise birthday party for himself: the surprise residing in what he and friends have managed to inflict on the house during their absence.

2.

On their flight home he reminds her of Herodotus Travel's imminent expansion to a second and third outlet. He sounds nervous, upbeat. *Pushing pushing.* He now has Bartlett on side, and possibly two old friends of his father's with nothing more exciting to do than sit around their downtown club wondering if capital locked up in bonds can lead to arteriosclerosis. He has tried to implant in each this unhealthy image of inactive money. Bartlett has agreed to remortgage his practice and invest in Herodotus. 'Why shouldn't his equity come our way, instead of going into granny bonds?'

'Because, sweetheart, when the profits come, if they come, they're already slated for one mother, one bank, one trust company – and apparently these two partridges in a pear tree at your dead father's club. Who knows who else you've been talking to.'

Stan Case. Orsetti.

'Who?'

'Your dance partner at the frat ball ... he wanted to take you to Brunei or someplace.'

She studies him. 'Our creditors, if they knew about your little secret, would raise their interest rates even higher. Or put revolvers to their temples. Your empire ... our empire ... theirs,' she says, 'is built on *sand.*'

He doesn't ask what might happen if their landlord should suddenly pull the plug, forcing them to look for a new place to live at four times their present rent – then where would they be, being in debt up to their eyes already?

November, 2060

Today my last at City Hall. Heavy rains. Looking down over the city discovered it to be missing. Would have preferred to go out on a sunbeam, I think, a piece of dust on a convective current blown across to the mountains. A fund has been launched to reincarnate me in bronze. This does lack earthiness. Better suits an upright civic mind than my scattered brain. A commemorative statue to Gwyn Potts can't help lacking qualities of character more evident in a rosebush. Including the manure to keep it in bloom. Would rather be remembered in a rosebush!

Am writing this before bed, with a headache from all the toasts answered this evening. After x many years voters will salute longevity even if they never voted for you. Simple secret: Retire from office before you're thrown out. Rise from the dust enough times, prove resilient in face of economic cycles, and everybody in the end will come to love you.

Don't know why I stayed so long, except for the feeling that someone else might do a less good job. This is the arrogance necessary to survive in public. I also liked listening to people, hearing where their ancestors came from, what for them constituted a family. I confess showoffiness was part of it too. Not a small part either.

Tributes from allies, enemies, the entire body politic. Flattering gush in media all week for our longest serving, beloved, et cetera. I am, they say, the city. The stinkers among them have asked for interviews, as if they'd never needled me, slammed me, written or broadcast libel. They probably don't even remember. But who cares now?

Am sought out to reflect on life in civic politics since my earliest days on council. What is your proudest accomplishment? Biggest disappointment? When did you first know you wanted to be Your Worship? How long did you expect to serve? Did the death of your husband keep you in office longer than intended (translation:

Were you compensating)?

None of these *political* questions. They seem human interest questions on a hungrier level. People look to people, I sensed quite early, out of the deepest curiosity about themselves, in the same way we watch the news for enlightenment but deeper down for simple entertainment. Maybe it's the same thing. To enlighten is to entertain, with all the compromise this entails, and all the longing this entails not to compensate. I don't know.

I don't feel successful. At seventy-nine I feel anonymous. It's what I always wanted to feel and the showoffiness was just something to attract admirers. The biggest mistake in public life starts to happen when you feel you can never get sufficient praise, notoriety, fame for your little victories. More you get the more you want,

until you crave bigger and bigger doses. Until it all ends in a hangover like tonight's. I fell for it.

Can't remember anything that might be called fulfilling. Oh projects, yes, public works. Heritage by-laws. Racial harmony. But little that hasn't been achieved without a less than clean feeling after inevitable compromises. How to explain this without explaining away my life? Private satisfaction is just harder to come by than public recognition. I think F. would have liked me to retire earlier, but who was to know these things? Who was to know?

Was always projecting ahead to crisis or bliss, whichever matched my agenda. Who understood time when the unities started to go? When you glanced back and noticed you'd replaced your family with a city?

Thirty years. My

secret was a capacity not to make enemies of my enemies. Not something I consciously strove for. Never thought about it. I usually liked people, which is probably why they liked me, or maybe it was the other way around. Can't think with this head.

Sound as if I'm dead and gone instead of tired and drunk. *Would describe the sound as being bronzed off.* And this in public would pass as wit?

My main companion has been a theatrical flair that sometimes went over well in public. That and B.S. Don't know if I inherited the flair from my father or my mother. True, have never been afraid to work hard. But listening to the tributes this evening am supposed to believe I brought us together like no one else ever did. Who among them is old enough to remember? To me we sound just as querulous as ever. But maybe that's the safest

way: to bicker instead of
butcher. No news in
Paradise is what must
make the evening news
there dull, just as the
weather report in Palm
Springs must sound
uneventful. The nature
of the political animal is
that it is what my
wayward son Renaldo
would call a good
mudder. I am a good
mudder. And I have
these roses tonight to
prove it.

Chapter 5

Songs of Travel

EXCITED BY THE WAY his own company is moving, Dwight wonders why he should trust a competitor who backhands himself to pee. Alan Babcock is a backhander, little finger high in the air above his foreskin. Dwight is more accustomed to a straight-handed opponent, a straight-ahead pincher: thumb on top and two fingers below. Not the perverse backhanded gripper, either side of his foreskin, as if holding somebody else's dick, gingerly, owing to possible contamination from suspicious-looking sores. He imagines the least trustful sort of guy would be a lefthanded backhander, with aspirations to the nursing profession. To his credit Babcock is righthanded, a budding brewer.

He may be trying to tempt Dwight in the wrong direction, finance-wise, and Dwight's trying just as hard to outflank him by talking like the initiator, enjoying a beer in the locker room, towelling down after their squash game.

'How'd I get into travel in the first place? Question of parlaying what capital I had, Alan, and getting into something with a good price earnings ratio and solid downside protection ... but with speculative potential.'

It amuses him to reel off this kind of jargon in front of somebody actually impressed by it. With travellers he speaks a different language, to do with 'pleasure' rather than 'upmarket potential'. He knows travellers prefer hearing 'your reward' to 'potential growth'. Not that he himself minds discussing potential growth: He's a business type too. It's like playing squash. By now, August, he has moved up the squash ladder as a result of his sheer will to climb, win, dominate. Without seeming to try. Now that tennis season is upon them, these hot inside courts are easy to come by. Not partners though. Alan Babcock, seeded number four, is a rare catch and well worth the effort Candice put into tracking him down with a challenge from her number twelve boss. After their match, which Dwight has narrowly but triumphantly won, three games to two, he and Alan are discussing market forces in the raw.

'With travel you've got a built-in support level,' he goes on, 'and nothing but beautiful numbers when the industry breaks out – which it did, which it's still doing. I think the leisure market is recession-proof, Alan. Since I got into it the travel business has just taken off. The volume we're doing is phenomenal. Remember, against the chains it's suicide for an independent to think of becoming numero uno. But, hey, HT fully intends to go national – that's a given, if I can keep talking money lenders into letting us expand, maybe franchise. Bankers hear profits when they hear "franchise", and I don't want to disappoint them. Our main goal right now is developing our marketing forces to attract the attention of suppliers.'

'Which means,' interprets Alan, 'you get yourself on the radio and in the papers to lure customers into your office, where you sell them a package of resort-sponsored initiatives.' He smiles at his own savvy.

He's nursing his beer, swilling it a little in his glass, holding it up to the light and examining its colour for flaws. Against club rules to drink in the locker room, but who's around in August to police the locker room? Not the Acer; he's pooling his medical doctor friends to buy a skiing condo. Babcock has brought glasses in his tote bag. Very suave. As if he tries to tempt every opponent into spilling his soul, pouring him an imported beer and leading him on, picking his brain. Dwight has refused the glass, to swig instead from the bottle. The locker room's no place for a glass, unless you're someone who backhands himself to pee.

'To survive in the travel game the secret's exceptional service, Alan. You create your own initiatives. A bit like squash. Got to be imaginative, innovative, automated. Capital A. I want the highest return for a minimum risk, but I'm not dumb. Nowadays I recognize I have to risk more than I might've in the past just to stay even, let alone get ahead.'

Babcock, he knows, is considering how to crack the local beer market with a new brand and fresh initiative. Dwight's aggressive account of his own success doesn't impress him. Neither has Dwight's slender victory on court. After all, the potential brewer's impatience with the competition is what got him to number four on the squash ladder.

'But ask yourself,' he tells Dwight, 'where the *big* profits in the leisure market are. In travel you think? Got news for you, Dwight, no offence. Travel is small potatoes. Ten percent … isn't that what you're working at? Except, hey, no one's paying you any salary up front. Waiters, Dwight, turn up their noses at ten percent. And they're already guaranteed pay cheques just for showing up at the restaurant. When a guy looks at the leisure market these days, and a lot of guys are, including this devil, ten percent just ain't worth the price of admission.'

Success has made Dwight circumspect enough not to bridle at such carping envy. Babcock's black eyes water a little, the eyes of a man who has never been circumcised. In Dwight's experience around locker rooms, the pointy uncircumcised penis usually belongs to the guy with moist eyes and hair that won't lie flat. He'd be willing to testify in court on this. He rubs a loose towel across his damp stomach, then swigs from his bottle.

'I'm sure you have it worked out, Alan. But look – right off the top – just to set yourself up in the beer market, just to give your public an inkling there's now one more local beer to choose from, just to get yourself off the *ground*: You got any idea what that's going to put you in the hole for, before you carry even one of these brown piggies to market?'

He wonders if this man appreciates how tough getting into *local* manufacturing really is. This year everybody's drinking imported beer and mineral water, wearing imported clothes and accessories, driving foreign cars, watching European films, and doing business with offshore money pouring into the city – basically for the purpose of buying it up. Dwight, for one, appreciates that you can do anything you wish with your money, or, better still, somebody else's. He listens to conventional wisdom and knows all the ways to handle and mishandle cash. You can bank it if you're foolish enough not to mind falling behind the rate of inflation. Or you can send it into foreign money markets to skirmish for you like a Salvadoran guerrilla unit, in the hope of a big return on your investment against the sliding Canadian buck. Listen. Buy up oil stocks and hold on for a nice ride. Or go on a spending spree – not just for the satisfying illusion of power this affords, but to hedge yourself in *things*, before prices shoot even higher: antiques, office towers, Haida carvings . . .

Or, if you listen to Dwight, you buy travellers' cheques and travel, the happiest hedge of them all.

He reads the business columnists. The worst scenario they tell him is to be liquid with simple cash. They tell him the best thing he can do is to borrow as much as he can against whatever he owns and speculate on adding to his equity. To be in debt is to emulate the creative financing of corporate giants. No wonder he feels large.

And here's Babcock, bless him, thinking of investing in something *local*.

Look at the clothes he's climbing into: French jeans, Italian tooled boots, a linen safari jacket. Dressed up in a Thai silk shirt, talking like an international financier, and spurning Dwight's travel industry as small potatoes yet ready to plunge himself into local beer. Psst, small beer! Well, give him his due, possibly not so small if his ideas for promoting this stuff he wants to call Salal ('real smooth name, with a local tie-in') ever flies in larger international markets. But has Alan Babcock the personal qualities to make it fly? He wonders.

He can't understand most of his ilk: promoters, financiers, concept men whose patience for the minutiae of promotion is less than steady, whose memory for facts is undervalued and thereby defective, whose concentration on details is less than ferocious. He himself is just as impatient with the competition as this would-be manufacturer. But he has a better *handle* on his ambition and is willing to bide his time. Pretty simple. He's in an expanding mode because he deserves to be. You can't fault success.

Alan can't conceal his interest in Reesa Potts, when Dwight casually drops this local celeb's name. *Pushing pushing.* Herodotus Tours is a joint company, he tells Babcock, both of them deserving credit when things fly, for better or worse and till death do them part.

'Listen, I'm looking for a bird myself,' says Alan. 'But I'm not sweating it, you know, if I don't happen to find Ms Right. Wouldn't want a relationship at this point in time if it's going to slow down my stroke. My thing is happening too fast right now to consider settling down.'

Cheers, Al. The world flying at them both from every which way, the speed of its game quicker than ever, and nobody's angle of return immune to another's enterprising stroke.

Today, pumped up after outclassing Babcock, he feels he might possibly approach his mother with the idea of persuading her to mortgage her house on behalf of Herodotus Tours. Help expedite her already successful son on his way up the travel ladder. Look, if his best friend Bartlett is willing to let him use his building as collateral, shouldn't his own mother stop objecting to him using his childhood home for the same thing?

Memo: Ask Lena to wrap Damon's birthday gift.

'That smile looks pretty cocky,' comments Alan. 'We'll have to tangle again.'

2.

As a generalist in the travel industry Dwight isn't willing to specialize in one group to the exclusion of another. He wants to be known as a travel consultant comfortable with the breadth of the population. He wants to expand his influence among ethnic, business and charter markets alike, become known as a mover and a shaker who expanded west to east, going against the flow of enterprise in Canada. Unlike Bartlett, who seems aimless these days, he's on track with his columns, board game, slide lectures, clients and a burgeoning staff of nine. He's also negotiating to convert a collapsed pizza parlour on Robson Street into a fourth travel office. He lets Candice handle hiring and other personnel problems, too busy himself creating fantasies to haggle over medical benefits for employees.

Hawaii, for examp, still *the* dream trip for anyone ignorant of the islands, and a reverie for all those who (unlike him) long to return: He sees Hawaii for the money tree it is, and a fantasy well worth encouraging: ... *floorshows, authentic Asian treasures, safe beaches, and designer swimming pools for the discriminating sunbather whose definition of a tall cool one isn't always a glassy wave gently breaking! Much pleasure awaits you in* MAUI ... *from rainforest drives to star-rich nights!*

August, the high season for local holidays, gives him breathing space for planning winter tour packages to entice future clients. How? By anticipating trends like swamp cruises, by creating unique journeys such as elephant rides across northern Thailand (or collecting sea shells on the Cook Islands), and by tarting up warhorse vacations to Florida and the Caribbean with his expert review of airfares and package options, luxury hotels and budget resorts. Voila. Such latitude requires swift lines of light across his screen, and a nimble mind unclouded by financial worry. Look, here's China opening up ... What've I got stored in the tank up on China: maybe a horse-drawn sleigh pilgrimage to — ?

Never mind Orsetti on the phone, wondering about his loan, please get me the atlas.

Lena comes in to his desk with 'Songs of Travel'. Her cadet-like figure seems to him enhanced by her subversive demeanour. She's tried, but she can't think of any more songs for this new sidelight to his radio spot, on the all-pervasive nature of travel in our lives, including travel music. He looks at her list. '"Passenger",' he reads. '"Iggy Pop".' This is the extent of her list.

'I also came up with "Faraway Places". Actually, Candice came up with it. She remembers that stuff.' Her punkish cute face betrays no recollection of songs prior to Iggy Pop's.

'How about "Early Morning Rain"?'

'Who sang that?'

'Gordon Lightfoot. Among others.'

She writes down the name. 'That a local group?'

'... *This old engine's got me down, in the early morning rain* ...'

She looks at him and shakes her head.

He takes her list and scribbles, 'Travellin' On' (Hank Snow), 'Hard Travellin'' (Limeliters), 'Up A Lazy River' (Mills Brothers, but stretching it?), 'The Long and Winding Road' (Beatles) ... He feels his producer could cue up a nice medley for his next appearance.

Lena squints at the list. 'How 'bout "Holiday"? I think the title's "Holiday". By the Sex Pistols? On their album *God Save the Queen?*'

He looks at her and shakes his head.

'Or,' she gamely suggests, 'there's that other song by DOA called "Holiday in Cambodia"... Maybe it's by the Dead Kennedys.'

Dwight suggests she go away and interline Mr Pestle's ticket to Tangier, since he has been phoning the office all day about his refusal to fly TAP from London.

'Poor man,' he reminds her. 'He's had terrible luck with us. You remember he had to accept denied booking compensation on his last flight – and when he finally got to Lisbon two days late, went DNS because the hotel where we booked him was too *noisy*. Be nice to him, Lena.'

'Why? He likes little boys.'

Dwight decides, after a little more reflection, that from now on he'll make 'Travellin' Man' (Rick Nelson) his radio theme song. He stares at his screen. He doesn't know how or why, but he has completely missed the Alaska cruise market this summer.

3.

Playing croquet with his brother he wonders how to broach the topic with his mother about using her house for collateral, persuade her to act as a guarantor, when she's still so het up about the break-in this afternoon, sitting out here on the patio with Reesa and rattling on with the rerun. Marlene Irving savours these turning points in her life, these crises, willing to discuss them ad noz. She was out shopping it seems when the burglar walked in the front door without so much as an If You Please. Damon was out here in the garden, helping the gardeners. He saw their burglar leaving through the basement door. The police are planning to take him downtown tomorrow to look at mugshots. His mother has since found all kinds of drawers and closets ransacked.

'If only Sylvia weren't still away on holiday! Really, Dwight, did you have to book our Owl all the way to Cape Breton?'

Damon spurns his mallet and returns to the patio, bends over and resumes tapping his new pocket calculator, watching the little screen. The afternoon sunshine makes him tip his plastic window at angles to let him see the numbers. He smiles at times, his hair slicked back from a recent swim. Sitting down he begins to jiggle his foot like he has a plantar wart.

'I feel violated,' Marlene is telling Reesa. 'A stranger walking around in my house? Then the fingerprint man sprinkling powder on the furniture. He didn't find one whorl, or whatever it is they look for. Was he wearing gloves, Damon? Was the burglar wearing gloves?' She pulls imaginary gloves down her fingers. 'Never mind, dear.'

She has fortified them all with gin and tonics, including Damon, who has already gulped his and sucked dry the lime wedge.

'Did he take the silver?' asks Dwight, coming over.

'I don't think he took anything. As far as I can tell he took a pair of new underpants I bought Damon, and a pewter vase. Things may start *not* showing up tonight after I've had time to look around. Owl comes back Monday. She has a sharp eye.'

Marlene lights up again. For a moment she stares at Dwight's yellow shoes, possibly wondering how any son of hers with his preference in footwear could be trusted to act responsibly as a consultant to the great travelling middle class. He offers to mix them all another drink, and carries their glasses inside. Nothing warming in the oven.

'It's awful what's happening,' he overhears her saying. 'Did you read last month about the Monster of the Andes?'

He has noticed in his mother a certain fondness lately for news of purple hue. He supposes anybody awaiting the Shroud of Turin to settle the question of Christ's resurrection is apt to follow all sorts of sensational stories. ('I still want someone to take me to see this film *The Elephant Man.*') Odd then she won't listen to the UFFI news about insulation undermining health from inside her own walls. She prefers hearing about *demonstrable* threats, spiritual and otherwise. These tickle her deep curiosity about miracles and evil.

When he returns with their drinks Marlene crosses her still shapely legs and adjusts her lemon sundress at the knees, butting out one Matinee and lighting up another.

She smiles at them both, touching her neck. 'If you two had let me know you were coming I'd have said bring bathing suits for a swim. Our earthquake cracked the pool, but so far no loss of water. You can see the line half way down the wall.'

'You'd think we'd have enough sense to bring bathing suits,' Dwight replies, 'on Damon's birthday.'

'Good heavens, I probably invited you to dinner. Did I?'

'We have a date elsewhere,' lies Reesa, checking her watch.

'Phew. Did I remember to buy Damon a cake, I wonder? Sylvia usually takes care of the parties. Half the time I'm too busy with meetings ...' She pats her hair. '"I guess I need another drink, after all the excitement around here ..."' Dangling her suddenly empty glass. Unpredictable woman, his mother. Elizabeth Taylor, he guesses, in *Who's Afraid of Marlene Irving?* and so finds himself back in the kitchen.

Through the windows he can see the rose garden and sweet peas, Da's Persian cat stroking itself against his brother's leg. Watching his older brother is like watching a roughly domesticated animal on a long journey nowhere. Who *did* Damon see leaving the house with his underpants? Anyone? Or did he have a bad-tempered outburst and go on a rampage by sacking the place himself? He's lost his temper before, bashing a coffee table to bits.

The air drifting in through the Dutch door smells exotic to Dwight. It wouldn't be like he was trying to move his mother *out* of her house. Remortgaging needn't even affect her. Not with him making the payments. Not like her selling her cottage on Bowen Island or their old cabin cruiser to help him launch Herodotus Tours. Or lending him cash, as earlier this year, to help him expand. Remortgaging her house would be like loosening up on his inheritance a bit earlier than expected: wouldn't cost her a cent. *Pushing pushing.* He adds an extra jigger of gin to the double he's already poured her.

Back outside a womanly discussion of matters in utero. How is Reesa feeling, seven months gone? Funny how his mother has always seemed to prefer motherhood by proxy.

'By the way, dear, I never miss your show. Mind you, with some of these abortionists you have on every other evening, I'll bet you aren't going to miss it either when you take your baby-leave in October.'

'I'm not allowed to miss it,' replies Reesa. 'We can't afford to, can we, sweetheart?'

Ask her now. He is sure their pregnancy has put his mother in a benevolent mood.

'... I don't suppose,' he says casually, handing over her drink, 'you'd be willing, Mrs Irving, as a mere formality, to sign a paper so Irving junior, yours truly, could borrow a little money against your house? As a way of helping his gold mine continue its smooth expansion?'

No reaction from Marlene. 'Be no question of you having to make payments,' he continues. 'Herodotus would take care of everything.'

Memo: Stay cool. Business is booming. Herodotus is booming. Who cares if interest rates are booming too?

'Incidentally, I should be able to start paying back your earlier loans before long. Cash flow is good.' He smiles, making his blue eyes twinkle like an altar boy's.

Marlene, resuming her puffing, chooses not to answer. He can tell she has put on her 'thinking hat', preferring to let the matter drift for the time being in the August humidity, along with her cigarette smoke.

Reesa changes the subject. She knows Marlene enjoys hearing tattle from behind the scenes at *City, City*. What her co-host Tom Whitelaw is really like and why his contract wasn't renewed. How wealthy the owner of the station is and who he knows in Hollywood. Dwight admires his wife's skills. At her job she knows how to defuse the little bombs of opinion that can damage interviews, and when she doesn't, how to set them off in a drum with the lid on. In and out with questions, standing back watchfully in her protective gear of unassailable fashion, listening to opinions go off harmlessly. Then she's back in to lift the lid and wave her hand with vivacious good humour at the smoke, refusing to be sucked in. A disposal expert of growing experience, Reesa Potts logs politicians, gay activists, hooker spokepersons, symphony conductors, Polish defectors, Egg Marketing Board representatives – a multitude of views and counterviews, sometimes clashing in the same interview. 'I don't know how you keep them all straight,' Marlene observes. 'You're my button for the news.' For entertainment she means. Male and female teamsters, extreme and moderate Sikhs, investment portfolio people.

Damon's attention has wandered in the direction of the birthday gift Dwight placed earlier on the patio table. His lip has drifted off to the left. Dwight loves Da's eyes, his father's round grey eyes. Yet the shine of curiosity he remembers in his father's eyes has never quite shone in Da's. His brother's flesh is encased in a child's suntan, marked off at the sleeves of one of Aloysius's Foreign Trade T-shirts. A soft unforced tan.

'Tell Mother what you have there, Damon!'

'It's for Damon's birthday!' responds Dwight.

A ritual, this pumping up the toddler's vague interest in what they think he should be thrilled about.

Damon casts aside his calculator, scaring the cat off its flagstone. He starts whittling away at his brother's small blue-papered gift. Once inside he pops the lid.

'Damon!' says his mother. 'A ring! My whangdoodle has never had a ring before!'

Dwight watches his brother's eyes brighten and hold their shine like a flare at sea. No one has ever thought to give him a ring before. His own ring. For a moment Marlene wonders if he knows what to do with it. But he knows. He extracts it from the red plush and begins trying it on, eventually arriving at his ring finger. The gold glistens in the sunshine.

'Look at the initials, Da,' Dwight tells him. '... Other side up. M.I. it says. It's a signet ring.'

The letters mean nothing to Damon, who turns and twists his new ring like a radio dial. Tuning himself in from the desert.

'That's very sweet of you, Dwight. I can tell he's pleased.'

'It was Dad's. When you gave it to me after he died, my fingers were too small to wear it. Then Reesa gave me a wedding ring. I had one of my secretaries find a box.'

Marlene is trying to remember. 'You know, I don't recall Matt having a ring. Isn't that awful? Did I give it to him? Back in thirty-four? *"Watch us roar in thirty-four, boys."* As Mae West *didn't* say, but should have. I think this gin of yours, Dwight, was the one too many.' She fusses modestly with her pouty cleavage, still puzzled.

'Did I tell you?' she says. 'Aloysius came past to see us the other day. He brought Damon a golf iron and a whiffle ball. He was showing your brother how to swing. I admire that boy.'

'Was his fee for the lesson included in the equipment rental?'

'Don't mind Dwight,' says Reesa. 'Aloysius has been pestering him at the office about this and that.'

Memo: Ask A. if his band has any travel songs on tape.

Marlene lights up again. 'I feel so guilty. I think I should give you a little more for his board and clothing ... And I was thinking: What about a nice church camp, before he goes back to school? I expect he needs a holiday.'

'Maybe to a Young Conservatives convention.'

'He told Da and me he's working very hard with refugees.'

'He's got travel plans for refugees even I can't figure out.'

Marlene nods her assent. 'I sense he's a clever boy. Is he getting to mass every Sunday? Dwight, you remember mass.'

'The smell of candlewax? Ask me the Latin responses.' He smiles. 'The Seven Gifts of the Holy Ghost ... I even remember what page of the Catechism we memorized them on.'

'You can smile, Dwight,' she says with a sniff, inhaling. Exhaling. The thought of his spiritual decline clearly saddens her. '... But I remember when you weren't too big and mighty to play mass with your brother and tell him your confession. Damon remembers, don't you Da. He still comes to mass twice a week to receive the Blessed Sacrament.'

Dwight's stomach is rumbling. The birthday boy will be lucky to get macaroni and cheese, the outer limits of Marlene Irving's cooking range.

'To answer your question, Dwight. I don't think it would be wise or beneficial just now for me to mortgage my house. I don't feel I want to carry that additional responsibility. I'm – '

'You'd have a good price-earnings ratio, if you wanted it, and solid downside protection. With speculative potential?'

She stares at him. A songbird trills in the apple tree.

Reesa reads the mood and proceeds to excuse them both, since they have a restaurant reservation at seven.

Saying goodbye he is disappointed but not bereft of hope, not by any means. As he tells Reesa in the car, these muffler shops on TV, claiming Everybody's a Somebody at Midas, are a little like the banks lately. Anybody can get a loan. And if you're a Somebody, as he has become, your touch is golden. He is amazed how loose the banks are compared to friends and family. The banks can't do enough for you. 'I guess it's the least they can do for their own, since they're already lending billions to countries like Brazil and Mexico. I'm not worried. Why shouldn't they come across for us again, in exchange for another promise of expansion and a persuasive position paper?'

'All you top guns,' she observes. 'I didn't know you had your father's ring.'

'I bought it,' he confesses. 'Yesterday.'

4.

A hot night in August. Barking dog. No breeze or moon. Forked lightning over coastal mountains. He listens through their bedroom window. Reesa once thought Herodotus Tours would be an ideal name for a company that thought of travel as fantastic; that planned on pinning up a lot of glossy posters, as a way to beat a lack of actual experience on the owner's part, or the desire for any except in his head. Herodotus as the Father of History was also known as the Father of Lies.

Smell of forest fires. He listens some more. Hawking youth taunting a dog. If there is domestic violence going on in apartments across the street, it's muffled by horse chestnuts and curtains.

'I'm exhausted,' he confesses. 'Herodotus is going to turn us either into millionaires or bums.'

'Baby feels ambitious tonight.'

'Kicking?'

'The odd jack boot, yes.'

They pretend to an equal interest in this progeny.

She shifts sideways and picks up the Dickens novel she's rereading, a page or two a night. But she has forgotten to remove her contact lenses, meant only for distance. So edging heavily out of bed, sitting down at her dressing table and spreading her legs, she unscrews the twin container lids, to deposit her clear dainty wafers in their chambers of solution.

'Today I was thinking,' she says, pinching her left eyeball to strip it, 'how like Plato's artist you are. With all your travelese and so much second-hand reality.'

'Alan Babcock would probably agree with you.'

She peers blindly at him. 'Friend of yours?'

'Locker room acquaintance. Thinks ten percent commission is for waiters. Backhands himself to pee.'

'I'm not sure I follow,' she says, turning away. 'Or want to.'

In the darkness now, whitened intermittently by lightning, he falls back, slowly counting. The models he used to count on do nothing for him anymore:

'Wisdom,' he mumbles, 'Understanding, Counsel, Fortitude, Knowledge, Piety and Fear of the Porridge ...'

'Top Guns?'

'... Seven Gifts of the Holy Ghost.'

Just then, or maybe it is some time later, he hears or maybe dreams he hears, Aloysius come home humming a May hymn to the Blessed Virgin Mary, some months following the Annunciation by the flying archangel M.I.

April, 2046

Stayed at office late, then taxied downtown in wig and power glasses to meet V. who was late. Theatre lobby abuzz in usual good cheer of a Friday night. Held back, unsure of my disguise, but resolved to wear it out again in less adulterous circumstances. Disguise lets a politician eavesdrop on the grassroots. Not that this glittering bunch could be accused of trucking with the grassroots. The Howe Street money crowd, turned out for a history play about one of its forebears, is like royalty on a fox hunt. I despise the attitude that buys its culture on margin.

Was watching for V. when a swishy young woman washed up alongside. The way she scrutinized me made me beat a retreat to the water fountain. I suppose she was appraising my wig. Face maybe, one too many familiar lines under my carefully arranged mask.

V. and I sat holding hands in the dark, in those few seconds between the house lights going out and the stage lights coming up. Counting down to a new world. Then we disentangled, I don't know why, like snakes in heat. Snakes wouldn't care. But we were two public figures in disguise, schooled to dodge scandal, yet cheeky enough to accept a pair of complimentary tickets to the theatrical event of the season. Do we want to be discovered? Crave to be the news? Maybe we were just glad to shed the spotlight.

Civic history is out of fashion just now, but this material has been beaten into a musical. *The Whiz* has its moments, all of them loud, full of those brassy Broadway voices always a hit with the striped suits. I can afford to condescend. My suit is cut to the specs of many styles calculated to blend in. One's campaign contributions come from all types. The political suit, says F., is unfortunately my strong one.

'The Whiz' himself was a happy buccaneer from the last century who first put our stock market on the map, and had a tummy the size of a mobster's. Broads, gold mines, insider trading, three dead Hollywood celebs who'd once sung cameo numbers to him at a charity roast, and a wedding dress the width of the stage. All wild west stuff. Actor playing the Whiz sang his songs very touchingly, especially one on why he was forced to manipulate stocks in a gold mine. His baritone brought the house down. He's meant to be a comic figure with short hair permed and tinted in the fashion of the time. If evening's performance was anything to go by, can see myself down the line being asked to attend the celebration of the play's one-thousandth performance. Raucous, tender songs. Good production values. Dead as drama.

V. and I fled by cab to Le Crocodile on Smythe. Everywhere and nowhere to go. Wanted to remove my hot droopy wig. V. also in a wig. What a ridiculous pair of eighteenth-century flowers! What gossip we would make in the morning's tabloid news: Two aging hothouse blossoms conduct affair as spouse slowly dies in clinic.

No wonder I feel the strain of deception. I'm sixty-four. I want it though. I want it. Have to remind myself how old we both are to be going around in costumes and having coiling conversation over oyster mushrooms.

'We've got the seeds of a play in *us*,' said V. '... But my lips are sealed. If yours are.' 'Except,' I said, 'I can see your tongue.' 'Can you?' said V. 'You don't miss a lick, do you, Gwyn?' *Arriba*.

A wonderful spring night. We walked for a while on the seawall holding hands. Embraced and kissed deeply by the tulip garden. Then we came back here. I had a message to phone the hospital. I knew what it was. Didn't want to know. F. was dead.

But no, my son's wife has just given birth to our first grandson. This morning I call Renaldo and extend our congratulations. Then come in here to sit down with my coffee before calling F. Feel like a mousetrap, abandoned in a summer cottage, just waiting to snap. Will have to dip into Mother's old boxes and rattle family skeletons for some possible understanding of my failing F. again and again.

Can't the doctors do anything to speed up the inevitable?

I should never have run again for mayor, but F. encouraged it. I have been running a long time. What it is that makes me run, administer, run again? Just to be invited to preside over a one-thousandth performance somewhere bright?

A diary remembers in the same way a tulip

remembers to close its
red brain nightly, and
reopen it in the
morning, long after stem
is severed from root and
brought inside to water.
These petals pressed
between lines can be
counted on in later years
to guide me back to
shallowness, vanity, fear
of aging, and a mind
capable of being seduced
by an audience.

Chapter 6

Travel by Proxy

HE HAS URGED HER to hang tough, but then a man would. The question for her is whether or not, should the pain get intense, she will accept an epidural. She wants everything to go as naturally as possible, but, unlike a vegetarian who'd rather starve than eat a hot dog, she isn't going to get doctrinaire about a drug to ease her birth pangs. Why tempt nature to go on a tear? His wife fears pain. *You must talk firmly but lovingly to your wife – give simple and precise directions. If she panics and momentarily loses control, speak to her in a firmer voice saying, 'Breathe in and out, keep it up, until the contraction is over.'*

He reads this over to himself at a busy sandwich bar in early October. He wonders if he can remember what to do when her time comes. They were told to 'practise' effleurage and shallow breathing at home. To 'coach' themselves through imaginary deliveries in preparation for the real event. 'All this getting set,' Reesa confessed, laughing at their drill, its second-handedness, 'makes it sound like a rugger scrum ... *Push* – out pops the ball.' Unlike him who can run on squash courts till he aches to breathe, she dislikes putting her own body through any but the laziest bike rides. If it weren't so trendy she'd prefer a Caesarean. As for a spinal drip, not to mention local anaesthetic for an episiotomy, she can't imagine refusing any suggestion made by her doctor. 'Or by you,' she's told him, amused. 'My travel guide. Just, please, don't tell me to *hang tough.*'

Dwight, standing at this downtown lunch counter, is rereading 'How You Can Help' (meaning him, the guide) on a mimeographed page from the City Health Department, peeling cellophane from his devilled egg sandwich to release it from an elbow of cardboard matting. These reminder sheets, stamped with a ring of tomato juice, make him feel like a student cramming for a biology exam. Seven days past due, and not much concerned, Reesa resents having to call his office every two hours to let his secretary know whether or not her water's broken. *She may become irritable and cross and may not want to be bothered with anyone or anything ...* Once her water breaks, he is supposed to coach her through early and active labour, to the hard or transitional stage of pushing – at which point (he reads) her cervix will have dilated from four to ten centimetres and effacement. How is he supposed to remember this stuff unless he uses cheat-sheets? *Notify your staff if your wife feels like pushing. It may be necessary to do transitional drill or panting at this time.* Panting?

Do PANT – BLOW *Breathing ... Puff-Puff-Puff-Puff ... Blow ...* Christ. Memo: Bring an Oh Henry to labour ward for self.

Up at dawn he's usually too played out to want to practise shallow breathing when he comes home. And Reesa (busy buying nursing bras, Penaten cream, bassinets) has told him she prefers to rely on her talent for improvisation anyway, not practice. Who's interested in practising for birth? Be like practising for death: hard to take the threat seriously when they are both busy living. These days his life, like her stomach, keeps expanding. For him, just keeping *up* in the world is a tireless, indigestive racing between engagements.

This afternoon, for examp, due at the airport for a two o'clock 'flight', he wonders how many unfinished tasks are left back on his desk. The books alone are a full-time job and he can't abide the financial end of business. Meanwhile four, and soon he hopes five, HT offices require a nudging visit from him every day or so, to ensure his new staff appreciate the importance of paying details the courtesy they unfailingly deserve. Taking calls, handling reservations, issuing tickets: Dwight conveys to his staff how much he relies on their taking care of this immediate business, not to mention assisting in visa and passport applications, car rentals and immunizations.

He himself has radio talks to prepare, slide lectures once or twice a month, and bank appointments. There's also his travel newsletter *Afar* to keep buoyant with hot tips and incisive suggestions. As well he is expected to market a prototype of JetSet soon, his game for armchair travellers. And he must read: far more than a normal travel consultant, because he doesn't travel himself. He spends more time poring over travel articles, promotional brochures and background guidebooks than wandering travel writers spend travelling. For a student who once preferred bridge to books, he's begun to worry about his eyes.

He's begun to worry about the roast-like carvings of an episiotomy *down there*, as in one of the 'birthing' films they saw last week at prenatal class.

Amusing that the more known he becomes the less ridiculous and endangered he feels: as if coming into the open about his Secret might do him no harm at all, possibly even enhance his entrepreneurial reputation.

Pushing pushing.

He glances up to discover the girl beside him at the lunch bar staring at his *puff-puffing* lips in the counter mirror.

2.

He knows on occasion when to let others in on the second-handedness of his reportedly first-hand experience. Like his flight this afternoon. He's planning to tell his radio listeners to *Where in the World?* all about it. Given the chance to fly a Boeing 747, he also plans to write a column on his experience as soon as he gets back to the office. It isn't the kind of experience he can afford to pass up. Born of curiosity about travel and pilots, his idea began on the phone, followed up by an invitation to come and experience for himself what the stresses of flying the biggest passenger plane in the world actually are.

Arriving at the airport by taxi Dwight senses he should have brought luggage, like an adulterer checking into a hotel. He soon narrows down his choice of destinations to Sydney, San Paulo, San Francisco ... before deciding the most glamorous, not to say dangerous, airport to fly into would be Hong Kong's Kaitak. So he selects Kaitak. He isn't disappointed. He has already picked up his 'flight' in the hangar. Climbing into the flight-training simulator he and Captain Daniels, who vows to stretch his new co-captain to the limit, take off down runway o8 in a barely vibrating cockpit, and climb a thousand metres before banking north where the gondola lights of Grouse Mountain tip into view. The realism of the video is astounding.

'All right,' his captain instructs him, 'let's take her higher.'

'You're the doctor.'

In no time they've crossed the International Dateline and are preparing their approach into Hong Kong. A busy checkdown before landing. He listens to Daniels tell him how to take the airliner in himself without computers. It's night again and he faces a two-hundred-foot ceiling, with visibility under a mile. The video is foggy. Dwight tenses. His palms dampen. He manages to bank smoothly (but unfortunately at too low an altitude) before losing his whole starboard wing and the lives of approximately four hundred and fifty people aboard. It's exactly the crash he was hoping to survive and talk about.

'Unlucky,' observes his co-pilot.

Daniels pushes buttons to reset the screen and restart their engines. 'Try her again.' This Old-Spiced coach, with the iron-grey hair and voice, who trains real pilots on his five-million-dollar video game, claims he's used to mistakes: maybe not to such spectacular mistakes: but mistakes in judgement when ambition or the stress of a bad situation (like trying to land this sucker at Kaitak in a rainstorm) makes things that much worse.

This time the captain punches in lightning, turbulence, a pair of crippled engines to port, and redirects their approach via Cheung Chau, through a mountain range of apartment towers.

Thus crippled Dwight bears down on the control wheel. He is delighted to feel his palms sweatier than ever, his stomach gastric, and his head starting to throb. He can even begin to reimagine the necessity of prayer. Daniels is flipping switches as they settle into their final approach. Dwight watches his IVSI dial, his Flap Indicators, his Altitude Director Indicator, and something Daniels calls his 'Approach Progress Display'. To deploy the wheels he's supposed to be on top of the Gear Selector Lever. When he does remember to look out the windshield – not really necessary, but what the heck – the metropolis is rushing up to greet them with stunning solidity.

'Nose up a hair,' suggests Daniels.

She may get a second wind and feel new energy and excitement.

'Lovely. Now hold her steady, right there ...'

She feels much pelvic pressure as the baby's head descends.

'Okay. Go for it ... That's the ticket ...'

A bump and they're down, straight down the middle, flashing by rain-mirrored runway lights, as tons of responsibility and steel suddenly lift from Dwight's tired shoulders. He feels fantastic.

'Beautiful,' Daniels dutifully acknowledges. '... But unless you reverse the engines pretty quick your party's over.'

When it *is* over Dwight sits back, very pleased with the authenticity of his experience. He imagines it as ten times better than the real thing. Especially now, at the end of a long day that has carried him into tomorrow, he won't have to disembark and wait with his fagged co-pilots in the rain for some hotel's mini-van with narrow seats. He won't have to endure the boredom of waiting round an unfamiliar city with irritable flight attendants, before turning back and flying all the way home into yesterday. Chinese food gives him indigestion anyway. He removes his headset.

Daniels is eating a dark scarlet tomato. Lapping its juices and sucking the flesh, he flips off the video screen. Dwight feels a strong attraction to this handsome, casual Father of Flight.

He ponders their journey. In his column and on the radio he thinks he'll focus on the not inconsequential stress of trying to duplicate somebody else's experience, and praise the authenticity of all this artificiality. Of travel by proxy. For once he can afford to be completely honest – which ought to amuse Reesa if nobody else. 'I certainly owe you an honourable mention,' he tells Daniels, 'especially for the lightning.' He tells him he intends to pronounce his simulator, which rents for $350 an hour but complimentary to Dwight, a bargain. Much less than for a real flight to Hong Kong, and at twenty times the thrill.

'That's the thing,' says Daniels, closing down the two engines they've come in on. 'Everybody raves about the reality factor. Afterwards, you can hear their hearts going pat-a-pat.'

He consumes the rest of his tomato.

Dwight, who hasn't eaten since he left Canada, begins to snack on his Oh Henry bar.

3.

JetSet has taken him forever to get right. He believes the end is finally in sight. Sort of. He's still labouring over notes for his ideal city, the enticement for dice-rolling players who must negotiate bad journeys to arrive at their reward. *Sidewalk cafés, of course, where Greek, French, Costa Rican coffee is served ... and good bread, piping bread.* Has to be a city where players will want to forget their pasts and take out citizenship. *Evening zocalos full of mynah birds, choiring brilliantly ...* A city where the modern world isn't excluded, but neither is its architectural past. Architecture harmonious, nothing higher than nineteenth-century buildings – though modern buildings of good design admitted, provided they blend in and speak of their own genius and time. *Climate? Temperate-tropical. Algarveish sea breezes, with hinterland of cork oaks and vineyards. A subway system with rubber wheels, sculptures on display from main museum ...*

Candice has been rapping on his door. He glances up from his screen. 'You want to include a "satisfaction-or-your-money-back" guarantee on this package to Venezuela? For the hotel and the rest of it?'

He acts surprised. 'Isn't that something we've built our rep on?'

'Yes ... but we don't know much about this place called – ' she has to check the sheets he has handed her – 'the Swann Hotel.'

'We go with our hunches, Candy. I bet the place'll be gorgeous.'

'Well, don't blame me.'

Doubting Thomas, he thinks. What grey eyes.

He longs to become a citizen of his ideal city (*name?*), climb through his screen and go walking streets and smelling air, find out secrets by visiting every room ... He has interwoven details for his players, local history to trade like gossip: *Inside the old opera house, pregnant Sonya the soprano longs for oysters and gets them. Handsome boys lounge at her rehearsals ...*

In imagining the urban melodramas, by way of familiarizing his players with the city, he welcomes Anna Noches, lying atop mail sacks on the marble floor of the post office, trying not to give birth before the ambulance arrives, as two citizens tear shirts off their backs. Meanwhile, dancing in the park has just received a nice boost from an anonymous millionaire, who wants to pay the city's orchestra out of his own pocket to perform on the lawn. And, what's this, the resolution of a court case has resulted in the judge's charge to a disgraced nursing home to fertilize and nurture the public rosebeds? No wonder the price of dying is coming down. Corruption has been stamped out.

Such genetic material Dwight tosses into the pot of his computer. He can't foresee yet how his players are going to interact with his imaginary citizens. But their response to his city is only part of the game.

The other part, the practical business part, is riskier. JetSet will never get off the ground without more infusion of capital. He's still scrambling on the money scene to borrow wherever he can. It gets harder by the month not to imagine the banks cancelling his performance if interest rates edge any higher. The end could always come as a complete surprise – although his understanding is banks don't care for surprises and would prefer to keep a game like his on the go. A lot easier if his mother would just agree to mortgage her house and let him take care of her monthly payments at the bank. The cash would help him solve his liquidity problem.

He rehearses his smile once or twice, wipes each eyelash in an upward direction, shakes his head to give his sandy hair a careless look, and prepares to welcome back into his presence Mr and Mrs Frank Conklin, who've evidently decided for their next trip to venture all the way to the South Seas.

He checks his watch. He flips open a gift box of Cuban cigars and positions it on his desk in front of Frank's chair. The hospital photograph of Reesa and his newborn daughter he carefully arranges to face Maureen.

His intercom buzzes on the minute. When he presses it to usher in his clients, he's mildly surprised to hear from Lena that the Conklins, who just phoned, apologize for having to cancel their interview in light of financial reconsiderations. The Conklins? A retired couple with a steady income? He has to wonder who might be next.

Memo: Strapped for cash? Don't be afraid to *borrow*, to invest in travel. Investment of a lifetime.

Memo: Start talking up credit.

Pushing pushing.

4.

On Thanksgiving Monday he drives his new family to his mother's for dinner. Both Bartlett and Aloysius have been good sports about the all-night squalling, about Reesa's postnatal depression, about the general untidiness of soiled diapers and burped-over sheets piling up in doorways. Theresa is still trying to get a handle on nannying. Theresa, a Salvadoran refugee from the basement of St. Sebastian's, is a girl of unsurpassed inability. Mrs Scobie, through Aloysius and Trudy, wasn't able to guarantee her competence beyond experience of growing up in a large, and lately persecuted, family of eight. He'd like to ask for a trade-in on Theresa but agrees with Reesa they should wait a little longer to see if she can stop feeling sorry for herself and figure out the purpose of disposable diapers.

Reesa's mom comes to help out, but she prefers talking on the phone to helping her daughter adjust to the new parameters. Her word, 'parameters'. Just as her grandmother did for her, she has passed on the family's lucky penny to her new granddaughter, thereby skipping Reesa's generation. An over-sandalled woman – with strap and trace climbing her unshaven legs like sweetpea nets – she has a certain charm, which Reesa has inherited in the musical timbre of voice. He would like her more if she didn't push garbanzo-bean casseroles so much. Tall and dark, very youthful, just like *her* mother, who has no reason to be in a nursing home.

'I just can't believe you haven't named her yet,' says Marlene Irving. Over sherry she has handed them *What Shall We Call Our Baby?* to help make up their minds. 'Take a peek at "Angela". I think Angela Irving would be a lovely name.'

Dwight wonders why Reesa doesn't stick up for her own name, Potts.

Thanks to Sylvia the house is meticulously dusted and the turkey smells delicious. Rooms open into other rooms without impediment, floors glisten, sinks sparkle. Damon is proud of the pearwood logs he has split and banked up like a blazing teepee in the fireplace. Even Aloysius is here. He agreed to come at Marlene's insistence and is lying like a chained-up mongrel on the hearth, scratching himself.

'"The angelic",' reads Reesa, 'or "heavenly messenger".' Dwight groans.

'It's from the Greek,' his mother tells him. 'It's not Catholic, if that's what you're thinking.' She holds her new granddaughter on the sofa, while Damon, who has given the fire a last poke, gazes at the baby. He was fascinated at the hospital, gazing through the nursery window. Now he clasps his hands and crosses the China carpet to play his new niece something on the baby grand. 'Pop Goes the Weasel.' Rusty technique, missing as many notes as he hits. They all applaud, except Aloysius, who rolls over on his back to stare at the ceiling. 'Sounded punk, Da.' His greatest compliment.

'*Pop!* goes the weasel,' repeats Marlene.

Reesa says to Dwight, 'I don't mind "Angela", sweetheart.'

He looks at her.

'Or "Vesta"?' She plays it with her teeth, lips, tongue. 'Vess-tah.'

'Are you serious?'

His mother looks at him. 'I didn't like your name either till I found out it meant "white" or "fair". It seemed to suit your snowy entrance.'

'I thought I meant "west" or "shining". What a disappointment.'

'"Vesta",' quotes Reesa, '"in Roman mythology was the goddess of hearth and home. She also guarded the sacred flame tended by the Vestal Virgins".'

'I think I prefer "Sappho",' says Dwight.

'I like "Angela",' says Marlene, firmly.

She plants a kiss on Angela Vesta Irving's forehead, closing her eyes to the sweet scent of her granddaughter's talc skin. He's surprised she can smell anything after decades of smoking. He wouldn't be surprised if she lit up now while still holding the child. And smoke isn't his only concern. He wonders how the toxic insulation lodged in her walls might affect the pink lungs of a newborn. The infant is safer in their own house, rented with few expectations and no insulation at all.

Conversation manages to skirt the two separate matters of the baby's baptism and her extra thumb. Neither he nor Reesa has any interest in returning the warranty (so far as christening implies) to ensure God's commiseration in case the product should fail to outgrow this trace of Original Sin. His mother remains circumspect for the time being. And if she has managed a peek inside the blanket, where the baby's hand lies hidden, she hasn't presumed to comment since their arrival. Maybe it's enough knowing her first grandchild is without any trace of Uncle Damon's odd deficiency. No trouble being *heard*, no.

Not even from upstairs, after Owl puts her down on Dwight's old bed.

Sitting them all for dinner Marlene makes a careful display of grace amid the silverware and crystal goblets. '... And P.S. Thank you, Lord, for delivering us Baby Angela safe and sound.'

She stubs out a Matinee and straightens a placemat for Sylvia to put down the turkey platter. Aloysius stubs out his Pall Mall. 'Dwight, dear, will you carve? Not a lot for Damon, he's been into Sylvia's bran muffins this morning. He snuck a whole tray of them when we were out shopping and now he's got the runs. That's all I have to say on that subject.'

Damon opens his mouth as if reluctant to acknowledge remorse, greediness, flatulence. Restless as a child, still restless as a man, he seldom sits long anywhere, least of all at the head of the table in his father's chair. After a few mouthfuls of stuffing, half a glass of milk, he's up again and banking his fire across the hall. 'Damon, dear! Don't overfeed the fire when we're not in the room! There's a good boy!'

At this enjoiner they hear a great *whack*.

'Oh dear,' says Marlene, rising apologetically and hurrying in to comfort her son, returning just as swiftly carrying the poker. She deposits it in the corner.

'He's started these temper fits lately when I ask him in the nicest way to do something. He gets over-excited on holidays. And now he's gone and taken a lump out of my mantelpiece. I think he's bored.'

Dwight notices his brother stretched out on the hearth, propped on his elbow, gazing into the fire. Little appears to have changed in twenty years. Owl blinking, his mother rambling, the house glowing.

'How do you like your turkey, Aloysius, dear?'

'A-1.'

'Now isn't that an interesting expression,' exclaims Marlene, encouraging him to eat more. 'You're picking up our idioms like a house on fire.'

Memo: Talk to A. again about his pyramid letter scam. Lay down the law.

Over dessert Dwight notices the empty hearth and excuses himself to look for Da.

Going upstairs he hears a vaguely familiar sound, not crying exactly, but a milder contented sound the baby makes after feeding. Inside his old bedroom he adjusts slowly to the dim light, and then sees Da lying on his elbow across the infant.

The baby is asleep.

It's Damon making the sound, from high up, somewhere inside his head.

The sound stuns Dwight: not the sound but the fact that he has never before heard his brother's voice. It comes as a revelation. *Hn Hn Hn Hn Hn Hn Hn Hn Hn Hn Hn Hn Hn* ... Is Da imitating pigeons in the eaves? The voice keeps on with little variation, not so much cooing as like some rundown car alarm, suggesting a thief in the night has been tampering with someone's ignition. Or a thirsty animal nearing a waterhole. The sound is eerie. Da, remembers Dwight, Da, Da ...

He senses this is what his older brother might have done over *him* as an infant, maybe to welcome him home from the hospital. Maybe to ... Then he notices what his brother is doing.

Holding the baby's hand, pinching it gently between his thumb and forefinger, gazing at the extra thumb. *Hn Hn Hn Hn* ... In Damon's fingers her tiny fish are wriggling, curling inward, struggling for their lives.

The child has awakened to his sound and begun to squawk. Something smells fishy. Diapers.

Downstairs, Marlene doesn't believe Damon has spoken.

'Go on, Da, show her!' Dwight is ready to celebrate. He wants Da to raise the roof.

His brother no longer seems interested. Dwight insists. He insists everybody ignore dessert to try all kinds of tests on his brother, including his handing the baby over to Da and forcing him to cuddle her, but she just cries louder. Her diapers stink. Damon looks bewildered.

'Don't upset him too much,' warns his mother.

'Shall I take her, Da?' offers Reesa. Damon returns to his fire and pokes it into a more responsible blaze. He adds a log, sweeps the hearth with the brass-handled broom, and settles back down on his elbow in a conscious imitation of Aloysius in his crotch chain.

'Dwight, really ...' Marlene's flustered. 'Da may have a voicebox but he's never *ever* made a sound ... Are you sure it wasn't Angela you heard upstairs?'

'Yes. I put my hand on his head and felt vibrations coming from inside.'

'Well, then, it's a miracle.' For a religious woman she doesn't exactly sound convinced. 'Your baby is responsible for a miracle, Reesa.'

Disappointed, he goes in to the hearth. He thinks of the mortgage proposal he was planning to reintroduce, the house, her acting as his guarantor. He's pissed off a great opportunity has disappeared to help enrich his cash flow in the wake of Da's indifference to a miracle.

'Maybe we could try Lourdes next, or Fatima,' he says. 'Till Da can babble on request.'

'Dwight, really!'

'Why does "a miracle" have to come into it? I heard him.'

His mother looks at him as if sorry for having such an atheist for a son on Thanksgiving Day.

5.

That night he is up till one, trying to understand the meaning of his brother's lapse into voice. He discusses the case with Bartlett, who listens carefully but has no explanation. Dwight, doing his daughter's laundry, is having to kick the spin dryer whenever it dies. 'I'll ask my old man to take a look at that,' remarks Bartlett. They're standing in the cubbyhole off the kitchen, swigging beer and badmouthing Theresa.

Bartlett's preference for a name is 'Gwyn.' Aloysius, making himself a sandwich, stops at the refrigerator to think. 'La Toya.' He's certain La Toya is the name she was born for. They all agree 'Vesta' ought to be thrown out with the bathwater.

Their rent by the way is scheduled to go up again November 1, and both Dwight and Bartlett think the landlord is trying to send them a message. They aren't sure what the message is. 'I couldn't afford regular rent,' says Dwight. 'I'm stretched as it is.' He doesn't mention the money he owes the bank via Bartlett. He inquires politely after Megan's disintegrating jawbone. Megan is Bartlett's girlfriend.

Before bed he asks Aloysius to join him in the den so they can have a word together about his chain letter scam. It doesn't go well.

'You need a break,' Reesa tells him upstairs. She's nursing Angela Vesta La Toya Gwyn Irving Potts. 'Sleep in tomorrow morning, sweetheart.'

'I just spoke to Aloysius about his fraudulent letter. Using my confidential list of clients. He proceeded to give me shit for selling sex junkets to Third-World countries!'

'How odd.'

'Where does he pick up this stuff?'

'Must be bad form to scold a punk rocker. Be glad he didn't spit on you.'

In the night it rains. The sound of windows being attacked with blown sand. The gutter is leaking onto shingles lower down where the pigeons shit.

Dwight doesn't sleep in that morning or any morning into the foreseeable future. He works flat out every day, declining to come home for dinner. One evening when he can no longer see straight he drives himself away from all the tower blocks in the West End, to collapse in the anonymous darkness of a second-run cinema in Kits. He finds himself stoking up on fatty foods he never used to eat, like Nanaimo bars and cookies. He sips a double espresso.

He drives home looking at the October night through his windshield like a filmmaker. *The Red Desert* had preceded *The Passenger*, full of rectangular images framed to look like abstract paintings: polluted ponds in the industrial wastelands of Ravenna, the rusting sides of freighters up close. Somehow both films seemed soft at the core: he can't put his finger on the failure. He liked the sunny deserts and the Gaudi architecture of the second feature. The façade of the unfinished cathedral in Barcelona. He makes a mental note to get cracking on a Spanish travel package, possibly a gay or lesbian tour, ahead of its time and defiant of the dead dictator, now that Franco's gone.

Reesa is lying in bed, not yet asleep.

'Enjoy yourself, shopping?'

'I bought a dress. I feel guilty.'

'You haven't bought any dresses for nine months.'

'I'm going to take it back. I don't really love it.' She sounds down, not her outgoing self since the baby's birth. 'My feminist mother makes me feel guilty buying smart clothes for work. Instead of sneakers and denim skirts.'

He slips into bed and falls asleep dreaming of Jack Nicholson in an undershirt. He's swapping his passport photo, for the corpse's on the bed. He wakes up at four, knowing Reesa is awake by the way her knees are sticking straight up under the duvet. She says she knows it's stupid but she's worried about spending too much money.

She is sleeping when he wakes up later. He shakes her gently. Hungry, the baby has been crying. 'I was dreaming about losing everything. The way I used to feel when my mother bought me clothes. That's the way she made me feel.'

He wonders if, by asking her who the father is, he might help her overcome the guilt of motherhood.

'What offer?' she asks him over breakfast.

'Gulfstream Travel. The giant is hungry. Or else jealous. Even wants to retain me at a fat salary after their proposed takeover, as a consultant in their national office.'

'That's wonderful news. Are you considering it?'

'What, move?'

'Where?'

'I wouldn't move east. Not when I'm in the business of turning us into the Crossroads of the Pacific. HT is going to fly a lot higher on its own.'

May, 2045

Official visit almost through, so we hung out on our terrace avoiding delegation. They could do as they pleased. We had upset stomachs and it wasn't the cheroots. V. and I agree we've got along well on our first trip together. Being abroad lets me say scandal doesn't worry us.

Recalled earlier junkets to Yokohama and Guangzhou, with Chamber of Commerce and symphony orchestra. We seem a family of seaport sisters inclined to one another out of narcissism. 'How we love mirrors,' I said.

'I love you on top of me,' said V.

Always a gap between what I imagine a city's going to be and what it is when I come. I wondered aloud if the two ever coincide. V. yawned.

As sometimes happens when I'm speaking off the cuff to Rotarians, I then made one of those observations I hadn't till that moment ever made, but which sounded like I'd been making all my life.

'... I often wonder what it might be like if the city I imagined were to match exactly the city I found. If over the map of a city I'm visiting I laid the map of the city in my head and found they fit precisely. Would this be paradise?'

V. responded by alluding to the local physician who'd surprised us by prescribing water to drink, out of a specially treated bottle on his shelf, with a promise of 'much happiness'. V. said, 'Talk about a holistic approach to travel. Yours, though, sounds a little scrappy.'

Debated lunch and decided since it was our final afternoon in Odessa we should order room service. The waiter uncorked a bottle of Rumanian red wine and we toasted ourselves.

'I would like to propose – because I want the city to get full value for the cost of sending me abroad, V. – a way of attracting esteem to our already international metropolis.'

'You will, I'm sure, put this into an electrifying motion before council. Why didn't we order food?'

'I'd like to propose

something over and beyond the town planners' notion of a city. I'd like to look at ours as a model city, in which we were to reinvest the clichés of its being the most liveable/ beautiful/ take your pick city in the world – you know, Board of Trade stuff I do my smartest to promulgate on these jaded junkets – with a new formula that would give us a different image to help guide around the tourists, no matter how much older and greater their cities may be than ours.'

V. lifted a puckered mouth. 'I can see I arouse you to the heights of hubris, Your Worship. Beats me why I've never had you in one of my films.' She lifted a bare foot and placed it on the table. A bird from the Black Sea started warbling in the potted tree below.

I poured more wine. And went on without spilling a drop. Why couldn't we take that old kitsch poster of the city, showing us before we actually existed – the one with a few strands of smoke rising from native fires hidden in huge conifers along the beaches, and the explorer's ship arriving in the bay – and press over this image a transparent sheet, upon which was imprinted a photograph of our skyscraping city, to create a kind of hologram floating in time.

V. grunted. I was cavorting with her big toe. I said, 'It'd be like one of your films, frozen in its frame. Except layered ... We could slip in transparent sheets of old photos, and with some hip-pocket technology and a little laser jazz, become time travellers.' I leaned forward. And tickled her toe with my tongue.

'Why don't you suck on a cheroot instead?' she asked.

'You'd still be whining about neglect, you floozy.'

To punish her, I pulled back and sucked a while on my extra thumb, hidden like a clitoris.

'My image would be portable,' I suggested. 'We could look into the costs of selling it in the map and guidebook section of bookstores ...'

'You're on a power trip,' said V., lifting her big toe to tap against my glasses. 'You should learn to think more like a gigolo.'

'You're not listening ... It wouldn't just be for the tourists, this hologram.'

'No, certainly not ...' She lifted her other foot to the table, since it was feeling left out, and began demanding equal attention for five more wriggling toes. 'Not if the hookers got wind of it,' she joked.

'By seeing ourselves in stereo, so to speak, we could pull the whole works into line in one floating image – centering the city we were living in now on top of sawmills, windjammers, the earliest Godforsaken immigrants – the wilderness itself, my dear V. – so we could listen in on whatever we decided to look for, strolling the city with all its time in our hands. We'd become our own guides to time. There wouldn't have to *come* a time when the reality of the place cancelled out the dream of it, when our memory of its image vanished.'

V. looked quite concerned for my mental health. 'Ream my toes,' she ordered.

I looked at my watch. I had an interview to give. I was feeling soused. I said, 'Instead of "my companion", I ought to be introducing you to our girthy Board of Traders as "my filthy-minded sounding board".'

'"Springboard", bikky. Pour me another glass of pinot noir. I *love* to be waited on. My husband never would.'

We're going home via Moscow, a city in the grip of self-romance, I understand, after much upheaval with whatever demons have long beguiled its civic body.

Must try to banish it from my imagination before landing.

Chapter 7

Float Therapy

A HITCH. His newest agency on Altamira he has had to shut down for lack of operating capital. His office on Robson, not exactly turning away clients at the door, could be next. The recession has begun to hurt, the new year is turning into a dog. The travelling public is looking elsewhere to put its money, staying home and paying down mortgages. How to persuade them to travel abroad when they haven't yet paid for home? Rather than flying to Portugal, they stroll instead to the Portuguese restaurant on Robson. He can't understand the universal contraction. Friendly bankers aren't as friendly as they used to be, nor are friends. Leo Orsetti (for examp) wants all his money back, like right now. And business loopholes are tightening up. Shrinking, disappearing.

'You bet they are,' agrees Alan Babcock, after beating his opponent in three straight games of noontime squash. The beer business is following a tougher game plan than he expected. 'Went to this business seminar last week, right? What d'you think, Dwight, is the biggest single killer in ninety-eight percent of all business failures? Lack of bread? Got news for you. Ignorance. Incompetence from lack of managerial skills and experience … And that's not the whole of it.'

Soaked, Babcock watches his partner dry off after their shower, while Dwight tries to prevent this by keeping his towel in a modest position – not because he cares if Alan Babcock has a gawk at his penis, but because of the shame he feels over his growing paunch. Babcock's own tool is a hawser.

'… Lots more where that comes from,' says Alan.

'What?'

'Failure. So many ways to fail it's a miracle every entrepreneur doesn't go belly up. Take what this guy from the Federal Business Development Bank was telling us. Besides ignorance, Christ, there's a list as long as your Tweetie Bird, like not enough money – or too much money, tied up in fixed assets – mismanaging your inventory, poor credit, too many profits going to the owner, stupid expansion plans ...'

'Yeah?' At his locker Dwight reaches for his shirt. He wonders for a moment if Babcock might be mocking him. Trying to undercut his success by going on about failure so much. Has Babcock some inkling of HT's current position? Has this guy got psychic powers coming up through a cloven foot? Maybe he's picked up some racy club gossip from a grudge-holder like Beardsley and is now twisting it to his advantage.

Dwight makes a big deal of decking out his neck in a flashy sunset tie from Hawaii. Trying to exude the kind of illicit confidence a colour like this allows in the world of business.

'Take me,' Babcock says. 'Organizational structure I'm fairly good at. Objectives. Physical plant needs, staff requirements – stuff I need to make a go of it in the early eighties. On paper I look good. I look like a solid credit risk the first go round, you know, when I pop up at my bank with projections and a battle plan. Suppose I can show some impressive security on a personal net worth statement ... let's say I get that far, right? I can show a banker how an independent like me can penetrate the local beer market, and I've done my homework: projected my costs, my gross margins, my inventory turns – so I look good on paper, Dwight, right?'

He sits down dripping on the bare bench by his locker, towel around his neck, cleaning out earwax with the tail of it. Dwight can't help feeling he's being teased, tempted to betray himself, when he's in a vulnerable position.

'... And suppose I basically know the difference between an incorporated company and a proprietorship. But for the sake of argument suppose I'm not interested in incorporating 'cause I can't take tax advantage of any spousal salary ... like you could, I imagine, if your wife didn't have a salary of her own. I'm guessing you're in a partnership, Dwight, a man in your position? ... Anyhow, here I am with a proprietorship, say. And in my early years, just suppose the tax bite hasn't chewed me up ...'

'So what's the problem?' says Dwight shortly, stepping into his trousers, reaching into his pocket. He studies his watch and flexes his expansion bracelet before snapping it on. Losing three straight games hasn't helped his sense of humour. He thought he might take at least a game from the number four seed to ease his sickening slide down the ladder. Last week he lost to Reg Lapwing, the number twenty-two. He's fallen back now to eighteen, where he was when he began his sudden rise.

'Problem,' says Babcock, 'is unlike you I'm not a good details man.' *Dee*tails. 'Hate keeping records and watching balance sheets. And I'm not sensitive enough to work real well with people.'

This is such a stark, even flattering confession, he again wonders if Alan is having him on, if maybe he's heard something on the grapevine. Or is his admission sincere? These days *in*sincerity is so much the ruling genre among wooers and competitors, sincerity is often hard to detect. He studies Babcock's moist eyes for a clue.

He asks, 'How do you know these things, Alan, if you haven't gone into business yet for yourself? What happened to Salal beer?'

'I'm getting cold feet.'

Is it advice he wants? Some managerial jargon to help ease him through his bank manager's door?

'Fact is,' Babcock says, 'I don't think I have what it takes to handle an empire. Decided I'd rather have a good time with my life. Carpay deeum. Don't want to be a slave to my own entrepreneurial wet dreams.'

'Is that what you think I am?'

'You, Dwight? Shit no. You're out there fucking them. I envy you the push. I really do. You can take a detail and run with it. Heard you on the radio. Don't know where you're coming from sometimes, but I'd buy a trip from you, sure. If Tanzania's the place, I'm off with bells on.'

Dwight does up his belt, then lets it out two, three notches. He relaxes. 'Well, Alan, we could use a few more clients like you ... Frankly, the slowdown's been a bitch.' He reaches into the locker for his soiled yellow shoes.

'Hey, mate, how d'ya like it? Tempt ya?'

Dwight turns, observes the uncircumcised Babcock now standing with a down-under stetson on his head, little baubles hanging from strings around its brim. They look like shrunken heads. Babcock grins and shakes his whole body. The baubles swing, bizarrely.

'Feel like I'm on *Saturday Night Live* every time I wear it. I'm giving consideration, mate, to targeting this bushman's beanie at the wild and crazy market. You know, socio-ec group our age? Less overhead than beer. Guys on the beach're just as likely to wear something like this as drink beer.'

The nude beach? 'It's January, Babcock. Despite El Niño.'

Alan shrugs, bends over to pluck argyle socks from his locker, shaking out one then the other before slipping into each from a one-footed stance, his penis and the hat's shrunken heads shaking in tandem with his balancing act.

'This is the other me, Dwight, the speculator. I don't feel chastened by the marketplace, not when I'm wearing my speculator's hat. You want the dope on becoming a speculator, ask me when I'm wearing this dingo hat.'

'You're wearing it.'

Alan eyes him, moistly. 'I'll tell you then,' his voice lower. '... Be prepared to get ruthless. Pay the price you think's too high. Junk assets that don't offer returns. Need be, junk yourself, Dwight. Beg, buy or borrow time. Lie to your creditors sans compunction. Take a bullish stance and watch for conclusive upside breakouts to give you buy signals.'

'Is that English?'

'Speculation.' He grins. 'Speculator's dream is to get in at the bottom. I call it the bugger's fantasy. Listen, mate, if you want advice on becoming a speculator, which I imagine frightens you a tad, I'd be only too glad to give you some tips on the futures market. Who to go to for a nice margin. Or for when the trade-off is coming? Whether to buy commercial paper, property, soybeans. *Comprenez?* How to profit from houses and antiques. Just ask Alan and I'll see you make your second million ... providing, natch, you're willing to second- and third-mortgage your business and keep your wife working till she drops. Tempting you at all?'

The thought recurs to Dwight that Babcock is mocking him, and he can't understand why. Revenge for Dwight's whipping him the last time they played? The bully on the block grown more sophisticated with his tongue? Does Alan sense his new soft underbelly, like one of these great white sharks his mother says are wrecking movies at the expense of the elephant men? He doesn't trust him, an uncircumcised guy who backhands himself to pee. Maybe he resents Dwight's success, the way Dwight patronized him last summer, an uppity lower seed amusing himself at Alan's expense with casual advice on how to expand.

Babcock towels off one-handed under his big balls, drops his towel on the bench he's straddling, before lifting his hat to remove a pair of yellow bikini briefs.

'But what's natural, Dwight? Denying yourself the natural human impulse to hedge? Hey, without a gold standard left we've got to survive its absence, no? Too much money chasing too little equity. That's the given. *Was* the given. Now our money's getting taken away. Devaluation looks cyclical and inevitable, like breakdown and bankruptcy. I've learned some-thing, Dwight. Unless you keep hedging against devaluation, using your brain power, like with this hat idea of mine – *hey, shake shake Sherry* – then you're going to sink into domestic depression … what used to be known as genteel starvation.'

'Alan, why're you telling me all this?'

'Offering you the world in a nutshell is all. World at your feet, Dwight, in return for becoming a man of the world. Not some guy dreaming about the world on posters.' (How does this man know so much about his business compared to the last time they tangled?) One leg into those bikini briefs now, still straddling the bench. 'Hell, Dwight, all it'll take is chewed finger-nails and thin spots in your hair. People hating you instead of thanking you. Current assets suddenly at the beck and call of current liabilities. But believe me,' stepping into his other leg, 'the rewards far outweigh the losses.'

Alan snaps the elastic round the cheeks of his briefs. Pretty hard not to feel teased again.

'What exactly are you talking about?' asks Dwight.

'Using your imagination till it develops bursitis. Know what a flight attendant friend tells me he does if he doesn't like a passenger in first class? Gobs in his food. He can be a demon for revenge. I guess we all can, freelancing. Everybody likes to win. But some people hate to lose more than they like to win. President Reagan, for example. Our current prime minis-ter.'

'With a seed like yourself, Alan, I'd have thought it was the other way around.'

'With me? I'm basically a son of a bitch.'

'Well, you said it.'

Babcock is looking at him moistly now. Then he laughs. 'Treat you to a Heineken? Winner's treat?'

Dwight is tying his shoelaces. 'Sorry, Alan. Got a radio interview. I'm flying.'

'Life still coming up concepts, eh? Listen, Dwight, work some more on that backstroke. I think you need more jump on the ball.'

Pushing pushing, the prick. To hell with him.

But he's still surprised Babcock knew right away in the shower he was using tar in his shampoo. 'Flaking scalp?' He wouldn't be surprised if Alan had put the hex on his nuts, too, which are itching again since he stepped back into his boxer shorts. Anxiety over Herodotus has started doing things to his skin, not to mention his backhand stroke down the left side of the box.

2.

'Didn't I tell you the Swann would be gorgeous?' he tells Candice, hanging up after hearing from a satisfied client back from two weeks in Venezuela. 'Undervalued, apparently. That'll teach you to be skeptical about our Third-World hotels.'

'Forgiveness, bwana.' Candice, in loose trousers and lowered eyes, bows out the door.

'See you listen to your G.O. next time!'

Barrel of laughs. Mr Travel, stressed out from wondering if HT should maybe be moving away from free-wheeling, whimsical pleasure markets, and deeper into *business* travel. Less scope but more dependable when rising interest rates are putting the screws to the economy. *Ethnic* travel, too, sending visiting families back to Greece, Hong Kong, India ... Steady flow of cash. Trouble is, other independent agencies have already divined the ethnic market and are two skips and a hop ahead of him.

His interim problem, with the Canadian buck sinking out of sight against the American, and with this growing recessionary slowdown, is to maintain the illusion that travel for pleasure is the most natural and accessible activity in the world. And, too, that it's smart to purchase this experience from Herodotus Tours, which stands for satisfied consumers, value for money, not to mention new concepts in travel for executives clear down to waitresses. He's afraid his clients are shrinking back into their shells at a time when he has put his own neck far out on the line, expanding. *Pushing.*

Fear (panic especially) releases fresh images of survival with every rush of adrenalin. The images of spas, say, to complement mineral water thirsts of a trendy generation. Step right up! Travel to springs! He hunches at his Apple to conjure up what the Romans discovered in Baden-Baden and Bath. He brings up Spa, Belgium, along with the ancient city of Liege and its spires close by. He frees up both the Valley of Less Boiling and the Valley of Greater Boiling, in Fuji-Hakone-Izu National Park, Japan. Closer to home maybe? He releases Hot Springs National Park, Arkansas, with its forty-seven springs; he lets Banff Springs, Alberta, come pumping in.

Concepts, Babcock? Finding himself cornered, Dwight's full of concepts. He pumps pictures.

Beach holidays still sell. For girl-watching try Bondi in Australia and Orient on St. Martin. The second a nude beach, the first semi-nude. How about those oranges, Alan? For watching fishermen, book into Kovalam in Kerala or Pao Pao in Moorea. Fish corralled at both beaches, and drawn to shore in nets. Or for delicious margaritas and white cabanas, reserve at Las Hadas, Manzanillo ... though for privacy and a pina colada don't forget Megan's Bay, St. Thomas. And for –

Afar, imminent issue, lots of beachy tips.

Along with these hot steers (he has never felt quite so desperate):

Q. *My husband and I are determined to holiday in Pago Pago before we become grandparents. Can you recommend one of your Best Beds there?*

A. *While I personally haven't stayed at the Pago Pago Rainmaker Hotel, on the harbour, it is reputed to offer the best available accommodation, at $42 (U.S.) for a double, and four dollars less for a single. You might also choose to stay in one of their fales (beach huts) at $38 for a double.*

Less expensive, and really quite good, is Herb and Sia's Pago Pago Hotel, where I have stayed in American Samoa, in one of their thirteen rooms. Etc.

Q. *This summer we hope to hike the Swiss Alpine paths. Can you tell us how many huts are along the paths? If we'll need reservations, and whether joining the Swiss Alpine Club is worth it for reductions in costs?*

A. *Members have priority, as well as a fifty percent reduction off the cost of a night's stay (a very comfortable stay, I found, if your varicose are behaving themselves) and off a basic meal (22 Swiss francs, or about $15). In all there are 173 rustic huts, but reservations are encouraged. Etc.*

Q. *Are whangdoodles allowed aboard cruises to Anchorage?*

A. *I don't know.*

He worries his keyboard, checks files, scribbles notes to himself in pencil. And he takes calls, which only serve to remind him how far overextended he is at the bank: how far the overhead of too many offices has started running ahead of his cash flow: how far –

'Lena!' he yells, hanging up. 'JetSet sounds like it's not going to fly!'

Lena in a short black skirt and black tights closes his door behind her. Must have a client at her desk. 'I don't *believe* it,' she commiserates. Reassuring or mocking him? 'Weren't you just waiting for the copyright to come through?'

'Doesn't rain but it pours.'

'Money?'

'Worse. Lawyers requiring "proof of originality for copyright".'

'Is that worse?'

He pinches his eyes to relax them from the emerald screen. He licks fur off his teeth. 'How do I know I didn't swipe the idea from a game I've forgotten? ... Just when the economy's contracting and a game like this is *the* answer to all the stay-at-homes?'

Candice pops in wondering about a new luxury hotel in Guatemala called Five Stars. She's carrying a colourful brochure with razor-thin creases.

'Book it, Candy.'

'The problem is we don't know anything about it,' she complains, 'except its glossy kit. The name's trying too hard or something.'

Irritated, he scratches his scalp. 'Have I been wrong yet? Trust me, Can. I have a nose for these places. I foresee a fine tour.'

'I agree the centrefold is nice. But the write-up is vague, what it says about –'

'Candice ...'

'Sorry I asked.' She shrugs meaningfully at Lena and walks out. Lena leaves too, black-booted, tugging down her mini-skirt.

He scratches again. His head, his elbows, his heart. He can't forbear from scratching at this dryness occasioned by the slightest thought of shrinkage. He refuses to consider shrinkage or shrivelling. He plans to maintain an expanding mode. Travel is *about* expansion. It's about imagination and a talent for avoiding turkeys. Money is his means, not the end. The end for the illusionist is about imagining well, even irresponsibly, if it means impacting better.

He switches diskettes, turning his energy to a new concept for holidaying executives and their wives, middle-management types with a hankering for a familiar time abroad, or else company employees being rewarded for superior performances with a vacation nonpareil. Ever since last summer, talking to Aloysius about his golf course job, Dwight has had it in mind to offer an unusual package tour that would permit play on some of the World's Most Exotic Golf Courses. He delves into his files for *Golf Vac*. (If the wives don't golf they might love to shop in exciting nearby towns, which he intends to describe along with local highlights.) A customized tour to the Princeville

Makai golf club on Kauai. Then on to the world's oldest golf club outside Great Britain, the Royal Calcutta (*Let the narrow fairways test you here, along with parading peacocks and scolding monkeys*), via the championship course just south of Bang Saen in Thailand ... *To be followed by the equally exotic Bombay Presidency Club, India's third Championship Course, beautifully groomed, a chance to treat yourself to service not known since the Raj!* He'll put out a brochure from Herodotus Tours. He'll talk it up at his lectures and on radio.

He pauses to scratch his scrotum before reapplying his fingers to the keyboard and to this concept he finds exciting, satisfying. He grins. He's into what he does best: bullshit to beat the band. Headhunting at the executive level. His molars click happily. A maker of journeys he intercoms Lena he's not to be disturbed. Then swivels round to look out his window and down over the city for deeper inspiration. He dreams from his high advantage of eventually feeling more at home with danger, risk, gratification.

He peers at anchored freighters in English Bay. Recently, didn't some Polish sailors seek asylum here, defecting because of conditions at home and wanting a new life in Canada? He allows himself this momentary diversion to let his brain freestyle. Anything in ship travel he's been missing? He swivels back and scribbles himself a memo to check into freighter schedules, determine if there might be a better market for such cruises than he previously thought. Through the Panama, say ...

Pushing pushing.

And before he forgets, as a follow-up to his golf tour, he keyboards himself an addendum about possible European and American courses, for a somewhat less exotic but also less costly package. The Algarve, for examp: Stay at either the Dom Pedro in Vilamoura, or the wonderful Quinta do Lago estate. Or the Florida Panhandle on the Emerald Coast: play the Cotton Creek club and then Perdido Bay, following on east to Tiger Point in Gulf Breeze and finally Sandestin. *As a sidelight, I especially loved the spa at Sandestin, and my favourite hole was the 466-yard par-four fourth (Dunes nine) with its intimate trees and elevated green. A bowl of delight.*

He could go on. He might never stop. Memo: Create a similar package, only this time with racetracks, for the other kind of handicappers, the horse bettors. He's less certain about *wives* here, about their caring to see husbands travel the world just to lose money. Memo (cont.): Needs a resort angle, similar to Reno/Vegas tours. No, better a big city angle. A West Coast tour say of San Francisco, L.A., San Diego – and their respective tracks ... Santa Anita et al.

'I'm away to the races, Lena. Don't want to see any clients just now.' He's repeating himself.

A pause. Then the intercom comes back on.

'Nobody's here, Mr Irving. The booking book is bare.'

3.

Driving home after rush hour Dwight happens to see Aloysius hurrying down the other side of Robson Street, a dark slim body passing through the light of shop windows given over to mannequins in silken sheaths and feathered hats. Escaping? He brakes.

He waves across the thinning traffic but the boy has vanished, no doubt into consuming affairs on his world-devouring mind. Does the kid ever have any *fun*? Can they ever believe what he *tells* them? He's like a spider spinning webs, the connections among which escape them. Their nanny he brought home one September night out of a heavy rainstorm, insisting she was the one. 'The one what, Aloysius?' Theresa, a young woman of sloppy habits, is still tending their daughter, yet who knows what resentment smoulders in her heart at being separated from her real family in El Salvador? What is it with Aloysius, promoting these victims of exile? These schemes of his that wander in from his brain ... Memo: Try being kind and patient: Fool him into a collaboration with civility. Then maybe he'll do more than frown and hand his foster father a poster from Foreign Trade's last dance. Maybe he'll *talk* about his band's last dance.

A window of opportunity had seemed to open up between them last Halloween when Gwyn's extra thumb was surgically removed. He really thought the boy's expression of concern, his hanging about for Reesa's return from the doctor's office, had signalled a shift in his allegiance to home. Alas. He was waiting for a phone call from Trudy, before allowing himself to show up at a band rehearsal. He still stays out to all hours of the night, ignoring house rules. They have to trust him ... hoping he might come to believe in home as a regulating principle.

The travel consultant waits patiently in the traffic. He refuses to fret, to allow sitting and being *un*consultant to rankle. Maybe at age thirty-three he's learning to live inside himself, as on bread and water? Maybe the moon is green cheese. Sitting here strapped in, he thinks isolation is a condition he'd understand and appreciate in utopia. For him isolation would *be* utopia. Peering out a window, making up cities. Seeing a miracle in the coherence of all the other rooms, those cells in a city's body.

He waits at Robson and Altamira, behind traffic still lined up to get down to Georgia and onto the causeway, through the park's dark forest and across the narrows to mountainside homes. He can see the window of the health food shop, alongside Bartlett's clinic on the corner, and he wonders if Bartlett colludes with this store by sending his patients in for Vitamin A, B, C ... how far up the alphabet do vitamins go these days – F? O? Dwight needs something to give him a lift, a jump on the ball. A holiday at home maybe.

'What you need,' Reesa will tell him when she comes in later this evening from the studio, 'is a good change of scene. To start believing what you preach.'

'You're being predictable.'

'Did you see my show tonight?'

'I was changing diapers.'

'I interviewed a float therapist.'

'A float therapist.'

'For seven dollars a float you can book yourself into a dark tank and float on your back till your head and body separate ...'

'Sounds like travel. What a headache.'

'You eventually reintegrate, at a new level of relaxation. That's the end result.'

'Sort of cruise while you stay home.'

'The water is heavily salted, so you don't sink.'

'Sounds Mormonic.'

Talking, he and Reesa will be lying separately in bed as they shiver in their uninsulated house, hoping for once their daughter sleeps through the night so they don't have to get up and lose the accumulated warmth of their protective duvet, to the deficit financing of unplanned parenthood.

But he's forgotten how mild it is. The unseasonable air is gentle on his cheek when he rolls open the window. He wheels left on Altamira, then right on Haro, searching for parking under the bare chestnuts two blocks down. He can't help it, he's peering into the glowing rooms of strangers in low-rise apartment blocks.

In minutes he'll be home himself. He keeps his thoughts from wandering back to Babcock and his teasing, his lousy triumph on court.

He'll greet the useless Theresa with a warm hug, take his daughter in arm and ask if she was a good girl today, smell the talc in her dark hair (and she the tar in his perhaps), kissing both her cheeks with a daddy's smooch.

Home: more fun to imagine than arrive?

The devil keeps him at it.

Lying in bed later he'll be thinking of his day, his day before that, and tomorrow. Is he happy? In the morning he'll be awakened by detectives at the door, inquiring after records, memoranda, anything an Aloysius Irving might have acquired from a Mr Singh that would link the two for possible prosecution. Maybe he'll be thinking, too, that when we think the lights in a house are all off the electricity really isn't. It's still humming in the darkness. Refrigerator in the kitchen, deep freezer in the basement. The instant-on tube keeping the TV warm, the pilot light in the furnace. He'll remember to count all these sheep at home like the digital clock radio counting at his bedside. And that silver disc outside, a carbuncle on the house, floating under glass, turning in its meter to measure electricity coursing like blood.

He's looking forward to a moment before sleep of such perfect bliss that his increasing anxiety will simply vanish.

He can't imagine being homeless. It would be like travel without reservations. It would be like travel with reservations. It would be awful.

September, 2044

'Your Worship,' announces my secretary, 'Police Chief on the line.' With this I learn, before the media do, that Renaldo has been charged with writing rubber cheques. I phone F. at home. We commiserate. Will our son never settle down, learn responsibility? F. thinks he never will. At twenty-eight he has no steady job and doesn't know any women. All his schemes seem to backfire. To relieve his remorse he goes to the track and loses money he has stolen. I regret my shortness with him, but –

A bad day. At a council meeting inadvertently humiliated a greedy developer named Erindale. Forgot my responsibilities to be even-handed and waved my little red flag. He's from the Mediterranean, reports Jenny, but for the same reason blacks will sometimes straighten their hair, has changed his name from Lazlo. She commiserates. A prick.

Stress with F. over our lack of life together goes on. Acrimony between us when our good intentions pass to bad again. Only vanity makes me think I alone am responsible for police and fire protection, subsidized housing, the water supply. It's me who has consolidated my empire in the whole metro region, and now must endure the chaos of conflicting local interests. I fear F. is relegated to one of these. I have no time for anything but dreaming up new pronouncements. Reports breed more reports, accounts accounts, coverage coverage.

Longing to be covered becomes an obsession when you accede to it. I did, long ago. Now can't think farther back than my own record spans. Does it matter? If good press means a good scrapbook I really can't complain. But in becoming my own press agent, covering my ass sometimes seems the only beat I've learned. That and hiring pretty secretaries.

Enemies, including my own spouse at times, are the baggage that comes with the job. They serve to remind me what I lack or have lost: a sense of perspective, my family, the murky past. The fucking building code encapsulates my dilemma. I am good in camera and efficient before council in enunciating and shaping recommendations to deal with the Erindales. But what of dealing with myself?

I do want a building code that's more responsible. An application to demolish a structure, to replace it with something more mod, should have to enumerate the reasons for dumping on an earlier generation's sense of space. If the applicant doesn't take into account the original building's intention and effect, its responsibilities and pleasures, he should have to undergo autopsy at the grassroots. Our wild west's penchant for fashion and preachiness – the trendiness and self-deceit of planners who lark their way to fancy reputations, by bulldozing the past – ought to see the writing on the wall. Literally. EEEEGOOOOOO (PLEASE GO!) as the latest graffiti rather politely puts it.

Erindale is a developer with architectural pretensions. The inelegance of his proposals is, he hopes, the blueprint of the future. Nursing homes as tower blocks? Gingerbread doodads as a bow to history? What have these to do with time?

Looks like I'll be adding the provincial jail to my beat, if the Chief is right about Renaldo's chances in court. His grandfather, my poor father, was once in jail too. In Costa Rica, Guatemala? I can't now remember. Families wax and wane.

Only this red rose in water is keeping up my spirits. A small thorn in a clear vase magnifies to the size of a hypodermic needle. I study the petals instead.

Chapter 8

Principles and Procedures

WHO CARES IF HE *is* an artist of travel? JetSet (or, as Lena now calls it, Jest-Set) has rolled over and sunk, before navigating through the ink and graphic designers, the red tape and lawyers, the sea of other debts now threatening Herodotus Tours. Dwight has had to sever all lines to his shining city. He feels bereft, sitting here with a pulsing cursor, where this city had once promised to shed its light on the marketplace.

No chance now for the successful traveller to find himself resident in an enchanting capital, choosing from among cellar wines of the countryside, pulling up to table with friends as accordion music washes in through louvered windows, to discuss some big quiz buster over veal *escalopes roman-ichel*, like, *What is the meaning of Here?*

He knows in his bones he was right about his ideal city, a place no tested traveller would've ever wanted to leave. None would've *had* to leave except those with insufficient imaginations. Those without enough stamina for long sessions of sitting and doing nothing, discussing the perfectibility of Time as they killed it in pleasant lapses over a vintage pinot noir. This was the end, the integration he foresaw in his board game, families rolling dice across hearths to win visas, the right of citizenship to his seductive city.

Creator and copyright holder, he, Dwight Irving, B. Comm. believes he could've gone on to dream up new variations on the old theme of quest, reconceiving the whole idea of travel for players who had reached their goal. The talk inside his city could have been so wonderful! He himself as mayor!

He sits gazing out at the mountains from his office tower. May now looks to be the cruellest month, until summer arrives and the bear market economy gets even worse. Interest rates are already out of sight. Money has hibernated.

Dwight tries to relax but his balls demand to be scratched raw. He undoes his belt for another go at them. He still bothers cultivating his façade of experience, but it's no longer enough. He despairs of Herodotus's decline over the last year, during which the economy inexplicably heated up and exploded. Dwight tries to forget a fundamental shift has occurred in the world. People now view travel as wildly extravagant. They look upon it now as they might upon Grand Tours of the nineteenth century. This hasn't stopped him from giving them advice on his radio show, in his newspaper columns and sparsely populated public lectures – but the results no longer justify his efforts. He still bothers to dream up tours when the ones on his books continue not to sell. He continues to retail his personal travels when many have forgotten who he is.

Sometimes his conscience dogpaddles to the surface. Makes an effort to call his Secret into moral question. So he schedules a date to exercise his body and overcome despair. To no avail. On his last visit to the Racquets Club he was beaten, by *Bartlett* of all people, three games out of four. Bartlett, who used to be plump, appears to have loaned his girth to Dwight. Last week in the shower he noticed for the first time his friend's trim figure, borrowing the chiropractor's Dial soap to scrub off. He felt envy. He now feels his accumulating bulk is responsible for his falling down the squash ladder so far that he might as well have let go of the rungs. He's smarting from the plunge. Feels scraped and bruised. Once as high as ninth seed, he's now twenty-eighth and sinking, soon to drift right through his pre-inflation level of forty-five.

Babcock now shuns games with his old rival because he can't get a workout. Ian Beardsley on the other hand, up from fourteenth seed to number six, and playing confidently on the secure salary of a middle management exec in a towel products company, really enjoyed the match he and Dwight played three weeks ago, thrashing the travel agent in straight games to revenge his unexpected loss over a year ago.

Bartlett is the only one who doesn't seem to care if he wins or not. His friend has been very considerate, even carrying Dwight's payments on his mortgaged practice, until Dwight can recover and square things with him soon. Bartlett isn't pestering him for the money, no. Quieter than he was, for sure not the animal he once was at frat parties. More thoughtful since he started travelling the world like a yo-yo. More generous, thinks Dwight. But distracted. He really ought to talk to his friend and housemate, not just about their loan but about travel and what it exactly *means* to Bartlett. Memo: Talk to B. Tell him how lucky we feel to have hooked up again, three years ago, when we offered him a share of our rambling old house Reesa found not far from his clinic. Kowtow.

He wishes his father's old friends at the City Club were as understanding as Bartlett, about how failure can befall travel like a hurricane. Those two have chosen to call *in* their loans (at least to 'renegotiate' them through lawyers) and he, like a developing nation in decline, finds himself having to accept whatever lifeline thrown him. Trouble is these creditors are not the IMF, worried the banking system might fail should he keep missing repayments: So they certainly won't offer him *more* money to help make them. A shame. He could benefit by the circular thinking at large in the world. The fact is his bank manager has liens against the two remaining HT outlets, having foreclosed on his third and fourth. His only relief right now (a blissful relief) consists in clawing his privates.

2.

Having wiped the last diskette marked *Ideal City* from existence he now mourns. He finds it impossible to believe his commitment to imagined playfulness, imperishable travel, has disappeared without a trace. Maybe he has a backup file ...

Why can't Stan Case and Leo Orsetti be his saviours? The answer he supposes is they were his patient creditors once already, having had to wait for their money in a way Bartlett, who refused to be bored playing frathouse bridge, never did. He hesitates to approach his mother again, to help him repay these same creditors, because of her still vivid recollection of being forced to bail him out of his student years when she had *no idea* how much debt he'd run up playing cards with his brothers. Brothers!

Cash is king, the creditor a sovereign. Who'd have thought so as recently as last summer? The common saver and her bankbook, once despised, are now back in fashion, conservative investors like Marlene Irving proving the visionary gurus of the eighties.

God help the world and its new love of dullness! The pundits' language is more depressing than a sauna. 'A turnaround' is the latest buzzword to surface, the hoped-for elixir to revive a polluted slough of economic jargon, including 'slowdown' and 'austerity', 'cutbacks' and 'restructuring'.

'What're you doing?' asks Candice at the door. 'Aren't you here?'

Embarrassed, he pushes his stomach up against his desk to hide the whereabouts of his scratching hand. He gives the keyboard a couple of smacks with his left hand. 'Damn screen's jammed.'

'Buzzer not working either? There's a call for the person who isn't here, on line two.'

'Who is it? The awful bank?'

'Spanish-speaking, by the sound of the accent.'

'Theresa. Probably wants permission to change a diaper. Say I'm not here.'

'It's a man.'

He ponders this. 'I don't know any Spanish-speaking men. Take a message, Candy. While you're at it get hold of CBC and find out if I'm still on coast to coast next week. They're talking about dropping *Where in the World?*'

She stands staring at his position, squashed up like a pervert.

'... They think I'm getting predictable.'

'Try sailing.'

She is soon back. 'I couldn't tell if our Spanish-speaker was the operator – or a spokesman for ... stars?' Trying to read her own writing. 'Movie stars?'

'Five Stars. Isn't that where our tour is staying?'

'Then you think he was phoning from Guatemala? I really couldn't understand him. 'Meesis Yones,' he kept saying. 'Meesis Yones.''

'Did we book a Jones?'

'To Guatemala? I'll check.'

'Maybe she's come down with *turista*.'

'You're supposed to phone back a number he gave me.'

Dwight wonders. 'Is the weather there supposed to be bad or anything? Hurricane brewing?'

'Not that I've heard.'

'Let's hold off then. Let Meesis Yones enjoy the beach for a while.'

She seldom smiles anymore, going out his door. Her sunny voice sounds eclipsed. What price loyalty these days?

The pair of them are probably looking for jobs with bigger, more secure chains. Not that anyone else is hiring with cutbacks pandemic in the industry. But a chain would look more attractive than Herodotus Tours does. Herodotus looks sick. Anxiety is causing its owner's scalp to shed like an arbutus tree. His nuts to smoulder and moult. The staff in his remaining branch office on Broadway hardly recognize him anymore when he ventures in.

Reaching for scripture he feels ravaged. *Principles and Procedures of Travel Counselling* is still his Bible for all seasons, guidebook of reaffirmation, source of the longer view. 'The travel agency is totally a service industry dealing in intangible products. The consumer pays for something which cannot be returned, unlike clothing or an appliance. The consumer has little opportunity to "examine the merchandise" before purchase. Often, he has no more than a glance at a picture of a hotel or a beautiful landscape.' In effect, not trusting a cover to tell the story, a client will rely on his counsellor for satisfaction. 'The capable travel counsellor must have current knowledge of ...' – his eye surveys fares, climates, currencies – 'and, often of prime importance, the current political situation.'

He pauses at this. He wonders if some recent coup in Guatemala City, of which he remains unaware, might have blindsided his package tour to the coast.

'The counsellor's personal travel experiences can be of great value ...' Here Dwight tries to recall what he said about his own trip to Guatemala in the public lecture he gave on touring that country while putting this package together. He considers then rejects culpability. This binder full of principles and procedures is quite correct on the importance of a counsellor's personal experience. He would never think of sending anyone anywhere unless he had thoroughly imagined their destination.

Later that afternoon he gets through to Guatemala. To whom is he speaking, please?

A courier, he gathers, whose story is straightforward and crushing.

The Five Stars is *not* the luxury hotel promised by Herodotus Tours. Rooms still under construction are full of mosquitoes, rats roam closets at will, toilets have ... anyway, showers are waterless. The whole package tour has become a debacle for irate clients of Herodotus Tours.

Dwight mutters reassurances. He 'understands completely' and is 'already on to the problem'. He drops his pants and scratches his testicles. He has the office to himself. The emptiness reminds him his lease is due again at month's end. He says goodbye to the exercised courier.

He is staring out the window when Leo Orsetti's lawyer calls. Dwight politely puts him on hold, does up his pants, and walks out the door. He locks it. He shares the empty elevator down with a toxic cloud of perfume. All weekend long, he thinks, that amber light will be winking on his desk.

3.

He might as well be travelling. He can't find it in him anymore, with so little to be cheerful about, to like himself at home. His scrotum has flared, his head throbs.

'You need a holiday.'

He lifts his head toward the cracked plaster ceiling of their bedroom and lets it fall back on his pillow. Bouncing it a couple of times for good measure.

'I've been reading your Herodotus homework,' says Reesa. 'There's a travel agents' convention next month in San Francisco. Why don't you go?'

'Alone?'

'Be good for you. Get you talking to other people with the same propensities. Find out if you're going to have to go on lying in public the rest of your life. You could surprise yourself, how well you cope with an exotic journey to San Francisco?'

Their voices have awakened Gwyn across the hall.

He tries keeping his hands above the covers. 'There's a bazaar this afternoon. I might take Gwyn along to see what the old convent where I used to serve mass looks like since it sold out to a private boys' school for Protestants. Want to come?'

'I have a date.'

He studies her face.

'Civic luncheon. Very boring.' She throws the brochure at him. 'Last one out of bed has to eat Theresa's breakfast.'

Over breakfast, she tells him the trouble with having great expectations is flying too far above familiar turf. He has made drip coffee and cut pumpernickel bread for toast. She's concerned how bad things at Herodotus could still become. She includes her other dependent in her admonition. 'As any good book will tell you, forget your domestic accounts and you'll collapse.'

'What book?' asks Aloysius.

'Any more papaya?' asks Dwight.

Upstairs, Bartlett is sleeping in and would've declined their invitation to breakfast anyway.

'He's with *her*,' says Aloysius. Megan.

When the young man exits, trailing vapours of ambition, his guardians sit on at the table in silence. Silence except for Gwyn suckling Reesa's breast, an insistent interlude between hunger and well-being. She's going to need glasses he thinks. His daughter has the myopic gaze of a bald soprano. Not his eyes, but brown like a Potts's.

'Bartlett has been the soul of discretion,' observes Reesa. She looks up from the feeding child, the way she does after her milk has dropped, with the look of happy encompassment. '... About our loan, sweetheart?'

'His business is probably booming.'

'Yes. He really is one of the lucky ones.'

4.

'I don't like to say it, dear, but you're getting fat.'

His mother's swimming pool has been cleaned and refilled, refiltering itself now in a steady hum, with no one to enjoy its pristine water. Damon seems preoccupied near the tennis court. Dwight's tempted, his balls need a dousing, but he forgot his bathing suit. 'I'm disappointed Aloysius couldn't come. How is he, dear, after all the courtroom ruckus?'

'Video. I don't know.'

Cocktails before dinner on the patio, except for Marlene, who continues to pour herself coffee. The red of her thermos is redder than the roses in her beds. 'I'm trying to cut down on alcohol for my systolic pressure.' She blows a monkey's tail with her smoke. 'That's all I have to say about me.'

Her Matinee-mellow voice sounds deeper this afternoon, huskier. Lines he has never noticed before have spread around her mouth like little fissures in a fly's wing. He suspects they have nothing to do with age. More to do with her buzzing mouth, talking so much she's wearing out the skin around it.

'You're not drinking a *lot* of cocktails these days, are you, Dwight?'

He crosses his legs in a vain attempt to generate some friction at the groin. Reesa interjects to say Victoria Day weekend seems to her a truer commencement of summer than June's solstice a month later.

A timer chimes in the kitchen where Sylvia is preparing dinner. A robin bursts into song. A pool's surface explodes in a splashy smack a distant house or two away. Then silence over the whole scene. Damon pads in their direction, across sand dunes separating him from family. His left foot drags. The heat lines in the intervening distance remind Dwight of some desert movie in which his brother is wrapped up like a mummy in blowing robes.

Marlene pats her yellowy-grey hair. Having scratched her imagination and discovered it endlessly theistic, she is unable to keep quiet about matters close to heart. But this is something new. A nasally Barbara Walters, her warhorse, interviewing Veronica at the sixth station of the cross, Veronica Wiping the Face of Jesus. 'Do you *reeeally* think your cloth is going to retain that imprint of His face, Veronica? Is there possibly, do you feel, a market for it in T-shirts?'

Her iconoclasm strikes him as something radical and unexpected. 'Encore,' he urges.

She stubs out her cigarette. Moving her performance right along to the final station, the Burial, she asks him to imagine for a moment Cher – Sonny Bono's ex – as Mary Magdalen enshrouding Jesus's crucified body with a wink and a bar or two of '*I got you babe* ...' She even sings it. Reesa snorts her approval.

His mother's standup impression of a slinky Cher is funny, one hand behind her back, tightening her silk dress over an ample midriff, the other pulling aside an imagined veil of long hair as she bobs and tilts in time to the music. Has he underrated Marlene's broadminded tolerance for skeptics and mockers? Might she still be open to the case of an unbelieving debtor like himself, sinking fast?

He notices how she's brought the subject within sniffing distance of the Shroud of Turin. He wonders if the next item on her list will be the Holy See's desire to give a lab leave to carbon-date the cloth and prove it the actual burial cloth of Our Lord.

'I wonder if you remember,' she asks him, sitting back down to pour herself more coffee and light another Matinee, '.. The Stations of the Cross really got started with the Franciscan friars wondering, well, if they couldn't make the long pilgrimage to the Holy Land in person, couldn't they just transport themselves there in spirit? They persuaded the Holy Father of the time, I don't recall his name – Pope Innocent? back then they were all so innocent, weren't they? – to grant them the same indulgences for visiting their own little *images* of the Crucifixion, as for travelling all the way to the Holy Land. And a later pope went even farther, dear. Luckily for us he decided *all* the faithful were eligible for the same indulgences as the Franciscans. That's the true story of our Stations.'

She seems to savour its authenticity. She puffs a while, fiddling with the turkey wattle at her neck.

'Dwight, I remember, used to say his Stations at home, reading them in his prayer book like he was studying a picture album. Nothing to be ashamed of exactly – even if he was cheating by not visiting them in church.'

'It was Lent. I was competing at school to see who could say the most rosaries and Stations. It seemed faster to stay home. Why ashamed?'

His sins of omission are the last thing he wants to get into when he's hoping for financial rescue of a foundering empire.

'Well, dear, sometimes you must wish you did act ashamed ...'

She appraises his wrinkled yellow shoes, in need of waxing or else burning in the barbecue pit, and she looks around for Da.

Dwight stands up as an excuse to scratch himself, on the sly, like a baseball pitcher preparing to throw a sinker.

'Earlier, Dwight, you were telling me what a lot of trouble Herodotus is in. Now I'm going let you in on a little secret about human nature. It isn't as if you don't have a sense of tradition ... you looked happier than I can remember in a long time, dear, telling me about your visit to the convent this afternoon. You can take the boy out of religion, but I don't think you can take ...'

Willing to appease, lie, he smiles agreeably and sits down again, reaching over to build himself a salmon cracker with two, three strips of smoked salmon, and a gob of cream cheese.

'That being the case –' she goes on, pinching the bone china handle of her coffee cup as she drags deeply on her cigarette – 'I don't see why there *has* to be a problem with your business, even with interest rates at umpteen percent ...' Coffee follows her smoke down the hatch.

What's she saying?

Christ, cheese on his knee.

'... Not if,' she continues, spouting smoke, 'you were to put your trust in an *adult* version of what you used to put it in, dear, as a Crusader making novenas and that kind of thing, asking for God's blessing in your school tests. And novenas for Daddy, do you remember, when he was ill?'

Dwight shifts uncomfortably in the cotton hammock of his deck chair, dabbing his white ducks with a serviette. What *is* she saying? Reesa has turned to watch Sylvia and Damon in the distance, where the little house-keeper has swooped out to brush off the large man's chinos, stained at the knee from his ignominious descent from the apple tree.

'Why need it be a burden to you?' wonders Marlene.

It? Does she mean Herodotus?

Her coiffed hair looks recently turned within an inch of its tinted life. She's fingering her string of pearls like a rosary. '… Even the odd novena, Dwight, made in the spirit of retreat and contemplation. In the same spirit I imagine you use to write up your tours …? Might be just the ticket to persuade the Sacred Heart to look kindly on your financial woes.'

She is offering him a business proposition he thinks.

'Did you know you can go to mass on Saturdays now, if you want to sleep in Sundays, which I know your hard-working generation likes to?'

He says nothing. Reesa isn't talking either. He stands up again to relieve the fire at his crotch. Something in the air reminds him of corruption. Bribery. The possible selling of his soul to save it. Memo: Clear the decks for a change in the weather.

A breeze wrinkles the pool's surface, also the lawn, brushing it away from them toward the greenhouse. A blackbird trills from the rushes by the lily pond. The sprinkler system next door begins pulsing like a heart. He can't explain it. He feels a headache coming on. He feels like he's abroad, leagues and leagues south.

'I guess,' he finally says. 'We have to go with what's in our own best interests.' He watches her satisfied smile spread. '… But I don't think religion is really in mine.'

He feels his headache actually retreat.

'You understand what I'm saying?' he asks his mother.

Reesa smiles one of her little consolation smiles: a smile he's noticed around Gwyn when the child can't find her nipple. Or doesn't want to.

His mother bridles, sweetly, 'You know, dear, sometimes when we're willing just to pay token service, this can be a move in the right direction too. Don't you think?'

To anyone conceivably teetering on the edge of belief she sounds more than ready to offer him the benefit of doubt.

What she appears to value is the trappings of the good heart. An impression of faith. An on-going concession on his part to the anointed past.

Her offer sounds like nothing less than a lucrative deal in exchange for returning to his roots. Tempting.

Memo: When is a principle a principle? Fool. Revise and get back to her.

Instead, he finds himself guiding the conversation away to more concrete matters like the greenhouse – 'the way the sun's striking it, see?' – this iron and glass palace calving four small arcades off the larger one, at the very centre of his childhood. Once he could always count on finding his father inside, adjusting nozzles, tending orchids, handfeeding colourful birds housed in humid foliage.

It was supposed to be a replica of the glass house in Kew Gardens, which his father had built as a retreat before the war, the memory of it afterward sustaining him through Japanese internment in Hong Kong. A Victorian world complete unto his father, who didn't live long enough to retire inside his passion full time.

Reesa is watching him eat hors d'oeuvres and hinting, because he continues to nibble compulsively, maybe he's had his share. Gin and tonic wash them down.

When she reveals his plan to go to San Francisco for a convention, his mother wonders why he'd want to bother. 'So noisy.' She confesses her own reluctance to travel back to San Francisco. While Marlene's proud to have come from San Francisco, sixty years ago, it isn't a city she feels great joy returning to these days now it has got so large. So gay, if they take her meaning.

Over veal cutlets they listen to the awakened Gwyn gurgling at her mother's breast. 'I insist you feed her with the rest of us,' says Marlene. And over dessert they're forced to listen to Damon across the hall playing *Home on the Range*. 'That gives me duckbumps every time he plays it,' says Marlene. '... One of Aloysius's expressions.'

'Does Da ever hum along like Glenn Gould when he plays?' Dwight is still curious about whether his brother has ever repeated his vocal utterances of last Thanksgiving, when he cooed upstairs over Gwyn.

'Mute as a church mouse. I think you were hearing things, dear.'

They listen politely, eating their pie, he on his third slice and scratching his balls under the table.

The timing of his brother's left hand is off, the rhythm moving slower than it should, lending the piece a discordant sweetness at the keyboard, possibly the source of his mother's duckbumps.

His headache has returned. He wonders if the toxic insulation in her walls could be responsible.

Damon's third repetition of *Home on the Range* tempts Marlene into comment on its homey theme.

'I suppose we should count our blessings when so many people are gravitating to *us* these days. Arriving here from their own homes – on the prairies in India and Timbuktu.'

Her parents had brought her here and gone on to make a fortune in hemlock, after the redwood supply had declined in California after 1920.

'*Oh give me a home ...*' she croons in a smoky mezzo voice. Gwyn laughs. Dwight scratches. His bathing suit wouldn't have fit him anyway, anymore.

He notices his brother's lips moving at the keyboard, but dragging behind the words, motion catching up with sound.

Even if Dwight felt like singing Gilbert and Sullivan this evening, in honour of Queen Victoria's birthday, his mother would encourage him to let Da keep the floor.

'You don't look at all well,' she tells him, leaving. 'Are you feeling all right?'

Hugs for Damon, hugs for Sylvia, and when his mother can be persuaded to give up the baby, hugs for Marlene too. Da, still hoping for a playtime with Gwyn, directs Reesa up the circular drive and out into the leafy crescent.

Reesa punches in a tape, heavy metal rock, one of Aloysius's contributions to her car. Ejected smartly. Zamfir kicks in. Out. Vivaldi's turn. The car perks up to the baroque and they listen ... whether to *Autumn* or *Winter* he can never tell. He scratches his balls for what feels like a decade of bliss. She accelerates.

Checking on the infant car seat in back he hears her say, 'You realize you could have had the money to refloat Herodotus.'

He caresses the sleeping child. The creator of an imaginary city caressing his imaginary daughter. He knows she isn't his, but then neither is his city anymore.

They rise smoothly to the centre of the cantilevered span over False Creek, carrying them home against a river of car lights coming the other way. The steel girders remind him of the framework of his father's greenhouse. When their car passes under them his headache vanishes.

'I can't believe I turned her down,' he says, rather pleased. 'That I didn't accept her bribe. I don't think she even cared if I'd been a hypocrite about it ...' In a wry British accent he adds, 'I do believe I'm losing the ability to tell lies about things I no longer believe in.'

She touches his elbow.

'I was proud of you.'

He looks at her, then twirls a finger at his own ear.

Three-alarm sunset, its embers still glowing up the Sunshine Coast. Silhouetted mountains, disappearing.

He stays up late to watch a black-and-white film starring Richard Attenborough, rented by Bartlett. Bartlett watches impassively as Dwight snacks on potato chips and dip. Dwight's toe is beginning to bother him. Maybe he ought to say something about his symptoms to Bartlett. They watch the screen in silence. Maybe he ought to divulge that his balls are now open for discussion by city council.

What does a chiropractor know?

5.

When he walks into the office after his long weekend Lena tells him their tour to Guatemala has gone badly.

'I know.'

He refuses to admit the hotel's brochure ought to have made him suspicious, before recommending the hotel highly to his clients.

At his desk he looks up 'Travel Counselling and the Law'. Not an encouraging chapter:

'... Thus, the customer can sue the travel agent, even though the error that led to the problem was the fault of the principal. If the principal is a Mexican hotel, a German tour operator or a Hawaiian bus operator, the customer will find it much easier to sue the travel agent down the street than the supplier a half a world away. Should you fail to disclose your principal, you may be giving a dissatisfied customer an opportunity to sue your agency successfully ...'

'But I *did* disclose my principal,' he says aloud. 'Five Stars Hotel. The hotel simply misrepresented itself. 'This fiasco isn't my fault.'

Lena, coughing politely, ducks out his door.

He has always prided himself on digging behind glittering brochures. Always followed faithfully the book on points of testimony: 'Be truthful, be complete, and be certain.' He had been. His imagination had testified to the accuracy of the hotel's claims. What happened?

Candice, arriving freshly tanned from sailing all weekend, resists any I-told-you-so remarks, though he can detect an undesirable tone in her muted conversation with Lena in the outer office.

She does offer one suggestion, between phone calls from a new boyfriend called Skipper: Why doesn't Dwight stop payment on his cheque for $11,000 to the hotel? He could use part of the money to compensate their returning clients for substandard accommodation, and what remains to pay the questionable management *down there* for such and any limited service as Dwight's clients consider owing (very little by the sound of it).

Sounds sensible.

She also suggests they contact all their travellers as soon as they return home tomorrow afternoon. This sounds sensible too. He asks her and Lena to take care of it. He compliments Candice on her suntan. By taking a strong position right away he believes HT can thwart a flood of complaints and possible lawsuits. He feels better already.

He ignores the cheese stain on his white ducks. These days he's trying his best to stay out of business suits.

That night in bed, hearing of the day's disaster, Reesa wants to know about his bird's nest as she calls it. His scrotum. 'Has this crisis made it worse?'

Surprised, he reaches under the covers. He hasn't felt the urge to scratch himself all day. This pleases him, having totally forgotten to scratch. *Having* to scratch.

'Hey, the rawness has disappeared.'

'That shows it wasn't worry.'

From under the duvet she fishes up the pair of boxer shorts he has just taken off. 'It was Downy,' she tells him drolly.

'Downy?' What's she talking about?

'Not this pair. This was the placebo pair, I snuck them into your clothes this morning.'

'Placebo.'

'I discovered Theresa has been lacing our laundry – not just the baby's – with fabric softener. Your skin is obviously allergic to the stuff.'

'I thought we used Tide. Cheer. All. One of those.'

'Downy's a chaser. It occurred to me she started adding it about the time your problem began.'

'How's Gwyn's skin?'

'She wears Luvs.'

'You're a genius.'

'You could probably handle San Francisco now.'

For a man going under, his life in travel still threatened, he sleeps very well that night. In the morning, two uniformed policemen knock early to ask if an Aloysius Irving at this address might be willing to answer some questions about a chain letter fraud.

Later that day, just before dinner, he overhears Reesa talking to her mother on the phone. 'If he doesn't, his scalp is never going to clear up. I need a dirty weekend myself.'

February, 2041

Mother's funeral a week ago today. A beautiful woman, Reesa Potts, even at ninety-two. Might have lived longer but for virulent new strain of streptococcus making its imported round of the city. Considered racist to mention where it comes from, but one country in Africa isn't above suspicion for its sad, incautious ways. She was among the later pioneers of public women, who overcame the death of my father and went on to become a respected film producer. No flowers by my request.

I have since received a rose.

Extended family of distant relatives and friends gathered to listen to the eulogy given by an old friend of Mother's, who once lent us his home to live in when we lost ours. I don't remember either the losing or the receiving, bereavement or gift. Never quite understood his relationship to us, but perhaps after sorting through her boxes full of family papers, videos, bric-à-brac, I will.

Requested a recording of 'A Wandering Minstrel I' for the service. I think she told me once it was after Daddy's singing this in a college production of *The Mikado* she first met him backstage with two long johns, a thermos of coffee, and a request to interview him for the campus newspaper. From such circumstances are we eventually to be remembered, reconceived, judged.

F. held my hand tightly. Lately we have had another family death. F.'s mother died when a ferry boat capsized during her trip to the Philippines. Body not recovered.

Was the hope someday of eulogizing all their lives why Mother squirreled away the history of our extended family like a pack rat? Into diaries like mine is where a family disappears, sans account sans fanfare.

I grieve. Renewed economic recession has left me susceptible to electoral grief as well, and I have permitted myself to wallow in the chance of it, privately if not publicly.

The old immigrant
eulogist and Member of
Parliament was the past
director and founder of
the MIDI chain of
halfway holding houses.
Corbin Irving spoke to
the gathering of Mother,
as well as of me, with
fond recollection. F.
listened and thought
afterward this MP may
have spent time in jail
for a mortgage scam,
forty or fifty years ago.
F. wasn't sure about the
scam, the sentence, or
for that matter the MP.
'Suppose I shouldn't
credit gossip. Memory,
even.'

Am beginning to feel
gossip might be the only
thing we should credit.
Thumbing through
Mother's
correspondence, for
example, I learn she
once had an affair with a
balding bigwig in
glasses. How to know for
sure whose child you
even are?

Chapter 9

Capital G Glass

AS SOON AS HE'S airborne, with the weight of ascent pressing him back on his tailbone, Dwight feels unaccountably happy, lighter than he has in months. The jet has climbed above an August drizzle, allowing a brilliant sun to flood in through cabin windows. He wonders if this weightlessness is the illusion travel confers on normal men. For a fat man, he begins to wonder whether travel might not be a better workout than squash or weight training. Memo: Travel and come back trim.

Isn't Bartlett the living example?

Landing in San Francisco, taxiing in from the airport, he feels enthusiastic in a way the recession had threatened to smoke out of him with August interest rates scaling the peaks at twenty-two and three-quarters percent. From the Westin St. Francis, on Union Square, he phones Reesa to give her his good news: 'I feel a lot better than Maui. Really relaxed. I actually like travel.'

He hangs up on their answering machine and looks out the window. As a tourist destination San Francisco is right up there with Mecca. Ur-city, mother lode, from which sufficient commissions flow to travel agents every year for them to buy, if they wished, an entire city like this one, to worship at leisure the icons of bridge, wharf and hills (what people in his industry pin as posters to their walls): where northern fog meets southern sunshine, and little cable cars climb halfway to the stars.

Mirrored in the sea.

It's now home that seems foreign and unappealing to him, a place of depressed markets and personal debts, unhappy clients and potential lawsuits. Abroad, eighty minutes down the coast, instead of discovering himself to be a man with retarded gross motor functions, coping lamely, he now decides he can afford to enjoy himself. Be physical and move about. The migraine and misanthropy he anticipated have not checked in. So he cancels room service. He changes into his yellow shoes. The freshness of being abroad has raised him up.

Thinking maybe he isn't here yet, that his heavy body has yet to catch up with his new sensibility, he floats up Nob Hill for a closer look at the white ornamented architecture and Mediterranean sky, before the bad news has a chance to overtake him. He doesn't even huff as he climbs. Are these really his shoes ascending this foreign mountain? He seems to take in details outside himself: fancier parking meters than those at home, less rounded curbs, zippier mailboxes ... He promises himself another hike up here this week to visit the stained-glass cathedral with the bronze doors, and maybe those swank hotels waving allegiance to the Republic with flags the size of tomato fields. It's so quiet and airy. He feels lighter, definitely.

Memo: Home is where the heart is. The heart is a moving target. Travel is home in motion.

Next morning, having descended from room to conference floor, Dwight meets a local travel counsellor who greets him by remembering what an awesome time she had visiting his city and Grouse Mountain with the cable car 'overlooking the whole scary world', Dwight, who's pinning on his nametag, reciprocates by mentioning how delighted he is by her own city. Something in his response causes her to wonder.

'This isn't your first visit ... ?' And he tells her, smiling to show his pearls, 'My mother was born here.' She smiles back. 'Oh, yes?' He then remarks on the extent of eye contact, even between men, strangers on sidewalks and in restaurants. Belou Snider, this svelte woman in her mid-thirties, is caught staring at him. 'Oh, eye contact is really big. Sometimes I just don't feel like it and walk by with my eyes down.' She glances curiously at his yellow shoes.

'Well, look who's here,' calls a take-charge voice. Its owner's tag says Dale Ludwig, L.A. 'When the cat's away ... Won't you excuse us, uh, Mr Irving?' The muscular young agent eyes him a little moistly, thinks Dwight, shepherding Ms Snider off toward the coffee urn. He notices how his sports jacket cleaves at the shoulders. Also, in a decade of short hair and little moustaches, how Dale's hair is a devilish ducktail.

He wonders how much time he has to visit the coffee shop for breakfast, before the first speaker starts in on 'Selling Techniques in a Recession'. He wants to get a feel for the grand ballroom, on the mezzanine level, where he is to speak later himself. The foyer overflows with delegates he hopes are just as susceptible to blond hair and blue eyes as his clients used to be. He hasn't forgotten how to sell himself, even when no one's buying.

Notice boards in the foyer offer delegates their choice of guided tours: by cable car to Fisherman's Wharf, followed by a boat ride to Alcatraz; or by chartered boat from the Ferry Terminal across to Sausalito, returning by bus to Golden Gate Park via the bridge and Presidio. Take your pick. An ideal city to dine out on the delicacies of the profession, but a smorgasbord of indigestion and heartburn too. Coit Tower, Mission Dolores, Chinatown, the North Beach and Pacific Heights Victorians, a sewer tour ... The great chance suddenly for travel counsellors to revel as tourists – like ski instructors on their own mountain, or car salesmen given keys to the car lot Jags. Between the lines, he can read invitations to engage escorts, spend promiscuously in restaurants, cavort like cadets and sleep in. It's a world he knows little about.

He searches the programme board for his own name, confirms the hour of his lecture, and heads for the cavernous coffee shop. Laughter spills from rooms and corridors. Streetwalkers, or else hotel guests without nametags, mingle with delegates in the semi-public lobby. He can spot them by their haircuts.

To feel really free to enjoy all this, he thinks, a traveller needs a sense of the forbidden. To find himself here and bereft of a sense of sin would be the worst kind of coincidence. Not a coincidence at all, a misfortune. Leading him back to migraines and confinement.

2.

At five minutes past two he begins his talk – 'you wouldn't call it a lecture,' he confesses to his audience of five hundred agents, 'though there may be a lesson in it, about survival in the Canadian travel industry, I don't know, from the point of view of a very lucky independent operator, who's maintained his unaffiliated status at some cost, but who soon hopes, in face of this current recession, to expand his market share.' (So far as he knows, most of these agents have never heard of Herodotus Tours, so he feels safe enough playing with the truth.)

His talk, something called the Thomas Cook Memorial lecture, represents a unique chance to place the Canadian industry on the international map. Until a second ago he was proud of this invitation to address the World Tourism Organization. Now he learns from his introducer, a frog-eyed man with hair parted down the middle, that he was one of just three delegates to apply for this talk (at Reesa's urging), the other two being a guidebook writer from Corpus Christi and an Egyptian who couldn't afford to come. According to Mr Bullfrog their guest was chosen for his 'outside perspective' and the 'integrity' of his C.V.

Pushing pushing.

Launching himself on an optimistic account of HT, Dwight narrates his history as a counsellor, columnist, tour operator and travel agent. He believes his credentials have been enhanced, he tells his audience, by the fact that as a tour operator Herodotus Tours has always prided itself on keeping its prices reasonable, and offering packages for intimate as well as larger groups. '... With a large group we prefer to command a hotel of our own abroad, instead of sharing it with other tour operators. This way we know the package offered is unique.'

He shares with his audience the fact he does his *own* research to ensure quality control. 'I don't see how you can know your product without going into the field yourself. Like a lot of you, I happen to travel a good deal. You probably share my feeling that unless you can see for yourself, you'll never know what to recommend. These trips help me dream up the sort of holidays and tours that competing companies might not have the time or inspiration to consider offering themselves ...'

He widens his blue eyes, smiling at the room. His hair is sandy enough to suggest regular familiarity with salt and sun. He leans forward and expands on his 'product line' via the beaches of south India. Then he lets them all in on Costa Rica and Guatemala, adding the beach potential of those countries is similarly overlooked. 'We went into Guatemala this year, and found the market there ready to explode. In Costa Rica ... listen, did you know more Canadians than Americans retire to Costa Rica? Is this our national secret? Let me whisper something into the mike: *Costa Rica is a country my country trusts.* What I'm really saying is no country, as most of you already know, is too small to overlook. *Listen, I'm bringing you the news.* My company happens to make its living trusting in small places like Costa Rica. The reality is we go out, if we have to, and conjure up details that make us a player. That may sound like boasting, ladies and gentlemen, and it *is* boasting. But my advice to you small independents and even you bigger fish is simple: *Don't overlook the overlooked markets. Don't be predictable. Don't repeat yourselves ...* Herodotus Tours, for examp, is concentrating its hedonism packages this year on the coasts of Third World countries. And we're in the black because of it!'

A self-congratulatory toast with his Perrier glass, and then a long sip for lubrication. He notices Dale Ludwig in the second row, alongside Belou Snider, his moist eyes like Alan Babcock's telling him, hey, he knows his Secret.

'When I listened to Mr Werner this morning, on maximizing our profits, I thought he could've stressed the extent to which hotels should be – are – dependent on *us* during this economic slowdown, and how at present we can drive hard bargains for our clients, who don't necessarily *want* to spend less overall, but who are definitely interested in first class accommodation at the best price!'

Here he unexpectedly bursts into song ... '"*There's a whole generation/ with a new explanation/ people in motion/ people in motion ...*"' a song he believes will reaffirm his audience's travelling instincts.

It gets a good slice of his audience clapping along in friendly recognition of their nomadic market. Dwight the tenor hasn't sung in public since he sang in *H.M.S. Pinafore* at college.

He goes on to speak about the pros and cons of affiliation by independents with chains and consortiums. He makes a persuasive case for remaining independent, for avoiding shares in a federation, for not selling out to a national enterprise and becoming a franchised hamburger outlet. All a fiction, of course. He really wishes he'd sold out when he had the offer from Gulfstream last year. But if he was willing to prosper by the legend of Herodotus (Father of History, Father of Lies) he should be prepared to drown by it, too. Or so Reesa tells him.

He considers another song, but decides to wrap up.

'Remember, my fellow travellers, we shouldn't have to take a cut in profits and commissions, just because of adverse recessionary conditions. With a little imaginative manoeuvring, panache, attention to details, we can ensure that our product is recession proof!'

He pauses, to show them his badge. He holds it aloft and blesses them. '... In conclusion, ladies and gentlemen, my company, Herodotus Tours, encourages you to make history and travel. Everywhere. Thank you.' He pins it to his own lapel.

Sipping from his glass he watches Dale Ludwig watching the audience applaud his performance. He regrets having missed the opportunity this morning to hand Dale his business card: Dwight Irving, B. Comm./Herodotus Tours, Independent.

'Book us for the Canary Islands,' he might've urged him.
He feels now like he could take on the world and its operators.

3.

Spurning available group tours the born-again traveller finds the Taraval line next morning, and solos in a streetcar, through a neighbourhood of row houses and chiropractors' offices, to the zoo off Sloat. The organ waltz of the carousel sounds like gypsy love, excessive in disappointment and poignant in lethargy, with kids pleading to be allowed onto the slowly turning horses. The zoo itself is a disappointment. The Big Cat House smells high; its fake rock cliffs look wan and cardboardy. Bears are hanging out on the other side of a sleazy moat. A wrinkled elephant, with a semaphoring trunk, opens up for peanuts. Imagine an animal this size bothering over a peanut.

'Rosemary's a gossip,' croaks a pensioner, pitching his peanuts far short of the outstretched trunk. Rosemary's ears shiver like sails. 'A real chatter-box,' says the old man fondly. 'Trumpet secrets'd make your mother blush.'

Later, in Golden Gate Park, Dwight comes upon a large conservatory rising out of the cypress trees like a wedding cake. This glass palace is set back on a terrace of irrigated lawns. Erected 1879 he reads. Like his father's greenhouse, it too is a replica of Kew. Hard not to conclude all glasshouses in the world, in every park and yard, are replicas of Kew: iron and glass spinoffs, smaller worlds, fragments of Capital G glass.

Memo: Research a glasshouse tour of Europe, starting London.

Mist greets him when he enters the palace. Wild birdsong. A pond is swimming with fat-headed goldfish. Waterpipes drip over begonias, palms, banana trees. Over orchids. And over more orchids under glass, which seems odd, a glass box inside a glasshouse. Glass, he thinks, responsible for the whole exotic world: mirrored shades, computer screens, his own reflection in the snake house.

A yellow canary flies by like a lost soul.

Not far away on Haight he finds himself glancing into shop windows. Here hippy prototypes once migrated with flowers in their hair, their stores turned into boutiques inviting perusal of the eighties' new fashions. Like archaeological signposts he imagines their names living on as memorials to the pioneers: Free Love, Flower Power, TokeEnds ...

Belou Snider, impressed by his lecture yesterday, declines an invitation to dinner when he runs into her again in the Westin St. Francis. She's busy with a delegation of Swedes, acting as the travel agent of travel agents, a position in keeping with her city as their host. 'The Germans are the real pain,' she complains. He confesses his surprise at the size of her international brigade. He wonders if Dale Ludwig, her sometime escort, might be available but refrains from asking. Actually, he's relieved not to be stuck with Belou for the evening.

He now calls Candice to inquire after legal developments against Herodotus. These (when she lists them) make no impression upon him at all. He says to her, 'Didn't we agree to withhold payment to the Five Stars Hotel, so we could eventually *compensate* these clients ...? Why are they irate?'

'It's not just the clients. The hotel too.'

'Shag the hotel.'

Dwight now remembers what the cathedral doors reminded him of the first day, and he wanders back up Nob Hill. Simple: the Bronze Baptistry Doors in Florence, or at least the tourist pictures he has seen of those doors. These doors of Grace Cathedral would be copies of the copies ... Old Testament scenes of the Garden of Eden, Cain and Abel, Isaac and Abraham ... depictions of the original stories. Reproductions just as removed as his father's greenhouse from Kew.

He enters the Gothic-looking church, stepping out of the afternoon August sun, into a cool interior filtered by blue and red stained-glass windows.

It's like coming home to a place he remembers but doesn't recognize. His Protestant father would've recognized it without remembering it. His father never went to church. He probably preferred the history of churches to churches themselves, just as he preferred medical books to his actual practice. This is what Marlene Irving always claimed, lamenting her husband's academic propensity. 'Matt's too quiet. I think he's hermetic.'

No doubt she knew this cathedral as a girl.

The sound of echoing shoes, bodies climbing out of pews, heels knocking wood: Mass in progress, people parading up to receive Holy Communion, returning down side aisles to whisper their thanksgivings.

For some reason he is surprised by their gullibility, their willingness to undertake celestial travel on a wing and a prayer. He's surprised by these parishioners' sloppy research. Travel is about correspondence: making palpable what you dream. You get your facts cold first.

He resists the urge to take communion himself, even as an act of revenge against his first seventeen years. Then reconsiders. He might rid himself of any further desire for petty reprisal, against having believed in this literal, fleshly assumption of Christ, by committing some kind of small outrage.

The thought pleases him. His daring travelling persona has settled in nicely. The double agent inside him decides he'd like to chew the Eucharist with his teeth, remove it from his tongue, roll the unleavened bread around like a piece of snot, and finally 'disappear' it with a casual flick of his fingers. He'd like to commit a sacrilege against the body and blood of an old oppressor.

Talk about petty protest.

He decides to go for it.

Joining the devout in line, shuffling toward the Chinese priest at the altar rail, he discovers this Thursday afternoon casualness feels alien to a cradle Catholic like himself, raised on Sunday-morning obligation. The indecorum of it oddly annoys him. He tries to compose himself, to look the part of a believer, instead of an impostor in yellow shoes about to commit serious sin.

He now notices something curious about the communicants walking back to their pews. They're – chewing. *He* grew up believing it a sin to touch the host with your teeth. He has to assume ecumenical common sense has since got rid of the petty apartheid stuff. But this new liturgical atmosphere reminds him of a cafeteria. He's disappointed by the irreverence.

The priest, dipping like a duck into his gold ciborium, is dressed in vestments slightly unfamiliar to Dwight. Obviously, as everywhere else, fashion now cuts its cloth in church. And there's no one to catch particles of the host on a plate, saving them from ignominy on the floor. (How far, he used to wonder as an altar boy, did the dust of these specks have to go before they became nothing? Were they infinite? In *his* universe a battalion of vacuum cleaners could never have recovered all the crumbs should he have accidentally spilled the plate.) Dogma these days definitely seems more casual: no doubt the price of doing business on a Thursday afternoon. Most of these middle-aged Catholics look downright uninterested, unmoved.

Where's their wonder?

The woman ahead mumbles something to the priest. The priest repeats himself to the next man in line, but Dwight doesn't catch the answer. Then it's his turn. 'Thanks be to God,' he mumbles, opening up and extending his tongue.

The host tastes precisely as he remembers. Yeastless, boneless. His eyes moisten a little in recollection of his First Communion. An entire circumference at first, melting to soggy pulp. All taste and touch.

Returning down a side aisle, he recognizes all these people sitting out communion can be identified as having souls in such racy conditions (stained and blotted with sins still unconfessed) they're forbidden to take the Eucharist out of threat of excommunication from the Church. Things were different when he was a boy. You couldn't be certain who was and wasn't in a state of grace, because in those years, before the Pope loosened up on dietary restrictions, you were ineligible to take morning communion if you'd eaten so much as a peanut after midnight.

Our Lord did not want to compete in your digestive tract with a peanut.

Swathed in stained-glass light, he finds an empty pew near the rear of the cathedral and kneels down on the riser, his elbows propped along the bench in front, folded hands in casual meditation at his mouth.

He opens one eye to peer around. He wants to conduct his sacrilege in absolute secrecy. This is between the past and him. He isn't out to insult the gullible.

The travel consultant now bites down on the consecrated host. He takes another bite, this time grinding away with his molars. Sweet revenge for his own erstwhile gullibility and mindless obedience. He finds himself chewing away on Christ's body like bubble gum.

This gives him a measure of satisfaction, until he remembers that chewing is no longer forbidden under pain of major sin, either.

So much for a quarter of his plan.

He hurriedly revises his schedule, working the host forward in his mouth. Since unleavened bread shrivels fast, he doesn't want to swallow the disappearing stuff accidentally. He does his best to dry it of saliva, by drawing air in over the pulp between his teeth. But the Eucharist remains a piece of used Kleenex – not at all firm enough to roll around in his fingers like snot.

He ends up dribbling the mushiness down between his praying hands, joined in thanksgiving. By the bored dry-eyed look of those around him, slowly digesting Superman, Creator of the Universe, not much chance they'd want to stone him, even if they should happen to catch him playing the sinner. Where's their wonder and closet rage? No wonder these days the Ayatollah's followers are getting all the press. This secret penetration of their ranks isn't turning out to be as satisfying as he'd hoped.

No choice now but to rub his sticky hands together and dry them off. He glances at the white gob in his palm, like a puddle of semen, and proceeds casually to put his hand in his pocket. He rubs away at his leg to get rid of the stickiness. He might've used his sock. This mortal sin feels mildly disappointing.

Before the priest leaves the altar Dwight is up and out of Grace Cathedral, his desire for revenge oddly exhausted.

He stands on the empty sidewalk like a man who has just said so long to a messy affair. The late afternoon sunshine greets him like a glass of chardonnay. He admires the deep blue sky. The view from up here, of his mother's city, makes him feel at home. An earthquake seems about as likely as a hurricane.

His sweeping glance happens to take in the cathedral's notice board, giving the hours for Holy Eucharist.

Episcopal it reads.

Seat of the Episcopal Bishop of California.

Episcopal?

Dwight studies the building. 'This isn't a Roman Catholic cathedral at all,' he says out loud. 'Christ fucking almighty.'

Ruefully, he smiles.

The imitation might not have fooled a practising Roman Catholic. But it fooled a lapsed one. Aren't the basics supposed to be as different as bread and cheese?

He feels annoyed at the Episcopalians' deliberate subterfuge. His error rather pisses him off. He feels cheated out of all proportion to his still untarnished innocence.

What good is a sacrilege when you discover it never had any chance of being blasphemous? You have to be Catholic (and a cradle one he surmises) to know what it feels like to sin against an icon. He worries that in moral matters he may no longer have the stuff to tell the difference between what's real and what's imitative. He's annoyed to see how the pleasure in committing sin, even a sin you no longer believe *is* a sin, can be completely wiped out by the imitative Protestant premise.

He spits, but misses the gutter. He feels obliged to rub the sidewalk with his shoe. Even the high Protestant, with his Roman trappings, lacks the true capacity for desecration. 'Do this in memory of me ...' said Christ to his

Apostles. He was *not* talking to Episcopalians in California. Dwight feels jerked around. He has put his faith in appearances and discovered himself to be one of the foolish virgins. It would be like him going to Bartlett's clinic, actually believing his friend could cure a broken bone.

Given the choice and an incentive for blasphemy, a Catholic would much rather break the stained glass of a cathedral in Italy than in any other country. You knew where you were headed, black day in July, if you smashed up stained glass in Italy.

Descending California, cheated out of a trip to Hell and deprived of his own profanity, he has begun to miss his daughter. This in the middle of the intersection at Powell, the street he then descends to Union Square and the Westin St. Francis. He dials home. He's coming home tomorrow.

'A woman called Mary Yip called by this morning with a letter. She claims to be Aloysius's "broker". She looked worried.' Reesa sounds uncomfortable.

'So he's playing the stock market, on top of producing videos?' asks Dwight.

'Not any more. He's in hock to her company and they want to talk to you about restructuring his debt.'

'My debt, you mean.'

'That was the implication.'

'So did you write her a cheque?'

'I could've written her a cheque, yes. But it would have bounced at the bank.'

'I'm not going to like the sum of this debt.'

'The restructuring bit sounded quite creative. I can see why you kowtow to these finance types. You get a juicy part in their ongoing little soap operas.'

'Is His Lowness home at present? I'd like to talk to him.'

'That's the other thing, sweetheart.'

'What, he sold the house?'

'He's gone.'

'He took your car.'

'He's living on the street,' she tells him. 'In a tent.'

She sounds strangely eager to emphasize the transformation of someone they used to know.

'He was on TV yesterday. With his protest. On the local news even.'

This latest youthful initiative strikes Dwight as possibly a sensible diversionary tactic. 'What's his beef?'

'Among other things, travel agents.'

'Come again?'

'Your treatment of women, apparently. He's forsaken the business world for virtue. I can't get through to him.'

'*Travel* agents? Women?'

'Why don't you stay away longer, sweetheart, since you're having such a good time?'

'Me? I can't even sin when I try.'

'Don't try so hard.'

'Hey, biscuit, I'll remember that for my trip to the poorhouse.'

On his flight back the illusionist remembers to note down on a napkin: *Home is where the heart is. The heart is a moving target. Travel is home in motion.* This for his future memoirs about a Life in Travel.

January, 2036

Plays about civic character seem the rage in our sesquicentennial year. F. and I go along to what he says is a kind of morality play for our own boom times.

F.'s new friend V. came in later for a nightcap and conversation about the film industry. She knows of Mother's old work so I suggested they meet. They'd enjoy each other. V. didn't suppose 'all that much has really changed. Our industry's appetite for stories is still here.'

'Really, then,' said F. to V, 'you'd have a whale of a story in *Scalpmania* ... if you could get the rights.'

V. hasn't seen it. Too busy at the moment producing and directing and starring in a lesbian film about a middle-aged gypsy with two kids and no income, except for her welfare cheque. F. wondered if the story wouldn't prove a little depressing, given everyone's current affluence. 'Who wants to look at poverty?'

I do, I said.

V. looked interested. She must be in her mid-fifties, my age. 'I'm only saying,' F. said to V., 'you have to be realistic. That's why you should go after the rights to this morality play. Somehow bring it up to date. Set it in our own boom times.'

I refilled V.'s glass. '*Arriba*,' said V. – I think as a compliment to F.

Why do I keep this diary? Because Mother encouraged me as a child to write myself down every day after school? 'String it together however you like. You'll never reread it. The point,' she used to say, 'is to give your life event.' *She* kept a diary, she claimed, to keep separate the things that happened to her and the things she thought happened to her. I think now, in public life, I know what she meant. After a while you crave the anonymity of the past.

Just like 'Sam' craved it in this evening's play. Myth gets mixed up with fact, as F. was explaining to V. This character attained mythical status, over half a century ago, and made national news. Resident of a boom city he embodied many people's aspirations in

⟨ 163 ⟩

those fractured times, flipping office towers at a pen's stroke, hockey teams, yachts, shopping centres. Leapt red tape at a single bound, dodged taxes, flew to the heart of deal after deal in a Lear jet with unerring instinct for credit lines stretching to the horizon and beyond. The economy was shattering. His empire went into traction.

'… And there'd still be old videotape you could insert,' suggested F., if V. should ever decide to do a film based on the play. 'Satellites once beamed this guy's image coast to coast. It'd make a natural film, Vicky. Everybody rooting for his comeback, including Revenue Canada, whose only hope of recovering its tax losses was to let him return to the line of work he seemed best at – bottom feeding and flipping.'

'Bottom feeding?'

'Smelling out the lowest prices.'

I was watching Vicky Casaqua, who seemed a little bored before F.'s enthusiasm. Too many laurels? Conceit? Always a let-down to meet the person behind the familiar and outspoken public figure. But then she might say the same about me. Her children must be Renaldo's age.

She said, 'The title makes it sound like a nasty play about aboriginal people.' F. disagreed. 'In *Scalpmania* the nasties are the white men. And scalps the properties they take.'

The real kicker in the drama, said F., is Sam's adieu at a benefit dinner hosted by his friends, where he declares undying love for his estranged wife, promises to honour financial obligations to his country by paying the back taxes he owes, and decides thereafter to shun notoriety and embrace anonymity.

'And does he?' asked V.

'Is a rose black?' I interjected.

Chapter 10

Bleak House

MARCH ALREADY, he thinks, and I continue to disappear. By which he means that his flaking skin condition, as bad as ever, has condemned him to vanish without a trace. He hardly recognizes the man in the mirror, a pale imitation of the fat man determined to charm his way into the heart of a Guatemalan hotelier last October. His falling skin has combined to undermine his identity. March already and I continue to disappear into someone else's story.

He is reading aloud to the commandante of St. Augustine's, a minimum-security prison constructed in a hill town outside San José as a late-sixties rehab project. ... *Full seven happy years I have been the mistress of Bleak House. The few words that I have to add to what I have written, are soon penned; then I, and the unknown friend to whom I write, will part for ever. Not without much dear remembrance on my side. Not without some, I hope, on his or hers ...*

He's been reading for approximately an hour, coming to the last chapter of a book the two men have shared for more than a month, him reading and the commandante listening, with sweet-F-all happening in final-appeal court to free the performer from his new jail. The commandante loves to be read to. Dickens with his food. Dickens with his coffee. A man seven years older than Dwight, in cowboy boots and a tan leather jacket. Gold bracelet. Spectacles. Not a strand of brown left in his prematurely grey hair. Every night the commandante 'invites' his Canadian inmate to his office for this unnatural practice of reading aloud to him for an hour, two hours. The perversion of a conceited autodidact, listening to improve his English.

Pablo Picasso Segura relaxes, nodding off sometimes over his coffee mug, then snapping awake to listen carefully to the good bits of Dwight's narrative. The coffee seems no impediment to his capacity to snooze. The commandante makes Dwight wonder. A self-improver, warden of men busy improving their own selves, he pays only lip service to institutional rehabilitation and doubts its outcome. He believes punishment pure and simple is what society should and does expect. Maybe it's because he can no longer get enough coffee into his largely immune system, that he grows teary and irritable on occasion. Dwight has noticed he dislikes sentimentality, in himself and anybody else. He's a determined man who knows how to get the most out of inmates.

An English drug peddler from Leeds, who managed to collect two shelves of worn English classics before leaving prison (Dwight isn't sure when or where to), had introduced Segura to Dickens. Dwight's luck, Dickens. The endless pages. The prisoner finds himself coughing to summon more push from his stomach muscles. The commandante's expectations have been chasing his syllables for weeks now, like silent threatening weasels. Memo: Plead laryngitis!

The commandante, a man in love with due procedure, and certainly accustomed to the bureaucracy of his own country, has found this particular Dickens about courts and legal hassles a revelation. Listening to it every night for a month, he has tracked the unfolding sentences of paragraphs, pages and chapters of what he dryly believes is Dwight's litigious world. 'El norte,' he grunts with satisfaction. A world in which, unless Pablo Picasso Segura is mistaken, the labyrinth of an English-speaking judiciary holds the lure of remorseless discovery. Prison in his own country is predictable: too lenient. His prisoners are free to lounge in the courtyard, see their girl friends, play ping pong. A womanizer himself, the commandante of St. Augustine's feels a strong need for stricter rules and fewer expectations, if incarceration is to count for anything. Dwight has studied him between sentences. Segura appears to have developed a very healthy respect for *el norte*. Attentive to his prisoner's performance, he enjoys farting away supper. Clearly, justice is elsewhere.

Dwight stops to sip from his own mug of coffee. The caffeine has depressed him, worsened his headache, scythed his nerve endings with a dull blade. He sips the liquid to lubricate his throat. He wonders whether he wasn't better off isolated in the ghastly penitentiary, where he could stay true to his own ramblings. Here he is expected to humour a sadist.

He hopes to be finished soon. Free soon.

A brief hospital stay in December had helped plug his dysentery, but returning to solitary confinement loosened it again. Following his friend Bartlett's visit his weight dropped further, skin collapsed on his bones, his skeleton sharpened. He was as good as gone. Then a reprieve. Transferred quite abruptly in February, to this minimum-security jail, he began his slow resurrection from the dead. He began to hope.

Until Reesa's letter arrived, that is, slipping through the bureaucratic post office without its usual look of having passed open across a dozen coffee-stained blotters. With this the noble prisoner's notion of homecoming suffered not one blow but two, suggesting his idea of home had become an anachronism.

... I try to write all this lightly, because my heart is full in drawing to an end; but when I write of him, my tears will have their way.

Sounds like Reesa's sad letter to do with houses, the lesser of which their landlord had decided to knock over in order to build a low highrise unit of condos '... as soon as interest rates come down. Meanwhile, Dwight, the scumbag plans to sit on a vacant lot. I plan to fight.' Just when she thought the recession had won them at least an amnesty against eviction. Gwyn, Bartlett, Theresa – '... you, if you're back – we're all supposed to be out by May 1. God, when are you coming back?' She didn't like to burden him in prison with this, but where were they going to live? She apologized. She planned to visit him, if she could only get away. *She hoped he was gradually getting over his mother's death.*

The other thing that had come to an end was his expectation of inheriting Marlene's property. Reesa was saving this in her letter. She hadn't wanted to depress me more than I already was, Your Worship. She and Bartlett had agreed Bartlett shouldn't mention the will during his visit after his mother's death.

And since her letter arrived shit has just kept hitting the fan. For examp, three weeks after his transfer here, as if in revenge, the lower court upheld Guatemala's request to have him extradited to Guatemala. Home retreated to another century. To debtor's prison and rats. J.R. Tocher suggested he appeal to the higher court right away; Dwight did. But he knows the decision promises to take still more months. Not that the Canadian embassy cares. His case is a stale one now, better left to the looping human cycle of erosion by neglect.

Consider his scaly skin and silver flakes. Chafing against neglect keeps causing his hair to itch, not to mention his elbows, hands, knees ... 'Keep reading, fool,' he tells himself, 'don't dwell on your epidermis.' The prisoner is determined to introduce the commandante to a new author; if only

Reesa could visit to tell him which paperbacks in his possession might humour this sadist.

'What's wrong with your hands?' the sadist interrupts.

'The doctor told me psoriasis.'

Segura nods, approvingly. The suffering of restitution. Ugly red lesions. White scales.

There's pressure on Dwight's bladder, but he can't afford to ask for a break so near the end of the story. The sadist is dying to hear what happens. *The people even praise Me as the doctor's wife. The people even like Me as I go about, and make so much of me that I am quite abashed. I owe it all to him, my love, my pride! They like me for his sake, as I do everything I do in life for his sake.*

Such worn-out sentiment. Did his mother ever talk to his father this way? His father was at the hospital so much of the time, the rest of his time sequestered in his greenhouse, she must've had to pretend to devotion.

The prisoner seems to remember his parents speaking less and less often, as if the influence of a dumb elder son had inclined them away from common language. As the younger son, Your Worship, I was left with the sense of a couple moving from room to room, shrub to hedge, spying on one another. Not till after her husband's unexpected death, leaving her alone with two sons, did his mother seem to discover the outside world as a more interesting manifestation of her religion: Elizabeth Fry, Save the Children, eventually Aloysius – even Cher. Her impression of Aloysius was by far the weakest in her repertoire. Her impression of a family didn't even count.

... But I know that my dearest little pets are very pretty, and that my darling is very beautiful, and that my husband is very handsome, and that my guardian has the brightest and most benevolent face that ever was seen; and that they can very well do without much beauty in me – even supposing – reads the womanly prisoner, with the resigned note of finality,

The End.

The commandante starts at the sudden silence. 'The end?' As if the configurations shaping this moment, the long narrative arc in a foreign tongue, he hasn't truly grasped. The family reconstituted. 'The end?'

'Si,' whispers Dwight. He would welcome a leak now.

Pablo Picasso Segura puts down his blue-glazed mug and picks it up again. He licks the rim of it several times. The fingers of his right hand grip and ungrip the handle. He seems to be considering their arrival at this point of sudden muteness. He wipes something, possibly a tear, from his cheek.

Confused, looking ripped off by the notion of any end, he scrapes a heel back across his desk. He looks anxious and dissatisfied but is trying not to show it.

'So. Tomorrow nights we start again.'

'If you like, of course ...'

The warden drains his coffee mug. He jiggles the gold chain at his throat. He jiggles the ring of keys attached to his belt loop. He runs a hand through his hair. He touches his spectacles.

'If I like, he say. I like, yes!'

'A new novel.'

'Diggens.'

'I was thinking of –'

'This one, again.'

Imagine poor Damon. Imagine his brother imprisoned here and dependent on this warden's good will for his release. Voiceless, poor Da couldn't transport the commandante anywhere.

The tenderness of this reflection graces more than the despair of jail. It suggests to him he still has a home.

Somewhere, somehow.

Pushing pushing.

2.

Green sheets of corrugated plastic cover the noisy courtyard, letting in sunlight by day and keeping off dew at night. Fig plants, hanging pothos, ferns, banana palms give the detention centre the look of a greenhouse. He waters the plants every day with a copper kettle, having volunteered upon his arrival. His hope was the sunlight would eventually cure his psoriasis, though he now wonders if the ultraviolet rays his skin needs might not be filtered out by the plastic. So he takes slow walks outside, to sit in the zocalo near the town's cathedral.

Tonight he unzips in the prison urinal and pees coffee to the count of one hundred and twenty-nine. This must include the Coke at dinner, before he showed up for his Diggens performance. From inside a cubicle someone's peering out at him, mumbling in Spanish as if in praise of his voiding bladder. Probably wanking thinks Dwight. He farts in the peeper's direction.

His empty room is no oasis, even with the door closed. In here he finds it hard to shut out the incessant courtyard voices, competing TV stations, confinement's jangle without a lull. Curfew will eventually bring the clamour indoors, turning the paddle-click of ping pong balls into masturbating whimpers; yakking voices into snores. He sags back in his bunk, pillow propping up his head, to consider his priorities. He discovers he has few of a practicable nature (less noise, more privacy), except to turn up another story than the Diggens he's supposed to start rereading tomorrow to PPS.

He reaches over to rummage through the drug peddler's bookshelf of dog-eared classics.

All around him pinups of blonde nude women paper the ceiling, walls, the undersides of bunk beds. Girls awaiting the return of their keepers. *Look at us looking at ourselves*, they whisper, keeping inmates content after their door is locked.

The atmosphere reminds him a little of his old frat house, where you were supposed to enjoy hanging out with the guys comparing tail you couldn't wait to get into, the house's papered walls a testimony to endless fucking desire. Similarly in here, he can watch his fellow inmates watching the walls. He can watch them watching the girls. Just like in Herodotus: as he once discovered, wondering what to name his new company: the good part when the king's watching his favourite courtesan, who's watching the queen undress, and Herodotus is watching all three ... and making it all up, figured Dwight.

He opens a paperback, wondering how he is going to appease Picasso the Asshole. Every night at this hour his migraine worsens and thoughts of home and the loss of home throw into relief the lack of communication between him and his jailer. What does the man want from him?

Ah! Vanitas vanitatum! *Which of us is happy in this world? Which of us has his desire? or, having it, is satisfied? – come children, let us shut up the box and the puppets, for our play is played out.*

He closes the ratty cover. He begins extracting and flipping randomly to other last pages of tattered paperbacks for some answer to his own feelings of dissatisfaction at being jerked around for the last six months in a foreign country with no news.

His forehead feels like someone's ripping foul balls back off the screen.

His forehead is the screen. Every jolt loosens more skin and hair. He rubs his temple; skin at the hairline flakes off. His joints, supported poorly by a worn-out mattress, ache like implanted semi-colons.

He's cheating now by skipping hundreds of pages. Cheating on the sadistic commandante. He wonders if endings to these narratives are ever happy, or just full of unfulfilled desire. He tries, without having read the hundreds of preceding pages, to imagine what events inside them could have driven their old-fashioned plots to these ends and not others. *She slipped his folded letter between the two buttons of her plain black bodice, and leaning her forehead against a window-pane remained there till dusk, perfectly motionless, giving him all the time she could spare. Gone! Was it possible? My God, was it possible? The blow had come softened by the spaces of the earth, by the years of absence. There had been whole days when she had not thought of him at all – had no time. But she had loved him after all.*

And their child, Gwyn? Whose was she?

These elegant endings seem like invitations to imagine himself in their sphere of influence. He tries to amuse himself, a prisoner fantasizing in his bunk, with last lines he imagines having reached after epic years of reading aloud to the commandante. Where will he end up?

They could always rent an apartment. In time he thinks he could even pay off his debts and resurface in the world as a man of his word. A man of his word would probably be redundant though. He can foresee being squeezed and strangled like a bankrupt case in the endless, bottomless hole of Chancery.

What an end! Why bother looking forward to a successful appeal to a higher court in Costa Rica, if he's merely destined for the courts of his own country?

Lately he has taken fewer walks in town. Citizens just stare at his skin, at his clothes. They poke fun at his rheumatic hobble. He walks like he has exclamation points up the ass, from so much reading to his jailer. He prefers watering his plants in the courtyard, napping, counting on his roommates staying lost. He itches his skin and his scales snow to the floor. He feels like some kind of dragon. Other inmates worry he has a communicable disease. The chill of winter is upon this man. He suits their idea of a Canadian to a T.

He pulls a Diggens from the bookshelf, a shorter Diggens, to gauge his chances of satisfying the sadist with it. Again he turns to the last pages: ...

such are the changes which a few years bring about, and so do things pass away, like a tale that is told! Another jab in the ass, but the commandante wouldn't be pleased with an ending that *ended*. '... What tings? No need.'

Not the sort of man who cares for codicils of any sort. It wouldn't surprise him if Pablo Picasso Segura intended to die intestate, so strenuously did he object to conclusions.

Not Dwight's mother though. Marlene Irving wasn't a sadist. But she was pretty perverse in willing her house to an orphan. He ponders this end. This *beginning* for the young man. Dwight, as her rightful heir, has just begun to understand (without having to accept) Reesa's explanation for his mother's queer bequest: that she did it to save her family from disintegrating. Had she willed her house to Dwight, the banks would then have had a claim on it should his company fail. His company did fail. In hindsight Reesa thought his mother's move made splendid sense. It helped Damon, for one thing, by not forcing him to move.

She thinks Dwight and she and Gwyn might possibly find themselves welcome in the house too. She thought she might ask 'the new owner' to help them out.

'Ask that little traitor? She must be bananas.'

He can't help feeling jealous. He remembers his mother's house, vividly, all its rooms adding up to a history of his first twenty-four years. He supposes the point of any house is to resist dissolution, by immortalizing its inhabitants' sojourns there. An arrogant point for an architect to make, Your Worship, every time he designs a house. In time an uncaring landlord like his and Reesa's will come along and demolish the place, just to punish such arrogance! Aloysius, too, could well decide to have the Irving house flattened, if it means money.

He lies in his bunk bed, trying to resist his own dissolution. As long as he can read aloud, he assumes he'll be safe from extradition to a hell-hole jail in Guatemala. He sometimes worries that is where his drug-peddling predecessor ended up, silenced by the commandante's refusal to accept his sentence was over. This could be a problem for Dwight too. Unless he accepts that as the commandante's reader he may never again be free. He can see the headlines at home: IMPOSTOR ENTERS PRISON IN REAL TIME, ENDS UP IN IMAGINARY TIME, READING TO A LUNATIC. A lunatic determined to punish his resistance.

He scratches his face and snow falls.

He's beginning to think the warden listens but makes no distinction between past and future. He's beginning to think whole worlds in these epics join each other in orbit, like travellers to an ideal city where silence is golden. Memo: What is the meaning of ...

The illusionist is going through book ends at a rapid rate now, moving forward with no notion of what has preceded these transfiguring finales, plots fallen from sight into darkness.

But no, he would not give in. Turning sharply, he walked towards the city's gold phosphorescence. His fists were shut, his mouth set fast. He would not take that direction, to the darkness, to follow her. He walked towards the faintly humming, glowing town, quickly.

Now there's a budding architect. Someone interested in civic transformation, Your Worship. An ambitious young man who can see things the way they might be.

The door opens. Enter the boy who stares too much. Tomas, a loner, who tries not to stare and stares moistly at Dwight anyway. At least his bad eye does, a wayward habit from some childhood disease, or possibly a street fight, the kind of shifty eye Dwight recalls in the face of an otherwise pretty man on Market Street last August in San Francisco.

Young Tomas sleeps up the ladder, in the bunk above his. Sometimes Dwight hears him masturbating, the overhead wooden platform creaking in steady response to the glossy wallpaper. He has no idea why this boy's in prison, and imagines all sorts of misadventures. Belly-up in the black-market. Street rackets gone bad. Protection scheme for small businessmen uncovered.

Soon their roommates will wander in, undress, pause in bed with throttled sighs and stabs at prayer. They'll all begin to meditate on their day in the sun, before the lights go out and the key in the door is turned.

One man is a chronic alcoholic, always neatly dressed in a sweater vest, who likes to fall asleep sipping hidden hair tonic. The other is a man Dwight's age who looks fifty, a wrinkled-faced coffee farmer who stiffed his brother in an uncontrollable fit of revenge. This is the drill. He refuses to visit the grave. Gets lower than the floor sometimes remembering, seeing his brother's face. Yelps in his sleep.

Where will they go, these men, once released from their roles as roommates, freed from the priorities of a commandante who expects them to be reimprisoned anyway? Dwight feels they're doomed to vanish and is uncontrollably sentimental, as if he will actually miss this configuration of bodies in a space the size of an enlarged tool shed.

He tries to forget bodies. He reaches for another novel. He reaches for the answer in something he can understand.

He senses someone looking down at him from on high, mumbling. He opens up again to last lines.

Teddy surveyed his charges with pride and affection. It was by means of them that he hoped one day to restore Hetton to the glory that it had enjoyed in the days of his ... guardian Dwight.

He looks up. Upstairs, Tomas is moving in tandem with his fantasy, a body of soft scented skin, the wanker at one with his imagination.

The Canadian looks to himself. His skin as usual is all over everything, snow from *el norte* on the bed, on the floor. He needs to become the object of someone's fantasy, soon, otherwise his skin will still be snowing as he sleeps. Still be snowing tomorrow, next week, next millennium, assuming he doesn't cave in sooner reading to a sadist in a hot country, his tale that is told of a Life in Travel.

December, 2030

Sworn in this morning as mayor, after four years on council. Far from youngest in history at forty-nine, but if the economy turns around needn't be briefest either. F. excited for me, but I wonder if this will hold when millstone of job comes knocking too heavily on my husband's good will? My loyal spouse. My chain of office really sparkles.

Massive unemployment, widespread dissatisfaction with housing, a pack of mad dogs on council ... winning by a landslide was easy. An educated horse could have defeated the incumbent donkey, hobbling out after a single term. These party hacks disgust me. My luck is

to have been the horse instead of the donkey. But can I last if the economy doesn't buck up?

I stumped okay. I lasted the course. I showed enough dash and flair for voters. Important for a candidate to sound on the edge of something interesting. Did fall back on bad habit of speaking in public like string, my sentence ends curling up – not in questions I suppose but desire. Desire for what, neat bows? Am afraid I've been promising too many gifts in the midst of our depression and with not much in my boxes.

We are taking the Christmas week off to visit Hawaii. At fourteen Renaldo thinks our

ocean not an ocean unless he can ride it the way he remembers it folding over him as an embryo in the womb – or wherever it is they've been taking him back to, with self-manipulated brainwaves. Brain surfing he calls it. F. worries about reefs – abroad, and at home in our son's head.

On return my first business will be to negotiate with the provincial government for a bigger fleet of commuter ferries round our harbour, to and from local islands, coastal towns. Our civic heritage is first and ever the sea. Let's 'refloat' ourselves, I told two million voters. 'We're a water city.'

But what of my other 'six Rs'? To 'relay'

watermains, 'repave' roads, 'rewire' transit, 'reequip' local pediatric clinics, 'relocate' ourselves among foreign sister cities … How to raise capital costs for all these projects and still find the way to prosperity?

I sound like an old-fashioned history book with its *de rigueur* chapter, 'Road to Prosperity'. Have been making much in public of time catching us on the backswing, of its going the other way if we don't look to the future.

I try to insist on a few minutes alone each evening at the piano, and a talk with F. Am lucky my small family is independent enough to manage without me when public functions call. We smile at how my old practice used to seem all-consuming. Campaigning has been a revelation in and of time, so it's no coincidence this diary has languished.

The coincidence is what F. chanced across the day of my election, a Royal Doulton figurine, something F.'s father had saved from his first wife, a couple sitting on a little slab bench. One of the figures is placing the Chain of Office – so the shells appear – around the neck of another, like a Hawaiian aloha. I think this would have decided us on Hawaii, if we hadn't already decided.

For a week am willing to forget the poor in our streets, the forlorn and the needful. But at what price? Impossible to justify selfishness. Only compromise.

Book Two

THE LIFE OF A TUXEDO

Brother Landlord

Chapter 11

Thin Ice

I HAVE HAD A DREAM. Lying in my own house, Mother, dreaming up the long climax when the day of tenants dawns, I, A.I., am everyone I wish to be. What are these burning ankles when my smile charms them so? So what if they hurt and sag inwards, or feel like a housemaid's knees, because how else will I learn ways to have fun and such like? Ankles burn when you ice skate. This is the given, Mother. I put up with burning to gain a purchase in my new society. Winter here is a bad proposition, but I have adaptable youth, a nice smile, I add up to a trophy for the Irvings when I barkeep. Did you ever see ice in Bombay, Mother, not counting drink ice?

These classmates rag me, so I try straightening my ankles but they flop outward and tilt to the shores of the lagoon. From a sag to a flop, flopping and sagging the circumference of the shoreline, I hug this ice between my legs. I have the world between my cold skinny legs. Teachers at school keep saying pay attention, Aloysius, you could be a doctor or anything else I don't want to be, if you applied your brain for sums and such like. But there is no time for the study of doctoring or lawyering or Bunsen burning. The Sisters of Hope thought I could add up to a bishop. But the time for bishoping is gone too. I know what I want and predict I will earn it soon. The House of the Lord, Mother, is what I want minus the landlord. Rad. The orphanage boosted my street talents for making oodles of schemes to finance a deed to the House of the Lord. Is this why I talk so much in a conversation that never takes place? You, Mother, help me fill my mouth to the rootbeams.

If I brag at school tomorrow, saying I was smooth today, my classmates have me cold, as we say in English, because everyone can see I ice skate like a substitute in life. Right now I wonder if their ragging is worth it, if cutting lines into this ice with razors on my feet can help me profit. Profit is what I stand on willy nilly. This question arises: Is being a good jock with classmates going to get me ahead? What point is there in circling and line cutting?

I need a rest from speculations, Mother, because they make my ankles burn. It is not razoring the ice that hurts them, no, but you throbbing in my bones to remind me. Forgive yours truly. Making icy lines is for having fun and passing the day. I interpret them so. I accept a useless endeavor as a way to joyful abandon. Trudy says I should learn to have more fun not less. This is the given, Mother. Sid Vicious and Nancy Spungen notwithstanding, I need to learn goodness and the right to justice. I am rotting into a bad apple.

My goals are therefore the following: To be rich as a magnate. To look more like Michael Jackson than Johnny Rotten. To be *amportant*. That is how we pronounce it in French class. I like the pushy 'am' from the French who think they centre the world, in a country the size of a licked stamp. C'est *amportant* to centre the world, Mother, if I hope to be awesome and such like. But with Michael Jackson's small nose I find my *amportant* sounds tinny. So I deepen the nasal 'ant' tacked to the end. *Amportaunt*. In English we undercut ourselves too often at the precise wrong termination.

I feel like climbing a bare naked willow on shore, to see what kind of writing all these blades are making over this huge frozen lagoon. A big mess is my guess, like a scribble picture of a preschooler like Chichi, you remember, Pearl's son? Ten thousand skaters in warm jackets and coloured scarves, dogs, hockey hoodlums, sleds, a population of citizens waltzing to break the band and going no place. This is okay too. Look at them all, Mother, taking a coast on their feet in the cold sun. Crowded they think, but nowhere half as crowded if a lagoon like this froze over in Bombay and Indians knew how to skate, wanted to skate, liked what a big pleasure it was, riding their feet in loops. Big pleasure, leisure, though I scoff it personally. I am everyone I want to be. But I will wait for spring to claim I skate like the Great Gretzky. Memories dim, but they are sharp in the short run for a performance like ice skating.

'Alawisshezz!! ...' this girl's floating voice down a long line of armlocked whipcrackers. The whip's tail comes hissing by, inches from my wobble, upsetting me in its wake of cold air. *Whap!* Face down, licking ice chips, me, hearing their wake of laughter, watching myself in distaste. Lying here on ice like a market herring, Mother, I unpocket a huge burning to get up and go fast, fly past them as they flew past me, darting insults as they darted them, also ragging the girls. I am the hottest skater on the lagoon! Why not, if desire counts, if being *amportant* is my foreordination? I have only to think I am the best skater and I *am*. I have only to believe in my genius for inveiglement. Everything is thinkable for Aloysius Irving. I can dissolve that dog moving faster than me by thinking Scram, Sniffer! and that dog is no more the memo of me skating like I have polio. I am a.k.a. Corbin, a name I lost on entering the orphanage. No one knows I was named after a raven, Mother. You must have had an attack of brain soggies to name me that. Where are my weeds?

Smoking, I wobble up the far shore where I remember bulrushes clogged the water last summer and a redwing blackbird gave me the notion for Foreign Trade. I wonder what gave John Lydon, a.k.a. Johnny Rotten, the notion for the Sex Pistols? *Ping*. Long gone the bulrushes, the blackbirds. Workers have axed this corner of the lagoon and a thousand, a million, water fowl are teeming. Birdbrains ... across the causeway they could swim in salt water free of ice from here to Honolulu. These skaters, too, could be home in a *hot bath*. Mother, why am I not home working on plans to enlarge my cash flow, instead of coughing like a furnace to keep myself thawed? Trudy says my dinky black jacket and ripped jeans are worse than zero to wear, but how would she know with her fatty layers? She is insured against winter. Home patrol would be better than this, even with Reesa telling me to groove myself into something better than collecting bottles, since I could be first in my class, or Dwight telling me pull up my socks or else face the music. I tell him the music I face is Foreign Trade's, and he groans remembering my band got suckered into kick fighting the boat kid gang at our last dance. As manager I should have kept better control Dwight says. I did not fight, I tell him. I went up on stage to say peacekeeping things in the mike. Mother, the socks he mentions? I never wore socks in my life, not till landing in Canada ten months ago in flip-flops. Now I wear black Velcro boots you could picture if you thought of two lips zippered without a zipper. It is a suction thing. I would give my lips to have invented Velcro because this franchise must be the Supreme Kiss awarded to a patenter in one lifetime.

What was I telling you? I was skimming *The Book of Daniel* for merchandising ideas and asking myself, versus Reesa, what percentage is there staying in school when the benefits are somewhere else? You would probably agree with Reesa. Not to worry, Mother, because if you could see my agenda for fiscal happiness you would have a great satisfaction. Here is my current list of possible good earners: Foreign Trade, bottled tap water with a French label to sell in the leisure market, crushed glass, and Mr Singh (I am hoping). The not so good list: perfume for high school girls, bootlegged mickeys at dances, trade in your skateboard scheme, selling jewellery out of my briefcase in the underground mall ... My failures are more teeming. High overhead and low cash flow, Mother, are twin debits of *amportance*. It is a problem with me, debits and such like.

My toes are numb. I would trade these ugly skates from Dwight's teenagehood for a cup of cocoa. Mother, if you could see me boxstep in them you would laugh out. Even fat Trudy can skate faster than yours truly. She feels bad passing me, poking my shoulder, hoping to be noticed in her old lady coat. Poor Trudy, she would love to get ragged as I get, as someone who counts enough for classmates to rag her growingly, but she is the outsider and wonders how I, A.I., charmed himself into pop regard with his haughtiness. *She* is like the refugee, not me. I feel sorry for Trudy and rag her sometimes in front of classmates, the way other boys rag pretty girls, just to tease. Noticed, she flowers, the whine falls from her voice, she starts floating weightless like a spacewoman. She owes me for these moments in the sun, Mother. I wonder what her typing speed is, because the day is approaching when I will require a secretary.

For example: Deliver me from icy fun! See no more of my time is wasted! A secretary would understand these orders and shield me from the circling scribble of teenagers at leisure. Teenagehood sucks in the pits. I want a profit from skating, if I *have* to skate, but see nothing to sell or patent except cocoa in a pushcart. This might make me a profit, if the lagoon did not melt in a rainstorm before winter does. Puffing my Pall Mall I keep one hand plugged in my black jeans, except to fall, and this tightness at the hips stunts my forward thrust. The small chain between my legs does not help thrusting either. Trudy thinks I keep my hand pocketed because I want to look more rad than anyone else, cutting over life's surface. She will make a good secretary from mind-reading alone. She knows I refuse to betray eagerness in grabbing grace these others already have. Mother, Reesa forgot to buy me gloves.

'Hey, wheeler dealer!' Andrew, flowing by me with a stick, clacking a black lump of rubber side to side, slapshoots it to shore. 'Where's your concession stand? Figured you'd be selling us barrels of hot chocolate!' I toss it back at him. 'I'm thinking Earth Rumblers!' But he dekes behind a long arm of hand-holding skaters swooping past like a compass pencil. *Whap!* I fall again, hands first, cigarette second, nose third. I hear my ash *sss* in the ice. Their bloody whips and compasses. I am burning to explode at the gross coldness of this winter country. 'Sorrrrry!' shouts a voice like Marcia's, laughing over a shoulder like Marcia's, puffy pink. I roll over on my elbow, smiling my dimple, pretending public amusement I do not feel in my liver. The ice creeps through the punk rips in my jeans. These scuffy skates, Mother, my guardian's skates he has not worn in more years than I have lived, too big for my feet. Too big to purchase a steady stride for gaining speed. They are also *brown*. All I can expect from short feet banging around inside brown banana boxes is slippage and blisters. I lie here. Lloyd powers sideways to a stop, showering me with ice chips, chuckling. 'How're they hanging, Wishes?' I stretch out and yawn. 'Cool, cool. Just resting in hammock here, recalling Uganda before Idi Amin kicked out lucky ones and killed less lucky.' He laughs. 'Thought you were from Bombay, pal.'

'I tell friends the truth.' I lean back farther on my elbow, tanning my Adam's apple in the dreamy sun. The truth is my indifference, Mother. I keep my cool from burning over with a dreamboat smile. 'Uganda was beautiful before killing started and soldiers stabbed my father to his death. He was coffee merchant and we drank coffee to the heart's content. Very cruel country now, but before Amin, before death, my country was welcome and green. We sipped coffee in hammocks like this. Then we put down cups and fled for our lives like the nobody's business.'

Lloyd is sharpening his blade edges on the ice in front of my voice. 'Awesome,' he says. 'Hey, I gotta catch the puck.' He is gone. I permit myself to brush his ice chips from my black jacket, prepare to rise up and renew my fun, to master the motion of scissoring my legs to cut the cold distance. But Trudy is returning again, letting her weight and pointed-in skates slow her to a drifty stop at my body. I refrain from rising farther. 'I need muffs!' she shouts down, banging green woollen mitts against her ears. Her plump face is red, nose dripping on my sleeve, earlobes white like two mushrooms. 'Not fair!' she shouts, thinking my ears are frozen too. 'You wear the dinkiest clothes alive, and an earring, and lie there looking like you're toasting at the beach! Wanna tug up?'

Her big chance to offer the helping hand to a refugee not grooving to local custom. Prettier girls than her, Mother, phone me out of the sky to talk about nothing. Marcia, as one example, is a flirt who hurts the hearts of boys like Lloyd. With her I keep my heart in an inside pocket though I let her fiddle with my soul. She can break it if she likes. Trudy will need to learn Marcia's phoning skills, like hanging up on bores, if she hopes to be my secretary. She is fat. Only the boat kids at school are less popular than Trudy. The fight was their fault, Mother. They thought my band looked too *rad*. They are so out of it. It is part of our punk look, looking like buttheads in a dining lounge. Ripped black jeans, red smears to look like blood. The blackbird's warble is not our sound, by any stretch.

Mother, you would find this outstretched limb of Trudy's thick, the way limbs are in Canada. Thicker arms and legs than we see at home. Bigger bones from French fries, Slurpees, jelly doughnuts. Pork. *Turkey*. Trudy knows she is heavier than furniture. To her benefit she is planning to be a Weight Watcher soon, in our Year of the Rooster. Maybe this will help tone down her voice too. She bellows like a gym mistress. 'Don't look like you even wanna stand up, Wishes! Look at Mr Cool with the crossed ankles! He's smiling! I bet he's been whistling! Waiting for Marcia or one of them to help him up!' Too loud, Mother, pleading for her own rescue by being let to help me. I let her. Marcia is a quarter mile away, skating with an escort under the willow limbs, probably Lloyd with the fucking fuck hips. He is porno the way he pumps on skates. I feel about his moves on Marcia the way I feel about the letter I saw on Dwight's desk, inviting sex tours, Mother, to Asian countries. Dwight and Lloyd deserve broken legs for taking liberties on pretty girls like you and Marcia. I respect Trudy. I would not take a liberty on her.

She is still hovering. She has offered her other green hand like she is saving one of the boat kids from drowning in the South China Sea. Trudy wants love like a whole country, Mother. I think this is her hope, to learn leanness in her aid to bad luckers like Aloysius Irving. Her jiggly white cheeks are stapled with moles and her skin looks sore. In the cold wind of January her brown eyes are tearing. I scramble up to avoid her eager fingers, then grab for them when my feet shoot off like ambulances. She is happy. We come together like waltzers. 'Aren't you the fresh one, Trudy.' She breaks out in a rash of poor teeth, retirement for a dentist. Everywhere this land of opportunity. 'What's wrong with your ears?' I say. She asks, 'Do they look awful? They feel dead!' I tell her, Mother, they look like pearl earrings and she blushes. Below the blood line this makes her lobes whiter, mushrooms growing in frigid air. I let her skate with me a furlong and give advice. 'That's the way!' she yells in my ear. 'Push yourself side to side! Relax more! You're getting used to it now! Sink or swim! Okay, you're swimming now!'

I have left Trudy behind. This sprint of speed surprises her. It surprises me. 'Wishes!' She can't catch me. I have had a dream. It has come to me how to match my feet to balance, like my mouth to brain, even sagging at the ankles. Even burning. Look, Mother, me moving across this foreign surface without falling on my face. I am on my way! I lift my eyes from the horrible white ice. I scissor my legs as other skaters scissor theirs, cross my thighs, turn up ice leaning into new directions. I am everyone I wish to be! My scissoring legs work like a dream, gliding now, letting me swing back my arms, cup my hands in a gentleman's fold. Pure pleasure! Man in motion, man flying, easier than bicycling, easy as dreaming! Pushing from one foot to the other I wonder who is going to believe this is my first time walking, sailing on frozen water? *All of them.* Who will guess how far I have come to prevail over a slippery world? *Everyone.* I am getting away with larceny in this trusting country. Canada Dry/Canada Trust ... Did I tell you, Mother, you would be surprised at my account book at Canada Trust? The transactions fill line after line, page after page. *Ping.* My business story is a pretty one, like these figure eights I am cutting in the ice. Landlording is my goal. You can hear the ice cracking, but it is safe, the pylons warn us of the chopped-open water. I forget on purpose to turn, to wave at my benefactress in the rising mists. My dream of a new city is flying me above this cold country.

May, 2016

Birth of our son last week. We intend to give him a Spanish name, in keeping with maternal half of F.'s family, but can't agree on what name. I like 'Renaldo'. Baby has olive skin like F.'s mother. F. thinks he looks like a bran muffin. We have even saved F.'s alpaca baby slippers for this moment, but of course they are sloppy on an infant. Look moth-eaten anyway. Need booties.

Married just three weeks ago, following the death of my dear Uncle Damon, who was supposed to toast us. Mother allowed as how our generation is fast about some things, we are very conservative rushing into others. F. and I have only known each other fifteen years and lived together one. Mother pretends social conventions don't matter to her, only to my grandmother.

This week she dug around in her archives for a photograph of me at three days old, my face like a dark tomato, so both families are now content their genes predominate. She's pleased, I think, at how her little family has knitted vague sadnesses of our past into a cheerful new pattern. My stepfather the banker has offered his congratulations in the shape of a cheque. This intended as a wedding gift, he said, to take us on a honeymoon once the baby came.

So we are planning to visit Peru when my practice allows and the child is stronger. F. says by then either pair of slippers ought to fit. We are suddenly no longer so close, if it could be said we ever really were, and I wonder which will prove our undoing – having a baby or finally tying the knot?

Chapter 12

Underground

MOTHER, SINCE I DAZZLED classmates at ice skating that day, the ice has cracked up and rotted in the attack of wet fronts lining up to needle it with rain. Today the fog is like old London town's. That is what Gord the weatherman predicted last night, the clash of warm and cold air, meaning fog, folks, minus coal smoke. This afternoon, downtown, I am not surprised rush hour is so slow, headlights drilling tunnels through the fog and brakelights spraying warnings like flowers. Mother, I walked downtown from the park ... now I am too rattled to walk home because I lost Reesa's car. Stole it this morning then lost it in Stanley Park. So the decision I must make is the following: whether to go home and face the music, or go back to live in the streets. With no tent to keep off fog drops the size of rosary beads, I have come underground to do my soul's inventory. I have even lost my briefcase for selling jewellery.

Underground this city is in another dream. Sunlight, flowering poinsettias, splashing fountains, like heaven fallen on top of Bombay. Shoppers drop their coats and walk this tunnel like tourists in a bazaar. We find ourselves mirrored in ceilings and windows, we ride unfolding steel stairs from one level to the next. It is even better than Safeway. We crowd the January sales, we lounge on low shiny benches, we sip Orange Julius from fake bottom cups, we gawk into windows piled up with ballroom slippers, LPs, crimson tea cosies and such like. Foreign Trade I think could wear crimson cosies for codpieces on stage. I listen, Mother, to music in the air, thinking how I might sell Foreign Trade's music into these hidden pipes and even, if I could dream up how, scents. Not FT's scents, but odours you used to wear like frangipani perfume, blown through these pipes with electric fans. So far I am a failure in selling to the nose, my perfume profits a washout. I even tried selling roses my talkless foster brother cut from his mother's garden. We got caught. Mrs Irving knew already I pilfered from her purse, skipped church, tried out her Audi. So how could she say she was sorry when I ran away to live with Dwight? But she did. She missed me, Damon missed me. Canadian people take me to their breasts like a water bottle.

Mother, why did you call me Corbin? 'My little raven,' you called me. At the orphanage Sister Anthony found it a grunty name and said from then on my name was Aloysius. 'Wash your face, Aloysius, it's black.' I missed you, Mother. You told me, 'Call me Rosy. I am too young for Mama.' Laughing, the three of you. I called Pearl and Lovina auntie, and did they hate that too? A taxi whisked us all to the cabaret whenever Tara forgot to come and care for me and Chichi, Pearl's boy. Did we all live in two rooms to save for the day you stopped dancing to live in your own country houses where no one knew you? Men in our building made sucking noises at your neon saris. Tara with the coughdrop eyes, where is she now? Where was she then? Chichi had a top he spun on his toe in the dressing room. You pinched your nose, Mother, to pee in the backstage lav. You waited your turn for the peeling door to open, the band to strike up, the men to clap, and then you went smiling into a glossy light. It was your turn to dance over the white mattress on the shiny floor. Chichi and I played on the roof where a waiter brought us colas and waved us down when you and Pearl and Lovina came up clutching men. Laughing and such like. Men in robes and suits, bare haircuts and turbans.

Mother, you were beautiful, not plump like Lovina and Pearl. Your smile flattened men dead in the cabaret. Chichi and I peeked through the door at you in your pink saree, threading the tables, smiling at the nicest men, bending down to their whispers. Rao the owner called me his Arab boy. My father had gone back to Arabia, he told me, but your lips were sealed. I wonder if my father owns the desert and maps lines in the sand to help him find gushers? The waiter brought supper to your dressing room and you smoked a cigarette and stroked my head. If you had your pick of who to murder, Mother, you could also pick who to eat your curry with. With me!

'Aloysius, you up?' Dwight's voice at my door this morning. I answered, 'Cold today.' He said, 'We're all cold, Aloysius, especially when we don't feel like getting up. What's the matter, got a quiz today?' 'No. No quiz. My nose is running a little bit.' He said, 'Shall I make you toast? You have to go to school.' I told him, 'For now, bed. Sleep is better.' 'Well,' said Dwight, drumming his fingers on the wood, 'when Reesa wakes up, you and she can have toast.' I listened for him to go away, down the creaking staircase, through the shutting doors. I waited, but none of these sounds came to my ears. 'Are you smoking, Aloysius? I smell smoke. Are you forgetting house rules?' Mother, I was dwelling on John Lennon's death last month.

No time for school, I had appointments today. I was waiting for Dwight to leave for work. Even when I first came here and grew happy with my own room on the third floor, full-service meals, an allowance of money every week, I still had my dream. Every night under new blankets I made schemes in my mind. This morning, Mother, I lay waiting for Dwight to leave before I could stir in the damp air and lay down a line of paste on my toothbrush. In the bathroom I foamed at the mouth like a poison dog, mad at my wasted time in bed, mad having to polish my mouth. You would tell me freshening the mouth is good for business but you did not have to pull waxed bean string through your molars like I do and twang it like a sitar. Mrs Irving showed me flossing after she showed me socks, and I will never floss again, once I retire.

I stepped onto Reesa's scales. One hundred and nine pounds, Mother. You can see how Canada has bulked me up into a football player. The coach at school is always asking me to try out for the team. He says, 'Aloysius, you look fast. C'mon out.' Mother, I would rather come out of the closet as a fruitcake. In the kitchen I opened a note from Dwight telling Reesa not to forget their appointment with Reynolds the bank manager at three-thirty, he would meet her at the bank, he loved her, Dwight. *Ping.* I was on my way to the basement when I heard this same ping I heard the morning we found Bartlett's canary dead. I think it is the metal cage bars warping in the winter air. But I feel sometimes it is my guilty reminder for not feeding Mikos after Bartlett asked me, then dumping in seed when Mikos was too weak, Mother, to peck it down. The bird made me homesick for tropical living. It made me homesick for you.

In the basement with a hammer, smashing one dozen beer bottles into shards on the concrete floor, I then smashed nine pop bottles, hating this slave work, checking my digital watch, looking out the door for Carl and Tony. Slave work, but I have no leeway to let these boys do hammer smashing too, if I wish to keep my overhead low. These grade sixers come three mornings a week before school, pushing a stolen Safeway basket full of bottles from boulevards and back alleys. I pay them market prices plus bonus. This morning they forgot to come, Mother, or else had no luck hunting. It happens with children. So I shut the door and reclimbed the stairs to write my letter at Dwight's desk.

Kiss Sum One you luv & make magick. This lettur has been sent to you for good luck. The orignal copy is in New England. It has been around the wurld 9 times. The luck has now been sent to you. Please send 20 copys of this lettur to you're friennds & associuts and see what hapens in 4 days. You will get a surprize. This is true even if you are not superstitus.

Do note the folowing: Constantine Diss receeved the chaine in 1975. He asked his seckretary to make 20 copys and send them out. A few days later he won a lottry of 2 million. This was not a coincidence. Arior Daddit an office employee recieved this lettur & forgot it had to leive his hands in 96 horus. He lossed his job. Dalien Fairchild recieved this letter in 1980, but not beleeveing it, threw it a way. 9 days later he died ... Plaese send no money. Except 15 dollars for handleing (to abuve addres). Do Not Ignore This.

It werks!

Reesa was still snoozing so I borrowed her Honda keys from the bedroom, Mother. She slept through our earthquake so I knew I was safe opening her purse. I had my appointment with Mr Singh, but I had Xerox copies of my letter to breed first, and envelopes to address and stamps to buy. Sometimes I am burning so much to succeed I forget things. Not this morning, Mother. I slipped the letter inside my briefcase and hurried up our foggy street to the community centre. I wore a toque to warm my head. I had the addresses of many clients of Dwight's travel company, who will *not* all send me back fifteen dollars, no. The lapse rate will be high, I expect lapsing, but the overhead is not so high I will go belly up if I am unable to earn a rightful return on my labours. This is the given, Mother.

If only I could gain a job at Safeway, I could dampen my cash flow with weekly wages. Bartlett has promised to talk to someone when he comes home from the moon. 'The manager owes me a favour, for curing his back spasms ... But your back, Aloysius, aren't you light for lifting boxes? Canned goods and the like?' No, I think of A.I. as large in the marketplace. I am older and stronger than they think me, Mother, disguised in a small person's body, cursed and blessed with a young person's face. This is the given, me lying, I accept it to gain an advantage along the road to landlordhood. I can count the years since my birth, but in Canada I have no wish to tell the truth. They would not believe me if I did. I have no beard. My smile is too cute for adulthood. My need is still for education, to get my dreaming language caught up to my spelling language. I am everyone I want to be, Mother, until I walk out of my bedroom in the morning. Then I must be on my wits.

I would be tickled to work part time at Safeway. I still like to go through that electric door and walk the aisles with a chrome shopping cart, filling it with ice cream, chicken drumsticks, soft drink cans and such like. Nobody cares how greedy I am because there is so much for every shopper. I have seen where the food comes from. It comes flying out of huge lorries, boxes whizzing down ramps of tiny steel wheels, into this store as big as a hockey rink. Mother, you roll along a shopping cart before you, filling it with cakes and jam tarts. The market is never crowded and dirty like Crawford Market. The aisles are valleys between food ghats. The floors are clean and the meat flyless. I am sometimes homesick for a fly. I never pay for the food by standing in this queue or that queue, for weighing and such like. Nobody cares if I just collect the food to see what it feels like in my cart piled high. Rad. I leave it all behind me near the yogurt case.

Mother, I had need of Reesa's car this morning to make a fine impression on the businessman I was meeting. I needed worldliness and my short legs needed length, so I levered her seat forward, and this was happiness, stepping on the fuel pedal, stepping on the brake pedal, as easy as ice skating. Power and glory at my toe tips, driving Reesa's Honda Accord into the park to investigate 'importing interests' with a man who had put the newspaper ad I answered. The fog was lifting. I wheeled past the rose garden and arrived at the Pavilion to find an empty parking lot. I thought the Pavilion would impress my contact as a breakfasting place for business interests. I found the lever to decline my seat, I popped a Pall Mall in my mouth, I punched in Reesa's tapedeck and heard a goatherder's panpipes. Mother, if I asked Foreign Trade to sing it they would make me eat their razor blades. Foreign Trade bloodlets its songs and I am proud and dizzy to be their manager. I am always stealing music to smuggle into Foreign Trade's act. But this was music from a Peruvian goat farm. I finally lost any hope for the Irving ears to learn music.

Mother, this piped-in music, underground tonight? It is just as gross. I sit in the mall, full of mirrors and bright faces, watching the angels shop, reliving two swollen faces popping up in the park this morning when I waited in Reesa's car, smoking my weed, being grossed up by the panpiper. Those faces in the shrubs did not look happy to be woken by a dude in a warm car. I knew what they were thinking, I used to sleep outside too. They were thinking vulture, fat cat, meat eater. I tilted upright and sprung my door, then remembered my seatbelt, closed the door to untangle my neck. I climbed out. I messed my spiked hair and scuffed my boots. I vaporized their envy. 'Hello, gentlemen! How're they hanging?' These tramps, thugs, studied their friendly prey. Then slid down from the shrubs over the stone wall by the parking stalls. They looked hungry for their breakfast. 'Aloysius,' I said, refusing fear any big say. 'I am up from Fiji a while, looking over your pretty city. People say I must be dotty visiting Canada in wintertime. But I like it. Very good country.' I charmed them with a smile I dimpled specially.

'Alla Wishes, eh?' The shorter dark one ignored my handshake offer. He was taller than me. 'What kinda name is Alla Wishes?' The taller one grabbed his own ponytail and tugged back his head so he was looking at fog in the treetops. Like a princess he said, '*I* figure he's scoffed this car. This is some family car this Paki's gone hotwired out of some garage someplace down a back alley somewheres.' His dark pal nodded. 'Have to agree with that there, Slopes, what you jist said. I wouldn't guess this here Honda Accord is Alla Wishes' car. How could it be? He don't look old enough to cross a street, let lone wee wee 'out his Pampers.' He was getting busy to do justice to a car thief. Mean justice, Mother.

I took my pack of Pall Malls and knocked three weeds straight up. The thug softened like a goatherder. 'Yeah, sure. We wouldn't say no to a fag, eh Slopes?' He grabbed the whole package. 'Pal Mals, huh? We don't git offered a lot of Pal Mals, do we Slopes?' Slopes refused a weed for himself, busy untying his ponytail and shaking out his hair like a girl. He said, 'I think this Paki's tryin to corrupt us, Kev.' Kev wiped his nose with his wrist, plucked out a weed, and inspected the suppository. 'You figure he's tryin to corrupt us, Slopes? With one of these?' So I said to both thugs, 'Look. Have as many as you wish. But save me two for this toothache. In Fiji we chew root for toothache, but smoking is good too. Smoke is good for numbing the gum.' They looked at me, Mother. 'Bloody bullshit artist,' said Kev. 'Lissen,' said Slopes. 'Maybe he's jist mixed up. You mixed up, Alla? That your problem?' He turned smirking to his friend. He was fingering my jacket. The punk rips had no vibes on his sympathy, nor on Kev's. Kev had liked Slopes's little diagnosis of my pickle. 'You got a light, Alla Wishes? Or is it gonna be my ass and your face?' He laughed sharply.

'Lighter,' I told him, 'in here.' Slopes intercepted me, playing a mind game. He opened the door and bent over inside. Hair covered his face when he turned back. He had my lighter in his filthy fingers. 'Good lighter,' I said.

'Top of the line.' 'Maybe,' answered Kev, 'if you're a Paki ... If you're a Paki you're impressed by cheap shit like plastic lighters. Here, Slopes. Flick my Bic.' Slopes flicked Kev's bic and watched him puff his weed into a bright glow. Kev coughed on the smoke, slammed the ground with his boot, beat his arms for warmth, tugged up his collar. I felt pity for them, Mother. Their coats shaped to their bodies by damp ground, twigs stuck in their hair, dirt in their pores so they looked chocolate. They looked too gross for the punk look. They stank. Kev said, 'Tobacco for breakfast is worse than a Cheezie.'

So I asked, 'You fellows sleeping in the park? I used to sleep out too.' Kev coughed again and squinted through his smoke. Slopes drew back his hair over one ear and held it there for a pose.

'This one's got all the answers, eh, Kev? Steal a car he'd probably steal a house. He's probably livin in a big house with all his Paki pals dumpin on the carpets, livin the life of a tuxedo. While we're on the outside mindin our own beeswax. Keepin our noses clean, not stickin em into garbage that don't concern us. Those who was born in Canada know our place. They know Pakis and Chinks and gooks are comin in tryin to burgle it away from us ...' This tune summed up Kev's thoughts too. 'Fuckin carpet jockey,' said Kev. 'That bein the reason,' Slopes trotted on, sucking a strand of greasy hair across his cheek, 'some lawbidin citizens oughta return this Honda Accord to its lawful owner, 'cause the problem as I see it is jist gonna get worse if we don't take a stand against the greedy nigs.'

'Amen,' said Kev.

Then they were into Reesa's car, Slopes screaming the engine out of his ignorance with engines, thumping it into reverse gear. I was on top of the windshield, Mother, banging it, then on the hood, then on the ground. A cloud of skunk smell lingered in their wake. My car vanished into tall firs and I was lying on the cold pavement without a dime to call Emergency. They had my briefcase full of costume jewellery. They had my black scarf I would wear to distinguish myself with Mr Singh. These clues pressed me to the pavement in dejection. When the police found my guardian's Honda Accord, the Irvings would know from a discarded briefcase and scarf the theft was mine. I had not been cool, Mother. Hence I did not phone.

Just then a Honda Accord rounded the corner from the rose garden into the naked parking lot. This was an older model than Reesa's, red not silver. Out of it came a greybeard in turban and tie, reading his watch. He looked up at the Pavilion holding a scrap of paper and did not see me lying on the ground. I rose up from the pavement as *amportant* as I could sound. 'Mr Singh?' I called. 'Sir?'

2.

I stop to take a Mars Bar from my ripped jacket. Should I tell you, Mother, I ripped my jacket on purpose because of fashion in Canada, and because I now manage Foreign Trade? Young people in Bombay would think I am marked for the lunatic bin. I would have thought this. I would have thought never would I be in another city like this one stealing cars and ripping my clothes. Or tinting my hair a little purple and wearing eyeliner and a nose stud. Or eating a chocolate bar and throwing half away. Tonight when the mall closes I escalate back up to the fog and listen to trolley buses lurch from the curb. They pick up speed from overhead wires sluicing juice down poles to their motors. I like it when poles clatter and spark blue at junctions, when trolley mouths lose their bite and bounce off wires, *thump*, toothless. I watch out for new acts to give Foreign Trade's electric guitars an extra punch. I have no money left for bus fare, owing to the thugs.

I walk up Granville, adding up the floors of towers still burning with electricity when the workers inside the buildings have all taken their powder. The low fog smothers my counting halfway up. This is another world, Mother, Dwight's world, compared to Bombay when I would pass the cabaret and see Lovina and Pearl arriving in a taxi. I did not go to them, talk to them, ask them about Chichi. The city had changed and so had your Corbin. They might have taken me home, but I was past Chichi, past Tara, making my own way and forgetting the child's life I had. I knew where to find scraps or a bandage, the best corners to beg baksheesh from office workers in higher echelons. I ran with a little batch of boys and slept in the street. I would make my own business in Bombay and have revenge, Mother, on the man who choked you dead.

One business I got was selling street tar to pilgrims leaving for Elephanta Island.

Use Deshi Vanspati
Ointment for all
SKIN
Diseases
TRY ONCE

Beggars and decaying lepers who needed ointment had no rupees to buy it and rich people were too wise. I would need to be wiser than rich people to expand in the world. Along Worli Seaface I bartered my ointment business for a sleeping pad, from a boy with boils on his neck, and retired to purse finding and other small enterprises. Night fell, the rats came out, I longed for monsoon rain to escape the heat.

Another business I did was guiding foreigners into jewellers' for changing money on the black market. Another, wiping dirty cloths across windscreens at red lights. Exhaust fumes blackened my snot. The pavement blackened my feet. I set up boxes to polish sandals, but the overhead for wax and brushes digested my profits. I went every day to apply for portering in Victoria Station. I also put in my name to be a dabawallah with the Union of Tiffin Boxers, to carry hot lunches between suburb wives and office husbands. I had little hope, Mother. None of us had hope. My friend Shankar dug himself a hole by the cricket grounds and placed his head inside. He filled in the loose dirt with his upside down feet. When he could keep his breath no longer he burst from the earth to find not one pedestrian had left him an anna. Shankar made better profits from his petrol trick. He stood in our best intersection for windscreen wiping. He swigged from a can and exhaled his breath in a three-foot flame. I ran around collecting his reward from startled drivers and taxi passengers.

I was losing my clothes to holes and rot, Mother. The homeless humps who lined my street slept under sheets and mothers' arms. The hotter the nights the louder the humps' crying and worse their smells. Little children squatted in gutters waiting for their insides to let go. Girls living five to a room shouted out their windows to passing men. They shouted vile things. They played loud music under yellow lightbulbs and ragged their pimps who yelled the dishes of the house. 'Filipino!' 'Japanese!' 'African!' One landlord owned all the houses, Mother. Here in Canada I have not yet found a row of houses like his. The hookers on Davie have their own palaces. They come and go as they please. They please themselves.

This moaning in the fog? It sounds like a freighter calling back sailors to the bay. I stop a headscarfed woman in Robson Street and she listens too. 'Probably the foghorn,' she says, turning away in the damp. I have never heard a foghorn, Mother, what is its reason? To trumpet the angels who lose their way in the clouds? I can see just ahead to a bank of faces, bright and beaming in a shop window, TV faces, the same face. Mother, Reesa's face! I stop. I watch her lips moving and hear only the moaning horn. She smiles her radiant smile, like yours, Mother, and does not look like a woman whose car was stolen. This is the meaning of purchased insurance I believe. I should look into selling insurance. If car insurance is such a comfort I can imagine the ointment of life insurance! Already there is talk of expelling me from high school for bad study practices, though I cannot afford to lose my life in high school yet, any more than give up Foreign Trade. They need me. Their heavy sound is no good without a business brain, Mother. This is the given.

The face changes. Reesa is interviewing a bald man in glasses with hair under his nose. I have seen him before, at our house party, flirting with her in a corner, a tall man who drinks tomato juice. I saw him touch her black-dressed hip. I saw Reesa lick her mouth, touch his mouth, laughing, with her fingers. I wanted to overhear their conversation. Now I am cut out, again. Sometimes he forgets to push the glasses up his nose and they divide his face and repeat it like the foghorn. His moustache brushes his silent words. It brushes and he blinks. I soon start down Robson again and feel my hair soaking from a cloud I am ghostwalking. I have never walked in a cloud and it is as easy as ice skating. It is moonwalking like Michael Jackson, Mother, home to Haro Street. Except my mind feels heavier than the curb. To be suckered by a pair of tramps! To sucker my own self! I deserve to face the music like a little child.

I must still be in the fog when I come close enough to see Reesa's silver Honda Accord parked under the street light. It is parked in the exact same space where I left two orange pylons this morning for the purpose of returning her car before she awoke. Rad. Did I dream the stealing like I dream you, Mother, stroking my hair? This is what it feels like, fog moving through my hair like a smoky hand, the foghorn warning me of wrong turns. How can her car be here and Reesa talking live on *City, City*? I push my face to the windshield to peer inside for my pigskin briefcase. Nothing, except my yellow BiC lighter lying on the carpet. This question arises: Am I damned or am I saved?

I need to prepare my defence, Mother. The Irvings have no idea of my expenses, or how much I need to expand in the world for seizing my dream. I have had a dream, yes. They think if I carry out garbage and clean their carpets my allowance is enough to take care of dreaming. A carpet jockey! I am sliding into a fog of financial decay. My guardians have no appreciation of the marketplace, Mother. Fatter returns need fatter investments, fatter risks. Like my risk in telephoning Mr Singh, then keeping mum over Reesa's stolen car as I quizzed him on his importing interests.

He was surprised I was Sikh, a Sikh orphan. He told me I might have a use to his business. 'You know, in spite your age.' He would be in communication with me soon. I had only two dollars to buy breakfast so we were having coffee only. 'You know, in spite your age,' he repeated, tapping his empty cream pouch, 'we have Sikhs in common.' I, Corbin Singh, a.k.a. Aloysius Irving, am everyone I want to be. 'Make way for the Legend!' they cry out at school. 'Make way for the hamburger!' They envy my *amportance*, Mother, do not mistake them.

I slip through the front door with my key and close it on the fog. Voices in the den. My eyes fall on a beautiful beach in the tropics, a picture postcard. *Ping*. PATTAYA BEACH, it says, in big letters as white as the fog outside.

Take a lot of this to destroy me, housemates. 1st class airconditioned room for $15, including breakfast. You have genius, D. Girls and water scooters for hire up and down beach. Bangkok an experience. But am not allowed to tell you WHY *I can't be home as soon as scheduled. No, am not heading to Phuket Island – but hear that's where the French flock.*

Bartlett

'... Oh, not at all, sir. Slopes and me was tryin to talk him into returnin the vehicle, sir. When he refuses like and runs off – scared I guess for what he done – we decided to return said vehicle to its registered owner. As I say, Mr Irving, we checked out your registration – your wife's like – in the glove compartment like, and brought it here straight off without botherin the cops none. That briefcase, too.'

Dwight's voice is low and muffled like the fog. It sounds tired, Mother. I am standing at the den door in the shadows looking at two little varnished-over initials carved in the oak door jamb: *S* underneath *F*. '... dollars satisfy you? As a token of our gratitude?' The tramps cough. 'Well, Mr Irving. That's generous of you like. Ain't it, Kev? We didn't bring your car back for no reward though. That's generous of you like. Ain't it, Kev?' I see the door jamb is missing two initials to say who *F.S.* loves, if he ever did. I, A.I., am already on my way upstairs to avoid exposure. In the morning I will tell Dwight the truth, that I never touched Reesa's car, that they made me turn over her keys after banging at the front door, this morning when ...

I will dream up something, Mother, as I sleep on the fruits of my foolishness. I hear their voices below, in the hallway, on the porch descending to the street. Those two belong in the street, shivering on a curb. I slide into Dwight's office and see my addressed envelopes sorted on his desk. He has lined up the names of his clients to question me on where I got these names and what I plan to mail in the envelopes. He will snoop inside my briefcase too. I have no trust in Dwight. This is the given, Mother. No rights for the tenants. Teenagehood sucks in the pits.

July, 2001

Beach party last night for the campaign workers. We lay around in the sand waiting for my fire to catch. Losing the election yesterday depressed us, but, as somebody remarked, at least we can return to classes come fall and renew our faith in idealism. 'But when you graduate, what then?' rejoined an earnest voice in the dark. 'Put your heads in the sand? Ignore the toxins killing the water?'

My own post mortem is that an environmental candidate these days is too narrowly regarded. She's now a dead duck. I think there's a split coming between those of us who went through high school together in the elite Voyager Programme, and those

who didn't. Now find myself siding with those who didn't.

The pouty Jill advised me my campfire was illegal and sending unprocessed hydrocarbons into the atmosphere. No one moved to stamp it out though. We sat in silence watching it, nourishing it with scraps of driftwood. It wasn't a bonfire. It felt like the most natural thing in the world. 'A beach party without a fire's like a mash without a squeeze ...' Same man's voice in the dark, this time without the earnestness. Jill almost barfed. She despises compromise. Has been working so long for the future she's worried it might not be as black as she imagines. She'd rather not face the

possibility.

I think our parents must have been just the opposite.

We can't move anymore without a recyling bag to catch our farts, before they escape to the ozone and wipe us out. Have even heard it said farters must share in blame for slow blackening of canvases in art galleries. And don't we chastise farmers for their cows' flatulence? Am amazed we don't get after the wild animals, too, and save nature from herself. Nature has become a sunset industry.

'That your tape playing?' Same voice as earlier. He looked dark in the firelight. 'Who is it?' he asked. I popped the cassette to check. '"Turn Me Loose",' I said. 'Jesus,' he said, 'that tiger stuff sounds fossilitic.' Trying to be witty.

But it's hard to tell anymore. Which is how I like it. I pulled out a cigarette and awaited his reaction. The others panicked and he stayed cool. I lit it. He got up and walked to the tide's edge, out of smokeshot.

I am usually taken for sixteen or seventeen and my odd taste in music seemed to confirm this boy's conviction I was too young to have developed any taste of my own. 'In fact,' I responded, when he returned to the fire and asked if I was planning on college, 'I'm twenty and in pre-med.' My tone surprised him.

'Why so testy?' he asked all innocent.

The sun was crumbling into embers over the gulf. His complexion and hair looked Latin in the dying light. Hadn't seen him before among our workers but he was probably younger than me.

'Here, wanna see something neat?' So up from the beach I soon found myself leaning on a huge concrete sculpture, an anchor or something, resting high on its side. He'd stopped in the dark to touch it. 'This all?' I inquired, politely. I was planning to return to the fire and have it out with Jill.

'Be prepared,' he said, flicking on a tiny flashlight and motioning me over to a nearby plaque that promised to explain his sculpture. He shone the light onto some words etched in brass. 'This is kind of about me.'

Wanted to laugh at his earnestness. The way he read out the words, the ancestor worship, all of it. Needed to put some daylight between us fast. Where was Jill?

A weeping willow nearby, but you couldn't see it, nor the wooded cliffs of Point Grey pumping out oxygen, eating up the emissions of cars passing along Marine Drive. Very peaceful. Distant city sparkled. Lights too from a movie set on Jericho Pier. God, I thought, he's going to kiss me.

Mentioning his name later to Mother she told me she thought she and my father had known his half-brother. 'What a coincidence!' she exclaimed. She thought she could document the fact he once wore alpaca baby slippers, from Peru, too. Not that she'd ever seen his.

'How fascinating,' I responded.

'You don't have to be contumacious, Gwyn.'

Remembering, she said this boy wouldn't have known his half-brother, their friend Bartlett, anyway. My mother and father had later learned from Bartlett's Peruvian wife that in India their friend had died when he accidentally dropped a hairdryer into his bath.

He was on his
honeymoon.
Electrocuted himself.
'Absurd,' said Mother,
shaking her head.

'Did he smoke?' I
wondered.

My new friend's
name is Fernando. He
wants to manufacture
ecologically sound pipe.
Plastic plus steel. Am
definitely not interested
in seeing him again,
although he asked me on
the beach. Has phoned
too. God save me.

Chapter 13

Foreign Trade

MOTHER, THE TEENAGEHOOD of this school caf is the given. 'Hey, Dimples!' Lloyd rags me from his table. 'Wanna sip?' He is offering me his chocolate milk carton in mock seriousness. I crumple my lunch bag to snowball size and hookshot it at the garbage barrel. 'After you backwashed inside? No way, Broccoli Breath!' I can rag as good as I take. Classmates have a nice enjoyment of this banter between the basketball captain and the manager of Foreign Trade. They would have a better one if I told them Marcia phones to flirt with me, after Lloyd walks her home. Andrew, prince of eunuchs, is my chief ragger at school. He is a mountain skier and a basketball forward who has money from his penthouse parents and is on his way to lawyering and the ownership of kayaks. 'Where you off to, Wishes? Time to collect rent and such like?' He keeps his teeth in a silver bracelet. I smile to butter them all. I am ragged so much because these classmates respect my power with the grade twelve punkers in Foreign Trade. They like my rad look. They listen to my hot buys. I moonwalk out of the caf to hoots of ragging regard. 'Buy gold!' they repeat. Sometimes they believe me.

The truth is not gold, Mother. It is true gold has blasted through eight hundred dollars per ounce and is heading for a thousand. Two thousand! You used to wear gold and would be in for a big shock weighing yourself, like Trudy at Weight Watchers, to find you could now afford a house in the country for retirement from cabaret men. No, the best gold is not metal gold, but people gold, and I am on my way to an appointment with Mr Singh. I am skipping school early to floss my brains in this warm spring sunshine. C'est *amportant* pour moi to floss my brains first, Mother, as I am working so hard at Safeway these days, at commissioning art students to paint the right bottle label for my local tap water to outsell Perrier water, at smaller and bigger wheels and deals. Walking down Altamira, puffing a Pall Mall, I see these new banks and suck pleasure from the business progress all around me in Canada. This is the given, Mother. I visited the stock exchange last month and sucked pleasure seeing men scream and throw paper in the air when a bell rang. The gravy was so thick it spilled off the train! Next morning I phoned up a house to place a buy order for three hundred shares of Great Hamil. It worked easily. I phoned up the woman again to sell my holdings in Great Hamil and asked her to mail me the difference between my entry level and my exit level, minus her commission. She sounded entertained, Mother, at such a small sale and never pressed me to deposit it in her house account. I needed the cheque to pay Carl and Tony for bottles outstanding.

A brokerage house is a house I would be pleased to landlord some day, the House of the Lord minus the Lord, having fun, throwing party paper, buying and selling. From newspaper clippings I have started to plot graphs tracking stock upsides and downsides, maybe for selling to young people with ready cash for investment options. I have many notions. I, A.I., am everyone I want to be. I have had a dream, Mother. I am burning to interpret for myself soon the difference between selling short and selling long.

At Davie Street, not heading up Hooker Hill to dope dealers and quick chickens, I cross Altamira to the beach. The hookers seep down on sunny afternoons like this one, girls with their own apartments. Some used to live in the Englesea, I know, before fire easily gutted it. The girls sit on benches now, staring across the bay. Sometimes I, A.I., will share my dream with them. I would even offer this one a Pall Mall, but she is licking a chocolate mocha cone from Swensen's on the corner. A plump hooker, no more than one or two years older than Trudy. 'Listen –' I am smiling at her – 'I also in peddling racket in Saigon, before I know what peddling is.' *Ping*. She looks at me, Mother, batless in the eye, so I go on.

'Nice party man in taxi roll down his window to suggest a bad deed. Friends on curb laugh and warn me then, so I back off it, the man roll up his window. But friends say I a fool not to rent my behind, my joss stick, whatever party man want.' Mother, I can mimic grass if there is the market for it. 'Gold was what we need to get out Vietnam. Lots gold. Grandmother gold, mother gold, dowry gold. My family pinch gold off dead baby once, just to buy family place in boat. No cabin, nothing clean. We have to sit on deck many day afterward. My grandmother die. We hungry. Worse nightmare still coming. You heard 'bout pirates?' The plump hooker is looking at me when I ask this, Mother, then she licks. She has pink pimples on her chin.

'Fishing boat in sea approaching, say to our tiny boat something, then men with machine gun come on deck, take away sisters, mothers, shoot fathers. My family is gone like that. I have nothing live for now. Get crazy mad. Floating like that many day after lots people die of thirst, I think what happen love ones? We bury more dead overboard. I put gold from them in pocket.' Listening, the girl on the bench is licking faster now.

'Pretty soon night storm swamp tiny boat and rest of living people thrown in ocean. If I wanna live, empty pockets. Gold sink. All night I near drowning. Waves smother face. I feel sick, sick. At dawn I wake up holding on a little bench from boat for infants. All alone, everybody drown, I see nobody. Ahead, what you think I see?' She stops licking, Mother, lipstick stained black with chocolate mocha. '... Beach. Palm trees. I rather drown I think. If this Vietnam return I rather drown.' Smiling at her. '... But this Thailand now. No more death. For two year then I live in refugee camp. After two year, proud, I come this emerald green city. Stay forever now.' I step on my cigarette, inhaling smoke deep inside after my oral climax. She has stopped licking. 'So,' she says. 'You're one of them boat people, huh?' She has licked a hole in her ice cream, right into her cone.

Whatever apartment this girl is from, Mother, it is ten times better than houses you never knew in Bombay, thank God, owned by Mr Pandernath. He payed protection rupees to police and hired older street boys to guard his investment of girls. He allowed his girls outside to buy tobacco and saris only. Or ghee to rub in their hair. I saw my future in a business of procurement. I, Corbin, took annas from pimps to bring men in way of Mr Pandernath's houses. He never let his girls keep the rupees they earned, except for necessities. He was a worse profiteer than your cabaret boss Mr Rao. Mother, you were free to quit dancing and buy your own house, once you had saved enough rupees. You were free to dance or not to dance, but dancing was your life, you loved dancing. You loved being beautiful. You could choose, but these girls were pestered animals. This was the given, Mother. You and I came to live in a flat on money from a man. We never guessed how matters would turn out to the bad.

The plump hooker gets up now to look elsewhere for a trick. This beach is where TV news shows Polar Bears swimming on New Year's Day drunk to a stupor. 'They're having fun,' Reesa told me. 'Don't be so earnest, Aloysius. Most of those revellers *do* have jobs.' I know I need more fun, like a Polar Bear, so I come walking in Stanley Park on pretty days like this to unwind myself. March air is blossoming in the streets. A pretty woman on a seawall bench regards me with close interest, so I strut and she writes in her notebook. Johnny Rotten she is writing. 'Death Disco.' A song Johnny wrote for his mother after she died. Mother, I too have had a dream song. I strut some more for the joggers in my black boots and torn jeans. They give space to the punk in spiked hair and nose stud, torn jacket and heavy chain between his legs. I remove my jacket and strut in my Foreign Trade T-shirt. I notice boat women picking seaweed off rocks and stuffing it in sacks. I would like to go down on the rocks to ask their scheme, but I remember my walk is for relaxing. Breathing and such like. Peace.

I remember my street, Mother, exploded in heat before the monsoon. Communal killing the police came too late to stop, revenge spilling into more streets, vehicles upturned, bonfires, a dead dog butchered. The smell of burning skin took away the smell of burning joss sticks stuck in our pavement against flies. Roaming gangs did atrocities, made people huddle in doorways and scream for loved ones, afraid for their lives. I, Corbin, ran through streets full of sliced Hindus, bleeding Muslims, in the short pants I was sleeping in. I longed in my heart for sweepers in brown, policemen in blue, small children selling jasmine necklaces, for garbage washing up the beach at Marine Drive. But I lost the way. The burning streets made my eyes blind. I was scared to stop, sit down. The smoke made my chest tight, tight. I fell down and cracked a knee joint. I crawled away and woke up, dreaming a woman in grey robes was touching my shoulder to raise me up from her stoop.

It took a year at her orphanage to forget I was a raven. 'Wash your face, Aloysius, it's black.' Another year to catch up in school with younger boys who looked older. These Sisters of Hope taught Bible reading and how to scrub floors. Sister Helen Anthony taught spelling. I was better at sums and Sister Thomas Kevin said my future was in counting rupees anyway. Sister Gertrude Monica couldn't understand why a beautiful boy like me had not been picked to emigrate, after mailing my photograph to charities in America. 'The older the boy the harder to find him a home. So let us subtract from your age, Aloysius. God will understand.' Mother, Corbin is now three years older than Aloysius. I, A.I., am a forgery.

Mrs Irving picked me from the orphanage to make her life happier and I made it worse landing in Canada and doing the wrong attitude. Four years in the orphanage made me want new opportunities, not the same jail as before. After four years a miracle happened and the sisters' novenas got answered for a foster mother.

Deer Mrs Erving;

I am to be you're new foster childe. Thanck you for pikking me from my pickture Sister supeeriur sent. I am 15 yeers old and at the end of my time. I would be bak liveing in streets agane if you did not seleckt me. I look forwerd to bieng your sun soon. My naime was Corbin before they changd it from the ravun to the sainte. God bye for this time bieing. you'rs truely:

Aloysius

Mother, the sisters made me rewrite it many times until I spelled it nicely, every word. In their excitement they posted the first copy. On my way to the airport these sisters patted my hair and cried they would miss my saint's face. I should always behave myself with good deportment, also read my Bible, so rich mothers in America would want more orphans like me from Bombay. They never said not to spike my hair in the airplane toilet. I thought Canadian teenagehood would never part its hair like my orphanage hair and I felt the punk look in an airplane magazine was the requirement in Canada from sea to sea.

It is on this same beach, Mother, I saw multitudinous teenagers last summer browning their skins, listening to their radios, zipping their frisbees. None had spiked haircuts. None wanted to look like Johnny Rotten. Not one looked uptight not looking for a job. This was their given, coolness. Coolness notwithstanding dependence on a job-holder's handout. I saw I needed coolness to disguise my ambitions, so I ripped my clothes and bought a chain. I persisted, Mother. Third Beach is still my favourite beach for relaxing. Indians before me paddled to this cove of high firs and lingered on the sand with the tide down.

I take off my boots to walk on the rocky reef, past mussels and pools of fingerlings. These tiny fish, I have an idea to profit from them in perch pie, through a gourmet restaurant. '*Scram!*' The crows are my rivals, Mother, they hate me for making them hop sideways from crab legs and mussels, from their punk dignity in the chain of food peckers. They rasp like Foreign Trade. They call me names. I think they hate me for changing mine. At the far end of the reef, little birds on nail legs rush all together one way, then back, as the waves wash in and out. I count seventy in my calculating way, but I think they are too skinny to be tasty. Whiskers like a dog's have popped up in the green water alongside. Another beast from the sea, gone. I am enthralled, Mother. Who else can relax like A.I. in the company of seals? I am standing on tiny clay rosebuds, cutting my bare soles, and I think of you wading with me in Bombay. Two ducks dunk for seaweed in the wrinkling water, green junk on the reef's flank, and I count two stars. The waves glass up their purple arms. Why do school authorities frown on purple hair when nature makes the colour?

Across the water highrises and houses quarrel up steep roads to the tree-line. Over that mountain, Mother, for a thousand miles north, are more mountains. I would like to be a tour guide for Herodotus Tours, but Dwight is slow to see his own city as a product for foreigners. Why? Canada begins at this city's shoreline and the tide is lowered every day like a welcome mat. Especially for sailors, the sun is shining on the exact acre where an aircraft carrier parked last year.

I walk through the forest to my *amportant* appointment at the Pavilion, smoking a Pall Mall. It is healthy to smoke in the forest, it blocks out the skunk smells and such like. Mother, a jogger stopped on the path is holding his nose like a skunk has stung him in the face, only it is bleeding. I feel dizzy, watching. He waves his fingers, playing me the flute with his nose. 'No problem. Nuisance juice. Maybe I oughta take up smoking instead of jogging.' Blood is caking in his naked chest hair. 'Don't ever get into forest products,' he warns me. '... Lunch hour's too short and there's hard times ahead.' He pushes his thumb against his good nostril and rocks forward, blowing a rusty clot into the underforest, followed by a second that speckles the little brook with wet blood. 'Sorry! Get you too?' Mother, I am in vertigo. He is worse than a punk rocker.

This park is a pocket of men from all walks, Mother. When I come to the huge forest's fringe I have men peddling their bums at me. I have seen them peddling them at Dwight, twitching like mice. To confuse them I puncture my cheeks with smiling dimples. They hate me for a punk rival, strutting. But I am a crow with feathers on the ruffle. They pay no attention to the old man in dirty white hair carrying Safeway bags. I, A.I., am everyone I want to be. I can hear mating birds beating on the lagoon. I am nervous this afternoon over putting a bad foot forward with Mr Singh. I have tried to relax by committing hooky. The blood has unsettled me.

2.

'Today I am taking you for your first real look, Corbin. I told you before, concerning Sikh special problems, coming to Canada and whatnot from Delhi is expensive business. Today I am driving us to meet some families and you can judge how much this problem of immigration is on minds of many Sikhs. Khalistan also. I came to Canada. You came. Others deserve our right too.' Mr Singh's toe on the gas pedal is chocolate with dried mud. He is wearing his tie, black turban, unclipped beard folded inside a hairnet. His porky fingers on the steering wheel have nicks and dirty cracks. He is smoking, I am smoking, both are smoking my Pall Malls. He tells me it is very fine to be winding up such a fiord on a pretty afternoon. He pushes a tape into his deck and it is terrible. Indian music with wavering sitars and sugary voices. 'Adjust seat back and relax, Corbin. I have this car for softness and a van for transporting in season my berry pickers.'

Mother, Mr Singh is a man to listen to. He talks and I pay him attention in my black scarf. 'Canada I don't care about, except for managing purposes. I am telling a heresy but this is true for all Sikhs, I believe. Sikhs don't love Canada. We love Khalistan, *nai*? Khalistan is like heaven with us. As Sikh orphan you remember Khalistan, I wager, but not family. Same thing. Family is Khalistan. My business overall is arranging Sikh happiness. If I make money for these efforts, Corbin, all to my good. In picking season I drive out vanfuls of Sikhs from city to farm. All day they pick and I drive them homewards. Some pickers who live in the ruralside want farms of their own one day. This is who we interview. I want to help many countrymen to have happiness, including Sikhs in India wanting to come here and build Khalistan at home.'

He looks to me from his steering. 'Yours is queer name for Sikh. You speak no Punjabi. Why keep claiming you are Sikh, eh?' He chuckles, Mother, tapping his weed in the tray. 'Christian!' he accuses. 'I know it from soap you use!' I deny this, because a nose like his full of smoke could never smell soap. He asks, 'Do you know what are duties of secretary?' 'To be recording?' 'Good, yes. Business first.' And so both of us puffing, eastward from saltwater, in a cloudy whiz past shopping malls carved from mountain forests. Then scrubby fields, a river, and off the highway into farms and a flood plain. It is nearing three o'clock. 'See peaks?' Mr Singh nods ahead at the snowy mountains in a dazzle. 'Golden,' he tells me. 'Golden when sun rises, golden when setting. Like Himalayas.'

Down here, Mother, I hate the ruralside where he has brought me. Broken fences, car carcasses, fields! On my first time outside the city I miss it after two minutes. 'Don't worry,' says Mr Singh, 'I am bringing you for look see only. Meet families to see how much problem of immigration is on their thoughts. Cow milking and blueberry picking are bad businesses. So they are open to some profit.'

A muddy lane leads past mushy pastures, empty outbuildings, a sad house with a falling down porch. Beside it is a panel lorry, green like the long grass. 'Look,' and Mr Singh points. 'Ram and goat fighting.' Butting heads, Mother, one horn broken off, ugly. Punk rocker goats, and I get a sudden idea for Foreign Trade. 'Crazy goats,' says Mr Singh, cutting his motor. 'All creatures fighting inflation, eh? You have notebook?' He beeps two times to announce us. The goats stop, stiffened to a truce by Mr Singh's announcement.

The house is quiet, puffing at the chimney. Cool air from the river has nothing on it but freshness and goose honks. No street fumes, no congestion, no trolley wires. I hate it, Mother. Peasant living is a big sacrifice compared to city adventures. '*Sss*, no smoking allowed,' whispers Mr Singh. 'Hide cigarettes!' Hide them, Mother? I feel homesick with a need to inhale my weed. Rips in my clothes feel wrong where goats have scab patches and the house peels paint. 'You have steno pad in briefcase?' I pat it. 'Take out. Listen closely to proceedings. Record all for files.' Mr Singh slips out from under his seat a Polaroid camera.

A fierce face has appeared on the porch in a black beard and saffron turban. *Helo Jagdish!* I stop to record Mr Singh's greeting. The landlord has a bad glare and nothing to respond. I smell his chapatis cooking, like a street dream, but it is coming from the farmhouse and this is why I know what I dream and what I interpret in my dream, Mother, is a divided truth. This fierce Sikh would destroy the dream of peace and prosperity I have in Canada. But Mr Singh has no worry of this warrior with his dagger. *All here Jagdish?* I write. *You recieved messege, excellant. This boy is my fresh asistent to keep recurd of our contracks today.* Jagdish glares at the assistant with a look I can hear, Mother. He has no love for spiked hair, for any hair not wrapped in a tent like his. I will not begin to record what he is thinking of purple hair. *I new every thing would be A-Wun when I saw your truck Jagdish. Shal we go insid?*

An old woman is cooking in a kitchen of men and young girls all staring, listening. Mr Singh before them is a very great visitor they do not trust. Or maybe it is me, A.I. *Sikhs all under stand one anuther and do bisness based on saime beleefs. ok?* The temperature between us stays at zero Celsius. 'Orthodox,' he whispers, stopping me from writing the word. 'Suspicious.' He widens his arms. *So. Pleese, befor eating this meal on my expens acount, I will take your naimes and dawhters naimes, to be rekorded by my seckretery at table here, where I will examin papers, pleese, startng one at a time with this side, ser, and your dawhter. Pleese come to table now. I wil also take photoe*

Mother, my fingers ache and I will never make Trudy write so fast as my own secretary. The first girl has a pretty face with a height taller than mine. She is staring at my hair. Her father in a white beard has the skinniness of a pencil. I am safe behind the kitchen table, beside Mr Singh. It is noiseless in the house except for the old woman tapping pots. Her cooking and our hot breath are fogging windows. *Ser, what is you're adress plese and do you have telaphone we can raech you?* Mr Singh turns his head, receives the girl's documents from Jagdish, his in-between gofer, holding passports and other papers in safekeeping. He compares the photo in the passport with the pretty face before us, asks this girl if she is who the passport says. She boggles her head. Mr Singh then points for me to copy down passport number, place of birth, height, colour of eyes and such like. 'Separate page for each girl.' When I start to copy her vitals he asks her father, *Does you're dawhter know proposels we are makeing for her mariage and boundrys that do and do not apertane?* So I am writing with both hands. Jagdish translates for Mr Singh and the old man boggles his head. *Good. Now plese, I will take photoe.*

The girl smiles, giggles after the flash explodes in her eyes. A little whirring sound in the camera is telling Mr Singh the pretty face of the girl is digesting well. He smiles reassurance when his camera ejects a very bad likeness of her. The next time I look it is sharper, Mother, and the next time, yes, it is the girl. Mr Singh takes a paper from his briefcase, hands it to the father, and asks the girl to sign their contract when her father is finished reading it. The old man looks to Jagdish. The turban tent nods. The old man does not bother reading the document or even looking. His daughter takes the pen and does her best signature. Afterward she giggles at my hair.

My last task for this first couple is a receipt, *Paymant in part*, requiring the father's signature, returned to Mr Singh's paperclip file of contract and photo, in exchange for six hundred dollars Mr Singh now counts below the table and gives the old man in hundred dollar bills, from a hidden pocket in his briefcase. *Followeing mariage, ser, and sucesfull immigraetion from Punjab of Sikh benefisary, a cheque of same sum is forthecoming in finel paymant.* The old man boggles his head and folds the cash into his shirt without counting. The same thing for each man and his daughter then, nine girls, seven fathers, two uncles. Mother, after one hour my hand is an arthritis web from the expectations of Mr Singh. I cannot handle the meal Jagdish's aunt over-cooks in a bad temper, waiting for us to finish our paperwork. Afterward, with fathers eating at our table, daughters in the other room, Mr Singh pays Jagdish one hundred twenty-five dollars for meal costs and asks me, A.I., to record their transaction in my steno pad.

I have no picture yet of the pieces and I await Mr Singh to say how it fits together, on our drive home. Darkness falling, stars showing. He shifts to overdrive and pretends I have it all calculated out. 'Tell me, Corbin Singh, you boast quickness with figures, what's profit going to be?' 'Profit?' 'Based on expenses today – subtract those – what would you say profit will be, roughly talking.' We are in a smokestack cloud of my Pall Malls again. He has unnotched his belt and hiked his balls for better comfort, pushing his music into the tapedeck again. For night driving he has fitted his nose with yellow goggles. I need to open up my steno pad, Mother, for precise remem-brance of our transactions. 'Expenses today … come to … $5,465.' 'Plus gas?' 'No, sir.' 'Plus your salary?' My salary we are still having to settle. 'Say two hundred dollars?' he asks. 'For your work today?' No more than four hours, Mother, two hundred dollars! 'Add on air fares,' he continues. 'My fare to Delhi back. Not to mention India expenses, bribes … for arrange-ment of marriages. Then nine fares more, one way to Canada.' I have had to stop writing. 'Say seven thousand total?' suggests Mr Singh. 'Seven thou-sand more expenses?' I ask. 'Precisely so.' I add in this figure: 'That leaves us … $12,565 in hole.' 'Plus gas,' he says. And then, 'But you also forget six hundred still owing fathei once daughter successfully carries out agreement at airport and so on. Nine guardians. Add fifty-four hundred to present total.' I add it in. I add up quickly. 'In hole then … altogether $17,965.'

Mr Singh turns to me now and winks once through his yellow goggles. 'I need to generate some profits, *nai?*' His voice deepens. 'How much you think I need charge each Sikh man who wishes to come to Canada? Come, Corbin, be generous to me …' I have no clue, Mother, but I am starting to see the *amportance* of imagination in the importing business. He reminds me, 'These are sons of prosperous Punjab merchants, suppose.' He is urging me to stab at a figure. I shrug and say, 'Three thousand each would leave you a profit of ... bit over nine thousand. Dollars.' 'Precisely so,' says Mr Singh. 'Not much profit for this much work and arranging, true? And risk. I am taking risk to help arrange sham marriages for purpose of illegal immigration to Canada. Most necessary to stress this with every prospective husband ...' Mother, I thought my profit estimation was a good one, but I am learning. 'This is reason,' says Mr Singh, 'I will charge every man more than three thousand dollars. I will charge him ten thousand.' Another yellow wink. 'American dollars, Corbin. No need to figure. I have sums up here in brain.' So I close my pad to hide further interest. To see better I open my window a crack to let out smoke. 'You see how, Mr Honorary Sikh, I will have over ninety thousand profit? Minus gas?' He blows smoke and butts out his weed in the ashtray. 'You are thinking,' he says, 'if that is so Mr Big Bucks could give me more than two hundred dollars. Is that what you are thinking?' 'No, no. I am pleased.' 'Maybe so. But I could give more ... I would expect more ...' He sounds dangerous and I enjoy it. 'Jagdish?' I ask, wanting to know more of the importing business. 'Jagdish? Jagdish is owed one hundred dollars each for every girl he brings us. It is enough for Jagdish. But I forgot him, true. Add nine hundred to expenses. I will take his cheque to temple.'

I am so much impressed with the importing business I light another Pall Mall and think what a shame, Mother, Canada will not open wider arms to newcomers, because of how many jobs they could do nobody wants. Waiting on tables, delivering porch flyers, selling subscriptions to widows and such like. Mr Singh is fumbling in the highway dark with his chin, still talking. *Ping*. I see my employer removing his whisker net, Mother. He tosses something on the dash comparing to a G-string. 'The upshot is win-win for everyone. Parents and girl get looksee at phony husband, when he lands in Canada with new married status. If family think he looks nice – nice catch for a poor girl – she has no need with legal divorce, not if his feeling is for her too, but instead they arrange courtship period, Sikh wedding at temple, and no dowry necessary. Poor girl has given him citizenship already. Everybody win-wins, *nai*?'

Mr Singh now pulls off his whole head, unravelling his black turban from his short hair. 'Khalistan wins, too. Young men work hard in Canada for Khalistan. Like you. Trick is learn immigration rules and follow to T, before breaking. Very risky business. A secretary must be cheek jowl with all rules. Yes, Mr Christian Hindu?' He looks at me in the dashlight of his green dials. He no longer looks like a Sikh. His beard has come right off. 'Am I going to be trusting you to secrecy?'

3.

Friday after school Foreign Trade rehearses in the tenement basement Arthur lives in. Grunt, butt, grunt. I knew it would sound natural, head butting the mike. I have a good ear, Mother, yours. Niggy butts his purple head, then it is Raoul's turn, but Raoul means it and gashes his forehead. Raoul never cares if it is rehearsal or concert, it is always performance with Raoul. Performance performance. His forehead bleeds into his eyes, the bleeding makes him crazy, he drives his electric guitar till a string breaks. This drives Arthur bloody on drums, Niggy and Sadie scream louder. I am dizzy at their bloodiness. Niggy and Sadie press fingers at Raoul's bloody forehead to smear their faces. Niggy wipes his crotch. Sadie wipes hers.

Trudy is listening with me for dead patches in their singing, but Foreign Trade is a punk band who live on dead patches. It is only a problem for a manager. Dizzy, I dictate to her an idea for better timing in *Piss n' Boots* and she writes it down, pleased to be my secretary. I, A.I., am everyone I want to be. But only for as long as Foreign Trade ceases any more fights with Asian gangs. I say nothing now. But I am secretly thinking of moving Foreign Trade away from the Sex Pistols' style toward Michael Jackson's. How, Mother?

Trudy has booked the community centre tonight, but I cannot arrive at the dance before 10:00 p.m. My new part-time duties at Safeway keep me wage earning Friday nights and all Saturday. I leave Trudy to hire fullback bouncers. Raoul and Iggy hate it when couples dance instead of listen, so they mock these dancers from the stage and their ranting back and forth makes bitterness sometimes. The band likes Trudy because she is as ugly as they are. They do not trust their manager so well, and I must not smile or show my dimple. I wipe off my eyeliner. I scowl. It is dangerous scowling at Safeway, where I am asked to perform courtesy service with a smile.

Tonight at coffee break I am listening to Warrick, the assistant manager, saying to me he is happy with his golf game, at an exclusive club on a mountainside course, if only he could hit the ball straighter in the clutch. '... But you're coordinated, Aloysius, by the look of that moonwalk of yours. I should take you out for a game someday. See how you do. Hit the ball right when you're young and you'll powder it straight when you're old. More business done on the golf course than any other place, including boardrooms.'

Warrick likes me, Mother, notwithstanding my hair spikes, he thinks I have getupandgo. But already, Mother, I am asking myself why the bloom is gone from the Safeway rose. I used to like dreaming in this paradise. Now it has faded to servicing customers, filling up the milk cooler, stocking shelf specials like apple juice and corn niblets. No incentive when pay is the same every hour, even when I hurry like a pageboy. Bartlett would be surprised I am looking forward to free enterprise so soon after he begged the favour of my wages from the manager.

'Hey, there's Wishes!' Lloyd and Marcia at the mixer shelf. 'Hey, man, what's with the smock?' Lloyd is impressed, Mother, I can hear it in his voice. 'Thought your band was playing the dance tonight.' I tell him it is. Marcia tells me, 'We're going, Aloysius, if it's safe.' Rad, I tell her. Foreign Trade will blow her mind out. Rehearsal went wild. I will be there, I tell her, after I am here. And I razor-knife open a carton of potato chips with a lightning slice to impress her. Also, I am afraid, some bags inside. She is taller than me, like you, Mother, a dancer's height on upswept calves. She is wearing black tights, black everything. I have had in mind to make her a present of some black lip gloss I found for Foreign Trade, once they move closer to M. Jackson's style. I wore some myself to school and I believe this has added to my expulsion file, even if Mr Blaylock liked it. 'Come to Andrew's penthouse for the after party,' she invites me. 'But don't bring those animals in your band,' warns Lloyd. 'We don't want the place trashed in two secs.' 'Andrew's parents are away skiing,' says Marcia. Lloyd says, 'If you want to invite the band, Wishes, throw your own party.'

At home, Mother, where I return to change into my black ripped clothes, Bartlett is watching himself on Reesa's VCR, being interviewed on *City, City*. He shakes his head. 'What am I telling her, anyway? It's just blab. That's not what happened. I sound like I'm talking and nothing's coming out. I sound like a gadfly.' I sit down to keep him company a moment in his worry over the bad country he came back from weeks ago. 'No,' he says to himself. He is not so fat anymore, Mother. His clothes are growing loose for him, like the morals of Foreign Trade are for Lloyd. My band is a delinquency machine. Maybe I should stay home. I worry over hearing from Trudy in a few minutes they have spat in the face of the community centre, defecating on stage and such like in their roles as goats and rams.

August, 1990

Daddy has died from red tide. Two weeks ago, so I can write about it now without crying. We've been very strong, Mother and me, although she was poisoned too. We all were. We feel better now. Granny has been nursing us with parsnip soup.

Our apartment was crowded with friends and relatives, but since the funeral they have left us alone. Mother has gone back to forecasting and Granny comes in to look after me. I will miss Daddy walking me to school next month, although I am old enough to walk myself now, and will do so, as I am almost nine. No one should blame Daddy for poisoning us. He was always very careful. He made me run the tap for fifteen seconds before I was allowed to brush my teeth or fill a glass. He'd say, 'Water picks up lead in the pipes if it sits too long.'

His new friend Nick taught him to be so pernickety, Mother claimed, because Nick is fussy about his own health. I like Nick's carrotty hair, but he's so thin.

Daddy would sit a whole day in this apartment without going outside. He'd got used to prison-sitting. Maybe this is why he never found a job, because he was always doing figures on paper as if he had one. He would never let me go outside alone. He imagined I might be kidnapped or smacked by a car. The East Side wasn't safe, he thought.

He still managed to poison us – but this wasn't his fault. He didn't know the clams he dug at the beach with Nick were infected.

At first we felt our lips tingle and tongues go numb. Then we agreed our faces and hands felt funny and I just threw up. I felt a little better then. Daddy felt worst, he couldn't breathe. Paralysed in his chair with the little fan on the window sill blowing his napkin ends. Mother jumped up and swept the clams on our plates to the floor. The ambulance came some time after, and that was the last time I saw him.

Granny and I have been looking at snapshots of him and Mother on a beach in Hawaii.

My fever felt good
almost. I felt a bone–
clean sensation inside
my head, rubbing there,
clean and white like a
shell. Warm, too. I don't
know if the August
weather has been hotter
than normal. Granny
says it has.

I think I have grown
up a lot since Daddy
passed away. For one
thing I practise my piano
without anybody asking.
Something else is the old
photographs we gaze at
to put our minds
elsewhere. We gaze at
photographs from long
ago. Granny told me
today her mother is the
second white child born
after the city was born.

Granny says
Fisheries has closed
down local waters to the
harvesting of mussels,
oysters, clams … 33,000
kilometres of coast now
closed because of our
experience at the dinner
table.

Chapter 14

The World is My Barbershop

MOTHER, MR. SINGH MAKES me write up profiles of each local bride and attach his photos taken in the ruralside for export to the Punjab. I know nothing of his girls but this has not mattered, not even when a right photo goes with the wrong story. Mr Singh's importing business is out of focus on purpose and this keeps me sharp to protect his interests in the legalities and such like of venture capital risk. Notwithstanding, the question arises have his paper marriages happened already, before he departs for Delhi to sell his brides to their highest bidders? I have been paid very high for accompanying Mr Singh to farms outside Vancouver, sometimes for fruit picking as well. I am no longer positive I once saw him pull off his turban, and anyway would never interpret the tangled importing business from one naked mirage in the green dashlight of a speeding car. Best sticking to passport facts.

Beside my secret profits from Mr Singh, Mother, I squeeze in wage earning this summer. For my goal of landlordship I am still condemned to labour. My bones feel gnawed in a stopgap job to help my cash flow. Every dawn I lean against a tire in the tractor shed, shooting the air with two college workers, hired like me to cut golf greens at 7:00 a.m. Five minutes till firing our Toros up with whipcords and I am tired, tired. For renewing my bones it helps to smoke a Pall Mall and unburden my past. 'To tell you a true story, friends, it is very hard for Sikhs to fit in with your country here, because in my country, Khalistan, our customs are Sikh customs, you see, and why we come to Canada is painful to confess appertaining to Indian government, who are throwing Sikhs in jail for wanting their own homeland. I myself hope to return as freedom fighter soon, even if I am not in belief of strict religion of fellow Sikhs.' At this I pat my spiked hair, Mother. I, A.I., am everyone I want to be. Gus and Terry snort in their noses. I tell them more. 'My father, you know, is in jail these three years. I must work to pay for food at home ...' My fellow workers have no comment so early in the morning, except *whhhaaaaaaaa* ...

My own mower is the hardest to fire up, Mother. I believe Mr Kymbach gave me it on purpose. Gus and Terry are already herding their islands of noise over dewy fairways, red mowers and grass catchers trailing fumes across the low sun. The greenskeeper, Mother, hates my earring and so charged me to cut his six highest greens. I put my Toro in gear and follow it up steep hills like a busboy to breakfast. I carry a rake on my skinny shoulder and a thirst for bottled water. To finish even steven with Gus and Terry, lower down on flat greens, I must drink sprinkler water and hurry all morning like a dog. An art, Mother, inside this picture postcard of mountain vistas.

At the clubhouse on top I stop to gaze down on the city glittering through mist. I am burning to conquer that city. Someday I will unify my corporation interests and find the sum of their pieces as a landlord. I will be begged into membership of a private clubhouse like this one, perched under peaks like these showing traces of snow and cool disdain. The landlord will prevail, Mother. He has had a dream. I watch landlords like Mr Singh discussing fairway deals every day, trading cigars. I am counting on Mr Singh to help me escape poverty and teenagehood.

'The players use your lines to line up their putts,' sour Mr Kymbach told me. 'Make sure you learn a steady hand pretty quick. Members can't putt on crooked stripes.' Mother, I have learned to cut a straight stripe on a rolling green, then a return stripe, back and forth on the counter grain starting each morning on a fresh diagonal. The world is my barbershop. I am prohibited to cut it in the punk image. Number thirteen, fourteen, up to number eighteen, greens as big as lakes and I polish off each with a pair of flanking cuts, clockwise and counterclockwise at the boundary. I am not permitted to waver like skate skids on a frozen lagoon. Every other morning Mr Kymbach lifts the sod core like an ore sample, to give club members a new goal by filling in their old one and moving the pin. It is the game of life, Mother, as it should be played. His tool is a corkscrew and my greens their lakes of champagne. I dream. I listen to the grass. To the hollow rattle when a golf ball tumbles in its cup. To the zipper on a bag in the still mountain air. Sounds, Mother, of the landlord's world.

I light a Pall Mall beside my vibrating Toro and breathe down to my socks after the long push uphill. I am wearing ripped cutoffs and a Foreign Trade T-shirt. The band's T-shirt with the built-in rips? I sell them at concerts to dancers. Also to street hookers and classmates at the beach. I have sold them to Gus and Terry. But I have other avenues for investment besides T-shirts, Mother. You would be pleased how I invest in penny stocks and have cash and margin accounts with Mary Yip. She calls to warn me not to jump in with board lot orders. I do anyway. I, A.I., am everyone I want to be. This is the given, Mother.

The bottles in our basement? They keep growing week to week from the beaches. I fall behind my suppliers with my hammer. 'Aloysius, dear,' Reesa will say, coming downstairs. 'Are you certain you have something ... in mind for all this glass? The bottles must be costing you Nebuchadnezzar's gold. Then you just smash them to smithereens! It doesn't make sense to the punkless like us.' Reesa enjoys ragging me, Mother, about *The Book of Daniel*, about dreaming. 'No sweat,' I tell her. 'I know a contractor who covets my shards once he hears my idea.' *Ping.* Her look darkens when she thinks I have slipped her an untruth. I would worry, Mother, if I did not know from her diary Reesa thinks I am A / OK. 'Lovable,' she writes. 'More or less.'

Dwight is the one not loving me. 'You up, Wishes? It's past six.' I was secretly reading his old Superman comics this morning in bed. He has no idea of their collector's worth and I will neglect to mention it when I sell them. Dwight has no nose for business, Mother, I think he is going to lose out on refugees totally. Learning to network is *amportant*, Mr Singh is *amportant*. But Dwight is careless, Mother. He thinks he can dismiss my Delhi offer to his travel company. I could hear him waiting at my door this morning. '... Get up and make yourself a lunch, okay? Or else join me for a cold shower and learn to go without.' He would like to discipline me like a scout master.

He thinks I am amazing. He is right for the wrong reason. Amazing, he thinks, is how much farther does Aloysius think he can slide before he falls flat on the ice? Far farther, Mother, because now I know how to cut dream lines on grass too. He shakes his head at yours truly collecting bottles and slaps it hearing I want to collect refugees also. 'Call Mr Singh, if you doubt this, Dwight. Here is his number.' Mother, I am trying to locate cheap Delhi tickets through Herodotus Tours, promising Mr Singh my travel agent will be in touch soon, if a one-way special fare can be worked out to assist his overhead for sponsoring Sikhs from Delhi. Mr Singh is secretive and shrugs my offer off. He is on his way to India, with or without Dwight's call. He is first class.

I mooch off these workers at the golf course. They give me waxpaper bundles of bread and cookies. Their wives would be angry, knowing a punk in a crotch chain mooches from their husbands. I smile and talk my way into their lunch pails. 'Foreign cities you don't mind hearing, but Beirut you are really sick of hearing, yes?' I smile again. 'Just my bad fortune to come from that cursed place, full of thugs popping away at the other man with no hoosegow to lock them in. I would clip their hair, why not, throw away the key. It is a very bad tragedy. Those Muslims killing Muslims. Those Muslims killing Christians and vice versa ...' I am outlining a truth they have seen with their own eyes, Mother, on TV. Car bombs, PLO and such like. Rad. Mr Kymbach is the only one to exit the lunchroom, not because he does not believe me, he just hates 'yappy coloured' kids. In the machine shed he will dab a pencil lead on his tongue to record my lateness this morning, on the work board hanging by a nail. He has a deep anger at Safeway Warrick for telling him I had mowed a golf course in Bombay. I wish Warrick had not. My future is in profit and loss, not wages, in wishing for a better risk of failure than labouring gives.

Mother, my listener, I love inflation. It is the engine of franchise growth. Money in things like video, if I could think how, or a product in the sex line, is the avenue to solicit on. C'est *amportant* to have smartness on my side, Mother, thank you. Gus and Terry look stupid from college, hooked on careers at the end of rainbows to pay back gold it took them to get there! I would like to *wear* my gold, like you did, Mother. I would like to take hold of inflation before it butts away my rainbow, and ride the marketplace saddle of good earners like Foreign Trade and bottled water. This is what I dream.

Nothing is safe. The rainbow could blind my parade and I could fall from the saddle. Risk could strangle me rolling over in my bed dreaming of rent revenues. Like you did, Mother, I would rather take my chance on a dimpled smile to increase my income and learn of happiness. Free enterprise will fight wages and such like from our beaches to the mountains. This is the given. My second summer in Canada is this long dream to get through. Superman was an orphan too.

2.

Mother, I want to be in on the basement floor when importing refugees gives some sign of welcoming franchise operators to its future opportunities. I have Mr Singh's example as an independent operator. If he branches out, or offers to share the opportunities of selling Canadian welcome mats, I need cash in a nest to seize that fortuity from the money tree. Meanwhile, I have made Trudy the following proposition: If she will keep her ears open around the boat kids, I promise her a commission on the network we will build in combo. She frowned, her brown eyes probing. 'I don't know what you're getting at, Wishes.' She does not know I am thinking gold and what that will buy off the high seas. 'That new Vietnamese restaurant, over from the library?' I asked her. 'Not dimeing and nickeling it, right? You need dollars to make dollars and they are making oodles.' Last winter when it opened, Mother, with tables of people eating and drinking, Bartlett took his girlfriend and me and we ate thirty dollars of food and alcohol. I was thinking, Mother, if Sikhs are interested in paying into the importing business, would not boat people also be interested, having money for restaurants and such like? Maybe Trudy could find out how these boat families paid for their restaurants, if not with smuggled gold. She frowned again and twiddled her liver-coloured hair. 'I don't know what you're getting at, Wishes.'

Then one day she asked, 'Did you read this?' And I knew, Mother, the importing business was bigger than I dreamed. 'It's kinda sad,' said Trudy. 'This clipping says outfits in Germany bring in women to get married. If you're a German man they give you an album of snaps to look through, and the vital stats of your potential wife.' She sucked at her bad teeth. 'A wife costs five thousand dollars, Wishes. And the man doesn't have to marry her. Girls from the Philippines, Latin America ... This says most end up without a husband or a passport, in debt to an agency.' And what happens to them, Mother? 'They start hooking on the streets.' 'Clubs?' I asked. Trudy said she hated Germans. 'I'd hate you, Wishes, if you imported girls.' Never, I swore. 'Mr Singh,' she said, 'I don't like him at all.' My secretary has never met Mr Singh, Mother. She only dislikes being secretary to a secretary.

I said nothing to her of Herodotus Tours, which I know is giving sex tours under the table like other travel agencies. Neither did I mention Bartlett went on a sex junket, thanks to Dwight's doing. I know, I switched on Bartlett's diary when he came home from Bangkok. Dwight is in the exporting business, but the importing business of Mr Singh's is more exciting, Mother. It unites the dream of people far away with the dream of people already here. I hope to be a landlord like Mr Singh someday.

Tonight I lie here in my bed thinking of Michael Jackson's glove. For

THE WORLD IS MY BARBERSHOP

Foreign Trade I think it could be modified from white to black, from crystal beaded to ripped and torn. This is the only way I could interest Niggy who hates M.J. the most. I have accidentally begun to wear a prototype, a worn-out golfer's glove fished from a litter barrel last week. This is the given, Mother, taking advantage of fate. Fate like Bartlett telling me last fall, at the kitchen tap pouring himself a glass of water, 'Beats that Perrier juice.' This put in my brain, Mother, a scheme for bottling the best water in the world, from right in our own taps and selling it with the French name, Jaillir.

Marcia has drawn a pretty label of a wishing well and I hope to market Jaillir as soon as my cash flow matches a little closer the rush of tap water. I save my wages and ask around. Bartlett shrugs and says he would be interested in investing in water, sure, but his money 'is tied up in travel right now.' I have not approached Mr Singh. He and I are too busy with his importing. Mr Singh says capital is ever and a day in flight from troubled places to safe ones. 'Biggest migrations of it come from countries needing it most and understanding it least. A shame, Corbin. But I am only middle man for filling up desires people have in their hearts.' I am learning strings from this importer, Mother, strings and such like for pulling operations smoothly through my head like dental floss.

Today, Sunday, after driving his pickers at dawn to the Fraser Valley and back at dusk, we visited the temple. All the Sikh contractors were there at Mr Singh's bidding to foil the new Farmworkers' Union. *You see,* I wrote keeping his minutes, *we must crushe this man who wants to sighn up our pepul. Othur wise, we are goeing to be cutt out from our just profets.* Mother, I worked today for my two hundred dollars, believe me. By sunset I was stiff from sitting and riding and totalling up in the ruralside. We delivered home whole families, from children to grandparents, jabbering away like nothing back-breaking in the raspberry canes had befallen their spines since dawn. The van was full, yet my employer kept loading in more bodies wrapped in coloured jodphurs, saris, turbans. Mr Singh contracts to supply farmers with pickers: fifteen, twenty-four, thirty-eight at my last count, packed inside his van, picking them up and dropping them off, many from the city. The saffron-turbaned Jagdish travels in his green lorry between Perumbur and Mission, Chilliwack and Langley, to rotate our pickers. He is Mr Singh's subcontractor. At dusk when Mr Singh and the farmer attend to flats, to scales, I mark down how many pounds each picker has scored. I give a copy to the farmer and a copy to the picker. My steno pad, Mother, looks like a carbon paper sandwich, and I thank the Orphanage of Hope for training me in sums. It is up to the farmer to pay Mr Singh when picking season ends, and Mr Singh to pay his pickers, based on my exact calculations. Mr Singh pays all in cash. '… Only way to guarantee loyalty.'

The new labour union wishes to outflank contractors like Mr Singh by telling pickers to count on the Farmworkers' Union to give them more benefits. It preaches that contractors reward themselves like princes. *Lies*, answered Mr Singh, tonight at temple. *You men knowe how much we do for thes poeple. Who else would drive them fourtie, sixtie miles befour brekfast?* FU *is agatation and comunism. I negoetiate price per pound with farmr. I garantee how meny pickers he wishes. I hire pickers, pickeing them up at dawn, takeing them home at nght late* … 'I could carry stick,' announced one contractor in his skyscraper turban, with fingers like wieners. Another said, 'No picket lines, or we will break them apart weddy badly.'

I scribbled down Mr Singh's oratoricals in respect of the hot plains of Khalistan, the nobility of Sikh holy history, and rights of fruit picking contractors. Not he or any of these other Mr Singhs sounded happy to be in Canada and all spoke badly of its spell. Except, Mother, my employer lightened up driving me home and I knew then I had not seen a mirage in the green dashlight the first time I went with him. He is his own entrepreneur. He would try to kill the union, yes. But he is not a frother at the mouth like some rads at temple who would kill people, he believes, to help Khalistan. 'Hotheads,' Mr Singh calls them. Mother, I think their brotherhood would love to give me the death blow for having spiked hair and a crotch chain. Only Mr Singh protects me. My boss and I smoked then for the first time since dawn. I buckled up my briefcase and we smoked ourselves into a cloud. I forgot to give him golf balls.

Tonight I have just telephoned Trudy. She has met a strong-willed woman at Weight Watchers, a Mrs Scobie, all gunged up on underground relief for Guatemalans and Salvadorans in the basement of St. Sebastian's atop Hooker Hill. A possible opportunity, Mother, if I dicker right for the franchise. I hear Central America is bursting with customers, dreaming of coming here like me, landing in a rainstorm and seeing the sun break out in walls of gold! They too burn to become landlords.

May, 1986

My head still sore from bursting stars. The fireworks last night made Mother's face light up on the beach. I was holding her hand and drinking apple juice from a box. We were all smeared with light and our feet felt cold. Granny said it was too cold to go swimming, but some of the yachters didn't think so, shooting up flares and hooting at anybody who jumped overboard in their clothes.

Barges offshore were competing to raise the most *ahs*. Daddy liked the Canadian stars best. The barges belonged to countries and so did the stars. The apple juice tasted bad because of gunpowder in the air. Who would think having a birthday party could throw up so much stardust? The city is a hundred. I just turned three and a half. I would like to go back to before my headache.

It took a long time to be over. The yachts seemed small with their sails down. Glass hulls mirrored the exploding colours. I must have fallen asleep on the blanket and got packed home in it. I can still feel the hammockiness round my shoulders.

Old Granny keeps a bottle of Beefeater gin in her room, and uses it to polish her teeth. They all had a glass of it.

Chapter 15

Thirst

SOMETHING THE MATTER IS happening to me, Mother. I moonwalk Safeway aisles, next to herbal teas, next to pickled relishes, thinking up new floating steps for Foreign Trade, and guess what is in my mind, what is in my wisdom, after one year of managing this band, knowing I am losing them to grossness and perversion? My punk rockers are mutilating themselves every time they play a concert, and will never outlast this Year of the Rooster. They have no Mick Jagger blood. This is the bottom line, I now see, the smirch in their ancestry. They are not roosters! They have no strut or smooth bridge between a thrust and a withdrawal. They remind me of mongrels, biting and yelping, scuffling and dumping. They hate my hints to them on moonwalking. Rhythm breaks across their butts. Mother, if I have one secret not unbosomed to the world it is this: I love dancing feet. I love my own feet when they dance. This is a dangerous divulgement in the manager of a punk band. FT mocks moonwalking, and if I spurn their shinhacking and such like they threaten to bash in my head with a guitar. They think it looks sissy, coming on like M. Jackson.

Mother, they hate the grace I learned from you! This is the given. I am a soaking dishrag from cleaning up bad feelings and wet furniture in wake of concert after concert. Niggy and Raoul hate any smooth move, any nice leg slide, any concert without barking and growling insults. They jerk and froth like bickering mutts. They chew up floorboards. They vomit on the dancers. Sadie bares her little teats on stage. Arthur pees on Sadie's boots, on anything red, on anything in need of cooling by his fire-hydrant ego. The band hates me for keeping them have-not underdogs, when the fees I haggle for their appearance evaporate into our deficit dances. Out of my own savings I pay down debts for broken lights and kicked-out windows. Thus Foreign Trade dries up its cash flow, notwithstanding my cash flow, and I have lost the hope to consolidate my loose spheres of business in the bigger sum of city music. The scene is not formulating to my ad, Mother.

Michael Jackson is a millionaire because he never lets himself lose grace in the body. This is *his* given. His voice as pure as water, his facelift in the direction of an angel. M. Jackson would never mutilate his nose with a safety pin. Maybe a pearl. With Foreign Trade, I am afraid, the negatives outbalance the positives. You know about me and debits, Mother, and how I used to care less about staying in the black. Since those days I have had a watershed. Now c'est *amportant* to keep my dream in the black before red ink makes all *ampossible*. The dance of my life is a balance in the making. Do I cancel the buy order or the sell order, and what will be my saving?

Money. The young Turk is a mark everywhere he walks. I have started dressing less ripped, less punk, more like M. Jackson but without sequins. I still spike my hair. I still wear an earring and gold nose stud. But the crotch chain is gone, Mother. My glove is a clue to my change. And I hang an epaulette off one shoulder. I look more heeled now and less like a flea bag. I have darkened my eyeliner. This afternoon the beggars can see me coming, as I hurry to Safeway toil, one begs my change for busfare to his job interview. He leans up against the hootch store on Robson, his raincoat filthy with rain stains from a hundred years of sidewalk saluting. In foggy November he lists like a torpedoed barley ship on an ocean of best intentions. I aid him with a quarter and a capsule of my best advice: 'Video.' He mock salutes me, Mother, without gratefulness for my generosity. 'Video. You bet, sonny ...' Smirking, estimating I mean X-rated video, as in bobbing boobs and wanking wieners from Red Hot Video across the street. He takes no hint of investing in the communication revolution. Only the sex one.

I keep on wage-earning at Safeway to help me in my dried-out condition. I thirst for profit, like Mr November thirsts to forget he is a shipwreck. I still burn to be a landlord. It is so hard for me, Mother, to have vanishing expectations, when I have street habits from boyhood making me raw material for a capitalist. I worry most over Mary Yip, whose brokerage house I am in hot water in. This is why I wag off my tail at Safeway, for as many hours as Warrick will employ me, and play hooky from school where assignments build higher. Mother, my broker is a panic nurse, ever since she met me, the young man behind my voice on her phone. She panics I will never earn enough to bail out her weakness in letting me buy shares without credit-checking me first, after my low price buy orders made big gains. When I thought a new penny stock called Sun Con would tumble, after start-up dust settled on its brightness, I shorted shares I did not own, Mother, I sold them. This is a licit practice of Howe Street wheelers, shorting to make money. Except, Mother, instead of tumbling, these shares I did not own kept climbing up in value, and I could not bail out by buying in, till I had dropped ten thousand big ones.

'Let that be lesson to you,' said Mary Yip, when I appeared at her office to spill the bean of my poverty. Pea? She was all set to phone my guardian, but she could not weasel his name from my lips, Mother. 'Oh no, por favore.' And between her coming-in calls, each asking Mary to move around their capital like air in a lorry tire, I sat saying: '... I doan got the money right now, but I get it pretty soon from jobs I got ...' Between these ringing clients I painted for her Guatemala before I fled it. She was staring from behind her files and furniture polish. 'I was drafted in army, from family village. Soldiers was killing poor people underneat my eyes. I come from poor family. Same like udder soldiers, who get asked to do killing ... First killing I seen happen outside San Mateo, like dat.' I swung my arm for her. 'The captain, he say to new boy soldier, cut off head of twelve men we find one night playing card. Captain laugh. The twelve apostle he say. We herd dem in truck. He give boy machete. If he doan kill, he will get a bullet his self. So boy go and did it. A true story. Dey doan do nudding bad, dose old men he kill, just play card. I seen dem. When he finish, his cloes got blood down all over dem ...'

Maybe she did not believe me, Mother, but my story was true. I did not lie on what is happening to people from Guatemala. I listen to Mrs Scobie translate talking in their church basement while Trudy takes notes. I hope soon for a large network in trafficking refugees like Mr Singh's. I am learning further and further from Mr Singh. I said to Mary Yip, 'I doan talk to priest, I ascared. I seen so many dings – you know, bad dings. *Capucha*, electric shock. Anudder time my time to do a bad ding. Captain tell me, walk inside dat shack and strangle the mudder and six children. Wit my own hand. He say he will shoot me through if I doan do it. Other soldiers, they doan say nudding. So I say to captain, I doan know how wit my hand. So he tell sergeant, teach him ...' I then bowed my head to Mary, like a crushed-down punk. She was open-eyed at what was sitting here in her busy, phoning office. I wiped my eye, Mother. I buttoned my both eyes to the floor. I took off my glove.

Mary Yip hates me, Mother, a bad debt, who has got her into trouble with her brokerage house. 'You sounded different on telephone, Aloysius.

Not Spanish ...' Maybe she felt sorry for me, because of immigrant relatives in her own closet, who started poor in this country too. *She stood up then and said I must promise not to buy one more share of any stock.* '... Meantime, I try cover for you.' She meant with her own money, Mother, monthly payments on my ten thousand dollars outstanding. I think she had no choice. Due to laziness on her part she is afraid of dishonourable discharge for letting a minor gamble in stocks through her house. Mother, I am now helping Mary service my debt from Safeway wages. And if I can incorporate a network of importing like Mr Singh's I may start to pay her back. I burn to pay her back and be free of my worst inveiglement.

Mr Singh tells me there is more money in the refugee business than I can dream ... if we do not get caught. Might we, Mother? I have sentences in my steno pad like *L.A. pipe line up and down caost, in and out throug Mexico, is one Sihks nead. Say nuthing, my guest Sihk, but bring me more bioughraphies* ... Mr Singh plans further marriages on direct Delhi flights and to keep pipelining his 'unmarriageable' refugees by other routes. I discover his tactics a mystery and have a suspicion he has misled me, Mother, like where his arranged marriages take place. In Delhi or here? My steno pad is a mash of crossovers and crossouts. My sums compute and do not compute in his refigurements and rearrangements. I have trouble with his places and dates, documents and schedules. He has pedalled sideways a thousand times. He chuckles at my confusion. I now think he is bringing over Sikh men to 'visit' first before 'marrying' them to clients. It is safer. I am puzzled by his 'convenience' talk and his 'love' talk. Since last summer, Mother, four girls, whose happy stories I wrote up for future husbands, have stayed with their imported men who chose them for convenience purposes. The remaining 'wives' are suing for divorce, just like we plotted last spring in the ruralside. Mr Singh promised them no problems, but I know he is having some, facing lawyers' costs or else an unmasking by his clients. Mr Singh now pulls his whisker net tight to his face.

But here is Mr November again. Skulking in my favourite moonwalking aisle, sliding a jar of Taster's Choice into his raincoat. 'Hey,' he calls, a startled little wave escaping his filthy fingers. 'Video, huh?' I say nothing, conflicted between my Safeway duty to bust him and my personal habit of loose turpitude. He thinks I am disapproving him and he squirms in his smelly beggar's pride. His resentment flares on me like a scratched match. It is beautiful to watch him, Mother. He reaches deep in his raincoat to give back the coffee jar to its shelf. His eyes rise to tea boxes on an upper shelf, overcome by pictures of hill plantations a million miles away. He confesses from the side of his mouth, 'I'm a little stuck this week for groceries, eh?' Rad. I never mind the truth. I shrug. My arms are full of Kleenex boxes bound for paper products, aisle three. 'Take it,' I tell him.

Mr November's eyes, Mother, drop from the hills to mine. He is surprised, totally. 'Yeah?' He sweeps his Taster's Death quickly back in his pocket, along with an orange jar of Coffee Mate to mix with his instant dust. How many kangaroo pockets has he inside that stinky raincoat, his woollen sweaters? He licks his purple lips. 'All I needs now is hot tap water from the Sally, eh, and I'm in business!' He smiles. He mock salutes me again, but means it this time. 'Much obliged, son, for the loan.' He is like a punk rocker, Mother, washed up from the cash flow of life. Holy crow. Cow?

'Isn't *that* an interesting expression,' said Mrs Irving, over roast turkey last month. I was rewarding her with a rare visit, Mother, for bringing me to Canada. Back to her house with Dwight and Reesa for Thanksgiving dinner. 'Is "holy cow" an expression you picked up in Canada, dear, or in Bombay? Forgive an old woman her little wonderings, but it's just the thing I'd expect to hear from a young Hindu ... before you converted, I mean. We need far more cross-fertilizings. Good for you.'

For a mile you pedaled upwerds, sweated, cursed her imprudant memry. You gulped til the canteen was dry. The sun fell from a blemish less sky and the air felt as thicke as rock. On the rode's shoulder lay a berd, white eyd and pupiless, blisturing from heat.

'Who's this?' Mrs Irving was asking, making her face look stupid, not saying one word to help us guess. Dwight sat there like a stone. 'Marcel Marceau!' she burst out. 'Just because he isn't American, Dwight, doesn't mean you're excused your ignorance!' Dwight said *he* was Canadian. 'Then you should know, dear, we're the imitators and never the imitated. Try to remember that.' Her wit tickled Reesa. I, A.I., sat waiting for a private moment with Mrs Irving, to make mention of boat people, for possible importing assistance from me. From her. 'I attend mass every Sunday,' I interrupted. She looked at me, her ex-orphan, blessedly. Dwight and Reesa looked at each other over my bald lie. 'I love the way Aloysius is attentive to Damon,' said Mrs Irving. 'Did you notice the pair of them playing checkers before dinner? Aloysius didn't let him win, either.' On our way home, I overheard Dwight tell Reesa his mother's impersonations were impersonations copied from impersonators. 'Like that reproduction she has hanging on the den wall. The Shroud of Turkey. Borrring ...'

Dwight and Reesa know of my bottle scheme going cockeyed up, Mother, but not yet the reason. They have watched my glass hills build in their basement. Now I am sticked. Stuck. My striking idea of selling shards as a new notion in Canadian security, something rich landlords employ in India, has not allured any contractors on building sites, who laugh off my idea of planting sharp glass atop walls to stop cat burglars. 'Not the way we do it in this country, son. We don't even build walls.' Fences, Mother? No, they will not entertain a possibility of sticking glass in wood either. No matter how many crushed bottles I have, of every colour for sale, at a price of outstanding moderation, contractors turn a blind ear. I have had to stop Carl and Tony from bringing any more empties from our beaches and streets. Dwight tells me these boys' parents are going to be 'after' me soon if I fail to pay my obligations. 'Listen, Aloysius. If you learn to meet a payroll now, it'll put you in good stead for the future. What seems to be the problem?' Dwight thinks I have lots of cash flow, from the golf course last summer, from my Safeway job still, that I am squirrelling my money to squeeze more interest at Canada Trust. He is in for a surprise, Mother, when I dry up and blow away.

Mother, the Safeway is no way to get ahead, but it is a place to dock my boat. I think the financial future is in refugees and video. I have no money to dream of real estate speculation, not yet, not before I disembark from high school. I am still trying to launch Jaillir water. Mr Singh says the scourge of inflation lashes only the weak, so it is *amportant* to stay strong by borrowing. Nothwithstanding my watershed, to keep my dream in the black, I think maybe Mr Singh is right. If only I could balance credit against debit, in a way inviting to a bottom line lender, I would be tempted to borrow too. *Ampossible.* Interest rates now are flying above us all. Only Mr Singh could advance me credit, but he is a landlord with budgetary cautions owing to his huge inventory of schemes for many tenants. Would he, Mother, have an impulse to invest in video?

This afternoon my Safeway shift is to serve mainly customers and I have lost my wonderment at this Shangri-la of food mountains. I am flat tired by six-thirty when I leave. 'Christ,' says Warrick, 'my day off tomorrow'll be too *wet* to swing a putter.' The street is shiny from rain, yes, slick with winter skin. 'Afernoonnn ... sp're change t'day?' Same beggar, Mr November, sloshed now to his gills, one touch closer to the dust of death. Why doesn't he ever recognize his benefactor, Mother, his saviour from the courts, his protector from shoplifting charges? I give him nothing. I advise him to brew a cup of instant coffee. 'Ohh ... hiii ... sssonny,' he slurs, remembering. 'Vi'eooo, huh? Them broads make me thirsty, thinkinn on their red hot bummmms ...' He grins, Mother, a wet tongue doozer. He is just an old tramp, living outside his dream.

2.

The story I am copying for class tomorrow is stolen, but I have no worry of sneaking it past Mr Blaylock, who thinks I have better work inside me waiting to be squeezed like golden syrup from the pus of teenagehood. Teenagehood sucks in the pits. High school is really a road to the poorhouse, Mother, to a job interview for janitor, when my ambition to be landlord is higher than Cypress Bowl. So I cheat, I have no time not to. Mr Blaylock will close a blind eye. He will buy the story I am copying from a library book as mine, Mother, when it does not sound mine. Blaylock will buy anything from Aloysius Irving. An igloo full of tents. Dream language in the nightmare of teenagehood.

You wer reborn with the monsoone explodeing off the tin. The monsoone was not due for weeks and so the lenhgth of you're deth gradually became cleer. Shivvring uncontrolably, you were thersty no more. You lay covered on a charpoy.

Trudy's alcoholic mom plays bingo Wednesday nights, so I come up here after wage earning at Safeway to plot refugee business with my secretary. These November days, because of schemes and such like, I am stretched tight like a guitar string. The pigeons would die at my pitch, cooing on their ledge outside Trudy's building with its stairwell pee smells. Not like our building, Mother, the tower on Marine Drive where we lived with an elevator view to Arabia. Short oily Mr Ghanai visited you there in his own building. You and I were kept till death did us part. After what he did to you, Mother, I promised us both that landlord would never fly again. It is a promise I am still keeping.

Trudy's pigeons are a big nuisance and I tell her she needs a pretend owl to scare them away. On birds she thinks it would be nice to have a canary but her mom sneers and says she already has a crow. Me, Mother, is the crow she wishes would leave her daughter alone. She hates the smoky smells I leave in her welfare furniture, smoky smells in her bed where she thinks I smoke a post hump Pall Mall. Mother, nothing could be so far from my dream, humping with a girl of Trudy's largeness. She would mash me under. Yes, Weight Watchers has reduced her overall by one-fifth, but she is still too vast, except maybe in a corner pocket, for A.I. Her mother's hope is for Trudy to stay fat and ugly.

She broils me wieners as I copy out my story on the kitchen table. Mrs Scobie has invited Trudy to move into a cobwebby house, near a brewery she says. 'My drunken mother should approve.' She says she will leave soon if her mother keeps sneering and smacking her around. Mrs Scobie promises to diet her and teach her things, not just about refugees, but about love and men. Trudy frowns. 'Marcia stuck up for you this afternoon, Wishes, when Andrew accidentally on purpose blurted out in Blaylock's class you were playing hooky. *She* said you had mono.' Trudy shakes her head, wondering. So I decide to tell her the truth. 'Sadie. Marcia thinks I do sex with Sadie.' 'And? Do you?' I flash my dimple. 'Wishes, do you? I have some right to know. That's my coffee cup you're drinking out of.' I deny Sadie has mono. 'Then why tell Marcia a lie?' Mother, I wanted Marcia to show me how bad she really wished to wear the black lip gloss I gave her for a present. If she wished to wear it even at all. 'You gave Marcia a lipstick?' Trudy is hurt. I sniff her burning wieners and copy some more in silence.

... She kept nurseing you til the monsoone stoped. Day by day you would study her movments, and silently predickt the way she would brush a fly off her rist, or make little gestchurs with her hands over meels.

'Want help with your spelling?' she asks from the oven. I tell her this time is different, I am trying to damage the spelling to pretend the story is mine. 'Blaylock will never believe you,' she says. Trudy thinks I will fail Mr Blaylock's class, my whole grade eleven, because I no longer care. 'Read me a sentence.' I read her a sentence, then another sentence. Listening, Mother, she scorches my wieners. '... You can't use that stuff, Wishes! You'll be toast as soon as he reads it!' I smile. 'He will love it.' 'You're shameless, Wishes. You deserve to be toast.' Toast is like chappatis, Mother, except it burns if the wiring gets crossed inside your toasting box. Trudy is jealous of Mr Blaylock, who has rushes near my person when I smile at him. Rushes or rashes, the exact same thing for Mr Blaylock, caused by my dimple flashing. 'You should learn to question your morals, Wishes.'

I eat one, two charred hot dogs, then Trudy bears me a huge wedge of apple pie supplied by her mother, cheese, chocolate ice cream, Coke. Mrs Macdonald hopes Trudy will grow into an elephant. She disapproves of Weight Watchers, of me, because we take away her domain over Trudy. But Trudy wishes to have control of her own body. She eats no more than sesame seeds she picks off hot dog buns. She eats like a bird, Mother. 'My mom says if I don't watch it, I'm going to screw up my constitution. She doesn't know anything about this other stuff, with you and that, eating me up inside.' This other stuff, Mother, is Mrs Scobie and her underground Latinos, hiding in the church basement at St. Sebastian's.

Trudy's slimming is not because of Weight Watchers, those clapping hands of fat women around her weigh-in scale, but because of Mrs Scobie, whose secret knowledge of refugees started Trudy's decline in appetite for no reason except fellow worry. Trudy visits them in St. Sebastian's, listens to their stories, taking me to listen too. I am interested for the importing business I am planning to incorporate, like Mr Singh's freelance business with the Sikhs, except I would include Latinos and such others who would be grateful. I wolf up my dessert. I light a Pall Mall.

Just one thing, I tell Trudy, about Mrs Scobie's Guats and Salvadorans. I think Mr Singh might be interested in names: of refugees already here and of others who wish to come: as a preliminary, Mother, to my own freelancing franchise, since I am in the red too much to finance a first stage of importing Latinos yet myself. I know Mrs Scobie has whispered in Trudy's ear that some refugees have nest eggs from dishwashing in L.A. on their way el norte. With these eggs I bet Mr Singh could think of a faster way than Mrs Scobie to scramble them up the coast! 'I don't like him,' answers Trudy. 'I don't trust him. You should watch out for his motives.' She means making dollars, Mother. Profits. I remind her Mr Singh, my part-time boss, is helping guide people to a new country for marriage and happiness. 'So you keep telling me, Wishes. Do you honestly believe that?' Mother, I tell her I would not have to include Mr Singh if I could capitalize the importing costs on my own flow charts. 'Are they like the water table,' she jokes, 'for your bottled H_2O?' I am patient with her. I want her to believe I have a good chance of being my own importer someday soon.

'You like to talk big, Wishes. I don't think Mrs Scobie is like Mr Singh at all. Zero comparison. She'd never cooperate with you to take money off refugees. Mrs Scobie's nice, even if she's a Catholic. For another thing she thinks men stink. I could learn something from her on getting jilted by men. I feel good helping Mrs Scobie, finding out stuff from her illegals, torture and that. It's scary what's happening down there. I can pocket their confidences, Wishes, but I could never take their money.'

I am an alien myself, Mother, still waiting to become a landlord. This is why I dream of my own importing business, profit-wise, to replace the Lord in His house. Mother, Christians and Canadians have no tolerance like Hindus and Indians for a whole house of idols, and this is my ambition, to moonwalk my own staircases in the Year of the Crow. Visiting my own tenants, collecting my own rent. That will be the year Asian youth gangs lie down with the skinheads. That will be the year debit equals credit. Am I dreaming? Is this the language I am always dreaming and never write, except in my dreams? Is this why I talk so much in a conversation that never takes place, Mother, filling my mouth to the roofbeams?

Mr Singh's profits will not be as fat as he told me. But he has a good portfolio and it will grow better soon. He tells me be ready for another drive into the ruralside to interview and document more 'wives'. Meanwhile, Mother, he has smuggled in fourteen Sikhs via Mexico. His pipeline is flowing. The importing business is flowing. No tourist visa is needed for a refugee who can reach Canada and claim status of a persecuted person. Many such persons are building up in the files of Mr Singh and Mrs Scobie. 'Many shall be purified, and made white, and tried ... Blessed is he that waiteth, and cometh to the thousand three hundred and five and thirty days.' It is a golden chance for Canada, Mother, it is a golden chance for refugees. I would interpret their opportunities as my reward too. My day will dawn.

One hitch notwithstanding. I fear I may not have the chance to include boat people in my importing business. They are fading badly in the picture. I have had no persuasion with Mrs Irving to tempt some officials into releasing refugees from detention camp. 'Why, which ones, Aloysius?' I did not know which ones, but I hoped ones with savings. With gold dust in little cloth bags. With gold jewellery wrapped in sarongs. I have had Trudy spying for me, to estimate at school which boat kids' families might be assisted in bringing relatives here. 'No,' said Mrs Irving. 'I can't help you. I'm not sure I know any officials. I'm not sure I even approve ... though Hong Kong camps remind me of Matthew, imprisoned in the war there. Did you know that?'

... Evenings, you are inspired to stand amung orange blossums and rescite to

her the storys of Bombay, to lie abed mornings to wunder as you awaik, encased in
tin, how anyone born insidhe walls like these could realiz the magnitud of a city.
Who wuold approve of you're mariage?

I have still four pages to copy. I light another Pall Mall. 'Are you still hoping,' she asks, 'for video dating?' I confess I am. She jumps on this. It gives
her job spice to mock me, Mother. 'I can just see you,' she says. 'Mr Date.'
But it will work, I tell her, my scheme for video. My scheme is for mixing
and matching videos after students talk to my video camera about his or her
sex tastes. 'Afterward, Trudy, he or she comes back to look at a tape of him
or her ... and if everything is swank we make the parties a date. You do.'
'Who was your servant last year, Wishes?' 'Okay, but I pay you ...' Trinkets,
Mother, costume bracelets and such like she forgets to wear. The truth is
Trudy will do anything to be secretary of a landlord in waiting. She would
be my private secretary even for nothing, just to hear the *amportant* schemes
I hide up my sleeve.

I look up to see her washing my dishes and her mother's dishes from
breakfast and lunch. A bird is crocheted in a wall hanging, a lacy bordered
bird. *Ping.* I have a stab of tenderness over my bad loyalty to Trudy. I think
of Sid Vicious stabbing to death his girl friend Nancy Spungen. I tell her
she is losing weight. '... Kids are saying so.' This pleases her. 'Who?' she
asks. I say I heard Lloyd telling Andrew the other day. 'Lloyd? B.S.,
Wishes.' But she is flattered all the same. So I launch my invitation. Does
she wish to come with me to the David Bowie concert? Mother, I have some
interest in seeing this old-fashioned singer, because of trickle-down effects
he could have on Foreign Trade to scrub up their act. But the band has
turned down my invitation. My managing days are counting down with my
persuasion powers. 'How'd you get tickets?' asks Trudy. I tell her, 'Scalping
for a friend.' She is suspicious. 'What's the catch?' *'Comment?'* 'You usually
want me to do something if you take me somewhere.' I say I owe her a salary.
'But you'd rather go to the concert with Marcia or somebody, wouldn't you
Wishes?' I deny this most poisonously. 'Honestly?' Mother, I can see I have
an unexpected favour coming so I put on my thinking hat.

'Maybe one thing, Trudy, about Mrs Scobie you could ask her advice for
...' I go on a little about two or three male Guats, who seem good prospects
for family reunions. Trudy brings me another piece of apple pie. I butt out
my Pall Mall. We talk like a boss and secretary in a business bigger than us
both. She looks away from my eating and talking mouth. Mother, will I ever

remember to practise table manners? Dwight says I should go and live with 'Kev' and 'Slopes' in the park or else learn to talk with my mouth closed. I mean chew with it closed, except when I am talking. I mean ... you know what I mean, Mother. The bald truth is Reesa's new baby keeps me awake these nights and I am tired from slaving all afternoon at Safeway. My guardians are lucky I talk at all. I am tired pretending to them I care if I do NOT become a doctor. I put down my pie fork. I push Trudy's plate from me and she bears it to the sink. I carry on my story to the finish line, the story of a young man named 'You,' leaving his mother in Bombay and one season later leaving his dream girl, for a dice-up future.

If she was sirprised when you left, her face refuzed to betray it. She evun laghed. Squinting in to the sun made litle lines acros her brow. As you left, her hiar was loose and in her white nailed fingrs she held hihg a flowuer, without moveing it onse.

Smoke was riseing from the bare brancshes.

You fantasized. Sati.

But a pyre would be an inawespicius ending for so tenuous a mariage as yours.

Upwerds, into the Ghats, sat werkers like lumps in the swerling dust, chipping at rocks to make the road bed even. You drank from you're canteen, the crooked roade curled up, on to the hier plain.

Here I scribble THE END. I know Mr Blaylock will believe me to be the composer, Mother. He will overlook anything stolen by yours truly. He beams at me, handing back my stories with little comments he dips in water like a naked man in a hot tub. 'I love your point, Aloysius. A good push to the finish. Keep it up.' What a geek, Mother. I think if I wanted I could make Mr Blaylock wear black lip gloss and sprinkle sequins in his bald hair, stick a pin up his nose. He looks on me as his special project for aiding and abetting in a new country. I, A.I., know I can count on him for special favours and such like, favours he will not give boat kids who struggle with their tongues like oars. 'Well, Chan, it's easy for you to say ...' In class they are drowning in Mr Blaylock's wit at a cost to their confidence, Mother. I keep remembering *The Book of Daniel*, from my orphanage days: 'And many of them that sleep in the dust of the earth shall awake, some to everlasting life, and some to shame and everlasting contempt.' I challenge Blaylock to find *me* out instead, Mother. I challenge him to punish me if he dares.

Mother, should I recopy this story and not bother unsmoothing its spelling? Should I challenge Mr Blaylock to accuse me? I am lazy tonight. I have no muscle of principle left. I am tired and blowing in the wind. I wonder: If this is the road to a landlord's reward then where is the boundary? I wonder because I go on dreaming up myself a place in the world without any homesickness for shame. I wonder if shame matters, Mother. Trudy glances at my pages. 'What's the title of your crime, Wishes?' I tell her. 'Thirst.' It could be my own story, Mother, your son leaving Bombay, but it is not. It is just someone peddling his silly adventure in the ruralside. I have nothing against the ruralside once the city smooths it under pavement. My love is the city. In a hundred years this one will be darker with people from my continent, Mother, our continent. The landlord will restore my soul. He will make me to lie down in green pastures. He will lead me beside the still waters. Yea ... my cup runneth over ... 'My father,' Trudy confesses, not getting the direction of my patriotism, 'was alcoholic too.'

October, 1983

Daddy came home from prison this morning, almost in time for my birthday. I said my first word. 'Caw.' Surprised everybody except Daddy, who was surprised I was even walking. I am surprised he was surprised, after a year.

I notice he has trouble walking after sitting in jail so long. He is as skinny as the other refugees and he shakes. The only thing different is he has no appetite. And trouble talking, too. Mother says he's voiceless from reading to a monster.

Everybody else surprised by my Caw. She's a crow they said. My rate of development is remarkable. I am learning so much. I love camel-riding Uncle Damon. I like to walk. I am going to adore talking. I –

I really have come into my own.

This house though hurts my ears. Have to plug them to get a bite to eat. Nobody this morning seemed to notice Daddy – nobody in the kitchen, nobody in the grounds. Everybody is me me me, no matter what language we jabber. It really is a zoo around this place. Some days I like it here. How do we all manage to get along in one house?

Our family has two rooms in the basement. We're the lucky ones. Mother can't imagine sleeping in the dining room or the garage, though I wouldn't mind trying a tent outside like some of them. Infants scattered through the house cry all night. Not me. The staircase landing is a house with a sheet roof. They've even opened up the attic and crawled in there to sleep and nose through our boxes. Some of them cook up there, thinks Mother, and get away with it.

Cooking keeps the kitchen a hothouse all day, from the stove and oven going non-stop and from long line-ups to use both.

Mother says Daddy is going to take care of the garden come spring. For one thing the lawn is brown and croaking. It's been a dry fall and the sprinklers haven't worked for ages.

Chapter 16

Video Dates and Dirty Luv

… Mother, my listener, now I am the centre of it all, dizzy in the whirl. I am not in a pickle, I am the pickle, smack dead in the middle of having my dream snuffed, shut off stage before I earn one hit from free enterprise, before I even land on the charts. The dance is over on a sour note. My big crunch is coming. My secretary thinks I will be dust before spring passes to summer, along with itchy blossom pollen corking her nose. Trudy thinks I make her hay fever worse with stress, but forgets she has got very happy on me, high, lining me up on a flat mirror to snort like snow. Because of me, Mother, Trudy has gotten popular at school. Because of Mrs Scobie, too, starting last Christmas when Trudy went to live with her new guardian and learned to eat less and be aggressive. Glamour sticks to her person now like little sequins dropped from Michael Jackson's glove. My glove, Mother.

She worries over my court show, like I have betrayed her diet and slipped her a box of disgusting chocolates. I feel hay fever has clogged her looking on the shiny side of working as secretary to a legend. 'Make way for the legend and his sec!' rags Andrew in school corridors. 'Make way for the hamburger and his triple O!' She should not begrudge my temporary decay in the public eye, Mother, owing to my court case as Mr Singh's assistant. It is on account of Mr Singh I am decaying, yes, but why forget loyalty to an employer in this loopy Year of the Dog? Trudy should not. My boundaries shrink with my widening debts. The dog circles the pig. I get dizzy with pleasure at my own turpitude, and sad at my best cash flow drying up. Dwight waves his finger at me, since I could be heading for the hoosegow any day soon.

So I sober up and look at my life. Winding down, burning up. *Ping*. Maybe, if I do not go to jail first, I will find myself revolving back to the streets. If Foreign Trade rockers have gone to jail, and for a less serious crime than mine, what hope for A.I.? Raoul and Iggy set matches to a stage curtain in the community centre, but no one died, or even got smoke poison.

It was part of their act. I interpret it so. I am just lucky to look underage and not have my true age printed on the orphanage certificate I carried to Canada. Mother, what is my true age? What boundaries should I claim while I crunch up again to a little beggar boy? I am still hoping for expansion, capital, but maybe it would be better not to count on my chances so much after the trial of Mr Singh's importing activities. Winning the success of a landlord is now a random turkey shoot. The odds against me have grown into a short drink of water in the desert. I am toast. My lines of credit are shrivelled to zeros. My cash flow is doing an evaporation trick before my ears. This is the given, Mother. I am everyone I want to be, except landlord in the House of the Lord. I am in trouble to my neck.

Mother, I have residence in the present only. This week I moonwalk into court with *amportance*, a not so good mistake if I hope the judge will grant lenience. I have trouble walking down to earth. Reesa makes me wear one of Dwight's ties and take off my glove. Dwight locked my epaulette in his desk upstairs. I know which drawer, because I have gone through his locked drawers with my key. Those two give me special guidance at breakfast every morning, not to swagger so much in and out of court, yet it is Mr Singh who is sucking up coverage. I am just a minor, think the media. I fail to receive my fair coverage, and I wish I had not lost my glove and such like to the guidance of Reesa and Dwight. They worry over 'having some control' on how I govern myself in 'striking the right note'. It is not like I still look like a punk, Mother, mangling a guitar. You would be pleased how my glove and my body cause friends at school to rag me for being Michael Jackson's clone brother. I have traced my eyes darker and darker with liner. I have grown out my last spike of hair, and with it my purple tint. Now braided hair glistens with a kink curl falling down my brow. Bartlett's girlfriend has permed me from a fan photo, especially for my court appearance. For once I am on the same wavelength with Megan, who values me as her work of art. I look like I could be bankable, maybe not in the pop market, Mother, but in a watershed with a risky slope. I have unpunked myself. I have closed my rips. I have plucked my nose stud and my earring, but not my dimple, it is unpluckable. The judge needs punctuation like my dimple to see where to put a stop to her verdict. I read between her lines!

We are hoping for the best, Mother, a suspended sentence for me, or else no sentence owing to my youth. Teenagehood sucks in the pits, for certain, but it can also save a delinquent from adult laws. This is just, and every day in court I feel Mr Singh watching me with envy. On our first day the judge told me to tell the court where I came from, before I came from Canada. Iran, Mother. '... Escaping revolution, Your Honour, where small business in the jewellery market is smothered. The Ayatollah police made me shut down my family welfare.' The judge looked at me. I had no time to go on about Shits called She/ites dumping on half the people of my country, on women like you, Mother. The judge cut me short. Did I understand what perjury was? The court knew full well who I was, the legal adopted son of Mrs Marlene Irving, where I lived and who with, and where I used to live. Mrs Irving was in court, said the judge, so were her son and daughter-in-law. She asked if I needed my family pointed out, sitting the other side of the glass where Mr Singh, the defendant, sat in the prisoner's dock. I was ashamed enough in my humility for the trial to proceed again from the same question: Where had I come from, in the beginning? Again I failed the quiz opener. I said Turkey, Mother. I said Lebanon also. I could not help myself. I could not let this chance tick by, to tell the court an earful of facts on where I came from.

Nothing to lose. The dream of my own importing franchise, of tapping into Mr Singh's L.A. pipeline, any pipeline, is already broken. I am left without my dream. The judge is going to find Mr Singh guilty of making up sham marriages for East Indian men who cheated to come here. Even if Mr Singh is found innocent, for lack of proof, he would never keep me on his payroll after I testified my notebook is the record, yes, the smoking knife of his conversations concerning charges before the court. '... But, Your Honour, we have Aloysius Irving claiming all manner of falsehoods in his opening testimony. Why should we believe him now? It is simply outrageous my client should be subjected to the whims and tall tales of an underaged pipe-dreamer. Mr Singh has testified he never set eyes on this boy in his life ...'

That lawyer for Mr Singh, as I tell Trudy at Carrots, having our Pall Malls and coffee when the trial adjourns, is a Sikh without a turban who speaks Canadian middle stream. To me it is no surprise Mr Singh keeps hidden under his own turban and whisker net. He needs the judge's sympathy as a man fighting for his people and their chance of dignity in Canada. Racism, he told me last summer, is like a cod liver oil enema given out in cocoa cups by a farmer to his pickers. It loosens their bowels. It is the shits. But the prosecutor had a witness up his shirt: Jagdish Singh Randhawa. He is the man in the tent turban I forgot to remind my employer to *pay*, Mother, after Mr Singh had forgotten that afternoon, one year ago in Perumbur. Jagdish has never forgiven Mr Singh. He was willing to testify against Mr Singh also for his anger regarding Mr Singh's temple influence with fellow contractors against the Khalistan militants in Babar Khalsa. Jagdish belongs to them. He looked very rad in court, in his saffron tent. He identified me, Corbin Irving, as being with Mr Singh that first afternoon. He denied under cross-examination having any promise of money from Mr Singh, or even working for him. But he forgot my steno notes, Mother, so his duck also is cooking a little, while the judge deliberates her verdict on Mr Singh. 'Fool,' I comment to Trudy. Her answer? 'Don't sound so high and mighty, Wishes,' breathing through her mouth, clogged up with smoke and pollen dust. 'You're not out of the oven either.'

Dwight would agree with Trudy. My guardians, Mother, think I could go to jail. 'Without passing Go,' says Dwight. They just say this. I know they think the worst that can happen to an underaged landed immigrant, unknowing about Canada and its immigration laws, a boy tricked by an older man, is a warning from the judge. I overheard Dwight saying this to his mother on the phone. But I am not against jail, so long as it is no more than two weeks. I think I could sell many cigarettes and such like inside. Condoms and drugs. I am always open to new avenues. 'Don't be a fool,' Trudy tells me, wading through traffic now to our deserted classroom, where girls wait near our latest project for improving my cash flow. Tomorrow the judge passes judgement. The doorlock evidence has come from one of Mr Singh's sham wives, whose arranged phony marriage with her father's blessing has wrecked her chances of a love marriage. Her lawyer insisted. To me it sounded crazy, Mother. But Trudy says men in general are so arrogant she is learning from Mrs Scobie not to trust them. 'Your fairy godmother,' I tell her, 'sounds just the opposite to mine. Mrs Irving likes men.' After four days, Mother, this trial is all whirled up in my mind like temple tom toms. I learned in court a union organizer was beaten by henchmen he swears were Mr Singh's. This was not a charge and got disallowed as evidence by Her Honour. So why was such a man allowed in court? He was telling of approaches made by Mr Singh to female members of the Farmworkers' Union about importing husbands.

'No sweat, I am not even an accessory,' I tell Trudy, entering our homeroom. 'You're not even a Sikh,' she answers. 'He's still a nig nog,' says

Andrew. Trudy turns on him. 'What's it to you, Bonerack?' The once ugly Trudy, Mother, turning on the school's basketball star with tart sarcasm! 'Mercy, oh white goddess!' he begs. Laughter from the waiting girls. 'You got a cold, Trudy? You sound all choked up.' To have shown up here Andrew must be curious about honing his dating chances through my new scheme. But today I am interviewing only girls. If he wanted to, Andrew could talk his penthouse parents into buying him a girlfriend in about two seconds. They must have paid two thousand for the silver bracelet for his teeth. I see Marcia, Lloyd's girl friend, here also. Why? She phoned to ask and I told her truly it was under her interest. At least a dozen girls are crowded at my video camera, kibitzing, and I am set to interview six who are interested in meeting boys from another high school 'for the object of friendship and dating,' reads my brochure, thanks to Trudy's spelling. I cannot tell them which high school, Mother, because I have not approached one yet. My idea is still in its caterpillar stage owing to courtroom melodramas swallowing me up. The girls, Mother, total two pretty cheerleaders, a tall shy girl with black hair and a reputation for piano, and three others with attachment to coral lips and eye shadow. They giggle, wondering whether to trust a boy who looks younger than them. They are slow to pay Trudy the fee. With Andrew shoving in his needle's worth, the girls are hawing and humming whether to pull out of my cash cow idea. Andrew asks if my interviews are open to the public and I tell him no way José, not even to other girls, who will have to wait outside in the corridor.

I, director and producer, now give some public instruction in the noisy classroom. I have the camera loaded on its tripod all set to roll. Jessica, a redhead with green eyes, I charm with a compliment about the way she pronounces 'good'. 'What are you talking about?' she asks, flattered. I say, 'Just be sure to use that word when I ask a question. If I ask, "What are you good at?" you answer, "I am good at ..." and tell the camera what.' The other girls laugh nervously, Mother, wondering how to answer this question when I aim it at them. Jessica says, 'But I don't *know* what I'm good at! Am I supposed to just say what I'm good at, like that? Tina, what am I good at? Don't start the camera till I find out!' Tina, the other cheerleader, is a popular girl with piled on mascara and a Chinese father who manufactures denim clothes for the leisure market. 'Hickies!' she tells Jessica. Much laughter, especially from Andrew, wetting his lips.

Andrew is critical of my whole scene. 'It's gonna sound so phony, Irving.

Wouldn't surprise me if you lose your shirt.' He is eyeing Jessica's crossed legs and fishnet stockings. He is wondering, star basketball forward, why should Jessica, a cheerleader, be interested in out-of-school studs when he is trying his best on court to defeat these studs, yelled on by Jessica? I answer him, 'Don't pester me, Andrew.' The girls laugh. This pricks him, Mother, a little nig nog like A.I. dismissing him in front of girls. He pokes my briefcase with his Nike toe. 'Pig skin,' he says slowly. 'Pig skin.' He has no coolness for all his big stature, no clue yet about compromise in life. Directing, Mother, is management decisions and compromise. I wanted to shoot my interviews in the park, on the Pavilion's porch with a leafy backdropping. But girls like total privacy, so Trudy and I have had to set up in a corner of our homeroom after school, telling the principal Mr Sweet this is an after school Social Studies project. Trudy's backdrop of a white sheet from Mrs Scobie's, plus daffodils I tore this afternoon from a bed near the law courts, make up our set. Cluttered with daffodils on an interviewee's desk, Mother, but Trudy says it gives a sweet touch. 'Your sheet, Trudy?' asks Andrew, squinting up close. 'Hey, whose yellow stains, huh? The nig nog's? Just kidding, don't hit me!'

Andrew is jealous of my *amportance* in his country, Mother. With the media coverage of Mr Singh's trial, and my popularity in school, he thinks I have been the middle of too much attention since I came to King George. As a basketball star he is defeated when girls think I am sexy like M. Jackson. I am different, Mother, but not mumbling different like the boat kids, so girls listen to me. Even Marcia said if she and Lloyd were not steadies she would pay me twenty dollars for the chance of an out-of-school date, 'sort of prestigious like,' through my video camera. 'Hey, who'd date a ratbag like you, Marcia, except maybe Captain Lloyd?' rags Andrew. The other girls laugh, touching their hair. But Marcia does not smile, Mother, so maybe she and Lloyd are having a spat. This must be Andrew's hope. It is tournament time in the basketball world and girlfriends and boyfriends are fluxing. Kids from city high schools wet themselves for a wider social scene. This is the given, Mother.

Groans when I shoo them all out before taping my first interview. I say to them it depends on Jessica if anybody gets to watch her video afterwards, and she says, 'No way! He's probably going to ask me about my sex life!' I am. But not in so few words. I skirt her edges like a prowler with questions to get her talking, like 'What is your idea of the perfect date?' and 'What is a turnoff for you in a guy?' and 'What kind of stuff turns you on, besides cheerleading?' Trudy has helped me make up questions. Then I listen, the way Reesa listens on TV, leaning a little forward, interested in answers. 'It's so good, like, to feel the connection with the crowd ...' Jessica cheers for football, volleyball, basketball. She wanders on through the seasons, winding up three minutes later, trying to sound funny. 'I know you're out there, big guy.' With a silly wave at the camera.

'Great,' I tell her. 'Yeah,' calls Trudy, from the closed door she is guarding. Jessica picks off a daffodil petal. 'I felt a little cruddy, especially till I warmed up. I wasn't the real Jessica.' I ask her if she would like to see Jessica the Pretender played back on the classroom monitor. 'Not with those guys watching.' Trudy promises her they will not get in. Jessica regards Trudy with new respect. 'Okay. But do I get my twenty bucks back if I hate myself?' When she is watching herself sounding so eager I snap a colour photo with Mr Singh's Polaroid, to clip to her profile form, so my male clients, when I find some, can see if they want to read about her particulars and maybe screen her video, just like these girls will do with the boys' profiles.

Mother, my listener, video is still a gamble and I require income *now*. So I am burning for a big song to market, or a cashable lottery ticket, to rescue my landlording potential. Jaillir Water has gone no place. Very few dollars trickle in from my chain letter anymore. Concert income with Foreign Trade has vanished but not its debts. I owe Mary Yip so much money I can never pay her back unless she frees me to play the market again. 'Let A.I. be A.I.,' I wish to tell her. Even Mr Blaylock is losing his patience with me in class. Maybe I am losing more touch than gaining it, Mother, and I wonder, how can I put things together in the best way to find a key to better success? I still burn to be a landlord. If I cannot balance my assets and my arrears soon I will feel a big need to torch my life and start over.

I polish the lens of my rented camera on its metal tripod. My eye to the viewfinder again I practise pulling back on Jessica's face as she watches herself on screen. I tap the microphone on top, I make the tripod go up and down. The list says my next client is the tall musician, Suzanne. I wonder, and I will ask her, could she record some music for us? What we need, Mother, is romantic music in the background and I do not think a tape of Foreign Trade's last concert is the answer. Punk is dying. Dating needs music to flow like water. Like a slippery kiss with cascading notes ...

Later, when Trudy and I are caravaning camera and such like back to Dwight's house, up Haro under leafing trees, she wonders what is the difference between my sexual trafficking and the kind going on in Dwight's travel agency. I scold her a little and tell her Dwight is in it for the money. My secretary looks at me, Mother. 'That's so funny, Wishes, I forgot to laugh. Hardy, har.' I tell her with us money is second. Our project belongs with friendship and such like. Trudy smirks. Okay, I confess. I hope to make some cash flow also. So does Reesa. She loaned me rental funds for composing a videotape library. She thinks my idea is better than selling booze at school on the black market. At this Trudy rolls her head back to look up into the trees. If elephants could swim. 'Look,' I point, 'squirrel. In Bombay, would it last a day?' I muffle my delight, Mother, in seeing squirrels daily outside our house. The entrepreneur inside me sees squirrel profits if this rodent could be marketed the right way. I do not know what way. I would never eat it personally, but I think its nut diet would make squirrel a delicious dish, with the bushy tail given as a garnish.

I am carried away in my imagination. The truth is I have no ounce of killer blood. It is the reason my life lags and I lap it time and again without a victory. I run and get so thirsty for wherewithal, I forget money does not grow on trees or spring up from the ground. I have failed at crushed glass, shoe polishing, selling Bibles and such like. I have no flair for squirrels or even canaries. I light a Pall Mall. The porch swallows are back for another springtime, rebuilding their mud nest on a beam. Trudy makes a big show of sidestepping their droppings with a dainty tiptoe across our rotting boards. She says she is getting used to old houses since Mrs Scobie's house is worse than this one. I use my key. The oak door whines on its hinges and we pass in with our video burden.

Such passing may be my only passing this year, Mother, because Trudy thinks I am doomed to fail grade eleven. 'Blaylock has had it with you, Wishes.' Tired of my cheating and bad spelling, spelling like a disorder. I wonder to myself if Bartlett's suppertime tale about one of his patients could connect to me. *Her brain is so sidetracked she smells words like 'Bless you' when she hears traffic and tastes yellow when she watches TV.* Is this my disease, Mother, applied to a spelling disorder? I would like to meet her. Trudy thinks Reesa was wrong to tell me spelling has zero connection to how smart I am. She says if she had not told me this I might feel shame for once and learn to spell. Might feel shame for feeling smarter than the rest of them. Mother, can I help what I feel? I feel my ear at an angle from other ears. This is my disease in a nutshell. It makes me dream in fire.

2.

I can burn but not hear. I can dream but not spell. I can imitate Theresa but decide not to, when we enter the kitchen with our equipment, frightening the baby to tears. I am handed the baby to comfort, because Trudy must comfort Theresa. Theresa falls to pieces every visit Trudy makes, since Trudy helped get her this job through Mrs Scobie, and Theresa thinks Trudy will understand her homesickness for El Salvador. Theresa has zero horsepower, Mother, and a daily record of breaking down. She has been living here six months and grows more weepy, not less, caring for Reesa's baby and keeping house. But the baby's diapers are loaded. The house is a filth sty. Theresa knows all the ways to get fired without knowing. She knows nothing of cooking, and will not cut her moustache even when I offer Dwight's electric shaver. Theresa is a basket case without a handle. I am supposed to help her with house chores to earn my allowance. Allowance, Mother? It is hardly enough to cover my time in carrying our garbage cans to the alley.

I hold the baby with this cigarette in my mouth. Reesa has declared her house 'a smoke free zone', but I think Gwyn's diapers make a smell zone worse than my Pall Malls. I smoke them to smokescreen the diaper smell. Theresa weeps so much she never smells when the baby needs changing. A throw away plastic milk pouch lies sucked out on the kitchen table and used nipples need scrubbing. She is trying to cook again. 'I ask Bartlett dis morning what he want. He say notting, he doan want make me trouble.' Trudy holds her as she sobs. 'He say he doan dink he has time if I make pancake. I make him anyways.' By the mess in the sink, Mother, it looks like a bad video since dawn. 'Pancakes was all over floor. Baby cry all day. Reesa alway stay home till afternoon, except dis week. She go in court all day to see what happen wit him. I doan know what happen wit me. I got someting matter in my skin, like some rash. I ascared to touch baby.' Not A.I., Mother, patting dis baby's back. Trudy give me eye. I ascared puff smoke. Smell so bad I cough on poop. I so sick on baby whining it make me homesick for live in street.

Bee bee bee bee … Climbing the stairs I make baby noises to hushabye my youngest relative. What relative, Mother? A family raffle has happened to me since coming to Canada. I carry baby Gwyn down the hallway, *bee beeing* to her ear, but her lungs are leather loud. I fail to know how she can be related to her quiet Uncle Damon. Her nursery has a crib and a changing table where I place her down, flat. Is it allowed to stuff cottonballs in a baby's mouth? Suddenly she halts bawling and is squinting a little. I think she needs glasses. I cannot guess how a baby can cry so much and not make tears, a mystery of the baby species.

Listen, Mother, to the filthy diaper ripping apart in my fingers. Theresa has fits when she hears a tape tab ripping open on a Luv. She is afraid of poop. This is why Mr Luv packs in talcum powder, to confuse a mother's nose, except when the poop grows so big it lumps out like papaya. Then it is disposed in two folds and a tuck. Easy, Mother. I think a gold mine has happened in the diaper market, except a diaper war has happened also, and I would never try a corporate raid before I had marketed an easier target product like mashed apple pablum. *Bee bee bee* – OUCH! My finger, Mother, is caught in the pink plastic teeth of the Wet Ones tub, trying to fish out a fresh tissue to wipe off this baby's bum! The pain of this unfair stabbing! Baby Gwyn, frightened, opens up again. Crying babies, crying nannies, crying girlfriends of Bartlett's: my ears need a new script, Mother, this house is feeding me up to here.

'Oh, Aloysius, how sweet of you! How are you coping? Poor baby, has Aloysius got you now, lovkins?' That is what I need to hear, not all this crying, but do you think I hear it? From Reesa entering the nursery, dark hair bouncing, eyes alight? No, Mother, I hear nothing except crying. My finger pain is smarting very sharply. I get no appreciation for my messy work. I am alone, smearing everything the wrong way, ending up with soiled knuckles and a streaky bum, because I forget how to hold up her legs, by the ankles maybe, with the undabbing hand. The legs kick, the lungs squawk, it is not a picnic giving care to a baby. I wish Theresa had showed me better how to do it. When do I cream her bum with a smear of paste in the blue tin? Where is this tin? I am staring at a mess of waste and crankiness. The smell! Her female apparatus, Mother, looks stranger to me than her extra thumb stump. I need an extra hand. How tight should I pull the tabs to keep in the next evacuation? That is why I would like to be a landlord, Mother, less messy by a landslide.

I feel I am rehearsing badly for a future I never want. I carry her dirty Luv at arm's length to the bathroom for flushing. I flush and carry my hands to the faucets for washing. In the mirror I see I am wearing still Dwight's tie, from the courtroom, and on one of the yellow swirls is baby business. Poop, Mother. I untie the tie, noticing my naked shoulder. I decide to steal back my epaulette from my guardian's locked drawer, but then I remember baby Gwyn, lying on the changing table. She could roll off it to the nursery floor! I forget, Mother, at five months she has pushing power in her thighs. I rush back to catch her up in my arms before she has the idea to roll. But I need a pee. So I bring her back to the bathroom, unzipper myself with spare fingers, and pee very hard in the toilet bowl, bouncing Gwyn in my arm and staring at anchors in the wallpaper. When I look down, an obstacle to my pee is in full sight. The Luv, Mother, has not flushed. It is still in the toilet bowl, too big for flushing, now covered in pee. My whip is hanging out, dribbling a little, and the baby is burping up on my naked shoulder. I am not in a pickle, Mother, I am the pickle, because if I flush again I could gag the plumbing. I got a bad warning about plumbing last year, after my party. I am puzzled why Luv's will not make streamlined diapers. Is this a gift horse idea staring me in the mouth, Mother? Where is a soiled diaper to vanish if not down a sewer line?

I have a decision to make. Do I try another flush to see if her diaper disappears? Try another flush to get rid of my pee anyway? But if the Luv also vanishes when I flush, gets stuck, a flooded floor could drown the ceiling below. Mother, I have no choice. I must follow a conscience the Sisters of Hope drummed me to follow, to help the helpless. And this helpless baby is staring at me, struck dumb. I clutch her to my breast and bend over, Mother, into my own smelly pee and raise out her diaper with two fingers. What now? I turn, dripping on the tiles, the diaper and my loose whip unzippered. I see myself in the mirror, smothering a baby who is stoking up her lungs again. What is this scream of anguish I feel cutting my own throat? I hate baby caring responsibilities. It is a joke the landlord plays on us, Mother, not allowing us to flush our waste, to remind us of our dependence on him. I place the Luv in the sink then wrap it in a towel. I pick up the towel in my free hand. I bear both bundles down, towel and baby, to the kitchen thinking this time I have lost my ball bearings. Domestic chores have flushed away my last chance to become a landlord.

I have been saddled, Mother, pricked and jabbed like an animal to the doom of poverty. My networking has disappeared with Mr Singh. All right, yes, maybe I could still make videos of things left in my head to do, like recording Mrs Scobie's refugees for possible profit, in the basement of St. Sebastian's Church where she hides them, then sell these to Reesa's station for a series on *City, City*, but it feels too late now, even to introduce Mrs Irving to Mrs Scobie. I am across the hill. Yes, maybe I could organize a charity foundation with a nice salary, making love to pretty girls from Guatemala, speaking up for Salvadorans with drained faces and ripped memories. But I am across the hill.

'Wishes! You changed a diaper!' In the kitchen, Trudy has turned, is looking amazed at my soaking present in the towel ... But no, she is looking amazed at my unzipped whip. She turns away, annoyed, and I must carry the diaper myself to the can under the sink. Facing the sink I zip up before Theresa sees and reports me to Reesa as a baby molester. Trudy is listening to Theresa pour out her heart over bad fairnesses in the world. '... I doan got time all day for dust and diaper, Trudy. One time a day I have to stroller baby in park. Cooking I doan like. I rather wear my new dresses *home* ...' The baby in my arms is slowly hushed by her nanny's whine.

'Shall I make us supper?' Trudy asks. She sounds stuffed up again. 'You sit down and comfort Theresa.' I sit down beside Theresa and cover up her pudgy hand with my leftover hand. The baby cradled in my crick is reaching for the M. Jackson forelock dangling in my eyes. 'I suppose to heat up beef stew,' says Theresa. 'I can handle that,' answers Trudy. 'I'll bake some spuds and make a salad.' Theresa says, 'Spuds is in stew. Reesa make dem.' Trudy asks if Bartlett and Dwight are expected for supper. Theresa should remember this from directions Reesa gave her this morning, but she remembers nutting. 'I just warm up for whoever,' she says. Trudy nods, sniffling, her eyes runny from hay fever. She has found a tin of crushed tomatoes in the cupboard to add to the stew. She is watching me. 'You're being very nice to Theresa, Wishes.'

I take away my hand to tickle the baby. I tell her Theresa makes me remember. Theresa is like lots of girls who get got at by other people. Trudy fits the electric can opener over the tin. 'Well,' she answers, breathing through her mouth, 'maybe you could've thought of that before you helped marry off those poor girls in Perumbur.' She presses down on the handle and the buzzing goes round in a little circle, carrying Theresa's eyes for a ride. I notice my secretary is wearing the bracelets I gave her. She unclips the tin and the lid sticks to the magnet. 'And who's supposedly getting at Theresa, Wishes? Reesa isn't using her, she and Dwight are helping her ...

like they're helping you, Wishes, giving you a place to live. Theresa is lucky. You both are.'

I tell her I could help Theresa more. I know what being an uproot is like. Helping people is the kind of thing Bruce Springsteen would do. When you get big enough you can afford to help people. This is why I wish to make a million dollars. 'You, Wishes, are on a power trip. But sometimes you're nice.' She studies me and Gwyn. '...Like now, I guess.' When I tell Trudy I am everyone I want to be she rolls her eyes. 'Listen, Wishes, you never told the judge what Mr Singh paid you two hundred dollars a day to *do*, when she asked you in court. You didn't help Sikhs beat up people, did you?' Murder and pillage, I answer. Just to see my picture on some wanted posters. She dumps the crushed tomatoes into the stew pot. 'You just want to be more famous than that asshole Andrew. Listen, do something useful and carry your camera some place safer. And scrub those sticky nipples for Theresa.' My secretary is teaching me aggression, Mother.

3.

Mother, my listener, what is the given? In my heart I will always live in the street, because that is where I have a better chance of dreaming what the House of the Lord looks like without the landlord. I owe so much, I will be back in the street quickly if the market drops me into bankruptcy. But a family cradles me. Socialism is their motive. This is why I want to be in an ownership position some day, not owing gratitude day and night. Teenage-hood sucks in the pits. I have had a dream, Mother. I would interpret it as acting my age, except I look younger instead of older. I know I am older but if I tell the judge she will have a different take on my treason and send me away for a long spell. Spell, Mother, an accidental joke. No sentence would be harder for A.I. than a long spell, writing lines in prison for a lifetime. Dwight knows I am the age he thinks I am, and he chuckles. He calls me two-faced, like Gilbert and Sullivan. Reesa tells Dwight he should know: '... You're the wandering minstrel ad noz.'

I think she means something, she sounds sarcastic. I know Dwight's kingdom is dividing, from the worry whispers I overhear at their bedroom door. But Dwight is a hoofer, even fat and heavy now, like a caribou on our quarter dollar. He thinks I am amazing, carrying on my businesses and not perishing in school. He sings in his deeper than normal voice: '*When I was a*

*lad I served a term / As office boy to an attorney's firm / I cleaned the windows
and swept the floors / And polished up the handle of the big front door …'* Then
some speedy repetition, Mother, before more heavy prancing. 'That's his
party piece,' Reesa told us, when Dwight's mother took us to lunch the first
day of my trial, and everybody was so nice to me, including Mrs Irving, over
my birth claims and such like on the stand. Dwight was dancing in the aisle
of this Spanish grill near the court house. 'Dwight was a star at college in
Pinafore and *Mikado*,' Reesa said. 'He's never recovered.' *'I grew so rich that I
was sent / By a pocket borough into Parliament …'*

'Oh, Dwight, dear, dry up, would you?' his mother told him. 'I want to
hear more about what Aloysius says he and Trudy are doing to help this Mrs
Scobie, Trudy's guardian … She's such an interesting-sounding woman I'd
love to meet her. What parish did you say she's with, dear?' She was showing
me patience, Mother, to help me start my rehabilitation. 'I want to hear all
about your refugees – and then I have to run, I'm late for Save the Children
…' On our walk back into court, Dwight told me if I played my cards right
and took in mass on Sundays, his mother would buy me a Toyota franchise.
He was being sarcastic. I know from inspecting Dwight's desk, Mother, he is
having cash flow problems at his tourist business and his own mother
refuses to assist him. I think he is jealous of me.

I look at this rented house of Dwight's. Living in it is like living on a
movie set. *Ping*. One day soon it will burn down, then where will I be? If our
landlord decides to profit from greed and hire an arsonist, where will I be? I
think I could be happy in the street again, directing my own entrances and
exits. From inside, these rooms are all just air and sky anyway. We can be
dumped on any time by our landlord. From outside, Mother, his windows
and doorways look real. I would feel more comfortable outside. I could
dream into my viewfinder without always having reminders from teachers
and creditors about spelling and debt. In the real film of life, babies would
never need changing, waterpipes never choke and burst, basements would
not clog up with broken glass.

Trudy and I are sitting in the living room, smoking. 'You won't even
cover the cost of your videotapes, Wishes, if more kids don't start showing
up with twenty dollars apiece …' She does not breathe the smoke down
inside her, but streams it instead at the old-fashioned cornices. She sounds
hoarse. I confess to her, Mother, I will soon have to declare bankruptcy if my
outgo and my income do not start to enjoy some repair. I will have to change

my whole attitude. Money is harder to keep here than in Bombay. The over-head here is high noon. I bounce the camera a little on the cushion, along-side my leg. I have had a dream but the law of the marketplace is catching up with it. 'You may have to go to jail, Wishes. After tomorrow. Have you thought about that?'

I look at her, past her watery eyes and nose, to notice her figure. Rad, I answer. Dreaming the wrong way so long, I forget to look and see the real reason for Trudy's new popularity. She has lost so much fat she is now almost a skinny binny, with teeth fixed up to make her smile pretty. The moles on her face and neck look like beauty dabs. I have treated Trudy poorly, Mother, this is a given. My bracelets were plastic. I think sometimes I should change our business dealings and start over. I tell her I may choose to announce bankruptcy. She stares at me. 'So you said.' I blow smoke that joins her smoke pressing the ceiling for some paint to kiss and blister. I tell her I could turn a new leaf and start making Vancouver listen to my ideas. No one wants to listen, I tell her, including Dwight. I ask her, how do you get business people to listen? Wear a T-shirt like Bruce Springsteen? 'Well, Wishes, maybe you should take off all your clothes instead.' I listen in a little state of shock. To be naked in public I know about from Bombay. I wonder if she means so much? I feel a tinglement. Mrs Scobie has been teaching Trudy from the heart, Mother, that breaking the law for a higher law is like obeying the simple law of the soul. It lets her hide refugees in a church base-ment.

I wonder how long the doodads and carvings are going to last before Dwight's landlord comes along to give us notice of peeling the ceiling off our heads. I am still at Safeway, Mother, dribbling away at debts with not a drop of cash flow. Why do I work for nothing? Why not stop work cold tur-key? I need more time to listen to the pop charts and read. I need more space for meditation purposes. I need more ... Listen, Mother, I have no more patience for the demand and supply of a city that fails to make me *ampor-tant*. It is nobody's fault. I still believe in the free market, yes, even when it fails me. But why work for peanuts? I will never get on TV working at Safe-way. I will never be a landlord. I light another Pall Mall. Trudy sniffles. The chandelier turns a little in the March draft. In like a lamb, Mother, round like a lamb. I can hear baby Gwyn beginning to blubber upstairs. I can hear Theresa too. 'I doan care. I doan like my life any more in dis house.' Waiting for her charge to fall asleep from hunger.

4.

I am saved from jail, Mother. This morning I heard, we heard, the verdict from the judge who was wearing her hair downside up and glasses on her nose. The judge talked about me, a callowness led wrong by Mr Singh, Mother, as if I was not happy to be led off like a goat. 'Mr Singh,' she read out in court, 'who profited from the avails of loveless and illegal marriage contracts, got rich while flouting the laws of his adopted country, and flew in the face of his oath by committing perjury.' She sentenced him to no more than three years in prison, and fined him, Mother, two hundred and fifty thousand dollars. As a contractor and entrepreneur, she declared, the court knew Mr Singh could afford this sum because of its access to his bank vault.

Alas, the *Sun* has failed to put me in its write-up again, where Mr Singh has his picture for the fifth or sixth time. I am under age they think. I should tell them, even if it means a sentence. But I am supposed to feel a little panic, owing to my close call with what Dwight says is my misspelled life. I am told to make a new leaf of myself at school, and my guardian wonders what boundaries I should have, once I shed my Michael Jackson epaulette and eyeliner. I wonder this too. I could become a Toyota salesman or a retirement franchiser in the pension market. Or I could just listen to the pop charts and read one of Reesa's books. Dwight wants me to forget land-lording dreams and channel into doctoring and such like at school. I wonder, Mother. I wonder if Michael Jackson would feel p.o.'ed if he heard I had ripped him off then put him down the toilet like a Luv.

Born today. What else can I say? Strange sensation, very strong sensation. How far to trust it? Have given this some thought and decided truth doesn't need to be demonstrable, just convincing. So I will describe it.

Sensation a smooth white pressure on my forehead. A loud bright entanglement. Quite pleasant, on the whole. A taste in the mouth of light. Everything else blank. Blankness is part of the sensation.

This doesn't sound very convincing. Isn't even coherent. So what should I do with the sensation, which as I say is strong? Try to remember it more coherently? My sense of the future would appear to be getting in the way.

Better forget about trying to sound convincing. I have no record, no video, no photograph taken at the moment of Daddy's first seeing me, to verify the possibility of the sensation.

Wait though. I was born. That is demonstrable. The question is whether the sensation I claim to have felt a few hours ago at birth can possibly be credited. Everything else surrounding my birth has already faded from memory.

The sensation, instead of growing indistinct, has remained quite constant, given my inclination to forget. My forehead still yearns for a sheet, a hand, *something* to rest against in this sudden vacuum.

Chapter 17

The Boss

THIS MORNING, MOTHER, the traffic woke me and I saw the spider eating the fly. This is the given, dog eat dog, what is my body doing in a stinking tent when my soul is having a shower bath? I beseech the monsoon to come. I beseech you, Mother, make it rain from your place in the sky! I unzippered my body bag to go outside and print a new number for Day 38 of my hunger strike. The tide in English Bay looked low, the blue waterslide sat high and sloping on seaweedy logs. I printed 8 with a black felt and taped it over the 7. Trudy asks why do I not reuse my numbers and save foolscap, and my answer is hunger stops me remembering little things. She had a hardy har at that. She thought I could do better than feeding her the same line I give interviewers. I gave her back a hardy har and also a private caress. The bottom line, Mother, is to remember plastic bags for my protest signs when the rain comes. I am looking forward to the rain. I listen to rock hits on a transistor, I read about expectations of Pip from Reesa. I feel very sorry for those days I was such a greed merchant.

Now I am a landlord, Mother, without a house. My Pathfinder can sleep two and a half, the entrance has a protective storm eve, the poles are shock corded. This is the given. The rainfly is heat reflective to keep the dweller cool inside. So why have I been using it as a pillow? Stupid. Ever since August 10, too busy protesting, I have missed the chance of making my dwelling better, notwithstanding any thought of soapscrubbing the walls to get rid of stink the skunks leave, circling me every night for garbage. Overripe fruit, greasy fry cartons, scraps. This corner park is a stopover oasis for them sneaking out of the real park, past the hotel, and they make me pay the cost of my hunger strike, the cost of cheating on it. Pests. I allow myself fruit juice in public, yes, to stop me shrivelling up in my fast. Trudy smuggles in food after dusk. Then we have our private time, underneath the noses of hookers and johns. Mother, I am already thin and have no wish to die from malnourishment.

I have a little picket fence of signs and a trip wire linking them to keep out skunks. END SEX JUNCKETS TO FILLIPINES. BOYCOTT TRAVELL AGUNCYS. And such like. This morning I printed a new sign. WAR IS PUTRED. I am in some risk of coming over like a Bible nut, so I made a decision to say which war out of a choice in the morning *Province*: Iran, Afghanistan, Angola ... END WAR IN BERMA. I am also protesting safaris in Africa, remembering Bartlett's silly holiday last winter in a tent. RICH TOURESTS STAY HOME AND GIV YOU'RE MONEY TO REFUGEES. Signs are *amportant* for liberation, Mother, mine and a million others. FORGIVE THE SIC NOT THE SHYSTURS. What end they will have is anybody's guess between a rock and a packed place.

Excuse me, Mother, another interviewer on the way, hunting for parking, his TV station in bright blue letters on his van. Reesa's letters. A chance he is only here to shoot hookers on Davie, or Shame the Johners, waving signs and chanting at the girls to beat it from their neighbourhood. Mother, I, A.I., started this campaign with my protest against sex junkets. I accidentally brought home a nearby problem of girls being used like you were, badly, by johns touring past them in a vehicular manner, smooth cars rolling in like skunks. I can tell you nothing pleases Huguette less than these protests of her customers, but she has not associated me to them, and still likes to hear me vituperate sex junkets abroad by rich tourists. 'Keep them home, sure.' She disagrees johns are a bunch of stinkers as Trudy thinks. 'I bet her slogan,' says Trudy, 'is "You Get More With Huguette".' I will tell you how I pleasure myself with Huguette in a minute, Mother, but it is not how Trudy thinks.

Trudy is truly for the movement to shame the johns: whether the local pickers-up of hookers like Huguette and Tracy, or travel agent customers on charter to Manila and Bangkok. I have also targeted the pimps in this, travel agents like Dwight, but without naming them. In my interviews I give out statistics Trudy has shovelled up. I imagine them sometimes, if I need an exact quote. I describe what happens on winter vacations south. I say, 'Spurn travel agencies like wine bottles from Chile.' If people want to travel, Mother, they should travel without the guiding help from pimps like Dwight. I have protest signs against mail-order brides also. I am united against injustice and Trudy helps my total package. A newspaper article said I date my conversion, 'from the world of free enterprise to the business of a free world,' since my first meeting with Mrs Scobie, the lady who hides refugees from Guatemala and El Salvador. I like that quote. I like it when I can make my interviews moonwalk in dream language, notwithstanding a) I am off Michael Jackson in any echo of walking or looks, and b) I did not say this, the interviewer put it kindly in my mouth. That is what interviewers do, Mother, sometimes to the good. I am sorry I mentioned St. Sebastian's. Trudy tells me they did not know Mrs Scobie's guests in their basement were illegals.

Mother, I have ripened a lot to see that Bruce Springsteen is where the truth is at, not M. Jackson, who is cute like me, admitted, but what is he interested in except buying bones of the Elephant Man for a million plus dollars? Who wants to be a freak freak? Michael is sexless, a slippery banana peel without a banana. I learn he had skin lifts and a relining of his face organs to mirror the smoothness of his moonwalking feet. But where does he *get* to, Mother, what does his music ever sound *P.O.ed* about? He is like a bank manager in his smoothness, minus pinstripes. Springsteen is nearer to Foreign Trade, before FT went to jail. Jerky and punkish, a straight aimer of his banana you could say. Fans respect the Boss. He is on the underside all the time of dogs in trouble. The Boss is the kind of landlord who would spit on a name like Daniel or Aloysius. Or Michael, Mother. He picked Bruce to sound like Bruise, I bet, except his parents picked it and he never changed it. Why change the given, unless an orphanage does it to you? The Boss would never dream of getting a face job. If you think of him singing in a bar then his name, Springsteen, is like the name of a beer made from good cold water. I would like to bottle water like his for export and call it Boss. He is what Canada needs, Mother, to be a better force in the world. We have the best water in the world, and no one to export it for our recognition. This is the given. The pop world is a better school for rethinking destiny. I use the Boss to leave my mark like an underdog.

My first interviewer had hair to her hips, thin lips, and a tooth gap the wideness of a pencil. That lady alone made me *amportant* for people like Mrs Scobie, eating supper in front of the News Hour. Why should somebody want to go on hunger strike? 'Homesick,' I told this reporter in my Boss T-shirt, Mother, these jeans. For the first time in my life I had beard stubble. 'I used to live on street in Calcutta. I love Vancouver. But I never forget my home town. Bruce Springsteen, when he sings "My Hometown", is singing to us in all our home towns. He stands up for what he personally believes ...' When my interviewer asked what *I* believed I said 'protest'. She vaulted her eyebrow. Then I said travel, I was against travel for exploiting purposes. I gave her some colour commentary about bicycling and thieves who sold me to a man who liked boys. I asked Trudy if the News Hour ever used my bicycle story. 'Nope.' '... Or what I said about reincarnation? You know, how citizens wish to come back as other people, like CEOs?' Trudy frowned. 'Translation?' 'Chief executive officers? Landlords? ...' No, she answered, that must have got chopped too. I get reincarnation from Huguette, Mother, who is interested in such like.

In the afternoon, when I am listening to Duran Duran or Boomtown Rats, sometimes Huguette will come by my tent for a snuggle talk. Hookers like Huguette or plump Tracy tempt me to lick their Swensen's cones, but I keep my fast unbroken for public consumption. Cinnamon raisin. Christ the landlord, cappuccino. I pretend I can hardly stand their ragging, and I hardly can. They idle down Davie to the bay when their johns are holing out at jobs. Huguette talks of *yin* and *yang*, what she calls the give and take of her own job, any job. She has had others so she knows, Mother, cashiering at the conservatory, taxi driving. 'There's positives and negatives to them all,' she will say with a lick. She is older than most hookers. 'I do Zen when I'm sacked out with a john. You have to sometimes, not to barf. Making you hungry, bub, licking my cone?' I bet she calls every john, every man, bub. 'I concentrate,' she says, 'on the Tantric symbol of the *yab yum* and meditate. The interpenetration of all existence.' Huguette thinks me sweet, Mother, but keeps a little space between herself and my tent, because of how it smells from skunk spray and such like, laughing, because the perfume she wears, Rose Something, heavy as a billy club, is manufactured from animal glands like the skunk's. 'What goes around comes around,' she says.

She wonders deep down what I am doing to myself. I am tanning my Adam's apple, lying near the rose bed, under a blue sky. She glances at Reesa's novel. 'You could do with a better guidebook than that one.' She has licked a divot in her cinnamon raisin cone. 'Only if you're really enlightened, bub, are you going to remember your previous lives. The best most of us can remember is a few déjà vus along the way.' She starts at her cone from the other end now, scratching her bra. 'All it comes down in the end to is sag. Who needs bonesetters anymore? Meditation isn't like thinking. It's just concentrating till you're still and emptied out. Calm inside like a seashell. I try to be resigned to what is.' Huguette has a fantastic pair of bubbers, Mother, this is what she calls them, sagging southward now.

'... Don't listen to me, bub. I think you've done the bright thing, giving up accumulation. The more you desire the more you've got to lose. Now you've got time for meditation. Too much maybe.' Mother, maybe my foreordination was always to be a street person like Huguette, burning with the need to be calm.

I meditate on her and the Boss. The nights go by. I fill my tent like a lung with smoke, Pall Malling my Pathfinder to smoke out the skunk odour in my nylon walls. My other visitors, not counting Trudy, are Dwight and Reesa. They came in August, squatting down in front of my flap, pretending not to hold their noses. Dwight had Gwyn in a packrack. I was listening to Wham! and thinking this is interpenetration, their visit and such like, Gwyn reminding me of bad diaper smells. '... Your debt load is massive!' Dwight was saying outside my flap. 'How are we supposed to pay off a stock market fiasco? We didn't know you were talking to *brokers*, Aloysius. We have debts ourselves. Does that make sense to you?' He did not sound angry, Mother, just very pumped up talking to a rad protester in a tent. 'What's with you anyhow, son? We saw you on TV telling more whoppers, about coming from some Gulf state. And what's all this about sex tours and travel agents? Am I supposed to be one of your *targets*?' He pointed at my signs. Gwyn pointed too. Reesa asked, 'Are you hungry, Aloysius?'

What did she think, Day 8, that I was lying down on my sleeping bag to keep up strength in my funny bone? I had to make it look good, Mother, so I took a sip of apple juice. I sucked in my cheeks to hollow them out. 'Can we bring you something, Aloysius? You can talk to us, we're your guardians. You wouldn't want us to ask the police to bring you home. We could, you know, make you see a doctor if you don't start taking care of yourself.' 'If the city doesn't clear him out first,' said Dwight, staring at my little patch of park. He looked like he thought I had turned the lawn brown myself. He and Reesa feared my hunger strike, Mother, the way people feared my tea cosies I got Foreign Trade for codpieces once. It spellbound and disgusted them. But it got their heed. I am like a rock star full of moodiness.

After their second visit, Dwight stopped coming. I told them what people like Theresa with no country and no family meant to me, A.I., compared to what *they* meant. They said I sounded ungrateful. '... Pew, what smells?' asked Dwight. I told them Mrs Scobie's example was better than Mr Singh's example, meaning if you break the law to help refugees, be naked when you break it, so you cannot stash money in your pockets. 'But you're not fooling anybody,' said Dwight. 'The real reason you're out here in a T-shirt is because you're bankrupt.' Reesa tried to referee. 'But he *was* carrying his debt without bothering us about it, sweetheart. All that time he was working at Safeway? And the golf course?' Dwight nodded. 'Uh huh. Then he quit. Put his last dollar in a tent, which you and I approach on our knees, I notice, why? He won't come outside for us, the way he will for every Brownie with a camera.' There was nothing more I could tell them, Mother. I smiled my best bony smile. 'You won't, will you, Wishes?' said Reesa. Total my health she meant. 'You still look not too bad. I'll ask Bartlett to drop by.' Through the mosquito mesh I watched them go off, shaking their heads. Then I peeled open a Coffee Crisp and ate it, Mother, watching them disappear up the street past the Sylvia. Where things now stood between me and the middle class was nowhere, I could see, minus barbwire. This is the given now. We all used to live in the Promised Land.

2.

I watch the TV man shoulder his camera and point this way. Rad. Before I crawl outside, Mother, halting a little to show my weakness, I look out my other window to make certain that pest woman is not around. She parades herself into my interviews on purpose, hoping to squeeze publicity for herself. We all believe she is eighty-seven, why does she think we do not believe her? The day Lloyd came by with Marcia she was here, asking me questions and exercising her neck, watching to see who was watching, before Andrew showed up to rag her. 'You look ninety, Gloria!' he called. 'How old *are* you, really?' Andrew's tooth brace is gone and he looks older himself, almost datable. She wandered off, across Beach Avenue, to talk to a hooker on a bathhouse bench. She tells everyone she has no reason to think of popping off, no home for God to call her back to. Huguette would love to debate this with her over ice cream and *yab yumming*. I have no home either, Mother, I shed it to become a refugee.

I say as much to this interviewer with balding hair and a Hawaii shirt. I, A.I., am everyone I want to be. He is sweating a little on the lip from the soupy air. Boy George is singing in my tent. I go on talking in the salty afternoon. '... Landlord changed in my country. Boom. Boom. Shells knocked down some walls of my village, my family lay buried when I came up from hiding in a well. I took with me a little water in a goat bladder. I was walking to Jalalabad. But instead some mujahedeen found me and took me higher in the mountains. They made me carry a big belt like this of bullets over my shoulder. Very cold in the mountains. My toes froze ... here, you can see some bad bunions in my foot ... I - I - I - I - I - I - I ...' I add this wail of hurt, Mother, to sound like a mullah. He stares at my foot. I do not know where the camera is aiming, but I smile a little to exercise my dimple and show I am forbearing pain.

'But where did you learn English?' *He* would rather throw curve balls, knowing his station has interviewed me before. He will remember I told another Afghan story to a rival station, not forgetting a Tibetan story, about when I escaped to a refugee school in Mussoorie. This is why he would rather throw me curve balls. Entertainment happens when the audience knows something they think the victim fails to know. I think my interviewer is supposed to be interviewing bikinis on the beach, to show his viewers this torrid September inside sweaty cleavages. To know for sure if he has tape running in his camera, I would have to peek inside. I could be the victim of a rag.

I wait every day for Trudy to come after school with junk food and apples, another Coffee Crisp, raisins for my energy level. To keep me alert, Mother, but not rad alert to stop me looking unwrecked by fasting, sipping nothing but fruit juice and resting in my tent to keep up pep. I keep a plastic garbage bag outside to toss in juice boxes for public show. Inside, I hide candy wrappers and such like in my pewter vase, till Trudy deposits them in her purse with hamburger wrappers, to carry away these snow job clues when she leaves. This afternoon I am listening to Dire Straits on the radio. The heavy air is a sweat bath. I swim every day in the bay and when the weather turns cold I will wash at a bathhouse sink. I dump in the bathhouse, where I am not supposed to dump because of my food strike, just pee, but how would the media find out if I go one or two in a private cubicle? Some-times, Mother, I need to be yabbed and yummed, so I take soap and carry my toothbrush in a towel. The gays, sitting on metal railings with their backs to the sea, are interested in this *amportant* hunger striker. They look at me like I am a doughnut. 'Or so you think,' Trudy will say. 'Not everybody's as hungry as you, Wishes.' Dwight is.

Trudy Macdonald is. I have this big confession, Mother, notwithstand-ing it is my secret history. I told you a bathroom secret, so now I will tell you a sex secret. When I took up Mrs Scobie's own custom of breaking the law to help less fortunates, and not myself alone, a naked liberation between Trudy and me just happened. What can I tell you further? I think when I was like Michael Jackson, the girls were more occupied by me than I was occupied by them. I treated them like mirrors. But now when I am closer to Bruce Springsteen I feel free to be a man. If I allowed myself to be rotten, Mother, I would easily resemble a Sex Pistol. Trudy likes to sleep with me in my sleeping bag, girdled by signs outside us like END HUNGER ALOW FREE FLOE OF IMIGRATION, because this is what Mrs Scobie teaches her is sexy. Trudy is like a groupie who comes across for Springsteen because Springsteen sings benefit concerts for out-of-work coal miners. Her weight watching is paying dividends. I taste her breasts, Mother, I blow air across her beauty marks. I wash her body with my tongue. I make her triangle of hair my campsite. This is the given. Another given is her voice. Dieting has made it lower, sweeter. I know she is more popular now at school than Marcia. She has new *amportance*. Her looks are changed and kids with no memories cannot remember her fat. They look at her like they look at a video game in 7 Eleven, to see what Trudy Macdonald's next bounce will be. *Ping*. She is outspoken and had her picture in the newspaper with A.I. as a social fighter.

I miss her when she flies too soon at night from my tent. We are like two glued together moths, hidden from the sex market and restaurants on Altamira. I keep my flaps tied and mosquito door zippered at our bare naked feet. I think a body like mine, so much in the camera eye, Mother, manufactures juices for export. Trudy's, too, makes me thirsty like mine makes her. She is why I spray with rose scent, to kill the skunk stink, to keep her here all night. But I cannot keep her, Mother. I hold aerosol cans till they rattle a last breath and die in my palm. I spray from inside, the skunks spray from outside, it is like I am landlord over park and city in one tent of interpenetrating odours.

Every day I wait for my secretary and girlfriend to come from school. School I would never go back to, even if some people like Reesa think I should for my future. My future is what I am having right now, Mother. Trudy told me one day she overheard school kids planning to come past just to look at my tent! 'Grade ten groupies, Wishes.' Is this not success, Mother? Grade ten groupies and up? Success is being my own landlord, taking off my clothes and walking naked in the truth. Truth is all around and we hardly see it, Mother. This morning, dialling for some music, I happened on Dwight and ended up hovering over his radio talk like a seagull, wondering where to land to gobble down a worm. Where he was saying he had travelled, Mother, magnetized me to his lies. I will ask Trudy to question his columns also. Why did I never know he talked like that, when he gave out tips and such like? How long has he pretended to be a traveller when he is secretly at home selling sex tours?

Mother, I wish to service the truth the way I service Trudy, with naked-ness. And I have this opportunity more and more. She says I am lucky I found Canada, where the media are so hungry I can become an item just by sleeping outside. 'Not like Bombay,' she says. 'You wouldn't get famous in Bombay for sleeping on the *sidewalk*. Would you, Wishes? Sweetheart?' Sometimes she sounds sarcastic, Mother, ragging me like this. I think she is still jealous of Huguette.

No, I would rather be sleeping in Stanley Park, hidden, not in this public trapezoid with four hawthorn trees. I do it here as my duty. The naked forest would give me oxygen, blot out these hot smells of souvlaki and suntan grease. I put up with drivers on Beach Avenue, tooting and such like, leaving behind fumes and popcorn. They have seen me protesting on TV, hungry. I discover protesting is like rock singing, saddled with aggravation. But I am glad to be liberating myself from vanity. Not like Dwight. His bird is frying. I have walked out on my own debts and vain ambitions to become naked again in the world. A T-shirt and jeans are my total costume. This is the given, Mother, living every day like my last, when city workers will arrive and pick my tent like a mushroom from its root. That is why I protest, like the Boss, to keep my hometown from vanishment.

When Bartlett came by he sat looking at the bay. Over there, he pointed, the Englesea Lodge used to stand before the city tore it down and grassed it over. I looked. You would never guess, Mother, a building was ever there. I hardly remember it, smouldering. Bartlett said his father told him a pier used to stand here also, sticking out to Asia. But it is toast too. Bartlett studied my little grass patch. He wondered if I had trouble sleeping, due to screeching rodents and such like. I told him crows are a big racket in the afternoons. How they rag me, Mother! And I told him sometimes, meditating, I can feel binoculars in the apartment towers looking down at my mushroom on a postage stamp, this tent on the parched lawn. I have an empty feeling these watchers would like to mail me on a raft out to sea.

3.

Trudy is clouded over in negative ions this afternoon, foreshadowing bad weather to come. Am I dreaming this, Mother? The crows are in a bad mood too. She will not take off her clothes to lie down with me, so we sit on the floor with the tent flaps up, fanning ourselves with playing cards. Playing cards! Robber is what Trudy plays with Mrs Scobie. The hot air is making the spider hang very still to digest the fly's bones. I am chewing what Trudy has brought me as a treat, an apple turnover, and a wish from Mrs Scobie. '... She wants me to give you up, Wishes. She says it breaks her heart to see me giving myself to useless grandstanding. "He's not helping to house one refugee," she says. So what am I supposed to tell her, Wishes? She hates me coming home late. And I owe her loyalty for taking me in.' I do not believe Trudy's fairy godmother would say this about me, Mother. Mrs Scobie supports my hunger vigil with her whole heart. I thought I was making impressions on her, like someone making sacrifices for injustice after being a foolish lounger for so long.

I pretend not to hear Trudy's question, and touch her cheek with my fingers to wipe away a sweat bead. I tell her I get no vibes in card-playing, compared to love-making, but if she commands me I will play Robber till the cows go home. Then I will ask her to do a job as my secretary. 'So what's the job?' She fans herself with a Queen. Notwithstanding sex tours, I tell her, Dwight is lying in public about his travels. I tell her this morning on radio he was saying he was in Jakarta and Kampala last month. I ask Trudy to uncover his newspaper column and read what it says. I think it could be saying Argentina and the Netherlands. Mother, my hope is to be a centre of Reuter facts. And I am thinking of a sign that would stop traffic in its skids: HARODUTUS TOURS TRAVELL OUWNER LIES ABOUT TRAVELL. This would illustrate to Mrs Scobie I am uncorrupted by friends and have given up the past. If she only knew, Warrick stopped past this morning to say if I was getting hungry I could have back my Safeway job. People like Warrick, Mother, just ignore watersheds in a life and will never twig. I wipe apple sauce from my mouth and light two Pall Malls. Rolling up my T-shirt sleeves I expect the Boss somewhere to be singing, 'I was *borrrnnnn* ...' I dial and dial but can only find Judas Priest, and the Cramps.

Trudy joins me blowing smoke at the skunk-sprayed walls. Our tent should have its own chimney, for lung cancer prevention. She is thinking about Dwight. 'You lie, too, Wishes, to make yourself a star just like him. Suppose for one awesome minute it *is* true he stays home more than he says he travels. It still sounds like you're making it up.' Mother, so help me I am not making it up, I am trying to find poor people a home when Dwight is selling suntans to rich people who want to leave home. He tells them how A/1 it is abroad, when I am telling them the opposite, and he is the liar because he has never been there. I have, Mother. I explain this and such like to Trudy, who forgets mine is a nakeder truth than Dwight's. Admitted, I have a need of white lies about my food strike, but this is to lure media attention for refugees who have nothing to eat and nowhere for living. Trudy listens, inhaling, her hair blonded and curled from swimming every afternoon. Not today though. She is in a negative space.

I find myself wishing her eyes were blue to go with her hair. I find myself singing of my hometown, just like Bruce Springsteen, but hometowns are also evil I tell Trudy. Dwight never promotes travel for people in those places, Mother. He must want to keep them shut out of Canada or locked up in camps. I want to boost travel for those people, just like Mrs Scobie does. 'Except, Wishes, you used to think Mr Singh's way was better. For profit. Now I think you think of profit as fame and glory. Not anonymity, like Mrs Scobie.' Mother, this puzzles me. What can I tell a lover who is suspicious of her lover's motives? It is like she is suspicious of me and Marcia or me and Huguette and wants to break my heart before I break hers. She knows I do not love Marcia, I love her, her blue eyes being windows to my soul. Her brown eyes, Mother. Why does she suffer carping like Mrs Scobie's? Teenagehood sucks in the pits. It is hard for Trudy to know who she is, when she lets herself be conflicted by Mrs Scobie. So it is I who suffer.

My protest, Mother, is a hymn. I want to benefit others, not Aloysius Irving. Why does Trudy doubt me? Dwight takes his hometown for granted. He is the flip side of the refugee trying to escape his or her country. He is the flip side also of the prostitute in her hometown waiting for the pleasure of tourists. My father, I tell Trudy, came from a rich country and kissed off my mother. Do you think he cared about anybody except his truly? She looks at me, exhaling her smoke. She does not know me, she thinks. She does not trust me. Love me! love me! love me! her eyes are saying, Mother, and I want to love her, but she no longer trusts me all the way.

She flicks her butt through my tent flap. I touch her cheek a second time.

I tell her my protest is against travel when refugees are *forbidden* to travel. So it is *amportant* to find Dwight's column in the newspaper, to use it as our ammunition. 'You say you care what Mrs Scobie thinks,' answers Trudy, 'but Theresa makes you mad. You don't really like Theresa.' Why should I like Theresa, Mother? 'She's not one of your groupies,' says Trudy, sounding jealous again. 'If you're so hungry for fame, Wishes, and I know you are, no matter what you say, why don't you run across Canada on a daily basis? You wouldn't have to pretend you weren't eating. You could collect a lot of money for refugees.'

Is this what she wants, Mother, a stunt? I quickly tell her the best protest is talking. 'And doing nothing?' she wonders. I am not doing nothing, Mother. I have become the lighthouse for people who have no hometowns. Becoming no bloody body, Mother, is a first step to becoming somebody. 'You admit it then, Wishes. You want everybody to think you're a somebody.' She wipes the sweat off her upper lip. 'You sound like a Midas muffler commercial.' But she wipes her fingers on my hand. She also pecks my earlobe on her way out. This tells me, Mother, Trudy still has a mind and heart of her own. I am so dependent on her now, like a CEO on a secretary headhunted by another CEO, I am glad she has not forsaken me. Not totally. I settle into my book again, instead of the bay. Times passes. The crows start ragging me, Mother, ragging me. And I think of what I used to be. Corbin at the orphanage, yes, plotting his revenge. If punk had punctured Bombay sooner I would have had an Iroquois in those years and listened to the Sic F*cks.

4.

Mother, my listener, look at the spider swallowed up by night, except when car lights rake across my thin walls and show its shadow. If city workers move in, as they keep saying, I will spring up in another park, away from intersections and streetlights, where I can see the stars from beside a bandstand. The stars are not seeable tonight, even if I could see them. I am waiting for the soupy air to cool with the first rain of summer. On my little radio is Power Plant, followed by Huey Lewis & the News, an ad for Burger King, a DOA number, then the Cars. The Boss, I think, will show up if I keep on this station, not dialhop and cut my chances with the Slits and such like. Thinking of chances, Mary Yip must be POed at A.I., skipping out of his promise to work hard on his debt for her brokerage house. And Mr Kym-bach, Mother, went totally to breakfast when I quit dead one afternoon at the end of July. It was my second summer at the golf course, mowing. His neck lit up like a barber pole. There. A lick of lightning? The air tonight is such I have hooded my protest signs with garbage bags to keep them dry from the monsoon I smell coming. I see out my door the black bay motionless, no white breaking waves, the waterslide in the dark as still as a house. No boat people yet, arriving in junks. Drown the Boat People sang my band, joking, before I dropped them.

My breath is bad. The only moving air is the smoke coming from my innards, drawing faint shadows on the walls, where car lights freeze it like an X-ray. I meditate inside this lung, breathing. A tent meant for mountain trips and clean air, for high meadows in a wilderness. How long can I keep up the stuffy company of a spider? The fly is gone. The fly digesting in the guts of the spider, I miss it, remembering how many days it lived off my cores and seeds. Suffering like me ghetto blasters, bouzouki music, rubber laid. This same fly, Mother, brushed from Mrs Irving's nose on her surprise visit last week. And stuck to Vaseline haircuts of a Chinese gang threatening me with razors, yes, if I did not piss off about boat people on TV. A fly tested with rose spray, clouds of it, till its perfumed wings drooped like two soaked tea leaves. For my spider, waiting for the Boss's music too, I turn the dial. I get Queen, the Sex Pistols, a Coke is It! jingle, then Bryan Ferry.

My eggs in one tent, Mother, was Mrs Irving's expression when she showed up to talk about responsibility. My broodiness she said came from hunger. Damon was picking park roses while she talked to me on her knees. Why had I given up all my good marketing ideas, she wanted to know, for this? 'This ... staring at the walls, starving, planting signs in the lawn. You might've worked your way up in Dwight's business, dear. Now I see you're criticizing travel agents for no reason at all!' Mother, she must know Dwight is a worse sex operator than all of them together. And a liar too. '... But, dear, I *do* think I approve of your support on TV for Mrs Scobie's work with poor refugees, I've heard so much about her work. And I was pleased to hear you say you go to mass with these people from those Spanish hot spots. If anything puts you back on the right track, the sacraments will.'

She paused a moment to watch Damon. To pull back from my tent and breathe clean air. 'I don't think I have anything more to say, dear. I heard you like to meditate away your hunger pangs. When you get sick of living outside there'll always be a room for you at our house.' She then waved at the smell, Mother. 'You might just as well be back in Bombay. At least in person you don't look as scrawny as you did in the paper. Meat still attached to your bones. I don't think trying to be another Mahatma is such a good idea, is it dear? That's all I have to say.' It was still not too late to bury myself in the ocean, Mother, to cool off. But the Irvings were not the end of my needling visitors.

'Hey, it's Alla Wishes! Hey, Alla Wishes, you asshole!'

To my surprise, rattling across the lawn came Reesa's car thieves pushing a Safeway cart full of bags stuffed with empty cans and blankets. These two tramps, dressed for winter, made a big show of strolling about like tourists, jeering to each other over my protest signs. Mother, they were not dazzled with my spelling. 'Listen here will ya, Slope's. I think what he's sayin like is we need more ragwinders in Canada. Lookit this sign ...' Kev tugged Slopes's ponytail, to get his friend's attention. Slopes said how did I like their luggage? He said on their last flight they lost it at the airport, so now they took it with them in cabin class. Kev smirked. Slopes said I was such a haywire wop I did not know how hunger ends up wiping you out. They both smirked. They said I was a good ad for Crease Clinic, protesting to bring more DPs into Canada. They smelled like they still live with skunks, Mother, but with a cat scared hatred of water.

Listen. Can you hear raindrops starting on the nylon? Thank you, Mother. Plus the Boss is on my radio at last. 'I was *borrrnnnn* ...' Music to my ears. I light another Pall Mall and wipe the sweat from my arms, lying back on my pillow. The skunks will not like this wet weather, no. Puff, puff, I coat my walls against them. In the smoke I notice my spider move for the first time, like it knows a danger is approaching. It is how we have our warnings, I believe, regarding earthquakes and electric storms, by how the smallest things move first in the grand design. Mother, this gas I breathe out reminds me of aldicarb pesticide, poor farmworkers breathing it at harvest time, followed by diarrhea, nervous twitchings, headaches. I will print a protest sign. I remember the labour union Mr Singh hated for pleading workers' compensation and such like. Even the lowest of the low insects know in their bones watermelons should not be sprayed. But skin rashes are a given, pickers get them, and what do pickers know about pesticide?

Mother, the knowledge I have about Dwight? It will be a traffic stopper: GEY HARODUTUS TOURS TRAVELL OUWNER LIES ABOUT TRAVELL.

Dwight is so stupid about the true direction of travel I cannot believe he is a counsellor at all. I cannot believe he has a leg to push on anymore. The rain falls heavier now, in a gust of wind. Mother, I see I am stupid too. I could get leaked on badly if a storm blows in off the gulf. This pillow of mine? The rainfly, yes. To raise it over a Pathfinder now I would need to read these instructions in the dark, getting soaked. The rain sounds like it is falling in drops the size of fir cones. The good thing is the dust of summer will soon wash south to the earth. But will the stink follow? This stuff is like insulation in a nightmare.

June, 1942

I - I - I ... Practising up for the big day. Have been snooping on couples, under the excuse of witnessing my own conception, or maybe willing it, I don't know.

Moped today. Felt aimless. After so long am getting irked at drifting around like dust, as shapeless as the now chlorinated water, everybody's and nobody's genetic material. *Whose?* if I may ask without sounding like a snoop. Whose cheek am I going to supply a talcum-powdered head for? Whose ears a whole night's cantankerous squawk? Whose nose a diaper full? And whose tongue a mouth to ... but why get so far ahead I forget to remember what's staring me in the face?

I speak figuratively for I have no face. No senses yet. No tongue, for crying out loud. A ghost from the future haunting this, haunting that. I check the stars every night for auspicious signs. I picket the birth announcements.

Not for a sign of myself, but for some configuration that lets me know things are more or less on track. You can't help wondering if your own parents are even conceived yet. You can't help thinking if not, then they must have more ants in their pants than you. Poor nameless souls. They look in mirrors and nobody is there. Does vanity exist if nobody is there? This is the thing about history. To see what you can't remember is impossible without a self to grieve for.

So you look around and take refuge in all possible conjunctions. Especially in a city at war. This one at present is full of refugees, all hoping against the probable, the improbable, the unthinkable. These citizens are to be shipped out by the trainful, to shack camps in the Interior. You sense their anguish. Rumours every day, every week since Pearl Harbor, don't convey the anguish. The coast is rife with rumours of where the war is headed.

'Marj, love. I'm going for a swim off the

dock.' A shack up the inlet, instead of one in the hinterland, would be paradise for any citizen threatened with confinement. If only some of them had guessed ...

Trust me, I would have any of them as my begetters.

Forbidden to be out after dusk a few at first were arrested. Then the police confiscated radios, in case Tokyo broadcasts, asking them to express patriotic zeal by preparing to welcome a Japanese invasion, should sway them to discover a guest bed.

Now the city has forsaken them. Fingerprinted Nisei, Issei, Sansei, closed down their language schools and newspapers. Homes have been seized, cars and trucks confiscated, fishboats tied up. Just like that, with a stroke of the pen, citizens have become refugees and their home alien. 'I' has been taken from them. So they haunt it as ghosts.

History in the making is really a dirty whistle. This is what it means to be unborn. I can look around from outside time and know the existence I hope for, take for granted, isn't the same as one struggled for inside. The voyeur has these advantages. I go whichever way the wind blows and never grieve. Can't. Nothing scares or surprises a speck like me, who has lived in the wings for aeons. These erstwhile citizens, though, are whistling in the dark, onstage where no one even sees them.

I see them. I also see the city's whole kit and caboodle.

Look at them all practising blackouts. Tarpaper over house windows, cut-out slits for car headlights, guards posted on darkened bridges and railway lines. Where are my parents hiding in this darkness? Is one or both to be born in a shack of some ghost town that once boasted a silver mine? Deprived of all properties, except hardened shells, are they being shucked like oysters?

I can see the advantage in having ancestors whose pearls remain ... intact.

Where are my grandparents? It is grandparents I need first, the way it used to be great grandparents, whom I never found either, giving up and moving on to what I hoped might be an easier sighting of those nearer me.

Shipyards, airplane factories, iron foundries: I visit so many. I have no single story, so the particle of speech I call me moves from nonentity to entity by every possible route, with no assurance of discovery. Skilled refugees from Europe are preoccupied casting boilers and condensers. Young couples, separated by draft and

service, defer having
families. So I can't even
hope to be *un*expected.
Everybody is rationed
meat, coffee, sugar ... I
only wish condoms too.

In the news a
submarine has just
shelled a lighthouse off
the coast, but no one's
thinking of injustice
done seamen whose
fishboats were
expropriated and resold
to whites.

Seems a sick
coincidence the sockeye
run this summer
promises to be the
biggest in living
memory. Not that my
memory is living, yet. I
really wish someone
would shake a leg.

Chapter 18

Love Prisoner

MOTHER, MY MEMORY, you are the engine of my dream. This is the given. Then how come you are pulling a nightmare out of me, like a tramp from a boxcar and I am abandoned to hobo my time in a sopping, smelly tent? Day 138 of my hunger strike, and I have run out of foolscap to print a new page every morning for passersby. No problem this morning, Mother, no traffic. Notwithstanding the foghorn, I think it is the quietest morning in my life. I keep my radio off, I hate Christmas carols. By preferment I count my pulse against grossness of the rich and jealous. And the overall sum total of this benefit protest? Close to zero. No one would care, Mother, if I starved or disappeared totally off city charts.

I think of dry things I would like to be doing this morning, and having breakfast at Mrs Irving's house would be my favourite thing, except I refused her dead when she came last week to plead. 'Please, Aloysius,' she said. She thinks I have done too much penance for my sins, that my long fast is Lent gone to seed. 'Why not end it with a warm bed on Christmas Eve, followed by French toast in the morning and cocoa? After all this skin and bones business, Our Blessed Saviour would take a very benevolent view of you eating turkey all day like a little pig, dear.' Mother, Mrs Irving approves my largest sign, standing up for our family, FREE TRAVIL AGUNT NOW! 'We can only pray,' she said, 'he'll be home for Christmas.' Shaking her head. 'Ten weeks now ...' She smiled, Mother. 'It would mean so much to Damon if you could come, Aloysius. It would mean a lot to me. Christmas is my loneliest day of the year. It's the day my husband fell into Japanese hands in Hong Kong over forty years ago.'

Crawling back up off her knees she looked as grey as the bay. 'God bless you, dear.' I was lying in my sleeping bag and she was talking through my mosquito netting. Confessing to me, Mother. I felt lonely to the max. Nut case sailors, sailboat racing in English Bay, I might as well have been a fly on the lamb of God for all they cared. How could a city go on yachting without one thought to suffering in other cities, where tourists like these nuts go frisking in the same peabrain way?

The media stopped coming to interview yours truly weeks ago. I am no longer a human interest item with exotic background and such like, notwithstanding the raft of stories I told of danger and escape. Trudy thinks I cried wolf once too much. So they cannot hear how Dwight is in bad danger, Mother, not when I, A.I., was the one who called him a liar. And since I fail to look thinner since last August, their curiosity in my hunger strike is dead meat. I am no longer everyone I want to be, left to rot like a mushroom on the lawn. Even the police, Mother, stopped watching my sagging shelter, the city workers quit waiting to bulldoze. I am hung out to dry! If only, but the rain since September never stops. I use garbage bags for slipping under my floor, drooping over my fly, catching water leaks all over me. Moss grows in my scalp. A headband to keep long hair from my eyes, like the Boss does, never stops it falling forward. Greasy worms humping on my cheeks. I have no succour. Crawling into this insomnia bag is like entering a waterslide tunnel, some days I never slip out except to use the bathhouse lav. Every day they lock it earlier and earlier. Today I went behind a log far down the beach. I hung my sign, GONE FOR A WAUCK, not that anyone except Trudy cares. If *she* cares, Mother. I think she is having it on with Andrew because she and I are drifting apart like two rafts. Mrs Scobie instructs her my prospects are bad, washed up in a bad dream of history where it pees so much my days shorten down to soggy butts in a winter toilet.

I was born for managing adulteration, Mother. Who can blame Trudy for not wanting anymore to sleep with me in my insomnia bag? Why would she want to smoke a Pall Mall with a wet wick? I smoke to burn out the smell but I cannot burn it out or scrub it off. The skunks love rain, they love it when it smears their glands deep in my walls. They love rubbing their soaking coats over pegs and strings. They find it a big joke that I live in a Pathfinder and cannot find my way to a dry bed. I am molested by skunks. By crows, too, ragging me, oozing sarcasm.

'Get up! Get up!' rag these garbage-pecking crows. Mother, remember these talking pests in Bombay? I think they are why you called me your little raven, because I talked so much to them, chattered loudly to you. They tell me 'Drown! Drown!' It is like yours truly has sailed his junk into freedom and found himself sinking in the bay. *Ping.* Have I capsized, Mother? Have I had it up to here? Tell me what I know, talk to me! It is too cold these days to skinny dip so I scrub my armpits at the bathhouse. I have sniffles. I station hop for the Boss, but my inspiration from him is now diluted in the max, his *amportance* is wearing me down. I think Foreign Trade made better music, Mother, before they landed in jail.

Guess what. I was listening to Freddie Mercury singing 'We Are the Champions' yesterday, when Reesa dropped by to bring my Christmas present. This big star of *City, City* also made an offer to wash my clothes and return them in a laundry bag. I think she is trying to oust Trudy as my underwear and such like washer, Mother, because I smell bad. Trudy acted a little jealous when I joked Reesa was trying to fire her. I told her Reesa thinks she is keeping me as her love prisoner. 'Then tell her the truth, Wishes.' The truth since Halloween, Mother, when the Chinese gang came back and tore down my tent on top of us, is Trudy and I have not slept together once. They pricked holes in my Pathfinder, like a Sheik condom, to rag me with worry when the rain drips through. And Mrs Scobie is teaching Trudy to break my heart. She is jealous. She thinks I am a negative publicity hound for refugee aid in her city. Trudy says her guardian is a most disappointed woman. Working in refugees has not sweetened her juices, after a husband forsook her for another woman. Now St. Sebastian's is also forsaking her, swearing to turn out the illegal Latinos she is hiding in its basement. Refugees have drained Mrs Scobie. She is near bankrupt, giving everything to them, but will not sell her house when its worth is still plunged down the toilet. Out of spite she wishes Trudy to reject me. Trudy is having a bad time with Mrs Scobie.

Maybe Reesa wants to rescue me from the smell of heartbreak. She used to talk of *City, City* profiling my cause, heaping praise where I deserved it, hoping then I would give up protesting and go back to school. She is old-fashioned, Mother, thinking I should live up to my doctoring potential when the world has changed into one for lawyering potential. I would not be a lawyer either. She forgot about my profile when Dwight became a conflict of interest, when I started campaigning for her husband's release from a stinking jail, notwithstanding I had unscaled the public eye about him lying between his cheeks in the first place. Reesa says her persuasion at the station has plunged anyway. Her programme has only a fifty-fifty chance of living on. With this economy she could lose her job. She told me, 'Theresa says she would press your laundry, Aloysius, if you decided to entrust it to us.' It was gross, Mother, a television personality grovelling to scrub my underwear. I was grateful for the offer, believe me.

I thanked her for her gift, a parcel the shape of a little tent that rattled when I shook it. I think it is cutlery and tins of gourmet food for Christmas dinner. She promised to drop by on the way to Mrs Irving's house for her own dinner. They are all hoping for Dwight's release from jail soon. She looked tired and jumpy. The shrinkage of Herodotus is second in her thoughts to stroking Dwight's suffering. Their days of party-giving look gone, their marriage too. A man I saw at a party was waiting for Reesa in her car. Mother, the world is shrinking in its betrayals, but if we remember our loyalties enough to care for the betrayed this is one small pace in the right road.

Even the hookers are jumpy at this end of our Year of the Dog. 'Business is supposed to firm up for Christmas rush,' Huguette told me, wrapped in a rabbit fur with a pretty hood and bow. 'This year it's damn soft, bubby. I might have to turn in my number and enroll in college as a mature student. No one's calling. Everybody's looking for a silver lining in the recession, thinking if they can't find it in Santa's stores they might spot it in the street. Joke, bub. The whole retail trade is tailspun. Where are all the Bugs Bunnies who want to jump in my hole?' Huguette shifted weight to her other heel. 'Like the colour of my new brolly? I needed something Indian to attract the sad sacks.' She sniffed the air, amazed. 'Have a stick of Trident. If things stay slow after Boxing Day, I really am going to enroll as a mature student and change my luck. No one's stopping here. All DOA. Morgue meat.' I asked her inside my tent to listen to Christmas carols. 'And have you muss the holiday hair? Bugger nuts to that, bub.'

Even Huguette is absent this morning. It is like a nuke alert has sucked streets bare, Mother. No fire could catch on a day like this, so dreamy, the fog threatens to muffle Vancouver in a soft shoe. Smoking, I fill this tent and cause my spider to run to a low corner near oxygen. What should I name him, Mother? I need a pet to help boost my protest. I need a dog called Bertram or Mohammed to mix it up with the skunks. I lie here listening for crows, but they are dreaming too. 'My little raven,' you would tell me, fingering the gold chain at your neck. 'You never call me Rosy. I am too young for Mama. Remember. Rosy.' Mother, c'est *amportant* I remember when you have no memory left, like my bank account without a sum. This is the given.

You gave in your notice to the nightclub owner, Rao, when we went back one morning to beg your pay. You were very happy. 'You are the best dancer

LOVE PRISONER

I have,' said Rao. 'Where can I get in touch with you?' You giggled, Mother, telling him you would never dance again. Rao patted me on the hair. 'My little Arab, found a father, yes?' Mother, your friends Pearl and Lovina teased and cried when we left them and Chichi for our flat over the sea. It was bigger, with a balcony, than the rooms we shared in the project. Mr Ghanai caged us in a lift and delivered us to the sky, staying that first afternoon to stroke you all over like a bird. And then went home to his family.

Mother, I wonder what Trudy will bring me to eat, if she will bring hot turkey in tinfoil from Mrs Scobie's church basement? I hate turkey. I hope Trudy smuggles a Big Mac. She wonders why I still fuss pretending I am on hunger strike. '... I mean nobody takes you seriously, anymore. Why should I "smuggle" stuff? You could walk to McDonald's yourself. It's no big deal, no big *secret*, Wishes.' But I am stubborn, Mother. A hermit is what my school friends think, if they still think of me, an awesome acid head doing his thing. I am tarnished in their eyes by my belief in a benefit protest. How are they to respect a tycoon who never eats, unless I have some secret contract with Sun Rype apple juice, keeping me alive X number of days before I cash the sponsorship cheque? This they would respect. But not starving myself for others, Mother, no. I wonder if they would understand it if Freddie Mercury, a.k.a. Frederick Bulsara, decided to sacrifice himself for poor people on Zanzibar? I think they would. That is his home, in the Indian Ocean. Fame buys respect. Queen rocks on.

Trudy no longer eats. Sometimes I ask if she ever has cravings for a pigout, up in Le Soleil Couchant maybe? No, she answers. My secretary grows more beautiful the less she eats. I think Mrs Scobie has schemed this from their Weight Watching days, causing me to fall in love with her protégée before plucking her from me forever. Mother, Mrs Scobie hates my grandstanding and hopes Trudy will soon drop me in the garbage can of history. She is why Trudy never feels like making love now, never a peck or a feel. I used to be a catch for her, the size of a killer whale, now I am lucky if I amount in her eyes to a salmon with some spawn to dribble.

I see fog creeping in from the ocean. It will suffocate everything except this tent, Mother. I would hardly know my tent smells, I am so used to it, except I remember what Trudy smells every time she comes. For this purpose I keep cedar boughs to crush in my hand, to cleanse my skunked nose. When Bartlett visited last month, with his patient who has unusual happenings with her own nose, I was surprised. He told me Trina Chase's boyfriend is gone and she is lonely for a friend. I would like to make Trudy jealous, Mother. I – Mother, over there, that dark van stopping, should I wave?

A cameraman and a reporter, Reesa, coming this way from the curb. No, not Reesa, only some woman with silly questions to ask A.I. after weeks of neglecting him. They must hate it, getting told to come down on Christmas Day to interview a gumsucker. She only has to wait for the camera to turn on and I am out of my tent talking to break the band. I have things bottled up and they fizz out like Pepsi when I flip my cap. '... As a Turk in Germany I could see things with these own eyes. I could see them for my own self, very bad. Poor girls from my country go to Germany because they think husbands wait to marry them. They are told this. They land up on streets, they –'

'No, no,' she interrupts. 'I wanted to ask you about –' 'Tamil Tigers,' I say. She can run me from any frame, Mother, I have no worry over garbaging her tape by not waiting for a silly question. I speak to the camera eye, hands flying. 'Tigers showed up in our village where my family sold pots and pans. We were all Tamils, the Tigers were our boys, yes. But just the same they made us line up in a street outside shops with our hands on our heads in hot sun. Who knows, maybe they were looking for some spy to the army. I was not knowing what was going on down the line. But my brother ... got led away. We stood for a long long time and Tigers poked into our shops and homes with machine rifles. That is when –'

But the cameraman, Mother, has shut down and lowered his camera. He never had turned it on. I feel strangulated, handcuffed. My interviewer is disgusted by a crankpot who will not wait to listen to one question. 'Let's gear over to see what the lagoon ducks are having for *their* dinner, Les.' She tosses tree ornaments she has in her ears. So I tell them, Mother, in a statement not so piping or singsongy as before, 'This is the day our External Affairs department should be really ashamed for not lifting one finger to help Dwight Irving, travel agent from this city in a Costa Rican prison.'

'Jesus Christ,' mutters Les. 'Let's shoot the ducks.' He is wearing earrings too. I shout after them, 'I don't have Christmas where I come from! We never worry what ducks are having! We worry getting out alive!' They reach their van. 'Crank!' answers the woman's muffled voice. 'Bauble!' I call, 'Grapevine!' I hear her hoot, climbing into her hearse, lifting red hoseried legs and tucking them inside. I call out, 'Do you wear garter belts too, with baby seal fur?' The door slams. A seagull appears through the fog to land in my little park. Scarlet dot, white head. Santa Claus with his mouth open. In all our rain the worms have risen and this gull has brought along its bib. But a crow hates and scolds my wormeater from a tree. *'Asshole! Get lost!'* The interviewer gives me the finger out her window. It looks like I can never escape Corbin, your little raven, Mother. Teenagehood sucks in the pits when you are left talking to yourself like I am. 'Shoo! Scram!' I cry. The mouth on a crow is bad news.

2.

Mother, were you pleased when you could stay at home all day waiting for Mr Ghanai in your new flat? I went to school now in a uniform and shoes. He came and you served him alcohol, nested with him in your bedroom giggling. You told me he was a big landlord who lived in a mansion. Mother, how could you go with a little man like that? An oily man with wet armpits, who burped. The boys at school were like what I thought Mr Ghanai's sons were, soft and obedient, except his sons were daughters. Did you wish to replace his wife? He was fat, you comely. Short and tall together. Men stared at you in your new sarees and made Mr Landlord jealous.

You were most lucky I did not run away when he came to have you those weeks. Coming home from school I could smell his armpits in the lift. His smell never left our flat. Our flat was full of his odour whenever I opened the door and heard you moaning. I was to leave you alone when you were moaning with Mr Ghanai. You wished for privacy and each other's accompaniment. That afternoon I boiled tea and turned on the radio. I heard no more from your bedroom and knew both were sleeping. He would be late for his supper, Mother. I looked in cupboards for our supper, but you had forgotten shopping. I liked you to forget because we would go to a restaurant when Mr Ghanai left. I sat and worked at my homework. It grew dark over the ocean. The odour of Mr Ghanai was still sticking to the air when I lay down from hunger on the sofa. He had never stayed all night, Mother. I woke up to turn on our fan, but the electricity was out.

We sweated such little things, you and I. In a tent I think about electricity ten times less than I think about skunks. Is skunk the smell making my mouth move, pretending I am still with that reporter, to take my mind off Trudy who hates to visit now? 'I come to city for a job or somethin, off the reserve where fuckin nothin was killin me like, and I ends up here with a busted nose from fightin downtown, and I don't remember if I lost my teeth then or what, only I was a mess like. Still can't smell nothin. Got no land left to smell a pine cone anyways. Stolen from us like.' 'Knock? Knock?' Trudy, Mother. 'What's the matter, Wishes, your batteries dead?' She is wearing eyeliner and lip gloss for Christmas. She is a vision out of the fog, entering my tent on her knees like Santa down the chimney. How I want to make love with her again! I have nowhere for love but a wet bag in a sagging tent. 'Merry Christmas, Wishes.' Her gift to me, Mother, two gifts. One feels like clothes, the other a box of chocolates. And she has brought a picnic in tin foil, to keep it warm from St. Sebastian's on her walk down Davie. I flash my dimple, but she shows no temptation for lying down. She has crawled inside and is sitting crosslegged in her jeans, grieving my smell. I can tell this by how she nuzzles her hand like a gas mask.

'It's totally impractical,' says Trudy when I rip open her bigger gift. 'You'll think I just bought it for the day you leave here.' Mother, the sweater is white with two grey stripes, and a maroon stripe in between. Getting a V-neck is like a rock singer getting a mandolin. 'I know it's a dorky colour for showing dirt,' she confesses. 'I thought you could wear it for a change. Off and on like for special occasions?' Is she trying to hint something, Mother? 'It's a small. Not cashmere, so you don't have to pore over the label.' I notice the tag reads 'Made in Thailand. 100% Acrylic. Club International, by Tip Top'. What did it cost? I ask. 'Aloysius!' Cheap? 'As a matter of fact,' she says, 'I got it on sale.' Mother, I feel a duty to point out to my sometime lover and secretary that a retailer can sell sweaters made in Bangkok 'on sale' because sweatshops making them pay only chicken seed to the Bangkok women who sew them. This one has an imitation crocodile over its heart and bespeaks ripoffness. She looks at me, Mother, wondering why she should be talking to a bozo. 'If women are prostituting themselves behind a sewing machine, Wishes, at least they're not doing it on the street. Not that you've got much against girls on the street I've noticed.' Poor Trudy, Mrs Scobie hardly gives her pocket money, and she has never earned anything from me except a hustler line of credit. She no longer wears my bracelets.

I brush the stripes with my hand, Mother. 'I like the sweater, Trudy. Nice lines.' I take off my patched nylon jacket, handed me the day I landed in Canada by Mrs Irving, and push my head and arms into her sweater. 'You could do with a scrub under the arms,' says Trudy. 'Wasn't your last swim in October?' She watches me, gas-masking her nose. 'You should join the Polar

Bears, Wishes, out front here on New Year's Day, with your little bar of soap and a deep breath.' I pull her sweater down over my flat stomach. A V-neck is not what Springsteen would wear dead, but Springsteen never shivers for days in a cold tent. *His* benefit protest is over and finished after a two-hour concert. '... I wouldn't wear it a lot till you buy a deodourant. Truly.' No? I think it better, Mother, not to forget where clothes come from and who is sweating for who. 'For whom,' corrects Trudy. She picks up her smaller package and hands this to me, the box of chocolates.

A Schick with batteries. 'A stocking stuffer, Wishes, to touch you up when you decide you need it. Cold water in the bathhouse isn't razor friendly I've noticed.' I am wondering next, Mother, if she has breath mints as another stocking stuffer for my mouth. The trouble with tent dwelling is I have no mirror to see if I look as bad as I feel some days. Or if I still look as handsome as the Boss. Designer stubble is supposed to be cool, Mother. So when your lover hands you a razor it is truly a downer. 'You don't like it?' I switch it on, the buzzing like a dentist drill. I feel as pleased as a punch I say. She sighs, sadly. I think it is near high time, Mother, for some straight talk about expectations from each other.

She looks around. 'Who's that gift from?' Reesa's gift in the corner, in blue striped paper. 'What is it, Wishes?' Food delicacies, I tell her. I open up Trudy's own hamper and the smell of warm turkey arises to my nostrils like skunk stink. As a cradle vegetarian I have no taste for meat, only hot dogs and Big Macs. I unpeel the tin foil, Mother, trapped like an orphanage Hindu by his ingratitude. But Trudy has turned to listen out my flap. 'There's a car stopping ...' My poor interviewers, finding no ducks in the fog, have come back to ask what I am eating for my Christmas meal. I hold no grudges, Mother. I will take it out and show them, let them shoot me making news, having my first meal since August. I will wobble out, a prisoner whiffing nourishment after his dungeon protest. But it is Reesa, Mother, hurrying out of the fog in sneakers over the emerald lawn, dressed in a black evening dress and a ratty shawl. 'Just starting to open your present,' I call out. 'Trudy came ...'

'Oh, Aloysius.' She sounds so excited I know for sure Dwight is released in time for turkey at his mother's. So I have not protested in vain. I have endured skunks and cold for this good end. Dwight could even have my turkey. 'I just heard,' she pants, red in the face from racing here with news. 'Dwight's mother. Sylvia phoned to say she found her lying by the fireplace with a log in her arms and a bruise on her head. She just collapsed. They pronounced her dead ten minutes ago, at the General ...' Trudy crawls out of the tent. 'I overheard ...' Reesa is wiping off cheek hair, hairs curling in the damp fog. 'I tried phoning the consulate in Costa Rica, with a message for Dwight, but it's Christmas Day ... So I'm on my way to comfort Damon and Sylvia, with Theresa and Gwyn in the car.' She wipes her face with a swipe of her shawl. 'Aloysius, will you come and help me with Damon?' She is asking this as a special favour, Mother, if I will come in her Honda Accord to give some succour.

I pretend to confer with my thoughts. I pretend to feel sadness for my fate, all our fates, especially Mrs Irving's. I stare out to where the sea waits on the underbelly of the fog. I have life swimming before my eyes, like a man drowning in futility. I foresee no junks and sampans arriving before night comes. Mrs Irving's warm house in Shaughnessy will not win me over, Mother. I will come back to my protest at nightfall and keep my dignity. Dignity? All the highrisers looking down from balconies can see what I am holding in my hands. It tells them at last I am breaking my hunger strike. Their smug satisfaction. I am wrong, though, if I think they can see down through this fog, to what I will do or not do with a turkey drumstick. Diners at Le Soleil Couchant, if it is open today, will barely see the hand in front of their mouths.

3.

Mother, I am back. Alone in my tent on New Year's Eve. I would welcome back sanity and sanitation if I knew how to *move* anymore, but the moonwalk has gone out of me. I have also worn out my ideas from Springsteen, who likes to *shout*, Mother, if I can tell this to you in secret, notwithstanding that he still sounds better than a Christmas carol. So I will spend the rest of this noisy night with my flashlight, reading in a wet sleeping bag. In benefit protesting I have had my get up and go sucked dry, and now I am at a loose end, not knowing which way to tie my tent flap shut. It makes no difference to anyone, let alone Trudy. Taxi headlights rake these walls like X-rays. For sure, Huguette will be happy for the work tonight, her busiest of the year. But I am dead meat, Mother. The odour I am wrapped up in is corpse odour that stops a protester from making his point. I am burning to make it, but no one cares if I grill myself to a crisp and blow away on the wind.

The funeral, Mother, did not unfold well. Mrs Scobie's refugees dropped Mrs Irving's casket almost in the aisle of St. Peter & Paul, before tilting it back, level. Mrs Irving was rolling over in her grave before she was in it. I got picked up by a funeral limousine with flip-down seats, to bear me to the church like a rock star. The chauffeur in a tail suit thought I was the body in question and closed the glass between us. Reesa whispered to me the driver's suit was called a morning suit, but not spelt the way I might think. Mother, this was like telling the arsonist his fire is not the colour he was hoping for. I do not think of spelling when I dream my way into a new country. The poor Guatemalans felt sheepy for jamming up Mrs Irving's bones in her casket. Reesa got these volunteers through Trudy. She had trouble finding pallbearers from Mrs Irving's old friends. They have all lost money to her son.

When the limousine returned me to my tent Reesa handed me a card that said Springsteen, LLD, or else Jaggers, LLD, and told me I was to show up next week for the reading of Mrs Irving's will. Mother, I will refuse a cash settlement and her Audi and such like. After this drippy tent I want her house. This is the given. I feel the given is what I deserve. I am tired of the landlord class in tenting. I burn for a better life than living in the street, when my benefit protest falls on blind ears like Trina Chase's. At least I interest Trina Chase, Bartlett's patient, Mother. My adopted city is not interested, honking in the new year, whining for a better year after this long nightmare for every debtor and his dog. At midnight fireworks will explode and try to wake me. People on balconies will try to wake me, waiting to see in the year with pots and pans to help them forget.

Mother, how long before I wakened on our sofa and stepped out to look down at the dark Arabian Sea? I should be happy, I thought, you never have to go out dancing anymore. There was just one man now, Mohammed Ghanai, whose armpit stink was a small sum to beat for changing your life, your sitting in a flat all day eating chocolate. Reading film mags and listening to stereo. The sky I saw was starting to brighten. Below on the beach I could make out sleeping lumps of cloth. We even had a toilet to take our waste down pipes out to sea. I could see lights burning on a freighter at anchor. I could see lights burning in Malabar Hill where Mr Ghanai lived. These burned between all the black spaces like stars. When the electricity came back, as it always did, I would go inside to make your morning tea.

When the sun came up I knocked on your door. I needed rupees for my lunch and such like at school. You did not answer, Mother, how could you and still keep your secret of Mr Ghanai? When I pushed open your door, I noticed the closet unshut and your wide bed untouched. You were lying on the floor in your pink sari. A little worm stem of blood had squeezed from your nose and dried on your lip. Your eyes were open, Mother, and you were cold when I touched you, gripping your suitcase handle. Your gold necklace lay crumpled in the carpet. I knew then no bonesetter could help, not with black bruises on your throat like stains. I could smell his sweat in your sari, your hair, covering you like little particles of petrol. My blood stopped moving and I felt condemned in that moment to dryness. To stiff movement through a dream, tearless. I was above you, thirsty for some love, looking down on a dead bird. I packed your suitcase, locked it, then forgot to take it away. I walked down many flights of stairs, hearing the lift cage rattle past me on its way up. In the street my mind was running everywhere at the same time. Chiefly, I would avenge your death, Mother. I would give you a pyre. I would burn to become a man.

'Knock? Knock?' Trudy. A surprise, Mother. I turn my flashlight back on. I close the book on my pillow. She is leaving me, I can tell. She is on her way to a funeral, dressed in black tights and a black skirt. Standing here, she is beautiful. 'You're invited to a New Year's party at Andrew's parents' penthouse, Wishes ... if you want to come.' To see in the Year of the Pig? Why bother, Mother. I know in my heart it is Andrew wanting her for his own date, so I will settle for a martyr's aloofness. I think she came here only from fading loyalty. She does not look happy with me. She looks pained from my disappearance as a person. Springsteen is singing 'Dancing in the Dark' and I turn him off. I ask her to come inside my Pathfinder, knowing she hates to, but saying nothing when she does, getting her knees wet. Then she says, 'Your sweater fit all right?' Yes, I tell her, a most warm and thoughtful Christmas present. I shine my flashlight along the stripes of my own chest in admiration. I apologize for having got her nothing, and she shrugs it off as *unamportant*. She smiles. 'Why don't you come to the party, Wishes, and see the year out? In?' She sneezes, twice. Here, I tell her. Lie back for a moment on my pillow. I hear her catching her death.

I rummage in the corner of my belongings pile, inside my black visiting bag. 'What're you doing, Wishes? Where'd you get the earphones?' I tell her they are my Christmas present from Reesa. Mother, this bag belonged to Dwight's father and Reesa wants me to remember him by thinking I will be a doctor some day. Trudy lies back and lets me have my way. A little. I fit the instrument to her rising and falling breast, delicately. I no longer hear the taxis, the sirens. Dr Irving listened through these same rubber knobs, I am positive, to sick prisoners in Hong Kong, and to Dwight's mother's heart when she had dizzy spells and such like down the years. Reesa thinks Mrs Irving suffered dizzy spells to catch a stroke.

Trudy lies back and lets me have my way. A little. I am like a burp tonight, repeating my heart's pleasure. I fit the instrument to her rising and falling breast, delicately. Then I know, listening. Leaving me, Mother, slipping out of my tent, she also squeezes my hand. I have thought since of her squeeze as a dream squeeze of the softest touch. I am very glad now to have had this interview, because in her face and touch she gave me an assurance her suffering is stronger than Mrs Scobie's teaching, yes, giving her a heart to understand what my heart used to be. Maybe, Mother, I should follow her advice to have a Polar Bear swim, tomorrow morning in the ocean.

June, 1936

Trying to make something of myself out of sheer impatience. A diary like mine is a valentine to ancestors, whoever they may be. I worry they may not exist. Then where will I be? Am governed by a growing urgency to discover a self. Not some whippet or a duck.

Was peeping on a parked couple in lover's lane, a dark leafy crescent where big houses can afford to leave lights burning in every room. Finding one set of grandparents is still only half the hunt, but I had a feeling about these two, in this tunnel of necking youth, a sense, though I have neither feelings nor senses, let alone a self, that wishing it to be so is half the battle of locating my soul.

Came upon this crescent full of hope that I should some day find myself the offspring of a classy purlieu. How a refugee from non-being will snoop without a blush!

My roadster had all the pheromones of a brothel on wheels. Rye whisky, Chanel perfume, cigarette smoke, with the addition of fried potato smells from the new drive-in, called White Spot, where young bucks with cars and girlfriends go to be envied. The slappy hands on this pair of possibles! The sucky lipsticked mouths! Could these be grandparents I *wanted*, absorbed as blotters?

Retreated from roadster to brood in a rhododendron bush like a yegg. Lawn here in the moonlight looked blue. Gravel driveway looped past the house in a crescent of its own. Boulevard trees blotted out streetlamps and made peeping safe. Heard a piano being played. Saw buttery light through canvas-awninged windows. Slipped into the backyard and paused. Towering shadows from a man moving inside a lighted glass house. He was watering plants.

Am afraid I made myself a pest.

'Take me in! Be my ancestor! Save me from drunken spooners, liable to kill themselves on the road, after conceiving me in their rumble seat!'

I pressed my case. I also wished to be saved

from a relief camp downtown. From the drifter's ejaculation into his hanky. From him dreaming a way home to his sweetheart in a one-elevator town on a bald prairie. 'I'm a city photon, thank you!'

He was listening to the trickling water, not me. The work camps wouldn't mean much anyway to a gentleman, nor would the thousands who've hoboed west looking for refuge and two-bits a day. I see them wandering the city, lost. I shouldn't whine so much for my own lack of life. In this book of life, what life have they?

Our new mayor has been trying to cheer up his citizens by spending money he doesn't have. A new city hall is rising to overlook his bankrupt city. A new fountain in the lagoon will soon spout our Golden Jubilee in a gush of coloured lights. He's tickled pink – and purple, as he drinks and blusters a good deal – a

fellow who has read the Riot Act to hunger marchers. Quite the crackerjack. Two daughters, so he has oats. Married money and lives in Point Grey. Plans a lavish military parade for the biggest party in city history, with fireworks and bonfires – even the Lord Mayor of London's voice on radio, to confirm our status as a city.

Downtown, young couples caught on film by street photographers can't afford to pick up their own images. I study these on walls of the developer's little shop. Part of my beat includes the White Lunch on Theatre Row. Rumour is Charlie Chaplin washed dishes here. So you never know who might be sipping a cherry Coke. Or spooning at a matinee. I prefer the Pantages farther downtown. All those coloured kerchiefs being pulled from hats? I just lounge and chuckle with the vagrants. You never know.

More anon.

Chapter 19

The Life of a Tuxedo

LISTENING FOR VOICES, Mother, how do I know anymore if I am awake or dreaming? Even the crows talk at dawn. The landlord is everyone he wants to be but still quarrels with the tenants in his ears. He is on overload like nobody's business. Like when his tenants plug in something as housebroken as a toaster, his wiring shorts out. How can he trust his nose anymore to make sure no one is burning garbage in the barbecue, or furniture and carpets in the fireplace? Tenants' wants, Mother, can tear him in six directions to breakfast. This is the given. The slum landlord tasting expectation in the air like smoke. He wants to scream sometimes when he should roll over and go back to sleep. In bed, if he smells something burning, he wonders what city he is in, whether he is back in Bombay, or if he has missed the New Jerusalem totally. Wonders never halt. Rooms wrangling in different languages, mouths by the dozen eating and sucking, chewing the breeze over dishwashing jobs and deportation. Some bequest, Mother. I, a.k.a. Corbin, keep to my daily round of sanity and sanitation. I give persistence and drop like a stone into bed.

Victoria Day dawns and singing birds in the May garden wake me. *Ping*. No, I am already awake from the talking crow. In the grey light Mrs Irving's crucifix is hanging somewhere over our bed. I say 'our' bed, Mother, because of who lies buried beside me after so long a separation. She whispers from the dead. '… back to sleep, Wishes.' Trudy takes no pleasure in my early risings or daybreak meditations. I worry she is drifting from me again like she did last winter. Then what, more heartache from vain longing? It is Andrew who suffers Trudy's loss now. My inheritance from Mrs Irving inveigled her to leave jealous Mrs Scobie and move in with me. I, A.I., inhale with pride. But the smell, what are these burning particles in my nostrils? 'All I smell,' she murmurs, 'is dust.' She is sleepy, not troubled by a landlord's liabilities.

I light a Pall Mall and pillow deeper. I meditate. Dwight, another refugee from Central America, arrives this evening via Mexico City and L.A. Coming home to live after seven months and a half in prison for his stubbornness. It took Reesa that long to scrape up cash enough for his 'exit visa' and to make him slide it to a commandante. I have told Reesa, who is living in my basement with Gwyn and Theresa, Dwight is welcome too: what else could I tell her, Mother, when her house burned down in March? I wonder what my ex-guardian will think of two Mozambique families squatting in his old bedroom. Since Dwight was a boy the world has filled in around the edges. The scene's shifted. Reesa thinks Dwight can be our gardener till he finds his feet again. I would never be a party dumper, Mother, but I need a gardener who knows where his feet are! These tenants are eroding my grounds into a slum. My Japanese gardeners left at the screaming point, crushed by emptiness after years of honest Irving toil.

Around here, Mother, I know the smell of expectation. 'You're obsessed, Wishes. Skunks ... wrecked your nose.' Hay fever has wrecked Trudy's nose, she sounds nasal. 'Come back to sleep,' she croaks. But smell is not all I must abide as the given, Mother. I hear water running and I have a gross time with water worries too. The swimming pool is half empty from water fighting and a crack in the side wall given by our earthquake. My Afghanis are the biggest water fighters because they fear water and have no clue how to swim. They like a shallow pool, these fools, so they beat the water down more. A person diving from the board would break his bones. Too little water is my curse, Mother. The Ugandans maltreated my underground pipes by snapping off sprinkler heads to make a smooth football field. The lawn is brown now. Too much water is also my curse. Do not ask who is responsbile for the last time the bathtub spilled over. Water leaked through the dining-room ceiling, to where three families were sleeping on the floor. A plasterless ceiling is the consequence, jagged holes and bad stains. And bad feelings in need of an ombudsman I think. If I had cash I would hire one.

C'est *amportant* for tenants to learn respect for property before inheriting their own Canadian house like me. I am not surprised to say the worst drawers of water come from landlocked countries. Yesterday, I heard a waterfall and looked up at Damon's window to witness the Laotian family dumping out his aquarium. Colored fish landed wriggling at my feet. Was money behind this deed, these spillers hoping to turn Damon's fish into circus acrobats, or hoping maybe to barbecue them fresh for selling as gourmet sardines? I have no clue to this family's joy, Mother. Nothing challenges my landlocked nationalities like water. The toilet plugs with diapers, so a communal latrine is their answer, dug out behind the carriage shed and hammered together with boards. Water seizures never worry my landlocked toilet pluggers. I just wish they would share the boat people's respect, who remember water as a saviour!

No, no wonder stress of landlording makes me smoke a Pall Mall before sunrise, to calm down the dripping water in my dreams. I can taste the noise like soggy wallpaper. If I tell Trudy this she will just say I have caught Trina Chase's disease, mixing up smells and sounds. But was it not this patient of Bartlett's who sniffed our leaking gas when she first came to visit? I see this now as a mixed blessing, Mother, if you will let me be a wit at Trina's cost. The mess from pulling apart my walls is radical. And the *money*, I am needing to rethink the cost of replastering. Do not mistake me. I think Trina did my house a good deed harping on infection she could hear in every room. *We* thought she needed padded walls, talking like that before she even sat down. I asked Owl and she said, well, is it UFFI the girl is on about? And she explained about UFFI, how pumping foam into old houses was once the way to insulate, till this poison was banned in the Year of the Monkey. We are now in the Year of the Pig. She says Mrs Irving tolerated leaking formaldahyde gas like she did cigarette smoke.

So how do we know, Mother, it was high blood and not bad gas that killed Mrs Irving? Notwithstanding plugged arteries, I think Mrs Irving died ahead of her time because she never removed the foam from her walls. On Trina's second visit we asked her to move in, as our gas detector. Nutters she said, trying to understand. She likes my tenants and says chaos makes her taste nice things when she visits, like mashed potatoes, so maybe I will ask her again when the UFFI is gutted out. Trina Chase has brought Mrs Irving's old house together in cooperation, even as we tear it apart.

Our purpose is to hang on, once my tenants outlast bad journeys to get here. The men help me an hour at a time, two maybe, and this is why the wall wrecking goes less fast than it should. For them survival means families first. They fence off living spaces on floors and landings, in rooms and closets, they struggle for cooking time and bathtub rights. They still need to learn *we* are a family, Mother, the house of us. We need more pulling together and gung-hoism. With weak cash flow we need more money. They have not dawned yet how hard it is to live in a rich country. Mrs Irving's legacy, for keeping Damon and Sylvia, is not enough to keep tenants who have no rent to pay for food and gutting. Therefore my two ideas for raising more operating cash flow are 1) a benefit reunion concert of Foreign Trade, now Iggy and Raoul have done their stick in jail, and 2) setting up a cartel with tenants for media rights to their stories. I already feel Idea One, with FT, is a no win. We hope to finish the wall work ourselves, Mother, before hiring in stuccoers. But the last five months have not gone fast.

My tenants come from countries where taking precautions in love and health is hard to gist. They are used to worse worries than wearing little mouth masks against plastic poison. It is cruel to say it, but I find workers I like best have the least worry for their bodies and pitch in with no health concerns. Mother, a landlord cannot play doctor too. He must take advantage when he can. Last week my best worker Thomas Joe was rehearsing, because he has heard the others. 'I come to city for a job or somethin, off the reserve where fuckin nothin was killin me like, and I ends up here with a busted nose from fightin downtown, and I don't remember if I lost my teeth then or what, only I was a mess like. Still can't smell nothin. Got no land left to smell a pine cone anyways. Stolen from us like.' Thomas sweats through his T-shirt in little islands of sweet odour. My workers are trying to get at our insulation from the outside in, instead of inside out, and this means balancing on ladders to chisel off stucco for mining UFFI between studs. Mother, the neighbourhood hates us for a hundred reasons, but tarpaper is the visible one, notwithstanding the shade of our skins.

My neighbours are clueless why some authority did not close down this halfway house after all their whining to City Hall. My secret weapon? The mayor, Mother, inside my pocket. I hope soon to put the media inside my other pocket, giving them access when I please, especially with Dwight the Knight coming home and the luscious Reesa Potts living in my basement. We will turn into an ongoing serial with no end to conflict on our horizon or gossip on our survival. This could be a mixed blessing, Mother. Because if it is found out the mayor likes to visit Reesa downstairs in secret, the whole balance could blow up in my pants.

2.

Trudy is asleep again, still as the window sheers. Sky has now brightened enough for any Tom Peeper to make out the crucified body overhead. I never have time to take it down. I hardly have time to smoke: once when I go to bed, once when I wake. Landlordhood sucks in the pits. Sometimes I have four emergencies in one night, a broken furnace and an unveiled adultery, stolen piano keys and a burning stove. Then I will smoke up to six Pall Malls to calm my pulse over a house that could freeze or explode, fall apart or burn down. Mother, I need smoke alarms. I am tired these mornings, keeping alert night after night. Last night was good, only one crisis to wake me. Alauddin and Ustad *still* arguing about Stanley Cup finals on TV. They hate ice hockey, but believe in cities. Our city is playing New York and Ustad thinks we should never be waving white towels of surrender. Alauddin laughed at his stupid thought so Ustad swung a butcher knife. The noise, Mother, my whole house punched the roof at this angry Iranian. I have put our two Khmer families in the library and shut its door, to muffle their troubled sleep. Maybe I could reinsulate my house with Dr Irving's medical books.

I like to speculate at dawn, meditate, before arising and climbing into my Indian landlord pajamas and dropping downstairs to the chaos. Huguette's example of *yin* and *yang* helps me rise above my problems, so I lie here before sunrise, skating the border line between chaos and relaxation. My dreaming improves when I do this. I am everyone I want to be. Alas, Mother. Having to read between lines of so many tenants, I grow deaf over jealousies they are having about fellow dwellers. Having to listen to so many stories, of how far away the horizon is to here, I grow blind thinking of their struggles. We communicate in broken dialects of English.

Yesterday, I asked Bahadur Puthli how he was hanging, thinking to shame him a little into helping gut out UFFI. But he was busy rehearsing. 'Cool, cool. Just resting in hammock here, recalling Uganda before Idi Amin kicked out lucky ones and killed less lucky.' He was once a merchant, now from Manchester, living with his 'sister' and three children in my carriage shed, along with Kumar Gandharva and his family of baby skinheads. Bahadur speaks with one forefinger against his nose, like he is warning listeners he has congestion, maybe sleeping sickness, telling me and Damon, who was holding his mother's red thermos, to refill his mug: 'Uganda was beautiful before killing started and soldiers stabbed my father to his death. He was coffee merchant and we drank coffee to the heart's content. Very cruel country now, but before Amin, before death, my country was welcome and green. We sipped coffee in hammocks like this. Then we put down cups and fled for our lives like the nobody's business.'

THE LIFE OF A TUXEDO

Once out of bed this morning, I know the landlord's duties will be endless and a reason for them not so clear as now. I perform them for their own sake, yes, to make plaster dust while the sun burns. But I also have my chance to perform a benefit protest from a landlord's perspective instead of a Springsteen's. My view will muddy as soon as I climb out of bed. My worries will collect in a puddle. Trudy plans to move out if her hay fever worsens more. She worries UFFI is locked up her nose. And she is drained from our lack of privacy, Mother. This room of Mrs Irving's is forbidden to the refugees, just like Damon's and Sylvia's rooms, and the two rooms where Reesa and Gwyn and Theresa live in my basement. But tenants visit any room, day or night, to change their babies and fornicate, to sleep or upset the goldfish. So this is another load on my back, hoping Trudy will stay, when her special privileges as the landlord's equal partner dribble away.

My duties are not so easy as I thought they would be when I said to Trudy last January, why not take in Mrs Scobie's illegals, when her church rejected them from hiding in the basement. 'We will have this whole house ourselves,' I said, 'except for Damon and Owl. We could take them.' My house filled up fast, Mother, when word went around the grape net. Latinos now are a minority of my tenants. My population is bursting and I worry on finding the right balance between control and chaos. I worry too on having to call the police or fire department, and what publicity could do to tenants squirrelling in here, rejected once already by Canada. The neighbours are screaming. And how long can I buy off the mayor? Once Dwight is home, good news, Reesa will take her secret rendezvousing to some hotel and I will not have a major story of blackmail to sell, bad news, though I never would. No. I am solely trying to hang on like everybody else, Mother. Solely trying to make a benefit protest for refugees. If our profile is too high it is my fault, for being a little generous.

Sylvia thinks I am toast. This week I see her beak gleam since she is counting on Dwight to restore saneness in his house. She is stung by what bee got inside her dead employer's mind, to forsake her rightful heir in favour of me, a.k.a. Corbin. She is suffering the snakes and ladders of Mrs Irving's will. She is shocked like our neighbours by what I am making Mrs Irving's home into, turning privacy inside out. She has trouble keeping a tail on Damon, who is tickled as punch by so many people. He wanders off like his cat to hear sob stories, to wrestle with the children, to vanish down the basement and show Gwyn how to spin a yoyo or play Chinese marbles.

Damon used to be lonely, Mother. But Owl wants him where she can groom him, deliver him to mass like her poodle, make his meals without elbowing for oven space. She keeps her pepper-coloured hair pinned up tight. She is scared of 'what things are coming to', and prays to the same faith now souring Mrs Scobie against it. For different reasons she and Mrs Scobie both hate Canada for making people suffer.

Trudy feels sorry for Mrs Scobie's conflicted shell and asks her for visits sometimes so her old guardian can see the Latinos in good hands, my hands. She hates my hands, Mother, she hates them on Trudy, too. Her face is the colour of rice pudding. She huddles at tea like the cleaning lady, if only we had one. I overhear her warning Trudy against putting her heart into smuggling aliens into a loveless country. She no longer goes to church. 'Do you know what I touch here?' she asks, laying her hands one upon the other on her left side. 'Yes, Mrs Scobie.' Trudy tells me the hands make her think of theatrical Latinos Mrs Scobie feels she let down. 'What do I touch?' 'Your heart.' 'Broken!' She utters the word with an eager look, a weird smile that has a boast in it. Trudy now pities her fairy godmother. And I worry. I, A.I., think Mrs Scobie would like some revenge for losing Trudy and her other dependents to my possession. If her bitterness bites to the wick, I think she could sound the whistle on us all. I know what it is to burn for revenge, Mother.

The burning smell comes and goes in my nose. Is this because I drift in and out of sleep, where I smell less? Maybe I smell more, dreaming. I could accidentally burn down the house. Dawn shows up the wedding picture of Dr and Mrs Irving, looking from a silver frame on their vanity. On the back the loopy handwriting reads *Fuimus*. And *Cor unum, via una*. Church Latin, Mother. *Our wedding day May 1, 1934*. The groom looks older than his bride, around Damon's age, silent. She with her hand on his arm is holding up flowers in her other hand, to peel the veil off her face. Was she imitating some actress? Were there actresses, Mother, forty-nine years ago? On these walls are yellowing ancestors of Dwight's and Damon's. I am planning to take them all down this morning and give them over to Dwight when he settles in tonight as my handyman. Trudy thinks we are sleeping in a time warp, Mother, with these portraits and cobwebs. She has no love either for peanut shells, bread crumbs, toenails. Sometimes she must think she is entitled to a starlet's privileges in a playboy's mansion. And she is, except the playboy is the staff and bottle washer too. She hated it when Huguette paid us a visit last March. Maybe she thought Huguette was looking too much for business.

Mother, Huguette helped me slow down my racing brain, recalling me to meditation. The new spring was warm, we were sitting on the patio listening to chaos. She smiled and said journeys should be to enlightenment, 'where we've always been, you know, if only we could see our own true beings? That's the grail, bub. We have to save ourselves from ego grubbing …' Mother, she is aware of her street addiction, repentant for emptiness in a sensual life. 'Retrieve your old life,' she told me, 'give up grubbiness and dreams of your own reality. Got that?' She was still smiling. As an Indian yogi I had a head start she said. 'In the beginning is your end.' Raising a glass of egg nog from Ustad's hidden carton in the fridge she said she was wondering more and more if her mask of words was a wall against seeing *stillness* in everything. '… You know, in the dead of night, bubby, the slack tide in the bay? Or that stillness in the sec before Creation, when I'm meditating my rebirth?' It sounded to me, Mother, she wanted to stay a hooker. Everything returns, she said, in the rest of death. Maybe she meant the death of rest. I pray so. She was listening to the house being pounded on its walls from ladders and platforms, being worn down by feet and tantrums. I could not keep my look off the line of her dress, Mother, the cut of her hair. She smelled like jasmine. I flashed my dimple.

Time passed, it looped back. Huguette sat listening for nirvana where I strained to hear the birds. She was a call girl, Mother, waiting for a ring. Cho Ng began his story of salvation, one of my boat people with thin limbs and a big heart. 'Listen,' Cho announced, stepping onto the patio with a bad-smelling cigarette. 'I also in peddling racket in Saigon, before I know what peddling is.' Huguette looked at him, batless in the eye, so Cho went on with his lines. 'Nice party man in taxi roll down his window to suggest a bad deed. Friends on curb laugh and warn me then, so I back off it, the man roll up his window. But friends say I a fool not to rent my behind, my joss stick, whatever party man want. Gold was what we need to get out Vietnam. Lots gold. Grandmother gold, mother gold, dowry gold. My family pinch gold off dead baby once, just to buy family place in boat. No cabin, nothing clean. We have to sit on deck many days afterward. My grandmother die. We hungry. Worse nightmare still coming. You heard 'bout pirates?' Huguette was waiting him out, Mother.

Trudy whispered to me in the kitchen, 'She's probably got her eye on offering in-house services, in exchange for gold she thinks Cho's got stuffed in his socks.' Mother, I have sometimes thought my Iranians are the tenants with gold in their socks. Alauddin had a passport forged in Bangkok for ten thousand dollars. I think, employ Huguette to finesse their bullion and she could return a share of the cost for keeping my house in food and such like. Is this an evil idea, Mother, regular visits from Huguette when we need more cash flow? The will lawyer keeps saying my maintenance money is solely to look after Damon and Sylvia. 'They are part of the estate, Mr Irving. Neglecting them ... for other pursuits could lead to a reconsideration of your inheritance.' Remember, he warns, I must never abuse Mrs Irving's trust in me.

On the patio sipping sour egg nog Huguette said the endless meals cooking in my kitchen impressed her. The hammering and racket, the flushing toilets and running taps, children stamping floors above us, babies crying, bodies moving in and out of rooms, back and forth across windows, through tree branches – not to say languages jangling at each other like bracelets on a clothesline '... everybody airing their laundry, bub, in the promised land? Bet you didn't expect so many smelly socks. I love the craziness.' Her tune had now changed a little from her stillness lust. She said she saw how my life was less free now, claustrophobic compared to my tent life, and she envied me my chance of a nice reincarnation for doing good deeds. She joked like a Buddhist, who would not mind 'returning' for a longer stay. Then left through the back door, the front being closed to traffic due to plaster removal.

'I can't imagine where we'd stuff her in,' said Trudy. I said Huguette would not be a burden, she likes meditation. 'So do your born-again Hong Kongers, Wishes, living in the attic. But Chinese Christians are way more trouble than Vietnamese Chinese, who maybe have trouble with Luvs, but at least they aren't trying to convert everybody with marathon Bible readings in the kitchen. Your friend's Zen shmem could make religion worse around here than it already is. And a free love colony isn't the answer, Wishes.'

What is, Mother? What I possess now is a dream house tangled up by my nightmare of running it. DOANT LET YOU'RE HAIR DOWN THE DRANES PLEESE. The hair, Mother, the breakage! MUTHERS > NO CHILDRUN IN THE GLAS HOUSE FOR SECURETIE PURPUSES. If only there was a glass house *left*, Mother, to endanger the baby Nazis who hang out there. These days I find I am having to print as many signs as I did at my tent. PLEESE RESPECKT YOU'RE NEIHGBORS RIGHT TO DIGNETY! Also, DIVEING OFF THE SWIMING BOURD PROHIBUTED BY FINE! And, SHAIR AND SHAIR A LIKE. I am dreaming if I think it can be any different than flying by the seat of my ear, like Damon does at his piano. I would rather fill my house with punk rock. But punkers are such ego heads, they could not tell a dream house from a mad house. They do not want to tell. I do, Mother, to save me losing Trudy a second time to her wilting respect for the dreamer on his skid. Me.

Foreign Trade loved chaos and I was too much trying to sort it out. A landlord who flunks sorting out his conflicting tenants is a landlord headed to the garbage can of history. I store up all their stories of rejection to learn which way my own story could rescue, sponsor you as my relative, Mother, to a lush country for reincarnates. This is patriotism my neighbours hate under any title. I burn up like a candle keeping memories alive, your memories, in the dawn like this, lying here in my double bed with Trudy Macdonald waiting for the sun. I listen with my nose for signs of burning down, confusing the smell of smouldering secrets with taste of Pall Mall smoke, rising above me on our mattress. I see ripping tape in my mind, a bad sign of –

'Was I talking in my sleep, Wishes?' I touch her and find she is sleeping as she talks, snoring to snuff the band. 'Just poke me.' Mother, the two of us are learning consideration for each other in sleeping, not wanting to lap our private troubles over to the partner, not wanting to pig the mattress first. We are learning how to be in bed par deux, on the same mattress of life, notwithstanding nightmares. I wish I could say our neighbours wish to learn this too, our forbearing, because I feel as much burden from them as from tenants. I am doing the best I can, Mother, only our neighbours have no wish to tolerate a house talking in its sleep at all hours of the clock. They think I am a wop orphan with his inheritance, and they are right, screwing up his life and theirs, in a country seduced by too many single view points.

I know this is what Sylvia Courtland thinks, keeping to her room these days like I have locked her in the attic. Not Damon though. With all his new friends he does not miss a game. I am thinking of naming my halfway house after Marlene Irving and Damon Irving, but this would have no benefit with the neighbours, except to make them hate us more. No, I have injured the real estate value of their houses, not so recession proof as they once thought.

They have given a frosty elbow to my tenants trying to better their lot by selling cut daffodils and tulips door to door. Especially the florist entrepreneur, she did not take a kind eye to their free enterprise, who can blame her? On election day, two weeks ago, when her party kept the socialists from power again, she was celebrating with hothouse lokelanis. I will not repeat which tenants offended her, Mother, cutting tulips in her yard, but they had the excellent scheme of carrying their own green wrapping paper for a fresh presentation at her door.

It is so hard to be a policeman I have stopped caring about my neighbours and such like. A bad mistake and I will soon owe the piper for being a bad ambassador. I know the mayor is on my side, being a socialist lawyer in real life, also in love with Reesa in this same life. If I cannot keep him on my side, inside my pocket, then I will have to answer compressions building up around my dike of refuge. I stick in fingers where I find holes, Mother, but it is a losing job when trees are cut down in neighbours' yards. What happens when the dike breaks? For example, I have bought a starling cannon from a blueberry foreman I met through Mr Singh, for keeping roosting pigeons from my eaves. Will the neighbours stick fingers in their ears very long over this bargain? *Ping.* They will have an outcry, before I have taught the pigeons with their acidy shit not to trespass. Maybe I could organize a window washing bee, sending envoys into our neighbourhood with soapy squeegees to make us allies and money. Trudy says I am dreaming. Or maybe a paper drive to help our neighbours get rid of old news? Still dreaming, she says.

It is true we are not worthy neighbours in the status quo of behaviour, in minding our neighbours' rights like our own, but most of us have no rights, Mother. Notwithstanding the fruit trees cut down for campfire wood, from my yard and theirs, I hear of many frogs trapped and cooked, goldfish gone missing from local ponds. I see the grasslands of my own house in peril and lacking a gardener. So much tramping through these crescents has turned the neighbourhood into a migrant's merry-go-round. We are noisy polluters who cheat and steal from a leaky refugee system, letting my neighbours drown in their rankling, Mother, as I try to restore the Irving house to its old peace and order. I wish I could be hopeful, but curdled cash flow and outside forces are making me think I am on my way out. The cedar hedge is in rags and the rose garden potatoes.

3.

I am learning from Reesa, Mother, after whining to her of my pressures. In Reesa's way she is loyal to her disgraced husband and does not think under *his* pressures he will sink at all. I think she is having a cigarette dream. Dwight has already sunk. But I listen to her like I listen to Huguette, for the conviction of herself. She says she is a big believer in the beginnings of things, like Dwight when Herodotus Tours first took off. She is a lot less interested in the ends of things.

'There's too much apocalypse,' she told Gwyn last Friday, plucking the child off her feet. A game, to make Gwyn listen to her mother for a change instead of Theresa, griping. 'Il pleut, Gwynnie, and suddenly the roof is on its way to falling in. N'est-ce pas?' She was speaking to me, too, Mother. 'You yourself are a classic victim, Aloysius, with your punk rock background. The media shape themselves more and more in their belief that crisis, any crisis so long as it's *our* crisis, is worse than all past crises, just so the present will look like the End of an Age. We're end crazy!' Then she let Gwyn down, so the child could get back to nursing dollies on the sofa. Both mothers were smiling. 'This recession of the early eighties is the Worst in Half a Century, for instance, and has to be seen growing worse every day. We can't wait till it *is* the worst! It makes us feel important to think we're living through it. Too bad the Hitler diaries turned out to be fakes this month.' Like Huguette Reesa sees cycles in existence, Mother, feeling very chirpy on Friday, giving Trudy and me coffee, expecting Dwight home in three days, thinking she would make him a good weather person. '... Literally. Have another muffin.'

Dressed in a maroon skirt and a navy blazer, Reesa Potts picked a muffin crumb from her napkin and announced her studio audition that morning, if she could just get her car to start. Otherwise, she said, she would have to borrow my Audi. 'I can't afford to be choosy about work, with the kind of money they're offering for a weather person's job. Besides, I fancy the idea of a new beginning. I never thought getting fired from my old job was the End of My Career. I think people *should* be fired, just to show them how beginnings open up. That's why I like your house, Aloysius, because everybody else is starting over too.'

After Reesa said goodbye, Mother, Trudy said to me, 'Is Dwight ever lucky to have somebody waiting for him with that outlook – no matter who she might be thinking of running off with.' My love was stuffed up in the nose. 'Dwight's so far down, the world probably looks up.' Theresa was rinsing out the bone china mugs, gifts from yours truly to Reesa, along with silverware and such like from upstairs. I have no need of family heirlooms, Mother, when you have none either. Theresa was bouncing them into the dishrack like Tupperware, P.O.ed to be left behind on a chance for shopping. 'When Dwight shows up,' Trudy went on, 'he'll still be seeing his whole life passing before his eyes. She'll put a stop to that.' Who, Theresa? 'Reesa, you git.'

Is this my job too, not letting my tenants quake before their futures? The house throbs day and night with untranslated talk and I know what each is asking the other about s.i.n. and such like. C'est *amportant* to know somebody who can forge a s.i.n. card. How much, Mother, for a good one? Holding a social insurance number lets the refugee look for a job right away, even a dishwasher's job. Five hundred dollars it costs. It lets you work underground, what Carmen from Chile calls 'undercover'. My tenants would like to rent cards from friends already living in Canada, to rent friends even. Everybody is looking for i.d., having got waved through Immigration after leaving i.d. behind. My telephone is busy, Mother, and tapped. A patient of Bartlett's knows where my illegals can buy birth certificates. She tells me breaking the law for non-commercial purposes is no crime, Mother. But she hangs up in a hurry. Her forger comes from Hong Kong, where the best work is done. I am not impressed. If I could only find a good printer, I would get into the forging and fudging business myself, to help our cash flow.

I have many refugees in my house, but I do not know where from for sure even when I know. Some flushed travel documents down toilets of Cathay Pacific and JAL, on flights starting in Karachi. Four Sri Lankans hiding here flew to Hong Kong via Manila, on Philippine Airlines, then waited in the Hong Kong transit lounge before sprinkling their fake passports onto mashed potatoes and eating them down over the North Pacific. These stories spread through the house, Mother, like smells and sounds. My economic refugees are Fijians and Mexicans, not wanted in Canada because they have queue-jumped to get in. The true claimants, persecuted at home, are just as poor. My tenants hang on for hearings, to confirm their stories of persecution. In these I assist them, knowing many good stories for the purposes of sympathy. They practise telling these to one another, taking free advice on the loopholes and how to wriggle through with a nice twist.

Fateh Singh, one of my Sikh bachelors, rehearses his story if I give him a Pall Mall. 'To tell you a true story, friends, it is very hard for Sikhs to fit in with your country here, because in my country, Khalistan, our customs are Sikh customs, you see, and why we come to Canada is painful to confess appertaining to Indian government, who are throwing Sikhs in jail for wanting their own homeland. I myself hope to return as freedom fighter soon, even if I am not in belief of strict religion of fellow Sikhs ...' Should Immigration not believe him, Mother, he will go AWOL, hoping for amnesty like the one they keep hearing of ten years past.

It is their stories I would like to bargain to the media for our groceries at Safeway, where Warrick lets us bulk order to save money, and gives free delivery for every expedition by Trudy and me to buy food. The refugees contribute what they can, next to nothing, Mother, if I am honest with you. Some of them, like Constantine, think the currency I give them is worthless, especially for the media market. But he tries it out. 'Foreign cities you don't mind hearing, but it is Beirut you are really sick of hearing, yes? Just my bad fortune to come from that cursed place, full of thugs popping away at the other man with no hoosegow to lock them in. I would clip their hair, why not, throw away the key. It is a very bad tragedy. Those Muslims killing Muslims. Those Muslims killing Christians and vice versa ...' Mother, I have calls from immigration consultants seeking refugees to coach in storytelling. You are a guaranteed deport if you have no story. These consultants know the system and do not care if you arrived from Ecuador or Togo, by plane or railroad, they will revise your story and help you win the lottery. They will show you how to receive free medical services. They will show you how to overcome shoplifting a jacket, if captured, or skipping your bond. The problem for my tenants is paying the consulting fee. They cannot even pay me, A.I., rent, and I have no expectation anymore of collecting my credit slips, now thick as a butcher's hand.

I am legitimate, Mother, my inheritance checks out. Some like Ernesto still sound like ramblers, practising for their hour in court. In the storytelling room, with Da at his piano, most keep it simple but Ernesto drags it out like a soap opera, and we wish he had some cigarette scars to show authorities, so he would not have to go on and on. The children are watchful, even when they do not understand his tale and whine a little. 'I was drafted in army, from family village. Soldiers was killing poor people underneat my eyes. I come from poor family. Same like udder soldiers, who get asked to do killing ... First killing I seen happen outside San Mateo, like dat.' He swings his arm for us. 'The captain, he say to new boy soldier, cut off head of twelve men we find one night playing card. Captain laugh. The twelve apostle he say ...' and say, Mother. We clap when he ends. The best stories quieten the room to a pin drop, *ping*, and no one claps. Ernesto will perk up in due time.

Damon plays two sad notes on his piano, *da dum*, to signal the next teller's turn. The man with the family of sisters, Rajaji, if he did not have hands could not tell us anything, the way he flaps them like wings out of jail. 'Tigers showed up in our village where my family sold pots and pans. We were all Tamils, the Tigers were our boys, yes. But just the same they made us line up in a street outside shops with our hands on our heads in hot sun. Who knows, maybe they were looking for some spy to the army. I was not knowing what was going on down the line. But my brother ...' It does not matter, Mother, if we have Africans talking, Turks telling, Argentines reciting, we listen to the vanishment of loved ones and such like with all our senses. I am proud of my tenants. It is *amportant* to tell a true story for acceptance in the House of the Lord, notwithstanding the Lord has gone away. Notwithstanding the proof is in the kindling. I respect what I hear, and sometimes hate what I suspect, Mother, when the real truth could help my house. I suspect the Iranians with gold in their socks could give us a helping foot up the food chain.

This chain stretches from our Safeway expeditions, through a never stopping kitchen, to dishwashing messes, and garbage day with delinquent idlers. I lie here this morning in my fog of smoke, worried over burning laws and such like city regulations. Last Friday was garbage collection day, after Reesa went for her interview, and I had a very hard time recalling whose garbage duty it was. Sometimes this house makes me want to scream, Mother, the lizard lounging and laziness! The name calling and bickering! My tenants have no thoughtfulness for a landlord's headaches. Trudy and I ended up degrading into anger ourselves, hauling cans to the street, helped by Constantine and his brother who will not take hospitality without giving back the favour, and by three children of a sickly Salvadoran family. The children watched, their noses running. Trudy's nose ran too. Her blue eyes looked red, either from pollen or plaster dust, her blonde hair stringy. Last week warm weather was sneaking up on us like a bad smell. Four cans over the four limit, and we could not stuff anymore into our legal four. We made a stinking performance, dragging eight spilling-over cans of vegetable peels, wet Kleenex, sanitary napkins and such like, used-up bottles of cooking oil, fish entrails, globules of rice, thrown-away sneakers and worthless pesos, torn up documents ... down my driveway to the crescent. Disgusted Mr Luce was staring from across the street. Trudy sneezed. 'If four of these cans have to wait a week on the curb, can you imagine the stink neighbours like him are going to raise?'

So now we are a week behind in garbage, Mother, trying to cut back two cans a week till we catch up, but it is a lost scuffle. We will have to start burying it. We do well for a populated house, but our size does not fit the neighbourhood. 'Burn it,' said Trudy. 'That'll settle it.' I said no, no garbage burning is one bylaw I will obey. To the Vietnamese, turning up our front yard sod to plant vegetables, I asked loudly could they help us compost our wet garbage? At that moment, Mother, the garbage of my past life shot past like a déjà vu, braked, and backed up in the middle of the crescent. Mr Luce was still watching. Two scrubby faces in a silver Nissan, not local faces, stared across to where I, a.k.a. Corbin, was standing in the centre of eight spilling garbage cans. The driver wound down his window. The passenger got out and squinted across the roof.

'Hey, Kev, look who's livin in a big house with all his Paki friends dumpin on the carpet, livin the life of a tuxedo. While we're on the outside mindin our own beeswax. Keepin our noses clean, not stickin em into garbage that don't concern us. Those who was born in Canada know our place. They know Pakis and Chinks and gooks are comin in tryin to burgle it away from us ...' 'Fuckin carpet jockey,' said the driver, gunning the engine. His partner climbed back inside and slammed his door. 'Creeps!' called Trudy. My friends took off. Not much different from our neighbours, I thought, like Mr Luce gawking from his garden. Trudy said our two tourists seemed in a big hurry. I told her landlording sucks in the pits.

Theresa came out to help us then, carrying a bag of garbage and walking backwards. She was bringing us used Luvs she said we forgot in the basement. She was hiding her face from the Ford Falcon, parked under an oak tree. She would not face the street. 'My mudder is die one year ago and I not go. Men like dat car want me go. Why doan dey go and leave us?' The gatekeepers from Immigration, Mother, peeling an eye on who comes and goes, pending hearings and such like. These men loomed up five months ago, when my house made news, owing to my sympathy for roofless Latinos expelled from Mrs Scobie's church basement.

Our gatekeepers are not the only oglers Theresa is tolerating, Mother. I will not name the country to you, but the Islamics overall are big oglers, you would remember this. Maybe they are used to wanting many wives. With Theresa it is really a tempest in a tea cosy. This is the given with Theresa. I only wish she would free up her room in a huff and go home, so I could fit in our Haitians who do not own a tent. They are sleeping still on the front porch, in the UFFI mess. 'I tell Reesa you tell me do dat,' she said. 'No, Theresa. Don't bother Reesa.' And I gave her hand a little kiss. 'I doan like you kiss my stinky hand from diaper.' Mother, Theresa never trusts us anymore to like her. She says Damon thinks she is doing a bad job with Gwyn, just because he wants to help feed her. She has no trust of Damon not to do violence on his niece, with evil lurking to jump out his dumb mouth. She is a basketcase, Mother, but Reesa is loyal, like she is loyal to another cripple, Dwight. She would never let gatekeepers arrest her illegal nanny without embarrassing them with an ear lashing. I do not know why. Theresa is homesick and would love to go home. But I say nothing to Reesa. Reesa likes failures, even Dwight. It pleases her to go against our age. It pleases me, to rehear their pillow pow pows from last year.

The gatekeepers think they have some goods on me, Mother, because of my trial with Mr Singh and his illegal profit-making off aliens. They would love to frog walk me to jail. Notwithstanding myself as a property owner, I cannot expect justice except my own justice. They cannot see I no longer have a profit lust, except for some windfall to cover my household operations. I worry. Often I envy Damon his *come see come sawness*. This is how I interpret his dreamy trust in the landlord. If he only knew, Mother. If a carpet is soaking from a flood, Damon loves to help us carry it outside to wring in the sunshine. 'How many Poles you need to squeeze a China carpet, Da?' asks Trudy. Damon holds up three fingers. 'Almost! Two to hold the carpet, two to turn the holders.' But would Trudy make fun of Poles if Solidarity had been a winner and not a loser this month at Gdansk? We make fun of losers, rooms in my house make fun of other rooms. In consequence, I worry. I puff and meditate every morning like a pyre. Not even Trudy can know the burden of a landlord's duties.

But no one rags Damon, except Sylvia, who calls him a whangdoodle. He is unmuffled by our invasion of his dead mother's house, and taps his ring on windowpanes, birdcode to the birds. He does not mind if Mrs Irving's French chairs get burned in the fireplace, if I forget to pay the furnace bill. If the dryer breaks down his laundry and ours dries on the hedge and shrubs. What does he care? It is camp and good times for Damon. He is swept up with the Ugandans in their football games. He takes his turn in the new latrine and under the hose. My tenants like Damon as the only white man they know not waiting to pepper them with questions. They think he is the landlord and I, a.k.a. Corbin, a pushy mouthpiece who lucked out as caretaker by bedding the white girl. To them life is ambition and corruption. They think they see in me a fellow grabber.

'Make love to me, Wishes.' Trudy, moaning in her underwater sleep, does not mean it. I know from her sleep talk she has been up half last night with the feverish Salvadoran baby. That burning smell, what is it, Mother? The baby? I notice the cigarette butt burning at my fingers but feel no pain. Skin is the smell, yes, like something bad entering our curtains from the barbecue pit. Some rotten meat maybe, frying in the kitchen. Mother, you can see the cause for my laziness this morning. Growing bedlam in the kitchen. My love of meditation. The sun is rising and I feel exhilarating uplift. The kind of start I like to my day, suffering tenants to come unto me, especially if they have some rent to water my cash flow. They never do. I hear feet on the diving board, clattering in the bright air, then a body slapping the half empty pool, an echo inside the cracked walls. I listen for a shout from the grass court, Mother, where the Tamils have their tents pitched inside the fading lines of white chalk. I wait and listen.

4.

I need aspirin, two or three, not for this vegetable pizza we are sharing with Reesa, but for bad news this morning of Miguel Artruro splitting open his head on the bottom of the swimming pool. 'I see tiles still blood,' says Theresa. Mother, I stay unbalanced at the sight of it in my mind, dizzy. The good news is Miguel will live, the hospital took an X-ray and plugged his fracture. Sadly, Mother, the gatekeepers have grabbed him, soon a deport back to El Salvador. The hospital had no duty but to report him, when the ambulance delivered him with no health card, no papers. Reesa is comforting me and Trudy with her charm and spirits. We are having an early supper in the basement, where my tenants will soon be four, after she picks up

Dwight and brings him home. Knowing I will be Dwight's new landlord, once he lands, I feel my headache grow a little louder.

Reesa is wary of the media finding out about our prodigal son's return. 'They can't wait to see how things turn out. For the worst they hope. So mum's the word, Aloysius, okay?' I swear, Mother. Their reunion is a private act as far as I care. Reesa is so calm in her musical chair with the mayor I should ask her secret to help me landlord my mansion with more cucumber coolness. If she has her weather person's job, this news will be a happy ending for somebody looking forward to a new start. She is still pretending she does not have it, because she auditioned on Friday like someone else already had the job. 'I didn't care, I gave them an audition I thought they'd detest!' 'Show it!' cries Theresa. 'Yes,' says Trudy, 'audition for us.'

Gwyn whimpers for attention and Reesa slices another pizza sliver for her bowl. With the bloody mess in the pool, and the whole house cleaning it up, Gwyn feels neglected today. Reesa gets up from the little table and goes to her handbag to fit something on her head. A party hat, Mother, from her dress rehearsal. 'Settle down, Gwyn, honey. Mummy will let you have her hat in a twinkle.' We are like a family of boat people on a raft, waiting with our mouths open. 'Okay, "The Weather",' she says.

'This evening, folks, I'm going to avoid forecasting chitchat. Seriously. On the news, you've just heard forecasts from an economist dreaming about an upswing, a sports commentator on who's finally going to win the Stanley Cup – as if anybody cared, with this summer weather – and a priest about your morals, if you don't have a change of heart pretty soon about the unborn. Besides, my anchorman has co-opted drought on the prairies and what the greenhouse effect is going to be on our own province ... as if acid rain, the national debt, a political collapse of the whole nation weren't enough for that guy. Right, Tony? Get a shot of Tony ... can't keep a straight face in the line of duty, can he? ...' Trudy chuckles her appreciation, she has a crush on Tony. Not Theresa, crushless as a handkerchief. 'Especially when yours truly's the one left high and dry and supposed to be funny,' continues Reesa. '... You find this funny? Come up here and try it for five minutes, when the weather's as bland and nice as it was today. That's how come the funny hat, folks, 'cause when I trace the satellite systems for you, you'll have something to hold your attention.' Here she pauses to lift the reflecting gold party hat off her hair in a little doff. Gwyn reaches from her highchair.

'This evening I take my hat off to all the municipalities up the valley,

THE LIFE OF A TUXEDO

where your weather is going to be exactly the same as it was today, sunny, and to our friends on the north coast, where ... See how a hat drops to the floor? ... Just like it's supposed to, in a studio devoted to the fall of things, like peace and the stock market? Look, for you folks at home, it's *hard* to compete with crises like those, even for a personality with her joker's licence. And while I'm at it, let me unload my pencils and pens ...' Suddenly she is dropping these from her blazer pocket onto the floor, Mother. Gywn throws her cheese topping at them, laughing. Then adds her plastic bowl, with a clatter. 'You didn't really say all this!' exclaims Trudy. 'Yes, everything falls, if you wait for it. Airliners and the price of gold, even the odd parkade, owing to corner cutting contractors. You wouldn't guess gravity is the weakest force, would you? But it is. Gravity's garden variety cheap, folks. Domestic entertainment in a nutshell.' Here Reesa checks her wristwatch for when she has to be at the airport. She screws up her eyes comically, searching for her crown up top like Nebuchadnezzar, Mother, trying to remember what else she said in her audition. Then throws up her hands. Gwyn, too, screaming to be picked up.

'... I guess I went on,' she tells us, taking off her hat and handing it to Gwyn. '... Being contumacious. Adlibbing like a loon about the New Ice Age and the New Warming Trend, and wondering if my debut were my dénouement. Isn't that what the weather forecast's supposed to be, a dénouement for the newscast? I could have kept expanding ad noz into a flat universe. I still don't think I got the job. I didn't act the part.' Trudy, nibbling her pizza like a mouse, picks off a mushroom. 'Well, I guess you were pretty deep for the likes of Tony and them.' Reesa sits down again, next to the highchair. Theresa, picking up Gwyn's mess off the floor, says, 'I tink she is worse dan notty diapers.' 'Tony wasn't in the studio,' Reesa tells Trudy. 'This was only an audition.' 'But whoever auditioned you was probably expecting you to gab on about "seasonal values". Isn't that what they call them? The fronts and stuff?'

'Values my hat. The report I was supposed to read said something like ...' and here she adopts her old *City, City* tone from a rival station, 'No change for tomorrow, the steady flow of westerly air will maintain sunny skies over the North Coast and Interior for the holiday weekend, and for the next several days, and here on the South Coast and Lower Mainland we can expect the same. Clear skies, Tony, and beach weather for the whole family. That's the weather picture. So enjoy.' I mean I could do that stuff in my sleep. So could Aloysius. The values in it are counterfeit. The nuclear family at its leisure.' Trudy has a little pile of mushrooms to the side of her plate. 'Don't you run a risk, though, admitting that to yourself?' Reesa looks at her. 'To myself? At this stage, Trudy, you forget I'm starting out with little to lose. My laundry is all hung out.' Not all of it, Mother, just hers and Dwight's. Hers and the mayor's is still hidden in my pocket. Gwyn is trying on the shiny party hat now, backwards. We spot ourselves in it, sitting round a square table. Over our heads someone is pounding on the floor, a slow pounding with no rhythm, like a punk band. 'It sounds like the axe is falling,' says Trudy. 'Probably poor Sylvia,' says Reesa, 'in despair.'

I am upstairs in a dart, Mother, to investigate destruction to my property and tenants. It is the fireplace poker, operated by the sickly Salvadoran child, Veronica, using it to attract attention on a bedsheet. Is she feverish again, or just bored? Her family is nowhere in sight. No one Spanish speaking is in the living room, just Amar Hoca, the man from Turkey, snoring on the sofa with a hole in his big toe. I see the child has chopped little craters in the oak floor, alongside her wasted body. It is the same poker Damon waves like a talking stick when he foams at being misunderstood. She watches me take it from her, touch her skin to see if she is still hot. My bedside manner, Mother, is not what it should be to gag a whimper, the sound that grates most on my eyelids. The sound that children leak when they are tired, or have a sliver festering from climbing in the treehouse Amar built them from my neighbour's fence. A sizeable treehouse, squatted in by the Chilean family. The city building inspector came last week to visit at the neighbour's request, to check out our treehouse, our UFFI removal, our outdoor latrine. We are in violation of several bylaws, I forget the ones, and I have not bothered to address myself to their obeyance. I might never. Emergencies like Veronica keep getting in the road.

Trudy hisses from the top of the stairs. She hears Veronica's mother in our bedroom, she thinks with a man. I climb up through the landing, through the encampment of bedsheet canopies there, to follow Trudy down the hallway to our closed door. We listen, Mother. 'Misericordia!' comes a woman's excited cry. I shrug to Trudy. I pat my pants for a piece of Trident, to take back down to the little girl with no rhythm in her bones. If the woman in our bed wants another birthing what can we do to stop her? Landlording sucks in the pits. Another round for us of nose wiping and keeping the lid on. Where is the *amportance*? Trudy, if she had another place to live, would like to slip out of here. I see it in her weariness. She says, 'I know what that burning is you were smelling this morning.'

The Sikhs and Guatemalans, against four or five UFFI removers with dirty hands, are all sweating in the sun at volleyball. Something is still smoking, Mother, the remains in the barbecue pit of what Trudy swears outside was a foetus. I do not believe this and neither does she. But the born-again Hong Kongers told her, in their annoyance at the boat women for wearing loose see-through dresses, it was a foetus. I have an idea it is Buster, the neighbourhood beagle, barbecued before dawn by the Hong Kongers. Trudy has not seen Buster either. Or else, Mother, the smell is the remains of somebody's garbage, burning in excess of my new limit on waste products from kitchen activity and such like. In the strong evening light the smouldering wisps have stirred Mustapha, the sandalled Afghani, to prac- tise his story on Omo our youngest Ugandan. They are both in mourning near the barbecue. Neither is watching the volleyball.

'... Landlord changed in my country. Boom. Boom. Shells knocked down some walls of my village, my family lay buried when I came up from down in a well. I took with me a little water in a goat bladder. I was walking to Jalalabad. But instead some mujahedeen found me and took me higher in the mountains. They made me carry a big belt like this of bullets over my shoulder. Very cold in the mountains. My toes froze ... here, you can see some bad bunions in my foot ...'

A window in the glass house bursts from someone's thrown croquet ball. So many broken windows, from cricket games and baby skinheads, the sur- prise is to hear any pane left unbroken! Amazed, I turn to listen, waiting to smell any tropical smell left inside to leak out. Any bird to fly out. I know what Dwight's father used to grow inside all winter, frangipani and lime blossom. In summer, said Mrs Irving, he would barbecue meat out here for his family and burn fruit leaves in the fall. The smells have changed a long way since then, to remind me of the new landlord's bad failings and radical family.

I do not know what happened to your body, Mother, lying on the floor, but I know what happened to Mr Ghanai's. I burned it. I stored up my revenge for when I could find his grand house, and I did find it, from the orphanage. I thought of a knife blade first. On my way back from Malabar Hill, I thought of cutting that assassin, until I saw my old street friend Shankar in an intersection, performing, and the sight of him gave me a new idea. It would have to be at night and he agreed, Mother, when I told him my story to help me finish it. He was the fire swallower. He brought along his can of petrol and some bottles. Lights were burning inside the grounds, inside the house, Mother. It was easy to hide in jasmine bushes till the rooms darkened, then to soak rags in Shankar's bottles to throw through open windows. Mr Ghanai perished in the flames. He burned up and perished. Rest assured, Mother. Ashes. In the end you had a bier from your grieving son.

I now felt no more guilt for running away and leaving you behind, a homeless body in an apartment tower, for the vultures and such like. My guilt vanished in the flames. I had done the son's duty for his mother with a roaring pyre. Even if it was not yours, the revenge was. I have no question he burned up like an oil slick. After three years I felt free for the first time. Except I did not feel free, Mother, when I heard in the newspaper our firebombs burned up his daughters in their beds. Back at the Orphanage of Hope, in Sister Helen Anthony's class, I had a horrible sadness for many days, fighting the evil accident I had committed. I tell this, Mother, so you will not miss me when I return in my next life as a dog or a cripple and can not talk to you, like Damon sniffing lily of the valley. I very badly wanted to be a man. Shankar and I cut ourselves, climbing the dead landlord's wall.

Damon is camel riding Gwyn on his shoulders, underneath the apple tree. Maybe he also at last is becoming a man. White smoke from the barbecue is still rising straight up in the air. I foresee another fine day tomorrow, but the day after we may need thunder to clear off the mugginess. High ridges can never fight off the fronts lining up and breaking down and building up, way out on the Pacific like fishboat navies. I stand beside tired Trudy, watching the world grinding down my lawn. You would like Trudy, Mother, notwithstanding how she broke my heart with Andrew. And you would find this noisy tenement comforting, the crying and conflicting bodies you missed moving in to your tower over Bombay. Hot pink peonies having a whipping from children rope skipping on my patio. The volleyball net made from bedsheets, bouncing ... Let us say there *is* this net, made from bedsheets or else curtains. Yes, you would like shrieks from the empty lily pond, where the Sri Lankans are having a tickling bee with Damon's cat. You would smile hearing a Laotian scolding his son not to spade up the cucumber garden. And Gwyn, I see, tugging Damon's hair and falling backwards, his hair in her hands, both of them opening up their mouths to ... A crow bursts from the apple leaves, Mother. 'I - I - I - I - I - I - I ...' This particle of speech, I know of no other word for evil we long to be crushed by more than I. I, a.k.a. Corbin, am a miracle and a dream. Sometimes, Mother, I give myself duckbumps. I take Trudy's hand in mine, to look over this ruined place, our place. She is wearing my plastic bracelets once more. Like those morning mists rising long ago, when I first skated the lagoon, moonwalked it, Mother, so these evening mists are rising now. In all this broad expanse of tranquil light they show me, I see no shadow of another parting from her.

Book Three

BONES

Pilgrim-in-Law

Chapter 20

A Time Traveller

BARTLETT DAY, D.C., was admitted into the prison through a gate in an edifice resembling the Alamo. Disneyland with turrets. January fourth. Fifth, he'd flown all night. James Tocher said goodbye at the door, warning him to expect a wait. The chiropractor waited an hour in a room surrounded by tropical scenes, probably the Costa Rican coastline, painted on the walls. Doors banged, voices shouted, a fly buzzed. A truck laboured uphill towards the prison before veering off. A hot morning. His hard bench sloped in favour of his left buttock and at cost to his right. *Whatever that means ... my right bun ached.* A dried smear of airplane butter attracted the fly to the matted hair on his wrist. Tired of giving it the brushoff he stood up and walked over to the barred paneless window.

He could see the city, down across the bridge with its striped barrier, empty oildrums and two guards, which he and the embassy man had just crossed to climb up here to the castle-like prison. The barranca acted as cleavage for a small stream and city garbage. By pressing his head against the bars, Bartlett could see the fleshy leaves of a vegetable garden flourishing in the pink volcanic soil next door to the red-and-white quarters of the Guardia Civil. A cannon from another era stood on ceremonial watch.

He thumbed one of the rusty bars and imagined his own incarceration, as the stink of burning garbage slowly intruded. Forced to escape, his nose flew from his face and came to nest outside in a trellis covered in magenta bougainvillaea. It started singing. The cannon had whitewall wheels of thin circumference and black spokes, a vintage vehicle with the equivalent of fins and ornaments.

He kept expecting Dwight to be led into the room. Instead, a guard with a carbine on his shoulder wandered by and summoned Bartlett deeper into the prison. First he frisked the visitor, sort of tapping his pants pocket with the back of one hand. He'd left his white lab coat at home, so the effect of his shirt and trousers, bagging freely like pyjamas, reminded him of the space his flesh used to require for spreading. The guard rummaged a bit in his shoulder bag, checking for concealed weapons, contraband, possibly a bribe.

They tramped up a dirt tunnel. This service road continued out into bright sunshine of a yard beyond. The visitor could see leafy limbs draping over a distant wall, lounging there in tropical air, beckoning. These must have given exercising inmates ponderable pleasure. Reach these, crawl along one of them to the tree trunk outside the wall, slither to the ground: Adios, amigos. *Wait ... am I embellishing here? Maybe there weren't any trees.*

He never reached the yard. The guard motioned him through a steel door into another empty room, this one with a table, two chairs and no window. Alone again, he had no choice but to settle in for another wait. He was surprised at how few guards and prisoners seemed resident in this decrepit penal colony. He and the guard had passed no one, except a janitor.

He collected himself. What Dwight was and wasn't to be told about his mother had already been decided between him and Reesa, talking it over, agonizing, delaying his departure south in order to check back with the estate lawyer to ensure Mrs Irving's will was legit, drawn up freely and of sound mind, that it was legally incontestable. They decided to break only the news of Mrs Irving's death – this, and her expressed wish to have her son set free from prison, for which she was more than willing to buy off the lamentable Five Stars Hotel, even from the grave.

He was carrying her money in travellers' cheques. Yet was doubtful now of signing them all over for their intended purpose. Not two hours ago at the airport, James Tocher had told him Dwight was still being stubborn 'on the principle of justice'. Yeah, so? Well, as a Canadian, the prisoner didn't seem to understand that Central American justice, even if you could count on it, which you couldn't, was *not* a protracted matter of waiting out indifference. This embassy hotshot told him in Costa Rica principles rarely interfered with whim and an expected bribe. They actually accompanied them.

After ten minutes a man was led into the visitors' room through an inner steel door. Bartlett was shocked. So recently a fat man, here now a skeleton. A bonerack. A scarecrow without a field, his clothes hanging on him like curtains, ditto his hair, long and foul, and his face scabby and encrusted with pus. In less than three months Dwight had degenerated from chief executive to bum. Beyond bum. *One glimpse and I saw where our youth had fallen off its high horse and begun to c-r-a-w-l.* Dwight was shaky but dignified, trying to suppress a nervous habit of scratching himself, only half succeeding.

The two old friends were allowed to shake hands and sit down at the table. They didn't speak. Bartlett dropped his shoulder bag to the floor, busying himself with squaring up his chair, at not looking Dwight in the eye. He looked instead at his friend's scabby hands. Then he surveyed the room as if cheerfully preparing himself for some routine board meeting. At either door a guard had squatted down on a three-legged stool, elbows on his knees, rifle barrel sticking up between them. The wall was flagged with a bony crucifix and no hint of tropical coastline.

'How are you, Dwight?'

A shrug. His fingers drummed the way an alcoholic's might, waiting for a drink to still them. He must have heard from Tocher to expect someone today, then guessed this person would try to persuade him to take his mother's money. He couldn't have guessed his mother was dead. 'I was in hospital two or three days over Christmas,' he conceded, smiling. 'Now the fucking diarrhea has come back.'

Bartlett nodded. He folded his hands on the deeply scored table and tried not to think of Dwight's diarrhea. The table might have come from the prison classroom, if the prison had a classroom. 'Fucking dysentery,' said Dwight.

'Dysentery.'

'Feels like it,' said Dwight.

His itching had worn away little patches of skin and left his flesh raw. His face's landscape had altered. His scalp too looked raw, where he'd been weeding out his hair. Flakes of skin lay on his shirt far thicker than dandruff.

'Reesa?'

'Oh, good,' answered Bartlett, a little eager in his desire not to seem alarmist. 'Gwyn's great too. Keeps asking for daddy. Everybody misses you, Dwight. Theresa ...' He didn't mention Aloysius. 'Any news,' he then asked, 'on a release date?' He knew the answer to this one too.

'Zero.'

'Son of a bitch,' said Bartlett.

Dwight suddenly gave in to his fingers, and allowed them one raking scrape to the back of his hand, followed by a prolonged harassment of his cheek. Flakes of skin drifted to the tabletop.

'Something cooking about a minimum-security place,' Dwight allowed, amidst the expansive relief afforded him by his scratching.

'Oh?'

Silence. Then: 'Tocher thought it might be a better place to wait out my time.'

'Far, this new place?'

'A hill town, somewhere near the capital.' He spoke as if the capital were somewhere else, not here where they were sitting.

'Well,' said Bartlett. 'Guess a smaller town would be a better place to wait out your time. Friendlier ...'

Dwight's fingers had moved on to another patch of his face. Protracted scratching, more falling skin. The bored guards had begun to leak spit onto the floorboards with barely audible ejaculations.

'Dwight. I have some sad news.'

'They keep me in solitary,' said Dwight. 'No mattress to speak of. Nothing a chiropractor would sanction.'

'Solitary?' Nobody had mentioned solitary to him.

'Except for half an hour a day. Then I feel too rickety to exercise in the yard. They have to help me outside.'

'Christ.'

The prisoner stopped scratching to savour the expression on Bartlett's face, before breaking into a sardonic smile. His blue eyes took on colour. So, unfortunately, did his teeth. Green. Bartlett smiled back.

His friend now confessed he'd been reading the Bible from cover to cover. 'Trying to survive in here. You can tell Reesa I've turned into a bookworm. No one does any serious reading till he goes to jail. I didn't.'

'Reesa wants you to know, Dwight, how much this has shocked all of us ... I mean, about your mother.'

Dwight was scratching again, his fingers raking his face like a harrow. He seemed absent.

'She had a stroke, Dwight ... out of left field. Totally unexpected.'

The prisoner seemed not to hear his visitor's news. Had the embassy already told him?

'We feel bad not telling you sooner,' explained Bartlett. 'Not being *able* to tell you, Dwight. Reesa wanted you told in person. She was thinking of conditions in here ... how you might need someone to talk to?' He was trying to confide, without striking the right note. 'It happened Christmas Day.'

The guard stood up and said something in Spanish.

'Don't touch me,' said Dwight.

'Sorry. What?'

'He's saying don't touch me ...'

The guard sat down again. Bartlett, suitably chastened, studied the table between them.

'Look, Dwight, this is terrible, having to tell you about your mother like this. I ... wanted to be a comfort. Some comfort, right?' He balled up his hands and bumped his knuckles, before entwining his fingers like a church full of people. *Here's the church, here's the ...*

'Your mother came to my office in November, Dwight, before she knew she was ill. She wanted to talk about you being in prison. It was her idea I should make this trip, back then. She even paid for it. She wanted me ... she wanted you to accept her willingness to pay off your debts down here.'

Dwight interrupted his scratching. 'I accept her willingness ...'

His concession pleased Bartlett. '... I'm glad, Dwight. That's what she hoped.' He bent over to retrieve his shoulder bag from the floor, saying he had the sum of her good faith right here.

'But not her money,' said Dwight. 'This place is something I have to handle for myself ...' Adding, strangely, 'She'll get over it.'

He tilted away from the table, cradling his elbows as if for warmth. Bartlett recognized his own mistake in having tried to soften the news of Marlene Irving's death.

'Dwight, listen, I'm sorry. Your mother ... is dead.'

The prisoner looked at him, before allowing his chair to come back down.

'She was dead on her arrival at the hospital, Dwight, on Christmas Day. The stroke I mentioned ...? I wish I'd explained it better. I'm sorry.'

The unexpected death of a mother was something of which Bartlett had personal recollection.

Dwight said nothing, turning his eyes to the table for solace, or else for some place to park them. He sat very still, unscratching. This news of his mother's death had noticeably calmed him. Bartlett thought he recognized the marrow of grief. Without it you were a –

The sudden silence caused the two guards to scrape boots over their little pools of spittle. One of them peered at his watch. A pair of flies landed and began to copulate on the table. Bartlett thought he should bring a bunch of bananas tomorrow. Something for his friend's diarrhea.

'Your brother's in good hands, Dwight. You can tell he misses your mother, but he isn't moping.'

Dwight said nothing.

'Sylvia's very good with Damon,' said Bartlett.

The prisoner was stoic.

Bartlett calculated his friend wouldn't be interested in hearing anything about Aloysius, but if asked he was prepared to lie. Reesa had suggested he lie unless he felt her husband looked strong enough for 'the total scene back here, including debtors and lawyers'. She was being kind. Dwight knew about the collapse of Herodotus, of course, in a general sort of way.

His eyes had dampened. Bartlett wanted to reach over and comfort him, but remembered the guard's warning. He reached over anyway. His friend's shoulder bone was sharp. 'The fuckers'll think you're trying to pass me a knife,' murmured Dwight.

'They can fuck themselves.'

The guard who'd warned him the first time stood up again, pissed off. If the visitor couldn't learn, time to stick Dwight back in his hole. The plank floor where his spittle was smeared looked like it hadn't been swept since nailed down in the last century. Dwight automatically stood up when the guard grunted, his customary signal: that and an impatient tip-tapping of the carbine's stock with his thumb. More skin fell away from the prisoner's face, drifting to the floor. His yellow shoes now looked genetically altered, the approximate colour of car tires on a boat dock.

'I can't take her money,' he repeated, sounding like an automaton. Did he sound persuadable though? *I felt like a dink. All this money I couldn't give away?* Bartlett felt miserable for his friend. He felt miserable in a way for himself.

'Dwight, I'll come back tomorrow, all right?' He was pushing back his chair. 'I'm in no hurry. I can talk over this money thing with the embassy, and report back to you ...'

Dwight said nothing, allowing himself to be turned away by a guard at either elbow. The one-time travel agent and visionary liar limped out through the door, his visitor left alone to find his own way back. He picked up his bag. What he would remember was a man disappearing through a door, resolved to confirm to his own satisfaction a dire dislike of travel.

2.

From prison the pilgrim crossed over into the capital, where he slept away the afternoon in solitary luxury. He dreamed and remembered little of his dreams, except for blank spaces he knew weren't empty of curiosities at the time of his dreaming them. He remembered having passed the way of these spaces, empty now of all identifying lines. He woke up thinking what a fuck-up Dwight had made of his life. Those who lived by illusion died by it. *What nonsense. Get up and try the tap water.* He put his diary aside.

Travel always left Bartlett with the feeling he'd been away from home longer than he really had. When he travelled, time passed at a much slower rate than it did at home. It was like getting lost in a book, say, on homeopathy. Time abroad slowed down as it did aboard a spaceship. A week was a month, a month six months. A year's travel would take infinitely longer than a year at home.

He ran the bathroom tap and filled a glass. He raised it. Abroad, he decided, new experience distanced you from habitual experience with even the most domestic gesture. A personal diary became romantic history. For the duration of any journey you became a character who could surprise even yourself. Bartlett could look back in his diary on progress and reversals with a vivid sense of lines between insight and decision. Travel time was imaginary time. It turned memory into a suitcase, *yes, that's it*, the encapsulated reminder of getting carried away with some other self. *The art is to travel light, you go home younger.* No wonder he'd grown thinner over the last two years.

When Sylvia handed him a large white envelope on Boxing Day, with his name printed on it, he and Reesa agreed he should fly down here and try to persuade Dwight to come to his senses. Enclosed was a cashier's cheque for US$19,000, for which Dr Day was to purchase travellers' cheques in his own name – as Mrs Irving instructed – fifteen thousand worth to be used to persuade the Guatemalan hotel to drop its charges against her luckless son. The rest of the money was to pay for Bartlett's trip and expenses, 'as discussed in your office'.

From Sylvia he'd learned Dwight's mom had had the cheque ready three weeks before her death, in the hope her son could be home for Christmas. Then for some reason she just sat on it. If Sylvia knew why, she didn't say. The envelope, given him the day after Mrs Irving's death, came as a surprise. But the real surprise came later. An unexpected call from Mrs Irving's lawyer to Reesa, made Reesa suggest he delay his trip south till after the reading of Mrs Irving's will. She hinted at dark matters, only because the lawyer had hinted at dark matters. She later wondered how Dwight might best be informed of his mother's bequest.

It took him ten days, from the time of her death, to reach Costa Rica and share with Dwight the news of her passing.

He went outside and bought bananas for tomorrow's visit. He returned these to his air-conditioned hotel room, hoping they'd remain firm.

After dinner in a Cantonese restaurant, where he and James Tocher discussed Dwight as well as Toronto, the two Canadians wandered into an old colonial house on Morazan Park, at Calle 7 and Avenida 3. Bartlett was reading his map. Tocher wondered if the building might once have been an embassy. It had a flagpole. Key Largo had been converted into a bar.

Outside, prostitutes tried to pick his pocket by pretending to feel him up. Fingers in his pockets, knuckles on his balls. *Not on my balls exactly, but in the groiny vicinity.* Kind of pleasant. He held onto his bag. Tocher shook his head. 'This may be the Switzerland of Central America,' he allowed, 'but less desirable things can work efficiently too.' Tocher, a bachelor in his late twenties, had brought Bartlett to Key Largo to finish their discussion of the prisoner's predicament. They made their way inside, minus the tarts.

Turned out he and Tocher had known the same landlady in Toronto, having lived in the same house on Howland Avenue at different times in their respective educations. In fact, suggested Tocher, they'd probably slept in the same bed. 'Fancy that,' he said archly. *Seems whenever a fag takes a shine to me, my elbow itches.* Bartlett asked him how many hockey games he'd seen at the Gardens. 'Oh, all of them.' Tocher had knocked down a first in Poli Sci, which condemned him to 'dull External Affairs', since diplomatic service was the only career he could discover with its own entry examinations – something in his favour, as all he was really good at were exams. 'Believe me, I'm useless with my hands.' He thought he must've slept in Bartlett's bed three or four years after Bartlett had earned his chiropractic ticket from Memorial.

Tocher reminded Bartlett of his father. *Wisdom, like desire, is knowing how to savour absence.* Both his father and the younger man knew how to hold their tongues, even in the business of deploying them, as chitchatters. His father was straight though. Which Bartlett knew Dwight wasn't, ever since his friend had tried to outfit him with a French tickler in the frat house can, at a drunken party when they were pledges. He sometimes wondered why Dwight had never come out, unless his sudden pursuit of the beautiful debating queen, Reesa Potts, had forced him into a spiralling deception. His frat brothers, who used to hound anyone in hock to their on-going game of bridge, would tease him mercilessly with suspicions.

Bartlett drifted in a suitcase toward the coastline of sleep, mike in hand, his diary the repository of more strange stuff for one day than he could imagine might sound convincing in the far-off country of inactive old age. *Erase inactive.* But he hadn't yet spoken it. Once memory failed him, and liver spots mottled his hands, he fancied the idea of filling in these blank spaces of his once having knocked about the world, this romantic self he would no longer recognize talking to a diary that sounded made up. *I'm going to bed.* But he was already here.

3.

The following afternoon, Saturday, he brought along money for the guards. This time only one guard stayed behind to keep watch in the visitors' room. Bartlett slipped him five hundred colons and pointed to his wristwatch. The man understood, and to show good faith shouldered his carbine, grunted in Spanish for the two friends to relax and have a conversation, gestured cheerfully and left the room.

The other guard promptly appeared and treaded water with the expectant air of a seal. Bartlett dug down and paid him off too. The man vanished.

He mentioned the coincidence to Dwight, of him and James Tocher having lived in the same house in Toronto, even the same room, in the seventies. 'I'm beginning to think,' said Bartlett, 'the whole world conspires to coincidence. If my brain was bigger I could see its shape better.'

Memo to the future: never disown a good line.

Dwight looked awful. He scratched himself every minute or so, like a flea-infested dog, then tasted a freckled banana. He hadn't consumed sugar in months and seemed to crave the exotic taste. *Seemed to, I like that.* It went straight to his brain, soothing his mumbles. He didn't look any worse than yesterday, but that may have been impossible. So Bartlett brightly suggested this might be a good time to talk him into coming home. '... Now that I have you under the intoxicating influence of food?' What did Dwight think about coming home with him? He, Bartlett, would look into the financial requirements of easing him out of prison.

Dwight just shook his head.

Bartlett confessed to his friend he felt the news of his mom's death might have softened his resistance to her last wishes. Was he wrong? He said the money was Dwight's now. Why should he go on declining it when he might use it to relieve his predicament?

My predicament I didn't mention.

Dwight mentioned a migraine. Did Bartlett have any professional remedy to relieve a headache?

'As a chiropractor you mean?' Bartlett made no attempt to disguise his doubt about the oddness of his friend's suggestion. 'You mean, like manipulating it?'

'Anything.'

'I'll give you a crank, sure. If you think it'll help. These days, actually, I'm more interested in homeopathy ...'

He stood up and brushed Dwight's moulting skin from the table. He pushed his banana peel to the floor. He was a little worried about breaking his friend's frail bones.

'Why don't we use this contraption for our adjusting table?' *Anything to ease him out of depression.* With difficulty he got Dwight to lie down on the table.

When the first guard looked in, he must have thought their position across the table explained Bartlett's bribe. The chiropractor stared him down. Discreetly, the guard closed the door in his own face.

Bartlett began to talk as he manipulated, only because the patient seemed reluctant to discuss his pain. Maybe the pain was too much. He told Dwight of the hookers outside Key Largo. Dwight had never been to Key Largo, or to any other bar in the city. He'd been thrown into the local dungeon quicker than bad milk. On Bartlett rambled, employing the fifth thoracic technique in the dusty prison room, using his knee as a fulcrum against Dwight's knobby spine. *Was trying to tell him something, anything ...* Then he took a breather.

A stiff and suffering Dwight staggered up to rotate his neck, but his migraine hadn't gone away. 'Still splitting,' he said. 'Got any manipulations for a skin condition?'

Bartlett took his snideness seriously. 'You,' he said, 'should consult a homeopath.' The miasm of his skin eruption could be quite a *hopeful* sign his disease had already been driven to the surface. 'Don't ask me how,' said Bartlett. He advised against any treatment for it now. 'I know enough homeopathy to know very little, except health isn't always what it looks like.'

Dwight slumped down on his chair. The buzzing of flies had increased noticeably in the vicinity of the remaining fruit, now forgotten on the floor.

The visit seemed over.

The story Dwight had been giving Tocher was that justice and patience would eventually conspire in his release. An obsessive fancy, believed Tocher, rooted in the prisoner's vision of some hopelessly ideal world. 'He's having to overcome a lot at once,' said Tocher.

Bartlett respected his friend's decision to tough it out alone, without giving in to corruption and extortion. But he now suggested, helping himself to a banana, that Dwight should come round to the logic of survival. He made it a point to mention Hong Kong, where Dwight's father had been held in Stanley Prison by the Japanese. He reminded him of his asking Bartlett to pay a visit to the cemetery of dead Canadian POWs, whom his father had barely survived. And Bartlett had. Dwight's eyes moistened.

So the visitor switched topics. He talked about his patients. His father's plans to remarry. Also about himself and Megan. *An awkward pause.* He disposed of his banana skin on the floor. Maybe, too, he should mention the drowning debt he was treading, because of Dwight's shipwrecked travel business. But Dwight was no longer listening. The prisoner was rubbing again at the scales he seemed determined to remove from his hands.

Bartlett said he'd be back Monday. Tomorrow he wanted to visit Poas Volcano and that was an all-day tour, the object of which was to peer down inside a mistless crater, he'd heard, and beyond the crater's rim as far as Nicaragua. 'Besides,' he suggested, 'you need time to reconsider your mother's sincerest wish.'

Dwight declined the rest of the fruit but accepted Bartlett's hand in friendship. Bartlett attempted to lighten the moment by giving the secret fourth- and fifth-finger squeeze of their old fraternity handshake. A puzzled, painful look passed across Dwight's face, possibly a spasm from his headache.

I felt silly, carrying off those bananas in my armpit ... Not even the guards wanted them.

4.

He'd had no expectation of seeing Costa Rica. He'd expected to be home within three days, having secured Dwight's permission to turn over Mrs Irving's money to the embassy, who would then arrange quietly for the prisoner's release in a week or two.

But because of Dwight's stubbornness he now had time to see the sights of San José. As well as those of Puntarenas on the Pacific, Limón on the Atlantic, not to mention Poas Volcano in the middle – where it rained – and Manuel Antonio National Park, south of Quepos, where he stayed overnight at an expensive hotel and swam in water the same green colour as the water on the wall of the prison waiting room. *Artificial.*

It turned into a holiday. He spent his holiday money. He did his best, between these side trips, to entice Dwight with stories about his travels. It was like talking elephants to an Eskimo. His friend couldn't understand the language. No luck whatever in convincing him to accept his dead mother's money in order to go free.

The more Bartlett thought about his own future the less free he felt himself.

There was a lot he wasn't telling Dwight, not complaining about: that his debt was Dwight's debt, that his father's debt was really Dwight's debt, and that his practice had declined. The other news he was concealing was about Dwight's disinheritance. Mrs Irving had unexpectedly willed her house to Aloysius, instead of to her son, cutting him out of its legacy entirely. *This still can't be right, can it?*

When he pondered how much farther Dwight had to sink, how far down his friend had sunk already, the perspective afforded by his friend's skeletal appearance resigned him to his own losses. He had little to grieve for in comparison. He was still a respectable quack. His losses, his threatened losses, didn't circumscribe him the way his friend's losses did, and wouldn't destroy his illusions the way they were suffocating Dwight's. He toured the little nation and thought about his friend's odd fate.

Sitting there resting his bones, his loneliness won't let him alone ...

Dwight had fashioned a career out of his imagination. And was now despised for not having told the truth. This truth was about travel, which Dwight had known in his bones to be hazardous. He'd withheld this knowledge in order to profit. Buyer beware. Yet apart from one miserable hotel, had any of his clients ever suffered from the ignorance of Dwight's experience? Or, to put it the other way, the wisdom of his non-experience? *Pride though. Hubris is despised.*

On Bartlett's final visit to prison, nine days after his arrival, James Tocher was sitting in the waiting room discouraging flies. 'Oh, hello,' said the diplomat. 'I thought you'd gone back to Canada.'

Bartlett mentioned how much he'd liked Puntarenas and disliked Limón.

'Most interesting,' said Tocher. 'And the Tincas?' He smiled mischievously, as if the reason for his prison visit was to deliver condoms and watermelon. He complimented Bartlett on his saddle shoes. When the two Canadians stepped into the visitors' room, the prisoner remarked dryly at the sight of them together, as if he'd been pondering their destinies in tandem. 'What a coincidence. I'm beginning to think the whole world conspires to coincidence.' Dwight's *sang-froid* should've sounded hopeful, but didn't. He sounded tired of seeing them both and resigned to his own company. His skin looked looser, more disfigured than ever. He slouched at the table like a disappeared person.

Tocher spoke up pleasantly. He characterized Dwight's case as difficult but not insurmountable. The embassy remained hopeful of relocating him to a minimum-security prison as the first step on his way to freedom. Why not, since the court had yet to decide on Guatemala's extradition request? Things weren't so black.

Bartlett tried to be upbeat too. Homeopathy is what he talked about. Incongruity and logic. About treating like with like. *Might as well've been gossiping about the porters.*

When they parted, he was sad to say goodbye. That night he dreamt of barred cells opening up into tunnels and wall-less deserts. He flew home oppressed with the knowledge of a shapeless future for them both.

5.

It was drizzling in Canada. And the house smelled stale when he walked in the door with his suitcase. To Bartlett, after long flights inside aluminum tubes, after perfume and pollution in foreign cities, home never smelled as he remembered it. His freshly travelled nose was unable to take for granted even its most familiar space. He didn't repress smells, just lost his awareness of them. Then time began to speed up again. Soon his nose would contrive to forget these incarcerating reminders of decay, and begin to fabricate home again, or at least its impression. You got used to home. *It's a struggle sometimes to remember you've ever been away.*

That afternoon he put on his white lab coat and shuffled out to the office. A shower of rain dumped on him. His scalp released oil it had been holding back under the burning Costa Rican sun. His hair grew long and stringy. The rain traced lines down his face. He was walking up Altamira on a Wednesday afternoon in mid-January and it was cold, miserable.

His office was deserted and locked. When he opened the door it swept back a pile of flyers. The heat had been turned off. The air smelled sour and dead. The blind on the door rattled like a skeleton, and he noticed again where a blade had fallen out, years before in the practice of his predecessor.

He walked over to examine his appointments book at the reception desk. Names entered here on the white pages of his chiropractic future seemed as rare as a condemned prisoner's hopes. He was losing his practice. It occurred to him, for the *nth* time, he'd already lost his vocation.

He puttered through drawers and files looking for Lois's phone number. He discovered a recent letter from Glassgraf advising him of nothing he didn't already know about that company's unavoidable delay in starting up its skeleton bank, in which his investment remained sunk. He was drowning. *I could do with a new self image.*

He came across an old video marked Bangkok, turned it over in his hand, remembered something and decided to take it home.

'Oh,' said Lois, when he got through on the phone, 'you're back. I expected you days ago. I stopped booking appointments when you didn't show up.'

'A lot of requests, were there?'

'Well, not exactly. I just stopped coming in till the afternoon.'

'This is the afternoon.'

The news seemed to surprise her. 'Well, I decided to skip a day. You don't have to pay me, Bartlett. But the phone really wasn't ringing. Did you hear what happened to one of our patients?'

'What happened to one of our patients?'

'He died. Mr Astapovo.'

'Needles?'

'Some guy from the depths came in to tell you all about it.'

'When?'

'When did he come in?'

'When did he die?'

'I don't think he imparted that piece of information. He just grunted a lot, like a little rodent. He also didn't say if it was exposure to the cold or an arrow through his neck. Probably old age. He was ancient, wasn't he? Just the opposite of Mrs Dawson.'

Bartlett hung up, locked the door, and walked home via Carrots where he had a cappuccino. He passed the bakery where he bought a loaf of Hovis, and down by the bay to see if Aloysius's tent still stood. It did, but Aloysius wasn't in. It looked abandoned. Everyone was losing their vocation.

The rain stopped. A north wind blowing from over the mountains sent the temperature still lower.

Bartlett rummaged in his room for the envelope Needles Astapovo had vouchsafed him. Couldn't find it. He checked all his drawers, cupboards, the pockets of unlaundered pants and jackets. Reesa was still out so he couldn't ask if she'd happened across it downstairs. Theresa wasn't home either. Where was everyone? He wondered if Gwyn might have toddled into his room, found it on the floor, and decided she liked the taste of it enough to eat. He unpacked his suitcase and went downstairs.

A fat cheque from a deceased recluse, in debt to his doctor, would be welcome at this point in the history of man's struggle with his mortgage. Or a map to buried treasure, in some dark and dirty corner of the park. *No, I'm making too much of this.* The bequest of a man who understood history was unlikely to be huge. Still, it might be something. A man who knew how to share a vision of trees wouldn't be ungenerous.

The house remained offensive to Bartlett's nose, but not his ears. The place was agreeably quiet. No one came home, no one went out. He sat in the den thinking. For just a moment he wondered if he was squatting in an abandoned house, its water and electricity cut off, and tried the lamp.

Later, waiting for Reesa to return from her show, which he watched eating a crust of stale toast, he replayed the video of himself in Bangkok.

There he suddenly was, in grainy colour, sounding tinny at the podium of the Kingdom Hotel, with Bea swinging from a coatrack. *Coordination is the principle of harmonious action of all parts of an organism, in fulfilling their offices and purposes ...* How could he've ever pretended to such certainty of profession? The public bullshitter. So full of principles he knew to be expedient. So willing to share knowledge tapped from cranks, instead of from patients with tales of painful experience.

Patients were their own best doctors.

Backache, like heartache, cured itself.

Talking soothed, time healed.

Upstairs he dug down in his sock drawer for the earliest tapes of his diary, from that same trip to Bangkok, and listened to the private man as he sounded two years ago. Two centuries ago. Here was the more authentic character, not the personality on video wound up to run down in public. Here was the private man, choosing from all possible things he might say about the world, these ones. He listened. The tape ran on like a delta. *Silt and sand, really. An endless mouth ...*

Listening, he felt appalled how often he lacked any urgency of obsession. *Obsession, yeah.* He felt chagrined at the lack of any urgency among his sad bones of contention. *The plump pilgrim ... and his progress to bankruptcy.*

November, 1918

What a snag. Am trying to be patient, but consider the odds against me.

No crowds allowed. Churches, theatres, dance halls – all closed while Spanish flu rages. City's death toll has neared five hundred. More hospital space needed, new cemetery.

Still. Regardless of official health order, crowds have clogged streets today, Armistice Day. What jubilation! Rattling pots and cans, dancing on streetcar tracks, shooting off mothballed pistols: all these possible forefathers. With bands and parades who would believe it's November?

Trying to locate self in this euphoric wave have lost sight of possible birth. Am the quintessence of dust. Exist and don't exist, depending on how I weigh what's still in the future. The uncertainty is a load. Destiny seems such a dicy affair given the stew of genes summing it up. Which celebrants, if any, will become great-grandparents?

Wounded vets have hobbled out of hospital beds to celebrate, within hollering distance of the new pavilion for flu victims. 11:00 a.m. Sawmills, factories, dockside steamers all whistling like there's no tomorrow.

The war has taken a huge bloody cut of possible ancestors. Impossible to know the grief of houses whose sons will never come back. I cannot know it.

If choice were mine, of knowing or not knowing, I would choose grief over ignorance, but at what price? Returning troop trains reach this coast last.

'Wallace will be home soon,' an old aunt reminds a shy niece living with her. 'Will you be seeing him, my dear? You've both been writing.'

I peep on the correspondence of survivors, secretary to my own future. Wallace, an army doctor stationed in Egypt, is bound to want children, as is she. She teaches the young. Would welcome a mother like her to closet me from war.

Hate to recall police combing dance halls last year, rooming houses, the skating arena, for

young men of cannon-
fodder age who'd failed
to check in under the
Military Service Act. So
many possible fathers
seized – now in
permanent separation
from home.

Don't even know
what sex I will be. Yet
am perversely willing to
predict the big clock
downtown will stop at
2:25 next month because
of an earthquake – p.m.?
Anything is possible in
imaginary time, where I
soon hope to close down
the loopholes and get on
with a life.

When? In what flesh?
To know whose story to
track would make things
easy as pie.

Chapter 21

The Elephant Is Slow to Mate

ON THE SAME EVENING as Dwight's house party back home, it was the morning after here in Bangkok. Bartlett's lungs felt like two Glad garbage bags tickling his ribs, refusing to ingest the traffic's hot fumes in the indecent heat. He was thirsty again. Soliloquizing hoarsely he walked back to his air-conditioned hotel room, showered, and lay back down on a round bed the size of a swimming pool. He was resolved to dream up a good talk, but not so resolved as to make the best use of his time. Opening *The Bangkok Post* to check recent NHL scores, he found himself among basketball stats from southern Bible colleges he never knew existed. He airmailed Sports to the floor.

... Cancel the foregoing. Maybe not in the same league as Captain Shrink – whose name's up there on the Stanley Cup of medical history. We're not talking historical watershed, with Palmer in the same league as Freud.

He stopped the spools by thumbing the mike button. Then restarted them, the battery-powered machine perched shakily atop his stomach ... *At the same time, fellow delegates, it's inspirational to remember even Freud started out like most of us at this conference ... as a quack.*

He'd been in Bangkok three days. But only up here in luxury, and sometimes down on the river where he caught the public riverboat behind the Kingdom – to chug up or down the meandering current, picking up and dropping off Thais too sensible to travel the city by tuk-tuk, bus or foot – only up here could he escape the feeling of rotting a little every time he breathed the polluted air. The city's small piers were hidden away behind narrow riverfront buildings, where the air was slightly cooler. He had visited the Grand Palace this way, on a river foray by himself, and Chinatown, where he watched people lining up to stoop to an elephant. *Waiting to traipse under an elephant. I deked over to inquire ...*

Turned out the practice was a kind of preventative medicine he thought he could adapt, offering his patients the widest possible openings to tell him of their hopes for pain-free happy lives. Made a note of this in the street, talking to his mike: *Item: elephant practice means listening to their...* Et cetera.

His talk at tomorrow morning's plenary session required a direct line of attack, yet he hesitated, still uncertain what to say. Did he believe in what he had to say? Abroad he seemed so open to suggestion, doubt. On his first trip to Asia he was storing his new diary in the refrigerator of his mini-bar at night, because the salesman had stipulated frigid air would help preserve his batteries in the tropics. *My batteries could do with preserving, but...* When he tried listening to his previous day's account, the air-conditioner's recorded hum compounded the air-conditioner's hum he was hearing live. Bartlett wasn't sure he could distinguish one hum from the other – whether it actually made listening harder or if the white noise was even noticeable.

He imagined this luxurious room remaining at a constant temperature through all of time. He felt protected here, pampered to the point of extinction. It prevented him from getting down to sharing his specialization with other delegates to this International Congress of Alternative Healing. *'My specialization' sounds a bit swank...* He grabbed a wide roll of stomach fat, like a handlebar, to steer himself in idle fashion to the left. Increasing doubt had to be squashed.

Irritation sharpened his attention. He was willing to go on record with this irritation.

Item: World-wide more than thirty thousand chiropractors treating fifteen million people a year. More or less. The medical monopoly would like to wipe us out. Look what it's done to the...

Maybe though instead of complaining about the monopoly of mainstream medicine, he should stick to explaining his own alternative. A little wryness wouldn't hurt either. He gave the mike a Gleasonish flick, but the tape recorder over-balanced, slid down his stomach and bounced off the mattress.

He climbed out of bed for the second time that morning, to gaze down on the Chao Phraya River. He could spell it and practically pronounce it. Hermetically sealed inside his hotel he could hear none of its water taxis, rice barges, or rackety motorcycle engines attached to the hang-yao gondolas. He was aware that Dwight, in sending him abroad with such attention to comfort and safety, was fulfilling what he loved most about travel himself: avoiding it.

He tapped on the window from five floors up. This glass was protecting him from disease, a bad accident, Asia itself. Sitting on the restaurant patio below, ignoring the river and eating breakfast, were men and women he took to be fellow delegates. Was it feeling thirsty for change that made him uncertain about manipulating bones for a living? Tested by a meter reader he figured his ambition would be found deficient of the kind of hustle favoured by chiropractors who flocked to conferences in Houston, say, on how to target a wider market share of manipulatable spines. He was no market groupie. Instead, at thirty-two, he found himself in Bangkok wondering if his elevator went all the way to the top.

The sun pedalled higher. The Gulf of Siam was somewhere over there.

He got out a cold Pepsi and chugalugged the can. He then removed two fresh tapes from the refrigerator to put in his bag, in case he got inspired. Why *tapes* in the fridge? He'd bought extra tapes in a department store he discovered last night in a district called Banglumpoo, streets choking with Thai teenagers, medicine shops, punk rock music, and garment stalls smothered in jeans and Jockey briefs. *Check that: imitation Jockey briefs, small j gaunchies.* He'd come upon Banglumpoo, grateful to have escaped the darkness of stinking khlongs and wide roads owned by crazy drivers who refused to waste their headlights by turning them on. In this cramped quarter he discovered the New World Department Store, opening up before him like Ali Baba's Cave, complete with air-conditioning, escalators, mirrors. A woman in a scarlet dress had even followed him floor to floor, making herself available to any invitation, suggestion, the merest hint. *A floor Jane?* He bought tapes and a cream-fudge pastry. He took his time. When he looked again the girl was gone.

The Pepsi made him belch. *What I think of diet colas in the nineteen-eighties:* ... and belched once more, this time for the record.

After hauling on his cutoffs, rubber thongs and Foreign Trade T-shirt, he put on his white lab coat but refrained from buttoning it. He dumped wallet and passport, travellers' cheques and shades, tapes and recorder into his shoulder bag, before removing the door key from its wall slot, hereby killing the air-conditioner. No more hum. To fill the vacuum he began whistling *Kisses Sweeter Than Wine* as he went out the door.

'You big body all ovah.'

A Thai girl, backing into the corridor from the room opposite, didn't strike him as discreet, not in the way he'd come to expect from call girls in the lobby. 'You big boy for a big time some more soon. Okay?' Her customer stood half hidden behind his door. Bartlett headed quickly for the elevator and nearly made it. He heard her sashaying after him, wrists brushing her silk-dressed hips like clappers at a rodeo. *Or so it sounded, to my hummed-out ears.*

He had to admire her entrepreneurial spirit, on their way down together, the way her frank stare appraised him as a possible investment in the future. In Bangkok the future stretched from the next minute to that evening, and its moments died and lit up again like numbers you watched in an elevator. Easy to make a return trip: just press a button, expectations nicely rise, the doors reopen and you stroll out arm in arm with your wish. Politics disappeared and the economy flourished. A country prospered in the shafts and passageways of its hotels.

'You wanna massage maybe, doctor?' The elevator doors slid open to the lobby.

Bartlett said he'd have to get back to her on that one, and entered the dining room with his coat tails flapping.

The sight of so much linen-cushioned crockery made him feel nothing in this place would meet a surface squarely. The tone of it was swank green, a restaurant that could've been anywhere overlooking a river short of the Volga. He recognized its generation of rattan furniture from hotel restaurants at home. Outside, delegates were eating at marble tables and waiters moved among them in white jackets far smarter than his own coat. In his cutoffs he was dressed for McDonald's.

The air-conditioned air on his bare legs felt chilly.

'Good morning, Dr Day.' The little homeopath from Bangalore, who seemed amused to see the fat man in his lab coat, was wearing a smart brown suit and blue tie. Bartlett walked over to shake his hand. 'In Bangkok, whenever I see a loose wire,' responded V.L., 'I think of Thomas Merton.' On his table stood a large water jug and two glasses.

A trickle down Bartlett's ear made him remember he hadn't dried his hair. *Who was this Thomas guy?* 'Seen many so far, loose wires?'

'Not one as yet, I will honestly tell you. But I am looking for one so I can warn you Thomas Merton was at a conference in Bangkok, just like us.' He smiled agreeably. V.L. often seemed amused by his own playful equations. Equations were what he called them. Here among the chosen V.L. looked amused by the very idea of salvation, as offered by so many conflicting alternatives.

He went on. 'There was a loose wire hanging from the ceiling in Merton's hotel room, not like this hotel, but a crumbbucket, I expect, somewhere less nice. Our philosopher,' said V.L., 'reached to touch it and the wire electrocuted him. It is ridiculous. He died on the spot of electric charge, Dr Day. Except he fell onto his bed, I believe, and no one realized he was a dead duck. The early reports went about he was sleeping only. I was reading this all.' The little homeopath's eyes twinkled. 'Or was I dreaming it?'

Bartlett had spent the better part of his first evening in Bangkok having a drink with V.L. and listening to someone who drank only water tell him how high he'd once got writing a song that should've been a hit in India, except a lawyer from a Delhi publisher heard it and claimed it owed too much to 'The Teddy Bears' Picnic'. V.L. claimed never to have heard the teddy-bear song. An American travesty of his own he politely suggested. 'I equate it so.' Had Bartlett ever heard a picnic song about bears? Bartlett thought he had. V.L. said he tried hitching his lyrics to another tune but the song never caught on. He was now standing behind his water jug. 'Will you join me for breakfast, Dr Day?'

'Love to. But I promised a Canadian guy. Your ice water looks inviting though. You don't appreciate good water till you can't drink the tap water.'

'Please then,' said the homeopath. 'Let me pour you a glass for your Canadian table. It is my duty. Two glasses. Very pure.' He tipped the jug forward and an ice cube plopped into the first glass.

'Cheers,' said Bartlett, sipping. He carried away both glasses of purified water.

Marcus was reading *The Bangkok Post* and didn't glance up when Bartlett set down the glass in front of him. 'Listen to this,' he said, shaking the page:

'Actor Len Cariou, a native of the Canadian prairies, says he had an affair with actress Lauren Bacall in the 1970s when they were both performing in the musical *Applause*. "We were playing lovers in the play anyway," said Cariou, as he relaxed with a coffee in a Winnipeg restaurant recently. Cariou, once a tailor's assistant in Winnipeg, also reminisced about Bacall being a strict taskmaster with colleagues during the one-year stint of the musical. "She was very, very demanding of everybody."'

Smiling, Marcus looked up at Bartlett.

'That's Canada for you,' he said. 'In a nutshell.'

'What is?'

'And another thing. The only time we're picked up by an international wire service is when we're fucking the Americans.' He peered over his newspaper at the glass of water. 'What's that, vodka?'

'From Brehznev's own river.'

Marcus Reambeault was a delegate from Nova Scotia, a fellow Canadian Bartlett had met at the newspaper kiosk his first morning here. To have met at all, concluded Marcus, it had been necessary for him to fly east and Bartlett west to a point on the globe neither of them had ever expected to come. 'A coincidence,' said Marcus, 'almost. Hey, this is water.'

He looked close to forty, not balding exactly, but his broad forehead and fair hair combined to give him the appearance of a man in whose genes lurked no hairless developments not clearly foreseen at a younger age. He carried with him, Bartlett soon found out, an impressive wad of testimonials to his energy and success as a faith healer. His portfolio of photographs, mainly of himself curing priests with cancer, housewives suffering valve disorders, children with asthma, suggested few cases came his way he wouldn't take on. Even talking at a table he radiated energy. *Talking is his sinew. The guy never stops flexing.*

Marcus's talk to the conference yesterday had pleased many. In telling them about faith healing he'd claimed to run his hands over patients, speaking to them quietly of force fields and God, till the opening he wanted would follow and the period of healing begin. He admitted to striking oil, sometimes right away, in the manner perfected by TV evangelists – not a claim he made very proudly. He said he tried to remain professional and circumspect about his calling. He didn't accept fees, only donations, and stated whatever psychic powers he possessed worked mainly through the medium of small encounter sessions conducted in the havens of suburban ecumenical chapels.

Earlier, Marcus Reambeault had mentioned to Bartlett he was independently wealthy, with debentures inherited from his father's cooking-ware factory. The only stipulation had been for him to go into the ministry. 'So I went.' Not into a monastery, though he wouldn't have minded finding out what hanky-panky went on in a monastery. '... Nothing stifles me, Bartlett.' Indeed, he remained the most hopeful man Bartlett had ever met, not least in the matter of vitamin pills, a coloured range of which he experimented with between courses at every meal, dispatching potential diseases and invigorating his body, despite the brisk disapproval here at the Congress of Alternative Healing over pills in any form.

'I'll have a large orange juice,' Bartlett told the waiter. 'Eggs easy over. Ham. Hash browns. Any porridge, by the way? Rolled oats?'

'Cream of wheat, sir, is good.'

'That too then. And coffee, please.'

'Pancakes, sir?'

'No ... but maybe bring me a couple of croissants with my toast. I'll think about the pancakes.'

'Sounds like something out of Dickens,' said Marcus. He'd turned the page. The police had just rescued fifty children from a Bangkok mosquito netting factory where they were forced to work eighteen-hour days, every day of the week, for the equivalent of two dollars a week.

Bartlett's juice arrived, on the double. He was wondering about Aloysius, how long before he would've organized these children and struck for higher wages.

Marcus finished his papaya and buttered a croissant. 'You coming on the bus trip today?'

Today, Sunday, delegates had a free day to do as they pleased. Later on a bus trip was planned to take the interested among them to a refugee border camp, where they could examine how folk doctors and modern physicians worked side by side for the common good. This happened to fit in with the implicit plea of their congress for wider recognition of the role alternative healers could and did play in today's evolving world. Before the bus trip Bartlett was planning to take himself to the zoo.

'I'm open to whatever comes along,' he replied.

'That means Thai kick-boxing tonight,' said Marcus. 'And after that some of the rolfers are recruiting delegates for a visit to Patpong to inspect the troops.'

'Oh. Yeah.' Bartlett confessed he might have to pass on both. He was on stage tomorrow morning and didn't have his speech ready. An evening with the troops might guarantee it stayed that way.

'Use that quote I showed you. You're an articulate guy. Make it up as you go along.' Marcus wiped his mouth with his serviette. 'I do.'

He began to mine his ear with a baby finger, nodding toward his newspaper. 'We don't have the depth they do ...'

'Pardon?'

His friend now swallowed another vitamin pill, this time a green one, with his coffee. He was working his way through a little row of pills across the tablecloth like an abbot at his beads.

'The Americans ... have a lot of country south of them to live in, come from, move to. Canadians only want to move horizontally. It shows up in our slim range of accents and climates. We're a line-type country, Bartlett. Countries are either lines or circles ... plus cones maybe. Circle countries like the States are more complete. Think of France or Britain. Australia is a line country, just like us, because it lives on the edge, along its shores. Like Brazil. I think instead of dividing the world into first, second, third, we ought to take lines and circles into account.'

'What's an example of a cone country?'

Marcus had to think. 'Norway. Those in-between Nordic countries, Bartlett. They're not afraid of their interiors the way we are, but they don't have the depth of circles. Kenya is a cone country. India is a circle country. Alignment has nothing to do with standards of living. It's basically about depth. They've got more to tell us. Like Thailand.'

More than Marcus the Canadian? Should've asked him.

'Fascinating.' Bartlett drained off his orange juice.

A delegate walked past in a mauve dress trailing French perfume. French, the chiropractor decided, because her nametag said France. He admired the way her arms swayed, from her shoulders. He hadn't caught the name.

He wondered if Aloysius would remember to feed Mikos and sprinkle gravel on the newsprint when he changed the cage.

When he finished his eggs and cereal, hash browns and ham, toast and croissants, he asked his friend if he was going to eat his orange because he needed something to quench his thirst at the zoo.

'Be sure to eat the peel,' said Marcus. 'Keeps your urine wholesome.'

Bartlett wiped his mouth. 'Isn't napkin,' he asked, 'the American word for serviette?'

He had decided to pass on the pancakes.

2.

He stepped out through the Kingdom's glass doors and into the first taxi in line. Why bother saving money inside an open tuk-tuk when his lungs, throat and ears would all ache after the cheaper ride, with its annoying whine of a coffee grinder?

The air-conditioned car sped him across Bangkok, just as hot and polluted on Sunday as on Saturday.

Last night after drinks Marcus Reambeault had guided him into the hotel's library, an alcove the size of a closet, to look at books by writers and utopists who'd once stayed at the Kingdom. *The guy relishes my partnership*, decided Bartlett. There were only a few books, and these of questionable jurisdiction.

'Melville didn't stay here,' said Marcus. 'He's here because he sailed to exotic places. Same with this guy, who only sailed as far as New Zealand and became a sheep farmer. But listen ...' And he opened up to a passage he'd discovered earlier, something he thought might be useful to Bartlett in explaining himself as 'a chiroquacktic' to the assembled delegates.

'"It is hardly necessary",' read Marcus, '"to say that the office of straightener is one which requires long and special training. It stands to reason that he who would cure a moral ailment must be practically acquainted with it in all its bearings. The student for the profession of straightener is required to set apart certain seasons for the practice of each vice in turn, as a religious duty. These seasons are called 'fasts', and are continued by the student until he finds that he can subdue all the more usual vices, and hence advise his patients from the results of his own experience."'

Bartlett didn't know whether to feel insulted by this suggestion. Fast? He found himself patting breasts he didn't have to be told needed shedding, along with a stomach. Marcus seemed to be suggesting he become a pilgrim.

Marcus smoothed the novel's page with a manicured hand. 'Wouldn't that be a sound statement of your commitment as a chiroquack? – you know, to put you in good with moral skeptics like the acapunks? Anyway,' he said, surveying his new friend with a certain critical affection, 'I fancy the coincidence ... Nobody starves if they *do* shed a few pounds. Though I fancy you're the kind of guy who cures his vices by indulging them. Right?' He actually sounded hopeful.

A little later back at the bar he'd overheard Marcus telling one of the Egyptians, 'Coincidence is the core of existence. You gentlemen read Lawrence of Arabia's *Seven Pills of Wisdom* ...?'

At the gates of Dusit Zoo no holiday crowds had yet gathered. Bartlett sat down on a bench and extracted his diary to record a personal, possibly useful note for his address: *When I was in school a chemistry teacher wanted to box my buns* ... Boy scouts, watching him in his white dress talking to his microphone, closed in. They were soliciting donations for their New Year's charity, stray dogs. Buddhists worshipped dogs. Frowning, tucking the machine into his shoulder bag, Bartlett quickly dropped ten baht in one of their cans. He was still wondering how personal his speech should be to delegates who'd never heard of him and who probably resented memoirs. Safer to go on the attack. Be political.

The elephants seemed glad to see him, or at least the wrinkled female did, lifting her trunk and coughing with delight, as if remembering him from the not so distant recesses of a good memory. Her name, according to the little biography printed in translation above her pen, was Belle. Born 1950. A year younger than him. Belle was tethered at the ankle with a steel cuff.

For Bartlett she swished hay into the air, swayed a little, flapped her pink-mottled ears like sails sensing wind. Her posture reminded him of a poem the student chiropractors used to pass around at Memorial – about what unknown ages of time the worn arch of an elephant's spine could support ... *Plod! Plod!* She swayed in the heat, maybe cooling herself, in the absence of shade or water to submerge her sun-ravaged skin. Her tusks were not yellow like piano keys. These glinted.

A couple of families smiled and pointed from Belle to him. They, too, sensed this elephant's recognition of the foreigner in the white coat, as an auspicious omen?

He threw up his arms in an expansive gesture.

'Bella! Bella! Bella!'

The old girl cocked her huge head to acknowledge his voice. She seemed prepared to perform.

'Belladonna, my love, how wonderful to see you again!'

The animal tossed her tusks like tuning forks. The Thais clapped and giggled. They threw peanuts at her. The prisoner coughed her delight. This behaviour made her two fellow inmates noticeably uneasy, and they tugged at their chained ankles in little four-footed shuffles.

'Are they taking good care of you, my sweet? How can I persuade them to unchain and let you go! *Bella*,' he called, '*Bella, Bella*' – blowing kisses from both his palms like a playful lunatic – 'believe me, I didn't abandon you, you were taken from me! I haven't lived a day without thinking of you! The stories you could tell us now!'

The Thais didn't know what to make of this foreign speech by a coat-flapping fat man in short pants, but they seemed to appreciate his friendly response to an animal begging for peanuts. They threw more peanuts. They laughed instead of giggled now. He took out his diary to record Belle's delighted squeals.

She was squealing loudly.

'You know that elephant?' asked a cultivated voice.

Turning, Bartlett saw it belonged to a dignified-looking man of advanced age and silvery complexion, who might properly have belonged to the impressive legislative buildings on the wide avenue outside the park.

'Evidently,' he said, his mike still extended.

'She is never like this,' said the man, clutching his own peanuts in a paper funnel, sold by the zoo for dispensation among inmates. '... Not flaring up so much like this.' He watched, pleasantly surprised at the unexpected grace of the fat foreigner, conducting his arms and bobbing at the knees for the benefit of a moth-eaten elephant.

Belle trumpeted fulsomely, her ears set full-sail like an old galleon heading home from the new world, her holds full of bullion. A triumphant sight! Frankly astonished by his own powers of persuasion, Bartlett paused. She was trying to tip her entire body back onto two legs – to shift the tremendous weight of all that gold – her toes sinking out of sight as she started back.

She had now raised herself above the other elephants, tucking her front legs under her tusks, but then, in an inspired moment, she delicately engineered one stumpy rear leg into the air, the unfettered one, till her whole body canted slightly forward onto a single foot.

In appreciation her audience went bananas.

'Bella, Bella, Bella!' urged Bartlett. 'Wonderful circus queen – you *remember* who taught you to sail!'

The little Thai legislator clapped the ringmaster's shoulder, egging him on. Belle seemed willing to exert herself to any heights on Bartlett Day's behalf.

Was he making up her performance as he went along, a maestro with his microphone? If only he could conduct his own show tomorrow as well as this, persuade fellow therapists he had something rousing to say about the chiropractic circus back home.

The sheer exertion of her display brought Belle into port huffing, her anchor unfurled in the dirt. Suddenly she looked winded, broken. Thirsty.

The families waited, expectant. Bartlett remembered how popular elephants in Thai culture were, letting people walk under their stomachs for luck and long lives, consolation from grief and broken bones.

He'd learned something the other day. *No, unlearned. I –* Actually, he had wondered if his own profession was becoming a 'white' elephant by ignoring the histories of its patients for the sake of making so many false claims about itself. Elephants in Thailand, he soon found out, no longer carried logs. These days their burdens seemed bigger and less defined. People plucked their hairs for good health and pregnant wombs. He even knew of one hotel that kept a baby elephant for the tourists.

From the exhausted Belle, now heaving like a stevedore, he passed on to a pair of bison from North America, nearly coatless in the heat. They looked old and unCanadian. He remembered an historical photo some crayoning wag had pinned to the wall of the lunch room at Memorial, piles of buffalo bones on the prairie outside a boxcar, ready for transportation to a fertilizer factory. 'Find the tibia,' it read.

Heat and humidity increased as the sun climbed. The park was filling up with families. Bartlett paused under a shade tree tagged 'Ficus' – a huge version of the same plant at home in offices of upwardly mobile chiropractors. Humming a bar of an old Animals' song, he was trying to recall the words. Crows seemed everywhere. He imagined them attracted to his bright belt buckle. He tried sucking it in.

The lake in the middle of the park felt concentric with his desire for an oasis. He was glad to find a bench he could sit down on and listen to the squeaky boats full of pedalling young couples under green-striped canopies circling the fountain. Thirsty, he was sweating in the heat.

He took out Marcus's orange and began peeling it, lining up the peel along his bare thigh. He was trying to remember: ... *shivers in my backbone, I got* ... A young couple sat down on the other end of his bench, speaking in familiar accents. They were talking about an elephant.

'Are you talking about Belle?' interrupted Bartlett. 'The crazy elephant doing tricks?'

'Tricks?' said the young man.

'Circus tricks. I had her going to beat the band.'

They scrutinized his white lab coat and bare plump legs, his rubber sandals and cutoffs. They were dressed in hiking boots and cotton T-shirts stamped Phuket Island. They looked thin, suntanned, possibly on drugs.

'The elephant you're probably talking about,' said the young man, 'just collapsed.'

The girl regarded his half-peeled orange. 'The poor thing was on its knees,' she said. 'Then it fell over and stopped breathing. We thought elephants even kept standing to sleep.'

'Can't be the same elephant,' said Bartlett.

'The tongue was fallen out. We saw it squashed up in the dust.'

'I'll check it out when I leave.'

Maybe he sounded officious, because after a while the girl asked, 'Are you … a vet?'

'Kind of a vet, yeah.' He chuckled.

'You're a doctor then.'

'D C.'

They stared at him.

'Doctor of chiropractic.' He nibbled some peel, offering them segments of his orange which they declined.

He learned they were Peace Corps volunteers, from Michigan.

'I like to think of countries,' said Bartlett, 'as either lines or circles. Plus cones maybe. Canada where I'm from is an example of a line-type country …'

They were soon on their way, excusing themselves politely.

On leaving the park himself he began to wonder where Bella – Belle – had travelled, how many tents and small towns she'd seen in her time, sailed to which foreign continents on what kind of tramp steamers, eaten her way through how many hectares of bad hay – and he wondered if Thailand was her home, or a country she'd got stuck in for a bad debt when the circus cleared out of town.

Her corpse lay there, just as the American couple had described it, and he studied it for a long time. A slowly decomposing hull of death-defying ribs, ready to stand up and be counted once her flesh melted away. He wondered if the zookeepers sitting in the shade would bother with an autopsy, surveying the wreck still chained by her foot and sucking their stubby little cigarettes. Or would they let nature take its rapid, putrescent course, letting her be carried away in the stomach of ants?

What could've clotted her heart, buckled her legs, crumpled her spine so suddenly? Something brackish and lethal in her water tank?

Bartlett tried with difficulty to breathe from the diaphragm, by opening his mouth like some fish in a sluggish school. His fingers were sticky with juice. He felt lousy and he wanted to wash. He was thirstier than ever.

3.

Heading east toward the border camp the air-conditioned bus was three-quarters full of delegates. He found a seat at the back where he planned to mumble undisturbed at his speech, cradling the tape recorder in his lap, trying to concentrate on chiropractic's history. The bus had yet to clear the capital's distractions and strike out along the expressway. Their driver had inserted a video cassette into a large TV set and turned up the volume, a British documentary about a primitive South American Indian tribe, roasting a tarantula and shooting arrows. Bartlett considered this and where he was: watching TV about Amerindians in a Thai bus, heading for some refugee camp along the border of a genocidal country. *No, rewind that ...* in a Thai bus full of quacks from around the world, driving down the wrong side of the road watching a British documentary about ... *I suppose this is what exotic means?*

At the sound of his mumbling a pair of Japanese 'naikan therapists', who were sharing a bottle of Black & White, possibly to immunize themselves from the passing slums, turned and held aloft their bottle with an invitation for him to join them in a slug. Very out of character, he thought, Japanese partying so openly around foreigners. He smiled demurely and shook his head.

Marcus Reambeault was making his way down the aisle, chatting up everybody who spoke English, dispensing box lunches supplied by the hotel. The naikans declined lunch till such time as they polished off their Scotch. They gestured as much to Marcus, who placed two boxes on the rack above their seats.

'And what're *you* doing back here? Speechifying, Dr Day?'

'What are naikan therapists?'

'Search me.'

'The alternative world is vast.'

'So is your appetite.' Marcus slapped his friend's wrist when he reached for a second box. 'Save room for tonight's dessert. Nudge, nudge.'

Putting aside tomorrow's address Bartlett ate his way through a roast beef sandwich, a cheese and tomato sandwich, three chocolate wafers and a celery stick. Lunch for a midget. Rice farms outside the tinted glass looked hot, flat, boring. Strange to an overweight guy like himself how guerrillas and soldiers would crawl through this heat to fight over anything more than some shade and the right to a bath. Who *cared* who controlled the plumbing? He supposed you might, if there was some chance you might get snuffed in the bathtub.

He washed down his food with a can of Sprite and switched on his diary again. *The medical profession*, he spoke, *accepted blindly by most people, drugs millions. Makes millions drugging millions, polluting citizens, carving them up. Tonsillectomies, appendectomies, hysterectomies...*

The naikan therapists had turned once more to listen. They bowed a little unsteadily in his direction, not understanding a word.

'Of course,' a loud Aussie voice up front was saying over the British voice of the South American documentary, 'one of the great disappointments of married life comes when the average bloke gets to a financial position where he can afford to buy his wife dresses for a fancy figure, and then discovers she's lost it.'

This was greeted by a gust of laughter from the other delegates. The naikans out of politeness joined in a moment later.

The guy was a rolfer, remembered Bartlett. What was there in that job-title suggestive of rolling them in the aisles – of bouncing them off the track to win a roller derby? Patients expected a little more depth to their healers. He flipped open a wrinkled scribbler to search for some chiropractic 'principles' he was supposed to have memorized as a student.

The twenty-fifth principle, he found, stated 'The forces of Innate Intelligence never injure or destroy the structures in which they work.' Obscure enough to sound sensible to him, once. But to fellow therapists, tomorrow morning? 'The intelligence of the educated mind is wholly acquired – learned by experience. The innate is not acquired. It is born within us and with us, and is capable of running all functions of the body at birth as in adult life.' So had spoken B.J. Palmer, D.D.'s weighty son, who'd brought chiropractic into the twentieth century following his father's odd invention of it. Bartlett paused to look out the window.

His profession was supposed to let the body's innate intelligence overcome interference to its health, when nerves were blocked or damaged because of dislocation in the spine. You just cranked the spine to better health. Wasn't alternative medicine usually based on this kind of neat answer to the invasive practices of allopathic physicians?

In his scribbler he noticed where he'd happened on the memoirs of a Frenchman who had gone against a promise to his father to become a doctor. The student had arrived in Paris in 1822 to study medicine. But upon entering the hospital's dissecting room his first morning, this future composer discovered he wasn't disposed to linger in the halls of his intended profession. 'Not by a long shot!' Bartlett had scrawled enthusiastically, alongside a passage he now felt, on rereading it, explained why so many on the bus had devoted their lives to holistic practices instead of mainstream butchery. He supposed, like vegetarians, they were all looking for something less carnivorous?

He read Berlioz's words into his machine, to try out as a possible intro to his speech:

'... At the sight of that terrible charnel-house – the fragments of limbs, the grinning heads and gaping skulls, the bloody quagmire underfoot and the atrocious smell it gave off, the swarms of sparrows wrangling over scraps of lung, the rats in their corner gnawing the bleeding vertebrae – such a feeling of revulsion possessed me that I leapt through the window of the dissecting-room and fled for home as though Death and all his hideous train were at my heels. The shock of that first impression lasted for twenty-four hours. I did not want to hear another word about anatomy, dissection or medicine, and I meditated a hundred mad schemes of escape from the future that hung over me.'

Amen, concluded Bartlett, letting his mike go limp. He loosened his belt buckle and spread his knees. He stared out at the sun-flattened landscape.

His meagre lunch had put him in mind of the caf at Memorial with its dubious concoctions. Palmer's Pudding. B.J.'s Beans. Oddly, no one had ever suggested the directors be keelhauled, only the cooks. Bartlett's tongue fell out with a seditious raspberry. The naikans turned.

They had begun eating their own lunches, which consisted of not eating anything but celery and searching their boxes for sushi. He wondered if they were not going to drink their pop, too.

4.

The refugee camp, some miles from the Cambodian frontier, was nobody's dream of refuge. After several hours their bus reached a tollgate in the rolling hills where the driver was expected to hand over official papers from Thai authorities in Bangkok. Plus unofficial envelopes containing 'maintenance taxes' for the soldiers.

'Well, everybody's got their expenses, right?' The rolfer was chuckling. 'Wonder what they charge the international rice caravans, the rotten s.o.b.s.'

Passing another checkpoint their bus was finally ushered through a barbwire fence into Khao-I-Dang.

Marcus came down the aisle and said he felt hot just looking out the window. He scratched himself underneath his pink golf shirt, purchased for the equivalent of two dollars in the lane outside the Kingdom. It had a little crocodile crest and looked like the real thing. The faith healer wondered if the heat would make them turn their air-conditioned bus around and beat it back to Bangkok.

'I'm thirsty,' said Bartlett. He wondered if his friend V.L. was carrying any ice water.

They disembarked.

To get to the Traditional Medical Center the delegates had to stumble through interlocking roads baked to red dust by the afternoon sun. They moved through a vast encampment of new tents and thatched bamboo huts, finished off with palm leaves and blue plastic tarps. Exactly how many persecuted refugees had already braved death to reach here, their guide, a graceful Thai man in a checked short-sleeve shirt, couldn't say. 'Maybe one hundred thousand. Biggest city of these peoples anywhere, including their own country.' He'd been employed by the International Committee of the Red Cross to welcome influential outsiders to his camp, and to direct their attention to areas in need of improvement. Food, sanitation, education ...

The one area of glut seemed medical, since the camp appeared host to more competing western medical teams than could be found, guessed Marcus, in the entire nation of Mozambique. Bamboo wards specializing in obstetrics, surgery, gynecology ...

This made the *krus* unique in such an allopathic camp and afforded some pride to visiting alternative healers. Under a thatched roof the visitors stood around and watched their brothers, these traditional folk doctors, exorcise unhappy children, massage mothers, and apply potions of betel and lime juice to men with running sores. Stuff M.D.s would never try.

Theirs was the most exotic healing Bartlett had yet seen.

'Betel leaf has eugenol,' explained their guide, 'the clove-oil compound? It is powerful antiseptic. And this tea here –' a kettle was steeping over the blue flame of a rusty campstove – 'this contains fifteen herbs for perking you up. The refugees drink it.'

'That'd give you a buzz,' Marcus told Bartlett.

Marcus was interested in the spiritual remedies, the exorcisms and performance of the head *kru*, who, in trying to make peace with the 'protective angel' of a young man having convulsions, lit candles, called up his dissatisfied spirit, and offered it a ceremonial meal of coconut and boiled chicken spread out on a straw mat.

'I've never used food,' admitted Marcus. 'Might be something to think about. Potluck prayers?'

The rolfer from Melbourne guffawed.

The delegation moved on like a progressive dinner.

The two Egyptian holists were startled to discover, among the numerous medical wards scattered through camp, a team of holistic healers from Marin County, California.

Andy and his fellow rolfer Marshall elbowed their way to the front. 'Jesus,' said Andy to the Americans. 'What's it like here, anyways? You guys in daily cahoots with the M.D.s, just like the *krus*? Or is it the same story's at home ... home in Oz, anyways, knocking your bleeding head against a wall?'

The holists confessed to finding themselves in the same competition for patients as they did at home. The meds, tolerant of far eastern quacks, saw no reason to go further and encourage quacks from California. They didn't at home.

'Same old story,' groaned Roach Lord, a naturopath from Atlantic City. Other delegates nodded sagely. Roach's armpits looked soggy and you could tell he was bushwhacked by the heat. *You could just tell he was a whiner,* Bartlett later recorded.

The delegates were anxious for the tour to wind up. The late afternoon humidity hung heavily over sloping acres of refugees, encouraging few of the visitors to feel much zeal to be out practising among the wretched.

Bartlett felt thirstier than ever. His back ached. He remembered something called ventilation and how his own vision for curing the sick was one free of flies. Standing alone in the road he stirred the air by fanning himself with the pockets of his open white coat. He wore no socks and his rubber thongs felt gritty with dust. Travel was work. Getting the drop on how the other half suffered took more energy, more curiosity than the tropics gave back. No wonder Dwight stayed home. The tropics preferred to dole out malaria, malnutrition, dysentery, *shock, too, I suppose ...*

A stray dog, lapping water from an open drain, growled menacingly. The chiropractor braced himself. Then thought to remove his tape recorder and extend its mike in the dog's direction. The bony animal growled louder.

'What's the drill, mate?' called Andy. Bartlett must've looked like he was fencing with the beast.

'I'm afraid of dogs.'

'Could've fooled me.'

A family, squatting under a temporary plastic tarpaulin, stared at him. Their clothes were rags and evidence of arrival in camp only a few hours earlier.

'A regular St. Francis,' said Roach Lord.

He watched Bartlett rewind his tape, then listened as the Canadian turned up the volume and played the dog back at itself.

The unexpected echo of its own bad temper caused the animal to growl ferociously, before erupting into a staccato of sharp obsessive barks. Bartlett stepped back to await some sign of success in his treatment. He looked around for V.L.

Andy said to him, 'You oughta be paying more attention to the endangered species, mate. In Oz they're night-hunting the 'roos, without a by-your-leave.'

The dog would not be cured. Their guide commented that if the owner didn't rescue it soon people would eat it. The starving family looked less interested in the dog, however, than in the plump man with his tape recorder ... *the plump man with his tape recorder. Me, Mr Elephant.* These refugees pressed backward into their shelter, staring out at him from sockety heads. Thailand was another world.

5.

The delegates had all shuffled back to the bus, now unbearable inside. V.L. gave Bartlett a wry twinkle, as if approving of the Canadian's sheer doggedness in view of his bulk. The naikans had drunk too much Black & White and seemed on their final legs. When the tour eventually departed camp, their open windows helped trash the airconditioner's effectiveness. The return journey south to Aranyaprathet, and then on to Bangkok, was a long soporific ride through the late afternoon.

'The high seas,' Marcus was saying across the aisle, 'full of boat people out there in the Gulf of Siam. Desperate for shore, Bartlett. Trying to avoid pirates. And here we both sit in mortal battle with drowsiness.' He yawned. 'Speeding back to the Kingdom.'

Marcus Reambeault closed his eyes. 'That's the rumour, anyway. Pirates.'

Up the aisle the homeopath from Bangalore was plugged in to a pair of earphones, listening happily to Handel. The naikans were snoring.

Bartlett began leafing through his scribbler again for notions, quotes, anecdotes – anything he might use in his address to the congress tomorrow morning. And he was singing. *Quivers down my thighbone ... I got the shakes in my thighbone ...*

He came to a note on the dying Louis Pasteur, too decrepit to talk to admirers who'd travelled from around the world to hear this former heretic on his deathbed, once scorned and ridiculed by the medical community, now vindicated and part of the mainstream. His son read out to these admirers what his father had written down for him to say:

'Young men, young men, whatever your profession may be, do not let yourself be touched by barren skepticism, nor discouraged by the sorrows of certain hours that pass over a nation.'

Bartlett didn't see how he could quote from the enemy, and turned the page.

History, he thought.

If history was going to serve his best interests tomorrow morning, which history? The internecine squabble of chiropractic, still split between 'straights' and 'mixers', and traceable from the Freudian rivalry of the profession's father and son? A hornets' nest. How about the founder's history: D.D. Palmer, fish peddler from Ontario, moving to Iowa as a young man in 1865 to practise phrenology and magnetic healing? They read D.D. at Memorial. His scribbler was full of D.D.

Hey, Palmer had been a guy impressed by results of any kind. Crutches, braces, canes – the abandonment of such pillars of old-fashioned medicine impressed Palmer. He'd delved into books on anatomy and physiology, yearning like crazy to make a contribution to medicine. In his one-thousand-page life story, required reading for every chiro student, Palmer told the now famous story of Harvey Lillard, the deaf janitor who couldn't hear a watch tick let alone the rumble of street wagons outside D.D.'s Davenport office. Harvey was telling him how he'd gone deaf at the same time his back went haywire, trying to lift ... Bartlett saw he'd smudged what Lillard was trying to lift, let's say a bucket of coal. When Palmer examined him he discovered a vertebra out of place, and reasoned if he could somehow set this right he might unblock dislocated nerve routes to the ear. It was a leap of scientific intuition. It took him half an hour to convince Harvey Lillard to let him fiddle with his spine, rack it back into place, but the result was history. The janitor leapt to his feet, crying, 'Doc! Doc! I hear!'

Who cares if it's *true*, one of Bartlett's classmates had punned, if the profession has never looked back?

Bartlett considered what he could and couldn't say tomorrow.

The omens at the turn of the century hadn't been jake for Palmer's new art. Even flush with success the founder was fined five hundred bucks for calling himself a doctor and imprisoned for practising without a licence.

6.

The sun had gone down before the delegation arrived back in Bangkok to shower, eat dinner at the Kingdom, then hire three taxis to take the interested among them to the kick-boxing matches in Ratchadamneon Stadium, where they discovered the card of nine matches was already half over.

The delegates trooped in to the sound of drums and cymbals rushing to a mad climax, as two boxers appeared to have lost control of themselves and were kicking, punching and kneeing each other to death. The crowd was shrill. Then the boxers stopped, bowed politely to one another, before one of them suddenly spun and caught his opponent with a foot to the ear, stunning him, followed by an elbow across the face and a quick knee to the stomach. The boy in red pants crumpled to the canvas. The stadium went quiet. 'That's all she wrote,' muttered Marcus. The betting for the next fight had already begun.

The victorious boy in green pants showed his respect for the fans, who ignored him now, by bowing to the four sides of the ring. The fighter in red, still stupefied, was hauled through the ropes as the next pair of boxers prepared to enter the ring.

'Bet *he* could do with a chiropractor right now,' cracked Andy.

Watching, Bartlett felt walloped. *No, violated.* But the band started up again, this time with a flute, and the madness seemed to evaporate on the strains of an ethereal tune.

'They're dancing,' he said.

'Ballet,' observed Marcus. 'Nice.'

'Evil spirits,' said Marshall, less artistically inclined. 'They're warding off evil spirits. I read that's how they keep away the head shit.'

They had all found seats by now. The Japanese naikans sat trading baht between themselves, as though they already appreciated the fine points of these pirouetting bodies and were about to place discriminating bets.

When the next fight began, and moved swiftly from round to round, the betting became more intense, with odds shortening on the wiry fighter out of some poor northern region near Chiang Mai, as he looked to be getting the better of an opponent afflicted with ugly blue boils across his shoulderblades.

'These boys really go at each other!' shouted Roach Lord. He was wearing a straw boater Bartlett thought made him look like a vaudeville clown.

'One a month,' Marshall shouted back, 'gets killed! I can see why!' He sounded excited at the prospect.

But the boxers never forgot traditional Thai respect and remembered to trade polite bows between particularly vicious blows. The Japanese naikans, whooping it up for the boy from the north, bowed when he bowed.

Marcus Reambeault laughed, possibly at himself. The smoky atmosphere of blood sport didn't seem much more endearing to him than it felt to Bartlett. *He looked pensive.* The faith healer looked like he wouldn't mind removing himself from audience participation with a thousand well-spoken words about non-contact sports like Scrabble or ballooning. But the racket from fans and orchestra stopped him from communicating this to his new friend. Instead, he shouted that he thought the naikans were guilt-trip therapists. He'd got the lowdown.

'What?' shouted Bartlett.

'Heavy-duty meds! In Japan you spend a week with a so-called naikan, locked up in a room talking about all the good things your mother did for you and why you should feel gratitude in life instead of narcissism!'

A roar. The favourite from the north had been kicked in the rib cage then punched in the face. He refused to go down. The ropes wouldn't let him. Saved by the bell, growling at himself, dabbing blood with his boxing glove … His handlers mirrored their boxer's anger, flapping towels and tongues in his face. The betting resumed, no longer in his favour.

'It's just the opposite of psychotherapy,' said Marcus, 'all our stress on the self-made man. These naikans put the accent on gratitude and service. Fits in, I suppose, with Japanese corporate philosophy.'

The fight ended in an upset. In the sixth round the boy from Chiang Mai was kicked dizzy by a totally unexpected pirouette from his opponent coming off the ropes. Whereupon, more or less gaga, he took a vicious kick to the nose, the *coup de grâce* that flipped him to the canvas.

The naikan therapists leapt to their feet as happy backers of the longshot. Bartlett was bewildered. He thought all their bets had been on the favourite, now pancaked. When the arena again fell quiet they sat down quickly, embarrassed by their outburst.

Bartlett hadn't bet the favourite either. Watching the humiliated handlers trying to bring their unconscious boxer back to life, he recalled the drawer of his filing cabinet that Lois would open and close to consult a patient's file. It always made him think about a body shelf in the morgue. *Sometimes about my income, too.* He wondered where to collect on his bet.

'What's it mean when I want to screw the teenage progeny of guys I went to high school with?' asked Marcus. 'You know, twenty-five years ago?' He leaned closer. 'It worries me, Bartlett.'

Bartlett looked at him. 'Bad?'

'These kids aren't old enough to be bad.'

'No. How bad do you want to screw them?'

'Wakes me up at night.' The faith healer was fingering the crocodile crest on his shirt and gently caressing his hint of a double chin.

A delay between matches had caused many fans to stand up, light cigarettes, abandon their seats and strut around like little warriors. The fans were all men.

'Their fathers are my age. Sometimes I'll dream about their dads and try to remember what we were like in high school, what I was like, with my own desires. How powerful my teenage sex drive must have been when it's still, you know, this bad after years of peaking, levelling out, so called declining.'

Obviously, he was thinking ahead to the rest of the evening in Patpong Road.

'That's what we always read,' said Bartlett, 'how we decline sexually … after twenty, is it?' It wasn't what he always read at all, but he thought it agreeable to say so.

So did Marcus. 'I believe you've put your finger on a social problem,

Bartlett.' He spoke confidentially now, preventing his friend from excusing himself. 'You see, I don't think I have levelled out. Let alone declined, no matter what I read. The way I see it is at seventeen, eighteen, I didn't know flesh the way I know it today. You understand what I'm saying? Ass and leg did it for you – who looked at skin? As a young guy, as a teenager, I didn't know anything about skin as an aphrodisiac. I didn't appreciate its nubility. I didn't know how skin *ages*, Bartlett. I had no clue about old skin compared to young skin, the way I do now.'

'Nobody knew the difference.'

'Not at that age. I didn't know how skin loses its shine. I never noticed how it sagged – with age, right?' Marcus was pinching his own cheek – 'wrinkled and fattened up. Stopped renewing itself, showed its veins, started tasting overripe ... am I turning you off? What else? Lost its very nice sensitivity, right?'

Bartlett was rubbing his elbow. 'You forgot dried out.'

'That too. Nothing like this should go without saying. Listen, Dr Day ...'

Marcus confessed he was moved by what he continued to observe in his restorative capacity as a faith healer. 'No, not moved exactly ... Well, maybe a bit.' And went on. For a middle-aged man like himself, his own faith was patently renewed by the sight of young skin in certain of his patients. This made it doubly necessary for him first to seduce minds, young minds, if Bartlett took his meaning. *I took it, or thought I did. I thought this explained why he talks so much. Always practising ... hoping to ingratiate himself.*

'... I probably sound like a crank, Bartlett. But listen. When skin starts to go it won't tuck in where it should and turns yellow in bad light. Right? With old age it droops farther till it melts off your bones, and what's left are jutting hips and oversize teeth. Your dick is no more than a string.'

'You're right. You do sound like a crank.'

Fresh boxers were preparing to enter the ring.

'All these young studs think about is lust.'

'Not us, though,' teased Bartlett.

'It may be lust, Bartlett, but it's informed lust. An appreciative lust, a loving, lasting, controlled lust. Ten times more powerful than any desire I knew at eighteen. At eighteen I might have snorted like a stallion. But I was just as thick and single-minded as a horse too.'

'And now?'

'I still feel my oats, Bartlett. I can still whinny. But it wouldn't bother me if I found myself in bed with the apple of my eye and couldn't get it up. The anticipation would only make it better. I think the middle-aged mind is vastly underrated. Written off with the mid-life crisis. The fact is my brain helps me appreciate how amazing young skin really is. It helps my own flesh feel young like it never felt when I was young. It helps keep me young.'

'You're an optimist.'

'I'm a survivor. Just look at the rewards.'

Two boxers had entered the ring and were about to begin their ritualistic, graceful ballet, before turning upon one another with death in their eyes. Their torsos, above the long colourful silk pants, glistened in anticipation, watched keenly by men preparing to bet on the one each believed more likely to prove explosive beneath his mask of exquisite politeness.

'I fancy the shorter one,' said Marcus.

Bartlett hoped his friend wasn't including his own among these middle-aged minds. At thirty-two he'd never thought of skin as much more inspiring to his sexual drive than an inner tube – crucial to getting there without a lot of friction, but not something to write home about en route. He'd never thought of skin as *exotic*.

7.

In the taxi on the way to Patpong, the Australians were saying Bangkok was a very interesting name. 'Given the 747s full of sex tours these days,' said Andy, 'Bangkok turned out to be kind of a prophetic label.' Marshall chuckled, adding, 'There's a tube stop in London called Cockfosters. Bet the bleeding poms swallow it, when they ask for a ticket to Cockfosters.' He pinched his mouth primly and raised his head. 'Co-fosters, please.' Both rolfers laughed.

Bartlett wondered if he should mention Banglumpoo.

The driver sped along the poorly lit avenues, without needing to be told their destination. For such a large congress it surprised Bartlett so few delegates had decided on this night out with the boys.

Alongside him in the backseat V.L. was speaking softly about homeopathy, equating it for his Canadian friend to a 'mirror image' of traditional medicine, where instead of neutralizing symptoms with drugs the homeopath aimed to make them worse by means of 'succussed' water. He too was speaking to the congress tomorrow morning, but he sounded more cheerful and confident of his material than the chiropractor did of his. This impressed Bartlett, in an envious sort of way. Like V.L. he too was a university dropout, yet his colleague carried a graduate's conviction about his rightful place in the world. He even invited Bartlett to pay him a visit in Bangalore. V.L. had left Bangalore as a Rhodes Scholar for Oxford. Then he met an Indian girl from Lambeth and dropped out of Oxford to marry her. Needing a profession to support his bride V.L. had fallen under the spell of water. He still equated the future with water.

The three taxis arrived together at the Mississippi Queen in Patpong Road. Except for the lone Indian they'd come in pairs: Egyptians, Australians, Canadians, Americans, Japanese. They all agreed to stick together as a cartel for their mutual defence. Inside, perched on bar stools, the girls watched them enter like boys with slingshots in their pockets. The girls were everywhere, Bangkok's natural resource, hundreds of thousands of them generating a cash flow that might have refloated the economy of an entire African nation ravaged by drought and a paralytic bureacracy.

'I don't know about you guys,' said Marshall, 'but I'm not planning to rush into anything too fast like.' He chuckled. '... So to speak.'

What surprised the delegates was the presence of so many of their fellow delegates from the conference, already here. They'd skipped the kickboxing to get a head start with the whores. So many delegates in attendance made V.L. suggest to Bartlett the two of them might be better off giving their speeches here than in the ballroom of the Kingdom. He twinkled.

Girls in bikinis, hot pants, and gowns slit up to their waists had flocked together and were preparing to descend. The delegates reclined themselves, expectantly. The birds flew at them now, messing with their hair, their pockets, their slingshots. Giggling, pecking, tapping tags, trying to pronounce names and professions. Bartlett managed to retrieve a menu from the table. In English and German, French and Arabic it read, 'Our go-go dancers are young, friendly, beautiful and way, way above average. Talk and drink with any you choose ... we're not just another nightclub. We'll sizzle, vibrate, shatter and amaze you!'

Bartlett already had a bird on each shoulder when another pair flew in to perch on his knees. He gave up on the menu and clung to his shoulder bag. Girls kept doing things to whet his appetite, while others sashayed past the table. Some danced provocatively in the distance to a grinding pop tune from speakers better suited to an outdoor stadium. 'I suppose it's like going to heaven,' said Marcus, doubtfully. For a man surrounded by young skin, and endowed with the inestimable aphrodisiac of a middle-aged mind, he sounded detached.

Roach Lord tipped back his straw boater and unknotted his polkadot bowtie. He looked very peckish, assessing the available dishes. He declared this to be free enterprise in its original guise.

The choice came down to renting a girl for eight hundred baht and leaving with her right away for your hotel, or hanging around for another hour and a half and taking her away at closing time for five hundred. 'Either way looks like it'll cost about the same,' figured Roach, 'since they're thirsty and we're expected to buy them drinks.' He personally felt they ought to see some more night life down the strip. 'Good chance I won't live through the night. I wanna make the most of it.'

So after two drinks each, and a couple each for the girls, the cartel agreed to tour Patpong and maybe find a massage parlour. The Japanese naikans looked disappointed, unable to follow the reasoning behind a retreat, yet reluctant to be left behind. They perked up when Marcus made massaging motions with his hands, across the slim tummy of the naikan named Seigo.

The girls pleaded with the delegates to stay, rubbing up very close and showing their tongues. Andy offered his own interpretation of this. 'They're telling us, "White men speak with forked tongues".'

V.L., still twinkling, said it felt very good to be wanted, even without his tie. 'I equate it with family.'

I knew what he meant. I could've come in cutoffs.

That night the bunch of them crawled through two more clubs where the music was disco, the girls cosmopolitan, and the atmosphere fun – except if you went to the can. 'It's the underbelly,' admitted Marshall. 'Pee in the street, mate, and save yourself the degradation of a visit.'

The massage parlour they found later by cab was the 'world's largest'. Several floors made it the size of a department store, and for a moment Bartlett wondered if the New World Store in Banglumpoo hadn't really been a massage parlour, complete with convenience shopping and a bakery, where families were welcome and ovens sold.

'It's like standing in line at McDonald's,' said Roach.

In a way, it was. The menu posted on the wall told them the one-hour basic massage would cost a hundred sixty baht. ('Let's see,' said Marshall.

'That's about nine dollars Australian. Jesus, I usually spend more on Fosters at the pub.') They learned the two-hour basic cost two hundred and forty baht ... the hour and a half 'B' (Body) Course three fifty ... and the Full Course, for as long as it took, would run you eight hundred baht.

'Those are just your upfront costs,' Roach warned them. 'Management takes most of that. My scouts tell me you've got your a la carte costs, once you're shacked up with a chick in her boudoir and decide you want more than your ankles tickled. Everything's extra. Like if you want her to take off her clothes, it's extra. Or if you want a hand job, or a soapy massage in her bathtub, or a fuck on her waterbed, every rung up the ladder is always a little more. Forewarned is forearmed.'

'Foreskinned,' said Marshall.

The delegates were all eyes now, ushered in with bells on, Amerindians helicoptored out of the Amazonian jungle and set down in their first shopping arcade. These delegates had reached the supermarket of sex, the pussy of Bangkok, the destination of chartered sex tours the world over. Bartlett stood gazing with the others through a two-way mirror, at about a hundred girls sitting on tiers. Just like the delegates each masseuse wore a plastic tag, pinned to her shoulder with a number. Each seemed immune to circumstance, *if that's the word. Shame might be better.* Dressed in miniskirts, lingerie, cocktail gowns, even a squaredance dress with a busy crinoline, the girls lounged to kill time. Sometimes a hand would lift and adjust a strap, dab an eyelash, plug in chewing gum ... a face might look into the mirror to prink. Most faces ignored the mirror, as if the world didn't exist on the other side of their bright fluorescent fantasy.

It turned out they were watching TV. Their faces frowned to give this up when their numbers were called out over the intercom.

'Beauty makes you sad,' observed Marcus.

'Horseshit,' replied Bartlett. *Surprised myself.*

Andy flung his arms across the pair of Japanese naikan shoulders. 'Hey, fellas, what's your pleasure?'

Bartlett had his eye on number fourteen. Did the number in any way reflect her age? He hoped not, but her delicate bone structure and not very tangible figure made him think it possible. She was dressed in an emerald party frock and a white bow as if to accentuate her youth. His desire embarrassed him. Structure, he thought, if our framework gets any worse we'll be unable to reproduce. He still didn't have tomorrow's speech, but imagined he was extending his research here. Man's getting bigger but his chest is getting flatter. His hips narrower, just like his face. Passages to his lungs are shrinking. *Elaborate on this...*

He thought he saw one of the naikans staring at number fourteen.

'We come from one of the most beautiful countries,' said Marcus, trying again. 'Arguable, but we've got it all – mountains, grasslands, oceans. The hard thing isn't how to understand Canada, but how to stand it. Canada is so beautiful it makes you sad.'

Marcus sounded sad. Maybe it was the watery gins from the Mississippi Queen. He shook out a green pill from a small bottle he carried in his pocket, placed it on his tongue, and downed it without water.

The naikans now consulted one another, bowing, bumping heads in their eagerness. Number fourteen? Number fourteen and number seventy-seven? A combination entrée? 'Seedy quacks,' mumbled Bartlett.

Roach Lord and V.L. were standing with their arms crossed – Roach, snapping a striped garter on his sleeve, V.L., a good foot and a half shorter than the American, looking serene. The Egyptian holists were smiling. The Australians had actually started rubbing up against the glass.

'We don't have enough images yet,' said Marcus. 'Only circle countries have enough images, which the rest of the world dreams about. Our own images don't travel. Americans don't sleep with our images like we do theirs. Their images penetrate us day and night. Their news is our news. They've got no idea how attractive we really are, because they never see us. A fact, Bartlett. We just don't possess the same lines of communication.'

'Yeah?' Bartlett wondered why he was standing here, listening to this stupid conversation in a whore house. He wanted number fourteen, he decided.

'Our patriotism,' said Marcus, staring into the bright room through the mirror, 'isn't a matter of winning and losing. I just can't imagine us with a national icon like the Statue of Liberty. That *torch* –'

'Beaver,' said Bartlett.

'What?'

'The beaver is *our* national icon.'

'Don't remind me, Dr Day, or I'll snicker. No, that torch is just a big finger signalling number one, number one, number – Listen, Bartlett, you and I hate losing just like everyone else does. But losing isn't our national phobia. No one's as sports-crazed as the Americans. Shuffleboard? Ever hear them pleading with their shoes at shuffleboard? 'Be good for me!' 'Oh baby!' 'Yes! Yes!' 'America!' These're the same shouts as their bedroom shouts, Bartlett. It's a questionable practice at best.'

Bartlett definitely felt he'd like to manipulate the spine of number fourteen – and cleared his pipes to announce this choice to the supervisor. '… We like sport too,' he reminded Marcus.

'But we're not obsessed. We don't yearn as much. That's why we're not great, Bartlett. We don't yearn hard enough.'

'Not even for young skin?'

'Why should we yearn? We've got the best of all worlds.' Marcus pressed his fingertips lightly together, an oddly evangelical gesture for a cat house, thought Bartlett.

'Speak for yourself,' he said.

'We don't yearn for justice – by and large we have it. And we don't yearn for utopia' – he was looking at the girls '– because we can't even imagine what it might be. Americans yearn for everything. In a perverse kind of way they're lucky. It makes them great.'

'Okay. But what number spins your wheels?'

He edged away from Marcus, who was beginning to give him a headache. Having walked through a zoo this morning, a refugee camp this afternoon, crowds at the stadium, nightclubs in Patpong Road, he felt tired and thirsty. His spine ached from the jetlag of travel. He yearned for a relaxing massage.

The naikans had just walked over to the beefy supervisor, who was writing down their numbers, sucking on his gold necklace. They bowed to confirm the numbers he read back at them. Then he removed his other hand from the microphone and spoke into it, so he was heard on both sides of the glass.

'Numba four tee two.'

Bartlett breathed easier. Number forty-two, when she stood up, looked like a holdover from R & R days of the American army. Her spike heels gave her the look of a post box, tricked out in a red sheath, open to invitations, special orders, requests to have your Maytag serviced when it was running just fine. She was bulky for a Thai.

Roach Lord grinned. He was peeling himself a piece of sugarless chewing gum. 'Don't make 'em like that in Tokyo, huh, guys?'

'Numba nine teen.'

'Hey,' said Andy. 'I had my eye on that scrubber!'

Roach laughed. 'Scrubber's right. Try fourteen, she looks like a little shagging machine. I'd be happy to supply her with a piston.'

Bartlett turned back to Marcus. 'You say we understand Americans. Why's Roach Lord such a jerk?'

The faith healer raised his eyebrow, as if to ask what else he expected of a naturopath from Atlantic City. Unfortunately, this led to more yap about Canada.

'... Bartlett, we see so much more of their culture than ours – there's so much of it to see – we don't have any choice but to defend ourselves looking at it.'

'Sad, Marcus.'

Roach looked like he was expecting number fourteen to start grinding his valves.

'It is sad. That's what I'm saying. We watch ourselves watching them, Bartlett, watching us – that's our ultimate dream – them watching us, only they never see us. Not as tourists, not as investors, not as movie actresses fucking kiss-and-tell Canucks. Not as anything. They don't even see us when they're giving us the eye. What a history.'

'I get it. We're on both sides of the glass at the same time. Is that it?'

'Bartlett, we're the hostesses.'

'Raunchy.'

'Hey,' said Roach. 'You guys pick a number yet? Or you want my hat to jerk off in?'

'I need a roulette wheel,' said V.L., smiling.

'Kinky,' said Roach.

That's the thing about Indians, Bartlett told his diary later that night, in genuine admiration. *They're from a circle country that doesn't feel threatened by quacks like naturopaths.*

The Thai was waiting. 'Number fourteen,' Bartlett quickly told him.

'Hey,' Roach Lord snorted.

8.

After most of the delegates had been rubbed, lathered, scoured, bounced off of, even ridden to death, they emerged refreshed and ready to roll. Roach the comedian said it was kind of like a car wash. You started off with your aerial collapsed, your gearshift in neutral and your motor barely turning over, till you got your wheels on track and the ritual started up, the soap and gush, followed by strange slapping rags all over your body, succeeded finally by the sucking mouth of a thumping machine anxious to be through with your chassis … 'with your skeleton, Day,' he added. 'You dog.' Roach's second choice had been a naughty number from Nong Khai, near Laotian border country. '… Talk about a rinser.'

Marcus quietly admitted he'd spent his time plying his girl's skin. 'She was so underage she had no hips.'

'They all are,' said Bartlett. 'A lot of them.'

'Village girls,' said Marshall.

A group of them, minus the Japanese naikans, who for some reason never reemerged from the carwash, had gathered in the street where a tout suggested a live show to relax them before bedtime. A joker, they agreed, and piled into three taxis for the short journey to a club where they took seats in front of a naked woman having a dextrous affair with ping-pong balls and a softdrink glass. 'Soft porn,' whispered Andy, popping a lifesaver into his mouth.

Marcus popped a black vitamin pill into his own mouth.

Spreadeagled, the woman had manoeuvred herself into position for an exhibition with a full bottle of Pepsi and two peeled bananas. 'How does she *do* it?' Roach asked, loud enough to be targeted and then sprayed with carbonated fuzz. They all laughed. 'Too bad the Jappies can't see you now,' said Andy.

The Egyptians holists were staring in the worldly way of those on a return junket to Sodom. Around the Kingdom they wore nomads' robes, where they lorded it over the rest of them like Bedouin sheiks. Elsewhere, as Marcus put it, they usually preferred the streetclothes of Shriners in Miami: blouses and pantaloons. One of them now yawned and sucked his teeth.

The warmup act of fruit and fuzz was followed by the two principals, a strikingly endowed Burmese couple, who put on a display of copulation, complete with an array of contorted positions so supple it made Bartlett, in his professional admiration of this suppleness, forget he was a voyeur. 'Jesus,' said Andy, 'the guy's control's amazing!'

'"The Burmese Bicycle",' repeated Roach.

'He can't come,' said Marshall matter-of-factly. 'It's just a rod implant. He probably came twenty minutes ago.'

Afterward, the pilgrim lay down on his bed, divested of his white doctor's coat, trousers and saddle shoes, to resume the search for his subject. The Kingdom's air conditioning hummed reassuringly.

Back to fundamentals, he announced, watching the silent screen on the shelf above. *'Cheir' means 'hand.' 'Praktikos' means 'to be done.' Thus chiropractic: 'Done by hand'* ...

He stopped the spools. Strange comfort afforded by a profession using *this* stuff: 'Christ, I can't say *that* tomorrow. Not in front of those guys tonight ... they'll laugh me out of the conference room.'

Did he want to admit he belonged to a profession that administered hand jobs and quick fixes? That he profited from a profession tarting itself up with Greek words to impress working-class youth like himself, desirous of becoming enterprising D.C.s catering to the dislocated?

He gulped from a cold can of Pepsi. He was already looking forward to the week Dwight had booked him down on the gulf. Bangkok was all heat and fumes. The seaside would be a good place to lose *weight*. Not that he didn't plan to treat himself every night to shrimp and oysters. He was looking forward to a leaner world. Sometimes he remembered home.

Trying to find the river again, after his visit to Banglumpoo last night, he'd wandered in the direction of the ferry slip, through a residential district of woodframe houses that made him think of the country he came from – not the style of houses but their material – the extremes dividing Canada off from its centre, where on either coast instead of solid brick structures the houses were wood.

The house he rented with Dwight and Reesa in Vancouver creaked when the wind blew and the coastal air leaked in. Their frame house didn't understand winter. Their decaying house was foreign to his country's heartland. It was closer to houses here. He and Dwight, Reesa and Aloysius: an extended family of which the Third World was full, each member contributing to the mutual incomprehension of the other. They all contributed in their own ways to helping the house function. Even Aloysius, with no agenda except his own, knew he needed a roof to sleep under.

The screen above his bed was shuffling through images of the day. The late news, or the early news – depending how close your earthly location to where this stuff originated – suggested to him politics were a vast stew of journalists flogging bylines to a camera. He had the sound turned off, not because the anchorwoman was speaking Thai, but because he was trying to concentrate on his speech, lying here, reflecting on how lines of communication with his own brain felt severed.

He juggled with lines for a while. You snorted a line of cocaine ... If Aloysius got a line on beer bottles, he made a bee line to his hammer ...

Similarly, *Similarly*, he went on, *the backbone as a line of time* ... but would the alternative world of quacks, to which he was messenger, want to be reminded of time so early in the morning?

The silent screen conveyed the same soap opera he was used to watching at home. A vicious car bombing in Lebanon. Polish immigrants scavenging in refuse bins for food in St. Louis, intercut with a couple enjoying a prosperous, big-church wedding. Yet another item on the recent assassination of John –

He rewound his diary and prepared to listen in to the day's entries, for some grabby passage to hang his speech on. As a voice-over, against the moving lips of the local King – belatedly delivering some soothing New Year's message to his nation – he heard himself for the first time today.

... The medical monopoly would like to wipe us out. Look what it's done to the tooth puller and the eye tester and the head shrinker. Plagiarized, monopolized, swallowed up. My fellow practitioners, it's all political. All chiropractors want is integrity. To be recognized and to receive referrals. To be treated as professionals...

After a glut of commercials for handsoap and soft drinks, an NFL game came bounding in from Dallas, whether live or prerecorded (today or yesterday) he couldn't say, so scrambled was his notion of tomorrow by meridians he'd lately crossed to get here.

Here he might have stopped listening to himself, plump man on his round Asian mattress – to insert a comment on the importance, the amazing importance in athletics of correct posture and straight spines – had he not already fallen asleep, dreaming of number fourteen's bad complexion, outcroppings of too many chocolate bars, too much yearning.

So he didn't hear the squeals, etched onto his magnetic tape as it revolved, of Belle, now dead to the world.

August, 1914

So angry I could spit. Could, could, could, if only someone would get about ancestoring me *toot sweet*. A shabby time for humour. I think the heat has got to me too, even *in vacuo*.

Because of heatwave decided to catch day-cruise steamship to Bowen Island, and so passed Japanese freighter in Coal Harbor full of Punjabis who'd mutinied the day before. Captain was trying to take them home, having got no permission to unload his cargo after two months at anchor.

We could see bearded men up close, defiant on gunwales, in riggings, wrapped in white and brown turbans, wearing the same suits they'd left Asia in. A party of two hundred constables was about to board their freighter from a funny-looking tugboat below. Our captain tried to warn us about too many to starboard, all urging on the police. What clowns!

Then it happened. The Sikhs began raining garbage down on the constables and immigration officers. Lumps of coal, iron pulleys, bamboo spears. Our ship thought the officers should use their pistols to 'shoot the Hindoos'. Instead they tried a firehose. One Sikh looked defiant, his turban flying and wet hair unravelled to his waist. I named him Ujjal.

It was all over fast. Tugboat backed off and the Sikhs volleyed with cheers, ecstatic to win a curt revenge for their long grim quarantine.

Police warned us away, and so we rumbled out through the narrows consigning these events to our wake. The bay was flat, the gulf empty of boats. We veered up the sound. I'm free to drift, if not always where I choose then still unanchored by genes. God, how I hate the emptiness!

On Bowen, searching for a couple with some purpose in its eyes, a little lust in its limbs, I flitted among picnicking employees from the Carpenters' and Printers' Union. Looking for great-grandparents of a descendant like me is hard when you don't know who you are. You chart a course and hope for the best.

Hot. Mentioned that. One couple, an elevator operator and a fireman, who had nothing to do with carpenters or printers, strolled down to the oyster beds. I followed them down from the Terminal Hotel. Salmon fishermen in rowboats were bobbing in Hotel Bay. Coastal peaks towered over the sound. I saw a gull's breast could cushion its wishbone in an enviable way. This couple sank down in the shell-strewn sand.

I love to peer at forbidden cargo in the world.

Ujjal, for example. Of almost four hundred of them you'd have thought at least one might have slipped overboard and swum ashore. I have to think Ujjal did. Discouraging to think my progenitor might have been aboard, a spunky Sikh, frightened away by Board of Traders and Crusaders of Labour.

Four days after my cruise, HCMS *Rainbow* levelled its rusted guns on the unwelcome *Komagata Maru* and encouraged it to sail forthwith for international waters. No choice for the Sikhs but to return to Calcutta without setting their feet ashore. The army had positioned soldiers on the docks.

I too feel excluded from citizenship. Yet this hasn't stopped my snooping presence at yachting regattas, afternoon teas or debutante balls, hammocky garden parties and beach picnics.

No sign of Ujjal, of course.

Have even ascended to the new roof garden of the Hotel Vancouver, from where the anchored freighter's waning days were watched by boa-hatted ladies taking tea in the pergola.

Quite a spectacle, our port making news throughout the Empire.

Black world knocking on white world's door, from a rusty bucket that stank downwind, full of men dying to enter a city that just wished them away.

Now, a few days later, what *The World* is calling the war to end all wars has broken out in Europe and news of our long standoff has become local again, diluted, close to forgotten on our own back page. A prouder reason for army and navy has taken over the front.

Am not hopeful for prospects in utero.

Chapter 22

Bones

Telling myself things in the dark because the light's rationed. And at home I worry after a storm if I have to reset an electric clock? We're all grateful about landing. The Belgian said an Ilyushin doesn't land, it gropes for earth like a shipwrecked sailor. This place really is something else. In the morning for sure I want a bath.

In the wake of war and French colonial cooking, Bartlett's omelette tasted of shell, his butter refused to spread, the milk substitute clotted in his coffee. Nothing dissolved.

After breakfast a soldier led away the terse Swiss adviser and this left their party at five, not counting the pretty guide who welcomed each of them with a handshake into the black limousine.

'Good morning, Dr Bartlett.'

Her holster rode high like a Mountie's under the right breast of her uniform. Asian, her breasts tripped demurely in bondage of their own.

'Just Bartlett, Miss. We all set?'

If you asked her to disco he bet she'd find out what it was and come back ready to shoot you for the frivolous invitation.

Something voyeuristic about his own profession made him feel slightly exposed here, like standing at a London Drugs' scanner with the name and price of his last purchase frozen above in bright green light – Sheik Condom – while the cashier takes her time wiping down the last litre of Ivory Snow, spilled and unwanted by other shoppers, with a bottle of Windex and a rag.

He still thought of the world in terms of home.

Along littered arteries of the capital no other traffic flowed and the passengers sat peering into deserted streets. Grass had taken over: grew in potholes, out of sidewalks, along curbs. Cars had lain down in the middle of roads and rusted through. Locks and shutters of shops bore the spreading rust of more than one monsoon season. Their limo's unexpected appearance startled a tattered trespasser into hiding down a side street. The Malaysian grunted. In response to the Romanian adviser, the pretty guide assured her the citizens would be permitted to return to their city soon. Rockets or angry elephants appeared to have gnawed away at entire buildings.

'Mortar eggs,' explained the guide in an alien locution.

The Romanian looked fifty and sensitive over a bad moult of dandruff or else psoriasis she kept ruffling from her blazer onto Bartlett's bare arms. He tried coughing to blow it off.

His arms had a flush of winter tan. A golden beach, bar girls, the fragrant frangipani nights. Agreeing to come here, cutting short his stay in Pattaya, booked by Dwight – Bartlett wondered again if his elevator went all the way to the top.

Walls around suburban mansions mouldered under lichen, not a stray dog could be seen. No one's woof or word broke the serenity until far out on the decaying highway a roadblock suddenly loomed. 'Trouble?' asked the Belgian. Soldiers stood around a cordoned-off patch of the cratered road. An armoured truck was the first vehicle they had encountered since jeeps at the airport.

Mr Strajik, the lanky Swede, spoke to the Malaysian first, who stepped out of the car with the Swedish official clapping his shoulder and returning his black suitcase. This Malaysian adviser they left behind in gesticulating conference with an officer.

Two decades ago their limousine was fit for a prince. Today it bumped and swayed with the grinding of age and a will to be liked. Bartlett put it down to shot shocks. He enjoyed the wily movement of this lover past her prime, a fine perversity. The air conditioner rattled on loyally, stubbornly, trying to be cool. For January the sun was getting hot.

The Belgian, who spoke excellent English, was telling everyone about his infant daughter. 'I like the way my wife can plunk her in front of an old Shirley Temple movie and be certain sooner or later the little actress will belt forth a song that nips crankiness in the whaa!' Like Mr Strajik he was a man used to addressing himself to the spaces between people. He knew about travelling.

The village on stilts they came to next looked lifeless and its rice fields parched. Dusty bicycles stood abandoned, not a hen clucked.

'I will see you later, please?' chirped the Romanian, opening her door reluctantly.

'Right,' said Bartlett, unfolding his arms. He smiled warmly. 'Break a leg.'

'No, never,' she replied, misunderstanding.

After introducing her to several peasants, emaciated and fervent, who emerged from a shed to shake her hand, Mr Strajik climbed back into his jump seat. He gave the woman his thumbs-up sign but she was busy nodding attentively at her welcomers.

A secondary route of even worse surface led through scrubby jungle and in time to a bombed-out bridge. At the riverbank was a little camp of huts and an old woman turning a pig on a spit. It was the Belgian's turn. Mr Strajik introduced him to a grim-looking soldier carrying large scrolls under either arm and a weariness that gave him a stoop. The Belgian walked him down to the river as he might a child whose walking stride was not his own. He listened carefully, thoughtfully, as the guide translated a summary of the project to hand – or something just as brief.

Alone now with his host and the pretty guide, Bartlett watched Mr Strajik spread his elongated limbs out on an empty seat as the driver turned the limousine around. Over the decades the leather seats had cracked into dried-up tributaries with the wear and rub of privileged backs.

'Dananga and I were going to drop you in the countryside,' said Mr Strajik in his Swedish lilt. 'Maybe, you know, to break in slowly?' Bartlett, curious about his role, knew nothing. He felt thirsty. 'But she insists priority is in the capital. So we are returning you to the city.'

'Okay by me,' said Bartlett. He relaxed, getting used to this escort service, wondering if Dananga was as unassailable as she appeared.

They reentered the capital, moving with black purposefulness to its dead heart, where the driver turned down a boulevard of large shade trees and stopped before a grand house – it looked to Bartlett like a reclaimed embassy.

The guide and Mr Strajik led him up steps and through a lavish vestibule into a ballroom of spectacular sunlight pouring in through open French doors.

Mr Strajik paused.

'This is where you come in,' he said.

Bartlett's eyes adjusted to the ballroom's unnatural brightness and saw one, then three million bones.

Fathoms of bones: hip, thigh, breast, collar, shin, jaw, rib, you name it. The piles seemed indiscriminate.

'Me?' said Bartlett. 'What is this place?'

'Your advice,' said the Swede.

'The Grief House,' said the guide.

'Where victims,' said Mr Strajik, 'of the government were debased and buried.'

'*N'est-ce pas?*' asked Dananga.

She introduced a civilian she called the curator, a short man with intense eyes in a moon face. She spoke French to him, moving her hands like budgies in distress. He might have been Bartlett's age, in his early thirties.

'He hopes you will show his workers all about skeletons,' said Mr Strajik.

'How to rebuild them,' suggested Dananga.

'Where to begin,' said Mr Strajik.

They were constructing, it turned out, a bone repository.

Bartlett was floored. There were thousands: thousands of shattered skeletons, it looked, hundreds of thousands of bones.

'Listen,' he said. 'I'm a chiropractor, okay?'

Mr Strajik studied his hot face closely. 'Yes, exactly.' To Bartlett he seemed to be saying, in a very concerned way, 'You don't play ball I'll close down your bingo hall.'

Workers with wheelbarrows were circling in through the French doors with more and more bones. Their soiled booty already covered the dance floor. Women with rags were wiping earth from these bones in a slow, dispirited way. Flies buzzed them, buzzed the remains. The gardens outside had been heaved up by relentless digging and implacable fatigue.

'Imagine,' said the Swede, 'if these neighbours' – he nodded in Dananga's direction – 'had not made their invasion and driven out the thugs …'

But Bartlett was having trouble imagining what he was looking at.

The pretty invader said to him, 'The survivors of the Grief House wish to commemorate the holocaust.'

Mr Strajik, wiping a hand through his thinning hair, glanced at his watch. 'Our Swiss banker at the exchequer will be wondering, yes?' He touched Bartlett's arm, politely. 'You will excuse me, Dr Day. I must see if he has all the records he requires? Thank you.'

'Hey,' piped Bartlett. 'What am I *doing* here? What am I *supposed* to be doing?'

Dananga pointed. 'Follow, please.'

She threaded a little path among the bones to a huge dining table around which the curator had gathered half a dozen assistants. 'Please,' she smiled, touching the table. 'A lesson.'

There were bones all over the once-gleaming surface. *Who'd eaten here?* he said later to his diary. *Who'd danced?*

'Listen,' said Bartlett. 'I manipulate backs.'

'Politics,' Dananga prodded him, a little curtly, 'is only medicine, I think, on the big scale?'

In Bangkok, when Mr Strajik had introduced himself at the International Congress of Alternative Healing, he'd said nothing of bones. 'It was the way you handled yourself, yes? I felt I should come and talk to you.'

Bartlett had beamed.

Mr Strajik was with the International Committee of the Red Cross, though reluctant to mention that particular organization 'at this congress', he'd said, his gaunt face smiling slyly. That evening over dinner he had asked Bartlett to delay his flight home in order to assist him with 'something of a nightmare'. Nightmare? Had invited him to a needy country, all expenses paid, a small delegation.

'What country?' asked Bartlett, painting his *gai yang* with a sharp Thai sauce. He was still all pumped up with the success of his lecture. 'Sir?'

'It's a secret,' replied Mr Strajk.

Bartlett chuckled. 'A secret?'

'Singapore. That's the first stop.'

'That's south a ways.'

'There we will meet up with the others at Raffles and wait for the Aeroflot flight.'

'That's Russian,' said Bartlett. When he swallowed, the chicken caught fire.

His new acquaintance said, 'Unfortunately, no one else is allowed to fly there.'

Bartlett drank off a glass of water. 'I'm no politico, okay?'

'You won't get us into trouble then.'

'Trouble's a possibility?'

'You're a man taken by history – I could tell that listening to you this morning. This is a chance to bear witness.' He leaned across the table. 'Dislocation?' He was reminding Bartlett of his speech to the congress. 'Doesn't dislocation *require* adjustment?'

Unimpressed, Bartlett had quoted Strajik's compliment in his diary that night. Then added, giving in to the revolving little spools in a fit of enthusiasm, *Hey I should consider it. I should just take off.* He could cut short his scheduled holiday in Pattycakes – however you pronounced it.

Dananga translated the moon-faced curator's question into English.

'He wishes, Doctor, that you show how to know bones and what bones to lay out to tell the awful stories of this mass grave.'

'Hey, listen,' said Bartlett.

'On the floor,' she said. 'In the fields.'

'I'm sorry. What?'

'You will please show these workers how to cope.' She spoke smartly. 'The driver will return for you in due time.'

With this she retreated across the bony reach of femur and clavicle, radius and tibia and sternum, phalange, humerus, metacarpal, fibula. Rafts of bones. Bones by the ton.

Bartlett gazed at the table where someone had placed a skull in the middle as though to confirm that every skeleton required one. He wondered if bone assemblage qualified for foreign aid in Ottawa. The shovels seemed to have set asunder every bone they aspired to raise.

After a while he said to the curator, 'Listen.' He was trying to sound sensible. 'I don't see any vertebrae here. Get me some vertebrae. All I see is ribs.'

But the museum workers only stared at Bartlett Day's white coat.

'I don't believe this,' he said. Turning, he heard a loud snap and discovered, looking down, his saddle shoe mashing a shoulder blade.

'Hey, listen,' he exclaimed. 'Where's Dananga?'

Their pretty translator appeared to have vanished in Mr Strajik's jump seat.

2.

Perhaps it was his bluff way of complaining only about the workers and not also the grave that made Bartlett's news more shocking to his fellow advisers. His seeming lack of anxiety when he told his story impressed them. They set down their forks, their reserve, and self-importance.

Comparing notes over dinner in their empty hotel, they were lamenting the bridges down, mines planted, farms in ruin, currency worthless and – after Bartlett spoke – the bones interred.

A time of interregnum, pleaded Mr Strajik. They must all please contribute what they could to national reconstruction. There were villages and towns to visit. To dally was immoral.

Mr Strajik was a guy with both oars in the water.

Of course they now realized what country he'd brought them to, descending by turbo-prop over pagodas and temples, ushered by an alien guide into an empty city. The rumours were confirmed. The tragic little nation was still out of bounds to international correspondents – its fate only suspected – and Bartlett refrained from mentioning the country's name in his diary in case their hosts, the invaders, should resent his blabbing and confiscate the recorder.

Instead he mumbled quietly, *The driven snow of history* ... The water had come back on, he was lying in a dark tepid bath trying to soak away slime from his hands and body. In Bangkok, like a beggar, the humidity had at least stayed outside. The Kingdom itself was barely a memory.

'"Coordination is the principle of harmonious action of all parts of an organism, in fulfilling their offices and purposes ..."'

Announcing this mothball text for his Bangkok speech, he'd patted his plastic skeleton on her backside, moving right into a joke by pretending his voice was hers, complaining about her spine.

'True,' he'd told his audience. 'Maybe you haven't heard about bipeds like ourselves, whose vertebrae were supposed to be flat, but whose brains tempted them to stand up on two legs instead of four. Right, so today our joints suffer. Our pelvic floors aren't what they used to be. Neither is anything else. Arteries bulge, sinuses clog. We get rickets and the runs, fallen arches and flat feet. That kind of stress isn't natural, it saps our energy. All because our brains told Mother Nature to buzz off.'

He was warming up the conference to his profession although pedigree was not a trait particularly valued among alternative healers. There were holists from Cairo, nutritionists from Buenos Aires, hypnotists from Marseilles and Perth, psychic surgeons and herbalists from Shanghai – God, body therapists from Bombay, biofeedback practitioners from Singapore and Cologne, naturopaths and iridologists out of Dacca, Kuala Lumpur and Atlantic City, all kinds of Indonesian and Burmese reflexologists, plus rolfers from Melbourne and a trichologist from Rhodes. Every country had its specialists. In one thing alone were they all united. They resented the worldwide clique of the drug and medical profession, with its germ-centred theory of disease.

'Know what I mean?' Bartlett had asked them from the podium. He sipped water from a glass. The conference room was large and panelled in expensive-looking tropical wood along the top of which ran, in a hidden runnel, diffuse golden light. 'Whenever it's a matter of deep pain I work hand in hand with Mother Nature. That's why I'm a chiropractor and not some vivisecting doctor. Out to restore the natural balance.' He looked at his audience. 'Like you. One of you comes into my office, say. I ask you when was the last time you had a spinal examination? You could have a dislocated spine and not know it. Razor back, for instance. A deviation of the thoracic vertebrae, some sort of structural disturbance, short leg, for example, or spasms in the shoulder girdle. You should make a date with me if you've been doing any improper lifting. Any bumps, jars. You might've slipped a disc, I'd tell you, and be wondering what the pain in your backside is. Know what I mean?'

Ever practical he'd rattled Bea his skeleton out of her sleep. 'Sometimes I just grab hold wherever I can. Right off the bat, by whatever hold I know. Bilateral transverse, the million-dollar roll, the shunt. If we had time, I could show you a full nelson, a knee chest drop, even a lower sacral thust.'

Bartlett raised an eyebrow and it got a laugh.

'In case anybody's skeptical, ask the Workers' Compensation Boards. I'm paid to get loggers and longshoremen back on the job. Ask the old ladies who come in, the athletes, the shoppers, I'm hand in glove with the whole population. Pop singers, cartoonists, boxers. Ask them.'

Leaving home seemed to have loosened his instinctive rein on fabrication there. Reality was just different when you travelled: What your nose detected in the air determined what you could get away with. Entering other people's houses you tested the air as a matter of course. *You never do this entering your own house. It seems the same with countries.*

Entering the ornate ballroom next morning, Bartlett met a man cautiously plastering the wall with unsmiling photograhs of men, women, sometimes children, posed before the same black curtain. Prisoners who had been processed and tortured in the Grief House – whose bones, said Dananga, Bartlett already knew. He stared at this luxation of time, breathing shallowly in his dirty white coat.

At the table the curator and his assistants awaited them mutely for the lugubrious lesson to commence.

In order not to feel queasy, Bartlett decided he would have to move, act, and be aggressive. Hollow in his eardrums he could detect the deep, repetitive sound elephants make with their teeth eating hay.

'Right,' he said cheerfully. 'Today we've got wire. Yesterday we named bones. Today we'll dangle this composite rascal from the chandelier. We'll wire her together.'

Dananga's translation puzzled his clients. Answering, the little curator sounded self-righteous.

'They think you are making light of the dead,' explained Dananga, deadpan.

'Pardon? Oh the chandelier, it's just a place to start, you know, to hang the specimen?' Bartlett was eager to please. To straighten up their stooping postures, charm, get a bearing on his situation.

He had a situation on his hands, no question. And he was thirsty.

Without a drill to thread an exact space between bones – ribs, for example – he set about wiring together yesterday's remains, lashing joint roughly to joint and sockets into place. Two and a half hours later he was ready, after tethering pelvis to torso, torso to eye orbits, to raise Rosemary to the chandelier and see if this makeshift method of knotting wire around bones could be used to suspend other approximations of skeletons in a similar manner. What did they want in this grief pit, boneracks on a thousand hooks? Stiff articulations for the sake of visitors? Bartlett asked his assistants to bear Rosemary – but on second thought he dropped his habit of naming every skeleton he met and referred simply to 'the victim' – to bear the victim by table into the centre of the ballroom.

The curator walked on bones in his haste to clear a way wide enough through their tide.

Bartlett studied as it moved this work of his upon a bier.

'Listen,' he finally muttered. 'It's buckshee.'

'Please?' inquired Dananga.

He ran one end of copper through the cavity of the absent nose, stepping onto the table daintily, for a plump man, to loop the rest through a crook in the chandelier. Warning the others back, he proceeded slowly to raise the victim off the table, skull followed by bones in more or less correct sequence like a toy train with dangling boxcars, until what tarsal and metatarsal bones they'd managed to find left the table, and Bartlett stood there in a hangman's muffled pride, the wire cutting into his palms with the collective weight of who knew how many victims' bones.

'Look upon me,' said the skeleton, protesting its hybrid composition. He pulled the wires.

Bartlett pulled the wires.

The curator and assistants applauded dutifully, as though saluting the winner of an Olympic contest whose flag they didn't recognize.

In the midst of this ceremony misfortune struck. Somewhere in his construction a knot slipped causing the victim to collapse with a ratatat on the table, leaving a few bones still hanging from the chandelier like fractured concrete at a demolition site. The squatting women with their rags glanced up at the racket.

'This is definitely dumb,' he said, standing at attention on the table.

The wheelbarrow men too were watching the show. But the curator and his assistants chose to stare at their feet rather than embarrass a foreign expert.

'This really is definitely dumb!' repeated Bartlett with feeling. Throwing up his hands he released the final remains and the skull plunged to the table, gouging the mahogany. It thudded like a cigar box.

'Jesus,' he exclaimed. 'The idea stank in the first place.' He felt preposterous. A tubby Canadian in a lab coat jumping off his platform, a quack.

Dananga commiserated but without much sympathy. She seemed to think his lack of persistence pretty childish.

Bartlett tramped up the curling rococo staircase to the second floor. From the balcony outside, a barren flagpole slanted toward the boulevard. He stood out here wanting water, thinking of his father. Turning abruptly, he travelled through the vast colonial mansion, Dananga following him room to room pointing out where inquisition and torture had gone on. '*Murder*,' she stressed.

Trying to recall home he couldn't get through.

She indicated iron cots where corpses had lain abandoned by the retreating murderers as brute evidence of their genocide. Of their tragedy. Used for eliciting confessions, electric wires dangled from ceilings. Leg chains hung from springless bedsteads. She tried to shock him with shreds of fried flesh scored to the metal, strands of hair, blood and brown stuff staining mattresses. Mouldy clothes thrown into corners.

'Primary exhibits,' warned Dananga. 'Touch nothing. We leave everything.'

Like any man in an awkward position, expected to deliver and unsure of the map, Bartlett could feel the shape of his jaw and set of his teeth. He detested the Grief House.

But she was on to something. He told her, 'No. Mixing and matching isn't where it's at, you're right.'

'Explain?'

He couldn't, not in so many words. But below in the ballroom he actually watched himself take the wirecutters to release his contorted victim from bondage. He was suddenly impatient. 'Nix the skeletons. Piles are where it's at.' Dananga did her best to translate. 'Just piles and piles. Skulls. Let's quit being fancy.'

He went at it bluntly, up to his elbows, pitching eagerly into bones. Bones that shed no clues of having danced inside bodies anywhere. He suggested to the curator that he order a halt to wheelbarrows dumping any more discoveries inside. The digging ceased.

Bartlett did not stop for lunch.

He was a willing pioneer.

Out of the crests and valleys he asked that all skulls be carried to the far wall. Here he coordinated their anchoring in rows, faces forward, one on top of another.

The humidity made everybody sweat like pigs. Bartlett longed for a glass of water. But the work's rhythm, the bending to salvage, the squatting to drop, felt good. The curator's intensity, instead of waxing in the turmoil, waned in phases. The mounting skulls spoke mutely without jawbones, in a chorus of death. Yet the clamouring silence dissolved none of their pain nor the house's grief. The walls wailed.

That night the bathwater spun slowly down his drain the colour of mud. The spools of his diary were spinning too. *Bones*, he spoke decisively, *are the driven snow of history.*

At dinner he avoided the Romanian agronomist keen to quiz him on the museum's infrastructure.

'Their goals, yes? Are the same as I describe in villages without tools and fertilizer?'

She dusted the tablecloth with anxious hands and tucked her elbows into the nest of her hips.

In the morning he fell mesmerically to work again. He avoided breakfast. When the workers had collected and stacked four thousand skulls plus, when no more skulls remained above ground that were not piled to the ceiling opposite the wall of photographs – buttressed along the floor with a low wooden paling – he began to contemplate the tens, hundreds of thousands of other bones of which the human frame is composed in such a mass grave.

Outside, the heaved-up earth would have to be levelled and returned to gardens.

Singing birds.

From home he had a sudden strange feeling about Mikos.

Inside, plotting his release, he wandered back and forth across the dance floor. He was coordinating a plan.

Starting with the kitchen, and working his way through other rooms on this floor, the curator could fill these up past the embassy's windows with undulating seas of bone, into which – as in rooms of a carefully preserved heritage house back home, where visitors are prevented from entering by a braided cord – future visitors might peer. Bewildered, they could also look in from the gardens. The little man understood and nodded at the unreality of it all.

'He says you are a shrewd adviser,' said Dananga.

That evening, avoiding the Belgian who wanted to play cards, Bartlett told Strajik his work was done. 'Ask Dananga,' he added.

Mr Strajik bridled. Had Bartlett not promised him two weeks? The Belgian agreed. Bartlett's claim to have completed his aid would single him out for the disapproval of his peers. Even envy. 'Work beyond imagination,' said Mr Strajik. 'There is no end of reconstruction, I'm afraid.' The spirit of the time would teach him patience. *Patience, who has time for that?*

There followed discussions of roads, villages and disarray. Foreign workers were expected soon to follow up Mr Strajik's advance guard with resident agencies of international rescue. In the meanwhile, stressed the Swede, cost of contribution was not a price you paid with ingenuity but the value you offered in time. The others agreed. They seemed used to thinking of themselves as interdependent citizens in a very compressed state of being.

At dawn, as if dreaming, Dr Bartlett Day found a message at his door to pack up and prepare to travel deeper into bones. A white Lada awaited him, driver and guide. He'd been all ready to go home.

3.

His progress north was slow. The pilgrim ate dust as the sun rose in the sky bathing dispossessed nomads. It was no country for old men. People evidently requiring the chiropractor's expertise made his guide stop everywhere.

Villagers were blighted.

Starving, actually.

'Supposed to eat, yuh, yuh,' said the decrepit guide, probably no more than forty, making eating noises with hand and mouth. His English relied on semaphore and could no more uncover idiom than a flag could shuck an oyster. In this country, it was enough.

People mopped the fields for blades of forgotten rice. Their forced labour had produced only years of sterile fields and ransacked souls. Bags of rice appeared and disappeared, bicycled in from a border, selling and reselling for profit. Nobody without means to barter could afford free Red Cross gifts.

These sterile fields turned out to be Bartlett's goal. Their excavation was leading to spontaneous catharsis all over the country. Liberation, if it had removed fear of murder, was also renewing the grief. He drank greedily from his canteen.

Each village uncovered its proof. The educated and disobedient, the suspected and despised: Their bones were bleaching upon every one of his arrivals. Wrist bones still bound with wire, skulls still blindfolded. Even better as graves than the rice fields were b-52 craters, saucers in the earth now overgrown with vegetation.

The simplicity of his advice made Bartlett's transmigration nimble. He took a stick, he drew in the dust. Long, two-shelved sheds open to the air. *Look*, he pointed, upper shelf for skulls, lower shelf for all these other bones...

Every village offered a variation of the same story. Five thousand, eight thousand, ten and more thousand in bigger towns, struck on the head with iron bars, pokers, rifle butts – anything to save bullets, said his guide – and buried by fellow villagers, after victims had dug their own graves.

And every night Bartlett the voyeur told this story to his diary. Record, tally, log of each pit's disclosure. It felt like a lie. Parched, he slept on dirt floors and ate infested rice. He was gnawed into lumps by mosquitoes. His quarters smelled. Dysentery touched him with the hand of hyperbole. Storing up memories deliberately for the first time in his life, he treated himself to new batteries and might've bartered dead ones for food.

News becomes news as it gets famous, he spoke sombrely into his machine. *I don't even recognize stuff I can't look at on a screen.*

These suddenly liberated people seemed to expect more of him than he could hope to deliver. They wanted hope for their lives, not advice about the dead. He was certainly hand in glove with the lot of them – or might've been had he any real relief to offer. They still felt enchained. They showed him trees where people had been tied and left for twisting hooks to extract their livers.

Back home, he recalled, his office was full of gadgets to keep suffering patients coming back. Technology soothed, so did tradition.

'"Look well to the spine",' he'd told delegates at the Congress of Alternative Healing, quoting a potted Hippocrates, '"for many diseases have their origin in dislocations of the vertebral column".'

He liked to tell the story of the human back, from ancient Egypt through the fall of the Roman Empire, the dark ages, the evolution of bonesetting in the Renaissance. This story of dislocation gave his profession a history.

By the time he got to the invention of chiropractic – and here he pressed home his facts – by a Canadian one September afternoon in 1895, who had to migrate south before he could overthrow the old ideas of taking care of bodies, Bartlett had quoted from ancient Chinese documents on tissue manipulation, cited examples of spinal adjustment by a number of cultures including the Inca, Toltec and Maya, plus the Sioux and Winnebago. Even today, he claimed, the Maori in New Zealand still walked across each other's backs to cure pain caused by nonaligned bones. Bone manipulation was a democratic phenomenon given international distinction by a Canadian.

He'd suggested this rather proudly, sipping water.

And concluded confidently, 'Bones are character. Bones helped our forefathers get to my country. Bones helped them make sails, splice ropes, hook fish. I know their secrets by the bones they kept. In the old country they kept bones for shuttlecocks and chastity belts. In Canada they turned them into clappers and pastry crimpers. Bangles and snow goggles. Earplugs and dog whistles. Bones,' he boasted, 'keep me in touch.'

He'd given his amanuensis another slap. Bea's slats shone as white as snow in the lights. Hubris made them both glow. He had hired an enterprising Thai to make a video of his address and planned to play it in the waiting room of his office at home. With Bea he even waltzed a bit and got a hand.

In this Bangkok hotel on the river, plied once by trading schooners and seafaring novelists, he was asked to dance that evening by the striking, pearl-necklaced hypnotist from Marseilles named Dr Legatt, and Bartlett told her he was going to Pattycakes – Pattaya – in the morning and she should come too.

'I feel,' she replied, in very limber English, 'your idea with me is the best thing since apple betty.' His heart had skipped at this domestic little allusion that was confident of, indeed pleased with itself as idiom. 'But my husband and I leave tomorrow for Rome.

'Not,' she added, hands on his chiropractor's shoulders, 'that my husband would mind.'

Reported Bartlett, later, *We could learn a lot from the French* ...

Now, on his last night in a fractured little country, he ended up in an abandoned luxury hotel, once a refuge for travellers from around the globe. Over the country's ancient ruins it had started to rain. The jungle smelled sour. Vast temple mountains, towers and courtyards, balustrades and moats, shrines and niches to ancestral kings of a dislocated future – a wonder of the world, claimed his guide, just beyond the window. Bartlett dutifully wondered.

He thought of home, the old house he and Dwight and Reesa shared, still standing between apartment buildings, and he imagined an empty city. The way a neighbour's rusted Pontiac no longer returned like a tired animal, tires scraping the curb, engine rumbling until kicked to charge it up for morning, then switched off, sounding like the last and unexpected breath of a buffalo.

In the morning a small plane would land at the unused airstrip and return him to the capital. He had no answer for the guide and driver who wanted to see the skyscrapers of Singapore.

Bones are the driven snow of history. Bones not stones were the real record, a nation's memory. The record of experience was bones.

And grief, he concluded.

Without it you were a quack.

Tuneless.

He got out of bed to close the shutters in the large, unelectrified suite. He felt his way back again in darkness.

The white dust of bones left out in the air would start falling years hence over this jungle, this country, this people. But no one would feel it, see it, know it. The dust would be falling over the ruins too. He heard the little spools of his diary dissolving in silence.

It'll never sink in anywhere, he added, killing the mike.

Against the wooden shutters the rain fell harder.

April, 1906

Me Me Me …
Rehearsing. What better place than the Opera House, with its looser ways? Overheard house manager bragging to his soprano, 'We have the whole world on our stage.' Perked up at his flirty tone.

Assuming he soon has his way with her, could these become my future great, or great-great-grandparents? Am willing to wait. I have as much shame as a fly on the wall. In my case the fourth wall, as it's known around here, as good a place as any to hang out when living in imaginary time. Living, my foot.

Wonder how many real flies have died in this house since construction fifteen years ago? Flies that just dried up and fell, after clinging a few weeks to the painted safety curtain of lakes and mountains. Dropped, unheard from again, off the undersides of sixteen hundred seats. Or, down in the orchestra pit, expired among floorboard cracks where bass players have tapped in crumbs of countless cheese sandwiches.

God, have become a fly on the wall even to flies! Shows how hard up I am for evidence of breeding. Spending my time watching insects copulate in the red plush draperies of private boxes, in dressing rooms across the autographed images of bustled starlets.

'You're a very intelligent girl,' said the house manager. '*I* don't have to woo you with a tenor's song do I?' Chuckling. A break in rehearsal of *The Yeoman of the Guard*, a seduction of potential interest to an ambitious piece of dust like me. 'You owe yourself my blandishments as well. Believe me. Why not stay on in town and see if you aren't well taken care of by my stage? Tea like this sails in from India regularly. Those silk pillows? China. I'm so busy taking care of my house, huffing and puffing it clean for beautiful voices like yours, sometimes I think I'm a Welsh stockhorn…. You've seen a Welsh stockhorn in your travels, Miss Spenser? The thigh bone of a sheep, with finger holes you blow into and a cow's horn at the other –? Why am I talking so much? Those eyes of yours give me stage fright, my dear. Anyway, say you'll come to supper with me at the Oyster Bar. Think about it and give me your reply when the orchestra goes home.'

Sipping his tea he went on to say he'd had Sarah Bernhardt pass through, the Emma Juch Grand English Opera Company, Mark Twain, and famous prima donnas who, like herself, had been astonished at the size and ornateness of his house on this soft rainforest edge of the world.

Overhearing him I understood what boosterism meant to his job. He thinks illusion is important in creating a city to resemble his grand theatre in size and popularity. Thinks the soft sell is part of his required manner.

But Magnus Hooper recognizes his deficiency. A wife to anchor any

extravagant illusions he might happen to entertain about his growing invincibleness. 'I fear nothing. Therefore I'm worried. Go on, eat up. These local oysters are the finest in the world. You won't get oysters like these anywhere in the old country. I bet a dollar.' Champagne bucket, white tablecloth, a rose in the buttonhole of his lintless suit. '... I worry it could all vanish tomorrow, my dear, without someone to appreciate it with me.'

He confessed he was thinking of bringing in a production of a new opera called *Mrs Butterfly*, or else staging a local production of same, if he could acquire rights and a knockout talent to sing it well. 'I imagine you would do it well ...'

She explained to him she was Catholic. Blinking, he released more lemon juice with his fork over his remaining oysters. He'd

probably have a better chance of bedding a Methodist or even a high Anglican. She was, however, a stage girl. He turned to watch a man in the street renewing the carbon of an electric-arc lamp. If worse came to worst he could rent a buggy from the livery stable and drive her into the park. He could lose his way in the evergreens for an afternoon.

He shifted again in his wicker chair, toasted her talent with champagne, and invited her up to his hotel suite for a look at Puccini's score. The shells had piled far higher on his plate than hers.

In his suite Hooper called down for another magnum of champagne to toast his guest's career on stage. His was a mellow-lit suite stuffed with mementos of fifteen years in theatre, including the Welsh stockhorn some waggish trombonist had unloaded here. For no

apparent reason,
suspended from the
ceiling on a string, was
the reconstructed
skeleton in flight of a
glaucous-winged gull.

It gave me the jim-
jams.

I waited, anticipating
the tremor of their
bodies in union beneath
her rococo petticoats, his
rolled moustaches silky
against her blossoming
cheeks, for already I was
polishing up my tiny
feet to help stick me to
the seagull's beak above
the divan.

Am condemned to
speak figuratively as a
shameless substitute for
living.

Good news I hope in
the morning.

Chapter 23

X-Rays

... Then Megan asks me, since you've lost all these pounds and look better, why don't you feel better about us? Aren't we both doing okay money-wise? We could scrounge up a mortgage on some starter home in the East End ... Not like this gross heirloom you share with those two, off enjoying themselves in Hawaii ...

Bartlett couldn't kick the habit of a travel diary once he got home to Canada. He found the act of rumination didn't really begin till he went to bed and ran over the events of his day just passed. Not till he pressed the button on his mike could he really even remember what day it was.

He'd come home from Asia feeling he might try living every day, diary in his holster, as if still travelling: forget about his appetite and learn to be more tolerant. This had helped him lose weight and listen with deeper sympathy to his patients. But it wasn't the same here. It was harder to discern the shape of home, when you were home.

This didn't stop his patients from trying to discern it for themselves, every time they came in. While some had seen Dr Day on TV, discussing his odd adventures abroad, nothing interested them deeply except their own painful lives. Lois's appointment book was crammed, his office crowded.

Megan, his girlfriend, had read in a magazine where bartenders, hairdressers and telephone operators should consider themselves 'gatekeepers', because they all worked at jobs where the emotional confidences of strangers could help the gatekeepers identify possible suicides. Megan was a hairdresser. *If she's the gatekeeper, I feel like the curator.* His was a whole gallery of tale-spouting strangers, ready and anxious to get things off their chests. *Actually, their backs.* None of his own clients seemed suicidal, but several resembled borderline manics. These tended to talk most. Maybe the inflationary spiral of the economy had pumped people up till they had to talk, or else burst and sink, thereby forcing the less well off to prefer chiropractors to psychiatrists. It was turning into a good decade for chiropractors. Backs inexplicably hurt, bones ached, and ordinary lives demanded release from pressures acquired in trying to keep afloat in the world.

It's a new world they'd all like to reach. Not one they know now. They want out of their rooms for a breather ...

Each sufferer's voyage to Bartlett's office seemed a brief rowing-out from home, from the feeling of dislocation in the main body of a life. The patient would arrive in a lifeboat, sans life preserver, with fishing pole casting a line over the unknown, tempting it. He felt this is what all of his patients did in his examining room, in launching themselves on another complaint, anecdote, daydream. What else could he do but listen to their sight-seeing gossip as he saw to their spines? Listen to their small, reconnoitring voices on the sea's lonely surface, never quite out-talking chronic luxations and so requiring another visit. His profession depended on repeat visits.

He X-rayed, manipulated, listened. He welcomed new patients despite statistical claims that if most backsufferers only rested at home, eighty-five percent would get better on their own. Sans treatment. A statistic kept quiet by chiropractors for obvious reasons. Yet Bartlett knew it wasn't so much bones his patients came in and came back to have straightened, but souls. Which gave his profession a spiritual dimension it preferred not to acknowledge, since its pride rested foursquare on what it claimed was a scientific foundation.

Doubt nagged him in ways he knew a true impostor would find irrelevant if not amusing. His oak-framed diploma on the wall didn't lessen his sense that rather than curing pain he was posturing instead. After six years of practice, and after his recent wrestle with bones in Asia, he thought the scientific terminology sounded dead. Subluxations. Skeletal balancing. Intervertebral foramen. Among his colleagues, respectability had become a driving force: Publicize or Perish. To draw attention to itself, to show that 'dis-ease' required prevention as well as manipulation, the Chiropractic Association had spread Posture Week across the nation. ('Gardening is no bed of roses when your back aches ... After a winter of inactivity the sun hits the garden and so do you. And the first crop you're likely to reap is pain – in spades: back ache, sore muscles, even a "slipped disc" ...') The four-eyed chiropractor, on the lookout for his patients' best interests, had eyes in the back of his head. He used his X-ray screen to turn their dark secrets into bright ones. Smack in the middle of Posture Week Bartlett had begun to feel again like a voyeur.

'Doc?'

'Doesn't look great, Mr Copithorne, this spine is giving you plenty of trouble ...'

He traced the line of his patient's thoracic vertebrae, on film up against the viewing screen. Spinographs legitimized diagnosis.

'Am I right?'

Did a branch bend? Weasel Copithorne enjoyed the winds of his unfortunate disability. Alone in the world, his wife dead, he could indulge his fairweather back in the office of a sympathetic healer. No matter how much walking he did, along cherry-blossom streets Weasel himself had helped to pave, it couldn't replace someone to talk to. He was still grieving after twenty years. This year he'd already used up his fifteen free visits under medicare, for patients over sixty-five, and was now paying eleven dollars a pop out of his own pocket convinced of the value. He knew Bartlett Day to be a soft touch and an excellent practitioner. Dr Day listened without hustling him out after two or three quick manoeuvres. *Why encourage the competition?*

'Well, Weasel, let's try bearing down on the unbearable, shall we?'

'Right you are, doc. Gimme the million-dollar roll.'

'Thought you liked to call it the slot machine.'

'I know when to stop kidding. This pain's no joke.'

'My nurse thinks *I* must be giving you the backache, Weasel, you're in so often. What do you think of that?'

'You didn't give it to me, doc. I had it festering for years. You just helped me locate and get a handle on it.'

Bartlett touched his fingers along Weasel's spine as he might have sounding, testing a flute. 'Tender?'

Weasel looked at him happily. 'Hurts like a son of a gun.'

He had laid himself face down on the adjusting table, speaking as was his custom into an armpit. 'It's the bejesus I want you to give me.' His chiropractor now lowered the electric table precisely to the horizontal. 'Work me over good.'

Bartlett went to work gently on Weasel Copithorne's back.

'I was thinking what you had to say back when about Asia, doc, and that there ...' Weasel was not some blurter-outer of whatever jumped into his head. He rehearsed his lines before coming in. Today, like every day, he'd decided on the truth.

'Why don't you come on a holiday, my wife used to say. Whenever she was in the dumps, whenever she felt locked up, she'd buy a timetable of the freighters in port. Where are we going I'd ask. The east, she'd say, Colombo. She'd get out books on them Sageery maidens and mongeese. Look at these, she'd say, why don't you look at these? You never look. She talked a blue streak, doc.'

Weasel was into his rhythm now. Bartlett moved sharply, Weasel winced.

'I couldn't have swung a trip like that, not a city worker like me, but money for her wasn't the thing and she went ahead with plans to book a sailing. So help me she booked one. Unlucky for us both she got sick ... headache, red spots, fever. She kept sweating. Doc, you haven't felt the half of it. I rang the hospital and an ambulance took us both away, me riding shotgun with the medics. She had typhoid like, the doctors prescribed antibiotics, she got worse. Dead within the week. Broke my heart. Cremated Friday, her ashes mine by Saturday. It was a weekend in August, nowhere else to go, so I came down to the park. She loved the park ... the grackles and things.'

Bartlett listened, pretending preoccupation with his patient's uncompromising bones.

'I strewed her ashes from a rowboat on the lagoon ... back when we *had* rowboats on the lagoon. Laid her to rest from a rowboat, Dr Day.'

Pause. Guess you had to be there the last time he came in, to know what was coming next ...

'Reckon I could of had her embalmed like, and laid to rest in a cemetery ...' He seemed doubtful of this burial of his wife at sea. 'Water's a variable, doc. Even the catfish've disappeared from that there lagoon.'

Another pause, then a new chapter.

'I never got away. Not like you, doc, not to the east like a roving deckhand. Mind you, after her death, on my holidays like, I bussed south to Reno, hoping the slots'd break the icejam in my heart. I reckon they did, in a manner of speaking. A young woman who was dispensing change introduced herself.'

'You don't say.'

Weasel lifted his head as if to position it for more dignified disclosure. 'When the coast was clear we went up to her room and bounced away the night. *Boing*, if you can believe it, *boing boing*. Hn!'

'Feeling better, Mr Copithorne?'

'Gimme another one of them.'

So Bartlett administered more coordinated magic to Weasel's spine.

'She kept talking about her husband,' said Weasel. 'Mowed down in a paddy field, fighting guerrillas in the jungle. I should of walked out on her. Instead I let her chew my ear off. Her husband was a dingaling who read Thomas Tray Herne and had hair in his nose. I kept thinking of him there in the sun, smelling to high heaven … excuse my French, doc. I don't know why I put up with her, especially with my own wife not that many months in the ground …'

'Homesickness?' inquired Bartlett.

'What amazed me,' said Weasel, 'was the patience I showed. I could of walked out on her. I definitely should of walked out.'

'I read somewhere,' said Bartlett, 'where the Thai peasants have a saying: He who has seen a white crow, the nest of a paddy bird, a straight coconut tree or a dead monkey, will live forever.'

Weasel sat up and reached back down his spine as far as he could bear to. Houdini with bursitis and a crick. Except he couldn't escape the bare facts.

'I'll be lucky to reach seventy, Dr Day. The city's going to save big on my pension. Inflation's eating me alive and I got no principal to dip into. You tell me what's fair like.'

Putting on his shirt Weasel grumped like a water buffalo. He'd given forty-some years to the city in roads and sewers. Something along the way, lifting manhole covers he figured, had done lasting damage to his lumbar. But those years of chronic pain were nothing compared to the economic erosion of his pension and the memory of his wife's death. Retirement was no beginning for Weasel Copithorne. Gone his hope of a cottage on a gulf island, salmon in a dipnet. Gone to more enterprising youth were fabulous trips to the far east.

Bartlett liked him. He liked most of his patients, although a bottom-line study might disclose less time spent with each patient would mean more income from the lot of them. In most, their resilience overcame the painful temptations to give up on rescue, give in to despair. He felt the island each endured was a self in need of love. Few felt the pressure of city life as responsible for their dislocated backs. *They couldn't afford to escape it anyway.* They viewed Vancouver as a prosperous city washed by Hawaiian currents and God's own tears. They had welfare, student loans, old age pension, mincome … What was a luxated back, compared to no TV in a foreign city, no medicare, no income at all?

2.

At lunch Bartlett's M.D. friend, Tom Cabot, was talking about physicians using X-ray machines, 'overusing them, like toys'. Cabot was one of the few medical doctors who didn't turn up his nose at consorting with chiropractors. And to prove he wasn't pinched-minded like his colleagues, once in a while referred a patient to Bartlett – Mrs Dawson, for example, after her complaining of aches in places where the M.D. could find nothing wrong. 'Now look at her,' Cabot liked to say, admiring Bartlett's progress. He was two years older than Bartlett, indulgent of his cures because he knew health depended on the mind anyway.

He was a new, if still rare, breed of mainstream physician.

'Listen, I've got patients who think snake venom's the answer to MS. Who am I to say Absolutely Not, if it doesn't make things worse? You've got colleagues, I've got colleagues ... we both know what the dinosaurs are like. Darth Vaders with X-ray machines.'

Bartlett was reading his paper placemat.

'You off fish and chips?' asked Cabot.

'Not hungry.' These days the chiropractor found chowder and a glass of water adequate. His white lab coat had begun to hang loosely. 'Says here,' he said, 'the world record for the walleyed pike is twenty-five pounds. Caught in the waters of Old Hickory Lake, Tennessee, in 1963.'

Sam Lung's small cafe specialized in fish and chips and was full of framed portraits of the Royal Family. Painted fish swam along the bottom half of his front window, through little blue waves resembling parentheses having a rest. The fish all swam in the direction of a British flag.

'In 1963,' said Cabot, 'I was panting to get my driver's licence. You?'

'Sock hops.'

'You could pant at those, I suppose.' Cabot sounded doubtful. '... You a good jiver, Day?'

'I had a pair of banana toes. I could slip and slide better than a lot of skinnier guys.'

'I always figured banana toes were for hardrocks. Those and gores.'

'You just grew up on the wrong side of town,' said Bartlett. 'You med-school types.'

'You guys are still wearing saddle shoes,' observed Cabot.

'Kids nowadays,' said Bartlett, 'wouldn't know a banker from a white buck.' He thought of Aloysius's black nylon Velcros. '*I* hardly know anymore.'

He did know about jiving. He could once jive like an octopus in heat, one of those fat kids who happened to move more gracefully than the odds would've predicted. His appearance on a basketball court always gave the Judas kiss to how smoothly he could pivot. The treason of his bulk was dismissed by other boys, who always picked him first for chink. *They didn't care if my gut wobbled ...*

'Why do we come to this place?' said Tom, waiting for his coffee. They looked at the empty tables, each one set with two paper placemats, edged with the same pair of pinking shears. Cabot claimed he could smell something like the coffee he ordered in the skein of smoke drifting in from the kitchen.

But diesel fumes from a Safeway truck washed in and expunged any trace of coffee, when the door opened and two hard-looking girls walked in wearing boots and crotch-pinching jeans. Tom regretted this. He felt lonely, he said, deprived of his pheromones. The women were licking ice cream cones.

His fish and chips arrived, stuck all over with packets of tartar sauce. 'I'm sorry,' he explained to Sam, 'we were having clam chowder ...'

'Yes, coming,' replied the proprietor, bobbing formally at his white-coated diners.

'You gotta ask for crackers,' said one of the girls, 'or he won't bring you crackers either.'

The doctors chuckled. Friendly types. No use getting shirty with Sam.

The newcomers had licked deep into their cones. Bartlett recognized the talkative, older one as a patient from two or three years ago, who'd come in once favouring her knee. *Her ankle maybe.* He noticed she was still wearing spike heels he must have warned were terrible for her coccyx. In the X-ray he'd taken of her bare back, he could still see her vertebrae curving gracefully like a mature gazelle's. She was a Buddhist or something. Chestnut eyes.

It was Dr Cabot she recognized. She raised her fingers in covert recognition. Tom nodded, nervously.

'Patient of mine,' he mumbled.

The plump younger girl let her whole cone slide down her throat.

Cabot's coffee arrived, conversation turned to billing practices and his allopathic colleagues, some of them more earnest than chiropractors he joked. Then their chowder was served. Cabot asked if Bartlett could guess the world record for the smallmouth bass. Bartlett, pushing aside his bowl for a better look, countered with the great blue sucker. Cabot, squeezing tartar sauce in the direction of his halibut, ended up squirting his friend's white sleeve.

'Here,' said Tom, 'let me wash it off.' Using his serviette and water glass, he pointed out that as professionals he and Bartlett didn't get enough time off for things like fishing – when the younger girl ... *maybe she had ice cream up her nose*, unexpectedly snorted at their palsy-walsy intimacy.

3.

In his office when he got back patients were waiting. Patients were always waiting. He noticed his chairs were identical to Sam Lung's, padded steel with wood veneer armrests, too thin to support an elbow without perfect balance. Slip and buzz your funnybone.

Bartlett had inherited his chairs, along with reliable patients like Weasel Copithorne, when he purchased his practice and building from the retiring A. Frey, D.C. He'd hung out his own sign, B. Day, D.C., without disturbing the furniture or changing the nurse. It might've helped the image of his office to redo it in strap and steel chairs and to hire a sexy receptionist. You probably learned this at marketing conferences in Houston: how you couldn't afford to let patients sense your practice wasn't at the leading edge of fashion in the medical profession. Anyway, he'd compromised. He called Lois 'Nurse' and she called him 'Doctor'. In the real sense of both names, neither was either. Society had only agreed to allow the chiropractor into medicare, and to call himself Doctor, if he agreed to caboose the appropriate letters after his name – to forewarn all except those in need of a quick fix, and indifferent to distinctions, of the exact nature of his whistle-stop kind of operation.

No wonder D.C.s are aggressive. Our train of thought makes us think we need to nab the whole family or starve.

Lois had just handed him the latest ad for Posture Week, from the morning paper. He read it through with distaste.

'You think we should target more kids?' he asked.

'I don't think kids have many backaches,' said Lois. 'We've got enough older types who think they invented it.'

He passed into his examining room to wash his hands and drink a glass of cold tapwater. Why should he be aggressive just to satisfy his association? Small cheques came in and business flourished. He showed patients out, he welcomed them back. He bent to his task and listened. The profession was founded in people's yearning to be whole, if only for a while, to escape into a harmonious world he could locate for them straight away as resident in their own skeletons. No wonder he was popular. They told him stories, obsessions of their lives.

He listened to their bones. He warned his patients to pay attention to what their own musculoskeletal structures were saying, or risk dislocation. Their choice? Live in pain or live. Sometimes he doubted his own diagnoses. He had begun to wonder why he wasn't happier. What did it matter if he fell back on smug spiels and spinographs time and again? So what if the shameless professional pedigree he boasted seemed flawed by ingenuity?

For instance, this brochure in the mail, an ad gimmick making use of the Thirty-Third Principle of Chiropractic to justify yet another conference on 'Free Enterprise and the D.C. in Transition'. Quoted like the Bible, in a handout at a revival rally: 'The Law of Demand & Supply is existent in the body of its ideal state; wherein the "clearing house" is the brain, Innate the virtuous "banker," & nerve cells "messengers".'

He reread it and it still didn't make sense, so he tossed it in the wastebasket. 'Who's next, Nurse?'

Lois wanted to know where to file the video of his Bangkok speech, since he no longer felt like setting up a monitor in the waiting room for the edification of his patients. 'Under B ...?' she wondered.

'N,' he told her, '... for Nostalgia. Who's next, please?'

Gloria Dawson strode into the examining room. He allowed her time alone to undress. Gloria was now into her 'ageproofing' so successfully it was impossible to guess she'd reached a very advanced age. Lois, filing her nails at the Selectric, whispered you couldn't guess she was the age she said she was – eighty-five.

Bartlett sipped from his glass of water. Nail dust was sifting into the keys.

Eighty-five, he knew, was the age Gloria was becoming famous for being and not looking. Lois regarded the closed door. *So what if she's suckered the media,'* she whispered. *'For years, women have been telling us they're younger than they are ... so when one comes along spurning all that, but still lying through her teeth, it's refreshing.* By rights,' she said aloud, 'she ought to look embalmed.'

A couple of waiting patients looked up. Bartlett buried his head in the appointments book. Gloria had been coming in for about a year, since Tom Cabot recommended her. With her marathoner's body Gloria had felt a chiropractic overhaul could help her learn to move more gracefully. Then, between her second and third visits, her imagination was stirred in a very peculiar way. She'd read a book. Not just any book, but one that changed her life. She returned to Bartlett with its message, and an extravagant claim meant to sweep away claims of any prior personal history she might have confided to him to do with her age. She'd suddenly changed the way she dressed. She wore smarter clothes, but of a more ancient cut. She'd even altered the way she spoke, sounding higher and brighter, in the manner of a very with-it senior. Her hair ...

'Don't forget to reassure her,' whispered Lois. *'Butter her up. She's good publicity.'* She was trying to keep her voice low, so the waiting patients wouldn't fret over an indiscreet nurse when it was their turn to go in and undress. *'Her so-called ageproofing is all relative – it's only a big success if you think she's eighty-five ...'*

'I forget, how old she's supposed to be?'

'Bet on the eyes. She's only as old as her eyes look.'

'Which is what, roughly?' He hadn't had a lot of time to study Gloria Dawson's eyes.

'Fifty-three, four.'

'B.S.!' He attracted more stares from his waiting patients. He whispered, *'Why would she claim to be thirty-one years older than she really is?'*

Lois raised an eyebrow. *'Because that way a relatively young bat gets famous as an old one who doesn't look it.'* She finished with her nail file and proceeded to blow the snow from her keys.

'Well,' he whispered, *'she looks a hell of a lot older than her early fifties.'*

'Exactly – but a lot younger than her mid-eighties. She'd be an 'ageproofed' failure if she let out her real age.'

'I think you're jealous, Lois.'

'No, I think it's great,' she whispered. *'I think she's great.'* She paused to pick up a pencil. *'I think she'd be even greater if she didn't ask for the senior's*

discount. Honestly, who else lies like she does? She's been on TV.'

Bartlett prepared himself to reenter the examining room, when a flat moan escaped it. Entering, he saw Gloria, who'd wrapped herself in a dressing gown, looking into the mirror and holding her head with overlapping arms, not unlike a hotcross bun. He waited for some explanation, but she was quiet now, though her lips continued to move.

He wondered if the roots of her hair had been dyed grey – whether her brown bun above these, streaked in silver wisps, wasn't her hair's natural colour got up to look dyed in a perverse, orange kind of way atop the dyed roots. It seemed like a lot of work, making yourself look older in order to look younger.

It exercised his imagination.

'I'm ageproofing my ears,' she said, turning to face him. He saw she was pulling up the tops of her ears with her criss-crossed arms. 'A woman is lucky, Dr Day. She can avoid droopy lobes if she stops wearing earrings. But even men can work off their vertical folds ... these things in front here. What I do is wiggle my ears. Then lift them for a count of fifteen. Try it ...'

Bartlett tried it and she began to count. They were both holding their ears with arms doubled over their heads.

'... Now relax. You repeat that ten times and feel the skin tighten up all over your skull.'

'I can feel it already.'

'Georgie Porgie,' said Gloria, 'kissed the girls and made them cry.'

She'd pitched her voice to mimic the drier vocal folds of an older woman, but without sacrificing the aggressive manner of a younger one. This made her sound more rambunctious and delightful than Nature probably intended her to sound thirty years hence. She had the timbre of an older woman, who sounded irrepressibly youthful.

'I'm a follower of Jane Ogle,' she said. 'She's quite a gal. If I see something in the mirror I don't like, I let myself know it. I look around at these old people my age, Dr Day, and I can't believe they don't *scream* at themselves. I still have lungs,' she said, 'like a vacuum cleaner.'

She then whooshed with laughter as if to prove it. Gloria Dawson relished her own vigour, the way any conceited pensioner might do with a captive audience of impressionable highschoolers, socking it to them with their own pep. She wanted to be admired for being with it. A regular time machine, with the latest microchip.

'Well,' said Bartlett. 'It doesn't look like you need much help from me ...'

'Stuff and nonsense, Dr Day.'

'Are you in any pain?'

'Fear,' said Gloria, 'of what could happen to my bones if I don't keep them limber. I come to you as the expert, same as I go to my dermatologist for skin and my dentist for teeth. I want to keep my bones in shape, and I want to ageproof the scallywags ...' Her language sounded intentionally seasoned and therefore, he thought, of even more interest to those in on the hoax. *Who, me?*

He looked into her eyes.

If she was fifty-four, as Lois thought, she looked like a unique specimen for gerontologists, but not in the way Gloria might have hoped. Her skin was old for a woman of fifty-four. Rough hands, ropy legs. She might have been anywhere from fifty-four to sixty-nine. If she *was* fifty-four, she had good reason to feel as tense as he now found her, when she dropped her dressing gown and lay down on his table.

He pressed the button to create a plane for her skeleton.

Everything in time seemed to depend on your perspective.

'... Yes, that feels looser, Dr Day. Tell me now. What kind of shape do you think they're in, my bones, for an eighty-five-year-old woman?' Shameless, her abiding need of compliments. 'On TV, I asked that Potts woman what she knew about demineralization, and she turned the question on me. I told her lots, but none of it any good, if you don't use your facts to eat right and exercise right. Menopause was the culprit. I lost masses of minerals – my bone minerals started disappearing, out from under my nose. If the wind was right, I could hear my spine crumble. I was lucky not to snap a hip, Dr Day. In those years who'd heard of osteoporosis? You accepted your dowager's hump and you bore it. Women did bear it and still do. But they don't have to – not if they drink milk and walk two miles a day. They can ageproof themselves ... just by lubing their joints. It's a conceit to say it, but I'm the living proof. Calcium, exercise, estrogen ...'

Bartlett was feeling her backbone. 'Probably a minor misalignment ...'

'Where?'

'... lower back vertebra. If it's not giving you too much discomfort, it'll probably correct on its own, if your surrounding tissues and muscles are as healthy as you say they are, Mrs Dawson.'

'Oh, they are. My trabecular and cortical bones testify to the health of my personal tissue. You know that, Dr Day. None of me has broken down – not yet. A team of these specialists are talking about doing a study on me, once I find them my birth certificate. One of them figures I could live another thirty or forty years. Break records.'

'An X-ray might help us establish, for sure, if there's any likelihood of osteoporosis,' said Bartlett. He wanted to play along. 'A woman can lose a third or half of her bone by the time she reaches eighty. The skeleton shrinks and lightens up.'

'Not black women.'

'Pardon?'

'The blacks have heavier bones to begin with. The ones at risk are us and the Orientals ... our bones are more birdlike.' She simpered a little, pleased with her command of the facts. 'The lighter your skin, the more chances of fractures and humps and snapped wrists. What's your feeling, honestly, about vitamin-D supplements?'

'I'm not –'

She smiled agreeably. 'Me neither. Better to trust the sun. I make it a rule to expose my skin a little bit every day. Yesterday was nice and warm, so I sat on the balcony in my halter. Carmen, my daughter, came over ... she's close to sixty and doesn't look twenty-five ... She swallows seventeen hundred milligrams of calcium every morning, before toast.'

'Do you ... is there a particular exercise you do for your back? I know a little –'

Gloria Dawson sat up, pleased her chiropractor might have something practical to suggest trying. Her bra was lifting her breasts in the same responsible way her fingers had earlier lifted her ears. Training and ageproofing them. For eighty-five, her breasts had stood up well to the gravity of time.

'Now you're talking,' she told him. 'What're you offering? Self manipulation?'

'First, let me see how you stand again, how your alignment looks ...'

She moved off the table to stand on the floor, very straight, shoulders square. She complained, twisting it behind her ear, of hair she needed to do something about, vitamin-wise. He noticed how her imaginary plumb line fell more or less through the centre of her knobs, joints and caps. Her alignment was good. Good, that is, for a woman of eighty-five. For a woman of fifty-four Bartlett needed to refine his diagnosis, alter his perspective. He suspected this was at the heart of diagnosis: Time in relation to the Evident.

'Very nice,' he told her. 'Now. Are you familiar, Mrs Dawson, with what I call the Bib and Tucker Jive ...? I wouldn't think, really, you were too old for it at all.'

'Show me,' she said eagerly. 'Is it something new, Dr Day?'

Exercise, he told all his female patients. Think motion. Any woman in her mid-twenties was losing bone, growing lighter in structure, more porous in her skeleton. She should pick up a pamphlet from his nurse on how much and what kind of minerals she required daily, to counteract Time's eraser. Pop a Tums, for extra calcium.

Bones are the driven snow of history.

That afternoon he welcomed back several housewives, from their twenties through their sixties, including a holdover from Dr Frey's practice, Anna Linde, with a long history of backache and a husband's neglect, who'd lately responded well to the manipulation of her atlanto-occipital joint – because, supposed Bartlett, she liked the sound of this name, and because it served to localize the pain. So he'd concentrated on this joint to the exclusion of other worthy candidates. But since her pain had now mostly vanished, she'd convinced herself she would soon be free of him.

'Though I'll miss our talks,' she said.

Not so much talks, he thought, as monologues. She was no different from most. From one week to the next he might hear about landlords and plugged sinks, plaster-of-paris rash, swans stoned by delinquents, sucking dicks vs. Popsicles, Truffaut films at The Bay, gays sharing budgets, thigh-stroking bosses, thunderstorms when you're living in a tent, kicking the habit of cats (an addiction ... cats, not kicking them), BCRIC shares, hoped-for weekends in Harrison Hot Springs, even murder. The murder turned out to be of the patient's own soul, in a lunge for upward mobility inside a townhouse he couldn't afford on the salary of an ad copy-editor.

Most patients had heard Bartlett's spiel about their luxations, some had heard it from Dr Frey, but a newcomer might sometimes ask for a pamphlet in support of her decision to try out this quacky-looking alternative to real medicine. A Greek-speaking diva, who'd lost her voice, requested treatment for whiplash, though she'd never been in a car accident. She thought it might reclaim her voice. She wanted Bartlett to find disc degeneration and exostoses. He'd done his best. She claimed her debut at the Met had already been ruined by pressing factors at home. It was all a fiction.

What matters, said Lois, is these patients have somewhere to come on a regular basis to talk out their troubles. And to have a knee X-rayed, then the left sacroiliac joint manipulated, till the pain disappeared. Or so they claimed. His patients usually wished to sound as agreeable as their credulity permitted. Lois was convinced this was a peculiarity of alternative medicine, the remarkable eagerness among patrons to support its claims.

Regularly, she suggested he hire somebody in a sandwich board to go to town for his business. 'Or hire an airplane,' she said.

'Yeah?'

'You pick a sunny day, when everybody's out enjoying a holiday, then the pilot takes off towing your line across the sky, so everybody in the city can read it.'

'What line?'

'You'd make up a short one. Like ... CHIROPRACTIC HABIT DR DAY.' She typed it out neatly on a filing card, her ringed fingers a sputter of motion. 'That translates,' she said, handing him the card, 'as, Get into the chiropractic habit of regular checkups with Dr Day.'

'Lois, I'm manipulating half the city already.'

'Why be happy with half a loaf?'

In her mid-forties, Lois had energy to burn and liked to pick out new wardrobes for her boss from Eaton's flyers. She thought he dressed like a shopping bag, jumping into whatever he found when he got up, before slipping into the worn-out white coat she called his 'coveralls' and his scuffed saddle shoes. Today she'd even sniffed the air and asked if he'd been camping out at home. 'As a matter of fact,' he began ... She favoured designer jeans for herself, at eighty-five dollars a pair. And confessed, from time to time, having a favourite spot to dab an indulgent perfume, but wouldn't say where and Bartlett never asked.

'Who's next?'

'Mr Astapovo.'

'What's that thing?'

'Rubik's Cube.' She picked it up. Her fingers moved with dexterity over this square lump of bright plastic. *Plastic has seen the future and knows how it works.* Plastic surgeons were just the beginning ... of what, Bartlett was reluctant to imagine. He recognized his instinctive mistrust of the mainstream world, in anything that smacked of injection, allopathy, capitalism.

'Mr Astapovo? Please, won't you come in?'

The white-bearded gentleman did so, hobbling with pain and supported by a stick.

Needles Astapovo was a man of genuinely advanced age who claimed to live in a tent. He claimed to have slept in every important and unimportant park in the world. As if to prove it he carried on his person an unmistakable gamey smell. Now retired from travel, a little reluctantly, he'd settled into Stanley Park. He lived nearby in the forest. His regular absence from a shower didn't cause Bartlett to overestimate the lavishness of his lair. Needles had severely injured his strong back last year, by tumbling down a cliff at the nudist beach on Point Grey. By trial and error, Bartlett had discovered the old man responded best to the second and third techniques for manipulations of his posterior innominate.

With Needles flat on his stomach, Bartlett would lift the right leg with his left hand, extending it fully, then thrust down sharply on the upper posterior to create a kind of twist in the sacroiliac joint of the lower spine.

'Yes,' said Needles. 'Again?' He claimed to cherish the pop.

Something reduced and simple about Needles gave the old man an aura of dignity in the teeth of chronic pain. He'd wanted nothing to do with X-rays, dismissing them quietly as immoral. 'Vile,' he said. 'Electromagnetic waves through the body make people magnets to death.' This put Bartlett back on his heels. But Needles was endlessly patient with him, and expected no miracle to improve his condition. Not overnight. He called Time a carving: Try to rush it, splinters in your hand. He liked to talk in pictures. This way he could feel his way into more abstract subjects like old age, the way a mortician, he suggested, works best surrounded by silence.

He wasn't a humourless man. He talked about parks and Bartlett listened with an interest whetted by his own recent travels. Needles knew of squares and parks of which the chiropractor had never heard.

'... Well, you know Kensington Gardens, don't you? I lived there for a month before they threw me out. I then found a hole in the fence in St. George's Square, down by the river, and crawled through there every night for a whole winter in a pup tent. Plus I lived on the heath for a year and a half. I knew parks and commons from Putney to Shoreditch.'

He'd slept in them all. The Bois in Paris, Chapultapec in Mexico City, Tigerbalm in Hong Kong, King's in Perth ... Running them together he sounded as rehearsed as Weasel Copithorne. He claimed nearly to have frozen to death during the big freeze in January. He hadn't slept a wink, as his 'coxitis' got worse.

His visit lengthened out like a shadow in the late April afternoon. His body rose and fell on the adjusting table.

'I say slept, Dr Bartlett. I meant snored. I can sleep anywhere there's a patch of grass and a water bottle ...' He had a dry soundless laugh, bracketed by teeth still his own. 'Don't know why I feel tired these days, after the years of sleeping I've done ... My tent's hidden in the middle of a forest, I can sleep till noon. I can read till the cows come home. Nobody's waiting to kick me out, no one knows I'm there. Come and visit me sometime, I'll show you the trees.' He gave another dry laugh through his white beard.

Needles always paid in cash. He felt buying on time was stealing from the future, and seemed never to have heard of medicare. He was a gentleman. He believed history had moulded us each in a lie. He hinted at a prosperous upbringing upon which, in carving out his eventual niche, he had turned his back.

'Kind of a reverse Howard Hughes,' suggested Lois, who thought he must be on OAP, though where the government would send his cheque she couldn't guess.

'No,' said Bartlett. 'He's out of a whole other ball game.'

'Well,' said Lois, switching on the fan, 'if b.o. is anything to go by, I don't doubt it for a sec.'

4.

Walking home that afternoon the pilgrim kept straight down Altamira for the bay, instead of turning for home. He was thinking of Megan, who wanted a house.

He noticed West End seniors besieging the community centre's restaurant at tea time, and knew the adjoining high school contributed just as many Pepsi-guzzling students at the same hour. Not Aloysius though, who was probably hustling red rinse to the bluerinsers this very moment over his own cup of Nabob.

He pressed on past Tom Cabot's office above the florist shop, past funky cafés, Ned's Halibut, a Chinese grocery and a pizzeria, the Racquets Club, barber shops. The local journey his patients made every day. He could still hear Marcus telling him about countries ... *Skin, for heaven's sake.*

The faith healer had made looking contagious. Yet at the beach Bartlett found himself paying no attention to the tide or to what colour the tulips were. Crossing the little park he forgot to smell the flowering hawthorns. He was studying his saddle shoes. *Looking through them, actually, to my bones.*

Long after shoestores had banned X-ray machines, his best high school friend, Butch Togg, had died.

The sudden connection startled him.

Let me try to dunk this.

Hadn't his dead friend once mentioned playing on those machines as a child in shoestores, peering through the Viewmaster doohickey at his bones – turning them on, turning them off?

Bartlett remembered his own father had never let him take pictures of his feet: Bert Day had read something, couldn't remember where, but it stuck with him. No monkey business on the foot machine, hear? No pictures. Bartlett nagged. His mom agreed with his dad. She stuck to the old way new shoes got checked for length, kneading them with her fingers like bread loaves.

When Bartlett was sixteen Butch was eighteen, dying, and didn't know it. No one did. One day on their way to school he fell on his bum and told Bartlett he was going home. A checkup uncovered leukemia. Two weeks later, during a blood transfusion, his friend died and Bartlett felt grief for the second time in his life.

He tried to recall whether his friend had worn bankers or banana toes. All he could see were white metatarsal bones. He felt thirsty.

On Beach Avenue he noticed they were tearing down the Englesea. This after a suspected case of arson a couple of months ago had closed the building. A crowd was watching the heavy ball swing its thunder. The back half of the old seven-floor structure lay in ruin, while the standing half, of jagged floors and cut-in-half kitchens, hung open to the air. One end of a bedroom looked untouched, fine to lie in: the other end was air. Like peering into a big dollhouse worked over by a Beirut terrorist force, then abandoned when the mortars ran out. Broken tubs and toilets, kitchen calendars two months behind, wallpaper clashing from one floor to the next. The earthquake he'd missed hadn't so much as budged the building.

'When council voted to *keep* the Englesea,' said a woman in nursing shoes, 'I'm willing to bet the condo owner on that side hired a delinquent to burn it down. It all comes down to I-want-this, you-can't-have-that.'

It was a theory he hadn't heard before.

She said on the prairies you at least didn't have to worry about the view.

'Krish!' She hauled smartly at a setter on a leash.

The building's pipes, twisted, broken and exposed to light like an X-ray, reminded Bartlett he was expected home. They'd had no running water in the house since Aloysius's party. He cut up the edge of the park, on the double now, and thought he saw Aloysius heading down to the ocean.

The sound of someone tapping pipes when he walked in arose from the basement. He went down.

'Bet your boots that gloomy Gus ain't figuring on replacing this dog's hind leg very quick. Surprised our earthquake didn't shake the whole works to bits. That would've fixed his wagon.'

Bert Day was inspecting the landlord's decrepit plumbing. 'You couldn't guess how much fug's inside this galvanized pipe, Bart. Surprises me you get enough pressure to water your coffee.' His father was holding a pipe wrench, standing in his shirtsleeves, ankle-deep in broken glass, touching a pipe. He had a gentle touch. He must've let himself in with no key.

'I take it personal. When you worked with pipe all your life, after a while you learn to look inside and ask yourself, Could this happen to my arteries if I keep eating the wrong kind of fat food? I'm talking about this new cholesterol thing. Stands to reason you take care of a home same as your body. If blood's squeezed through narrower and narrower mazes, what guarantee the pressure on the pump won't all of a sudden rupture like a balloon, *kapowee*, pieces of heart speckling the inside of your chest? Rust buildup in these old pipes makes you wonder. Leaks come the size of pinpricks. No explosion as such. But water's water. It rises just the same. The mice clear out, the cat swims.'

He was wading round in the broken glass, pointing with his pipe wrench. 'If I was to replumb this place, Bart, it'd take me three days to figure out where the hind leg goes. And maybe one minute to call on Moses to divide the Red Sea, when I started tearing it out, and the fug come down like the curse of Jonah. No,' he told his son, 'if you're counting on squatting here any length of time, copper's my obvious advice. Cost an arm and a leg to do right, all four floors. But then it's done and you've got water for a century. Pressure you can count on. No more leaks. Not like the galvanized.'

'We'd have to pay for it ourselves,' said Bartlett. 'Dwight's got a lease saying he has to pay repairs, in exchange for cheap rent and subletting rights.

We're safe as long as the landlord's agreeable. If he decides to sell, a developer'd demolish the house, including any squatters and your new copper pipes.'

His father shook his head, doubtfully. 'Who knows when the whole house won't just float away some night, irregardless? Water's got a mind of its own. Remembers where it wants to go when it's let loose.' Bert Day took a last knock at the pipes. 'Listen, I made sure the water ain't going to come back on before we want it. Let's go up and survey the damage. Kids did all that themselves?'

He was referring to the upstairs bathroom.

What Aloysius's friends had done was see how many of them could take a bath at the same time. *Something like that. Give them credit for starting out with harmless intent.* Three pairs of Jockey shorts and a pair of panties were later used trying to staunch the resulting tidal wave. He thought these must've belonged to Aloysius's band, till he realized punk rockers wouldn't wear underwear. On closer inspection the shorts and panties turned out to belong to Dwight and Reesa.

The party, which according to Aloysius he had no choice but to agree to when threatened by two older boys with shivs, had happened with Bartlett dining out with Megan. It evolved upstairs, into the bathroom, where both tub handles got snapped off, faucets on the sink jimmied free, and the float in the toilet tank ripped out, all for a lark. *Looks quite punkish, especially the soaped-up mirrors. I suppose graffiti's better than splinters?* Besides damaging rugs and staining furniture, as the water seeped through ceilings, it also left behind the residue of the cholesterol Bert Day was talking about. Fug.

Aloysius had hired workmen the next day to come in and start mopping up the mess.

'Kid hired them on his own?' asked Bert, climbing up to the third floor. He was more impressed by Aloysius's proprietorship than surprised by his partying. 'You got to hand it to these boat-type people. Maybe they skedaddled outta one country with the gold, but they've put it to work in this one like nobody's business. I'm thinking of the restaurants they're starting, for one thing. You watch. Their kids are going to be sailing through medical school just like you did. Maybe not him, owing to his business predilections and that, but kids just like him.'

His father had been tickled by Bartlett's appearance on *City, City*, in connection with his medical duties and whatnot abroad with the Red Cross.

Bert Day was proud of the fact his son had a practice he could afford to leave, to be part of the news scene in distant corners of the globe. Bert Day was a news junkie. He watched every evening as the world turned.

It took him the rest of the afternoon and well into the night to weld and replace the damaged fixtures. Blow torches glowed, solder dripped, new pipe ends were threaded on a machine straddling Reesa's Persian carpet, over which his father had carefully laid a tarp. He made frequent trips to his truck in the alley for joints and cut-off valves. Bartlett ordered a pineapple pizza, which his father nibbled at to be polite. Retired, he found he worked and ate at a lot slower pace now. Father and son watched the news in a blue, edgy glow. Electricity was being sucked into the house, but no water yet.

'I told Aloysius I had a patient living with more dignity in a tent than we lived with here.'

When Bert Day finally went down to turn on the water, he remarked on the sea of broken glass for the first time. 'Somebody hammering bottles into their constituent parts?'

Bartlett shook his head. 'Aloysius.'

'Sure is a sight,' said Bert, wiping his hands on his overalls. 'Guess if he was my kid I'd put my foot down.'

'I think it's supposed to be a money-making scheme.'

'Be hard to justify as a hobby,' said Bert, toeing shards with his boot.

5.

That night the house had running water for the first time in living memory. It seemed to Bartlett he hadn't turned on a tap or flushed a toilet since childhood. He thought he could remember a pattern of movement his hands once made splashing water on his face and neck. But he wasn't sure. Water con cealed the past, making it as mysterious as radiation.

To help him celebrate, Megan drove over at midnight to cut his hair after washing it for him in the shower. She trimmed and feathered it, wet. They were alone in his dishevelled room, she in his white lab coat with nothing on underneath, he on a chair beside the heat register, naked. The air, arriving from the old furnace three floors below, lost much of its heat in passage. Chilled, Bartlett asked her for the towel to put around his shoulders. He felt like one of his patients attended to in loving detail and wooed by a sympathetic ear. Except Megan, weary of listening to her own customers, was doing most of the talking. He remained the gatekeeper.

She was a small-boned but shapely girl, not at all beautiful like Reesa, yet pretty in a kitchen-sink sort of way like Glenda Jackson. She was punkish, after the fashion, an orange tint to her hair, strategic rips to her discarded jeans. 'The more you watch her face,' observed Megan, 'the more she grows on you.' They were watching a film the other night on TV, starring the British actress, set in London and the Costa Something. 'Costa the Earth,' said Bartlett. The resort reminded him of Pattycakes, he told her, where you could get the same luxury suite on the Gulf of Thailand for a third the price.

Megan shared an apartment with a waitress-painter, above a grocery store on a busy corner in Kits. Nothing to distinguish the building, except its high rent and noisy proximity to the beach. This was why she wanted to move out of it and into something with Bartlett. Not *this* messy heirloom. This house gave her disease.

'It's cold and creaky ... Besides, I'm not snazzy like Reesa and Dwight, Bee, I wouldn't feel at home here.' She spat an imaginary raspberry on his imitation Turkish rug.

He couldn't remember asking if she *would* feel at home here, let alone if she'd care to move in. *I still like her, though ...*

'I think it was wrong, Bee, you offering to lend Dwight that money. Except I guess if it turns out good you'll have the last word on that one ...' She'd begun to blow-dry his scalp, buffing his dark tangled hair aggressively with her brush, shaping it with efficient ease.

She wanted him to choose her over his house friends. But his work or something was getting to him she felt. He seemed distant these days. A lot slimmer, but what good was slim if you disappeared *into* yourself? She had trouble raising her voice over the motor and its stormy air, an effort that seemed to cost her. He strained to hear what he knew was coming next.

'... Ever since your big trip, your practice seems to've taken you over, like it's the only thing in your life? Where's your priorities, Bee? If you're not on a diet, then what are you on, snort? You don't eat anymore. You don't *talk* anymore. How long've we been sleeping together? ... and these days when I suggest commitment you tell me you're not sure? That's okay – I'm not trying to spook you – except ... if what you told me's true, about wanting to travel some more on your own before you settle down, then I wish you'd take off and get it over with.'

She switched off the hairdryer. 'Like all I want, is to know where I stand ...'

They made love in his brass bed, tenderly, with not a lot of noise since he wasn't sure if Aloysius was in or out. 'That's the trouble,' she whispered. 'It's like living in a dormitory here.' All the sexier, he suggested. On top of her, playfully forcing her hands against the unpolished bars, he proceeded to conduct a medical examination of her ear whorls with his tongue. Her hands struggled in patient compliance. Releasing them, he began to massage her shoulders, caress her neck. Her bones felt springy. 'In your hands now, doctor ...' She'd already closed her eyes to the mess and stuff around her, when something began poking her in the spine. 'Birdcage,' he whispered. 'Sorry.' He was storing the empty cage under his bed.

He presently informed his patient he would soon be knocking on her gate. 'Knock, knock?' Squeezing, he went at her hipbones with his teeth, grazing on muscle and ribs. The bedframe creaked. Her knees lifted, widened. His ankle snapped. Their teeth bumped.

Deep inside one another, something clicked. *No, that's not right –*

Megan had turned aside in pain. With her mouth stuck open, she was moaning, her hands moving helplessly in her hair. '*Yiyahhh,*' she whimpered. He lifted his head. He put his hand to her mouth. '*Yiiyahhhh!*'

Locked open, her jaw refused to close. *My jaw,* she was saying. Having opened it too wide, she had dislodged its hinge again. Her pain was acute. He had no idea how to respond, stiff inside her, unwilling to come no matter how much her involuntary motion tantalized his cock. He took her head and rolled it gently side to side. This seemed to help her jawbone. Her moaning ebbed as the pain went away. Her mouth closed, her language returned.

'Oh, God,' she gasped.

Uncomfortable, upset with herself, she could only whisper: 'Your tree has gone away ...'

She lamented the death of his sheathed erection, and could only lie in miserable recollection of its promise, breathing shallowly.

6.

When she left they sidestepped the fresh swallow shit and pizza flyers on the front porch and embraced. On his way back upstairs, Bartlett grabbed a magazine from the pile in the den. He listened at Aloysius's door, then returned to his own bed. The air was still cool. It took hours to heat a house this size, and then it never really heated. Dwight had said spending the whole spring in Maui would cost everyone less than keeping their decrepit oil furnace going for a week.

His magazine revealed X-ray photographs of the Shroud of Turin. Someone had been ticking off clues to its mystery in red ink.

'Excellent point.'

'Consider!'

'Dead right.'

He read where the secret of the shroud's origins had been buried with the bones of a French nobleman in the fourteenth century. Where *he'd* discovered the burial cloth no one knew. But if the shroud was a hoax the evidence seemed decidedly against it.

Bartlett found himself reading carefully. The nail wounds were in the right place: through the wrist, where the bone could support a body's weight, not through the palm where it couldn't. A doctor in Paris had demonstrated this crucial fact by nailing up cadavers. The recent discovery of a first-century skeleton showed its wristbone had been scraped by a nail, thus confirming the no-hands theory.

The point was medieval artists had depicted the Crucifixion with nails in the palms. There was no record of an artist studying anatomy till Donatello's time, and Donatello wasn't even born when the shroud turned up in France. So if the shroud *was* forged, its artist must have had a very sophisticated anatomical knowledge, at a time when dissections were rare.

Bartlett scratched his moist scrotum.

The image on the cloth resembled one of his own X-rays, only full-length, including head and feet. He peered at the image. It revealed little you wouldn't have to make up if you wanted to tell its story. Yet a close examination by one coroner had given *him* a plot he claimed *not* to be making up. Its victim had been whipped nude by two men with a Roman scourge, one man shorter than the other. Then the sufferer's heart had failed, killing him, not long before a Roman spear punctured his chest between the fifth and sixth ribs. This coroner wasn't inexperienced in the way bodies hung, for he'd suspended himself from a crucifix, using leather straps, and recalled the pain in his muscles as agonizing. *Grief through mimicry ...*

Bartlett lay back on his pillow, tired. When he turned out his lamp the streetlight shone in through the window.

He began to reimagine his love-making with Megan, positioning her in slightly altered ways, fitting her into a pair of spike heels, and in this manner brought himself slowly off. The birdcage underneath him twanged. He gasped as he came, switching abruptly to the girl in Bangkok, the image of her unpinning number fourteen from her breast.

For lack of a Kleenex he smeared his palmful of semen over his scrotum and rubbed till it was dry enough not to dribble on the sheet. In the morning he could treat himself to another shower. He could immerse himself in hot water for as long as the tank held out. What joy!

No more camping out.

No more water on a sponge.

In the end, maybe the beginning, life came down to water. Didn't water run in and out of life through the house? It did, at least in this lucky country. In his head he X-rayed the house's bones: water pipes, patched and tourniqued most of their lengths, swinging loose from beams, joists, webbed like spider routes, clogged and reducing pressure in summer to the trickle of an old man's urine.

He reached for his diary in the dark. He felt a sudden wish to thank his father for his shoes and life. He switched it on.

Pilgrims who felt like verifying tall tales seemed condemned to wander from the beaten track. He wondered how long before his own wandering caused him to walk away from his profession.

Below he heard a door open. It would be weeks down there before the damp smell went away.

Soon swimmers would come out. Sunbathers already had. *Tulips come up, then roses bloom. This afternoon I saw a catamaran* ... Times every day when he thought of his hair sailing in a stiff breeze, getting wet when it showered, blotting up salt smells blowing in off the gulf. It would grow longer. The sun stronger.

His patients would continue to wait in silence, for a chance to tell him of the pain their hyperbole seemed to lighten. His doubts would grow.

For some reason, the junk mail arriving on the front porch that spring was already heavier than normal.

June, 1898

Have been tracking a young sawmill worker named Frank Seaton. Has come from London to make a new life for himself. Happened on him at the roller rink Saturday night, talking to two girls, both simpering, and I had to fancy my chances a little more round an enterprising young man like Frank.

My dossier on him is incomplete. Boasted to girls he would have his own house and family inside two years. 'Guaranteed. By the turn of the century I want to be sitting pretty.' Already has a building lot in Fairview, paying one hundred and fifty for it during the real estate boom. Fifteen down. Told them he is building his own workingman's cottage out of lumber he buys at discount from the mill. Avoids poker games. Wants a poultry run and a small garden for potatoes once he destumps his yard. Girls exploded into giggles.

Not me, I'm desperate for an ancestor. As yet am related to nothing but a city.

Mill is his main job. Then after ten hours' labour he takes the streetcar to a building lot near the park where a master carpenter named Hud works overtime on a mansion for rich people with three floors, a large reception room, gingerbread doodads, a turret or two. Frank works with Hud to learn carpentry. In these long evenings he fetches for him: levels, chisels, special saws for the mouldings.

I appreciate Frank's ambition but wonder how long he can keep up the pace. At twenty-six he looks thirty-seven. Walks with a slight limp. May wear out before he finds a girl to love. Skates slower than younger men who pump past him on the plank floor buzzing girls like honeybees. Finding time for romance is hard for Frank – and finding it keeping it. Are his chances for a family slim? Am thinking of dumping him.

Truth is his job in the sawmill smells. Smelly clothes make courtship exacting. Air bronchial with sawdust. Noise infernal. Head and trimmer saws screaming all day, from whistle at seven a.m. when his greenchain cranks up, to five when men plod home stinking. Stench from beehive burners will saturate any bachelor from his hair to his socks.

Over lunch on docks, astride a fir beam bound for Peru, Bruce James says he's thinking of heading up to the Klondike.

'You got enough for a dog team?' Frank asks. Bruce answers, 'You mean them mutts for sale on Cordova? I'm a greenhorn, Frank, but I ain't stupid. Touch wood.'

Compared to him Frank is a plodder. Am tempted to conclude all plodders a waste of time, as nothing so far has sparked in me recognition of a family line.

Unborn, I pause to reconsider.

Being outside time is like being outside Hastings Mill Store. Too easy to conclude it can

be summed up in a glance.

Inside, a thousand elixirs line the store's shelves. Jamaica Ginger, Pains Celery Compound, Wizard Oil … Along with carpet sweepers, pickle kegs, Foster's plug tobacco with a jewel-encrusted tapper. This dome-stic scene strikes me as exotic.

By contrast scene outside looks simple. Plodding even. Mill buildings, a few horse-pulled wagons with firewood, a power pole. Smoke. As if everything history will never know is waiting *inside* the store. As if the eye of the man under a black cloth over there is reducing figures outside to props, his lens useless in weaker light.

No wonder he can't picture *me*.

Decided to give Frank another chance. It's plodders after all building the city and having families. Working himself to death even,

Frank Seaton may yet prove a Proteus. Sailed so far to reach the new world, could be he's still tired from the voyage. Has yet to unpack his trunks.

Unlike me, unlike water, Frank has a past that should help to plant the memory of someone like me in his future.

Chapter 24

The Hand of Hyperbole

WEASEL COPITHORNE couldn't face death and talked around it as a dog might worry a bone, to soften his dear wife's passing. *I may be coming at this sideways*, related Bartlett to his diary. *Maybe I'm wrong.* Maybe Weasel's was a more direct story than it sounded. Saga or not, the gist of it seemed to lie in the loose ends he refused to tie, the shadows he was avoiding face-down on the table. On his most recent visit he was telling Dr Day of a young woman he'd met over the summer.

'... She said to me, I seen you before, somewhere, where? I said was it by the bandstand sitting on the grass? Now I remember, she said, yeah. You were in denim slacks. I had to laugh, really. I was never on the grass by the bandstand in my life.'

He winced gladly when Bartlett tugged.

'No, the truth is, we'd met once in a Punjabi restaurant ordering mango chutney. In Water Street like. When the waiter came by I asked him if the chutney was hot. This young lady pipes up from across the way, it isn't even warm. So I ordered some. I was bone-dry so I ordered a glass of beer. She smiled and did the same. There we were, two strangers, dressed to dance and not a soul to eat with. So I decided to show my hand. I asked her, she said all right, I moved over to her table and we started drinking beer. Playing footsie sort of. That got us talking about turbans and the Punjab. The whole subcontinent. It was like supper at the UN. After that we walked down to the harbour ...'

Dislocations, thought Bartlett, made a widower's grief the way to shape his world. He wanted to understand how. If you knew where to look for them, when to listen, bones revealed the shape of everything. *A penny for my brilliance.* The skeleton in the closet, the dinosaur in the badlands, probably the universe in an equation. Given doubts about his own profession he was still willing to answer others' needs to have their shapes – in pain of one kind or another – confirmed. In this he figured he was like Marcus Reambeault, the Nova Scotian faith healer, answering the profoundest questions with a meagre repertoire: his hands, and laying them on. Bartlett had no choice but to go along with a philosophy he felt to be in jeopardy. It was a living. Constantly rewriting its past, he felt, just to maintain its status quo.

At a time when he wanted to make up his mind about the future, when he didn't feel hungry anymore in the normal sense of ambition, chiropractic was sticking by its claims. Exaggeration seemed the normal state of obsession. Health was all.

He ran tap water till it was cold and free of fug. He was often thirsty these days, and wondered if he had something the matter with him. The city's obsession with health in its new body factories and ballet mirrors seemed a sickness. The anxiety it gave rise to distorted the way citizens like him tried to stay robust. They risked everything when it came to health, making them prey to charlatans and earnestness. The chiropractor, the impostor, could order his credulous patients to roll over, play with wool, or have their claws clipped. *Kittens love a fascist ... Maybe I should declare the health craze to be over? Tow a sign across the sky?* He'd begun to wonder, *I'm beginning to ask*, if genuinely ill people now didn't feel they'd fallen, like bank robbers at large, into a state of immorality. He preferred to listen rather than prescribe.

Chiropractic threw new light on nothing and he sometimes wondered if he wasn't going blind to please capitalism. Americans, especially, appreciated any go-getting chiropractor who'd worked his way up from sweeping factory floors. The working-class fellow whose dream wasn't a deadend after all. A guy who has seen the world round and seen it whole. *A salesman, not a sob sister. Three cheers for his enterprise!*

One patient, Trina Chase, was just the opposite of obsessed about health, and he wanted to consult with Tom Cabot about her charming indifference to distortions she experienced in her touch, hearing, taste ... *take your pick.* Cabot had referred Ms Chase to his good friend in alternative medicine, not unlike the way he'd also referred Gloria Dawson, as being hopelessly beyond his own powers of amelioration. Bartlett wondered in this case if his friend's referral hadn't bordered on professional dereliction, since Bartlett presumed no chiropractor had ever treated a case like hers. He was intending to bring up the matter with Cabot when they met this evening in the Sylvia lounge, but professional discussion took off instead in an unsettling direction at their small, coaster-covered table.

2.

He'd expected to find Tom alone, not with his mentor Rowland Storey, M.D., a silver-haired man with a drinker's complexion and a gold wrist-watch. Retired, Storey was the past owner of Cabot's practice on Altamira. The three men sat down after introductions at a corner table, looking out to where the Englesea Waterfront Lodge had stood until last spring.

'... Tell us then,' Storey said expansively, ordering another round of drinks. 'What kind of questions does the chiropractor pop at the devoted who come to see him? There must be hundreds. Hundreds of customers? Hundreds of questions?' He was sipping his second or fifth martini. Bartlett smiled, expecting him to drop the wiseguy act as soon as he established allo-pathic dominance.

Cabot played along. 'Urine, maybe? Is your urine the colour of a chest-nut?'

'That chestnut, yes.' The elder M.D. thought a moment, then adopting his professional tone asked the chiropractor: 'Are you discharging from your nipples?' And: 'When you exert yourself, do you experience discomfort in the chest, which is relieved by belching?' He turned back to Cabot. 'I ask you, Tom, who asks these questions of themselves anymore?'

Their drinks arrived.

'We're trained to address silence,' answered Tom. 'To act as we see fit.'

'But not always to believe our own eyes,' said Storey, returning his gaze to Bartlett. 'Wouldn't you agree, Dr Day, or are you what I gather your pro-fession calls one of the straights? Not a mixed practitioner of the art at all?' He savoured his fresh martini. 'To be absolutely blunt, but fair, isn't your profession for hookers? I mean aren't you all tugging the same bones, listen-ing for identical cracks? Would that be a reasonable assessment of your pro-fession?'

'Witty,' said Bartlett. 'Look, if –'

Somehow he'd ended up with a second beer before having had a third swallow from his first. He was falling behind.

Storey smirked. The good doctor drank his martinis straight up with a twist. Life seemed to offer him no finer moment than this one, just prior to gobbling his olive in the company of a quack. He fingered the stem of his glass. 'The problem is you're a charlatan aren't you?' He sounded very calm.

'Don't get me wrong. It's just that you deny more than you accept, don't you, scientifically speaking?'

Unfortunately, I straightened up and answered this windbag. Reverting to his professional spiel with more relish than he'd felt since Bangkok:

'Haven't M.D.s drugged millions? Made millions drugging millions, polluting the body, carving it up? Tonsillectomies, appendectomies, hysterectomies ... Most of them a waste of time. Look at Louis Pasteur. Look at the ridicule he met. When he was young he sounded like a heretic. Then when he was too decrepit to talk – like when the last thing he needed was recognition – these guys came from around the world to pay homage ... I try to remember that. Chiropractors are still spurned and persecuted. Know what I mean?'

Rowland Storey broke into a smile. 'Louis Pasteur was a chemist.'

'At least it didn't stop him from telling the truth.'

'That was the truth he told.'

'What was?'

'That little organisms cause putrefaction. Disease? You've heard of disease, Dr Bartlett. Pasteur believed in chemistry. Tapped the spines of mad dogs and inoculated bunnies. Theatre of the Absurd.'

Cabot, quietly sipping his martini on ice, spoke up to say Bartlett had had some outstanding successes with patients he himself couldn't treat and had referred to his friend. Like Trina Chase –

'Really?' remarked Storey, doubtfully. 'Mind you, the College of Physicians and Surgeons might look askance.'

He took a long sip now, returning his empty glass to the precise spot from which he'd lifted it. This appeared to please him, the soft landing of his slim glass in the exact centre of a round coaster. In heavy weather the movement demonstrated his immaculate control from a fogged-in cockpit. He looked up.

'Suppose,' he said to Bartlett, 'I come into your office complaining about my lumbar. What would you do?'

The chiropractor paused. 'If it was worn out, I'd want to see what was separated. Do some traction, rotate your leg.'

At this Storey slapped the table in triumph. 'The chiropractor's art! Pulling my leg!' Very pleased with himself. 'How do we know, Dr Day, you just don't improvise as you go along?'

'You don't.'

'No?'

'In fact I'd be the first to admit I'm working through misrepresentation,' said Bartlett.

Rowland Storey raised his eyebrows. His young antagonist was willing to go even further. 'Doesn't bother me in the least,' he said. 'I don't mind talking about thin blood with people. Or about a double joint or a pinched nerve. All those misnomers. According to you guys, no such things. Same with tennis elbows and slipped discs. What your College calls a slipped disc, quote, is "a posterior herniation of the annulus fibroses" – right? – "with a protrusion of the nucleus pulposes into the spinal canal". I like the misnomer better.'

'Which leaves you open to charges, I suppose,' said Storey.

Bartlett turned to his friend then, with whom he was still hoping to discuss Trina Chase. 'This guy's a quack.'

Tom laughed. Storey chuckled, and ordered two more martinis and Bartlett a third beer. Bartlett took another swallow from his first.

'No one outlasts his bones,' he said. 'They're where you end up.'

'Don't you mean down?' asked Storey. 'Six feet under?'

'Same thing. Bones are history. They keep you in touch.'

'Like Chinese ancestors …'

Bartlett wiped his mouth. 'I'm trained to tell when bones start breaking down. When it's taking them longer to mend … When they can't stand the strain like they used to, old bones getting porous. They get brittle and break. Down.'

'That's gravity, is it?'

'Dislocation.'

'Sounds like politics,' said Storey. 'Can't you just see it?' he asked Tom, sounding squiffy. 'Socialized chiropractic breaking up our whole profession? Mammologists and dermatologists, obstetricians and orthopods – all of us out of work? The whole country on the rocks? The only place left for us the States, to the sun-kissed south … to the blessed right?'

He saluted Bartlett with his empty glass. 'A toast to con artists! Here's to these backbreaking men in white … to the backward language they speak … to their behind-the-back manoeuvrings! To chiropractors everywhere!'

The entire lounge had swung around to listen, amused. Tom was laughing. Storey's glass refused to yield another drop and Rowland was licking it for moisture. Bartlett felt a strong urge to talk back to him like a schoolboy.

'You kind of get carried away, don't you?'

'Just watch me,' said Storey, delighted with the evening so far.

It continued downhill from there. Bartlett closed his ears. He shrugged off Storey's mockery as coming from a man who'd retired from listening and was now free, at least in his own mind, to tell it like he saw it. America was full of such men. They were also called chiropractors. Bartlett knew as long as he kept going to conferences and speaking out for chiropractic as the be-all and end-all, he would never understand dislocation.

3.

Labour Day sun was hot at the beach. A blue heron slouched overhead in a fir tree. He and Megan lay nude between logs, listening to waves wash up the stones. Officially, this beach didn't exist, because otherwise the city would have to patrol it against public nudity. Unofficially, it was known as the healing beach. Alternative sun worshippers came down leafy trails to relax, shed clothes, renew themselves. He watched the way their bodies moved and how shapes, any shapes, took up position in the world: frisbees, a juggler's oranges, kites. Men and women ambled or lay along several miles of foreshore cliffs, from the Musqueam reservation around to tidier family beaches in eyeshot of the city. He scratched the mole beside his nose and ordered a strawberry yoghurt from the passing vendor.

The vendor had a Slavic accent and a St. Christopher medal gleaming from the oiled hair on his chest. This entrepreneur of sand and logs let his Alsatian run free, an alligator on the prowl. Bartlett wished he had a gun.

He placed the yoghurt on the blanket behind Megan's head. 'You can at least eat yoghurt,' he said.

She turned her other cheek to the blanket. 'Unh *uh* ...'

He ran his hand gently across her bare bum and up her spine. Massaging her body seemed to unknot the muscles in her neck. She stopped crying. Her thin buttocks, squeezing tightly, shuddered once, and then under his other hand, relaxed.

'Like to come to my dad's house for supper?' he asked.

She bunched up a towel and lowered her forehead into it, to relieve pressure on her jaw. She shook her head. 'Don't think so. Taking a painkiller and going to bed early.'

Her conversation was restricted. 'Lots of VLH,' she might murmur, in observation of a nearby naked lady. She'd then explain, with more difficulty than it was worth, 'Visible leg hair?' For someone in the hair business, she couldn't help noticing razors weren't popular around the legs and armpits of nude sunbathers.

Bartlett's body was turning pink. He touched it to make sure of this. He knew you couldn't tan before you burned. He'd learned this epidermic fact as a teenager and never wavered in its belief. He would probably die of melanoma.

'When I was young,' he said, flicking a piece of bark toward the flat waves, 'the hair on my head took all day. To tell you the truth, Meg, I lacked a nifty head of hair. Everybody wanted the swept-back look. I wanted it too, only my hair wouldn't sweep. I tried everything. Vaseline. Hair nets and women's hairspray. I spent hours in bed with my hair over the side getting gravity to train it, backwards. It worked for the morning, but it didn't last past lunch.'

He pushed the yoghurt away. 'Know what I mean?'

Megan nodded. He was making an effort, she could see that, trying to cheer her up. This made her irritable. She reached for her tube of sunscreen, rolled over, and following a healthy squeeze began to reoil her breasts. Aggressively. They were small, freckled, Glenda Jackson breasts. He looked across to Cape Cowan and thought of summer frat parties on Dwight's cabin cruiser. Booze cruises, bottle bashes, juice jags. Ski sprees.

He wasn't hungry enough to eat the yoghurt himself. And it would go rancid in the heat. Megan plucked a hair from her nipple, wincing with the pluck.

These days she was unhappy with him, unhappy with her jaw. The one unhappiness encouraged the other: She could count the ways. *He* wanted to travel before settling down, and had been invited abroad again without her. Plus he was being as clear as grease about how much money he'd loaned Dwight, not to mention whether he was even interested anymore in pooling his and her savings to buy a house – make a down payment on one. Did he really want to go on living in the same house with Reesa and Dwight, after his friends had their baby? With the foster foreigner still living there too? Bartlett was paying a third of the rent but would soon be settling for a fifth, a sixth of the house ... didn't they plan to hire a nanny?

She kept after him and he had nothing to tell her one way or the other. *Her lovely bones in my arms I like, but not enough to whisk her away to a rose-covered bungalow.* She didn't understand what was happening to him. He didn't understand himself.

He wanted to understand what was happening to her. He tried to set up his rubber thongs as a pillow for her head. She resisted the overture.

He knew she'd gone over to the enemy, that much he knew. He'd listened dully to her tales of journeying among medical specialists who, it sounded to him, had no better solution to her pain than a chiropractor or a masseuse. 'At least they care about my problem,' she countered. 'I care,' he answered. But she doubted it. She'd come to him as a patient, that was how they met. Two years ago she'd come suffering from backache, headache, and a sore jaw. Her wiry frame had attracted him. The strange angles. The subversive punkishness, punctured in odd places like her nose with a pin. Four months later, seeing one another socially, she'd got worse, with trouble eating meat and apples. It was just fortunate, in her opinion, she had happened to have a dentist appointment.

Her dentist diagnosed TMJ, dislocation of the jaw's 'temporomandibular joint', caused by slow deterioration of her cushioning disc. Bartlett told her a chiropractor might've diagnosed the same, if his training hadn't focused on the spine. In treating her the dentist had no more success than Bartlett had. He too manipulated her jaw. He too recommended jaw exercises. And prescribed drugs, splints, physiotherapy, ultra-sound stimulation of the nerves, hydraulic pressure on the joint and a soft diet.

'It still hurts,' Megan later complained. Bartlett couldn't smother a small feeling of professional satisfaction.

Her deterioration got worse. Her mouth began to close in response to painful muscle spasms in her jaw. She'd lost twenty pounds since spring, now ate puréed meals with a baby's spoon, drank though a straw, and never expected to sleep through another night. Her love habits had become odd reflexes she blamed on uncertainty. His. If only he could commit himself, she would feel a lot better, she thought. Not cured, but she might sleep better nights, knowing he was with her.

'I'm with you.'

'In a mosquito's eye.'

The oral surgeon who supervised her orthogram, injecting dye to trace the lines of her disc and joint, *he* told her she had no cartilage left, that her disc was worthless, that her pain was the dire result of bone on bone at the joint. Unless she had surgery to reconstruct her jaw, she could expect it to keep shifting, closing, clamping down, till she could no longer speak or eat.

It was serious – almost unbelievable. Worse, the operation had only a fifty-fifty chance of success.

... This afternoon I fed her yoghurt from a dixie cup, cajoling. Seade jae bcxe budfa coos, I said, cida eliursade lasdk rdies opwesz dkieur, joweo eurtyt deel mideijd? ... She smiled. I said this was how she was soon going to sound, like a baby, if she didn't stop crying about her jaw. About us. About relocating our lives ... But I felt bad. Her pain's real. I think the beach helped. The yoghurt curdled.

About the time Reesa was due to go in and give birth, Megan was scheduled to enter hospital to have her jaw broken and repositioned. It was going to cost her hundreds and hundreds of dollars, because her medical insurance didn't cover TMJ, though it would've having a baby. She seemed to blame Bartlett for this. She would've liked a baby, but knew they couldn't afford a baby and a house too. First she wanted a house. No, first she wanted Bartlett.

She had fallen asleep now.

The notion of bringing Megan to Wreck Beach had occurred to him after manipulating one of his patients. Poppy Nybo had been dreaming of a woman who looked like her mother used to, and as he worked at her inflamed hip joint she told him what she'd dreamed.

'... This woman in my dream said she felt sorry for anyone who'd never come to this beach. "No one's strutting and showing off," she said. "No one needs to peep. It's all out in the open," she said, "why don't you take off your suit?" She was well-preserved, really.'

'Did you know her?' he'd asked.

She had sounded as obsessed at Weasel Copithorne. Dressed in white, like morning glory, she clung to him in a whispery voice.

'... When I opened my eyes,' said Poppy, 'this woman was kneeling and rubbing sand up and down her face. Blood was seeping through the sand, through her fingers. After a while her hands stopped moving. When they fell from her face, there was a hole there.'

Bartlett had paused, his palms still on Ms Nybo's hips.

'You – she – dreamed this?'

'It's the most horrible dream I can remember, Dr Day. I practically woke up with sunstroke. My hip felt paralysed ...' Where did obsession end, or was it contagious? He'd liked the peeping part, and the fact she hadn't made herself the woman kneeling in the sand. Not wholly. The self split like a mussel the crow drops: this took an artist. But who could distinguish between the reflecting mirrors of self-obsession? *Carried on, regardless. Listening in like a gatekeeper ...*

Megan woke up to him wiping the perspiration from her upper lip, with a corner of his towel. 'You were grinding your teeth,' he said.

'It's all sore along here,' she mumbled.

'I know.'

He didn't know. It seemed hard to credit the pain of those nearest home when no genocidal regime, no grinding poverty, no slum landlord had inflicted their suffering. Being home took more imagination than being abroad, he thought. Especially for patients, who wanted to understand the shadow world in their own mirrors. They sought out alternative therapists like him. They wanted him to touch them with the hand of hyperbole.

She put on her sunglasses and peered at her towel. 'Look, a moth. Flew all this way from somebody's closet.'

'Care for a dip?'

She prodded his stomach with her finger. He was still losing weight she said. And his skin was burning from no sunscreen. 'Nearly said "sunscream",' she said, brightening a little. 'I was listening to my jaw, Bee.'

They held hands and sank into the green gulf. They were seals. Fish. The water made them holler and hug. He hollered, she hugged. They remembered another life, another time. Their naked groins remembered and mimicked one another under water, thrusting home. Bone on bone.

A year ago last month, Hurricane Allen had killed three hundred in the Caribbean. He recalled the reports on his birthday. Extreme weather happened elsewhere. Here a flotilla of sawdust scows was always in passage, leery of so much as a whitecap. 'Look, a cloud,' said Megan. He looked. She cupped his underwater testicles and told him to cough.

Drying off in the sun, on their blanket, she bent down and proceeded to lick his elbow. His armpits. The salt made her thirsty she said, continuing to lick. He offered her a cup of cold thermos water but she kept on licking. Stop it, he warned. 'Make me, doctor.' A seagull with one foot was standing on a nearby rock posing for a handout. Bartlett planted the half-eaten yoghurt in the sand. The seagull flew away.

He dug himself a hole under the blanket for his hip. She fingered the wet ends of his hair, watching. She asked if it ever occurred to him that in saving all his haircuts since childhood, let's say piled up in the bathtub, there'd be enough hair to stuff a double mattress for him and his wife, two pillows, with enough left over to fill a jumping bag for their kids.

He ignored the hint, the allusion to love in a bungalow, to the possibility of a bungalow. 'Hair,' he said, 'is about the worst thing you can sleep on for your back ... except maybe sand.' He shifted his hip in the hole. 'A water mattress is what you want.'

So she answered: 'All my water then. If I had all my tears in a bathtub, Bee, I could show you what I meant.'

4.

When he phoned his father to say Megan couldn't come, Bert Day wanted to know how come. She was a welcome lady. 'I'm planning to serve up fresh beets and a salmon. Labour Day ought to be celebrated. Everybody's forgotten what it means.' 'Her jaw's sore.' 'Well, why d'you think I cooked soft food?' His son apologized. 'No big deal,' said Bert. 'I'll wrap some fish in tinfoil and you can take it to her afterward like.'

Bartlett drove his aging Mustang several miles across the city, to his father's house on a treeless East End street of neat bungalows and narrow lots. Italians, who'd introduced gnomes to the neighbourhood when Bartlett was growing up, had given way to vegetable gardens and Chinese, who were now giving way to crabpots and Vietnamese, along with young couples like his father and mother thirty years ago. It was a circle observed by his father.

'Cept these kids drive nice cars with baby seats. We couldn't hardly afford the streetcar. Buggies was *verboten* 'cause they didn't collapse like the rigs today.'

Bert Day guessed everybody's dream was still to own their own home. He refused to call it a house. Until lately, when things had started climbing out of sight, this dream was more or less a right. 'Not the dream, the home.' He hated dogs dumping on his lawn, and wondered if one of these chainlink fences you saw in the neighbourhood might be the answer to dogs.

His front room smelled of rubber. Bartlett noticed balloons taped to the cheap chandelier. 'I'm celebrating Labour Day,' said his father. 'Least that's what I'm telling you now, since I forgot to blow them up last June for Tony's birthday.'

A typical weekend supper at Bert Day's house. Bartlett's younger sister, her two kids, the table neatly set a good hour and a half before supper, and his father busy in the kitchen punching down bread dough. 'So how's the doctoring business?' he asked his son. 'How many patients you got for a grand total now?'

Bartlett couldn't exactly tell him.

'Modest,' said Bert Day. 'Like your mother was. If you had too few of them you'd know exactly how many you had. So I guess you're doing good.'

'I don't know,' said Bartlett. 'I think I'm losing it. My interest.'

'Fed up, are you?'

Bartlett looked at Betty, darning a hole in her father's sock. 'I'd like to travel more,' he replied.

'Boy, wouldn't we all.' His father rabbit-punched his dough inside a scarred wooden bowl. 'But I guess if you look at it close like, how much travel does one man need? Not that many places worth going to. You found that out yourself, Bart. Skullduggery's depressing. If you're losing interest, travelling won't find it. Take it from me. Vacations are just a way to get you more dissatisfied when you come back. Your friend Dwight what's-his-face … I hear him on the radio sometimes. Trying to talk people into spending their money. He's somebody, that Dwight twerp, who likes talking through his hat. Another thing is the investment angle. Seeing as how doctors are always looking for tax shelters and that, how do you justify travel to Timbuktu as a write-off?'

'I don't.'

'You can't.'

'I don't think I'm following you, Dad.'

'I put out that dip for you. Goes with the Old Dutch cholesterol. To battle the cholesterol I put artichoke in the dip and garlic in the salmon. Medicinal properties of garlic will also assist my circulation and blood pressure. Help yourself to a brew in the fridge.'

The defeated bread dough he now proceeded to pull apart. He was greasing five oblong pans with a piece of buttered waxpaper, preparing to drop loaves into each. The pans resembled shoeboxes.

'On the other hand,' he said, 'if it's inflation killing your interest in doctoring, maybe travel's not such a lousy notion. Way to beat inflation ain't to live like an investor. A lot better to take off when you feel like it. Take pleasure in impulsives. Like when it's sunny, take off your shirt, and don't take your hands off a woman till she squawks. Heh, heh.' Betty looked at him.

'Best thing, Bet, is take whatever comes along. Like peas in the pod or slippers on special. Take me, Bart. I took your mother at her word and look where it got me – plumber's blisters and happiness money couldn't buy. I was away to the races. This is what I'm saying. You young doctors have life ahead of you and you're investing it in hedges like nobody's business. Maybe I'm wrong. But the impression I get is you're looking out for the future. I think it's wrong as all get out to be looking that way. Trying to see your way clear through to my age is a futility.'

He was studying his loaves in pans. 'I sure hope this Plasticine rises. You kids like Plasticine?'

Tony shook his head. 'Is that real Plasticine, Mommy?'

'Grampy's just teasing, lovey.'

'You kids are sure good kids to sit so quiet while Grampy's grumping,' said Bert. He lowered his oven door to slip in his pans, two at a time, before shutting it to wait for the dough to rise. He wasn't going to fuss with the dial till later.

'My friend Dwight?' said Bartlett, getting up to run a glass of cold water. 'Might surprise you, listening to him on the radio, but he's never been near any of those places he's always talking about visiting.'

'Don't surprise me one whisker. You can tell, listening to him, Irving's a blowhard.'

Bartlett watched his father dump his beets in the sink and start scrubbing them. 'You have to hand it to him though, Dad. He's taking a calculated risk.'

'I wouldn't hand him nothing. You bet on the wrong horse and he breaks a leg.' He topped and diced the beets, then went to the refrigerator for cabbage and potatoes in the crisper. 'Listen, Bart,' he said. 'You going to break that diet of yours and eat a potato chip? Lookit Betty.'

Betty, overweight, told her father to mind his own beeswax.

'That's right,' he told her. 'Eat me out of house and home. My own progeny. My progeny's progeny. Here, Tony. You hold this here grater for me while I shred us some coleslaw. Coleslaw'll help curl your hair.'

'It's curly already,' said the child.

'Ain't curly enough to catch a cutie's eye.'

By suppertime the loaves had risen, got baked, been tapped out of their aluminum pans to lie upside down on the sideboard. His father served warm bread and butter with broiled salmon, diced beets, mashed potatoes and coleslaw. The kids liked the bread. 'True, it don't taste like an old sock,' admitted Bert. Mary picked crumbs off her bib to put in her mouth. Betty said to her dad, 'You're not my father. No father knows how to cook this good.'

'Course I'm your father, Bet.' Bert Day was happy to defend his paternity. 'Who'd you think brought you up, a Mexican gaucho?' Eating his own cooking encouraged pride of reflection. 'Remember me, wiping away the tears, pinching your cheeks? Wiping your rear end when you were a spat, telling you the facts of life years on? You remember. Those years when I was an open-a-tin-of-beans, heartbroken father? Till I bought myself *The Joy of Cooking* ...? Say, Bart, I hear there's *A Joy of Something Else* out now. Big bestseller.' He winked at his son. 'Read it?'

'Yeah, I read it,' said Bartlett. 'By the way,' he said to his sister. 'Where did you say Kirk was?'

'Fishing. I'm a fishing widow these days. Kirk's fish-crazy.'

'He sure is,' said their father. 'Can't even talk him into eating his own salmon like.'

'Oh, Dad. He wanted to come ...' Bartlett thought he detected the patient in her voice, rowing out to tempt the unknown. Only in this case she'd been left behind. 'He just likes fishing is all,' said his sister, looking away to Tony. The child had a whippet face, like his father's, staring at his plate.

'No harm in that, Bet. Coho tasty as this, worth going after. Ask me about cholesterol and I'd say the Indians had the right idea eating salmon and nothing but. I hear fish oil's better for you now than molasses.' He reached over to the highchair and removed a bone from Mary's supper. His granddaughter had already made it plain she wouldn't be eating any fish, by dumping her bowl on his carpet. 'Butterfingers, just like her Uncle Barty used to have.' As for her skimpy appetite, Uncle Barty must've given her that too. Uncle Barty was going to waste away to a broom handle if he didn't stop fasting like one of these bulimics.

After supper they watched the local news, eating ice cream. The kids hugged their balloons and licked Revels. His father apologized for the dessert, pistachio-flavoured, sprinkled with blueberries. 'Can't do pastry.'

The day's top stories were a shapeless mix Bert Day found soothing to imbibe every evening of the week. He would relax into his chair like a bishop, to receive all the secular information of the world. If he had a plumbing job, he liked to make sure he was home in time to see everything that had befallen the world since dawn.

'Lookit the lead story,' he said in disgust. 'Report on how many at the jam-packed beaches today. Doggone, I thought this was Labour Day ...'

'Dad,' said Betty, 'workers are off today. The beaches are where they go.'

'Didn't they have a parade or nothing? Floats and clowns to help celebrate? Workers ashamed of themselves or something?' He was enjoying himself. 'Our movement is taking a bashing. Labour Day has sunk to disrepute.'

Bartlett watched.

A local warehouse fire burned hotter and longer on screen than a fire in Texas killing seven in a mobile home. The nearer an event to the domestic market, he thought, the longer it was allowed to run on. Even more popular than the local fire were a beauty contest and the weather. His father had begun to worry over how trivial it was all getting.

'Same old story. Don't respect ourselves enough to know why we're important. Ain't important, we think, till we're picked up on the national news, or the international. Our earthquake wasn't capital N news till we saw it reported on NBC outta New York. Our real news ends up coming from elsewhere like ... Speaking of which,' he glanced at his watch. 'Don't mind the old man,' standing up to collect their dessert bowls and the children's Revel sticks. It was time to change channels.

An explosion made Betty jump. Tony's face had collapsed. She scolded her son harshly for biting his balloon. Sobbing, the child buried his head in Bartlett's lap.

World News Tonight came at them now from farther away.

... Still, when you checked it out, local too. He couldn't help himself, comparing. Like preparations for a corruption hearing in Washington, filling the screen far longer than the map of an African country where seventy-five people were feared massacred, in a Marxist attack on a country town identified by a dot. He wondered. If stories by definition originated at local levels, local levels were seldom equal. A Simon and Garfunkel reunion concert in Central Park got more attention this evening than the massacre. By about ten times to one.

He soothed his convulsive nephew. And sensed how having his father and family around kept sane the hyperbole of his shadowy profession of dreams and X-rays. Maybe his life belonged with Megan after all.

Another dot on a map, marking a coal mine behind the Iron Curtain, made him wonder why 'reliable sources' were always associated with stories without pictures. The stories *with* pictures never seemed to require such sources. Pictures seemed more real than words, whether they told the whole story or not. This is probably why Bert Day spent so little time on his throne anymore reading newspapers, and found it pained him to listen to his radio. Only pictures mattered.

... *Shroud syndrome keeps father glued to seat* is the headline Bartlett reported later to his diary.

He drove home that evening with a fresh loaf of bread and a piece of broiled salmon to drop off at Megan's – along with a fresh loaf of bread for himself. He'd vowed not to see Megan for a while, so he decided to donate her share of loot to the communal kitchen. *If it pleases the court, I have nothing to say in my own defence.* By way of sentence, he pictured himself tomorrow evening feeding everybody in his house from the loaves and fishes in his Mustang.

5.

Nobody was home. He passed up a Bogart movie, found the fat weekend edition of the *Sun*, and climbed the landings to his room. Every day ended in this same stuffy room, atop the same mattress where his day had begun, him opening his eyes on a dogwood tree. To how many patients had he stressed that a mattress was their most important investment? He prodded his. It sagged the way his principles had. He needed a firmer mattress, a chiropractic mattress. Removing his cutoffs and thongs, underpants and sweat shirt, he prodded his sunburned skin in the mirror and foresaw an uncomfortable night enclosed in his swale.

And so to the beach ... he began, after inserting a fresh cassette and shaking loose his mike. Used tapes lined his bookcase. He planned to start reusing these soon and shell out no more for fresh ones. But the backlog kept growing. His diary seemed to interest him only in the moment of utterance, yet he was saving it, why? As his own anchorman he coordinated daily reports from all points of a compass he called home. Was this why its archives got neglected?

History, as he understood it, was a lie anyway.

He wondered how many millions were yearning for the Shroud of Turin to be dated back two thousand years, for science to authenticate faith. Could it, without lying?

The story of chiropractic was the evolution to brass numbers on a cedar door. Ferns in the reception room. *A shell game.* What was the point of upgrading himself except for prestige and money? His boxy office still had a mirror on the wall and Venetian blinds on the windows. Not a great location either ... panhandlers from the local liquor store, cut-rate travel agencies, traffic passing through to a better lifestyle on the west shore, rebate Tax shops with walnutty interiors, gallivanting men in fishnet stockings and blonde wigs.

He no longer shared his profession's wish to become part of mainstream, middle-class medicine: to receive referrals, be allowed into hospitals, sign death certificates. Maybe he never had. Chiropractors like veterinarians could act as guarantors on passport applications, and Bartlett was content with this, although no patient had ever asked him, except Dwight, who owned a passport with no entries and was not a patient.

Who needed death certificates?

In the newspaper, beside him in bed, he knew death at a distance was reduced to little boxes of black ink on the third page under 'Briefly'. The shape of bad news from far away. From nowhere, really. The paper, like his father's TV, lied through its lack of *body* in its reports. He opened it.

Item: at least twenty-seven farmworkers killed in Mexico, when train hits truck on way to pick strawberries.

Item: half a village swept away by landslide in Peruvian Andes, killing one hundred twenty, another two hundred missing.

Every week ferries capsized, trains disappeared off bridges killing unmentioned hundreds. Floods and earthquakes struck. More real to him was Gloria Dawson, asking Dr Day to count the bumps on her spine in the style to which she was accustomed, and then pressing them till they popped like buttons.

He slapped the page. Which brief black box would he happen to *remember*?

This one: A fifty-six-year-old Englishman had suffered a fatal heart attack after scaling the fence of a nudist colony in southern England. He'd been found dead with binoculars still in hand. *Binoculars or X-ray machines, God, we're all peepers at heart ...*

'If he'd waited till Saturday,' a nudist in camp was quoted as saying, 'he could've visited us legally and gotten a glimpse. That's when we have open house.'

Bartlett's own mother had died of rabies. An absurd, preventable death. Dying in fear and spasms.

Mothers weren't supposed to die this way. They weren't supposed to die unexpectedly, or even expected to die, not with children as young as Bart and Betty. Death was supposed to visit mothers in other countries, other times.

My own history's a lack of grief. The feeling of grief. I need more faith in a cure. He reached for an old textbook by his bed, and turned up a passage he noticed marked in red ink from his student days at Memorial. '... There is no other activity except, perhaps, the playing of a musical instrument, in which practice is more necessary than in spinal adjusting. And the spinologist like the musician is and – notwithstanding his scientific background – must always remain an artist.'

The chiropractor as liar was about all he *could* believe. And this put him in a bind: How could he stick at a profession he cared about, at least for his patients, if it had come to hold as many grave doubts for him as mainstream medicine? He was swimming over his head.

For example, with Trina Chase. Her problem, when he talked to her about it, seemed to be she saw what he was saying – literally. Her senses were jumbled and he didn't see how manipulating her spine was going to relocate them. Make her whole. She told him she saw yellow when a car started, and peach melba ice cream when her boyfriend, Harlow, kissed her. And when she looked at the off-white paint on Dr Day's examining-room wall she heard music. She didn't tell him what tune, but was a little surprised to hear him call it white when it definitely smelled green. 'It *is* green,' she said, staring at it. He just figured she was having him on. And Cabot had passed her on to a chiropractor? Maybe he should've asked Rowland Storey, M.D. for an outside opinion.

Bartlett mimicked Storey's pompous tone, into his mike.

'*Coming to the likes of you, Dr Day, all Miss Chase wants is a placebo. You can't honestly expect to talk turkey with her ... with us, when what it is coming out of your trap is polio! Understand, chiroquacktor, what I'm saying?*'

Tonight, as if in rebuttal, the chiropractor promptly decided to accept invitations to speak at successive quack conferences in Hong Kong and Nairobi, and would ask Dwight to book him a cut-rate, long-distance ticket. If in nothing else, he thought, a pilgrim should put his faith in flexibility. Did Dwight? How flexible was Herodotus? B. Day, D.C. had more invested in Herodotus Travel than he cared to admit to Megan, or even to himself.

He tacked toward sleep, lying on his side to avoid direct pressure on his sunburned stomach. He felt like a child, grimacing each time he tried to shift position in the small world of a messy room. He could either call in his mom to rub him down with salve, or he could keep hoping for sleep.

Dwight was supposed to make his monthly payments. So far, meticulously, Dwight had. But if he failed, Bartlett would need a healthier income than he enjoyed at present to make them himself and survive. He'd need a lucky moonlighting junket to Reno to boost his treasury. In spite of his friend's rep as a spendthrift at college, he trusted Dwight's entrepreneurial aggressiveness as something lacking in himself. This is why, faced with Irving's confident euphoria over burgeoning sales and the opportunity to expand – to earn investors in Herodotus Tours their money back and lots more – Bartlett had offered to mortgage his building and practice to help out with the expansion. He'd finished paying off his own mortgage last year. 'You must be a dope ...' said Megan. 'He's Napoleon reincarnate.'

He thought of Megan trying to sleep with her painful jaw. He thought of his father alone in front of his TV. Of people like his sister whose husband was seeing other women. And people in surrounding apartment blocks with backache. He decided pain lived for them all in the shadows between words they picked to tell their news.

Their stories probably merged somewhere, but Bartlett didn't believe in a gatekeeper in the sky.

Did *World News Tonight* understand the way seagull tracks in the sand resembled a sailboat tacking?

From his mother long dead he seemed to be picking up static, snow falling, as he settled into his swale of a mattress to replay his day at the beach.

The human body he recalled was ninety-eight percent water, ten gallons of the stuff. Bones, by comparison, barely came into it.

November, 1894

Have been haunting the new hospital wondering if my interest in Dr Richardson is justified given his singularities. Otherwise, could be up the creek, lost. I *am* lost.

Homesick.

Today the Sisters of Charity were beside themselves. 'A miracle,' Mother Superior was explaining to His Worship. Recovery of her new hospital's first patient on the very day of its official opening was surely a sign from God! Possibly a double sign, she now whispered, *because this smallpox victim was brought in from Keefer Street.* Her pustular spots had vanished overnight *and possibly her past too.* Would the mayor care to visit the isolation ward and see for himself?

The official delegation shuffled timidly to the door of a room where an oily-haired girl without spots was holding a Crucifix in her hands.

Mother Superior confessed she was impressed with the cowpox vaccine used elsewhere in countering smallpox. In this case however *it had not been used.* Carbolic acid had been used, along with chloride lime, to scour the walls and floors of the isolation ward by two dedicated nursing sisters. The girl in bed just stared.

Dr Richardson now appeared on the scene. Beaming, the handsome little physician was glad to welcome the mayor, as well as to extend his own range of local conquests. '... Your Worship. With due deference to the Almighty, I am slightly less inclined than the good sisters to put the dramatic cure down to the purgative effects of prayer than to those cleaning acids of which I must plead St. Paul's main and tiresome proponent. The goddess of health works in entirely predictable ways. Let me explain ...'

I like him. He's the sort to know whether he wants offspring or not, and what good breeding stock is about. I don't get the same little shock of recognition from hanging round the mayor.

'... I confess I don't believe in germs so much as a lack of outer equilibrium, something

I can observe myself, as the cause of disease.'

Mother Superior stood tactfully aside as her resident physician, a new arrival from a spotless British hospital, proceeded to discourse to the civic delegation about the efficacy of a city built of brick instead of lumber. Brick could better be kept scrubbed, he suggested. Its walls could, which should be left free of pictures and wallpaper, incidentally, as these collect dust and mould.

The mayor and aldermen began their tour of other beds, all so far empty, with Richardson at their side. They had nineteen rooms to visit and a ribbon to snip. As they strolled, the bright little doctor went on talking.

'A model city has no place for drinking or smoking, not to mention –' and he did not, though it was clear from his glance back to the room they'd come from he meant prostitution.

'... And the city's dead should be allowed to return to dust without coffins to encumber their passage, or gravestones to commemorate what really, after all, Your Worship, is just a recycling of soil.'

He didn't go so far as to impugn the after-life. He had to balance his own beliefs against those of his new employer, Mother Superior.

The mayor coughed and checked his pocket watch. He must have wondered how the good sisters had managed to saddle themselves with a quack. He took a deep breath. And heard how the doctor would eliminate pollution and noise from the city. How roads ought to be paved and wooden sidewalks eliminated because they harboured dirt between cracks. How sewer lines should be extended and roads regularly washed down.

The mayor smiled briefly at his flagging aldermen. 'I am an idealist, too, Dr Richardson, in that I have ideals. But a politician soon learns the price of believing in their practicableness.' He looked out the window. Rain. The present business depression may have added to his gloom. He looked flatulent. 'Mother Superior, might I trouble you for my umbrella and congratulate you on your splendid new facility for our city's use?'

I overheard Richardson saying to him at the door, 'Pasteur was a bit of a Frenchman, eh?' Explaining he himself believed sickness was really the evidence of moral imbalance in human nature ...

The mayor tipped his umbrella formally in bidding St. Paul's resident physician adieu.

Thus and so Dr Richardson. Upon his arrival in May this forthright man was dismayed by much,

including severe flooding
seen in the Valley from
his transcontinental
train. Bloated carcasses
of sheep and cattle
floating downstream.
Human refugees pouring
into the city. Disease, he
thought, rampant.

Yet he's hopeful
about Vancouver. It has
the potential for healthy
seafood and cricket. Our
recent fog he believes is
the product of smoke
from the satanic
sawmills. This is a hell
he hopes to reform. He
takes extensive notes on
a city into which he
worries about bringing
offspring.

More tomorrow, I
hope, regarding his
proposal of marriage to
the tall, red-haired
daughter of a banker.
Her father has had the
misfortune of being
discovered light-fingered
with other people's
money – nothing time
won't cure. His health
like hers is excellent.

Chapter 25

Dr Death & Co.

'IT SUCKS ...' he wrote to Megan at the end of his disastrous detour via Calcutta. In a cramped hand, because stamps with Hindi script covered nearly half the card. He also wired home a begging telegram to his father, a necessary but distasteful task. In his diary he summed up the Bengali city this way: *Makes me think of a jampacked arena, when the home hockey team has just stunk the place out ...* A confining comparison he then erased to let the hole, the gap, speak more eloquently. And he had to be honest: ... *What use the syndicate sees in Chandar is a big puzzle to me. He didn't mention crate costs. Nobody mentioned Chandar's expectations. I've been had.*

When Bartlett got offered the job, handed an unexpected stopover between Hong Kong and Nairobi, three nights here had seemed like plenty of time to dicker for bones and complete his commission. It was, if not exactly in the way he expected, enough time to negotiate a transaction. His employer in Hong Kong, a cultivated Dean of a New England medical school, on a trip to investigate acupuncture in China, had simply failed to prepare him for the lesser costs. Maybe he was counting on Dr Chandar to do this. Dr Morgan L. Cheaver had mainly been interested in Bartlett's reliability and trustworthiness. He'd made a Calcutta detour sound very straightforward, not to mention profitable. Bartlett equivocated, at first.

'Profitable ...' urged Marcus Reambeault. 'Wasn't it Mae West who said "Whenever I'm caught between two evils, I take the one I've never tried?" She may have died a year or two ago, but her philosophy lives on.'

Marcus was attending this same post-Xmas conference in Hong Kong, together with orthomolecularists and aroma therapists, spreading his own enthusiasm for faith healing, while Bartlett continued to mull over the weird proposition to cash in on Calcutta.

'Aren't you a chiropractor?' said Marcus.

'What's that got to do with it?'

They'd been strolling the path around Victoria Peak, with the skyscrapers, the harbour, a population of millions – another billion or so over the horizon – at their feet. By way of an answer Marcus went on to discuss clothes. He was in the market for three or four custom-made silk suits and had an appointment for his first fitting in Lee Yuen Street, just before dinnertime.

'Deciding what to wear is always a deeper matter than we give it credit, Bartlett. Assuming, of course, you have the choice qua choice and you're not a beggar. It's like deciding how to live. I think the answer's to look ordinary. No matter what you wear, it's always a costume. Picking a costume that looks ordinary reflects a man who believes in what he tells you. Roles are more serious than dressing carelessly. They should be.'

Bartlett was wearing his white lab coat and saddle shoes – which made him look very alternative, said Marcus. 'Just the ticket.' The faith healer didn't believe for one minute this is what his friend wore at home. Marcus had on the pink golf shirt he'd bought in Bangkok, with the crocodile crest, as fresh as the day it was minted. He unzipped his jacket to demonstrate cosmic coincidence to his friend. 'This shirt's come home. Hong Kong's where the sweat shops copy good labels, the brand names, before exporting these fakes around the world.' He unpocketed a large brown pill as they walked, a gift from a megavitamin specialist at the conference, and gulped it. The *suits* made here were different. Authentic, if you were careful where you shopped and paid a reasonable price. A cheap suit would rumple fast and unravel. 'It can't be faked up to the standard of a cheap shirt,' he told Bartlett. 'So they don't bother to the same degree.' Marcus had decided the colours of his new suits would be variations on the colour grey.

He smiled. A perfect disguise for a faith healer.

Meanwhile, he thought Bartlett looked very fit. He admired 'the real you', previously obscure to him in Bangkok, 'the thin man inside the fat one'. Bartlett's bones were far nearer the surface of his skin now. The Nova Scotian suggested for better or worse Bartlett had shed his dubious distinction as an unhealthy looking specimen, for whom the picture of health had dwelled solely in the spine. 'For the better, I think ... yes ... very trim.' Bartlett replied he wasn't on any fancy diet, if that's what Marcus was thinking.

A comely European woman then jogged by them on the circuitous path, heading in the direction of the funicular tram. 'Not as easy-going either,' observed Marcus. 'Why not look into a local escort service? Have a

Susie Wong sandal up to your room at teatime? I like your mole. That new?'

Up here in the cleaner, lighter air, where houses of the colony's wealthiest entrepreneurs capped the peak, winter hadn't stopped gardens from flowering or leaves from staying green. It was different below. Below, the exhaust fumes stank. Oases among skyscrapers were as scarce as wild deer. So was charm. So were queues. He and Marcus descended the slope by tram, an elevator that went all the way to the top of the very shrewdest minds in international trade.

For a few cents they rode the Star Ferry back to Kowloon. Junks plunged past them through the green choppy harbour, vultures circled on thermals of humid air. Bartlett sat back. He ran his memory over these worn ropes, these varnished benches on the upper deck, over the cream and white paint on steel decks and trusses. *The memory of our voyage over...*

'Not vultures,' Marcus pointed out, 'kites.' He placed a hand on his countryman's sleeve. 'We'll probably see them covering us in Nairobi. Give your same talk there, by the way, and you'll probably earn another commission to the glue factory. But nothing's better than experience. I'd go.' To Calcutta he meant, en route.

Thus had it been decided that Bartlett should accept the offered detour via Calcutta.

First you were in one city, then another. Kites followed, memories trailing, while your baggage as a chiropractor proceeded you.

2.

In Calcutta the pilgrim was surprised at what a living skeleton could fetch in down payment on its own eventual collapse – very little – compared to what he'd been given by Dean Cheaver to bargain for dead ones and have exported to a North American syndicate of schools for study and medical research. This was his injunction. To select and arrange skeletons for export, which in life had no idea they'd be emigrating to the New World in death. To be examined there by future doctors, but too late to avoid their having to emigrate at all.

His contact in Calcutta was a gentle ophthalmologist, whose interest in bones appeared to be disinterested. Bartlett thought of Dr Chandar straight off as a colleague with philanthropic interests. He was right, but in the wrong way. Entering into a transaction too soon, how could a Canadian in Calcutta have known it was too soon for his own good?

A profitable business, bones, and the supply in India seemed inexhaustible. *India would harvest hair if it could sell it, maybe does ... and it bottles sweat, I bet, for the mineral water market overseas ...* The twin threats of inflation and a possible ban on bone exports had conspired to push up prices and increase international demand for the Indian product. Bartlett's job, apart from negotiating price, was to make sure the quality of this year's crop didn't suffer with respect to his syndicate's share of it. He was expected to feel proprietary. He knew bones and was expected to be discerning. 'You know – quality control, that sort of thing.' He nodded. Dean Cheaver, dressed in a blue Oxford shirt and pinstriped suit, not exactly camouflaged amidst the alternative therapists, had stipulated so many children's skeletons, so many adult, and a few crooked or diseased ones – 'you understand, the interesting exceptions to prove the rule' – oh, and if Bartlett could find, say, an 'elephant man', so much the better. 'Another drink?'

The chiropractor's performance before delegates in Hong Kong must have sounded persuasive – *Listen, the structure of the world* DEPENDS *on bones, blah blah* – and made a favourable impression on the busy Dean, who wasn't very interested in getting his own hands dirty in Calcutta. 'I'm expected in China.' He seemed more interested in the frontiers of acupuncture than in his profession's anatomical mainstream. Possibly he saw the borders of both medicines as belonging to the same country, but still too far apart for a joint journey. Introducing himself, Cheaver reminded Bartlett of Mr Strajik, the Swede. 'It was the way you handled yourself, yes? I felt I should come and talk to you.'

Thus another spinoff abroad, seeming to offer him a practical alternative to the theory he professed to espouse at home. Enough to make his doubts worse. *Me a bone merchant, an agent? Should've had my meter read ...* This commission had looked like an unexpected gift to cover the cost of his round-the-world ticket. More. A cushion. If, for example, Dwight were to start missing payments on the mortgage taken out by Bartlett against himself, a possibility this winter, a Calcutta commission could shield him against foreclosure. This clincher occurred to him in Hong Kong as the best reason for accepting the side trip .

No illusions, only a preconception that his knowledge mattered to the world. It didn't. He discovered the skeleton industry in Calcutta was a proud one and knew more about human frames than he did. The industry regulated itself according to the high standard of markets it exported to. He quickly saw its dependence on exports was too high for any dealer to countenance slipshod work. The craftsmen lived their profession, used to labelling every bone. The bespectacled Dr Chandar, the chiropractor's contact and introduction to the Calcutta bazaar, had briefed the Canadian in his clinic before Bartlett plunged into his rounds. 'Ask me any more questions,' urged Chandar.

'I'm probably on top of it now,' said Bartlett. 'Sounds straightforward.' Professional pride, however misplaced, had bolstered his can-do attitude. He wanted to wrap up his job in a hurry and jet on to Nairobi. *Listen…* Free enterprise was letting him create his own pace.

His abrupt appearance in the bone warehouse, the morning after he arrived in Calcutta, impressed not a soul. Made no difference to anybody except maybe Bartlett and his own understanding of the ongoing life of bones. He ordered and agreed to pay for six hundred skeletons, inspecting barely half a dozen, along with a few curiosity pieces the man in white overalls agreed to throw into the bargain. No elephant men to be had. Few aberrations. Didn't matter. The sickening stench of the place was too much to stomach any more shopping among similar companies for a better deal. Bartlett let it be known – he was entitled to say this, and it made him feel important as a go-between *to* say it – if the quality of this shipment was good, then another, larger order would be forthcoming from the American syndicate he represented. Did an indifferent boggle of the head, from the man in white overalls, disguise his surprise at a lack of any bargaining from Dr Day, D.C.?

This sombre assistant had hooked a sucker and seemed reluctant to shake him loose with any eager movement. Languidly, he adjusted his black-framed spectacles, confident in his knowledge of an endless appetite abroad for India's dead. In a seller's market he could afford to be reserved, dealing with a ravenous fish.

Bartlett had swallowed bait and line. But the real reason he hadn't bothered nosing around among the dozen or so other dealers, for a better price, was that while the price for the sort of top-of-the-line articulated adult skeletons he desired did vary, a company like V.K. Hyatt & Co., according to his contact, had very good quality. He could check for himself, visit every other company in the city. 'Probably good idea,' suggested Dr Chandar. 'Although please, for quality of workmanship, expect what you pay for. It is straight-forward business. Cut corners,' he warned, 'be burned.'

Too true, it turned out. If Bartlett had known then what he found out later, about the accommodation between Chandar and Hyatt & Co., he might've been willing to swim through the stench of a few more warehouses. *Stench, that's the word for this business.*

He inspected a few suspended skeletons articulated with metal and had agreed to pay Hyatt an average of three hundred dollars U.S. each. 'Less than top price for largest skeletons,' insisted the bespectacled assistant in overalls, with the voice of an undertaker, 'but only on agreement that entire shipment will contain a mixture of sizes.' Bartlett agreed, but stipulated no more than fifteen percent children's skeletons. No skulls on their own, no loose bones, except those thrown into the bargain.

He'd felt in charge.

He enjoyed a certain latitude to negotiate his purchase, on the under-standing his commission would be fifty percent of any residual balance under the two hundred thousand dollars he had in trust from Dean Cheaver to draw on at American Express. His homework had been done for him in Hong Kong. The syndicate's ingenious policy was supposed to encourage saving. It merely spooked Bartlett, anxious to close the deal, into foreseeing a fat commission after a single visit.

The workmanship of all the purchased skeletons, agreed the undertaker, would be up to the standard on display. His head barely boggled. He instructed his customer to return tomorrow, for 'inspection of freighting' and to meet Mr Hyatt himself.

'No sweat,' said Bartlett, calculating he'd made ten thousand American dollars for half a day's work. Travel certainly exaggerated more than the lag time between continents. He felt like Mae West, caught between two evils, and enjoying both.

3.

If inflation's got a home town, it's one like Calcutta. Obsessed with survival, this city could only scramble for its life by knowing the price of everything and the value of nothing. Calcutta helped explain to him where Aloysius was coming from. Calcutta probably explained where most refugees in the world wanted to be. In Canada, with Aloysius. Maybe this was why

Canadians seemed dull to them. Canadians weren't dying to leave their own land. Most of them could afford to be burned or buried in it. The cost was complacency, of course, but millions abroad would kill to pay this price of home. *Dear Diary* ...

He witnessed bodies, live ones, together with bullock carts, buses, taxis and rickshaws, mashed up in the worst traffic jams he'd ever seen. *The customary manner of death must be by asphyxiation* ... But the city had a dream. He read they were building a subway. The Calcutta Metro Railway. The platforms would gleam, there would be chandeliers and potted plants, Hindu hymns would play on loudspeakers – and no beggars, sleeping families, or litter of any kind would be allowed underground on the spotless tiles. Aloysius would enjoy reading this pipedream ... a city's underside cleaner, brighter, more wholesome than its topside! He addressed a hotel envelope that first evening, stuffed in the newspaper clipping, and rang down for half a page of stamps.

'But it's true,' protested Dr Chandar, who'd accepted without opening it Bartlett's letter of introduction from Dean Cheaver, dropping it on the examining table in his shabby surgery. 'This dream is costing a half billion American dollars, more. But is good to have a dream. You have just come in a taxi from A to B, Dr Day, and know how bad it is this morning. So a dream is our A-1 priority.'

Bartlett must have looked skeptical.

'You are thinking what a waste of money, when we have so much misery to erase with more hospitals.' Chandar was peering closely into the cataracted eyes of a ragged child, whose shy mother was standing silently in the doorway with a veil across her face. Behind her a line-up of patients snaked out into the courtyard, down a corridor and into the street. It continued up the street. For the miracle of vision, the blind were willing to wait patiently in the darkness of hot bright days.

'Who,' asked Chandar, 'will give us dollars for erasing simple misery? Foreign banks must fund *monuments*. Thus our Underground. Why worry, Dr Day? Never can we pay them back. But if some new train whisks us along, like rest of world is whisked, why should we not have a whisker too?'

Chandar had gone about his business of preparing the blind boy to meet his dream. He'd removed his spectacles and was now looking into his patient's eyes with an ocular instrument that reminded Bartlett of a sextant. Chandar changed the subject to the nature of the chiropractor's visit.

'I am myself not a believer in reincarnation, Dr Day. I ask you does it matter if we burn or not burn our corpses? Of what importance is it if *Dom* procurers fish corpses from Hooghly? Or steal them from pyres? Bones are bones. Our exports help your students in America know anatomy, and India's balance of trade is assisted.'

He pressed back the boy's head to peer aggressively into his iris, as if he expected to discover the secret of the universe. His greying hair fell forward.

'On other hand, I am unhappy when these procurers procure skeletons still living. It is same as hospital orderlies removing eyes from dying patients in mental hospitals to sell to eye banks. Repulsive.' The boy's mother was squinting over top of her veil, trying to see into her son's eyes from her station in the doorway. Her posture already resembled a grandmother's. 'You say you have chiropractice, Dr Day? I will introduce you to one young acquaintance of mine whose condition will interest a chiropractor. He has sold his skeleton on the instalment plan.'

So Bartlett had reluctantly promised to come again tomorrow, once he was free of syndicate busines.

Clinic to charnel house to bank. He later fled the charnel house in his cutoffs and thongs. All that remained was to return tomorrow, inspect the packing cases and pay for his bones. Then he was through with aiding and abetting the mainstream enemies of his own profession in America, ensconced in their medical schools and earnest to a man. His chiropractic training was embedded deep in opposition. Still, he was enjoying this betrayal. He expected a comfortable payoff for his treason.

Looking out of the taxi on his way to American Express, he noticed a dog on the sidewalk, at home among the forests of legs and probably planning future attacks at its own sniffing pace. Thirsty, Bartlett promised to indulge himself later in the hotel lounge, feet up, as soon as his paperwork was done and the junket complete.

Indian banking proved complicated. Unlike V.K. Hyatt & Co., the banks offered no one-stop shopping, and commuting between different banks for financial transactions took him the rest of the day. The Bank of India kept certain transaction rights to itself, but not others. And line-ups proved incurable, except with patience, this slowest of medicines and hardest on the feet. The bank reminded him of some late nineteenth-century British hospital. It functioned on the premise that its patients were never to be coddled. He limped home and had the bellhop draw him a bath. In his suite he reexamined the canopy over his bed, the bell pull, the copper spittoons in the bathroom. On somebody else's money he could afford to spit far, tip extravagantly, and command relief. No mini-fridge for his batteries. He was back in the nineteenth century.

Come up and see me sometime ... He was soaking himself in bubbles, recording his day. *It's not the women in my life, it's the life in my women that counts.* He could hear the voice of Marcus Reambeault. He couldn't hear any traffic outside on Chowringhee. Calcutta didn't exist. Sympathetic as he was with Ram Chandar's work in giving sight to the blind, the thought of another taxi trip miles across Calcutta to visit his clinic didn't turn Bartlett's crank. He had, however, promised. *It's the life in my word that counts, too, I guess.* He was lucky not to drop his tape recorder into the bathtub, when he fumbled the shampoo and things got hairy when he fell.

4.

In the morning he taxied back to the slums. He knew from his first brief visit that Dr Chandar had the reputation of a saint among his patients. Every year he restored the sight of hundreds. Possibly thousands.

When Bartlett arrived the line-up of pilgrims was even thicker than on the first day and his driver declined to wait. Hundreds were sitting in the street, stuffed into the corridor, camped out in the courtyard. Children, old men, blankets, cooking pots ... The small three-storey building was a hospital crammed to the nines. To get into it people were willing to camp weeks.

'Back already,' observed Chandar, looking up from a patient whose bandaged head he was unwrapping. 'In time for a dream to come true. Please, watch?'

At first the young girl failed to register the significance of light flooding into view when he uncovered her eyes. She looked too frightened to move. Her eyes were watering. Then gradually the blur sharpened into better focus, her tears dried and lines converged.

Her whole face lit up like a sunlamp.

'Ah,' said Dr Chandar, pleased. 'You see, Dr Day. A miracle never fails to move its creator.'

'You bet,' said Bartlett, glad now he'd come back. The child was beaming. Chandar was resplendent. The child's mother laughed. Never had Bartlett seen a patient so dramatically cured. The mother looked willing to toast away the morning with crystal goblets, had she owned any.

'Our surgery is only this small torch against much darkness. You are bone specialist, I am eye specialist. I am sure neither can ever do enough to cure our countries' disabled.'

To be acknowledged as a peer made Bartlett uneasy. Yet here they both stood in their white coats. He knew an eye operation cost just twenty-five American dollars. He felt pleased to be doing his bit. Cataracts vanished, thanks in part to donations from the syndicate he represented.

'Of course,' said Dr Chandar, examining the next patient's eyes with his sextant, 'we all hear reports of unscrupulous who injure our professions by preying on defenceless people's … eyes, bones.'

Bartlett nodded solemnly.

When the ophthalmologist finished examining the old woman in a scrappy sari, he put his spectacles back on and spoke to Dr Seth, his assistant, in Hindi. This young man with striking cheekbones nodded, turning back to the woman to explain something in Bengali, as Ram Chandar led Bartlett out of his surgery, through the courtyard of beseeching petitioners, and down the corridor to his office.

Here supporting himself on a pair of sticks was a young man who stumbled in his eagerness to greet Bartlett. He had been standing like this, volunteered Chandar's servant, an old man with patchy red hair, for one hour. He had refused to sit down. He had refused to take tea.

To Bartlett Chandar said, by way of introducing the young cripple, 'Waiting for you is this person who no longer owns his living bones. Meet Dhuniya.' Dhuniya, had he been able to bend over, appeared willing to kiss Bartlett's saddle shoes in gratitude for his audience. Chandar wanted the chiropractor to listen to Dhuniya's story. Bartlett the voyeur seemed back in business.

Unfortunately, a bad body odour had engulfed the room.

Dhuniya had 'lathyrism', said Chandar, his spine was 'degenerate'. The two practitioners stood on either side of the young man, 'only twenty-five, Dr Day, but already old and crumbling.' Obviously incapable of bathing. Bartlett could see he had no backbone, only a kind of stiff hope in his eager eyes.

'His legs, you see how twisted are his legs that make him walk like a drunkard? What is worse for a man, Dr Day – not to see or not to walk? Can it be said? I promised this poor man you would examine him. Please, possibly you know of procedures to use with him to alleviate some pain? Maybe help him hope he will not be exported to one of your medical schools? I think your students would not prefer his twisted skeleton.'

The crippled man's eyes followed their conversation in eager agreement with everything Dr Chandar seemed to urge on his behalf. Bartlett felt like a charlatan ... *In over my head, drowning in professional fabrication.* He was listening to Chandar, to a medical doctor who actually seemed to believe a chiropractor possessed the means to straighten crooked bones. Far worse than Rowland Storey M.D. calling him a quack. Bartlett had never heard of lathyrism. 'No cure for it,' admitted Chandar, 'so far.' And briefly he related Dhuniya's history as a bonded village labourer, slowly dying of paralysis. Lathyrism. Once or twice he consulted Dhuniya in halting Bengali, but knew the young man's story well enough to relay it fluently.

When Dhuniya could no longer earn his food at home, he had come to beg on Calcutta's pavements. He had sold his blood seven, ten times. But his bones he could sell just once. A procurer promised him five hundred rupees – minus one hundred rupees because of twisted legs. Dhuniya was progressing on schedule. He expected to collect his second instalment soon.

'But this kesari dal they eat, why doesn't the government ban it?'

'Three years ago, yes. Banned. Since then production has doubled.' Ram Chandar shrugged. 'I am ophthalmologist who specializes in eyes. I have concluded our worst blind people are those who can see.' He meant landlords who grew this crippling legume for profit, and labourers forced to eat it out of hunger.

Dhuniya's eyes never left Bartlett's face, searching for some sign to justify his hopes.

The chiropractor suddenly felt weighed down with all the goddamn claims his profession had made since D.D. Palmer's story of racking the spine of poor Harvey Lillard to cure the infamous janitor of his deafness. Henceforth, chiropractors had seen life was good and spinal luxations the source of all history, all disease. It stood to reason, if nerves to each and every limb travelled from brain to spine, and if one of those limbs should start to suffer, that you could cure the pain once you located misalignment in the spine. Fundamental plumbing. *And as a student I came close to believing the romance of a duck who quacked like* THIS?

Out of politeness, and to stall for time, Bartlett asked the ophthalmologist: 'Where did you meet Dhuniya?'

'At V.K. Hyatt and Company. I was briefing them on your arrival. This man was led in off street. Such desperation, his third tour of inspection, when Hyatt's man finally agreed to pay him first instalment. One hundred rupees. Can you imagine, Dr Day? Dhuniya had to look near death before qualifying for one hundred rupees.'

Bartlett was having to tread water now, drowning in his own barren profession. Water, water everywhere ... his chiropractic nose barely above the surface of the Hooghly. Why were thin legs and torsos in Canadian society evidence of the good life, but in this country clues to an unwholesome existence? *Bad health as a condition of shame ... To sell or not to sell your bones ... twin evils, cruel dilemma.*

If you ended up with enough rupees to pay your daughter's dowry, figured Bartlett, you had none left over to buy wood for your pyre. But you weren't allowed to have a pyre if you decided to sell your bones. Except if you didn't sell them you'd end up with no grandchildren and your daughter shamed. Thus dignity: none in life, none in death.

No different than selling your body for pleasure, he supposed. Selling yourself for survival, and neither pleasure nor survival likely.

'Dr Day?' Chandar removed his pocket watch, refusing to glance at it out of politeness to his colleague. 'Can you do anything out of charity for this living skeleton?'

Bartlett didn't think he had a choice. That night he ended up telling his diary Dhuniya looked so trusting he'd felt obliged to examine the man's back. Legs. Arms. He moved them all very gently, without favouritism.

Dr Chandar was nodding agreeably as he left the room.

Bartlett was afraid to apply pressure for fear of breaking his patient in half. He tried putting Dhuniya at his ease by talking to him in English. But he felt bad, seditious ... Felt, too, blind eyes at the window peering in at his dilemma they could smell, these eyes of beggars.

A mirror over the desk mocked him.

His humiliation was complete when Chandar, returning abruptly for a scope, which no doubt made the microscopic very large, noticed Dhuniya crying tears of happiness, *kissing my manipulating hands ...*, poor twisted cripple, believing a few feeble probes had set him on the road to recovery. A road no cart, no horse, no arm need ever help him down again, once he allowed his walking sticks to fall. Dr Chandar, used to miracles, boggled his head approvingly and headed back out the door.

5.

The next morning when he returned to inspect packing cases at V.K. Hyatt & Co., to ensure the safe freightage of his purchases, he came to realize the vanity of his hasty calculations over profit. Cashier's cheque in tow, he reentered the stinking warehouse, welcomed by the same deep-voiced assistant, Mr Hyatt's spokesman, who looked through the caller to his skeleton. He wore thick lenses to accomplish this feat. He wore white overalls as if to signify clinical detachment from the real labour going on in here. Dr Death. His building seemed to swallow its breath again, to press its bones in on Bartlett like ... *like entering a ballroom after a death dance.* Reason required grief, and without it you were a quack. Dr Death had all the sorrow of a rabid dog.

Bartlett saw again the thousands of bones lining shelves, covering tables. Lumps of vertebrae – cervical, sacrum, coccyx ... And skulls, thoraxes, clavicles, humeruses ... pectoral girdles and patellas. *The comic names of our fundamental plumbing.* Bones for sale and export. *The driven snow of history.*

Complete and polished skeletons in an extended family of sizes lined the walls of the emporium. Naked lightbulbs dangled over them every thirty feet, in an odd display of economy and shadowy jurisdiction.

The hellish stink of glue arose from a boiling cauldron of rejected bones, just like yesterday, fed first through a machine like his father's wringer washer crushing them to dust. This aphrodisiac of bookbinders and librarians was an example, he supposed, of new life emerging from compost. The bone mafia laundering its money. This time he dug a tissue out of his white coat and held it to his nose as he and Dr Death passed the kitchen. His plan was to check out the packing cases and take a fast powder.

His guide led him again through the gallery of artisans bent over bones like painters and sculptors. Before bringing his bones to market an exporter first had to strip away their flesh. The procedure, once begun, was cumulative and reformative. Here artisans sat scraping off dry residual membrane. Out of chaotic piles of calcium and marrow they sought to reassemble the integrity of death. Variations from skeleton to skeleton commanded their respect. Pliers and chisels, wirecutters and saws: each tool manipulated with deft gestures in the direction of recognition and wholeness. Restorers, these men recreated articulations of joints, jaws and digits. Hammers tapped, drills pierced, brushes polished. Men reassembling anatomies out of the fragments of strangers. Men unable, for all their skill, experience and devotion, to breathe life into the most pliant of sockets. Their gallery, he now noticed, was silent of voices. Their instruments of re-creation were all. He wondered if these quick, delicate artisans were tuned in to some news from nowhere, hunched over skulls as over conch shells, knowing the spoken word, like loose flesh, was their impediment to perfection.

Listen here, bone.

Speak. Sing.

Tides ebb, affairs cease.

Voices drown.

'This way to Mr Hyatt's office,' spoke Dr Death. But Bartlett remembered the way.

Today the room was occupied.

The man seated behind the desk ignored them as they entered. He too wore heavy glasses in black frames, his desk buried in invoices and papers. He wore long-sleeved white pyjamas open at the neck. Dressed in white, surrounded by white, he sat amidst papers and bones. A fan in the ceiling created no stir, not a page trembled. The naked lightbulb overhead cast a weak light the approximate colour of margarine. Dwight's yellow shoes, thought Bartlett. Except for Mr Hyatt's presence, and a packing crate on the floor beside his desk, the visit was a repetition of yesterday's. 'Very Fragile,' the label read. 'Handle with Care.'

Dr Death stepped back to await acknowledgement.

Mr Hyatt ignored him. Deaf to the intrusion of both men, he didn't look up from behind his raised black quill.

Bartlett now sensed what trying to sell his skeleton on the hoof might be like. First looked through, then ignored. He looked around for a chair. Because of the humidity he considered sitting down on the coffin to rest his feet. He was sweating like a supplicant. He'd gladly give any packing arrangements his earliest blessing, just to be allowed to rejoin the city of the living. If 'living' was the word for Calcutta. Two days in Calcutta felt like years. Hong Kong was in another orbit. Vancouver occupied a different galaxy.

In Hong Kong he'd learned from Marcus how deeply the Chinese *worshipped* bones. Chinese cemeteries were crowded places, bones the source of prosperity and good luck. Marcus described *feng shui* to him, the ancient philosophy of 'wind and water' used to arrange graveyards in a proper balance with nature. But the faith healer also knew something else. Skulls were *imported* into China, Tibet, Nepal for ancestor worship. Either, he suggested, religious fervour was in excess of the bone harvest there, or else all this worshipping wore out bone at such a clip these circle-type countries were required to import it holus-bolus. Few poor countries, especially of the line-type, knew anything of the potential market abroad for ancestor worship. India was the exception, because in Marcus's atlas it was a circle country without a bone fetish.

So Mr Hyatt here, the exporter, was responsible for wealth and luck abroad, not to mention the education of doctors and dentists, in countries reluctant to desecrate their own dead. This same guy, who welcomed death at home. Odd how the disenfranchised of Mr Hyatt's country should end up the focus of such studious devotion abroad. Their bones replenished the world's anatomical understanding.

Bartlett was glad to have hanging in the closet at his hotel, in a suitbag, the plastic skeleton he employed in public speeches as his prop. Bea. Because his memory of the dying Dhuniya was still too much with him.

He thought he now understood the necessary illusion of religion.

'You have paid Dr Chandar his fee?' inquired Mr Hyatt, without glancing up.

Bartlett thought he must be addressing his assistant, Dr Death. When silence ensued, he thought to speak up. 'Pardon me?'

'Please,' interjected the assistant, in a deeply soothing way. 'Look here first.' Dr Death dipped down to raise the packing case lid for his inspection. Inside was another case, a cardboard box. At this revelation Dr Death held up his palms like a magician to indicate he had nothing to hide. He boggled his head, then proceeded to raise a second lid, voila, to reveal a linen shroud. With a supple two-handed gesture he then flipped open the shroud, by tearing through its stitches. Inside the shroud was a long, articulated skeleton, scrubbed very white and nestling against a cotton pad.

'Yes?' asked this magician in white overalls. A pause for maximum effect. Then, cupping palm behind skull, he lifted the skull a few inches in order to prod the underlying pad – it looked like a sponge – with his middle finger to show the client how attention to detail went right through to the floor of his purchase.

'Yeah, good. Fine.'

'Another ten dollars, we will give one extra layer of cotton pad ...' The words rolled up effortlessly from deep inside Dr Death's stooping diaphragm.

'No, no ... Whatever's adequate for overseas shipments.' Bartlett shuddered to think how far six hundred cotton pads would eat into his commission.

Mr Hyatt's assistant boggled his head and laid the skull delicately back down on the single pad. He rewound the linen shroud and closed the cardboard box. Then he replaced the wooden lid of the coffin, indicating with a hammering motion that he would later nail it down, once a customs inspection sticker had been attached.

Mr Hyatt had yet to glance up from the paperwork over which his quill pen circled. He was calculating his angle of descent. 'You approve our arrangements then?' he asked in an aloof, not unpleasant voice. Higher and mellower than his assistant's.

'... Yes,' said Bartlett. 'Things seem in order here. Very good.'

'Good,' said the bone trader, lifting his face to look Bartlett square in the belt buckle. He seemed diverted by the glint. 'I will be one moment, please,' and with his quill dove to the figures on his desk. Bartlett stood there with Dr Death at his side. They could hear the fan revolving faintly overhead, the artisans' tools whirring in the gallery, a distant wringer washer grinding the rejected bones away to powder. He had just died. They were toting up his ledger.

He dug into his pocket for more tissue. He noticed how his old cords now hung on his hips and needed taking in. His white coat bore fresh smudges of Calcutta. His saddle shoes would need a shoeshine boy to bring them back to life. The Kleenex reminded him. In Hong Kong, having promised Dwight to remember his father imprisoned there by the Japanese, he'd visited the Stanley prison camp. It was still a prison. He hadn't gone inside. In the adjacent cemetery he came across tombstones clumsily carved by prisoners, possibly even Dr Irving, tending the sick and dead. 'Here Lie the Bones of T.L. Dawson, April 1943' / 'Skull of Unknown, December 1941.' Bartlett was still using the same tissue he had with him on Boxing Day. He stuffed the tissue back in his pocket without wiping his brow.

Mr Hyatt picked up a blotter and Bartlett noticed his gold wristwatch for the first time. A tiara. The owner squared the blotter to his page, pressed down for several seconds as if to suffocate any trace of moisture from the buried lines, then lifted it like a coffin lid to extract a page.

'Your bill, sir.' He was looking through his glasses at Bartlett's buckle.

Bartlett saw it was in triplicate. He stepped closer and took the invoice in hand. 'Costs Outstanding,' he saw, came to 'US$198,600.00'.

'I don't understand.'

The bone dealer was kind enough to take to the air again, in order to direct his black quill to his precise calculations. Reaching, he pecked the page in Bartlett's hand with an inky nib. Six hundred skeletons at three hundred dollars per. And six hundred coffins times thirty dollars each, material and labour. He rested his quill.

They were soaking me for coffins plus the skeletons ...

'Hang on. I don't know what your arithmetic is all about, but we had an agreement yesterday and I drew you a cashier's cheque for a hundred eighty thousand dollars ... I have it here ...' He patted the shoulder bag at his hip.

The vast sum made him nervous to be carrying it. That it might not be enough now terrified him.

Mr Hyatt simply nodded, reaching for another file to occupy himself while the chiropractor pondered his position. His assistant, Dr Death, looked at his hands as though determined to avoid any unsavoury commerce with the world.

'We agreed that you'd ship six hundred skeletons to the U.S.' said Bartlett. 'That was the deal, right?'

Mr Hyatt was silent.

'Yes,' he finally said. 'Is there some problem? Some reason you feel we have dishonoured our agreement?'

'Well, yeah. Now you're trying to nail me for an extra eighteen thou six hundred for shipping.'

Mr Hyatt appeared surprised. His eyebrows lifted. He glanced at his assistant for confirmation of their visitor's unreasonableness. Receiving none, he turned back and spoke softly to the visitor.

'There must be misunderstanding, sir. The cost of freighting bones was not included. It is never included. Freighting, brokerage, warehouse charges, customs bribes ...'

'Bribes?'

Mr Hyatt paused. He would not be drawn into disagreement, or, for that matter, into looking his customer in the eye.

When he spoke again it was patiently and without aggression to Bartlett's belt buckle. 'If you wish, sir, we can show you invoices signed by other agents, such as yourself, for similar transactions with America.'

'… All right. Sure.'

Dr Death now joined his hands. Mr Hyatt paused again. He then exhaled with a measured patience, accosted by this tiresome child he would have to appease. 'Wait, please.'

His heavy black-rimmed glasses lifted toward the ceiling. For a second his lenses went opaque in the lightbulb's two reflected images. Then the eyes resurfaced briefly between the fan's rotating blades, while the fingers, Mr Hyatt's manicured fingers, pulled down his pyjama sleeves to adjust the French cuffs he didn't have. At this point he promptly disappeared.

Rummaging among his records, Mr Hyatt sounded to be in search of transactions conducted with more experienced agents. Swollen from years of humidity his lower drawers gave way with scritching reluctance. Excavated papers surfaced slowly. Slim entrepreneurial fingers, shaped like his quill, unwrapped fading ribbons in the search through excavated bundles. Mummified folders fell apart in his hands. He squinted at them, he sifted their pages. His gold watch snagged the unnatural light, sweat beaded his brow, the fan afforded him no relief.

All this toil on his behalf pleased Bartlett. He waited.

In vain. Mr Hyatt produced at last the coffin costs of half a dozen, a dozen, purchases. They ranged all the way up to two hundred twenty-seven thousand dollars for a single order of nine hundred skeletons, six months ago, bound for Los Angeles. Costs outstanding did indeed appear to include coffins *in addition to* skeletons. He could see the figures for himself.

His consignors waited. Dull fan blades chopped at the muggy air, without so much as scratching its surface.

'I don't have the money …' he lied. 'The freightage, I mean.' He dug into his shoulder bag for his wallet. 'I figured I'd covered the works. Here's my cheque for the skeletons. A cashier's cheque …'

Was he hoping they might give in to this bird in the hand? He let it glide down to Mr Hyatt's desk, tempting him.

Both Bengalis were examining their fingernails. Patient men, used to waiting for their cash crop on the instalment plan. Suddenly, Mr Hyatt swooped to pluck the cheque, and, without looking at it, dropped it into a drawer, slammed the drawer, and stood up.

Bartlett now saw his mistake. He ought to have held on to the cheque as his bargaining chip. No way now could he escape their clutches, without coughing up more money or else abandoning purchases already made. They had him on the rack, crying uncle, before he even knew he was a prisoner.

His hubris had assumed the deal closed, once it put ten thousand bucks' commission in his pockets. Now this commission was going to get swallowed up, along with most of the balance, leaving him 'half' – of what, fourteen hundred? Barely enough to cover the expense of his hotel, the cost of rewriting his plane ticket to make the detour, the cost … And who knew about bribes?

Mr Hyatt read his mind and proceeded to turn the screws. 'You have not forgotten Dr Chandar, of course.'

'You mentioned Chandar, yes. I'll never forget Dr Chandar, thank you.'

Mr Hyatt had begun returning his ancient records to their graves. 'His good work,' he suggested, disappearing himself into a drawer, 'deserves support.'

Bartlett still didn't understand. He preferred to bracket Chandar with Cheaver, part of the shuttle network set up in Hong Kong to land him gently here, in the dead middle of the bloody moon.

The Dean must've seen in him a much sharper fellow than he really was. Cheaver must've seen a typical chiropractor, in fact, attracted to some supposed built-in incentive to bargain, a ploy intended to save the syndicate as much as the chiropractor made in profit himself. Bartlett now estimated had he been greedier and bargained for a better price, for such a large shipment of skeletons, he could've *still* covered the unexpected cost of coffins and earned himself a significant commission. Why hadn't Chandar warned him about unexpected costs?

Here he stood, the innocent pilgrim, left holding an invoice for money that in Hong Kong he'd been assured was in healthy excess of what was required to make his purchases. He supposed now he had no recourse but to pay the bastards for their coffins, go back to the bank for another cheque … unless he washed his hands of the whole scene, in which case, the mainstream medical schools he represented – *me, a chiropractor!* – would probably prosecute him for absconding with funds. Not, of course, the first time orthodox medicine would've gone after a chiropractor for dubious practices.

And Chandar?

He elaborately excused himself from the presence of Mr Hyatt and Dr

Death – promising to return next morning with a cheque for their outstanding sum. His hosts watched him go without comment. They knew he would return. What choice had he?

6.

When he did find a free taxi, after walking blocks through fetid vegetable peelings and hawked spume, the driver refused to take him all the way to the eye clinic unless he paid twice the going rate.

'Terrific,' muttered Bartlett.

'Traffic,' reasoned the Sikh. 'What I lose in many delays over such distance I could make double, three times, in many small fares.'

Bartlett believed him. From the back seat of the Ambassador he could only ponder this black hole of a city, sucking him in and then spitting him out like a backwoods rube. Far from a teddy bear's picnic. He wondered if Bangalore was as bad. He wondered if the reason India was a country full of homeopaths, as he understood it to be, was because desperation made them thirsty for change. Maybe the drier the land the more a country's interest in water showed, and what that water meant to life. He recalled his friend V.L.'s talk in Bangkok, a challenge to the complacency of the *rest* of their challenges to the mainstream. His had seemed an especially enlightened talk, given the low calibre of competition among phrenologists and colon flushers.

Amidst the traffic chaos, stifling late-morning air, and beggars banging on the taxi's dirty windows for baksheesh, he took refuge in a catalogue of what he knew the world traveller B.J. Palmer had managed to harvest from his own journeys. The hustling son of D.D. had managed to bring chiropractic into the twentieth century, by introducing new, unorthodox practices – including the use of X-rays – and he'd proselytized abroad. Bartlett had had to acknowledge in his Hong Kong talk his predecessor's panache as a traveller. B.J.'s mementos were reputed to include Chinese Foo dogs, a ninety-ton Buddha, a bench from King Tut's tomb, eight Hindu idols carved from lava, a pair of record-setting clamshells, a gate from a Japanese temple, satsuma vases, cast-iron elks … and evidently a replica of the Black Hole of Calcutta. Bartlett now decided he was visiting the original model. The collector himself had deposited his mementos on campus, in the college he'd founded in opposition to his father's original school. Unlike father, son had a world view. Chiropractor as archaeologist.

'He was a screwball mixture,' Bartlett had readily admitted to his audience. From his missionary world travels, B.J. had also brought back a substantial flood of *brio* and shrunken heads. But strangest of his deeds, to Bartlett, was choosing to be *cremated*, then enshrined under a granite bust of himself in a bronze urn. B.J. had also had his father cremated and enshrined in ashes under *his* bust.

I doubted aloud in Hong Kong: a chiropractic Thomas, asking if destiny shouldn't have included the preservation of these men's bones in display cases, say, for future generations of students to learn chiropractic from its founders. He was trying to be honest, and historically shrewd. His profession had required those relics for its integrity. All it had now was dust. He was frank with his audience. Think of the Buddha's enshrined bones, he told them. Rarely did any creator of followers escape his disciples, nor should he, if consequences mattered. If the emblematic mattered.

If bones mattered.

Dean Cheaver had been listening.

'Ah, Dr Day,' said Ram Chandar, through a mask on his way into surgery. 'Please make yourself welcome in my office.'

His taxi had gone. So he had no choice but to watch the surgeon, touched by many hands, disappear down the corridor. The hands now turned to the chiropractor. In his white coat he became for the moment their new saviour. The sighted as well as blind pressed him for favour. Bartlett remained unmoved. He needed to be mean, resolved anyway, if he hoped to get to the bottom of this debacle over Chandar's role as his adviser.

Half an hour later the ophthalmologist reappeared, his mask dangling at his throat, a new trail of petitioners in his wake. They hovered on the threshold. Chandar accepted a cup of tea from his barefoot servant, who'd brewed Bartlett a cup with a red hair in it. Chandar looked weary, probably worn out from his fifteenth operation that morning. Bartlett didn't care. 'What's all this about extra freight costs?' he asked. The oculist was setting down his tea.

'Please explain,' urged Chandar, removing his spectacles to clean them on his soiled sleeve.

Bartlett elaborated on what had happened at the warehouse, saying he thought Chandar was supposed to have advised, not hosed him. 'Hosed? This means?' Ripped him off. Led him down the garden path. What was going on? Plus, what was this about a fee for Chandar himself? *Did* he expect a fee? Why hadn't Dean Cheaver mentioned him as part of the pipeline?

The surgeon was silent for a time. Bartlett regretted sounding so uppity. When Chandar did speak he said only, 'My young friend Dhuniya was very grateful for your kindness.'

Bartlett looked at him.

'I did nothing for that man,' he said.

'We all contribute something.'

'Tell me then. What am I supposed to contribute to Dr Chandar?'

He felt ambivalent, challenging this doctor so obviously devoted to good work.

The grey-headed surgeon replaced his glasses and began to pour tea into his saucer, blowing on it. He blew several times. He added a drop of milk. He picked out a hair. Then he set down his saucer without sipping from it and put his hands on the desk beside his cup.

He was matter of fact. 'Five thousand dollars is your usual donation to this clinic.'

'Really? That cheap?' said Bartlett.

'Your syndicate is very generous. Not for me, you understand. For us all.' He indicated the blind people at the open door to his office. 'In return for me supporting your exports, smoothing away wrinkles and such, with certain necessary certificates of origin ... my word here, my bribe there ... officials will release your bones to cross the ocean. It is necessary corruption.'

Five more thousand. Bartlett began to see red. *As in debt, alas.* How much of all this was crap? If Dean Cheaver was as financially meticulous as he'd been sartorially, wouldn't he have mentioned this fee? If Chandar was supposed to fill him in, why hadn't he?

What a country.

Chandar took up his saucer and began to sip. Between sips he said to his visitor, 'I suggested you try several dealers, did I not? V.K. Hyatt was one name only ... You need not have accepted Hyatt price.'

Like most Canadians, Bartlett was used to dealing up front, fair and square. He – *I* ...

What use disagreement now? He needed Chandar's understanding, not excuses, if he was going to talk his way out of this one. Pleading bankruptcy.

But Chandar disappointed him. 'I will send in my assistant to look after details.' He was looking at his pocket watch again. 'I have many patients to see. Yes,' he said, and smiled gently at his own pun. He repositioned the gauze mask, quietly retying it behind his grey head.

'Now, listen ...' began Bartlett.

Chandar pointed to his covered face, indicating his isolation from further speech or contamination. He exited at a brisk pace, down the corridor, toward his surgery where miracles mattered more than dickering for peanuts.

'Hey, listen ...' Bartlett called after, like some blind petitioner. And was left holding the tab for his own misadventure.

Not till Dr Seth entered, the assistant with sharp cheekbones, did he learn the clinic also expected a commission from the Hyatt Company itself for directing the American medical establishment its way. This news emerged after several pushy questions from Bartlett. It was the final punch in the head.

The young ophthalmologist paused when he noticed the chiropractor's drained expression. 'I have said something of a surprise, maybe?' His cheekbones flattened.

As Bartlett put it to himself that evening, from the blank canvas of his baroque bed: *Explained problem Cheekbones* STOP *Returned hotel to raise Chandar fee abroad* STOP ... His cassette turned. He'd just wired his father for financial assistance and felt stunted for having to beg.

He was a little afraid of falling asleep and deciding, in a dream, how he *wouldn't* pay his moral debt to an institution that gave vision to the poor and unwitting. Chandar actually trusted him to turn over five thousand dollars! *What am I doing here? What am I supposed to be doing?*

He still had his ticket for Africa.

He was such a late bloomer he felt invisible to the world of recorded history. He only wanted to report on how travel seemed to scuttle his voice ... how he needed to raise it every night by sounding for it. His dreams were responsible for carrying him into loneliness abroad, a country whose language he couldn't yet converse in.

... The next evening when he found out his flight would be delayed a day, on account of a strike by firemen at Dum Dum Airport, it wearied him to talk at all to the airline official who called, and he thought of Megan's slow recovery from the operation on her jaw. So many cripples. So full was he of ash in his soul, he felt unable to eat.

He rang down for a thermos of water.

He dropped a postcard to Megan, hinting of his mixed-up state: 'It sucks ... Blinded by greed, have nothing envious to report. Which should help your recovery and make you feel better. Love, Bee.'

The water arrived at his door long after he'd fallen asleep, dreaming of crows burning up on a beach brushed by hurricanes.

September, 1891

I - I - I ... just practising. How much longer before I find my way?

John Foster, amateur botanist and philosopher from Boston, was explaining passion to his wife. 'Once upon a time, Molly, say your friendly ...' Molly blushed rose. 'That, my bud, is how I begin a tale to catch your interest.'

He went on, 'I come to you and I touch your friendly. It starts to open. I can't get enough of the happiness it gives when I inhale it, Molly. I finally pluck it for my own.'

That was Sunday a month. I confess a weakness for bedroom conversations, following their lines so carefully my beatless heart is often in my voiceless throat. I could have done worse than spy on these two, wondering if their climax, when it came, might be the moment to claim recognition of my ancestors. And so discover, if not my own link, at least the chain that contains it.

Felt nothing, however. No telltale shudder. Nothing to give me a clue. Will it never be possible to know which chain to follow? So many possible chains ... Uncertainty overwhelms, unless I can go on pretending that someday I'll exist. I consider my chances. The probability of discovering where I might finally intersect with *myself* by adding up the chains associated with every couple ... Absurd!

I poke my nose into one generation after another, looking for activity in the bedchamber, hints from any likely source. By pretending that some day I'll exist, this allows me to predict a number of possible endings. The most likely I hope being birth. So many loose strands in a diary.

So many new lines in the city. Where do they go? In loops, that's where, for a nickel. On the new streetcars you can travel through space at six miles per hour. We are now among the advanced cities of the continent, so few years since Incorporation that ashes from the Big Fire are scarcely cold. Now Molly can ride to stores she used to go on foot to.

Electricity astonishes

her. Suddenly everywhere, coursing overhead through lines for the trolleys, telephones, lights. Four years since its arrival, says Molly, already we see and hear better because of it. We travel by interurban through bog and bear.

Where the streetcar doesn't run is to the hollow tree in the park, where people pose and picnic inside a cedar cave. This is where John comes with his tripod Sunday afternoons, to await holiday-makers from the beach below.

Unlike his other hobbies of botany and philosophy, he can foresee financial remuneration in photography. For example, he has studiously shot each of the new white *Empress* liners, from high in the park, hoping to sell his prints of terminating voyages to crowds watching the silk ships dock. The sleek liners linking Vancouver with

Shanghai, Yokohama – cities interested in exporting their teas and silk across the Pacific in record time. Then by fast trains to Montreal and New York. John sees a wide market for his prints.

He's a remittance man but stoops to odd jobs, such as roofing, to supplement his income for buying photographic equipment, new books on empiricism, and rhododendron cuttings from Darjeeling for his small flower garden.

He believes getting his hands dirty squares the mind for thoughtful conversation with his wife. I listen closely. I yearn for some clue. The city itself yearns for the future, understandable in a place still so young it smells of stump-burning, garbage, a bracing sea and the coniferous forest. *I* can't smell anything.

John's *a posteriori* reasoning leads him to believe the disease of

ambition is in making too much of moving ahead. 'All these new buildings, Molly, this boom in real estate and the accompanying greed … The race here for the dollar is worse than it was in Boston.'

Water he believes is timeless. You look at it and it offers no clue. It is as it will be and was. Lines appear abruptly in water then vanish. 'My name is written in it,' he confides to her on Labour Day, 'vis à vis a career, I guess, at my age …' 'We're just lucky to be expecting,' answers Molly. John looks surprised, pleased. 'Elsie Green and her husband are as barren as thistles.' 'Thistles aren't barren, Molly.' 'Well, she has never been up the stump, Mr Foster. You account for that with one of your flowers.'

Chapter 26

Man's Creation

BACK IN NAIROBI he said goodbye to Marcus, who was going on a two-day sex tour to Mombasa. 'The coast is guaranteed sybaritic. My treat, Bartlett, if you'd like to come. The experience of Patpong shouldn't be lost on you.' Marcus Reambeault couldn't understand why his friend would want to head west to a country shot out like some game park by sadistic soldiers. *Obviously, has no recollection of his advice to me in Bangkok.* '... Why be a masochist? The bones are hardly cold.' But he agreed to lend his friend the airfare, just as he had the cost of the safari they were returning from in the Masai Mara, to help Bartlett over his notable Calcutta losses. Bartlett thought if it came down to experience that mattered in the long run his own excursion would probably be more interesting than the flesh-pots of Mombasa. His was an invitation to help examine bones in Uganda. *A rerun?* A coincidence even of dubious distinction he felt Marcus should approve.

They shook hands. Marcus was sympathetic. He'd detected in his friend disillusionment with conferences at which the chiropractor spoke forcefully about an alternative medicine he didn't really trust. The faith healer could read his doubt, his aimlessness, even interpret in his body language clear signs of fraudulence. Marcus still seemed to trust his own faith-healing medicine and enjoy its artifice. It took him effortlessly back to creation. *Mine always takes me, it seems, in the direction of death.*

From the air it looked like a beautiful country, and it was, from the air ... *the shoreline of Lake Victoria, the far-off line of peaks in the Ruwenzori Range, then the rolling loam hills of the capital.* From the ground, well ... line-ups, soldiers, poverty. And worse, when he saw them, bones ... *not old ones, like a skull up Lake Turkana way, some roaming brother of Lucy's* ... No, these came from fresh graves, for use against the old regime, as if any more evidence were needed to condemn it. His mouth felt dry, his throat parched. The parallel evolution of tyrannical countries was no less obvious for his seeing such countries in different years. Up close their unwritten histories looked the same.

He rubbed his fingers back and forth over the crown of a skull piled up with other skulls in a vacant lot. In the sun it felt grainy and warm. Dogs sniffing the pile cowered, except for a hairless bitch, which turned on him. *I regretted coming, almost from the start.*

'Cheer up,' urged Chris Atkins, convinced the Canadian had done the right thing by joining him. 'Weren't you *doubting* in your lecture anybody could tell the true story of bones? I'd like to show you otherwise.' The short stocky American was a forensic expert specializing in large-city crime. Skeletal remains were his on-going specialty. 'This junket will end up costing you nothing, Dr Day, compared to what you'll pick up fee-wise in future lectures. Experience on the ground's invaluable.' This had sounded okay in Nairobi – not the fee, which Atkins presumed about, but the perspective the pilgrim might gain in another war-ruined country, as he continued to rethink his profession. Now in Kampala, alas, it sounded foolish. This city mocked his presumption.

Dr Aliamba, the host arranged for them by the American consular representative, was just as pessimistic as Bartlett. 'One army has supplanted another, this is all. It is the same immorality all over. Rape, tribal slaughter, revenge. Our resistance hiding in the bush gives citizens in town their only hope. The children's army is there in the bush. An army of boys who have lost their families in the last ten years ...'

Aliamba was a native pediatrician trained in Manchester. Like Bartlett he also wore his white coat outside his clinic, but for a starker reason: It afforded him safety, now that half his country's doctors had fled or died. Doctors were an endangered species and his white coat signalled non-aggression, neutrality, disinterest.

All of course lies. For this doctor confessed to a rebellious heart: 'I have committed many crimes of passion against this regime in my breast.'

It was Aliamba who pointed out the circling kites when the three men set out by taxi from the Speke Hotel. They were following the birds. Bartlett could detect traces of northern English dialect in his speech, and watched his hands for signs of distress. The pediatrician confessed to exhaustion.

I think I saw why ... Having shared the cost of a five-thousand-shilling ride with Chris Atkins from the airport, Bartlett soon discovered monetary inflation was nothing here compared to the hyperinflation of death. This time the ride was short, while the journey itself began to feel interminable. The three men, plus the taxi driver, stood in a vacant lot under the hot afternoon sun. The dead people all around them, their bones, buzzed steadily with flies.

The chiropractor gaped. *Felt destitute…*

In a less murderous time these dead would be walking about, their bones would, buying milk or chewing glazed candy. Worrying about chiggers under toenails. Tying up yellow bandanas, back-slapping a surprised lottery winner, scolding disobedient children in front of their cousins. Instead, dug up for the gaze of those left to gaze, they lay in a heap to discredit a fat stupid general who'd fled abroad to escape his crimes. Memento Brute.

Still. The guy who'd chased him out, and encouraged this digging-up, couldn't stop the slaughter. Was even rumoured to encourage it, the premature decay of flesh into bone. So the past continued in the future.

'Who can say for certain when these people were killed?' Dr Aliamba asked Atkins. He was watching the American writing quietly in his notebook. 'The foreign soldiers are just as evil as our own were, roaming game parks, the towns, poaching life. The killing continues. Life does not go on.'

Indeed, once-prosperous coffee and cotton plantations stayed ravaged, tea and sugar exports stayed cancelled. And the capital's Indian merchants remained in exile, because the former dictator, now rumoured to be in Arab hands, was talking about a comeback. Milton Aliamba thought the refugees from his country were adding to a new configuration of the world.

On this first stop the stocky steak-fed Atkins closed his notebook and commented only briefly. 'I'd have to say they're probably a mixed bag, these skulls here.' He tugged the bill of his Mets cap. 'Mostly killed at different times. My guess is a show dump. Not very organic. Not a lot of clues without the rest of the skeletal framework.'

This dump was more or less in the centre of Kampala. For the purposes of his research Atkins believed they'd have to get farther out.

Interested in skeletal 'markers', the American was writing a study of appendicular stress and he appreciated Milton's cooperation in showing them around the capital's available bone piles – in exchange for listening to the pediatrician's recitation of medical needs. He only half listened. He'd promised to do what he could when he got back to the States, talk up the desperate situation here to some charity folk he knew with access to badly needed medicines. 'I'll get on to it, Milton.'

I don't dislike him exactly, but he doesn't see the forest for the trees. Flesh, Bartlett meant, for the bones.

Few real trees remained.

Their taxi sped them toward more bone deposits on the outskirts of the capital, this time unofficial and undisturbed deposits. Maybe it was the heat, but he saw fewer citizens in the streets than he expected to. As they drove Milton Aliamba discussed measles and tuberculosis, ignoring the fly that took up residence on his sideburn. He scratched his black cheek. Apart from homicide, measles were now his country's main killer. Measles and T.B.

'Ten years ago, three-quarters of our children were immunized against tuberculosis ... today less than one-tenth. I feel what our children need most is immunization of hope ...'

'Yeah, I agree,' said Atkins. 'That's a main requirement.' He didn't sound in the least down about the prospect for hope. A member of the New York City Police Department, he was spending his entire holiday abroad doing field research. He was looking ahead. His devotion to bones made it impossible for him to impose speed bumps on his enthusiasm for a country that helped to drive his work.

Grief. Without it you're a quack. Bartlett needed water. He was thirsty.

On the capital's outskirts they learned the curfew was in looser effect and night-time murders consequently more frequent. The driver drew up beside a nondescript field of leafless scrub. He pointed to the sun, unstuck his shirt at the armpits, and made no move to get out of the car. He did suggest the victims here would be fresher and more noisome. Not even the kites had shown up yet. The air was very still.

Chiropractor and forensicist climbed out of the taxi, immediately up to their knees in brambles. Like being on safari, thought Bartlett, but with the game all vanished. They wandered off in their own directions, until Atkins disappeared. Bartlett found nothing untoward and began to think they'd come to the wrong place. A smell of earth carried him back to his father's small vegetable plot. 'Hey, Dr Day, lookit this,' called the American, suddenly erect in the scrub.

He went over. Atkins had been examining some half-buried bones and had discovered several abnormal facets. He knelt down again to tap a spinal column with his pen.

'... This woman was maybe twenty-seven, eight.' He was sounding pleased with his deduction. 'If you know about African women, Dr Day, this one likely came to the city from her village, where she carried children on her back. These markers, see? ... show pressure at the bottom of her spine.' The stocky forensicist opened up his notebook to record her story. 'Axial stress is always interesting.'

It was like being with a detective, which is what Atkins had become before realizing it, studying paleontology and physical anthropology in Chicago, along with criminology as a minor. He'd come to believe characterizing bones could be a useful tool for specialists, because up till now criminology had never paid enough attention to victims' remains. You could learn a lot from bones. You could learn a lot from Africa.

'Every one of these bones,' he continued, 'has its own tale, if you know where to look.' He now led the chiropractor eight feet west. He knew it was west because he was using a compass.

'Take this guy who squatted a lot – how can I tell? I can tell by different markers, Dr Day, here at the bottom of the shinbone, here at the knee, and at the hip. Like those fellas –' he pointed to two or three squatting children Bartlett hadn't noticed. They had appeared out of nowhere to watch the visitors from a little mound. The children looked kindergarten age and parentless. 'Squatting is common from here back to Kingdom Come. A normal way to sit, only we're not used to it. Just like talking to police academies feels weird till you get used to that.'

He spoke with assurance, accustomed to cities and crowds. *He has the ease of a vegetable vendor.* Barrel-chested, he wore a cotton golf shirt that seemed to Bartlett beloved of off-duty police detectives, the ones in TV shows, and on-duty newspaper reporters in the same shows. Not to mention faith healers.

'... Most folks, even chiropractors I'll bet, never see human remains. That's how come I figured you needed bucking up after that lecture. Don't misunderstand, I enjoyed what you had to say, I just thought you should have a chance to press some real bones instead of your plastic dummy.'

Singing birds.

'I hate to say it,' he said, making sure Milton was out of earshot, 'but this country is the mother lode. That's what I was trying to tell you in a roundabout way over dinner in Nairobi. The places I like to visit, a normal traveller wouldn't be caught dead in. Holidays are my work.'

They wandered farther afield, to find the remains of a more recent victim, face down, with scraps of dried skin and clothing still stuck to its bones. Bartlett watched the other man poke and prod for some time, pausing to take notes. He was kneeling on the ground, indifferent to the dust.

Then, in a confidential voice, he indicated to Bartlett where a bullet had entered the victim's back. 'See, second rib, smooth round chip through the top half? The bone break is back to front ...'

He looked up. 'Things follow backwards from this. You go on to guess the velocity of the bullet, which then lets you say if the victim was running away, or standing still when struck. Care to guess?'

'Standing still.'

'Standing still, sir, you're talking pointblank, and I don't think that's what you mean.'

'No.'

'Up close, see, a bullet penetrating the rib cage from behind – assuming it misses the spine altogether, which is clearly the case with these vertebrae – is going to blast hairline fractures up and down this rib like spaghetti fossils. Not the case here, is it?'

'Just a smooth chip.'

'Right. Plus, don't forget the logic factor. If I was going to execute a man from behind, I'd do it through the head. Certain death. Less certain, otherwise. So what we're looking at is standard plot. A bullet in the back is always a basic clue to the victim's trying to escape ... I guess you don't read many murder mysteries.'

'Fewer and fewer.'

'No problem.' He removed his baseball cap and wiped the band inside with a handkerchief. '... Because – and this'll come as pleasant news to you, Dr Day – in *this* case the books'd be wrong and you'd be right.'

'Right.'

Atkins leant closer to peer with a magnifying glass, to touch the rib with his pen nib. 'My opinion's based on the oblique angle of entry. I don't know ... maybe you noticed this first?'

'Right.'

Atkins regarded him, dubiously. 'Well, I take my hat off to you. 'Cause my considered opinion's this victim was shot up close and from the blind side. The bullet probably ripped through the lung and managed to nip the rib on its way out the front door. Here, take a look at the kneecap.'

Bartlett, curious, squatted down beside the American.

'Note the clue I've turned up on this left cap. See it?' He offered his guest the magnifying glass. 'Barest hint of scraping. That tells me something. This guy crawled for a good hundred feet, is my guess, from the highway into this field, trying to hide. You could probably reconstruct the murder. Guy is brought by vehicular transport out here, pushed out the door, has his blindfold removed, then told to run for his life. Hoo boy. Pow. Except this guy ran faster than his assassin could get off a decent shot, right?'

Dr Aliamba joined them, hands behind his back, sombre.

Atkins shook his head and stood up. 'Hard to date these stories inside two or three years, unless the skin's still hanging.' He looked back down. 'Which it is, in this case. Six months ago, maybe.' He made another note before clipping his ballpoint pen to his spiral binding.

He walked thirty feet deeper into the field, stooped, picked up a skull and studied it.

Bartlett listened for birds. *Not even a baobab tree in this dump.* Nothing in the sky. He still expected kites.

'This is interesting,' called Atkins. 'Look here.' Bartlett and Milton trekked over. 'See where this skull's worn away at the sides? We're into heavy weather, sir, with this sort of squeezing. Probably a vice, poor sod.'

He knelt down in the dust to examine the disturbed nest of bones at his feet. Posthumously gnawed by dogs, he suggested. He took off his watch and handed the heavy black expansion bracelet to Bartlett, who noted the wiry hairs sprouting from his wrist. Atkins handed him his notebook and pen, his magnifying glass and compass.

'Hey, check this out,' he said. 'The shoulder joints …? Looks like the heavy-duty boys suspended this lady from the doorjamb and ruined her balls and sockets. You don't see these markings in the States.'

He looked grimly satisfied by his discovery. 'Have to travel to find this kind of stuff.' It was exactly the kind of stuff he'd come to East Africa to discover.

Recovering time and notebook, glass and compass, he began to peer and scribble, pry and write. The sun baked the sterile field as he wrote. 'Hate to have to say it, Dr Day, in such a sad state of affairs, but human rights activists might find my study very telling. Not to say useful.'

His enthusiasm made Bartlett thirstier. He felt an urgent need to check out of this country, but was going to have to hang around for the return flight Atkins had reserved. He regretted coming. The American had perfected a divorce from grief and a way to profit from bones that boosted his self-esteem. His profession cultivated detachment. He was headed in another direction from Bartlett.

The Canadian decided to swear off any more foreign lectures on chiropractic. With the state his finances were in this wouldn't be any problem. He owed his father, he owed Marcus. This whole trip, including the debacle in Calcutta, was costing him a bundle. He had his ticket home, true, yet once there he would have to confront the dilemma of making chiropractic more profitable to pay off his debts.

As he lost his faith in it, his profession seemed a growing trap.

2.

That evening the dim dining room of their hotel reminded him how much better conditions had been on safari in the Serengeti earlier that week. Even listening to Marcus going on about the Big Bang, waving his hand at the crepuscular sky, with the stars popping out like rabbits over Masai Mara, was a lot better than this powercut. Snatches of Swahili had been heard coming from the cook tent, where a throng of baboons capered under an acacia tree and the smell of pot roast settled on the evening air.

'This is the answer,' Marcus had exclaimed of the vast preserve and its dome. 'Five hundred dollars for two and a half days ... a bargain. If we think inflation's ruining us, we should think again. It's made us what we are to enjoy all this. The exploding stars –'

He'd listened to the faith healer telling them all at the campfire the story of Creation. 'Snap, crackle ... pop – symmetry breaking like a bone, Bartlett, sending everybody and their dog off booking cabins, two by two, on the Ark? Yea, brethren, pain arose but who understood it? Soap operas flourished. Shipboard romances. Healers like Dr Day and me were discovered onboard working the deck. It's stormy and folks are seasick. *We* do our best to dispense cures with limited means. We ask one thing: "Here, love, tell me where it hurts, take a load off your mind." *My* advantage is I believe in the Book of Life. You know, "In the beginning was the Word ..." We're both appreciated for our cures. Dr Day here once had an elephant in Bangkok remember him from somewhere else. Right, Bart? Then it rolled over and died.'

Marcus had gone on to the assembled party about a sense of wonder.

How his father used to call him Markle-Sparkle, because of his wonder at the stars. '... I suppose this became the story of my life. I could've been an astronomer, or an American. My whole life cries out for circles and sometimes it hurts.' He was drinking gin and tonic. 'If I talk coincidence sometimes, I'm talking coinciding centres in concentric circles, at the heart of things. I'm talking a hole in the middle of my clock.'

It seemed an odd confession to make ...

'... A handless clock that keeps us on our toes – wondering? I'm beginning to think the whole world conspires to coincidence. If my brain was bigger I could see its shape better. Like the mind of God, holding Time in His head at the second of Creation. I could see how things tied in, found each other – blessedly, how yearning disappeared.'

Everybody was listening to the fire. Whether or not they saw the hole in Marcus's clock they gave no clue, except to pay him the compliment, or rather the indifference, of their stillness.

'It's my humble belief, which basically accounts for my being a faith healer, folks, all our worlds are looking for a single centre. Like this campfire. At home my job's trying to find a hearth like this one for the faithful. I have them hold hands around me in a circle. I place my hands on their heads, one at a time, and we listen together. I take them back to Genesis. I tell them *listen. Yearn.* I press down and sometimes, if the vibes are right, we strike oil. Somebody's suffering matches his yearning – with so much symmetry his pain disappears.'

He'd lifted his glass. 'Coincidence, I feel, is definitely a force ...' He sipped from his drink. 'There's a sum,' he told them, 'over and beyond history. I'm uncertain about its total effect on my wallet, or even on where I'm supposed to end up. I travel from soup to nuts by every imaginable airline. How fast I'm going makes me forget where I'm at. I get homesick and don't know what for. Even at home I feel fractured. I'm always yearning to be somewhere else.'

'This ees somewhere else,' said the widow from Paris, the only woman among them. She was wearing jodhpurs.

In the two days that had followed, jackal and ostrich, kongoni and eland, buffalo and topi, had come forth upon the grasslands, just as the Cheetah Tracks brochure had promised. The chiropractor marvelled at the extended vertebrae of the reticulated giraffe, at how well – in what harmony with its limbs, for all the rocking stress at its joints – this animal galloped. Their guide told them stories of wildebeest appearing in their millions between August and November from the dry Tanzanian plains. The little safari spotted lions and zebra. With his new video camera from Hong Hong Marcus recorded Masai men spear-dancing in weird hairdos for the tourists. *The man is everywhere ...*

Retiring to his tent each night, in dread of the noisy courtship of the tree hyrax, Bartlett had slumbered uneasily with debt in mind. He recorded the night, by letting the rest of his cassette run out on the unnatural noises of a continent. He lacked the heart of a lion. A tsetse fly or something was chewing his elbow.

On their last morning, at the balloon base in Little Governor's Camp, the faith healer recorded his most interesting sighting so far in Paradise: the spectacular swelling of the three balloons their party was to drift in over the savannah, eating breakfast west of the Mara River.

Marcus had been shooting it all, preparing to climb into his basket for the reverse angle, where he could peer back down on creation. The bulging spheres impressed him.

'I happen to believe a genius, Bartlett, can keep in mind the grain of sand and the whole beach at the same time. But the guy who thrills me is the one who remembers to bring the beachball. Bill's brought the beachball!'

'Full of hot air,' answered Bill Sands, their rugged guide. 'You ought to be able to find an elephant to shoot from up there, Reambeault.'

For an hour and a half they floated like planets over a pristine country, from where Bartlett thought they must have looked gloriously beside the point. He and Marcus shared a gondola. They shared Marcus's binoculars, peering down on the wrinkles they could read in the grey backs of the African elephants. These galleons were moving west, undisturbed by heavenly bodies, ears like sails catching the faintest savannah winds.

'I should tell you, for what it's worth,' said Marcus, recording the Cradle of Creation in all its Edenic splendour. 'Our first night? Madame Laflame showed up at the tent and I had to pretend to be asleep ...' *He threw the line away.* 'Look, a water buffalo.' Bartlett was scratching his elbow and missed it.

In the afternoon they'd all climbed back into Land Cruisers and Land Rovers – servants and guests, chiropractors and faith healers – to return across the Great Rift Valley, east again to Nairobi. *And so it was, very Heaven.*

3.

Here now over dinner, after the lights went out, the waiters brought in candles. They were used to powercuts. The long shadows seemed to suit their cravings for anonymity. 'You don't eat a lot, do you?' said Atkins, offering to help himself to Dr Day's uneaten steak. They'd already had to cancel showers before dinner because of the disrupted water supply. The visitors felt gamey, not having showered since this morning at the Intercontinental in Nairobi. Their dinner guest, Dr Aliamba, said he was used to showering at three a.m., when the water supply at his house could better be counted on. He ate up everything on his plate.

The American was expressing satisfaction at how his research was going. He stopped chewing his meat to fill them in. As *the* expert on bone markers, or so he let them know, he was counting on this study to make his reputation – in the area of sports med and the workplace, and in his own field, crime. The variety here would help him at home. At home he was inundated with stress markers, and any new experiences abroad would help him with victims' stories back there. At home they were always fishing bones out of the Hudson. He was expected to reconstruct their histories: murdered, drowned – maybe both? How old was the victim? And lifestyle?

'… Like an enlarged forearm might suggest a tennis player or a baseball pitcher. Maybe, by remote chance, a javelin thrower. You never know: any missing javelin throwers in the New York area? How 'bout Cleveland? These kind of connections go with the job, ipso facto. You've got other clues too. In the jaw, for instance, an irregularity could tell me the victim was a tuba player. Or that he'd broken his jaw once in a fistfight. There's bowler's ankle, carpenter's elbow, even a jockey's instep. An individual's experience of the world creates his or her own bone marker. I don't want to get cute with the fingers – but you wouldn't rule out mud-wrestling when the temptation would be to fall for the cello, right? An open take on all kinds of case histories is part of the job.'

He looked at Dr Aliamba in the candlelight. 'With my kind of background in paleontology, Milton, I have to handle a lot of questions on diet and childhood diseases. I'll do spectroscopic analyses, if I have to … But it's just more interesting to see how the bone by itself can tell a story. More responsible, too. Science is more subjective than you might think.'

He now mopped up the gravy in his plate with his last piece of steak. He was intending to call his study *Once upon a Bone: Resetting Life from the Skeleton*.

'... You know, light and heavy at the same time. That's because there's no such thing as typical death. Markers abound, if you know where to look for the buggers. You just have to want to look. Violent death is the given. It's always pretty absurd. What I do is work backwards from there.'

After dinner Milton suggested a visit to the adjoining bar, called the Veranda, where he repeated how glad he was the other two had chosen to visit his country. He ordered himself a Shirley Temple. *If that's the right name for water and water.* He didn't sound very hopeful about his ability to cut through red tape in order to land the medical supplies his clinic needed from abroad, and which Chris had promised to look into.

'Judas Priest,' he suddenly swore.

The waiter had spilled something on his white coat. The pediatrician sounded peevish and tired. 'I'm going to small pieces in a handbasket,' he explained. 'This country. No water to even wash my coat.' Milton Aliamba laughed. 'We have even lost the capacity to train our own waiters. How can we ever hope to produce our own chiropractors and forensic people?'

Bartlett had been trained to expect irony from M.D.s. He heard no trace of it now in Milton's lament. Instead, an invitation from him to tea tomorrow afternoon at the Lake Victoria Hotel. Then they might all try a stroll in the Botanical Gardens, except Milton thought the birds there probably dead from drought. The view from Wireless Hill might still be pleasant though. They could visit there too.

The next morning Bartlett wished his flight back to Nairobi was today and not tomorrow. He declined Chris Atkins's offer to accompany him farther into the countryside, explaining how he felt feverish and unlikely to relish the pounding promised by bad roads. Besides, Milton wanted him to drop into his clinic, if he could find the time.

'No problem,' said the American. 'I'm used to drudgery like this.'

The chiropractor stayed in bed until eleven. When he went downstairs for breakfast he ran into Mr Strajik who did not, at first, recognize Bartlett.

'Yes,' said Bartlett, reminding him, 'you must still be with the Red Cross.'

'Of course,' said Mr Strajik, 'now I recall, you were fatter. How is it we find ourselves together again in the same hurricane's eye? You are with what agency now, please?'

4.

In Nairobi he ran into Marcus at the airport, awaiting his own connecting flight out of Kenya. If the chance meeting appealed to the faith healer's sense of wonder, he didn't mention it, eager instead to expand on the young black skin he'd been enjoying in Mombasa. 'It's more *alive*, that's the only way to put it, Bartlett. You can smuggle it into your room, into your dreams, like fresh fruit. I don't buy the sex-fear thing one guy was talking about on the beach. V.D. can't kill you. Eden is stained but it's inhabitable. You should've been there, mon ami, I swear. The Nyali Beach Hotel bent over backwards.'

So they said goodbye a second time in Nairobi. Marcus was flying home via London, and Bartlett was flying home on Dwight's cut-rate ticket via Rome. 'You'd think we were multinational tycoons,' said Marcus. 'Let's plan to meet at the next conference, wherever. Lima.'

When Bartlett replied doubtfully, the faith healer shrugged, convinced they'd run into one another again soon enough. 'Time is funny that way. Africa used to be the only place you could come for a decent cup of coffee. Now we've got so many continents to jet to for coffee, Bartlett, we never see each other at home. That's the price of Canada. Continents creep back together, we stay apart. Arrivederci!'

Such a cosmic view, I don't see how God has time for the competition.

The next morning in Rome he went along to the crypt of Santa Maria della Concezione, near the Palazzo Barberini. It meant a short taxi ride of tens of thousands of lire, whose dilapidated colours bore no relation to any value he could determine, except to the way his driver's temper moderated as he added more and more notes to the ones already in his palm. His talk became friendlier, and no less voluble.

Italians never stopped talking. Those inside the crypt's iron-gated chapels sounded like they'd come to a wiener roast. The framed memento mori on one door, in four languages, did not intimidate these pilgrims in the least:

That which you now are, we were,

That which we now are, you will be.

What these words personified, he discovered, were the mute bones of four thousand friars. From whitewashed ceilings and walls their bones hung in rococo designs through half a dozen chapels, where skeletons compiled whole altars and alcoves.

I don't know ... maybe I'm searching for a mate for Bea.

His life had turned into a picaresque journey and he felt faintly ridiculous, hounding grief. Truth seemed to languish in abeyance. *And me in my profession, a dinosaur.* The chief potboiling message of this dusty place – 'to remind visitors of the drama of life which ends in death' – had somehow lost its capacity to discover God.

Skipping a frankfurter in favour of mineral water in St. Peter's Square, he entered the Vatican Museums refreshed. In the long Gallery of the Maps, he came on visitors crowded round a table where a slender old woman in a smock was painting from a chair sanctioned with a papal insignia. Her canvas was tiny. She was working, glasses on the end of her nose, with a magnifying glass in one hand and a brush of microscropic hairs in the other. Perpetually poised, her hand never appeared to move. He could make out she was copying a picture, itself a copy, onto a brooch. The chiropractor twisted through the onlookers for a closer peek.

The woman was explaining her ... Michelangelo's ... *Man's Creation* ... *Eve's Temptation* ... selling piece by ... in the gallery shop.

He'd been on his way to the Sistine Chapel, for a reclining look at the ceiling in all its cosmic glory. But it was this miniature, the practically invisible, that fascinated Bartlett for the brief time he was gathered with his fellow tourists squinting at the tiny ivory.

He soon realized he'd thought little of Megan since Calcutta. He wondered, upon arriving at the noisy chapel, if he should return and buy her one of the painter's brooches to hang between her breasts.

... but when I brought back that old woman's skill with her tools, her eternal patience with customers, her firm hands ... I was remembering not the woman who cuts my hair, but artisans at Hyatt & Co., indistinguishable from the Master.

He told this later to his diary, abed above motorbikes whining in the Eternal City's streets.

Eve's eyes, he discovered, were looking sideways in *Man's Creation*, expansive white spaces the brush must have placed in an instant, and her lips, yet unkissed, in an arabesque wiggle. It was hard to see what the fuss was about without knowing, he supposed, lying here in the noise, whether you were looking at a mere detail or at the very centre of the world.

May, 1887

My memory, if only I could find one. A telescope

Today, closeted with the superintendent's young wife, thought I saw my great-grandfather on the tracks below. Who can say? I saw this boy bend down to place a penny on the rail. Wanted badly for it to be him.

He must have been hoping to flatten it into a sheet. The boy wavered in the heat rising from the railbed. He was awaiting a return on his investment. The entire city was awaiting the train's arrival.

Listened jealously to a baby whimpering in an upstairs bedroom, and to the tall mother gone up to comfort it, clucking the way mothers do when their egg has

hatched. Lost sight of the boy.

Had sidled into this parlour on my way down to the terminal. Houses draped in flags and cedar boughs to celebrate arrival of first transcontinental train. Beribboned horses, abandoned to nosebags, had finished their mash and started sneezing into jute. No one to water them.

Then we heard the whistle. 'She's coming!' People poured down the bluff to the decorated arch. Festooned boats whistled in the harbour. Sawmills whistled. The train itself shrieked and commenced clanging from a great distance. The band struck up. The crowd cheered.

For a locomotive that had just puffed across

the entire Dominion, linking Atlantic to Pacific, it seemed spry. Somewhere underneath its wheels an image of the queen was being flattened for a souvenir. The decorated locomotive shook and thundered into the station.

Could see the mayor preening grandly for his speech of welcome, near a banner announcing OCCIDENT GREETS ORIENT and CONFEDERATION ACCOMPLISHED. On the platform he prepared to address his remarks to the railway's superintendent, to arriving passengers, to the crowd.

'It is the nature of our city, barely a year old, ladies and gentlemen, that

< 478 >

everybody here comes from somewhere else ...' Cheers from all the immigrants. Am imagining what he said for the mayor's words didn't carry up the bluff. Could see his lips moving, however. He nodded toward the superintendent.

'We may take it, sir, that the CPR is the wave of the future. This great line of yours, Mr Superintendent, now becomes a world line, as soon as promised ships from Japan begin unloading their ...'

Applause.

'We are thus both the terminal city and the originating city. The sun sets here on Her Majesty's empire. But ladies and gentlemen, boys and girls, it rises too! Today a magnificent line has crossed Canada and we intend to prosper!'

His Worship's lips fluttered on. Observing with mock gravity, I believe, that while it might be impossible to say where a train would be at any given time – or even how fast such a wonder might be speeding across yellow prairie and over purple mountain – we had the superintendent's word the train's schedule would allow us to know of its arrival to the *minute*. Today, the time of 12:45 p.m. had been a truly remarkable prediction, and the first beyond number, His Worship trusted, of arrivals and departures foretold.

He noted in closing that across the locomotive he had observed the words 'Arcadia' and 'Eldorado' – placed there he presumed in honour of its destination.

'Well, who among us will argue with such perspicacity? We are the ideal destination of a continent! It is we who have within us the formula for uniting east and west in a model city! Let us rejoice at our destiny today!'

The band struck up, and there was a rush on board by men and boys to swank in the red plush seats of a Pullman coach. Nowhere in sight was my youthful ancestor.

I could see smoke from stump fires in the distance. The tracks in that direction were now empty. The baby upstairs had stopped whimpering. The mother descended to the dining room, where she was expecting her superintendent husband and the mayor for lunch.

Was already on my way out for a souvenir. My vanished forebear had placed that coin on the track, doubtless wondering how big a sheet the train would forge when all wheels had ground it down. I doubted it could have avoided dislodgement by the very first wheel, and descended for a look under boxcars.

Chapter 27

Wisdom, Like Desire

HE THOUGHT THE SKIN on his glans in the morning looked like a wrinkled acorn if he fell asleep wearing a condom the night before. His ejaculated sperm conked out there, shrivelled up and died, and it took two or three days when he remembered, bathing, to pick off this false skin in patches, where his real skin would reemerge with the satin texture of a new shoot. So he tried not to forget, before falling asleep, to remove his equipment and drape it like a herniated eel over the clock radio, where it slowly expired in the green digital light.

'Equipment' was Megan's name for a condom, and she would reach over for its plastic pouch from flat on her back, extracting the wafer before pinching its teat, rolling the rubber down with the hand of a strumpet. She stroked it to get the wrinkles out. She wet it all over with the mouth of hunger.

She suffered.

She could no longer open her jaw comfortably wider than one knuckle's width. So, while her mouth for him was a blissful fit, for her it hurt to suck, though she preferred sucking to licking. Fellatio let her think she could impersonate desire without him knowing. And he tried to reciprocate her good intentions. He conducted what he imagined to be the secret overtures of her hairdresser's dreams. He ran fingers along her arteries with his refined sense of anatomy, brought her nerve ends to the surface like feeding fish, emerged dripping from every dark place he could think to visit with his tongue. She offered him her world. Bartlett travelled overland.

No destination short of marriage would really satisfy Megan. Did he love her? *She has* ... he'd concede *the skin of nubility*. He had no problem praising her skin, its elasticity, petal softness, willingness to dimple where it ought not when he cupped it with an adoring palm. He told her so. He praised her Glenda Jackson cheekbones.

These dogged ruses saved him from having to say what he didn't feel.

His diary encouraged something closer to what he did feel: a remembrance of matters too much with him. He rambled in it like a traveller, because of where it always led, back to sleep with another day of sightseeing done, with maybe one memory per dozen to cherish into dream. He worried about his practice. He reviewed his patients. He reported on his love life, looking to reformulate its basic chemistry.

Megan's favourite part of *him*, even more attended to than his oak tree, was his hair. 'Too thick, too oily,' she'd cluck in jealous humour, pestering him to let her wash and cut it. Pleased to have her do this, he lapsed lazily into the role of customer, patient, beneficiary of her blowdriven shaping. His hair, as a result, was the only part of him to appear unvagrant and spruce, instead of the natural crown for his habitual untidiness. She offered him her world. It surprised him it was no longer enough.

The trouble with all her sucking and washing was Megan no longer shared herself, which put him off. It was just easier for her, whether at her place or his, if he played guest and did all the talking. She could no longer converse the way she used to, because of her jaw. The bone had refused to set right, even after a second operation to insert artificial bone chips. She found toothpaste acted more like glue than lubricant. It hurt her to talk, except through clenched teeth.

She no longer talked, for example, of a bungalow of their own. That dream was gone – gone even had her jaw been normal. No one in their positions, even pooling incomes, could hope to buy more than a shanty with mortgage rates now on the moon. In theory a small window of opportunity had existed last year, which might've allowed them to finance a small East End house, after Bartlett paid off the mortgage on his practice. But as a favour to the Irvings, and to be in on the travel explosion, he'd gone and ... and that was the end of the house hope, which was Megan's hope anyway. The window of opportunity got boarded up

His own city and Dwight's were different. True, both men believed in gratification for people willing to pay, but his patients didn't travel and were inclined to believe in miracles. Dwight's customers were skeptical and better off. The kind of party guests downstairs, people Reesa might mingle with as an interviewer – alderpersons, indicted rock stars, young financiers, fellow broadcasters – weren't the sort to come and see a chiropractor. Their bones were taken care of by body shops full of mirrors and punchy music. They could afford to holiday outside their country.

It was Megan who believed East Side people ought to go their own way. 'Us – you, Bee – we don't belong in the same house as the Irvings and upscale party people. We're from the other side of Main.'

At this class-scarred snit, they both laughed. The motion causing his cock to tingle nicely, then make a flatulent noise when it encountered the air pocket inside her body, making them laugh louder, at the rude air trying to squeeze out past his rubberized plug. *Plug. Joke. Mortgage rates are drowning me, what's to laugh about?* His pain like Megan's had come without warning or justice. Nothing conspired to cure it. A whole dike had burst. They sometimes thought each other's shoulders would keep them afloat.

Not quite. They'd seen one another less often after her first operation, because circumstances of her recuperation discouraged it. Then later, when he was away chasing lions and bones, and after that when her jawbone refused to heal, he tried to decide if he wanted to go on seeing someone who had marriage so much in mind, as a cure for her own cheerless attitude. Their conversations no longer outlasted haircuts. At her salon this wouldn't have mattered. There, she could escape expectation by listening, asking customers some question to get them talking, keep them going. But with him, also a listener by profession, she revealed herself as having nothing to say. She'd grown vague, like mist.

By mist he meant Megan's sense of wonder, finding no particular articulation. It refused to particularize the world ... *Seade jae bcxe budfa coos. Conversation should take us somewhere, but with Megan I never feel like we leave home.*

Poor Megan, he kept thinking, and recognized this as fatal. The leather ankle boots she wore, aping Brixton fashion, and her little razor blade dangling from one ear. A safety pin to keep together an old brassiere he happened to favour, and his cameo-of-Eve gift between her breasts, stubbornly scratching skin. Her oil of patchouli too freely applied. The little scar on her thumb, where she was once bitten by a child who didn't want as much off the top as his mother had asked her to take. He felt tender toward Megan in fragmented ways. Like a child she took her parts for granted but was unable, or unwilling, to see herself whole. Maybe this was at the marrow of her punkish fashion. The fashion current in the West, which to him seemed sad. She seemed vaguely in the business of revenge.

Sad.

I worry about becoming a prig.

He was still losing weight.

He fretted about compromise, as he continued taking her to bed, a place where her mouth in motion pleased him a lot more than in a restaurant, where neither of them had boo to say over a scampi dinner of intended conciliation. He knew the way he felt about Megan wasn't how he wanted to feel about the woman he was going to bed with. He felt he was taking her for granted.

No longer felt, as he came, her skeleton in his arms, or grief imagining her dead. She offered no history of experience he felt he could cherish.

As a lover, listening for an empty cage, he felt like an impersonator.

2.

Maybe because of what else was on his mind, he felt distracted from telling her the truth and ending their affair. An investment scheme now occupied him like a foreign army. He'd given in to the idea of collaboration, not so much out of greed as the need to survive. He'd tried ignoring the temptation to get in deeper than he was already, and discovered he couldn't. Couldn't afford to ignore the odds against rescue if he didn't collaborate, not to mention the chance of getting ahead if he did. Bartlett wanted out of chiropractic. But he needed to raise capital in order to be free.

It made him feel like an aging Aloysius, scrambling to take advantage of what he could see just dimly down the road. He'd put Lois on standby for calls and bought himself a beeper. It all seemed so futile.

Not that he felt disloyal acting important. He thought expanding his life at a time of general contraction, plotting to get further into the marketplace when his doubts about it inclined him to withdraw, might help to ... *who knows?*

The truth was ugly. He was having trouble meeting payments on his remortgaged practice, which weren't supposed to be *his* payments at all. Dwight had intended to conquer the world. Instead he seemed to have caved in to it and shrunk. By having to suspend payments, temporarily, Dwight was no longer covering his loan. So Bartlett was carrying him month to month.

Rates were now twenty percent and rising. It was unbelievable. Everybody said so. Yet no amount of published or broadcast outrage made any difference: The economy was being strangled. Some said it was already comatose. Inflation, the villain, still twitched, but seemed as likely to rise again as a used condom. Speculators were no longer bullish. Demand for goods and services had gone flat. *Gone ape is what they did during the boom.* A root change in the sum of reality had taken everybody, previously impressed with the rampant meltdown of the economy, by surprise. Loss and sterility were in ascendancy. Fallout was spreading fast.

His mortgage was an open one, which meant it floated higher every Thursday when the Bank of Canada set its weekly rate. Businesses without life rafts were going under. *Banks are putting the squeeze on collaborators like me.* It was weird, carrying a friend you trusted to know his market, who'd always sounded like he knew the earth and how to see it from the brightest angles, seeing him destroyed. Christ, pouring money into a dark hole, with no prospect of Herodotus Travel ever shining again.

Dwight shrank, even as he grew heavier with debt. Bartlett watched him grow heavier. *I thrash him at squash now. Jowls wiggle when he runs. Gets his boxer shorts tangled in the locker room, stepping into them.* With the dislocation of once common expectations, things were turning inside out for Dwight. *A cruel joke.*

The Irvings were swearing to pay him back with interest as soon as possible. But the possible had begun to look more and more unlikely. If he should default on his mortgage – their mortgage – he'd face foreclosure from the bank with no legal recourse. Farmers were going under, dress shops, why not chiropractors? The number of patients in this recession, like the number of travellers, had fallen sharply.

So he was left with the inverted logic of a new proposition: by investing in skeletons, this time plastic skeletons, he might save his collapsing practice. By going still further into debt, and taking a flyer on plastic, he might survive as a chiropractor.

He didn't want to survive as a chiropractor.

Instead, I should be getting off the train.

He felt trapped wading deeper into bones (which weren't bones at all) when what he really wanted was to quit the profession. But he couldn't afford to quit. After his fiasco in Calcutta he needed to finish paying off his father. He'd also borrowed money from Marcus in Africa. And now his credit line was frayed. *Frayed? Listen, B. Day, D.C. It's hanging by a thread ...* He couldn't even sell out now for what his building and practice were mortgaged for. The return on selling out was dropping everywhere.

If he did nothing, and held on till rates came down, he could possibly pull through if no more patients decided to abandon him for lack of faith and ready cash. *I felt like a walnut cone today, but the feeling passed* ... As he rationalized his savings his indifferent appetite didn't let him down.

The pilgrim grew slimmer still.

One benefit in being rational about the irrational was a flatter stomach. He thought he should patent his discovery: *You don't feed anxiety ... you feed off it instead.* He'd talked this over with his diary till it showed. A clutter of cassettes on his bedspread, like a thorax of ribs Megan might count, seemed like figures from a bone company he was trying to fathom.

'... And you're thinking of borrowing more money?' asked Tom Cabot.

Bartlett was telling his M.D. friend about the reproduction scheme, one warm June afternoon over lunch.

'They want my expertise on their letterhead.'

'What expertise?'

'Witty, Tom.' He savoured his glass of water and wondered the same thing. 'Anyhow, the Indian government's moving to cut off the export of human remains. Genocidal countries are out of the picture. So things are bleak. The world's skeleton supply is falling off at the same time it's increasing. Reproductions might be the only way to go.'

'So what's their pitch?'

'Urethane plastic ...' Playing with his cracker package, Bartlett elaborated.

In Hong Kong an American couple travelling with his recent employer, Dean Cheaver, had wanted to start manufacturing bones in Iowa. This couple had mentioned to Bartlett how devoted Iowa already was to the human skeleton, because of chiropractic roots there, and how they themselves owned property in the state. They were struck by the plastic skeleton he'd used in his demonstration lecture. In fact, they already had offers to purchase plastic skeletons from medical schools and clinics, chiropractors and physical therapists, hospitals and medical libraries, in about a dozen countries. The thing was, their factory could sell a full skeleton for a fifth what it cost to import a live one.

'... A real one,' he explained to Cabot. 'Handmade bones from original moulds, screwed and wired into full skeletons ... Plus this company is talking of replicating arteries and nerves too.'

Tom picked up his soup spoon. 'A breakthrough it sounds like. Your big opportunity.' He tasted his chowder and made a face resembling a clown's. 'Why do we keep coming here?'

Bartlett sat back in his chair, surveying the cheekbones in Princess Anne's face. 'I hoped to discuss your old patient Trina Chase.'

A look of puzzlement replaced Cabot's clown face.

'Recall the case you referred to me last year? With her senses haywire?'

'Haywire. I love the medical exactitude.'

'Scrambled.'

'I remember some sort of dysfunctional.'

'She's back again.' Bartlett swallowed some water. 'I don't know what to do with her. She tells me she smells ponies when I touch her backbone.'

Cabot was trying to place her. 'What exactly are her symptoms?'

'Her boyfriend can't talk to her, because the sound of his voice has started to give her a potato taste.'

The M.D. coughed politely and glanced round in a humorous way to see who might be listening. He already knew they were alone. A little electric fan spun without consequence. The door to the street stood open, possibly to allow in traffic smells to soften the kitchen smoke.

'... Those are her symptoms,' Bartlett insisted. 'Weird stuff like that.'

Cabot slid his full chowder bowl off the paper placemat of coloured fish, and replaced it with a plate of fish and chips Sam Lung had left there to chill, along with his coffee. The proprietor had perfected the one-stop delivery of an entire lunch.

'Is she in pain?'

'More like blissed out. Confused, I guess.' Bartlett swallowed more water. 'She has a couple of luxated vertebrae ... but then so do the healthiest spines, as you M.D.s like to point out.'

'Basically, she's idiopathic then.'

'I ... what?'

'No apparent cause?'

'That's why I'm asking, Tom.'

'... And I suppose why I sent her to you.'

'You didn't see much the matter with her then?'

'I don't honestly recall the symptoms, Bartlett.' He stabbed a French fry.

'She the type to sue for malpractice?'

'She's young.'

'Sounds like a space cadet. Better send her back.'

Bartlett's beeper went off, the kind of echo tonier restaurants welcomed with a house phone for patrons to call in for messages. His office was half a block down Altamira. He supposed the advantage in eating at a Chinese establishment, masquerading as a British one, on a West End street that catered as much to visiting tourists as local pensioners, was it kept you close to home.

He canned the beeps. 'I like the subversion of her body, Tom. It's telling her real loud not to take the backbone for granted.'

'How many skeletons can your proposed factory turn out?'

'My factory?' He thought. 'A dozen, fifteen, a day. That's the projection. Employing two dozen.'

'You might get Rowland to invest.'

Bartlett's turn to look puzzled.

'Raucous Rowland, my predecessor ...? Martini M.D.? He thinks the time to invest aggressively is when everybody else is running for cover.'

'I'd rather ask Dr Jekyll,' said Bartlett.

Cabot knew his halibut was chewier with tartar sauce, and smeared the second pouch of this paste around with his fork, wiping the tines on his fish. 'I'm no good for a loan,' he said. 'I'm getting stung on MURBs.'

'I never understood what MURBs were,' said Bartlett.

'A tax dodge for lottery winners and doctors. Condo blocks, basically.'

'Your predecessor get you into that?'

'He didn't help matters.'

Ou-boum. The once echoing boom of real estate, reduced these days to the scratch of matches. The pain seemed universal. Worms coiling, pyres smoking. Shadowy figures hired to torch buildings ... *am half-wondering about Aloysius and a smell of kerosene in his room* ... now that values had sunk to less than the mortgages taken out to buy them.

If you can't stand the heat, I guess, stay out of the bank.

He drank some more water. For guys like him, it was already too late.

'How do I requisition another tartar sauce?' asked Cabot.

'You remember to tip the head waiter on your way in?'

3.

He learned from Lois that Mr Weldon from the replica company had called, needing to know by Monday latest if Dr Day was in or out. If in, then

G.H. Glassgraf Co. would require a cashier's cheque by the end of July, as per the original proposal. Lois smiled. 'I told him you were broke.'

'Yeah?' He suddenly felt relieved.

She laughed. 'I should have. I see life ahead on welfare.'

'Lois, you get paid before the bank does. Who's in the waiting room?'

She regarded his white coat the way she might a wolf pelt dropped off at the pound for incineration. 'I think your duds need a scrub.' She rolled up her eyes on her way way out, stopping to straighten his sign. 'This should double as your laundry notice.'

GET THE ONCE-A-MONTH
CHIROPRACTIC
CHECK-UP HABIT

He removed the frame and dusted it with his sleeve. Getting out the word was something pioneers of chiropractic had believed in: D.D. Palmer, with his fat textbook on bony discoveries; B.J. Palmer, employing commercial slogans to convince his followers of the advantages of self-promotion in the marketplace. EARLY TO BED, EARLY TO RISE; WORK LIKE HELL AND ADVERTISE. From his student days, Bartlett remembered B.J. had also written: 'Our school is on a business, not a professional, basis. We manufacture chiropractors.' This guy, coming to maturity in a new century, had used words more bluntly than his father: 'Q. What are the principal functions of the spine? A. 1) To support the head. 2) To support the ribs. 3) To support the chiropractor.'

He rapped the glassy slogan with his knuckles.

B.J. had turned chiropractic into a commercial empire and invented mail-order diplomas. All the mixers had descended from B.J.: all their heat therapies, enemas, electrical stimulants, pills, X-rays, gadgets ... all employed by chiropractors not strict about their provenance. This son of the father had forgotten about straightforward manipulation of the spine, as the one key to a healthy nervous system. The slogan on his campus greenhouse used to read (before *his* son had taken over and removed such slogans) 'ANYTHING I DO YOU DON'T IS QUEER. QUEER ISN'T IT?' Signed 'B.J.' He'd become an embarrassment over time. Had even taken to going to M.D.s for his health.

Bartlett reread the notice in his hands, then slipped it into a drawer full of exposed film from his old X-ray machine. He was buttoning up his coat when Gloria Dawson strode into his room in walking shorts.

'Good afternoon, Dr Day. Happen to see me on TV?'

'I must have missed you, Mrs Dawson.'

'Serves me right for asking.'

As far as Gloria was concerned she was still news. She wanted it known, by a public given over to the must of political gossip, that she was an enduring source of youth. She was the immediate heiress of Adam's right rib: wiry proof that bones needn't outlast the flesh, if flesh would only cooperate. She had yet to leave the Garden of Eden.

She really thinks she has it all together.

Maybe she did have it all together. 'Let's have a look at those earlobes.'

'Have a gander at my throat, while you're at it. Ever see such tight skin on an old crone?'

'Very commendable, Mrs Dawson.'

For a woman who'd just turned eighty-seven she had no trouble shaping physical reality according to an ongoing sense of self. It changed the way you saw Gloria, the way she saw herself. If she was a fraud he figured she'd absorbed this truth into the illusion of her robust self-image.

Gloria liked her chiropractor to be rambunctious with her, to reinforce this idea of herself as anything but brittle-boned and inflexible. So he did his best to practise preventive medicine, by attending to her minor luxations: correction of vertebrae, release of joint compression, improvement of nerve transmission. Here was a woman who wanted to feel life flow anew through her body at every visit. She loved her body, and Bartlett's manoeuvres made her love it even more.

If only Megan had one pint of Gloria Dawson's life force.

Who cared if this nut was thirty years younger than she claimed? Or a closet hypochondriac. She knew everything about her latest interest, osteoarthritis.

'On my birthday – did you hear me on the radio? – it's proper exercise I told them. That's the ticket, Dr Day. Exercise thickens the cartilage. Situps are good for any bony degradation in my lower back.' She touched her lumbar and smiled her ageproofed smile of inferior caps. 'You said you played racquet ball?' she asked him.

'Squash.'

'Too fast, if you don't mind my telling you. Abuse your joints – a chiropractor knows this – over-compress them, have to pay the piper. Let your cartilage go, your ligaments – bye-bye bounce, hello osteoarthritis! I'll tell you a big thing I've found out. Ninety-eight percent of Canadians past sixty get osteoarthritis from abusing themselves as *younger people*. What's this mystery, Dr Day, is it cartilage disintegrating at the ends of bones, fraying out and making little holes? My feeling is it's jelly. Drying up so your joints hurt when you perambulate. Abuse them young, that's what happens. I must have avoided self-abuse before I knew what it was. Now I do situps and come to see you.'

'You're in remarkable shape.'

'Thank you. The movement is good for my cartilage. Keeps my synovial fluid sticky.'

'Oh?'

'That lube and oil stuff. You're the one who knows how much nourishment cartilage needs. Active joints send oxygen straight to your tissue.'

He felt he always learned something when Gloria visited. And he took professional pride in his skill with her, in how he manipulated her body, if only because she seemed so appreciative. In the unlikely event she *was* eighty-seven, he went easy on the force and pressure applied in each manipulation's line of drive. If he applied sufficient speed in his corrections, he needed little force.

Against her scoliosis, both patient and practitioner could hear her vertebrae pop pleasantly. It was like cracking knuckles, as his professor at Memorial used to say, 'but don't tell the patient that,' since it was possible to keep her coming back for months, sometimes years, on a regular programme of pretending to correct this natural curvature of the spine.

Gloria liked to hear *all* her joints pop. Had made up her mind manipulation should be part of her preventative exercise, along with situps, walking, and Highland dancing in the park. Whenever interviewed – a not infrequent event as her youthful reputation spread – she was a public booster of chiropractic. She believed in its ameliorative powers.

'God bless it, Dr Day!'

Who can afford to discourage her?

Once a week she lay down on her right side first, bending her left leg forward, left foot tucked behind right knee, keeping it in place like a well-travelled hooker, while Bartlett made contact with the middle finger of his right hand, holding her lumbar spine before lifting – as he applied pressure with his right knee downward on her left leg – at the same time pressuring her left shoulder with his left hand, pulling upward with his contact hand and finger.

This was the million-dollar roll, the missionary position of chiropractic, a source of great relief for millions with lower back pain.

'... Crackle, pop,' said Gloria, pleased. 'The whole shebang. Always a lovely sensation for a battleaxe like me. Other side now?'

She chatted, she teased. She knew the formula for youth. Her stiffness lessened as he administered to her different regions. Youth and vitality flowed through her as ageproofing continued. He moved on to correct her vertebrae from thoracic one through lumbar five ... cervical vertebrae ... her atlas ... her whole world. Her bones popped with satisfying regularity. She was made whole.

Finished, Gloria would regularly delight in making a show of asking Lois for her senior's discount with a gnomic smirk. And just as regularly Lois would complain afterward Mrs Dawson was cheating them, because she wasn't yet, and probably never would be, sixty-five.

'Well,' said Bartlett, 'she's publicity for my genius.'

Lois was shaking her finger, irritated by a broken nail. He could smell traces of nailpolish on the air, the memory of nailpolish.

Another sign on his wall: GET KNOWLEDGE OF THE SPINE, FOR THIS IS THE REQUISITE FOR MANY DISEASES. HIPPOCRATES.

Did he really say this? Who said he said it?

Chiropractors, that's who, redecorating their offices with chrome and leather chairs, lobbying for respect. *History with its shallow voice* ... Chiropractors, still seen as dangerous, too close to their working-class origins of janitors and fish peddlers, hated their past. They grabbed at straws. Their thinning list of famous patients needed bolstering: Thomas Edison, Eleanor Roosevelt, J.D. Rockefeller, Rocky Marciano ...

Weasel Copithorne

'Backache,' said Weasel, hobbling in the door. 'Next to motion sickness, I hear backache's an astronaut's worst complaint.'

Weasel continued to envy anyone who travelled.

'Listen, doc, the body grows an inch up there, which accounts for the pain. Me, I feel like I'm in space all the time.' He stripped off his shirt and lay down on the adjusting table. 'Give it to me good.'

Bartlett tapped his spine, listening to the covert grief Weasel still felt over the premature death of his wife. Along with his recent retirement, her death remained the most stressful event in his life. This was twenty years ago. Bartlett listened to the pleasure Weasel Copithorne took in narrating the rehearsed story of his wife, including the patent lie of faded affluence.

'... I was thinking of redoing the summer cottage, doc. I wanted her advice. I might turn the whole works into cedar and glass, what did she think? I might even lay in an Indian carpet to please her. Hang some Oriental pictures ...'

He went on, his memory for invention good.

Every story Bartlett heard in his ministrations seemed to him an approximation of some larger whole. *Which is why I no longer bother taking X-rays.* He trusted patients to tell him how they felt, where it hurt. Luxated bones weren't what turned up on a screen but what was articulated from the heart. His profession was founded on the illusory truth of the spine, a pathway of electrical impulses difficult to pin down. He could try, but a patient's pain often popped up in another guise. A chiropractor had to listen.

'I was also thinking of scuttling the sloop. Of building a schooner, doc, to take the crossing with a bone in her teeth. 'Course, I'd need help sailing a schooner. Somebody to unplug the scuppers, somebody to take the wheel. Even a cook. With the cottage being rebuilt we'd have to live at anchor, in the bay, keeping tabs on the workmen. We were going to dive for oysters, she and me, coming up to a teak deck with salt on our tongues. Cleaning mussels off the hull so the whole boat went faster.'

He asked Bartlett, over his shoulder, 'In your view, doc, should I have bothered? I mean with the scuttling.'

'No.'

'How 'bout the cottage?'

'What did you decide?'

'The problem was red tide. And spawning time. Oyster flesh is thin around spawning, you get sick. My wife did. She died eating contaminated oysters.'

He shuddered when Bartlett cracked his spine and the plot climaxed.

'I spread her ashes all over the Spanish Main. Check any closet you want to, she's been swimming for years. Travelling, doc, you probably saw her on one of the seven seas drifting by in the current ...'

'I thought you spread her ashes on Lost Lagoon.'

'What a lunatic, pestering the oysters to spawn with a jigger. A jigger!

Got herself drenched, ruined her nails, flummoxed the oysters.'

'She didn't walk out on you then.'

'I told you, doc. I threw her out. Of an urn. Winter depressed her. She was lonely like.'

Like, thought Bartlett. Wasn't treating like with like the foundation for homeopathy? He was looking into homeopathy and considering the option of presenting a talk on his deductions. A conference next year in Lima had him thinking ...

He had no money, but wanted to go. Travel had got into his bloodstream. So had leaving chiropractic behind: the faith it required, the suspension of incredulity.

Patients were believers in a way few chiropractors were. Tell a patient like Anna Linde the tenth dorsal vertebra was luxated in cases of kidney disease – and she was all ears for the knowledge. Ditto the second lumbar vertebra in cases of constipation; or a luxation in the upper cervical and upper dorsal regions, with any interference in the motion of the heart.

Heart and Soul. Jan and Dean ...

She had loosened up a lot since her first visit, many visits ago, to admit her dependence on help for a very painful back. She climbed onto his table stroking her purse. A small gesture she was learning to control, by leaving her wallet at the desk, where Lois agreed to tuck it in a drawer for safekeeping.

'I think that's so true, Doctor, what you told me to do at home by way of situps.' The neglected housewife took pieces of greying hair in two fingers and wove them back into her bun. She no longer felt quite so neglected, so lost, when she had situps to fall back on.

Sad, he thought, her need of contact with a chiropractor when she had no reason to see him, unless all reason was physical and in need of exercise. In which case, her coming to him suggested his quackery might have a rational basis.

Spinal column, cord, pathway ... *My life line to nonsense.* Except maybe it had a shape he couldn't see? He felt like a quester for science, who couldn't read the map.

When she left, twenty minutes later, he had time on his hands. Friday afternoons in June were even slower this year than Friday mornings in June.

He suggested to Lois she take off the rest of the afternoon and hit the beach. He thought he'd drive across town to visit his father. He had her telephone ahead to announce his coming. This always gave Bert Day a charge, hearing from his busy son's nurse.

'He didn't sound that enthusiastic,' remarked Lois.

'I've been neglecting him.'

4.

He walked home in the sunshine to pick up his car. Few would mistake him for a mainstream doctor, sauntering home in the middle of a working day, wrinkled white coat fluttering like a butcher's smock on a flagpole. After six years of squeezing into it, the coat was now much too big, and his pants flapped like blankets. He wore saddle shoes when black wingtips were called for, and he didn't care who thought they needed polish. He'd inherited the untidy habits of his mother.

Upstairs his bedroom overflowed with junk. Empty cassette boxes, a broken shoehorn, pennies on the sill. A used condom on the clock radio, a safari brochure he'd brought home for Aloysius, pocketbooks on homeopathy. Peeling posters and a model airplane with a broken wing. He put on his Foreign Trade T-shirt, cutoff jeans, then changed into thongs.

It was time he changed his life.

His rusted-out Mustang was no stranger to detritus either. Surrounding it, orange peel littered the ground. Inside, forgotten shirts on their way to the dry cleaner were stuffed into plastic Safeway bags. Airing along the back window were court shoes, unlaundered squash shorts and mismatched sweat socks. Hoping the oven would cool, he held open the door. A miniature spine – gimmick from the proposed new bone company – dangled from his rearview mirror. The dashboard supported a broken frost scraper, a worn-down whisk, a tire gauge that rolled in tandem with a golf ball going round corners. Everything was collecting dust. Chiropractic literature selling the latest props, and an empty Kleenex box. The dash clock read 2:25 ... in perpetuity, unless he happened to move its hands like a picture every year, to change the perspective. The windshield needed a good tornado to clean off the crow shit.

Bartlett sank into the hot leather seat. A cloud of black exhaust enveloped the car when he switched on the ignition.

He buckled up.

The sunroof didn't leak exactly, but the seal was no longer kissing its opposite number, and hadn't for two winters. He cranked open the roof, clunked his automatic transmission into drive, and spun the power steering like a top. He knew this car better than he knew Megan. The disc brakes in front needed replacing. The rearview mirror was loose on the windshield. The trunk was full of rayon hot pants hauled home from a rummage sale, as a favour to Aloysius, who no longer wanted them. In there was also a run-down car battery, leaking acid in the dark.

He punched a rock 'n' roll station specializing in the classics. 'Bad Moon Rising' ... Sometimes he wished he was so good-looking people fainted when they looked at him. The music poured out through his roof. People on sidewalks turned, drivers glanced across, bus passengers peered down. He was a regular dreamboat. Here sat a romantic guy. Here sat a man who'd gone shopping for skeletons in Calcutta.

He'd forgotten his shades. You couldn't be cool in a black T-shirt and a Mustang without shades.

His aerial, which brought smiles from other drivers, was a rearranged coat hanger. It worked well, if you kept it jammed in at the right angle.

Tall buildings, Dwight's building, drifted past in the sky.

At the commercial he punched a new station. 'Rafe, the main problem in health today is digestology ...' A hotline host was interviewing a naturopath.

Every quack with his answer to disease, the threat of disease, yet another outsider and heretic thinking time would turn him into a butterfly.

Crossing Main he swerved to avoid a drunk teetering off the sidewalk. This near miss caused Bartlett to reconsider his profession's tawdry origins. How the discoverer of the 'fountainhead' of all medical science, what old Palmer liked to call his recovery of chiropractic from the Greeks, had spent time in jail for fraudulent practice. How the son later bought out the father, in time embittering D.D. at his son's heretical direction into orthodoxy. (And how, before losing his marbles, D.D. came to hate B.J. and every other chiropractor, once dashing out of a crowd to attack his son's car in a public parade, dying estranged three months later in hospital with strict orders to keep his son away.)

No wonder the profession yearns for respectability. Trying to forget its ...

He hoped his father wouldn't cook supper. Too hot to eat he felt thirsty for a cold Pepsi.

On Hastings he pulled over to a Chinese grocery, stepped out, and left his motor running in the faint hope a bored drunk with nothing better to do might help him collect theft insurance on an irreplaceable classic Mustang.

A passing Safeway truck rattled bottles in the store's old water cooler. Back in his car the little plastic spine was still swaying in the truck's wake. He sat watching it, sipping Pepsi, waiting for the diesel fumes to clear.

He'd dithered over plastic. A compact demonstration model like Bea was one thing; another to offer students of anatomy plastic skeletons scrubbed free of the wear and tear of time. This was supposedly an advantage: skeletons that would no longer crumble after prolonged student handling. But what of their stories? *Bones are the driven snow of history* ... What advantage in scrubbing away grief, suffering, longing? A student's knowledge should include these extrapolations. Shouldn't it?

He suspected from the rumbling of his muffler that the cavity in it had grown to the size of a horse's turd.

He reached for his seat belt and punched the radio again. Otis Redding ... He gunned away from the curb and his golf ball spun off the dashboard to the floor.

At Commercial he braked for a stoplight and nothing happened. Then the shoes warmed up and saved him one more time. Maybe his fluid was leaking. He kept his mind circling above his frayed linings. He touched the spine on his rearview mirror for luck. He stepped on the gas.

Reconstruction, the Iowa bone factory's goal, consisted of make-believe bones arising from the moulds of real bones. According to the prospectus, Glassgraf would offer surgeons the choice of a plastic bone over a metal pin in replacing your father's hip bone.

The city ran on. At night it ran up and down hills, in lines of light you could see from its western summit of Point Grey, edging the gulf, to Capitol Hill with better but less fashionable views. The East End always brought him back to what permanence in his life remained. Not just to his father, or to the house he was conceived in, but to the memory of summer mornings a quarter century ago, to the smell of cat, clink of milk bottles, a golden freshness every morning, before afternoon breezes brought food and sawdust smells from the PNE, *onion smells ... something like that*, and at night gaudy reflections of a Ferris wheel staining the sky.

The afternoon air stuck him to his seat. He came to the little neighbourhood park, with its new rubber-tire swing and plastic corkscrew slide, deserted now at nap-time. He turned left at a street he knew better than his

‹ 496 ›

own face. A dog was scratching grass into the air. His father hated dogs fouling his lawn. Next door, the sight of a child's abandoned rocking horse encouraged in Bartlett a tenderness born of nostalgia for himself. He pulled up, his valves in need of repair.

His history was so simple compared to history.

5.

In the basement, Bert Day was nailing cedar lasts to a frame of one-by-twos he was planning to erect on the back deck for his climbing rose. Bartlett could smell little sachets of red cedar, released when his father tapped each shingle nail into the wood. He watched the bones in his father's hands rearranging the sawhorses, bones worn into view through years of manipulating tools. He was going to paint his creation with a semi-transparent stain called Fruitwood, in a can from Color Your World. He had a new brush set aside and a fresh stir stick. He wasn't planning to paint indoors.

'I'll be an artist outside, after I nail my trellis to the porch. Cripes, why risk cancer ingesting fumes? Plumbers are healthier than painters by a long shot – only they don't know it.'

His father kept nails and screws, hooks and eyes, in jam and peanut-butter jars scrubbed clear of labels and screwed into their lids. These lids were nailed to the bottom side of a shelf above his workbench. His jars ran in a slanting row, biggest to smallest, like ascending staffs of musical notation. If you ran a screwdriver along the glass sides, guessed Bartlett, you'd hear scales. *Dick Powell, maybe, warming up with Tommy Dorsey, or one of those bands from the age before Golden Oldies.*

'You got into the health industry at the exact right time, Bart. Medical science, that's where it's at today, paying attention to my arteries for cholesterol purposes. It sure ain't unplugging the other guy's sewer with an auger.'

Bert was measuring the space for his next last with an inch-wide measuring stick. His knuckly fingers played with the space against the cedar last already in place, till he created an exact square with the last on top. He then nailed this top one with two and a half taps of his hammer at either end. Bartlett noticed he wasn't wearing his wedding ring.

Bert glanced at his finger. 'No, that's right.'

Perspiring, he laid down his hammer without picking up the next last.

The sun outside felt intense, the basement a humidity trap. His father's breasts sagged inside his damp undershirt, yet for a man who enjoyed cooking his stomach was lean. Bartlett's mom had been the heavy one, large-boned and stout.

Bert Day turned to him. 'I got a girlfriend,' he blurted.

'Yeah? She the jealous type?'

His father returned to his composition.

'I just felt funny wearing it. Different with you young people.'

'C'mon, Dad. Who is she?'

'Met her at my pastry course. Community centre.'

Bartlett felt like a father ferreting details from an embarrassed son. 'I love it,' he teased. 'Pastry?'

'What's the matter with pastry?'

'Nothing, nothing.'

'She's different.'

'Good.'

'Young.'

'Bull's-eye.'

'Lets me run her home is all.'

'Yeah?'

Bert Day looked up from his last. 'Asiatic.'

'Nice.'

'Twenty-odd.'

'Hard to tell sometimes.'

'In the vicinity. I ain't proud of it.' He seemed to think he ought to be ashamed of himself, a dirty old man. ''Cept who cares, if she doesn't?'

'Now you're talking.'

'Filipino. No raspberry blonde.'

Bartlett kept quiet. His father went on. 'Somebody's domestic help, in a big house up Springer way. Puts in two years, gets her landed immigrancy papers. Good deal, if you don't have relatives here to sponsor you, like she don't. Minimum wage and all found ...'

His father wanted to finish up the trellis and have it in place, on his deck, before it was time to take his bread out of the oven. He checked his watch. He was also planning to bake a strawberry pie. A special dessert for which he'd purchased strawberries from the greengrocer this morning.

'This pastry business's all new to me. Haven't had pastry in the house since Mary died.' He regarded his son's thin torso. 'From the looks of you, you could do with some pie. Lost your sweet tooth?'

'Know what I'm trying to get into?' answered Bartlett.

'No.'

'Plastic.'

'That some kind of jumpsuit?'

'Plastic bones.'

'You mean, like one of them Halloween costumes?'

'Here, let me give you a hand with this.'

Later on they bumped a few dozen petals to the porch erecting the new trellis, a massacre for which time would forgive them. When his father began staining the wood, Bartlett sat and sipped beer in the shade. Bert Day intended to tie the climbing shoots to the lasts with Safeway twists, till he had time to train them properly with butcher's twine. *My father lets me in on so much, who'd guess he had a secret in the world?*

He yelled from the kitchen, rolling his pie crust. The roses he claimed were Golden Ransoms.

Bartlett had another beer.

'By the way, I stopped using aluminum pans for my bread, so you won't get cancer anymore.'

Over dessert they watched the news. Who else was there to eat his strawberry pie, his father wanted to know. He'd had the ingredients all ready, so he was tickled Bart had come. The dining room table had been set with emerald placemats and white cloth napkins. Bert stared at the rips in his son's T-shirt but said nothing.

'It's delicious,' said Bartlett.

'I won't deny it.'

'The pastry is very successful.'

'All in what you don't use. People put in too much flour.' He'd whipped a cup of cream then forgotten it in the fridge. He went out and came back.

'Slow evening for news. That there footage of the Royal Family means they don't have much on tap about the Falklands. New heir to the throne, big deal.' By 'they' he meant self-important meatheads who brought them news from a factory called a studio. It was the way they manufactured the news, when you thought about it, that got his goat.

'One smug chinwag's all it is, Bart, with pretty faces. It's got a gossip component we forget. And the pundits. Pundits make me sick. Who invented TV news? And the desk for all them faces. I watch, sure. What else've I got to do at suppertime 'cept find out what they're dishing up in Ottawa. Somebody bringing home the constitution. Somebody else imposing metric. And who raised sports to news status, Bart? You can bet if women was running things sports wouldn't be news, and I'd be in total sympathy with the libbers on that one. Whatever happened to news, capital N?'

He seemed to think the genre had been corrupted.

'Let's switch channels ... I'll make coffee.'

The beans were new, the grinder was new. Bartlett had never before been offered fresh ground coffee at his father's. Bert Day unfolded the cone filter like a diaper in the hands of a bishop. When his boiling water hit the beans it let go an exotic aroma. The coffee lover's equivalent of talcum powder. Incense.

'Glad you came,' Bert called from the kitchen, mist rising. 'Gives me a chance to put on the dog. Somebody to eat my poor pie.'

He brought in a bottle of Kahlua to go with the coffee.

'Capital N news is like original sin,' he said, putting down the bottle. 'Real news, if you follow me. Hardball stuff.' An item about the new movie *E. T.* was playing on NBC. '... Generally speaking, I mean.'

He went back to the kitchen to remove his filter.

'Mostly,' said Bert, 'there's just offshoots of real news – rehash and leftovers, the media shoving these pictures at us of guilt and whatnot. Why compare happiness with money, Bart? We supposed to cough up money for people living the other side of the Gobi Desert, so they can live exactly like us? Who says the Peruvian family living in a road pipe ain't as happy as me? Maybe they ain't. But money won't guarantee them. We ship millions to countries like Calcutta – has it made a difference? You been there. They're just as bad off as before the ship come in ... and they're laughing up their turbans at us for sending it. I don't blame 'em for laughing. Us with our latest grinders and wave ovens and colour TVs – nothing like this stuff twenty years ago – and all of a jiffy, the pundits are telling us no one else can be happy without the same doohickies. It's paranormal, Bart.'

At his father's mention of Calcutta he'd shifted uneasily. Bert, meanwhile, was pouring hot water into a new blue thermos, to warm it up.

'People've always taken care of their own. No one's starving who's hungry enough to eat, any more than anyone who wants a job's out of work.'

'You're wrong there.'

'Am I?'

'The UI lineup now goes up the block and around the dog.'

'Poor buggers,' said Bert, meaning it. He emptied his thermos into the sink, then began to pour in coffee from the pot.

Bartlett raised his voice to be heard over the closing commercials. '*Lots* of my patients in this recession out of work ...'

The news was over and light entertainment followed.

'One show I can't stand,' said his father, 'is that *Lifestyles of the Rich and Famous*. Lookit it.'

'Guess you'd have to be a suave diplomat to talk to those types,' said Bartlett.

'Dripping with sincerity, yeah.'

His father went over and snapped off the set, coming back to pour them each coffee from his new thermos. He tightened the lid, then sat down to try his cup, as if tasting real coffee for the first time. He looked pleased with his experiment. 'Costa Rican,' he said.

No air moved through the house. The screen doors acted like tea strainers, letting in hot wet air and keeping out any leafy breezes. The picture tube let out a loud clack, cooling.

'You was wondering 'bout my wedding ring? Better I should mention your sister's. Betty's going through a bad patch of road just now. Life of a rubber boot depends on how you use it. I gather Kirk's running around with another woman.' He sipped his coffee. 'That's something I never did. Even now, I still feel sleazy stepping out ... to dos at the centre, shindigs like that. That's why I take it off.' He rubbed his finger.

Bartlett felt close to his father this evening. *Thought I knew what he was thinking, waiting for him to call his new girlfriend 'a dilly' ... Anyway, decided to confide in him about my practice.* He spoke quietly, looking at his cup. His father listened. Bert Day was a good listener, for a man who liked to talk.

He'd had no idea his son's practice was so shaky. Bartlett went on to tell him how his patients were falling off. How, with the shrinking econony, patients were hanging back on appointments they needed, *he* needed, to stay healthy. How summer was a poor time for chiropractic anyway.

How – and this was his point – he wanted to pay off his Calcutta debt to his father as soon as possible.

'Why? I'm not hurting none,' said Bert. 'You done what you thought was right, and took it on the chin over there.'

His son saved his worst-case scenario for last. The prospect of having to fold up his tent and go out of business.

'... Because,' and here he rubbed the back of his neck, 'of a stupid mortgage I assumed on my building, to help out Dwight. How can I put it ...'

His father put down his cup. 'I'm not following.'

'I'm close to the edge.'

'Mean that Dwight twerp ain't paying you back ...?'

'He's near the edge too. We both expected his company'd be making oodles on expansion. But ... seems he's having problems with his timing.'

Bert Day pushed his cup and saucer aside. He was having problems with what he was hearing.

'You agreed to invest in that phoney?'

'It didn't look bad. I'd get my money back to cover bank payments every month, plus an interest in Herodotus Travel. You know, as it grew?'

'It ain't growing.'

'No.'

'It ain't making money.'

'No.'

'Losing money.'

'Right.'

'It's going down the sewer.'

'Well, I wouldn't –'

'Sounds like it's been flushed. Talk about cash flow. Look, Bart, if he can't pay back his friends he won't be paying back the banks.'

Bartlett didn't answer.

'Don't worry yourself about my loan,' said his father. 'I ain't going to foreclose you.'

Bartlett shook his head. 'The weird thing now is, I find myself with a new business opportunity.'

His father pulled his saucer closer and rearranged his cup. 'Yeah?' He was curious. Could his son's practice not be so bad off after all?

'Plastic.'

'You keep mentioning it.'

'Well, it's now history. The opportunity I mean.'

'Finished before it started.'

'Plastic skeletons.'

His father frowned. 'You been talking to Irving about this?'

'Dwight's the reason I thought of getting into plastic. Might help bail me out.'

'You got the inside dope?'

Bartlett shrugged.

He reminded Bert where skeletons for medical schools usually came from. Imported like blackmarket sculptures. Death had no dominion. His father listened, interested in the kind of news he couldn't get from TV. He now found out why the supply of skeletons was probably going to dry up in India. What the alternatives might be. What the prospects for profit were, if you could get in on the ground floor of plastic replicas.

'Your doings in Calcutta. Were they homework for all this?'

'I got taken to the cleaners in Calcutta.'

'So you want your own back. To make them suppliers obsolete like …?'

To his father it sounded like a very bright takeover move. A 'white-knight' kind of move. 'When nobody's buying, that's when the smart cookie makes his move … in an economic downturn.' Bert Day had this on trust. 'My advice is go for it, Bart. How much they want?'

Bartlett told him.

He was sorry for his father's sake it was so much. Bert Day's enthusiasm suddenly, out of necessity, waned. He usually enjoyed this kind of wheeling with his son, hypothetical deal-making. That he could never afford such a proposition now hit him like a joke.

They both stared out the front screen door. Children across the street were playing Go-Go-Stop with explosive ecstasy on the final word. '*Stop!*' came the cry with all the same insincerity of twenty-five years ago.

His father must have spotted a dog, because he grew excited again. He stood up.

'I might mortgage the house for you.' This surprised Bartlett. 'Wouldn't bring me as much as when the market was buoyant, but it might help jumpstart you.'

'This place?'

The trouble was his father meant it. He actually sounded willing to go to the bank come Monday and borrow money to help his son buy into plastic bones. His son should be in on the revolution in bone. That simple.

He fetched two little glasses from the sideboard and poured them both Kahlua from the bottle.

'Here's to it,' he said. 'Pie in your eye.'

Bartlett rolled a thread on his cotton napkin, reluctant to hoist his glass. He listened to the kids. No choice but to decline his father's generous offer.

'... Too risky,' he explained gently. 'Startup in production too far down the road. I couldn't meet monthly payments on another mortgage ... But, hey, thanks a lot.'

'I got my pensions coming in,' said Bert. 'Savings. Work when I want it. I'm hunkydory. I could even carry the bank awhile myself like.' He took another sip and studied the bottle's label. 'You want the money or not, Bart?' He sounded impatient.

'I appreciate the offer, Dad. Believe me. But no.'

'Well, think about it. You'd be doing me a favour.' He looked down. 'More pie?'

He wasn't hungry. But felt it ungracious to refuse.

'Back in a jiffy.'

Bartlett's eyes wandered to the gas fireplace and the mantel above. His mother's porcelain figurines had been neatly grouped in pairs before the big mirror, resting on little islands of embroidered lace. The girl of one couple was accepting a necklace of yellow shells.

The room's windows he saw were caulked and clean. The house's small rooms had all been reinsulated and their windows double-glazed. The attic would be cool in summer, dry and warm in winter. Once a year the concrete floor in the basement got scrubbed and painted. Bartlett knew the roof was no more than three years old, the house's aluminum siding guaranteed a lifetime. The small lawn and garden were weedless, the cherry tree now heavy with fruit because of efficient pruning in February. A rustless panel truck, full of neat lengths of copper pipe, sat freshly lubed and oiled in the carport.

No, he couldn't wish on his father any replacement for his home, should the risk of Glassgraf overtake the return, and force Bert Day into a one-room basement when a bank repossessed his world.

Bartlett drove home with the evening sun still high over the mountains. In the traffic drifted smells of other summer nights – tires, fumes, tar – and in his teeth the taste of strawberries. A piece of pie wrapped in wax paper rode in the other bucket seat, for Megan. And a fresh loaf of bread for each of them. Love in a bungalow wasn't just Megan's hope, but his father's too.

He began to wonder. Were strawberries the reason his father hadn't sounded wild on the phone to see him this afternoon? He slowed down, nearing Victoria Drive ...

He began to reconstruct his day in a new light.

Say Bert Day had been planning to have over his new girlfriend for the first time. Say he'd invited her to come and have supper on her night off. Say he planned to bake her a pie full of fresh strawberries, something she'd never had. Say the coffee beans were for her. The new placemats. Likewise the bottle of Kahlua, an exotic treat for an exotic visitor.

... *Fuck.*

And after all his father's shopping and planning, say he'd had to phone her at the last moment to postpone her coming, you see, because his son –

Bartlett's foot rose from the gas pedal. A bus passed him.

How wonderful this sudden knowledge made him feel!

Not because his father had given him priority over this girl ... but because his father was a diplomat, a gracious man, who knew instinctively how to welcome his son's intrusive world, when the guy hadn't felt like welcoming it at all. *But telling his son how glad he was to have somebody to eat his pie with him ... Come off it, Dad!*

This was news from nowhere.

His father's gracious forbearing, his working away at another level, when to Bartlett he'd always seemed to live at the local level of smalltalk. A diplomat, one who'd never travelled, knowing how to hold his tongue even as he deployed it.

Unlike the offer to remortgage his house, this smaller sacrifice of reticence and privacy, a calculated diplomatic deception, seemed to his son by far the greater sacrifice.

Bartlett stopped at an unmarked intersection on Powell for a teenage boy with thin legs and worn-out sneakers. He noticed in his rearview mirror how he was holding up traffic.

Wisdom, like desire, is knowing how to savour absence. He felt humble in his innocence. The mirror-side of knowledge was seldom up front.

Rarely symmetrical.

That night, alone except for Aloysius, who for all he knew was in his room figuring out how to import tree hyraxes for an all-night disco, the chiropractor recorded the following obit in his diary.

His father might have hounded his mother about her untidiness. Her sloppiness. Her indifference. But he was a good person. A person for whom, in the ordinary course of life, evil didn't exist. He didn't expect to be robbed, spat at or fingered. He paid hydro and telephone bills without a second notice, would've gladly done jury duty if selected. Death would come, but gently. He liked people. He greeted strangers on the street with a hello and a smile. He appreciated sunshine and roses: teenagers laughing and playing tag: Italians dribbling soccer balls: kids on roundabouts and high on candy. Parks were what he liked. He believed in old concrete swimming pools on sunny afternoons at the season's brink. He believed people everywhere could be good, if only others accorded them respect. He didn't trust the disadvantaged, or what he heard of them on TV. Yet he'd give anybody – not in the larger picture of the world, but in its cameo – the shirt off his back ... *Or his son, the house he lives in.* He was one of the city's last pioneers.

Bartlett lay among the cassettes of his life, piled up around him on his unmade bed. He lay wondering how widespread were monologues like his – among fellow chiropractors who'd inherited the autobiographical impulse of their collective father, D.D. Palmer – spilling out like nocturnal emissions.

Wisdom, like desire, was knowing how to savour absence.

The mirror-side of knowledge was seldom up front.

This knowledge got scrambled. It was in the air.

You could never go too far, because the truth was always beyond that.

He put down his mike and removed the tape. He picked up a cassette at random and stuck it in the machine. He was surprised to hear Gwyn trying to talk. He'd forgotten the city had other voices besides his.

He'd watched her grow, crawl, try to walk. He'd cuddled and dandled her like a daughter. Over the unspoken objections of Reesa's mother, who watched him bending over Gwyn and speaking like a ranter to her grandchild.

'... *I've heard her talk. She knows how to talk. Let's hear you talk, Gwyn, sweetheart. Yeah, she knows how to talk. There's a big girl.*'

Even the grandmother's mother was still living. A long-lived line, these Pottses. It pleased him tonight to be a part of ... such a long line of bones, compared to his.

The common knowledge of bones fascinated him. He longed to be the citizen of a city that required its body of common knowledge be uncommonly held. Clasping any body, even with his eyes, he wanted to see how it leaned on bones like a tent its poles. Tonight, earlier, he'd watched Reesa relaxing on TV, entwining her legs and folding her hands, effortlessly moving her jawbone.

He always saw her in the child.

'Time won't let meee ...' The Outsiders? He turned off the radio, then his diary.

Time would let him watch Aloysius bend to the winds of opportunity. Let him watch Dwight grow incautious, reckless in the manner of his claims and ambition. Let him watch Megan move in response to his love thrusts. The way he treated her, what did she see in him, a lamb in wolf's clothing? It was inverted knowledge he wished he understood. This news from elsewhere, the extreme shape of home, where the flesh might be willing yet the spirit grew weak.

February, 1887

If having their pigtails tied to other men's pigtails is to be their fate, why was I snooping in Carrall Street the other day for ancestors? His name was Ling. I miss him. Driven out of town two mornings ago by the Knights of Labour.

Came away shaken from the loading scene. Ling owns a laundry so it was unclear whose job he was stealing, when no one else will wash and press dirty clothes. In frigid air the victims sat twitching, seething and humiliated, shipped out in horse-drawn drays and banished by steamer to the capital.

I would feel heartsick recounting this, if I had a heart to feel anything. If I had a nose to pick or a bum to itch I might feel shame. I want to feel embarrassed.

To insist on my own I. Am nothing more than an imaginary citizen of a city whose future is still unimagined. Moping. I remember the future as I do home, an arrow that pierces hearts of nostalgic Oriental men. This keeps me going.

Had happened upon a bird cage hanging inside the small steamed-up laundry. A domed bamboo cage with a finch inside, all the way from China.

The owner was whispering to it, in vigils stolen from his steaming vats of clothes. Asking the sunny-chested little bird why it had refused its perch and flopped down on the befouled bottom of its cage. He

spoke in Wu, for I imagine it to be Wu and not Cantonese, though it might have been Mandarin or even Foochow. Am more familiar with what's spoken than how. More proof of how mixed up I feel, a ghost from the future. Feathers were moulting like dead skin.

Not more than an hour later the thrashing began. A sudden beating of wings against the cage's floor. By the time Ling hurried back the bird had flopped over and – in a last convulsion, eyes sealed, heart mad for one beat more – died.

I watched Ling staring at his bird. Last closing of the beak, infolding of wings, final twitch of claws curling shut. He could do nothing. Too late to reach in, even if he could have brought himself to pinch the windpipe. 'Oak. Poor Oak.' Oak's feet had each shrivelled up as if returning to the egg. A tear ran sideways across Ling's cheek.

His stoicism was the stoicism of a father I wanted for myself. I could learn sorrow from this man. Resolve, too.

Ling is a survivor. Found out from eavesdropping on him and the rice importer next door, his first job was roadbuilding in the Interior, also panning for gold in old tailings of white prospectors. Both men knew – know – the railway is coming soon. They could both remember, homesick, hauling rock away in baskets and laying ties.

At age thirty-four Ling had become owner of a new laundry, but they carted him away two days ago granny-knotted by the hair to the rice importer. The Knights had painted white Xs on the plank sidewalk to identify these yellow vermin in need of removal.

I must believe he will be back.

Today, having connived against the Asiatic plague, the city has had to forfeit the right to employ its own constables. The provincial government has shipped over three dozen special policemen to keep us from each others' throats.

Chapter 28

Mirror-Side of Knowledge

LOIS INTERRUPTED HIS interview. '... She says it's urgent.' The way she pronounced 'Mrs Herodotus' made the caller's name sound conniving and slightly pornographic.

He learned Dwight had been detained in Costa Rica. 'Our embassy has been trying to reach me for two days,' said Reesa. 'Guatemala wants to extradite him. I'm concerned, Bartlett.'

Puzzled and surprised he listened.

'Not one word from Dwight,' she said.

'Diplomats are slow.'

'Bartlett? I think the shit has finally hit the fan. His company's cooked ...'

These subluxed observations crying out to be straightened. He wanted to commiserate, but felt cooked himself. 'Let's go into it this evening,' he told her. 'Think up a game plan or whatever and sock it to them.'

Trina Chase was wriggling her toes when he returned to the examining room. This gave her a delicious taste of mint or something. He couldn't remember if it was mint. Chocolate pudding he knew came into the picture if he tried any move on her right shoulder. He'd thought of documenting her symptoms the way Hahnemann and his disciples did a century and a half ago for homeopathy. He felt a growing attraction to homeopathy. As a result he felt a growing attraction to Trina Chase. Except Trina had no symptoms. Within the rooms of her own house she was entirely normal. Her skin glowed, her eyes shone. She looked neither sick nor haywire.

His young patient appeared to live with windows that were really mirrors. Her house reflected a brain of unconventional circuitry, carrying tales of mixed-up senses and odd perceptions. She'd refused to return to Dr Cabot, M.D. for diagnosis. In fact she had no recollection of who Dr Cabot was. Trina Chase claimed she was committed to Dr Day, someone who had time to listen to her wiring.

This was how she talked. 'Listen to my wiring.' This was so literally how her brain worked she sounded figurative without knowing it. She seemed to remember without any abstract connectors. Like finding her way to his office. Lois might locate her in the health shop next door gazing at red and green bottles of vitamin pills. Her logic was sensual and therefore promiscuous: constantly forging new associations. Ms Chase, a pert young redhead, claimed the look of these bottles made her hear banjos in an old Burt Reynolds movie about 'trout hunting'. For the trivia of the past she possessed a completely normal memory. *She just can't recall what in everybody else depends on habit.* Nothing seemed likely or about to cure her short circuiting; she appeared unable even to mourn the missing links. He knew this was a guise.

'... And when you see ink,' he asked, 'does it make you feel sorry he's no longer touching your skin?'

'It can't be helped, can it,' she replied in a steady voice.

Studying his white coat she thought today his garment sounded like a stream in the wilderness. She was trying to divert the doctor from getting too near her grief. Wilderness? He knew she was a twenty-year-old woman who'd never been outside her own city. For her the city seemed enough of a distraction and perennially exotic. She heard bitterness, tasted colours. Saw sounds, felt aromas. Smelled voices. Any such sensuous combination one could imagine, and she missed the whole.

He took a break and strode into the outer office to review her file. His research at the public library had discovered her condition to be a rare disease of the senses called synaesthesia.

'"Synaesthesia",' he read aloud to Lois, '"may be the way early man viewed the world before his cortex opened, grew more complex and began separating his senses ..."'

The waiting room was empty and Lois was attacking her hair with a brush of plastic spikes. She felt he'd strayed a little far outside his area of expertise. 'Damn this dry air,' she said of the crackling halo around her head.

He drummed his fingers on her desk and reread himself the page. 'Look, Lois. If your cortex and mine opened up like petals once, in our own garden-variety brains, how come not in hers?'

'I think her own bouquet is kind of wonderful,' said Lois.

'Do you? Even when her boyfriend has scuttled her?'

'Oh ... is this the latest?'

Trina Chase's boyfriend had cleared out because the things he did to pleasure her left sour tastes on her tongue, and the things she wished to hear he never learned to say with his hand in the right place. 'In this respect,' said Bartlett, 'she seems quite normal.'

'Speak for yourself,' said Lois, placing her green embroidered tam just so in the mirror. 'I'm off to shop. Ciao.'

Unlike Megan, whom Bartlett was no longer seeing, Trina was willing to discuss her senses or any other subject he introduced, assuming her tongue had time to catch up with her jumbled perceptions. She was a chore some visits. But her extreme case was fascinating to someone whose living depended every day on the hand of hyperbole. To a story as mixed up as hers he felt especially attracted ... *the way I'm not attracted to stories that are all bone and no skin.* When Trina did manage to make the linkage between some object and its name, to perceive a tiny equation of everyday shorthand that his other patients took for granted, the revelation for her was like a dead person's upon coming back to life. She'd glimpsed life whole! Ecstasy! He couldn't imagine her horror, if she should ever travel into bones and understand them as murder.

He suspected the real reason Trina's boyfriend had left was because she couldn't converse in any abstract way. She was the most concrete person Bartlett had ever met. He knew she couldn't read and eat at the same time, because words got in the way of her taste and vice versa.

Her addled perceptions stirred an askew appetite within himself. The same appetite he supposed that first attracted him to alternative medicine: a craving for a knowledge beyond knowledge. For better or worse, holists like him were condemned to figuring out the world in oblique ways.

He sat listening to her hopeless entanglements, her sensual geography going nowhere.

Housebound, with no feeling for the city at large, she confessed to looking for herself in toasters and glass-oven doors, yearning for a reflection.

He found himself pondering her case long after he should've packed it in.

At night, studying homeopathy, he wondered if homeopathy could possibly treat a disease like hers. Such a disease of the imagination seemed to cry out for a cure in keeping with a corresponding root. He knew treating 'like with like' had proved to be Hahnemann's fundamental equation in treating disease. He just couldn't imagine, in Trina Chase's case, what this might mean.

He'd pause between chapters to talk to his diary. He speculated about cures in the Third World where modern homeopathy had found a home. He wondered if V.L., the little homeopath at the conference in Bangkok, still lived in Bangalore. He went on pondering the structure of Trina Chase's brain. He kept refining his image of her brain and confiding it to his diary. *It's like this, really* ... And it wasn't. Until one night he thought of an amusement park.

As a house of mirrors her imagination gave off reflections distorted by a sixth sense running through her entire being. Trina's sixth sense was her third eye. Her second nose, third ear, second tongue, third hand ... For every sense he decided she had a mirror sense. Her poor jumbled brain remained underdeveloped, in an exotic way, which made him feel impertinent practising on her bones. So he gave this up.

His breakthrough never came, because nothing he could do finally made any difference to her condition. He just sat and listened now. Trina Chase experienced grief, even when she appeared to shrug grief off. She needed time, he decided, to reconcile the space between what she saw and what she thought.

It was as if in coming in to see him over and over she kept applying for a job as gardener without knowing what a lawn mower looked like. The rejection, every time she applied, was cruel. She *knew* she was qualified. She also sensed she was lost.

The lack of a job and thus independence kept her living inside the confines of her family. She was suffocating.

When her boyfriend disappeared, Trina was stricken and kept him closeted inside her heart.

2.

By the following week Dwight still wasn't free from jail. 'Prison' is what the embassy was calling it in this unusual travesty of justice by an otherwise responsible country. The bad news had its lighter side. A respectable businessman flies south on his own initiative to negotiate with a scuzzy hotel in Guatemala, and a neighbouring country sends him directly to jail for not paying his bill in the country he hasn't yet reached. To Bartlett it sounded like a board game. Not to be taken seriously.

Reesa would get through to the embassy in San José about once every two days. The official assigned to Dwight's case had little new information.

Incredibly, he was still trying to secure permission to interview the prisoner. He assured Ms Potts the embassy was doing everything possible in the unusual circumstances of the case. Could she perhaps supply him with a few more facts? So she repeated the story:

Unworried, Dwight had flown south on a charge card to see if he could work out a compromise with the Guatemalan hotel he'd booked for his abortive tour last spring. His pride was at stake. Herodotus Travel had been tainted. He'd taken a stand and flatly refused to pay the hotel for its failure to deliver a product. Still, he was willing to negotiate, although his irate clients thought he was crazy for contemplating any negotiation with this irresponsible hotel. Instead he should negotiate entirely with them. So as an entrepreneur who liked to be on good terms with everyone, he had ended up pleasing no one.

'It's a joke,' she told Bartlett. She was forced to carry on as if everything were peachy. On *City, City* she spoke calmly to guests and studio audiences. In the evenings he made tea and awaited her return. Beautiful, breezy, she came in like a woman of the world and collapsed in a small pile. She clutched her chipped mug with worried hands. He told her not to get upset about things here at home: Theresa was coping with Gwyn, who seemed happy and oblivious to the turmoil.

Reesa wondered if they couldn't make use of Theresa's Spanish. 'With the authorities down there? I don't know how, except to stick her on at this end and see what she comes up with.' This sounded to Bartlett like if you had bananas in the house you might want to give some thought to basting a roast. Logic, he noticed, went out the window in times of stress. In its place misadventure seemed to await them at the door.

... I wonder how long the house is ours, before we're torched or knocked over? He plotted his understanding of the facts. And his diary began to sound like one of Theresa's soaps looked on TV. By the middle of October he was in debt to the bank and in debt to his father, worried about Aloysius who was in debt to Dwight, and worried about Dwight who was in debt to everyone. *'Dallas' has nothing on this family.*

Dwight was now out of the picture even if he should suddenly reenter it trailing remorse. His loose ends had multiplied. A brokerage house, for example, hoped to take him to court for the loss sustained by an underage client in selling stock short he never owned. The company felt it had a case against the guardian.

So debt was a spreading web. And Aloysius had abandoned the web, for-saking their house for a tent. There was something to be said for freedom. The boy's tent had no windows, just a flap for a door. Such tenancy seemed to fertilize his imagination as he printed his libellous slogans and held forth, a sound-byte celebrity, on local TV. *What a picture, what a craving we have for what we'd like to be true. The chance of the little guy becoming somebody.*

Bartlett's own windows remained his patients. Some cracked, others opaque, a few thinly curtained. Most were port-hole in size, with the odd plate-glass thrown in to make him gawk at what he heard ... *to mix my per-ceptions, Trina-fashion.* His patients didn't live in houses. They came from apartment blocks and rented rooms. A house for most of them remained a luxury of imagination, toward which they wandered in endless migration.

When another week went by and Dwight still wasn't free, Dwight's secretaries started calling up Reesa to say they had no authority to make decisions about Herodotus's advertised tours. Were they still Go? Broad-casts, columns, tours ... Deadlines for these required extension or post-ponement. They asked her what they should do. Running low on petty cash they hadn't bought doughnuts in ten days.

Reesa conveyed these reports to Bartlett, who heard about bank manag-ers ringing up HT and learning of Mr Irving's extended absence abroad. Where exactly was he? Why was he out of the country? Wasn't he account-able to them for the on-going restructuring of his debts? Lena wanted to know if she was allowed to say Dwight was in the can in Latin America.

Office morale had touched bottom.

At home it was another story. While the house hungered for news of Dwight, it was full up with news of Aloysius and his hunger strike. His girlfriend Trudy told Bartlett not to worry, Wishes wasn't starving himself. Seemed Aloysius had lost none of his craftiness, just dressed it up as virtue. Even Theresa had taken to watching the lunchtime news for reports of his campaign.

So the soap opera went on in expanding circles:

Dwight owed Bartlett who owed the bank, which held the collateral mort-gage on his practice, taken out to help Irving finesse his national expansion.

Bartlett still owed his father. Now, more than ever.

His father was in debt to the bank, for remortgaging his house to help Bartlett invest in a plastic bone company, which his son had hoped to use to offset his losses to Dwight.

So far, with no return from Glassgraf, there was no chance to pay off his father for the Calcutta loan, or even help him with monthly payments on his refinanced house.

N.B: Aloysius wants his Jockey shorts.

3.

'I take my pleasure in trees,' said Needles Astapovo. He was trying to relax by reflecting on why he'd spent his entire adult life living in parks around the world. The old man in the white beard was in pain and struggling to keep his mind above it.

'I lie back to watch trees in motion. I pretend the wind up high doesn't exist, Dr Bartlett. It's the tree moving on its own. Its own bones is what a doctor like you might say, a picture of the unmoved mover. Whatever we mean by that.'

Needles could barely move himself. He almost hadn't made it in today. After his fall down the cliff two years ago, he'd been on the mend and staying away from doctors for over a year. Now he was wondering if Bartlett made house calls. When the manipulations on his posterior innominate were finished, he drew his practitioner a map.

'I don't make it in next week you'll find me here.' He sounded serious. He seemed to expect his chiropractor to visit him in Stanley Park, should he fail to appear for his next appointment. 'Here' was an X in the middle of much white space. He drew lines to indicate forest trails connecting the urban outsider to his tent.

'This pain comes on me like a coffin now.' Laughing dryly, paying in cash, he handed the doctor two ten-dollar bills, both John A. Macdonald's heads noosed in black ink, noticed Bartlett. 'Credit my account with the balance.'

Like Lois he wondered where this philosopher of trees had the government mail his OAP and his income assistance. Needles used to safari into town every Wednesday on his stick, to have his back adjusted and do his business. Maybe he had a bank account in town, thousands salted away out of money saved from living rough and without bills. Maybe –

'Your father on the line,' interrupted Lois.

He helped Needles on with his shirt and vet jacket, their odour redolent of the young man cripped with lathyrism in Calcutta. The smell filled the office and made Bartlett queasy. Lois popped through the door to conduct Mr Astapovo out with the same delicate consideration she had given to conducting him in. The patient waiting, the Greek soprano, must have wondered what Bartlett had done to the poor man. This woman, still dreaming of a comeback, pulled the kerchief at her throat closer to her nose.

He picked up the receiver: His father had marriage news. Bartlett's sister Betty was going to divorce her husband Kirk. 'Normally, Bart, I wouldn't bother you at work with how the world turns. But I figured it might be decent if you could ring Bet just to say hello like. She feels like a dog.'

'Right. Call Bet.'

'... Saw you on the local news last night.'

'Yeah?'

'Holding a pair of underpants. That kid is news for nothing I can see 'cept protesting. Why's he telling so many dotty stories? Hope you told him to start eating, then head back for the schoolyard. He's trying to make us all feel guilty for nothing.' Bert Day paused. 'Actually, he makes me proud to be a Canadian ...'

He didn't sound sarcastic.

'Maybe it's the girl I'm seeing.'

'Still seeing her?'

'The Filipino.'

'Going good?'

'Could be worse.'

'Thick and heavy it sounds.'

'Incidentally ... he's kinda making that Dwight friend of yours a back number, ain't he?' Bert Day spoke confidentially. 'Letting it be known in public Irving's a fraud? How's his travel outfit supposed to survive like that?'

'Maybe it isn't.'

'That's what I wonder.'

'Dwight's in jail.'

This news caused his father to give a quiet whistle. 'The kid did that?'

'No, Guatemala. Authorities in Costa Rica threw him in jail as a favour to their neighbours.' He heard his father taking in the news that had yet to become news. 'Something to do with a hotel bill,' he added.

'... Stuck in the slammer.'

'Right.'

'Sounds to me then like you're in deeper than ever now, Bart.'

He waited for his father to tell him not to sweat it, about his debts to the old man and all.

Bert Day said instead, 'I wonder when something's going to happen with them urethane plastic people?'

Bartlett hesitated. '... Well. Glassgraf keeps talking more cash. You know, before they can get the manufacturing end started up?' Glassgraf was supposed to be his investment in the future, his ace in the hole.

'Ain't that what they were saying last summer?'

'Right.'

'Assholes,' said Bert Day.

The word startled Bartlett. Coming from his father.

'Doggone assholes.'

Not the language he expected from his father. He felt betrayed by this collapse of diplomacy. *If collapsed is the word. Rearrangement ...?* For the first time he sensed in a small way what Dwight must be feeling, forsaken by his own kind. The saving illusion collapsing in a curse.

At precisely one o'clock he walked halfway up the block to meet Tom Cabot for lunch.

'... I did suggest you try Rowland Storey,' said Tom, when Bartlett confessed his anxiety over the investment of his father's money in the American plastic company.

'Storey,' repeated Bartlett. 'Trying to fathom that quack's personality would turn me into a Trina Chase.'

'How is Ms Chase?'

'Ask me about a tree. About unmoved movers.'

The two friends still met once a week over lunch to compare their careers in medicine.

'Scallops,' suggested Bartlett. 'Why don't you ever order scallops?' He looked down at his own uneaten lunch. 'Wish I could stomach the fries.'

'When I see scallops in the market,' said Cabot, 'they remind me of yellow cadaver fat. I was never a proponent of the dissecting kit at college. I resented the scalpel and hacksaw.'

'So did what's-his-name ...'

'My fingers buzzing from the phenol.'

'Cheerios ... Berlioz.'

'You going to eat your fries or what?'

Bartlett looked across to the other table. *Still wearing the same high heels, I think. Doesn't recognize either of us.*

'Speaking of medicine,' said the chiropractor, 'what d'you know about homeopathy? Like what it purports and so on.'

'I wouldn't want to bet the bulldog on it,' said Tom. 'Water's an important ingredient. I doubt it's the answer to bone cancer.'

'Answer to surgery though? With its holistic approach?'

Tom speared a cold fried potato off the chiropractor's plate. 'You're talking to a G.P. who's talking to a D.C. Aren't we both holists?'

'Tom, both of us know we don't know anything. We memorized the parts at college.' A snicker from the other table caused him to lower his voice. '... I think the whole picture's another story. We're quacks. We can't cure Trina Chase. We don't even understand what's the *matter* with Trina Chase.'

'Exotic dancing, Dr Day, is probably just as good for what ails Trina Chase as homeopathy.' Cabot managed to impart this cynicism in a confidential tone.

Bartlett responded in kind. 'I promise not to report your sexism to the College of Physicians and Surgeons.'

'In my defence, Your Honour, let me say I haven't had time for visits to the interesting-looking dives and back alleys abroad like my learned colleague here. As much as I might like to wander ...'

Bartlett sipped his water as the woman opened her purse, tossed a five and a two-dollar bill onto the table, scraped back her chair and butted out her cigarette. Sam Lung bowed from the kitchen door as she strolled out.

'I've got this patient who sleeps in the park,' said Bartlett. 'He's coming from every park around the world. Claims he's *slept* in every park ...'

'What's *his* problem, chilblains?' Tom watched her stroll by the window. *A patient of his. Or used to be ...*

'That's just it,' said Bartlett 'I don't know.'

'Either his back hurts or it doesn't hurt.'

'Yes, but is he at home here or isn't he?'

'What difference does that make?'

'Have the whole plate.' Bartlett pushed his fries across the table. He sipped more water. His jug needed a refill. 'My patients, Tom, like yours, call where they live home. And it's home they're sick of. The habits of the bloody place. Where's my real home is what they're asking when they're asking us to cure them. They want to feel exotic, not run-down and domestic. This is the problem. This guy from the park is already exotic. Like poor Trina.'

'And still suffering.'

'You got it.'

Cabot sprinkled vinegar from the square bottle over Bartlett's uneaten plate. 'Basically,' he said, offering a little flourish of his wrist, 'I'm a fish-and-chip guy when it comes to lunch. Fast food suits my personality.' He replaced the bottle in its chrome rack.

'You feel at home in an English fish and chip shop run by a Vietnamese Chinese? You might be more exotic than you thought.'

'Think there's hope for me then, Dr Day?'

'I think allopathic medicine is too confining. Look, Tom, it's rooted in materialism ...'

'And chiropractic?'

'Quacksville.'

Cabot shrugged. 'You said it.'

'Mine tries,' said Bartlett, 'in its reactionary way. I'm not sure about homeopathy though ... A homeopath may know more than either of us knows, without knowing he knows it. Like your illusion that disease is caused by bacteria.'

Tom rolled his eyes. He put down his fork and wiped his mouth with a serviette. He felt called upon to rebut the illusion bit.

'Look,' he said, studying his watch. '... I've got a plantar wart coming by at two. Very infectious. You know, bacteria? Extremely painful. It's the only surgery I do.'

'The Butcher of Altamira.'

'I use electrolysis to drill into a frozen foot. The athletic patient is very grateful for my getting in and out inside half an hour. It's like coming by for tea.'

'There you go, being exotic.'

'I think the kind of medicine *you* want is whatever's cooking the other side of the fence.'

'Listen, Tom. I'm just trying to figure out what it'd be like if there was no fence.'

His friend looked at him like he thought here was a case who had just stepped off the elevator between floors.

Finally, noticing the empty water jug, he said, 'You polydipsic or something?'

4.

The D.C. listens … the M.D. prescribes. *Don't know if this is true. But feels proverbial.* He was scrambling now for conviction. No longer sure he understood his patients enough anymore to comment on their afflictions, Bartlett felt his crisis of faith meant fewer remedies than ever to suggest their trying.
    Listen.
    With Poppy Nybo, the dreamer, he mentally went out to coffee whenever she floated in. He had no idea what he was supposed to do for such a woman. He no longer wished to indulge what he felt at heart was fraudulent in her. Her breathy obsessions only seemed a way of attracting attention to herself. These days the weirder her story the less it concerned him. Courage in the face of decline interested him more. But Ms Nybo didn't acknowledge the possibility of decline. She resembled Gloria Dawson in this. Neither had the depth he sensed but couldn't plumb in Trina Chase.
    He phoned his sister Betty the next afternoon to commiserate. He listened to her uninflected voice, then congratulated her on having the courage of her conviction.
    'What courage?'
    'Deciding to divorce Kirk.'
    'Wasn't my decision,' she said. 'His.' So she was deprived of even this.
    And the future frightened her. Supposing she did get a job, how could she afford daycare? Kirk wouldn't support the kids. 'I ain't a happy camper,' she said. 'Scared's what I am, Bartlett. For the kids.'
    'I hear what you're saying.' And heard himself urging upon her the kind of bland consolation he offered patients. He could only listen and promise to call back.
    He was rereading a note on Lois's desk. 'Dr Bartlett. Can you come? N. Astapovo.' Written in black ink, in a firm almost elegant hand. It had arrived this morning, delivered by a scruffy, forelock-tugging acquaintance of Needles', who promptly vanished, leaving behind him, according to Lois, the pewy call of the wild. She waved a hand in front of her nose. Bartlett held the inky lines to the light. Digging among coins and pencil stubs in his white coat he located the map Needles had sketched him.
    'I still think you should get a plane to tow us an ad,' said Lois. She indicated the blank appointment page for the rest of the day. 'Nobody.'

'Good. I'm off on safari.' He waved the note with the kind of air he usually reserved for his invitations abroad.

He then left the office to outfit himself with supplies from the 7-Eleven, a handful of two-cent Dubble Bubbles, preparing to make a house call on behalf of a profession he now held to be dishonourable.

5.

October in the park wasn't unlike April in the park, except tiny maple leaves, springing across space with no apparent support, had turned crimson and you could see their veins against the sky. The conifers like the ferns never varied from season to season. The rain forest seemed constant and reassuring ... *Generic names, no need to get personal, no tedious details.*

He blew a bubble.

On the first trail a young man glanced at his saddle shoes then looked away. Scratching his elbow, Bartlett recaptured the bubble and studied his wrinkled map. He suspected Dwight the jogger knew this territory better than he.

Other men paced the trail's fringe, stepping away to light up in the undergrowth, pretending not to notice him. Kleenex wads, rotting cigarette boxes, butts. The yellow sun through the trees lit up dark secret tunnels for field mice in the salal. Deeper in, where the trail forked, the sex market fell away.

The chiropractor took the trail to the left, wearing only his white cotton lab coat and feeling chilly. He carried no bag, no pills, no syringes. *Natural medicine penetrating the natural world, what a combo ...* The first house call he'd ever made.

The pilgrim wound deeper into the forest, away from distant traffic, looking for the creek where he was to pivot and discover a small path through the underbrush. The map was precise about the path. When he found it he was to follow on, though it might sometimes disappear – as the broken line indicated – keeping his 'lookout' for a tall dead spire with a 'crow's nest'.

Felt like the Kon-Tiki voyage minus raft.

A gauze of morning fog, unvaporized by the sun, had snagged in some fir boughs.

He found what he thought was the creek, but no path. A trickle of water irrigating skunk cabbages, which smelled fetid. He decided to relieve himself and reconsider his journey.

No one was in sight when he stepped off the trail. He carefully unzipped some feet from the creek, where his urine splashed the forest floor with a thudding sound. He was sure this had happened to him before. Hand on his cock, urine steaming in the shadows, the uplifting smell of fallen fir needles in his nostrils. He was sure it had happened to his ancestors: to any man who'd ever progressed through a forest. He could smell woodsmoke.

When he glanced up he noticed a middle-aged man in jogging shorts, standing on the main trail holding a bloody Kleenex to his nose. Penis in hand, Bartlett didn't know whether to reveal himself or remain motionless and risk the more embarrassing discovery as a peeping Tom. *Quiet now, a few last dribbles* ... He stopped chewing his gum. Maybe his best bet was to stroll out of the underbrush like some dislocated polar bear. Why be shy about having a pee?

He listened to the muttering jogger, no more than fifteen feet away, breathing deeply through his nose and exhaling through the mouth. In, out ... testing for fresh blood, little suspecting the presence of a doctor reluctant to assist him.

The man would take a step down the trail, stop, dab his nose, then another step. In this fashion it took him five minutes to disappear ... and probably half a day to get back to the Y.

Only when Bartlett stepped back onto the trail did he discover he'd been looking for his route on the wrong side of the path. He popped a bubble. Either his sense of direction was defective or Needles' cartography required a compass. He pressed forward into the brush, along a thin line of worn ground.

A discarded scrap of paper, part of a bank deposit slip, made him stop and pick it up. On the back was listed 'Toilet paper, O.J., Eggs, Chicken, Yams, Beer, Paprika.' Not in Needles' hand. The slantless letters came from a hand needing concentration to manipulate a pencil. A man on a dietician's list at the community centre, with an indifference to pastry: a hermit, an ex-con, a pedophile.

He went farther into this shadow world. Crossing a fallen tree he noticed smoke rising in a glade. Sunlight angled down, intersecting it at different levels. He could hear voices rising and falling. Rising, falling. A camp of hobos. A camp of men who could peer into the city without being seen, who could listen in whenever they liked. Make forays into enemy territory to suit their desires.

So what was the big thrill for me, standing there?

Being a peeper, he supposed, of the peepers. Peering in on them murmuring in the soft October sunshine. Listening in without being seen. He couldn't distinguish words.

He could taste woodsmoke.

Then a head turned. An arm went up. Fearing dogs he slipped deeper into the forest. Decked out in white he could always claim Red Cross immunity, if captured, make known his status as a doctor. The shadows spooked him. He pressed on and thought of returning to his office.

He was searching the sky for a spire topped with a crow's nest. Heading in the direction intimated by his map, he could pick up little correspondence to its intermittent line. Compared to the paper in his hand the unmarked ground, without fern or weed, looked blank to the untrained eye. The traveller spat out his gum and concentrated closely on where to place his feet. He bent lower and lower under limbs, as roots came up to meet him. He felt stones through his shoes. A man with back pain would wince through here. A man without back pain would soon acquire it.

At last something like a tall tree rose off to the right, a hundred yards, five hundred yards, Bartlett couldn't tell without gauging its height in relation to the earth. He could see no crows in the spire. Just a remote clot of sticks. Keeping this in view he abandoned his map.

He spotted a tent when he entered the grassy glade. It was standing underneath the dead spire. No smoke rose, no man sat over a campfire, no dog barked. The white-bearded inhabitant was dead. Bartlett knew he was going to peel open the tent like a bodybag and discover his former patient stiff from exposure, pickled in time, having failed painfully to get out of bed and build himself a fire.

He felt like an archaeologist, polite enough to inquire before he excavated. He tried to remember who he was looking for.

'Mr Astapovo?'

Silence, except for a distant river. Wilderness, dead at the heart ... *the 'X' in X-ray, and what buried treasure I wondered.*

The dead tree resembled the spire of a cathedral, abandoned before a nave could be attached. The tent, not a new alpine one like Aloysius's, but stitched together out of old sails, had a fly suspended above it on a rope, tied to the tree trunk at one end and a sapling at the other. The fly itself, like the tent, was pegged down taut as a drum. You could have played dirges on it with a spoon.

Across the clearing a white-bearded figure appeared. 'Over here,' it spoke, before vanishing again behind the vast trunk.

Bartlett wasn't certain he'd seen or heard anything. Listening, he moved through the long grass and skirted the tent. Behind the tree he expected to find Needles preparing tea. He found him in fact flat up against the trunk.

Hanging from a rope.

The rope had been passed through an eye, screwed into the tree higher up, and suspended with two hand loops, to which Needles was attached like a gymnast on rings, his knees bent to free his feet from the ground.

'My back ...' grunted the old goat with great difficulty. 'Lifts the vertebrae ... stops them ... squeezing my cord.'

Bartlett was impressed by this solution to the ancient problem of gravity-induced back pain. Ingenious.

'Any help?'

'Trade ... off. Kills ... my arms.'

'No wonder.'

The old man then unbent his knees and let his feet slowly retouch the earth. He waited, head bowed, to catch his breath. Bartlett waited too. If his patient had to hang like this to relieve his pain, the pain of not hanging must be considerably worse. Even with Needles' bones growing lighter with age, porous, the diminishment seemed to have made no difference. He still hung like a carcass. It hurt to watch him reach for the loops a second time and drag his feet into the air. The old man hung for ten seconds, fifteen, counting. Then slowly returned to earth.

'I got the feeling from your message,' said Bartlett, 'you were on your deathbed.'

'Can't ... walk. Hobbleong Cassidy.' Needles gave a dry little laugh.

Bartlett had intended to explain he couldn't do anything without his adjusting table. He couldn't do anything of course with his table. He could listen, but would Needles feel like talking? The old man stood there, head bowed, puffing.

'Friends of yours?' inquired Bartlett. '... Guys back in the glade? Couple of blocks back, as the crow flies?'

Needles looked up.

'Depends. I just make sure the police know me. Must've reported four bodies to them, in my years here. Bones I've come across, down between logs. Murders and suicides are stories the tourists don't hear. The park is a graveyard.'

This was news to Bartlett.

'The sleeping rough. The dope crowd. Nothing touches tourists except the spruced-up bits, the flowerbeds at the zoo. They come for the beaches. Swim and play frisbee.'

Needles fell back a step on his rope, before resuming his measured conversation.

'The park has a secret life. Hides more than it gives away. Like this tree. I like to imagine the rings inside it.'

The rope slapped the trunk when he released it.

'Inside ...' he said. 'Have a gander.'

He grunted painfully, hobbling round to the tree's other side, before bending over to vanish through a narrow entrance Bartlett hadn't noticed.

He'd vanished quicker than one of the wild rabbits. Jabbed by Pasteur?

Bartlett ducked down and peered inside. Black. The trunk was hollow. He inched forward. His main sense was the smell of mouldering wood. The expected seemed the unexpected. He felt splinters scratching at his fingertips.

Then a light flared, fire in the hand of his patient, coupled to a candle.

A spacious cave had revealed itself, the rib-like circumference of the inner tree vanishing up into a darkness of tapered air. The cave was pitched high with rotting cardboard boxes, against which a wooden stepladder, leaning, cast an elongated shadow.

Bartlett felt like a small animal in a children's story. Across the earthen floor lay spilled a hundred, a thousand, books. 'Welcome to the library wing,' said Needles.

God, books in boxes. Books on top of boxes. Boxes split and bearded with mould.

The old man's dark secret confounded his visitor, who had trouble comprehending the conceit.

Needles lifted his candle stiffly, as if looking for some lost volume promising him release from back pain.

The chiropractor bent over to examine the plastic-covered books scattered on the floor. Waterstained cards bore faint stamps of dates: Oct 23,

Aug 10, Dec 8, July 7 … none stamped with a year. They were stuck inside little pouches announcing the cost of overdue fines, some as ancient as two cents a day. The shape of cards and style of print varied with the decade of each card's issuance.

Needles chuckled into his beard. 'You imagine the sum of my fines?'

Boxfuls of books about economy, wars, people … Hundreds, thousands of books, borrowed three and four at a time, filed into cartons and forgotten.

The web of disguises, pseudonyms, addresses needed to keep his cards current, as older cards got cut off, must have piqued the old man's imagination.

'Shifting boxes is a pain, Dr Bartlett. Can't put my hands on what I want anymore. You like history?'

'Bones,' said Bartlett, '… are the driven snow of history.'

Needles considered this, his candle dripping wax down his knuckles. 'I guess you'd be the right one to say so. But what history?'

Bartlett checked his watch.

'A locomotive moves,' said the old man. 'We ask, What makes it move? Force? What force? The hero? The movement of the wheels?' He smiled. 'God, maybe?'

'At least we know what makes the boxcars move,' joked Bartlett. He smiled foolishly in the flickering candlelight.

'… I'm a drifter,' said Needles. 'I don't believe in the great man. Those guys are all motherfuckers. History's about the mothers who got fucked. It's about the cooks.'

Bartlett felt the mole beside his nose begin to itch.

'Louis Pasteur?' he said.

Needles stared at him. So Bartlett recanted his facetiousness. 'Idi Amin?'

'Example of what I'm talking about. An event takes place at the will of one man or a few. So it seems. But think about time. The long line of events, Doctor Bartlett. History's an example of lots of cooks. The cooks doing most of the cooking end up as stew. Who's to say the chef even remembers what's in the pot?'

Needles licked his lips. 'Why events happen we don't know. Endless curve of accidents with peacetime just as historical as war. Things happen. Things don't happen. Like being up the stump. "Accidentally on purpose" is what we used to say as kids. We're still free, Dr Bartlett. But history isn't.'

He looked up into the dark tree, his white beard close to the candle flame.

Then Bartlett looked up, wondering what he was doing here. *Listening? Or wishing I was in Timbuktu?* Over the years he'd degenerated from a take-charge kind of guy to a passive listener inside a tree stump. Needles Astapovo was a crank.

He foresaw the old man's end in a declining body temperature, and the loss of his ability to keep himself warm with fire. Simplicity, dignity, no longer seemed enough. *A guy needs to retain his capacity for embarrassment as well.*

'... History doesn't have an ending,' said Needles.

'I guess it'd like to.'

'Can't. Future's history too.'

Locked in mortal debate.

Needles shuffled a few steps, peering into the gloom. He picked up three or four volumes, discarding each in turn. He failed to find the book he was looking for. The candle wax had begun to run down his wrist, disappearing up his sleeve. The flame singed his beard making him slap at it from time to time. The smoke caused his eyes to water. He said his 'coxitis' had begun bothering his hip again.

'... Need to get back to my rope.' He coughed. The candle guttered. He said, 'Reminds me of a Chinese fortune cookie: "We don't see things the way they are. We see them the way *we* are". Problem with that cookie, Dr Bartlett, is we've got illusions about ourselves. But at least we trust them. Historians are afraid to trust themselves. Scared to venture out in the world, so they feed off each other. As one example, take all the volumes in this beehive. They don't tell history. They tell the history of histories. The tree is dead. You can see that for yourself. Think what that says about the books.'

The candle guttered again and went out. The two men could do nothing but feel their way back to daylight, where the air seemed fresh and liquid.

Bartlett offered to manipulate the old man's back, if they could find a table. But Needles's feet had already left the ground.

'That's ... not ... why I ...'

Fifteen ... twenty seconds, distending his skeleton to relieve the pain, man strung out like a monkey, before regaining the earth. Breathless.

The old man waited a full minute before attempting to resume his hobble, a step at a time, reborn to the world.

He made his way round to the door of his tent, pausing to clear his throat of phlegm and spit it out, before disappearing inside. His stick was leaning against the canvas.

He reappeared with two deckchairs. These caused him pain, just dragging them outside.

'Here,' said Bartlett. 'Let me ...'

'Herbal tea? Water's simmering inside.'

Courteously, painfully, he unfolded the chairs to make his guest comfortable under the fly. Bartlett felt like he was back in Kenya.

'In that case,' he responded, 'I'd like some tea. Thank you.'

'A case of cases is it?' Needles chuckled. He said if he ever needed the favour returned, Bartlett could be a guarantor for his passport.

'You thinking of renewing it?'

'Never had one. Never will, I suppose, now.'

The chiropractor decided he didn't know anything in the end about his patients. He expected Needles would've collected as many expiry dates in old passports by now as in his borrowed books. His succession of parks, his chain of island homes in foreign cities, his gulag of –

'Never been abroad. Hoboed rails in the States some. That's about it.' He stood there fingering his beard, amused. 'Tell me which is stranger, Dr Bartlett, history or history?'

Bartlett would pause more than once that evening over his diary. Here was a patient whose notions of responsibility to the past seemed unbounded by the usual conventions of time. He was disappearing into his tent again. Bartlett sat down in a deckchair, for the first time since his African safari.

The packages of bubble gum in his pocket no longer came wrapped, he noticed, in coloured comic strips. The pink gum wasn't as thick either as it used to be. The only unchanged item was the price. Dubble Bubble Inc. had found the answer to inflation over time with the simplest of formulas. Maximize your product line by minimizing the product. *Something banal like that* ... Smaller mouthful, smaller bubbles.

Needles returned with two mugs of Red Zinger tea, offering one to his guest and spilling half the other on his woollen trousers. The hot tea scalded him but he uttered no cry. He was trying to settle into a canvas chair without destroying his vertebrae. Bartlett held his wooden armrest steady.

Neither man spoke. Together they listened to the forest. Bartlett tried hard to see the moving trees as their own movers. He watched them, listening to their silences. He tasted the air. Sniffed his tea.

'Listen,' said Needles.

Sometimes, if the breeze cooperated, the sound of a distant river of traffic would blow their way. The sound, said Needles, of the dead. '... Sum total of my entertainment, sitting here immobilized. Reeling in the past. Guessing civilization's speed. Can you believe it?'

He said his dream was to live on grasslands somewhere. Somewhere he'd no longer be able to hide. Trees gave him privacy but you got tired of privacy. Sometimes you just wanted to sit down and wet your whistle with a friend.

The patient reached painfully inside his vet surplus jacket and pulled something out. A plain white envelope.

'Something happens to me,' said Needles Astapovo, 'open it.' He handed the envelope to his guest.

The chiropractor saw 'Dr Bartlett' printed across it in black ink. Bartlett nodded, careful to accept all this attitudinizing quite solemnly.

He deposited the envelope in the pocket of his white coat, beside his bubble gum, without any inquiry into all the other parks in the world the old man had told him stories about. They must have existed, the visitor now figured, in his dream of grasslands.

6.

With the new month it began to rain. Vancouver's annual shrinkage had begun, sea fog and sunlight giving way to eastern fronts and the gloomiest patch of the year. November led nowhere but down to darker days, wrapped in the bright camouflage of Christmas.

By now Dwight had written three terse, unhappy letters home. This was the grand total. Reesa was still writing to him every day, with enough assurance from the local embassy that her mail was getting through. She felt she could tell him gently but in detail of the likely collapse of his travel company.

She avoided saying it had collapsed.

Lena and Candice had stopped calling the house for advice. Instead the banks called, claiming to have had enough. Even old friends of Dwight's and Dwight's father had had enough and were scheduling court action against Herodotus. Official-looking letters arrived Special Delivery and Reesa readdressed them to the legal firm she and Dwight retained.

'Jaundice and Jaundice,' she called it. The fate of Herodotus Tours definitely appeared sealed. At the height of the travel season, when citizens resented the city, its wet-dog look and its surrender to homeliness – when those with money were glad to escape it at any cost – the company had virtually ceased to function.

As if Dwight never mattered. He's history now. No more self to come home to.

Maybe this explained Dwight's continuing refusal to accept his mother's offer, relayed through Reesa, to pay off the Guatemalan hotel and so buy his quick release from prison. He just didn't seem interested in relocating himself inside his larger failure.

Aloysius had changed his tune and was now campaigning against Dwight's unfair imprisonment. Dwight had become one in a long line of refugees he was championing, or thought he was, in the public eye. *Seeing us the way we are, the way he thinks we don't see ourselves, and maybe he's right ...* Reesa, less interested in her appearance these days, concurred. She was surprised by her husband's stubbornness and expected him to drop his self-deception. *She's still disappointed over him deceiving her, I bet, since even before they were married.*

When Lois announced Mrs Irving one afternoon she wasn't who he expected. She had disguised herself as Dwight's mother. She was Dwight's mother. Flushed from the blowing rain and raw atmosphere, she was puffing like a lion with heat prostration.

'I don't think ... we've actually met. I'm Marlene Irving ... Dwight's mother. Very kind ... of you to fit me ... in on such short notice.'

'Not at all. Won't you sit down?'

At the door Lois was fanning the air in front of her nose in case he'd missed this gal's perfume. Expensive perfume, he decided, could smell very loud. *A subluxed observation worthy of a young patient I happen to know.*

Without prompting, Mrs Irving began telling him how she'd been feeling lately. Unsettled. Worried. And not just because of what was happening to her son. She removed her kid gloves and placed them in her handbag.

'It's like a high dizziness. And don't ask me what I mean by high. Not intoxicated ...' She then dropped the lay description and admitted to arterial sclerosis. She had it. High blood pressure. She had this too. 'Is this where my dizziness is coming from, Dr Day?'

It sounded like a foregone diagnosis.

'My M.D. tells me I'm a prime target. For one thing I drink too much coffee. I haven't told her about my sweet tooth but she suspects it. She's one of these health nuts. Excuse me, you're not, are you?'

'No,' he replied. 'I mean I can take it or leave it. I find health just gets in the way of business.'

She smiled and began playing with the corner of a smart London Fog raincoat, wet from where her umbrella hadn't protected it in the driving rain. She had yet to take it off. 'I know my husband wasn't very trustful of chiropractors. He practised internal medicine, you know.'

'Yes, Dwight –'

'He went routinely to the hospital. To the university ...'

Establishing her allopathic pedigree ...

He decided he'd charge her as much as her kind of traffic would bear. The well-off with their worn facet joints and pelvic tilts should pay hand-somely for presuming to slum it with a chiropractor. The middle class deserved to pay a premium.

'I think I also heard,' he said, smiling, 'you're interested in the Shroud of Turin.'

She was pleasantly surprised by his knowledge. She stopped fiddling with her raincoat and relaxed. The silk scarf at her throat was allowed to droop, and he noticed she used it to hide a wobbly red neck.

'Is it true the anatomy is quite precise?' he asked. 'The image's?'

She folded her hands comfortably in her lap. 'Well, do you know, scien-tists are just now finding the language to describe the cloth –' she spoke of 'the cloth' as proudly as a Hong Kong tailor might describe a suit to his mainland cousin – 'and how what *scored* it must have happened in a flash of hot light. They find it all a big mystery. I'm very hopeful.'

'Hopeful ...'

'About the authenticity. X-rays haven't spilled a bean against it. It doesn't appear anything is going to. In my opinion, just the opposite is going to hap-pen.'

'So you're convinced it was the burial cloth of Christ.'

'I am, yes.' She compressed her lips and released them. 'Many are.'

Bartlett admitted he liked the notion that all these scientists couldn't dis-count the possibility of the unaccountable.

'Yes! That *is* satisfying,' she said. 'It's a breakthrough. The Church isn't against carbon dating, by any means. They only want to be careful the cloth doesn't fall into the wrong hands.'

She was studying him carefully, kneading the fingers of her ring hand as if to relieve an arthritic condition.

'... Tell me, Dr Day. You travel. Would you consider paying a visit to my son? If I were to pay your fare and expenses – there and back?'

Did she mean a house call?

'You have to understand,' she went on, 'and perhaps you already know this from Reesa. I can't persuade Dwight to accept my money to get himself released. And I'm not up to travelling down there myself, not to a horrible country like that one. I gather though you've made bad journeys something of a specialty ...'

'Well, not – '

She was looking at his wall. 'I would naturally expect to compensate your practice for loss of revenue while you were away. Say, for a week or ten days?' Her eyes had settled upon his chiropractic diploma framed in oak. 'Yes, I think if his best friend were to talk some sense to Dwight ...'

'You want me to fly to Costa Rica, just to talk to him?'

'Or listen, depending on his frame of mind. It's important for him to know we all care and want him out of prison. He has to understand, Dr Day, his family needs him. His company needs him. It's just criminal to think what's happening to my son in the name of Latin American justice.'

She then confessed the thought of his incarceration sickened her. 'Not to put too fine a point on it, I would expect to supply enough travellers' cheques for you to buy him out of jail. At any cost.'

Bartlett nodded at this, took a sip of water from a glass by his little sink, parted his coat tails and sat himself down on the adjusting table.

'By the way,' she said, 'I wonder if you know – but I confess I haven't even spoken to Reesa about this ...'

No sooner had he relaxed into the idea of a free trip with compensation, than she was inquiring, 'delicately', as she put it, into whether he might happen to know who else Dwight and his company were in debt to, besides herself.

Well, let me –

She confessed to Dr Day she was now willing, in the circumstances, to write off Dwight's debt to herself. As she once had done, he might remember, Dwight's bridge debts at the university to his friends. She wasn't telling any tales out of school she hoped.

'Of course,' she added, 'he's changed a lot since those days.' Meaning, he supposed, she felt her son was now more responsible.

He crossed his legs and adjusted his coat over one knee. Locked his hands together and held on to his shank, rocking imperceptibly, looking like he was prepared to launch an anecdote. He was actually getting ready to be rescued from financial ruin.

He paused. She was telling him she didn't want Herodotus Travel to fail just because Dwight wasn't home to see to its continuing success, and therefore ability, to keep up with its bills. She certainly didn't want that.

'I see ...' said Bartlett.

What he saw was Reesa hadn't said a word to her mother-in-law about the terminal condition of Herodotus, thus insulating her from the truth.

He had paid the price of Dwight's ambition, and his father had paid it too. Both of them were still paying the price of Dwight's ambition.

'Well, in answer to your inquiry, Mrs Irving, maybe I could mention a couple of things ...'

He was careful to spill the beans slowly.

It *was* possible, he suggested, Herodotus Travel could collapse. Hovering, persistent banks seemed ready to pounce. And other –

The news perplexed Marlene Irving, altering her complexion to a deeper veinier flush. 'I hadn't known that,' she told him. 'What banks?' A hand lifted to adjust her blue silk scarf.

He professed ignorance of details, but expressed surprise that she hadn't been informed.

She said nothing to this, looking instead at his wall. He wondered if he ought to bring up his own desperate case, or hope Reesa would fill her in on the details. *She'll have no choice, after this little chat.*

'This shines a new light on things,' said Mrs Irving. '... On everything, really.' She looked tired now. He wondered if he'd somehow blown his chance of rescue. She sounded more business-like now, dropping the confidential tone of a friend's mother.

She admitted Dr Day's news surprised but didn't shock her. She had come here today expecting the worst. Frankly, she'd been surprised by Aloysius's strange campaign against Dwight. 'I didn't know what to make of that. Oh, I admit I knew Dwight was more an imaginative traveller than ... well, an actual one.' But she felt his flying off to Central America was a sign he and his company were going to ride out the recession in style.

'... And now, you see, Aloysius is back on Dwight's side, calling for his release.'

At least this knowledge was a consolation to her. She worried a lot about Aloysius as well as Dwight. She offered up novenas for all three of her sons.

She was sounding confidential again.

'I confess I'm really here under false pretences. Though I wonder what true pretences would be ... Anyway, Dr Day, I appreciate what you've had to say, and ... I don't suppose you have any health pills you especially recommend?'

'Health pills?'

'Something regular doctors won't touch?' She patted her yellowy-grey hair. 'Unapproved Mexican jumping beans?' She uttered this in an exaggerated voice. 'Richard Widmark? I just don't know what chiropractors prescribe. I know you jiggle bones. You could jiggle mine if you liked, if you felt it would do me some good. I don't imagine it would do me any harm ...?' She raised her voice suggestively, in case she'd unintentionally offended him and felt he needed soothing.

'You look as fit as an antelope.'

'In that case I really can't be excused for taking up any more of your valuable time.' She stood up. 'I'll have to talk to Reesa about this family business.'

She held out her hand to him. 'On my way out I'll square things with your nurse.' She opened her purse. 'I don't suppose you're on medicare are you?' Her budget for health sounded like a tight one. 'I happen to have my medicare card right here.'

She would get back to him about Dwight. She really wanted to help her son clear his name and hoped Dr Day could help out. It would be wonderful, if he could.

'Yes,' said Bartlett. 'Help is everyone's hope.'

7.

He phoned his father with the news that Marlene Irving, Dwight's mother, might be willing to square her son's debts. This pleased Bert Day. His son's information threw a new light on things. He had a scoop of his own. 'I've been thinking of asking my Filipino girlfriend to marry me. This news'll encourage me to pop the question.'

'I kind of thought there might be something cooking between you two ...'

His father chuckled. 'Yeah. Pastry.' He accepted his son's congratulations. The world turned.

But the weather continued rotten. Drizzle had become the city's permanent condition. Impossible anymore to believe in sun. It no longer existed, and no one could believe either in civic enlightenment. The city sagged.

Only Trina Chase seemed unaffected by the weather. 'I hear this sound of old Cadillac fins,' she said, 'when I visit the bakery.' Her condition was a standoff. Her raids on the world continued, or was it the world's raids on Trina?

Bartlett said nothing to Reesa of his interview with Mrs Irving. He was still counting on Dwight's mother to pay off his mortgage, once she discovered the fortune he'd already poured into her son's interest payments.

He decided to treat himself to a businessman's lunch.

He ended up downtown at the art gallery, for a travelling exhibition of Norwegian paintings, reading an excerpt reproduced in the catalogue, from Edvard Munch's diary: *One evening I was walking along a path. On one side lay the city and below me the fjord. I was tired and ill. I stopped and looked out across the fjord. The sun was setting, the clouds were dyed red like blood ...* This plot of Munch's featured painting didn't stir his interest, till he reached the climax: *I felt a scream pass through nature; it seemed to me that I could hear the scream. I painted this picture, painted the clouds as real blood. The colours were screaming.*

He studied the canvas up close. The opened-mouthed, hollow-eyed figure standing on a bridge, hands over ears, trying to shut out a shrieking sky, had the effect of forcing him back into the room. He made himself reenter the artist's nightmare, thinking of Trina Chase.

Like the wake of a meteor, lines radiated everywhere. Colours echoed concussion. He saw sound waves in the sky, the seascape. He heard light waves through the paint. The shoreline, look at it, was shifting. Trees had vanished. This portrait of grief was moving fast. It seemed impossible to have pinned it to a wall.

Compound *The Scream* with three more senses, he wondered, and would he have a better idea of his patient's story as she lived it every day? The literal horror of being unable to step back from the picture? The closer you came to diagnosing one aberration the more likely seemed another. What an illusion, he thought, a reality like hers. Or Needles Astopov's, or Dwight Irving's, or ...

On his walk home down Robson, the rain and cloud prevented him from testing his diagnosis against a canvas full of red sun.

He thought ahead. By December, when sun was a mere memory, the national rate of inflation was expected to fall below ten percent for the first time in two years. It was on long winter evenings such as those he planned to replay his diary ... *The mirror-side of knowledge is seldom up front. It gets scrambled. It's in the air. You can never go too far because the truth is always beyond that ...*

A gust of rain against a shop window made him shiver.

He would listen to his diary and then start in again, shaping fragments as best he could, talking. Whenever he felt a new entry coming on he'd line up a fresh Memorex tape, aware of going down in history as the man who kept Radio Shack in business during the great recession of the eighties. He was losing his profession. He planned – he longed – to talk his story out.

8.

Home from Costa Rica in January, he woke up at two the next morning lamenting Dwight's incarceration and dreaming of Needles Astapovo. He switched off his diary. It had switched itself off. He'd suddenly filled in the blank space where the old man's last will and testament was stashed: in the glove compartment of his Mustang, along with Visa receipts and outdated insurance slips. He dreamed this. Of the candy in there, donated to Aloysius by a hooker on Halloween, which the young man had made a big show of turning over to Bartlett as his hunger strike reached toward a fourth month. The candy would be rotten by now. *Was any of this true?*

He put on his lab coat, his saddle shoes, and went downstairs in the dark. Outside it had begun to snow. The wet blanket of it on the ground made the world seem brighter. Snow was falling over the city, its buildings, its sleepers. No one knew it was falling. Bartlett was the very first to see it. It was falling on his car, on his neighbour's rusty Pontiac, on all the cars of the city. The city was without sound.

The Mustang smelled cold and worn-out inside. His breath looked like puffs of dust in the freezing air. He pulled the reluctant door closed after him. He was inside a cocoon. The snow had dusted his entire windshield and the world through this scrim looked uniformly white. The street light was keeping it white, yet as the snow thickened toward dawn it would grow darker. *I was a time traveller, flying by the seat of my pants, freezing to death.*

He grew younger in anticipation. With his key he entered the glove compartment and began to remove mouldy jujubes, licorice sticks, Mars bars Megan used to suck – shrivelled now in their wrappers. An apple had rotted through and dried up. The fibre of peanut shells felt soft and frail.

He went deeper. He discovered unpaid parking tickets, a defective tire gauge, burned-out fuses the shape of cold capsules. He located a white envelope at last beneath a pair of wirecutters.

He sat shivering, watching his breath. *Every breath I take...* He dared not turn on his radio for fear of running down the battery. Hell, with the contents of this envelope he'd buy himself a new car.

In the face of good fortune he suddenly felt generous. He felt a surge of grief for Needles, for Dwight, for victims everywhere. He considered what he owed them: an apology to Megan for love that had died. Loyalty to his father for a debt he couldn't so far repay ...

He tore off one end of the white envelope and extracted a single sheet of thick bond paper, the weight of paper he knew banks used. Unfolding it, he held it up to the white scrim. He read the simple black inscription in a familiar, elegant hand:

My love is a red red rose
Love life see death

The snow deepened till dawn, when it stopped. At breakfast there were happy greetings all round. Theresa said she and Gwyn were about to take their first steps in a new world. They gazed out happily, excited by the snow. Reesa, as he expected, was saddened by his news from prison. The condition of her husband's bony health grieved her. The injustice of his solitary confinement angered and chastened her. That afternoon the snow resumed and fell till morning, when a warm frontal assault, which the weather person in front of a colour-enhanced image from deep space called the Pineapple Express, washed it all away.

June, 1886

On Sunday the new city disappeared. Suddenly and without warning found ourselves on ships and planks. On foot and wading into creeks. Had got used to smoke this spring, to daily slash burning west of town, to constant dust from stump blastings. Now cinders falling everywhere, and half an hour later you couldn't recognize the past.

Not that I have a past to recognize, let alone mourn. It's the future I yearn for.

Had been spying on a woman making love after lunch to her husband, when a sheet of flame engulfed their frame house and changed her view from blue to red. Her window burst inwards from the heat. Her husband exploded.

'Alice! Forget that corset!'

Saved his beloved's life. Even so, plank sidewalk burned up behind us faster than we could run. Me, Alice, Arnold ... Veered off for the harbour and waded in.

Waded out to examine smoking ruins, my own hopes ash. Alice bawled for a while in her sleeve.

Before dark a refugee camp sprouted in tents and lean-tos. Alice and Arnold slept on the ground, without one lustful thought between them. I was still hoping, of course, waiting. In the morning Arnold did an accounting. What remains of the city is a sawmill and two hotels plus Spratt's herring oilery. What we have lost is six hundred to a thousand buildings, with three thousand homeless. 'A terrible price to pay for building with wood,' says Arnold.

Charred stumps and logs litter the landscape. The Union Jack has not flapped once, raised to half-mast on a charred pole. Melted iron wheels from consumed wagons are still warm to the touch; nails lie black and shrivelled in warm ash. Nothing green or growing seems left.

The refugees have pitched in to make the present disresemble itself as quickly as possible. But my couple has yet to show any sign of desire, apart from reassuring hugs. So I have been keeping a watch on the mayor.

Does my lack of substance compel in me a desire to make even civic events a private snoop? Arnold, a cloth merchant, says he doesn't trust MacLean. He's a real estate agent.

Elected five weeks ago, by stuffing the ballot box in his own favour, he was presiding a week later over the first council meeting, one month after incorporation. The fire has redoubled his enthusiasm for the city as a capital for investors and gamblers.

City Hall now a tent on the waterfront. At anchor, waiting, are lumber schooners from Great Britain, China, Peru. At the first council meeting since the conflagration one cheery alderman said, 'The past began again with the fire, Your Worship. The fire got us launched with a bigger bang. The Chinamen couldn't have done it better with their fireworks.'

'Hear, Hear.'

Reconstruction has been explosive, but so far love-making has taken a back seat. Why? My only hope of possibility is still carnal knowledge, somewhere down the line. Where though? When? I wait, sniffing the air for romance.

Arnold wants to employ the first available carpenters to rebuild his house and shop to exacting specifications. He and Alice are the new hotel's first couple. I just wish their privacy could be guaranteed. Din of hammers and saws has accounted for the scantling of a hundred houses and stores.

This end seems the city's true beginning. And the mayor was right. Charred lots selling for twice what they were last week with buildings. A gambler's paradise. I know my own chances will improve as time goes by, with or without the cloth merchant. *He*, Arnold, is starting to remind me of a pernickety fellow. Alice can't get his mind off dresses – to help him take off hers. A diary should be a place of hope.

Fallers in longjohns and suspenders, bouncing. Outside town their springboards entrance me, slotted into notches in the huge flanks.

Am fervent for some glimpse of coitus. The thought of a woman's cocked thigh fills me with the impatience of a faller.

Chapter 29

Nazca

Fifty-second day, fog until dawn. Three flames ate the sun and the big stars were seen. Solemn stuff from Marcus Reambeault, on a cliff in Miraflores, overlooking the fogbound sea. *Revise: not from Marcus, from his new and desperate interest in bones ...*

Summer and dry in the coastal capital, wet and winter in the Andes. Everything backwards. He could now add December in Peru to his travelling inventory of Third-World reversals, along with inflation and repression, poverty and persecution. Time had stretched out for him once more – slowed – a fact he now learned from Marcus wasn't limited to a drawer in his traveller's imagination. *No: to put it positively.*

Marcus coughed and rubbed his thin gooseflesh arms. He was emaciated. The two friends had come by taxi from the medical conference downtown, to end up here on a cliff with the *garua* rolling in, the coastal fog that happened to remind Marcus of what he'd been reading ... fog, and not in a guidebook: *I think in an esoteric science journal, trying to diagnose himself.* It didn't concern El Niño or anything local. No, scientists at the Jet Propulsion Lab in California had been studying the inscription on an ancient Chinese 'oracle bone' – a kind of tortoise-shell diary, said Marcus – and from daytime stars and coronal streamers, licking out from the sun, had concluded the earth's rotation had slowed, the length of a day now .047 seconds longer than it used to be in 1302 BC.

'Big deal,' said the faith healer. 'Who'll be around to worry when time dies in its orbit? Least of all me. David Niven died this year. And Reagan, God help him, launches Star Wars.'

Marcus looked wasted in the weird air, a ghost of his former self, his thin hair greying. But it hadn't stopped him talking. In his now reedy voice he said it only took *him* about .047 seconds to decide to come to this conference, all the way to South America, despite how crappy he felt. He was on the lookout for cures, hoping for something out of left field, from a travelling *hakim*, say, you never knew. He was even willing to visit Timbuktu, if guava skin or papaya juice promised anything at all.

'On second thought, that's Africa.' He didn't care for Africa again.

His clothes appeared to have given up on him some time ago, for lack of fulfilment. You noticed them for the wrong reason. Similarly his words, loose too, whereas once, or so Bartlett remembered, they fitted his obsessions like a new suit. Between sentences he popped pills – green ones, white ones, brown ones – and had trouble walking any distance without wobbles in his trunk and legs. He teetered in this moist, sea-smelling light and remarked on the roiling indifference of the pearl hue everywhere. 'Just us chickens in the fog ...'

He said his eyesight was going anyway.

It had shocked Bartlett to meet up with his friend again last night, not two years since Hong Kong. *Felt my toes curl ...* They'd talked at their hotel, ignoring other delegates at the bar, and Marcus had refused the American dollars Bartlett offered in repayment for his unexpected side trips from Nairobi. 'Don't need 'em,' said Marcus. 'What I need ...' And went on to confess no specialist so far had been able to diagnose his illness, but if Bartlett could this was the only repayment he wanted. 'I've heard rumours. I need facts.' He was weak and caught colds easily, felt lymphatic and mutable. Supposed he was fading, yet seemed unwilling to compromise his sense of wonder for the sake of saving his life. He still loved to ramble.

His complexion had a yellow hue and he looked a little like Dwight, when Dwight came home from prison. But Dwight had recovered, though not his chatter. Dwight hardly talked anymore, at least to Bartlett. Whereas Marcus never stopped. *Pause, breath, wobble.*

Anxious to try any remedy, perhaps even God, the faith healer wondered why Bartlett had abandoned chiropractic. He sounded disappointed, a man clutching for straws he knew couldn't support even his bony weight. 'I mean you had the spiel down pat. You sounded passionate in Bangkok, Hong Kong, Nairobi ... I felt you cared.'

'An act, Reverend Reambeault. You of all healers should recognize a performance.' They retreated from the fog, slowly up the street to where traffic was heavier and sunshine constant. This wealthy suburb promised any number of attractive sidewalk cafés to rescue them from having to go on farther with the sights. Bartlett was sweating and thirsty.

In a capital of bones, where you couldn't escape bones, Marcus settled in as a willing prisoner. They'd been busy tourists this morning. Not far from the Museo de Ciencias de la Salud – site of their conference on 'Healing Methodologies and Integration' – the two Canadians had visited the catacombs of the church and monastery of San Francisco. In the Cathedral in Plaza de Armas they'd happened upon the now-authenticated bones of the conquistador, Francisco Pizarro. From here they had crossed Abancay to the museum of the Spanish Inquisition, where wax dummies, stretched on the rack or lifted by a pulley, contributed to the dislocation and disarticulation of the bones on display. A Grief House that fascinated the faith healer, who wavered along its narrow walkways above the exhibits.

He clung to Bartlett's arm, a drowning man.

Talking, though, talking.

They now ordered themselves chocolate milkshakes, in a sidewalk café off Miraflores Plaza, full of palm trees and Sunday painters. Bartlett was wearing his saddle shoes, the object of mirthful competition among poor shoeshine boys who welcomed the challenge of going to town on two colours of a single shoe. At home he never polished these scuffed shoes from one season to the next. Here, who could afford not to have them polished twice, three times a day? It pleased so many others besides himself. The dust of poverty settled down on his toes like the scum of pollution. It was the scum of pollution. Poor boys were willing to scour it away for a few cents and the chance to snicker at shoes crisscrossed with diagonal lines. *These guys with their rinky-dink stands, snickering at me...?*

2.

Marcus spoke at the museum of health sciences the next morning. The museum was an old colonial mansion downtown, with exhibit rooms on the second floor and above these a library and workrooms. The two Canadians had already toured the disease room, which included diseased bones on display in glass cases. 'Interesting,' said Marcus feeling these would fit in nicely as a backdrop for his lecture. 'Take my arm and help me back out to the foyer, in case my audience has shown up.'

No one had, yet. He sat down on a white wrought-iron chair below the skylit dome, where chairs and a lectern had been set up for daily talks on alternative medicines. This small rotunda sat at the top of a winding staircase. Its wallpaper consisted of huge black-and-white photographs of old

Lima. They reminded Marcus. 'Our own cities add up to something like sixth in national economic productivity. So what?' He meant it. His indifference to chauvinism sounded heartfelt.

He decided to conserve his energy while he waited. He tapped his sandal on the tile floor, then turned to Bartlett. 'Check out the library upstairs, why don't you, and let me think over my speech.' He needed to cast himself ahead, to the state of medicine in the twenty-first century, to the coming together of the spiritual and the scientific in health and healing. 'My grand finale.' He was picking lint off a silk Hong Kong suit that fit him like a body bag.

On the third floor Bartlett peered into a small windowless room, with skulls all over the floor. A woman inside was knitting, he thought. Something about the way disease was viewed in pre-Columbian Peru struck an echo in him. Disease or 'onccoy' was supposed to reveal a patient's moral condition.

Downstairs, Marcus was perched sideways on the speaker's stool, addressing thirty or forty delegates from his lectern in the softly echoing rotunda. The decline in his performance since Bangkok struck Bartlett with some force. His reedy voice was full of dry air, hampered by a kind of osteoporosis of the vocal column. He was discussing meditation, commending euphoric states as good medicine, foreseeing the laying on of hands among various religions as more and more acceptable, and predicting that faith healing, already popular enough to attract vast numbers of people round the world, would eventually be welcomed into the medical community as part of mainstream therapy.

Reaching out, touching ... his way to health and wholeness. 'Listen ...' He tried to sound upbeat, forecasting a medical apocalypse and concluding his prophecy by quoting from the book of Ezekiel. He hoped to possess himself by the strength of the prophet's plea. He had unperched himself to conclude his speech, by holding on to the lectern and declaiming from memory:

'The hand of the Lord was upon me, and carried me out in the spirit of the Lord, and set me down in the midst of the valley which was full of bones,

'And caused me to pass by them round about: and, behold, there were very many in the open valley; and, lo, they were very dry.

'And he said unto me, Son of man, can these bones live? And I answered, O Lord God, thou knowest ...'

A sad, strained note to end on. He received ragged applause, from the delegates who came from poor Latin American countries like Paraguay and Guatemala, persecuted more by the ravages of inflation than by orthodox medicine, or by self-doubt as fringe therapists.

The lecture following his, by a Pakistani herbalist from Sheffield, included a tour of the rooftop garden, where an array of plants used in herbal healing flourished in the polluted sunshine of the old city. These plants interested Bartlett more than the antiquated surgical instruments on the floor below, more than X-ray photographs of diseased mummies, more than petrified foods displayed in the food room. Scholars in the library downstairs could delve all they wished into the history of diseases. He, like Marcus, preferred to consider the future of healing – and, in tune with the conference – the possibilities for integration.

He was trying to put chiropractic behind him, for his talk on homeopathy tomorrow. He wanted to see what the drug exported from Lima to Europe in the seventeenth century, the source of quinine, looked like in its natural state. Cinchona: Peruvian bark. The very first drug to enter Western medicine and be used for a particular disease. Malaria.

The herbalist, unfortunately, looked blank. So Bartlett decided to shut up for the rest of their rooftop tour. Later, overhearing him claim lily-of-the-valley good for a lazy tongue, he wondered if his silence had offended the herbalist.

Peruvian bark he happened to know was the first drug Samuel Hahnemann had experimented with, before making his discovery leading to the principles of homeopathy. Peruvian bark was equivalent to the janitor's backbone D.D. Palmer dallied with half a century later ... except Hahnemann wasn't a quack. He spoke five languages, read medical history, and had actually given up a reputable career as a doctor because he no longer believed in the butchery practised by conventional medicine of his day.

Instead, the guy tinkered. Swallowed doses of Peruvian bark himself. He recorded the feverish symptoms it produced in him, similar to malaria. From this he'd come to his momentous conclusion: A substance that causes particular symptoms in a healthy body will cure those same symptoms in a sick body.

Like, in other words, cured like. The Law of Similars.

Today it still made sense. A hot drink on a hot day cooled you faster than a cold one. Too much aspirin could raise your temperature, whereas just enough could bring down a fever. X-rays gave you cancer, but they were also used to treat cancer. Funny how health and disease balanced one another, were one another, the way dung and a rose were ... not to mention the history and fiction of so many old patients like Needles.

3.

The next morning he wandered across the river into Rimac, saw how poor was the first church he entered with holes in its roof, wire mesh blocking off the rotting steps to the pulpit, and left. Those desperate enough would worship anywhere, even staring at discoloured walls and pigeon shit. Or pouring out their souls in a doctor's office. He was thirsty. He wandered back across the bridge.

In the Hada Tours office, in shabby Plaza San Martin, where his hotel and the illegal money changers stood side by side, he chatted up the girl arranging his Aero Peru ticket to Cuzco and Arequipa. Not at all like Dwight's old office, in his swank tower. She spoke idiomatic English and wore a pretty green scarf over her sand-coloured uniform. Her nametag said Marilyn Casaqua. Indian, unlike the lighter-skinned girls with their disinterested Spanish bearing. She quoted him prices and jauntily prepared his ticket between phone calls. *On a whim, I asked her to lunch.*

'Sure.'

He passed an hour thumbing through his *South American Handbook*, learning how to cover his toes at night against rabid vampire bats, before the office was quiet enough to let her go. He soon discovered, despite her worldly assurance on the job, Marilyn Casaqua was less poised on her own, the daughter of a woman who sold soap and chewing gum in the streets till midnight. Travel-office girls usually came from Miraflores, he learned, intimate with air routes to Orlando and L.A. where they'd visited Disneyland and Disney World with their families. She had got her job only because she spoke English. She'd never been anywhere.

Turned out she was planning to be in Cuzco at the same time he was, on a weekend junket. Her first trip outside Lima. It was her dream. She rolled her 'r's' in a sound he found Canadian.

He discussed Canada as a line-type country, similar to hers. She confessed she would do anything to get out of Peru. He thought she was telling him something. Their hands accidentally touched, over a chicken fricassee.

That afternoon, the last of the conference, the audience for his talk had diminished by a third. Out sightseeing? Marcus showed up but looked exhausted, weak from too much attitudinizing at breakfast. A Lima conference on fringe medicine was bound to be a poor copy of past meetings Bartlett remembered in other cities. It wasn't just the calibre of missing quacks – a contradiction in terms anyway. No, something seedy about Lima limited the city as an international centre for quacks of all calibres. In the world-wide recession few healers seemed tempted to travel this far to share alternatives in a place that made them feel even less important than they felt at home. He didn't care. He was really on his way to India, in search of more knowledge about homeopathy. The meeting had seemed a good chance to launch himself on what he hoped was a new career, *help me sort through to its essence.*

He began by pouring himself a glass of water, out of a French bottle that reminded him of Aloysius's aborted scheme for selling water at home. Switching on his tape recorder then, he introduced himself to the audience by confessing the bankruptcy of his old speciality, chiropractic. '... It's all a fraud. Which is why ...' He spoke slowly, sincerely, trying to decipher his scribbled cards while distracted by a stain the colour of tartar sauce on the sleeve of his white coat.

'The weapons of past surgery, those we've all seen in a nearby room, testify to the zeal of the "heroic" medicine *each* of us is in reaction to. Those weapons are still *at it*, as you know ...'

Indeed most delegates had visited reluctantly the historical array of saws and pliers, syringes and hypodermic needles, tubes and waffle irons ('molde de bronce para supositorios para hemorroides'), wheels and presses, drills and extractors. He had noted these on his first day, speaking softly into his diary. *The blow torches resemble pastry pumps...*

'... My topic today is water.' And he paused to take his first swallow at the lectern. *Go on, be passionate,* he'd later urge himself with revisionist fervour, listening to this tape upon which he would shortly be begging indulgence from the one or two healers here who knew homeopathy's potted history better than he. *Nix the historical nitter natter.* His earlier self must've been listening. He temporarily put aside his cards and spoke directly to the delegates.

'Water is the big *unifier.* I think we underestimate its properties. It holds answers to health … *wholeness*. Right? Believe me, fellow colleagues, somebody's going to come along and find a formula that'll unlock water's code – so why shouldn't homeopaths be in on the leading edge, along with the physicists?'

At this he thought he heard a little grunt of approval from Marcus.

'Homeopaths look to the *origin* of disease, to its idea in *time*, then they try to cure it from the inside, see, at the molecular level where laws have to be imagined.' He hesitated. '… Sort of with creative uncertainty, because water has magical properties. Magical because we don't understand them yet, right? Healing comes from inside anyway. Homeopaths aren't happy just to *suppress* symptoms, not like allopaths and chiropractors …'

He went on, surveying the rotunda, lit from on high by its glass dome upon which the fumes of Lima were settling down in a new layer of daily skin. A wonder any light at all got through, after decades of combustion.

He'd planned to circle back to dilutions and the underpinnings of ortho-dox science, which dumped on any idea of water's capacity to astonish us. But he'd got het up about water a little too soon and messed up the order of his cards. 'The *memory* of water …' he was saying. 'The *mimicry* of water … How else account for the biochemical impossibility of water not retaining any *molecular* trace of an enzyme beyond the …' finding his place, 'Avogadro limit? Eh?'

Drooping eyes, blank lids. He could only think to rub his palms together, as if he couldn't wait to get to the good stuff. *You always have to pretend there's good stuff …* He mentioned the olfactory hormones of insects, in par-ticular the moth. The sexual attraction of the goddamn moth.

No reaction.

'Prince Charles and his mom – the Queen of England? *They* believe in homeopathy, *they* consult homeopaths regularly …' Eyes opening, feet stir-ring. 'Mother Teresa? Tina Turner?'

The ex-bonesetter wanted them all to appreciate the more you diluted the structure of your original material in the solvent world, the stronger the reaction, the more dramatic the end result. In the watery world, patterns and relationships changed. Spaces got rearranged. Naturally, you couldn't see any one of these changes till the world reappeared in a new shape. An aberration of the original.

'… This actually *happens* in the real world. Homeopathy's a mirror image of orthodox medicine.'

He was remembering Trina Chase. He imagined he could've gone on for-ever trying to shake Trina Chase to her senses and not got anywhere, as a chiropractor. But she was probably immune to homeopaths too. Her senses were diluted and succussed already, over countless generations, till their potency was many times more acute than the senses of her own parents. She seemed imprinted with the memory of remote ancestors, with a heightened animal awareness of the world. As a homeopath he couldn't have treated Trina because he had no idea what the 'like' was she required – what, in other words, the 'healthy' person might take to produce the same symptoms as in her.

A rose perhaps? The essence of rose ground up?

Trina Chase, in a way, embodied the science as its martyr.

He waded on, 'Homeopathy is a *reversal* of the world …' Its remedies were ultimately immaterial, other-worldly, spiritual. But concrete, too. This was the 'unity' he was seeking, between the materialism of allopathic drugs and the idealistic principles of chiropractic theory.

Could've fooled your audience.

'My friends, homeopaths go on treating disease with the molecular *mem-ory* of that disease …' *Just pray V.L. doesn't disappoint me, by turning out to be a quack.* 'As I was saying earlier, some moths are attracted over miles of empty air by the littlest hint of pheromones in the atmosphere. *My* sugges-tion, for what it's worth, is the preparation of drugs by allopathic companies should definitely change. They could do worse, in my opinion, than try water. Try dilution, try succussion. Try eliminating drugs altogether, by treating disease in a new way – using like to cure like? When I think of water I think of –' *What did I think of …?*

The truth was, he thought of his dead mother.

He said loudly, 'The fact that *lots* of Third World countries now practise homeopathy seems to disqualify western countries from even considering what *they* figure is quackery, practised by old-fashioned medicine men. So far, and it sticks out a mile, there's an unreconcilable gulf between under-developed medicines like acupuncture and homeopathy, on one side, and allopathy and brain surgery on the other. How to unite them? How to open *up* the narrowness of the drug-centred world …?'

'Hear, hear,' he heard a reedy voice call out.

4.

That night he dreamt of his mother's death. An absurd death. From dog bite
– they learned too late – its virus taking a long time to travel her nerve fibres
from calf to brain: a journey she never suspected, in the deterioration of her
once mild temperament. 'Who'd of suspected rabies was something to catch
from a neighbourhood pet?' wondered his father. At first Mary Bartlett had
blamed herself, for giving in to strange eruptions, irrational rages, those
marks and scratches on her son. In calmer, wonderful moments she would
kiss his wounds – her saliva more dangerous, it turned out, than her
scratches...

He woke up and wondered about his father.

News of his marriage hadn't surprised his son in the same way news of
selling his house had. What would he do now without his kitchen, his work-
shop, his own garden and fruit trees? Bartlett felt like a traitor. 'Pipe down,
would you?' said his father, kindly. 'Sounds like you're trying to bonyize the
market on sorrow. We all fall on our fundamentals sometimes, so what?
Ain't your fault. Me, I plan on swishing into the future like a young buck,
not some weepy Miss Tuffet. Just sorry I have to turn you out is all.'

Guitar music welled up from below in Plaza San Martin. *Nothing else to
report: Bert turns out Bart.*

Turned out of his house, since Bartlett had been living there after he and
Reesa got forced out of their shared house by the landlord ... who, for good
measure, had it torched before they could appeal their eviction. Bert Day
had cooked him supper every night and Bartlett found himself full of the
past: his father putting on good clothes to go out with his sweetheart ...
then a Catholic priest marrying him five months ago, and his son feeling like
a peeper privy to his own conception. *Weird.*

Rosa Segura was everything his father could have dreamed. He
deserved happiness after the strange death of his first wife, her sudden
fits of calm and rage, delirious convulsions neither he nor the twelve-
year-old Bartlett could account for. And in the end, whenever she craved
water, her hydrophobia bringing on painful spasms of the larynx. She
never finished reading him *Kon-Tiki*. His father had finally called in a
doctor – 'not a psychiatrist, Bart ...' – too late though for the painful
injections he gave her, the boy deciding these were what killed her. The

enemy's syringe. His feelings about drugs changed abruptly as he came into puberty.

His father contended he'd had no choice about selling out, and apologized to his son. He just couldn't afford to marry and keep paying on a house he was supposed to own. And he was helping out Betty with daycare costs, so she could waitress at the minimum wage and still support her kids without caving in to welfare. He'd had to sell out at the bottom of the market. And then move into an apartment like any young husband with his bride and the future to screw around with. He hoped with his pension, and what was left over from paying off his house a second time, he could keep cracking for the foreseeable future.

'Rosa wants to go on working, as a daytime nanny, and I didn't say no. I should of maybe. But I ain't sure with the economy in the toilet how much work I can count on, plumbing. She wants to bring her family to Canada.'

It all sounded so absurd. His father selling his house and coming out of retirement, Bartlett counting on the plastic bone company to bail himself out of Dwight's company, after borrowing against his father's house to counter the mortgage on his own dying practice. Ridiculous. A practice forcing him to ponder his future, after his having let Lois go in June. *My one and only experience as a terminator.*

He'd ended up sleeping in his office, on the examining table, eating Vietnamese food in take-out containers, and bathing in English Bay like a crab-infested tramp. When the ocean cooled in October he swam at the Aquatic Centre. He taught himself to butterfly, sucking in chlorine as he pulled his arms like racing oars. He thought about water. He lunched from time to time with Tom Cabot, to talk insolvency and heroics. The news didn't change.

Not, that is, till Dwight came home after twelve months in prison – four months later than expected – and Bartlett visited him at Aloysius's. Over Thanksgiving dinner Reesa unexpectedly announced Bartlett should keep the rest of Mrs Irving's travellers' cheques, since he had these coming to him anyway, and a lot more than the Irvings could afford to pay him back right now. He got his idea, soon after she handed the cheques over in an envelope, of walking out on his bloodsucking mortgage, the falseness of his practice, and letting the bank repossess his building and table. He knew where he could travel to make his windfall last. He said nothing to the bank of his good fortune, nothing of his plans to visit India.

He waited till December, before the conference in Lima, then sold his

Mustang and cancelled three or four appointments in his book, withdrew his last savings and packed his travellers' cheques. He wrote a letter to the bank explaining his intention to default on his mortgage. He apologized for causing them this trouble. Then locked his office, dropped the key in an envelope, posted it to the bank and caught a wet cab to Peru. *Never thought to say goodbye to Bea, lying somewhere in Aloysius's attic.*

He had the clothes on his back and some in his suitcase, including his white lab coat, cutoffs and thongs. His clothes flapped in the wind. He was wearing his saddle shoes, but the rain had soaked them. Flying out to another world, the pilgrim didn't know, didn't want to know, when he might be back.

5.

In the morning, Marcus tried his best to be cheerful, torn between the rubberiness of his legs and his desire to keep talking, keep buoyant. They taxied to the zoo. By now the faith healer was an expert on local taxis, chatting up drivers on long and short rides across the capital, inquiring in broken Spanish whether *this* VW was German- or Brazilian-made, where exactly the driver lived, how many children he had and which hours of the night he drove – confessing that in Canada it was 'mucho frio', an idea every driver seemed pleased to have confirmed. Cold himself, Marcus massaged his scrawny arms.

It was baking at the zoo, a heat presided over by crows leashed to the shade of trees. They were too dark for Marcus to see. Bartlett's mole felt sunburnt, and he pressed his finger to it as they made their way from pen to pen in the parched gardens. The zoo was thick with sprawling, picnicking families. Marcus depended on his friend for locomotion. For sympathy, too, especially as he seemed intent on reviewing the world since they'd last met, but recognized his own lack of gusto. The Americans had invaded Grenada this year to recover pride lost in Beirut. 'Is their pride inseparable from power?' Sir Ralph Richardson had died. Marcus was very sombre about this death of the stage.

The elephants looked in need of some Canadian frio. The three beasts tottered in the heat like boulders. Bartlett unshouldered his bag. He looked for a pink mottled ear.

'Bella!' he belted, jolting Marcus Reambeault into cool surprise. 'Bella, Bella, Bella!' He pulled out his tape recorder, and pressed a button to await her reply.

Marcus was polite. 'That's a sour-looking tub of water. No wonder there's lichen growing in her skin.' He wiped his face with a handkerchief. 'Try succussing *that* water, my friend, you'll still end up with typhoid. Canadians may be dull, but our water's –'

'I'm glad she didn't answer,' said Bartlett, tucking away his mike.

'Really? … That's the thing,' said Marcus, disappointed. 'I'm infected with blank spots now. I can remember the news, sort of. But if you once told me an elephant tale, I've forgotten it. Did you?'

'Nah. Just checking to see if I could still carry a tune.' Bartlett dismissed his own odd behaviour. 'The coincidence would've forced me into religion.'

The sun was torrid. Marcus, breathing heavily, was watching a shabby family watching Bartlett watching the elephants. They were also watching Marcus. Bartlett would later rearrange it so he was watching them all. The family probably lived in a road pipe, miles from the zoo. He now propped his emaciated friend up against the fence. The wire mesh was soon gnawing at his fleshless back. But Marcus refused to complain.

'Unofficially,' he said, 'Lima's afloat on cocaine dollars. The anti-cities account for the real economy. Officially, like poufs in the Church, they don't exist. Lima is the national soul and it's bankrupt. Flying apart as it hyperinflates. No wonder poor migrants like them are attracted to the slums. Except when they come to the zoo.'

'No more treasure left,' said Bartlett, watching the detusked animals.

Marcus breathed deeply. He caught a smell from the other side of the moat. Could it be true, he asked, that elephants recognized the bodies and bones of dead elephants? Smelling, touching, even moving them? Elephant graveyards were probably a myth. Bill Sands, in Kenya, had told him they were a myth.

Later, when the two friends said goodbye, Marcus looked doleful. He was flying home via Mexico City, where he hoped to scout up some dubious pills not officially approved in Canada. 'Also, you made me think I ought to give homeopathy a shot.' He'd been picked clean, he said. 'No roses left in my cheeks. Why do I bother hoping?'

Bartlett hugged him, gathering in the frail skeleton as he used to Bea, for the mock formality of a waltz. *We held on with true affection. He's dying. God knows of cancer deeper than a sunburnt mole. He needs a friend.* The law of similars, in Marcus's case, might have saved him. Instead, it seemed to be killing him. 'I'm gay,' the faith healer confessed, 'as if you didn't know. I've always felt forsaken.' Bartlett felt that if he himself died abroad, searching for a remedy, he didn't want to be alone like some monk.

Marcus handed him a box. The video of their time together in paradise. Bartlett on safari, he said, Bartlett in a balloon. 'A memento. I'm going to miss our meetings in all the old familiar places.' He wiped away a tear. 'Not much to leave behind, is it, a video?'

That afternoon, walking five miles up Avenida Arequipa from another visit to Miraflores, Bartlett thought no wonder Canada looked straight and 'frio' from abroad. Marilyn Casaqua, travel agent, had about as much chance of qualifying for Canada as a belly dancer, and much less chance than a money launderer. As a traveller, even on a cut-rate ticket, she couldn't afford it, and as an immigrant she wouldn't qualify.

As a wife...?

He reflected on his own city. Like Lima it had the sea, coastal mountains, a river, even earthquakes. Mirror cities of opposing hemispheres, both hugging the Pacific, sharing Christmas in opposite seasons and drain water that danced differently to the same gravity. But Lima seemed exotic without being memorable.

He sat down on a bench to remove his pair of zoo-dusty saddle shoes and massage his sore feet. From abroad he remembered Vancouver as invaded by the natural world ... inlets, beaches, harbours. Peaks and sounds. By a curvaceous world, pressing in from all sides, making it far more than a city of domestic gridlock. *Through the exhaust fumes of Avenida Arequipa, I had an image of my city as it is ...* The only city in the world where it seemed possible to feel exotic *and* at home at the same time. *So why've I left?*

He was thinking of V.L. when he arrived in Plaza de Armas, the little homeopath who'd invited him by return mail to come on a study visit to Bangalore and learn the practice of curing disease with water. Bartlett intended to be away indefinitely.

He noticed soldiers hooked up to Mace cans. These, the batons and automatic rifles meant guerrillas, who strolled up very close in Lima to cause mayhem, would pay a price. Blood for the Sendero Luminoso was the 'manure' of liberty. He wondered if violence by the army, who'd promised free elections, could ever cure violence by the Senderos? Treating like with like had worked out badly in two countries he'd visited in the aftermaths of civil wars. Violence was like an undiluted drug, applied without reference to individual differences, homeopathy's lament, to produce a chronic condition. Here, neither side believed free elections would do much to cure Peru.

6.

In Cuzco, he ran into Marilyn Casaqua on the tourist train to Machu Picchu, where it rained and he was miserable. She was with a girl friend from Hada and seemed delighted by her first adventure abroad. He'd been counting on seeing her again, recalling their simultaneous trips to the Inca capital. Returning in the train she looked soaked and happy. Anita, her girl friend, gave up her seat so he and Marilyn could 'share a conversation'. The taped music that cut in when Cuzco's lights appeared – and the coach lights were killed to enhance the panpiped romance – made him wish she didn't have to return so soon to Lima. Their hands touched, this time on purpose.

In the rain he walked her back to the Colonial Palace and said he was sorry to say adios. He meant it. He kissed her hair and thought of Ruth, in the Bible, homesick.

Anita had already scooted inside.

In the arcade outside his own more respectable hotel he bought a pair of alpaca slippers to send to Gwyn. He wondered if he ought to buy a second pair, for his unborn half-brother, expected some time in the spring.

At thirty-five he now found himself wishing for a family of his own.

She wasn't a pretty woman, she wasn't even as attractive as Megan. Walking together in the ruins he'd noticed a little roll of fat on her dark-haired neck. She was short and had a pimple on her nose. When she opened her mouth, he'd seen little braces on her eye teeth anchoring a plate for her two front teeth. She had the beginnings of a moustache. No wonder, stripped of youthful bloom, she was sometimes called señora, as she disarmingly claimed. At twenty-five she had begun to resemble these peasant women who sold slippers.

He packed his suitcase for Arequipa in the morning. Bringing his diary up to date, he concentrated on her good features, her flashing dimple and dark eyes. *She could pass for Aloysius's older sister. I actually asked her to come with me to Arequipa* ... Taping, he couldn't help recording the unexpected knock on his door.

There, standing with her knapsack in hand, was Marilyn. 'You will let me come in?'

He closed the door and so became her porter. Her dimple flashed, this piece of punctuation a hesitant, nervous addition to her declaration that she must return to Lima in the morning.

She came up to his throat. Her alien hair brought her scalp's scent to his nose, carrying to his lungs the exotic smell of ripe corn. This aphrodisiac sent oxygen tingling to his cock and fingertips. *The most domestic of substances, hair ...* Domestic? When he felt this expansive, nothing seemed domestic. Even kitchen tea came from abroad, its water from the sea. *Think where love must come from ...* with its passport of entry stamps, its bearer's vulnerable photo, its wild visas pinned to the page. He buried his nose deeper in her black, aboriginal scalp.

He sensed he might take her anywhere. She trusted him as she would a coyote, hired to smuggle her into a foreign country. She didn't trust him at all. He found himself biting her neck's black fuzz. He found himself licking her skin sleek. He found himself putting his tongue in her ear, daring her to flinch. He found himself ... *I found myself* inside her mouth, discovering her virgin history by how she flinched at his tongue. By how she sucked it, surprised.

She understood from his hand on her breast, his thigh inside hers, from her own fingers landing on his bare shoulder, that he might take her by any route. The bedside lamp shone weakly, where the dead mike waited to be wrapped. He could hear the rain falling on red roof tiles, swilling down gutters, making rusty mud in Cuzco's cobbled streets.

They traded intimacies, negotiating pleasure. They bartered far longer than he and Megan had ever bartered, were ever complicit about the smallest details of carnal knowledge. He and this strange Peruvian woman struck new bargains over a dimple, a cleft, each other's hair, oh, each other's hair.

'Vamp me,' he whispered.

'What is the meaning ...'

The love moth, something had accosted him, as he stripped off her blouse and cheap jeans, sandals and bra. From calves to eyelids he blew on her damp brown skin, peeling off the nylon panties with his teeth, painting her virgin territory with his tongue in the bright colours of an Andean blanket. Buttocks, elbows, raisin-dark nipples ... She was slow, rapturously slow, determined to be taken anywhere, pinching the thin gold chain at her throat with the demure gesture of a vagrant thief.

They slept. And the second time he came inside her she erupted –

against her past, *as I imagined, slicing my back with her nails.* She lifted him above her in the darkness, from where he could see his saliva tracing her body like phosphorescent lines. She cried out like a bird.

At dawn his eyes accosted her. Feeling them, she awoke to discover her bones in his hands.

He showed her how to cant her chin, close her eyes, hunch her shoulder like a piece of coral, loosen her knees. To come open like an oyster.

A rose.

Her labial petals. His rooting love.

He turned on his diary, introducing her to magnetic tape and microphones. *'Blow into it.'* She did. *'Now kiss.'* She kissed his mike with chewing lips. *'Lick.'* She licked. *'Swallow,'* he urged her.

Putting themselves on record for the prurient interest of Ezekiel's time travellers ...

He played back the interview and they listened to the absurd sounds of love. He entered her and the phone rang. All flights into and out of Cuzco now cancelled because of cloud cover. So he decided he was free to spend the rest of Monday tying her up with tape. He had old tape to burn. He might as well burn it, or deploy it in bondage.

'Hang on, please,' he said, handing her over to the desk clerk. She asked in Spanish to be put through to the local Hada office. She blew into the mouthpiece, comically, and stuck her finger in his ear to prick it with a sharpened nail. A fairy godmother's voice confirmed her luck: All flights grounded.

She hung up. She could lose her job.

She didn't care.

Bartlett travelled overland. He made love to the back of her knees. He asked her to draw him in from behind, holding his cock between her fingers like a cigar. He asked her to remove her two front teeth, to let him slip in his tongue and probe her vacant gum. He asked if she felt roots throbbing, desiccated, no longer there. 'Si.' There was nothing he didn't want to know, want her to know.

He let her study his cigar. He introduced her to smoking. She learned to inhale and soon he was ash. She spat him out and lay back. They both lay back. The sky brightened, a storm passed. He studied the blemish on her nose. Then, when she smiled toothlessly, he painted her face. Traced her moustache with his tongue. Defaced her as she connived, holding up her little plastic dental plate, making him lick this too, thrusting herself high on the sheet, clamping her short thighs around him like flower pots.

They fell asleep in her garden. They woke up in Cuzco. He shared his toothbrush with her, his bottled water. His handfuls of her buttocks bobbed as she scrubbed at her mouth. He coated his glans with Colgate and nudged playfully inside her from behind. She grinned in the mirror, her mouth foaming in a rabid look of love. He came in her bum, as she bit down on the silver loops that guaranteed her smile.

Weak sunshine appeared as they stepped from the shower. She scratched him again with her nails, believing this is what men loved. Men did, sometimes. Men sometimes bit back. The pair of them filed reports of love gone berserk. He wondered how far it should go, the tattooing with teeth and nails of news across their skins. He let sanity be guided. He drew up her toes to ream the Cuzco mud, the Dial soap, her phalanx. He fitted her toenails inside his nostrils and snorted.

'That tickles, Dr Day.'

'Lovers should paint their nails red,' he said. 'These smell purple.'

'My friend had some, so I did it.'

'Your friend had Dubble Bubble, would you do that too?'

'You tell me is what and I would make you love it.'

She pressed his body like a map. 'I see what I do last night, you never said ...'

'Don't be sorry. Your blood on the bedsheet belongs to my ancestors' habit of screwing yours.'

She blushed, for the first time since knocking on his door. He was holding her by the ankles, had her on the rack daring her to meet his eyes, defying her to reaffirm their complicity. She arched for him, he entered her. Their locked eyes never wavered.

Over breakfast she offered to guide him on a mini-bus tour of the local ruins. She wanted to see them herself. She wanted to see so much.

She soon learned the cost of an inflationary world, unsticking his Dubble Bubble when it stuck to her dental plate. 'At least the colour matches,' he consoled, burying his nose in her hair. He had something alarming to show her. 'You're a fire wagon,' she said. They cut breakfast short, pushing into the elevator for him to show her how long his hose had got. She bit it badly, on her knees. In their room she marked him further with her nails. They showered again, and he switched on her hairdryer. This overheated and threatened to blow up, slithering wildly on the floor. The chamber maid, overhearing violence, knocked loudly to change the sheets.

Marilyn Casaqua took pleasure as his guide. The sun had broken through, blue sky prevailed. Tambo, with its mauve wildflowers and running water, wild mountain air and silence, planted the scent of her scalp forever in his brain.

Sacsayhuaman, known by the mnemonic Sexy Woman, he might have mocked on his own, making its chaste observations his narrative: *Stunning walls, expanse and light, a view of Cuzco's red roofs below. Dogbarks and kids' cries washing up the mountainside...*

Instead, he gave her his solemn word among the gigantic fortifying rocks to find her again in Lima. She looked skeptical.

'I *want* to see you,' he said. She wondered why. 'I want to make love to you,' he said. Then saw this was the wrong thing to say. Her Hada look of confidence had vanished somewhere among the boulders. She was no longer his travel guide. 'I'm dumpy.' He caressed her hip. 'So am I, Señorita.' She told him, 'No. You're thin as bones. I felt them when I scratch you bad.'

True, his back against the hot stone smarted. He extracted his handbook to read back to her her history, this site of the Inca defeat by Juan Pizarro's fifty Spanish cavalry, who penetrated the ramparts to leave a thousand rotting Indians for condors to pick to the bone.

The source of the eight condors, in Cuzco's coat-of-arms.

Condors, not bones, her nation's record.

'I also want to teach you my name.'

'Bartlett?'

'Si.'

7.

Next day alone in Arequipa, Bartlett found himself outside the story he wanted to record, wondering how to get back in. He was obsessed with thinking of her. So he did his best not to, concentrating instead on the White City's churches, their side porches dating to 1654, and on – ... *I can't go on lying to my diary. Travel babble, potted history! I'm more interested in the future.* He missed her. He wanted her. How much did he want her? Like forever? He was already circling back to Lima.

In his hotel he discovered he couldn't make the toilet refill, having flushed it once. The metal linkage rattled in his hand. He wondered what practical talents he could possibly bring to homeopathy. Son of a plumber, he lacked the skill around water to ensure its reliable passage even through a toilet tank.

He found himself backing into the future, cradled inside the pages of *The South American Handbook.*

He hurried north up the coast, this time by bus, a thumping all-night journey next to a farting young man who smoked stale cigarettes when he wasn't snoring, his head in Bartlett's lap. The hump of the front wheel prevented the ex-chiropractor from stretching out his legs, and he envied the mother and baby sleeping in the aisle. Thirsty from the desert air, he shifted his saddle shoes. The moonlighting driver had squeezed his reserved bus full of illegal passengers.

The bus growled, swinging out on mountain curves to overtake trucks, stopping in dark villages. Children attached to lantern-lit fruit stalls slept on sacks. On the dry air lay the smell of diesel fumes. Passengers relieved themselves, squatting and standing under the faint stars. The road ran on full of potholes. He came to at dawn, hearing surf through the fog, their bus stuck in sand somewhere along the Pacific. His journey had come to this. Wind-driven dunes had buried the Pan-American highway, and held up trucks and buses coming south. Miles of them. He didn't reach Nazca till the desert temperatures were climbing. It was eight a.m. He was thirstier than ever.

But then in a whirl he was in the blue sky over Nazca. Checked into a hotel, booked on a flight, transported to the little airfield by Aero Condor, and squeezed into a Cessna beside a hairy-legged daughter of a fat army officer, in front of a young Italian couple on their honeymoon. They all bumped down the unpaved runway and banked clear of earth. Unnatural lines were cutting up the desert floor for miles. The engine hummed, the struts vibrated, the coastal desert ran away between flattened mountains.

They saw a fish in the desert – it looked like a whale. The hair-oiled pilot made two passes above it, tipping his cargo first to port, then starboard, to reveal the creature's sinuous pattern. Two other Cessnas zipped back and forth at lower elevations like insects.

'On the desert floor,' shouted the pilot, over his dandruffy shoulder, 'you don't know the lines are there! Cannot even see them!'

These were the mysterious lines of which he'd never heard until paging his way into town. No historian could account for them. Why, when ancient artisans couldn't see these huge images close up, from where they conceived and scraped them into the earth, should they have bothered scraping them at all? Had they already invented hot air balloons, as one theory went, allowing them to view their own work from the necessary elevation? Or were the lines really star calendars?

Anonymous artisans, just squirts ... Needles Astapovo would've approved.

Their Cessna buzzed off on tangents, around in circles, down close to what the ducktailed pilot called a spaceship runway, and back up into the sky. He tipped and wagged their wings at the hot horizon. Bartlett felt rash, high on love and no sleep. Maybe the pilot was too.

Bartlett promptly decided the old theories were pie in the sky. These vast scrapings hadn't been read for what they were. They were just plain time. A way to read time. *He* could read time in these images of sand and rock. In the like of them. In the is of them. He was reading history at its source instead of in his handbook.

Actually, I was expecting to barf down the next air pocket. Things in retrospect ...

Into the skin of this earth had been scratched images of monkeys, hummingbirds, flowers ... the Cessna buzzed them all, like a honey bee. He held on. Lines as images. Lines as lines. Straight lines running to the horizon as evidence of dogged industry. Circles, too, incongruous ... but when he pondered them they kept coming together in this simple picture of time.

Is this what yearning does to your eyes, after a long night? Lines you can't see earthbound you catch for a minute miles above? Then kaput – unless you can remember them? Having to imagine what's staring you in the face?

He was hypothesizing from lust.

The Italians were holding hands. The fat army officer had one eye on his daughter, seated next to Bartlett, the other on Bartlett. The Canadian peered down ...

Couldn't be reduced or destroyed, though some day these dusty images would disappear. Pretty simple declaration. *That's the word, simple.* Adding not one molecule to the desert floor, these lines added everything. The pilgrim squinted. Guys scratching away with hoes from their memory of the world. Mimicking the world, inventing these lines to mirror time. *Maybe to slow it down?*

You felt like a voyeur, staring at their love bites. Didn't Marcus once call their kind of sandy imagination genius? *I'd have called it patience.* And nobody, as far as Bartlett could tell, had asked them to do it. Their lines were given freely. Scratching the same message generation after generation: We're here, look, mirrored in our dust! He sensed they were signalling the future. Him!

Her hairy legs, dear me: here today ... The father was staring at him aggressively now, ignoring the lines.

The years it had taken his own lover's forebears to hoe a shallow trench was exactly what they were trying to uncover.

Time itself.

Dust as the collective memory.

Dust as the nation's business. Groovy.

These artisans had guaranteed their anonymity with monuments of dust. With it, through it, in it. It made him thirsty to think about.

He had a bottle of pop back at his hotel. He had two bottles of pop. He would've had a swim had the swimming pool any water in it. He sat by the empty pool, taping his diary in the shade of an acacia tree, watching his spools circle like toy ducks. The hotel's laundry woman came and went, the only living creature with access to water. The hotel plumbing had been turned off, just as the desert sun began to burn before noon.

In the afternoon heat, unable to sleep or shower, he shuffled into town in thongs. He was thinking of Marilyn, wishing he could give her this desert as a memento. Machu Picchu with its stone monuments seemed so forgettable ... *Must've filed it under flashbulbs. I don't remember.* But the desert, like live flesh yearning to be scratched, was something else. Her ancestors had turned desire into an art, mimicking the horizon line, which they couldn't hope to get over except by dreaming themselves into flight.

He found a little plaza downtown that looked shady and empty. Under a pepper tree he sat and studied the blank screen of a TV set atop a concrete pillar, locked inside a tabernacle behind chicken wire. A ladder leant against the pillar. He bet children came to this altar to watch cartoons beamed down from a satellite. Images reaching them through the air. From the capital would come evening news of exotic places, to which these children of an oasis already yearned to go.

8.

Pierre and Barbara, the Italian honeymooners, had persuaded him to share the cost of a car with them to the Cemetery of Chauchilla. The desert was supposed to cool down around four. He couldn't imagine anyone else except Marcus shelling out to inspect a cemetery. Carlos, a Nazcan as young as the Italians, turned up late wearing floral bathing trunks, a mauve T-shirt, white sneakers and wrap-around shades. The pilgrim had changed back into his saddle shoes.

Their yellow Beetle headed thirty kilometres outside Nazca, into the surrounding hills. Handsome Carlos spoke three or four languages and longed like everyone else his age to leave Peru. The country was dying. A gust of desert wind rocked the little car. 'Brazilian Beetle,' he admitted, ruefully.

Pierre in the back seat with his bride told Bartlett he was an apprenticing architect in Milan and that his wife was a fine arts major.

'Design,' she confessed. 'A trendy Italian.'

'Like the lines,' said Pierre, trying to be helpful. 'She and I make structures from a confusion.'

'*He* calls it art,' teased his bride.

'Fractals,' said Pierre, 'if nature makes them. Yes?'

The couple was travelling south from Lima, heading to Machu Picchu via Arequipa. 'You should visit the museum in Ica,' Pierre advised him. 'Skulls, mummies ...'

'A rehydrated hand,' added Barbara, wagging her own ringed hand.

'Probably from heat,' said Pierre. 'Very hot in Ica.'

'Nazca cold in winter?' Bartlett asked Carlos.

'Nazca is almost the same, summer and winter.'

'You're lucky. In California, they'd turn it into another Palm Springs.'

Carlos smiled to indulge this remark. His wardrobe suggested a strong sympathy for Californian resorts.

Bartlett felt thirsty again. According to Carlos the Cemetery of Chauchilla dated from the late Nazca period, 500 to 700 AD, possibly concurrent with the famous lines.

The air-cooled engine climbed poorly, before carrying them from the paved road onto a dirt track that wound three miles into a lunar plain, dotted by an occasional thorn tree. They bounced, shivered, rattled to the graveyard on worn Brazilian springs.

At the edge of what turned out to be several acres of bones, littering the sand everywhere, the solitary tourists got out and prepared to begin their visit, watching carefully where they stepped.

A steady wind was sweeping down from the lunar Andes at their backs. The whole surface of the cemetery seemed tilted toward a green fertile valley. The visitors faced into the valley, toward which the warm wind was blowing as the late sun cast shadows of sharp contrast against the valley's tan and purple mountains. *I didn't expect anything half so ... rhetorical.*

The constant wind of centuries had gradually eroded the salty sand to expose acres of mummified corpses: bleached ribs and skulls, femurs, vertebrae, a sandal strap. Entombed mummies were emerging, rising up slowly from hollows and depressions, eventually to be sandblasted to dust and carried on the wind like pollen to the valley below.

Nothing he could see, apart from the terrible track in, indicated the cemetery had ever been discovered. No signboards, no other tourists ... It was like stumbling over ruins in a rain forest – except these ruins had got uncovered by wind instead of smothered in jungle. Bones, not stones, were the record, crumbling to dust.

This news from nowhere.

At home dust stayed buried, whereas here it covered him all over, microscopic in his pores, his hair, his teeth. He could taste the sand. Relentless, the wind covered each of them as it uncovered the dead. Barbara's hair was turning white.

Carlos told them no one had guessed of the cemetery's existence till twenty years ago, when the wind gradually began 'doing it to the graves' after 'thousands of years' of blowing away the surface. The 'queen mummy' was now in a Lima museum. All the other relics had been left to rot, without a boundary to demark cemetery from desert. 'Look,' he said. Braids of hair strewn like stains on the sand. And cotton fabric, once used to wrap the mummies, now inseparable from parched skin. A place, said Carlos, for tourists to come and be ghoulish. The way he said 'ghoulish' suggested he knew something of the graveyard's effect on visitors, who enjoyed a good murder mystery.

Maybe, because he felt like singing, Bartlett thought there should be birds here. The site had unexpectedly elated him and he wasn't sure why, till he felt his soul lift a little on the wind, fly tentatively in the direction of home, out of this nothingness of a landscape into the green valley below. *How melodramatic an end, mountains shining back at me.*

He expected this is how he was supposed to feel, the cemetery located in such a place as to offer hope by contrast, a *memento mori* on earth scale, where dead souls were certain to be blown from this waterless cemetery into the fertile valley beyond. Was he reading this right? The barren cemetery gave him flight, standing stock still on its revolving plain. *See you around, old soul...*

Barbara wandered off to look for shade. He admired the effortless way she strolled through the sand without stepping on a bone. Not even looking.

What these ancients couldn't have foreseen was the wind disinterring their remains, their bones arising after centuries to disappear as dust. He stopped for a jawbone. *They must've been kind of naive*, to believe in mummification, in such a Band-Aid illusion, hiding from them the real news about fragmentation ... *all these pieces of themselves, now in disarray?*

He watched Pierre gazing at Barbara. Their hair and clothes had whitened. Maybe it was the line-drawers who'd foreseen the rearrangements of the world, living on in their own images of dust. Ezekiel sure hadn't. The prophet had denied dust, just like these mummies had. Marcus had lost the string on his outboard if he thought Ezekiel's story the one to drag in his wake. *I doubt he does ...* His sense of wonder, like Needles Astapovo's, was really what kept him buoyant as his flesh melted away. He'd be curious about the lines, seeing them as if from the future, flying over monkeys, spiders, fish ... *'We're lucky if a few lines last, to remind us of ourselves.'* He could hear Marcus going on like this, curing himself of death and the healing illusions of Old Testament news.

Bones didn't last, only dust did.

The ex-chiropractor thought of the wife still alive in Weasel Copithorne's imagination.

He tramped off by himself through the undulating sand, in his all-white saddle shoes. He was trying to imagine what, if anything, dust like this was yearning for.

He slipped the jawbone into his shoulder bag, then stooped to pick up a stray half-pack of vertebrae still glued to some mummified skin. *Hold the phone, Pedro, our cameras have just spotted a little hanky panky, over at the cemetery ...* A grave robber, worshipper of relics, he felt reproached from miles above by the powerful lens of a watchdog satellite.

He looked around for the others.

Blowing sand was nibbling harder now at his bare legs. Was it shame that overcame his plunderous desire to lay hold of the harmony here? He slowly spilled the bones back onto the surface, where they settled again into a rootless state.

It was later, when Carlos drove the three dusty tourists down to look at an underground aqueduct in the valley – amid green cotton fields, where sacks were grown once to stitch the mummies in – that Bartlett realized what was missing back at the cemetery.

Its absence was behind everything meant to last uncorrupted there. And because it was missing it allowed no roots, no worms, into the landscape of the dead.

Water.

What his mother had died in fear of, embroidering a pillowcase and pricking her finger amidst the distractions of red and green threads, sometimes screaming at him for no reason a boy could understand.

Water was the unifying force. Absent in a landscape of no measurable rainfall, yet part of it, imprinted deeper than memory.

He opened the car door and stepped out.

In the presence of life, why not, these ancient people all knew water as inseparable from dust, but separable from dust in their understanding of time.

This news from nowhere was so commonplace it made him stop to ponder the sand glaciers in the mountains above.

Living bone deprived of water hardened and died. Phosphate, calcium carbonate, salt … Difficult for him to imagine being as dry as a bone, as he felt now, and still having the time of his life!

But he was having just that.

Carlos called them 'eyes' – where he guided them down to view the aqueduct – visible signs of an underground stream, flowing from the mountains, still in use after centuries and giving life to the surrounding cotton fields. This stream, he said, gave anyone who drank from it the heart of a lion.

Bartlett followed Carlos into a deep hole where the clear water ran, exposed briefly to the sky in passage. The white dust on his saddle shoes turned to mud. His toes felt yeasty. Then he, too, scooped up water in his palm and dared, as Samuel Hahnemann before him had, to taste. *Aude sapere* – as he'd scribbled on one of his unused cards.

He quenched his thirst.

The two men washed their faces.

Their hearts grew large.

That night Bartlett recalled another Latin tag, when he came to etch his voice onto tape for the last time.

Non inutilis vixi. I did not live in vain ...

He must have miles of tape by now, crisscrossing the globe, like those flight lines plotted inside airline brochures he plucked from seat pockets on long journeys. Where did it go, memory, the vibrations of it growing fainter down the years? Most of it he thought was stashed in the attic of what was now Aloysius Irving's house, attracting dust, along with his old bed and his model airplane.

The night encouraged reflection. He wasn't tired at all.

He talked on. He'd had a day to remember.

In the cemetery he'd decided to ask Marilyn Casaqua to come with him to India. After that, who knew? He was already hoping to share with her his news from nowhere, which he now diagnosed as common knowledge uncommonly held. Her peasant body was exotic to him. Their children ... *listen to me, but go on, Day* ... would have both hemispheres in their genes.

A tenuous future, putting his fish in one pond.

He didn't expect to discover his future in homeopathy misplaced, but if he did, if quackery had somehow seduced him again, he would retain the memory of Nazca to remind him of the deepest properties of water. *That's a plus.* To remind him of grief too ... that when a person's ten gallons of water evaporated, his blood, her bones, their cells turned to dust.

Pronto.

The white dust of their bones left out in the air would start falling years hence over this desert, this country, this people. But no one would feel it, see it, know it. The dust would be falling over the lines too. It would become the lines. It would become the news.

He heard the little spools of his diary dissolving in silence ... not one, but two still points in the turning world. Two holes in the middle of his clock.

It'll sink in everywhere, he added hopefully, killing his mike. The desert darkness was starry.

Night moths drifted through his window on the century's hot air, and on the air of the century after. This hotel in time just vanished.

Afterword

After the death of my grandmother, I was expected to claim her things at Hygeia. On a hot Thursday in early July I made my way by SkyTrain from my West End apartment to her tower block in Point Grey. Many passengers, to judge by their seashore attire, were ready to compete for space, no doubt with rented umbrellas they would plant in the sand like flags. I too was dressed for the beach.

This city is another world from the one my grandmother grew up in, became a pediatrician and later a politician in, flowered and died, aged 110. The city, distrustful of age and illness, is no longer innocent. Her death was treated as a non-event, in effect covered up, because of her suspected attacker's senility. (Where could you put a hundred-year-old murderer but straight back into a nursing home?) His advanced age suggested the statute of limitations had expired the moment he reached out with his stick to strike her.

– Toodle ... on over, she had called to say two weeks earlier, when we last talked. I watched on screen her slow, liver-spotted hands, folding themselves in her lap like bony doves. She wanted me to take her down to the beach, for an anniversay. Could I take the afternoon off? – We'll taxi ... to the beach, before the old viper ... here does me ... in from odium. I do ... believe he would like to snuff me.

After her cremation service, attended by dignitaries including the mayor, the sanitarium's head nurse gave me what she called *the facts.*

– We found her lying in the corridor. She was trying to walk without supervision, when the lights went out. It could only have happened in the dark. We had another powercut. She was conscious when we found her, but mute. Then she just seemed to decide it was her time to go. Before we had time to contact anyone ... even her doctor ... she slipped away.

She wanted to blame the Americans, for another unscheduled

powercut, since the electricity supply has been greatly overestimated by engineers rerouting still more of our power and water to California.

The tubular sign over the glass doors was glowing coolly in the heat: HYGEIA. I removed my dark glasses in the temperature-controlled lobby and the lift arrived.

– Mr Day? The nurse on duty seemed distressed by my garb, my bare, sweat-stained toes.

She herself was wearing old-fashioned nurse's shoes, stout snow-white heels, and a starched dress. In one of those tiara hats she conspired to look like Florence Nightingale. *Conspired*, yes, since Nan had told me of recent legal threats from the Red Cross over Hygeia's appropriation of its name and emblem on stationery used to solicit donations.

Nurse Nightingale led me down the same corridor my grandmother had travelled a thousand times. Two moppers were busy ... they travelled to every floor, disinfecting one an hour. In all, twenty-four floors. Coincidence? Nan claimed there was a huge cuckoo on the roof of this sanitarium set to go mad on the dot of every mop rotation. She'd lived on the fourteenth floor of this sterile tower for the last twenty years.

My guide paused at the rec room, where residents sat in wheelchairs and a few, who still operated walkers and canes, had parked themselves on hard benches intended to encourage youthful posture. She seemed to be looking for evidence of aging to use against them. I believe Hygeia's treatment, with its discouragement of comfort and iconography, explains a little of the indignation and fury a patient like the murderer might feel toward another's perceived trespass against the institutional philosophy he'd absorbed ... prolier-than-thou, my grandmother (his victim) called it. It bemused her. Crumbling public health-care had left her little choice but a private home like this one.

I knew Hygeia was in debt to a two-century-old vision of a utopian city. Strange, since they presume the future and not the past deserves to be maintained as the status quo. Health before all. Keep illness at bay. Scrub scrub. Germs, yes, but just as responsible for disease are weak moral tendencies. No wonder illness is punished. A sick person is ostracized and forbidden to mix with other residents. Old age itself is a kind of catchable disease, so it isn't encouraged either. Walks are; prunes are; uprightness.

I spotted her murderer wheeling down the corridor, his cane across his armrests. Nightingale accosted him. – It's time for your haircut, Mr Lazlo. Where have you been skulking? The old man, by no means gaga, regarded her malevolently through old-fashioned rims.

– Have you washed your face, Mr Lazlo? He'd had pigeon pie or something for lunch, the feathers still stuck to his mouth. His bottom lip moved and with it a dental plate. He refused to answer and pushed his chair right by us, hands wired to his wrists. – The barber is coming! she sang out in his wake.

1401 GWYN POTTS

Her name on the closed door looked forlorn. When we entered, a large coffin was resting in the centre of the room. I raised my eyes to the view. Her corner-window view of the city, bay and mountains seemed to work as a sedative against the tower's stark aura.

– We've laid out everything, said Nurse Nightingale. She gestured at the bare mattress of the waterbed upon which laundered clothes and eye glasses lay neatly arranged, along with half a bottle of pinot noir ... evidence, I guessed, to be used against Nan in case the manner of her fall should come under suspicion by family.

– You may wish to donate her dresses and sweaters, I don't know. We can't have them here. You might find the Salvation Army would come and remove them for the poor.

– A good idea, yes.

She looked down at the trunk. – We haven't touched that, except to move it from her closet.

– No.

– It will have to be arranged for. She appraised with distaste this large steamer trunk covered in a skin of grey dust. – It will take professional movers. With block-and-tackle she seemed to suggest. I agreed to send someone over after I checked through it for anything worth keeping.

She smiled unhappily. – Yes, well. I will leave you to your task. Lines around her eyes gave her the slightly raccoonish look of a housebreaker. – We require the room soon ... for our next occupant, you understand.

With this she vanished in a white puff. The smell of carbolic acid was in the air. Likewise the white noise of the building's ventilating system in perpetual transfusion.

I spent a few moments running my hands over the trunk, tracing its bulk under the dust, its dome and shoulders, its brass hinges and peculiar buckles, the fitted brass toes of the four corners, and its wooden slats battened to the hide.

I tried lifting one end with its leather handle. She must have been hoarding gold bars inside. I had no success either in raising the lid. I thought of fiddling the lock with a credit card, when I noticed at her desk a key resting on her black address book and concluded from its archaic size this should fit the trunk.

I turned it, the lock snapped, the domed lid bumped open from the pressure I imagined within. It creaked as I raised it with both hands.

Inside were hundreds of mementos, moulded to fit the vault of the closed lid, a wonderful feat of stowage. Or was it that the years had shaped these things to make them inseparable from her growing memory of them? The trunk was lined with cedar, yet everything smelled zooish, the very opposite of Hygeia. I wondered where in the world to dip in, what if anything to discard.

On top were menus and awards, unframed photos of her younger self, often chained and robed, all a little bent by the lid's pressure of years. I dug down and discovered two wigs and a Russian Easter egg. Tulip petals fell from a theatre program. Some sketches for an unfinished poster had been folded away. I dug deeper. Letters of condolence; a ring. Figurines and baby slippers. Clamshells, an ivory brooch, a pewter vase ...

By digging straight down I could see things I was missing to every side. Some spilled onto the floor as I pulled up photo albums from below. I sifted down through passports of ancestors with fading mug shots and funny haircuts. An ancient pistol-like apparatus, possibly for drying hair, stuffed inside a disintegrating brown box from Bangalore, addressed to *Albert C. Day, Esq.* A relative I concluded.

Wills and more wills. A child's party hat. A torn golfer's glove. Scores of ancient video cassettes marked *City, City* on bits of metal tape. Others, identified in different hands, on scraps of yellow adhesive: *Masai Flight, Dating Interviews, Bangkok Talk* ... And dozens of audio tapes, numbered but out of sequence. Similarly deeds, plumbing invoices, mortgage papers and IOUs, a pigskin valise. Somebody's school exercises long since in tatters.

I fished up marriage contracts. The wing of a model airplane and a pocket calculator. Hotel receipts from Rome, Calcutta ... Big old floppy diskettes marked *JetSet* and *Golf.Hols*. A black boxy briefcase with a built-in dial lock, smashed to a noticeable degree on one corner. Even – as

I saw, by lifting to let it unfold – a plastic skeleton, lacking ribs and connective string, which clattered to the floor. Two packages of fish food had petrified. A blue-and-white lapel badge said HERODOTUS TOURS / MAKE HISTORY / TRAVEL. Paperback novels and sheet music from Gilbert and Sullivan ... *Tempo: Razzle-dazzle.*

Her whole world, thrown together in such a small place, made a midden of my senses. Had she ever listened to these tapes? Watched the videos or lingered over the snapshots? Read the school exercises or booted up the diskettes? Studied ...

Why do families cling to flotsam when they are all drowning anyway? Perhaps because they are drowning? I was abashed. I decided whatever her trunk held, it certainly lacked any real treasure beyond its shipshape stowage – a feat I would soon see couldn't be repeated.

The contents did offer one possibility. Instead of transferring them to my separated wife's basement, where I'd planned to forget them, I might clear a space in my apartment and have the trunk delivered there. I could sift through it some weekend when my daughter Minna came to stay and got bored watching VR. A challenge to find the hardware to play these antique cassettes and let the pair of us listen in on the voices of our forefathers. I had no idea yet that Nan had scripted them all, by reconstructing her world.

I'd gone more or less straight down, tossing up objects as I dug, so the floor surrounding the trunk was now awash in spoils. I struck a bony hornpipe, a flattened penny in an envelope, and glanced off a bamboo birdcage stuffed with sepia photographs and the score for *Madama Butterfly.* I had no time to excavate this cage, nestling in dresses and a Union Jack.

At the very bottom of the trunk my fingers hit on something round, like a leather barrel, fat

Wiggling it free and drawing it to the surface I saw what it was. Its hide had cracked round the brass tubing. Its size and weight had none of the compactness of today's specifications; in this it resembled the trunk. Unfolding it, I marvelled at its length, the size of a safari gun.

I stood up and aimed it at the window. The shimmering bay bounced below me, the mountains jiggled. There was nothing to focus with, till I discovered how to twist the sliding tubes. A sail or wing appeared briefly, then vanished in fuzz. Static.

I collapsed the telescope and stepped over to the waterbed, where I unzipped my bag and laid it inside. The zipper made a silky swish. The bed gently rippled.

I added the address book, surprisingly heavy, to the pile of objects on the floor. Then squatted and began returning her things to the trunk. Reaching the brim, trying to round off the remaining items, I discovered I had too little space for the lid to close. I removed her address book and placed it in my bag. To repack things properly, roughly as I remembered removing them, might take the rest of the afternoon.

Nurse Nightingale looked in when I was leaning on the dome, trying to press it into place. – Trying, I muttered, to get the latches to catch. Her smile seemed to suggest I try reordering my priorities. At the sound of senile bellowing up the corridor, she vanished through the door in the white puff she had perfected.

I relifted the lid, hoping to remember how Nan had had matters arranged. *Had* they been arranged or was her order an illusion? I climbed aboard like a mahout, straddling the lid to ride it into submission, feeling it sink only slightly, then stop. Neither lock nor latches would catch, and clearly the straps had shrunk.

I dismounted to try another manoeuvre, retrieving the cord of her dressing gown from the waterbed. I stripped the laces from her walking shoes, knotting these end-for-end with the cord, before proceeding to encircle most of the trunk's girth with a noose.

– Up, old girl, up! I couldn't even lift the handle to slip my line under.

No choice then but to remove many of the same items as before, to make the trunk light enough to lift and lower again for refilling. I lost track of the hour, and wondered if Nightingale might not return soon with a mop handle to remind me Hygeia was a cuckoo-driven building.

The lid in the end continued to resist, refusing to close all the way. So I cinched the cord as tightly as possible to prevent spillage. Then tossed the key into my bag.

A wall calendar was still showing June. I flipped up July with its blue sky and rainbow-coloured sails of beached catamarans. The city's skyline closely rivalled the encircling mountains. I was a little surprised to find this copy of a photograph allowed on the wall. It was like stumbling across a girlie calendar in a morgue.

Underneath the photo, in the box with today's date, I noticed

Pedro/ Beach inked with the spidery black letters of her tiny hand. I knew she'd wanted me to take her to the seashore today, and out of respect I was planning to take myself there and round off my visit with a swim. I tried her phone but the screen had been disconnected.

The beach was crowded with umbrellas, as were sandbars where the tide had temporarily vanished to deeper channels. Four miles across the bay, towers and condos climbed to the highest ridges ... a nonexistent winter snowline no longer the deterrent it used to be in her day. The same intense light off the sand I could recall from my inculpable years of volleyball, burnt feet and netted girls.

I was thinking: My dark looks are slowly turning grey. My once thick hair is thinning, unaccountably, since my father isn't bald nor was my grandfather. How many generations can genes jump? After forty-five years my leg muscles feel slack. My hands lie at loose ends wormy with veins. My breasts belong to some other man. My stomach ... what has happened to my stomach that it now makes decisions about its own movements like a distant satrap?

Nostalgia for myself as husband and father was making my hands tingle. Separation reaped by middle age and ambition had put me at a distance from any unifying principle I was able to call home.

I made my way up the beach on sweaty sandals, a mile or more toward the end of Spanish Banks. Water rolled off my face and dripped to the path, lined with benches bearing plaques to silver anniversaries and dead people ('And when the fragrant day is done, / Night – and a shoal of stars' etc.). I plodded on in the heat, past acacia trees, bag slapping hip. The numbers of bathers declined farther west, where the foreshore looked less manicured, a little wilder. A stray dog peed on a lump of driftwood. Windshields glinted from the road. A grassy plain swept over to the bosky cliffs, and in the distance large weeping willows hung as straight as Nan's hair.

Among these I nearly missed the decaying concrete anchor, lying on its side as if washed up in the trees. I remembered this sculpture, mouldering and cracked now, and could make out its once sharp hook shaped to suggest a sail. It lay on a small knoll, pointing up to the cliffs like an arrow eroded by time.

I hunted dutifully in the grass to locate the plaque she'd wanted me to see, its brass tarnished, but inscription still readable: ... *honours the accomplishment of Spanish explorer Don José Narvaez/ the first European to visit these waters/ on July 5, 1791, aboard the schooner Santa Saturnina.* I studied the dead artist's name, and a facsimile of the navigator's chart below, etched into brass and described as *Islas de Valparaiso (now known as Point Grey) / as mapped by Navigator Narvaez.*

I turned to look out to sea. Her little surprise. Three hundred years ago today, this afternoon, this hour perhaps, a schooner, probably no more than thirty or forty feet, had sailed in on the tide, discovered no harbour worth charting, and sailed out again. Missing the Narrows completely. A very quirky piece of navigation. She obviously thought it worth my while taking the afternoon off to celebrate my Spanish heritage. Help me remember my stake in the city. How the Spanish had once claimed the Pacific, from Valparaiso the whole way north.

– It's important to feel foreign, she told me, on my last visit to Hygeia, even ... when you're not. To see yourself ... differently. Make you ... appreciate ... what you, Pedro ... lack. Glasses on the tip of her nose.

Nan had married the son of a Filipino woman, Fernando Day. My grandmother, with not a drop of Spanish blood, had kept her mother's English surname ... but agreed to name their son Renaldo. My father named me after an immigrant uncle of his father's. I should have felt kinship with the past. But my link in the chain felt weak to the point of broken.

I spread my towel on the beach, buried watch and wallet under sand, and walked out nude through shallow green tide pools. I required deeper water to float my stomach. Black clamholes sent bubbles of gas to the surface.

Up to my thighs now, the seawater scurling shoreward on the flood, I noticed a tidemarker holding the distance like a steeple. Why not cast her ashes here, I thought, bring her to the beach as she wished one last time? I wanted a galleon to appear, trumpeting itself shoreward under sail, holds full of bullion and silver plate, to commemorate the end of Nan's long life.

She deserved a baroque departure and this took my own mind off separation, homelessness, a daughter I seldom saw. I missed my daughter.

Back on the beach I lay down on my towel between two logs to let the sun tan my back. Digging up my watch I noticed it was after three; the worst UV had passed.

When I awoke my shoulders felt burned and I reached into my bag for more aloe cream. I sat up, opened the bottle and lubricated my skin. An old girl friend with chestnut hair and chapped lips was working me over like a masseuse. I smiled and closed my eyes. I reopened them and checked my watch: not yet two. The hot magnetic sand had done something to reset the digits. Perhaps it was my eyes. A galleon was sailing straight for shore. I saw its masts topple, her crow's-nest vanish. The sea washed in. The white sails drowned.

My skin colour had deepened.

Replacing the bottle I happened to touch a smooth surface, as featureless as a piece of glass. My grandmother's address book. I drew it out, impressed by its smallness for a woman who had known everyone, yet surprised again by its heft. Where it fell open I discovered no addresses at all, but rather three columns under Addresses, Area Codes, Telphone Numbers, dense with stringy handwriting. Into it she appeared to have poured the endless mass of her life and many other lives. I seemed to be holding their album in my hands. The more I read the more fractured grew the world.

I closed it. I opened it. The inky lines drew in the last pages till they waved before my eyes. I removed my shades and squinted at her collapsing life: *Suddenly here, out of nothing ...*

I spoke slowly, like my daughter learning to read.

A breath of wind lifted my hair. I adjusted my shades and went on:

... The floating world. Have nothing to compare to the weightlessness of it. It just is, as I am. Yet I am not, as I hope to be, after finding a line forward to myself. Yesterday fell into search for ancestors, found none. Just families curling off every way but mine. Will I recognize my direction when it appears, drawn out in the stars or limned in sand? Don't yet see how. My need for a familiar signature is like the arrow's for trajectory. How else to report this condition? Seem tainted with comparisons that do little to explain the floating.

Up here in the branches, mosquitoes get blown limb from limb. Dustballs too. Scaly cones toss in the sea's breeze. Such meagre things make me happy to learn of their presence. To me, though, nostalgia eats at their substance in lieu of any stuffing of my own. A cry baby.

These trees are numberless like the constellations. The

forest mirrored in the sea spreads smooth and even in all directions, full of animals as the saltwater is full of fish. From up here I know the world is everywhere the same, a climate of evergreens and tree-covered mountains, a dog barking in the village below. I am sure the world has no edge, no matter what Little Far teaches his children at the fire.

How can I sound so positive about the world when I'm still uncertain about a local riddle like falling? No matter how light an object, it falls. *Splot.* Things go down, not up. Falling is not a thing in itself, as I am not, sliding down a strand of smoke, say, through the smoke hole of the longhouse for a snoop inside.

People inside fill me with envy. The way they have bodies and move, suck air and spit, eat shellfish, carve yellow paddles, copulate and twitch in their sleep.

May the world's wonders surprise and keep me buoyant. May they grant me a *me*.

This cedar tree. Is a house. Jacket, cradle, blanket, basket. These aren't comparisons. The people weave and wear its bark. They eat and play with its shapes. They lay their dead in its wood. They honour the tree as themselves, as they do the raven in its limbs.

But I wander. Something has happened and I would be derelict not to say it has changed things considerably in the village. This occurred yesterday, just as the afternoon air was dampening to a salty breeze. A little island with two dead trees, enshrouded in fog, floated round the point and stopped offshore.

Suddenly here, out of nothing.

The Musqueam grew agitated at the apparition of islanders who lowered a canoe and proceeded

to paddle it ashore. They relaxed when these strangers began digging, far out in the sand.

Women and children hanging back, the men headed out over furrowed salt flats, through tide pools, to reach the foreigners in their tall hats and black clothes, who greeted them in a strange tongue.

The men grabbed their naked bellies and fell down dead in the sand. The visitors smiled and ignored their warnings. They laughed. Eventually, after further digging with odd tools of quick efficiency, the hairy-faced foreigners returned with their hats full of clams to the canoe. Sitting backwards they set off for their island, shouting as they pulled away, still facing shore. Maybe they were shouting greetings. It made sense, their manner of paddling, for in the end they arrived where they had come from, alongside the cliff they now reclimbed, up a rope ladder.

They soon departed, standing on shore. Leaving, they rehung white blankets from the dead trees, which the wind caught, and away they drifted into the gulf. I now saw it was not an island but a great canoe, inside which these men must have cooked, eaten and lived. The tree it was carved from is impossible for me to picture. By comparison the grandest trees here can only be saplings.

This unexpected visit has made me reconsider my certainties. The world must not be the same at its extremities. Not if clams are always good to eat where these strangers come from. They may not even have clams, of course. I presume nothing. Before yesterday I thought I understood the world.

Today the villagers have been decorating their canoes with dogskin blankets, hoisted on poles. The idea seems irresistible to them, though so far the wind has resisted their offerings. The men have tried paddling backwards, too. Nothing.

The women and children have been watching all this through a hollow stick. This is thought to be a peace offering, left behind by the pink men in black clothes. But what kind of peace that excites and calms at the same time?

Everyone keeps looking through it for clues, sensing energy in it. The stick is hollow and not hollow. They cannot, for example, push an arrow through it because of ice trapped inside. They wonder, when the ice melts, which way should the arrow go?

They compete to tell whoppers about the purpose of the stick. It is Little Far who bosses it at dusk but can't decide which end to let his daughter peek through.

Speaking Ear tells him it depends on what he wants her to see.

'Can it help us make peace with the Haida?'

'No, only identify our friends.' This from Little Far's daughter who snatches the seeing stick from her father to study the sea. They all stop talking in admiration. Maybe the stick is not as useless as they thought, if it can bring friends close and keep enemies a long way off.

The darkening sky makes it hard to tell them apart at the fire. The stick passes in and out of their hands. They encircle the moon with it. A dogfish is caught in the stars. One of them does not know if he has snared a mosquito or a fishing heron. The others laugh and slap his shoulder.

Ahead and back he collapses and uncollapses the stick, peering through it. Mosquito or heron? 'Comparisons decay,' he claims. 'Embers in the sky are reflected in our dying fire. The nesting raven has just folded herself into night ...'

So far he's pleased with his story. The others goad him on. He will soon have to decide what he sees, they tease. Does it prey on the skin of the world? Does it have wings to bear off the world in darkness?

He will not escape easily unless he can report answers.

So he discloses to them the fading light will soon collapse differences between here and there, in favour of a new figure. Gamble or a ruse? The others at the fire grumble in disappointment at this convenient manoeuvre down his own windpipe. He even has the audacity to tell them the figure he has in mind reflects this collapse and predicts their downfall.

Does he mean as rival storytellers? Or is he talking the figure of a foreigner? His tale will need more flesh if he plans to satisfy their appetites.

I sense from expressions on faces I can no longer see that others think *he* thinks his is the story of everything. The mystery of the universe in a clamshell. Poor man, he acts so certain, his performance is doomed to founder. Let him go down like a stone.

It's such a good-natured night morning will soon come from the other direction, on the same wings of the raven he has dissolved into darkness.

Acknowledgements

Chapter 21 and several of the interludes appeared previously in *The Malahat Review*, in somewhat different form. I am grateful to the magazine's editor of the time, Constance Rooke, as well as to my current editor, John Metcalf, for his considered judgements. Indebtedness also to the Canada Council and to the Cultural Services Branch of British Columbia, for financial assistance in completing this novel. And I would like to acknowledge the following articles and books: *Futurehype* (1989) by Max Dublin, for 'Futurehype in Health'; *The Sense of an Ending* (1967), by Frank Kermode, for 'Solitary Confinement'; *The City of Joy* (1985) by Dominique Lapierre, for Chapter 64; *Portrait of India* (1970) by Ved Mehta, p. 454; 'Shreds of Evidence,' by Cullen Murphy, *Harper's*, November 1981. Credit also to *Ageproofing* (1984) by Jane Ogle, and *Principles and Procedures of Travel Counselling*, ed. David Wright, n.d. (Canadian Institutes of Travel Counsellors). The content and protagonists in this novel are imaginary. Any resemblance to living persons or actual events is coincidental.